# HIDEAWAY COVE

## COLLECTION 1

### ZOE CHANT

# THE GRIFFIN'S MATE

I

# LAINIE

"Oh, no, no, *no*." Lainie groaned as the car engine whined to a halt. "*Please* don't die, car. I seriously don't need this today. Not on top of everything else."

The car's engine, deaf to her pleas, gave one final croak and fell silent.

"*Shit.*"

Lainie coasted to the side of the road, coming to a stop under a worn wooden sign. In faded red script, the sign read: *Hideaway Cove: Population---*

The sign was so old that the number was completely worn away. Lainie sighed.

*Population, one less family than there should be*, she thought. Her grandparents had been the last Eaves to live in Hideaway Cove, and after her grandmother's death one month before, that wasn't likely to change.

Lainie tried to feel angry about it, but what was the point? She'd resigned herself to her situation years ago. Her problems weren't going to change just because circumstances were finally forcing her to face them head-on.

*Just one night,* she told herself. *One afternoon, one night, one morning. And then I can leave again.*

She shielded her eyes from the afternoon sun and looked down the hill toward the cluster of buildings that made up Hideaway Cove.

The small coastal town in the bay below her was almost cartoonishly cute. Old Victorian-era buildings lined the wide main street, and a shallow sandy beach swept down into the sheltered cove. A small marina at the end of town nearest the highway held a handful of small fishing and leisure boats, and at the other end of the crescent-shaped bay, a hill jutted up from the waves, protecting the town from the northerly winds.

And from the top of the hill, a house built at the base of an old lighthouse stared back down at the town.

Lainie looked straight across at it. Her grandparents' house.

Her stomach twisted.

It had been fifteen years since Lainie last stepped foot in Hideaway Cove. Fifteen years since the last long, dream-like summer vacation she'd spent at her paternal grandparents' rambling old house on the hill. A month of fishing, and swimming, and gorging herself on ice cream.

Fifteen years since the late-night fights she'd had to pretend she couldn't hear. Since her grandparents started to sigh and purse their lips when they looked at her. Since the vacation that had ended with her grandparents telling Lainie and her mom and dad never to come back. That they were no longer welcome in Hideaway, and never would be.

Fourteen-and-a-half years since her father walked out on Lainie and her mother forever. Anywhere between fourteen and nine years ago that Lainie's granddad had died. She didn't know exactly, because no one had bothered to notify her or her mother, who were by then living in a small apartment in the city.

Eight years since Lainie's grandmother had gone into a care home. And four weeks since she'd died.

Lainie groaned. Counting down like this usually helped. Separating a problem into little squares and looking them one at a time made her feel more in control. But breaking up her life like this just left Lainie with more questions.

The biggest question of all was the one she'd never dared speak. Not to her Mom, not to her Dad before he left, not even in her own diary.

*What did I do wrong?*

She gripped the steering wheel. *It's too late to worry about that now,* she told herself sternly. *Granddad's dead. Grandma's dead. Dad's gone—who knows whether he's alive or not, but he disappeared so completely he's been declared legally dead. Whatever reasons they had for what they did have gone with them.*

Her grandmother's will had come as a shock. The news had been delivered by a neat little lawyer in a fussy suit and shiny shoes, who'd clearly spent some time preparing his explanation of the situation.

Mrs. Iris Eaves had left her entire estate to her only son, Mr. Anton Eaves. As Mr. Anton Eaves had been declared dead *in absentia*, the inheritance fell to his only child, Ms. Lainie Eaves.

After fifteen years of being completely stonewalled by her father's side of the family, suddenly, Lainie had inherited everything they had owned.

Which was what had brought her back to Hideaway Cove.

Lainie took a deep breath. *You can do this,* she told herself, mouthing the words. *You're a grown woman now. And this is business. You're* good *at business.*

"And as for you," Lainie said out loud, glaring at the steering wheel, "I did *not* pay through the nose for a rental just to have it die on me! Come on…"

Holding her breath, Lainie turned the key in the ignition. The engine revved—and revved—and turned over. She sighed with relief.

"One night, and then you can leave all of this behind you," she promised herself. "A fresh start without Hideaway Cove."

2

# HARRISON

Harrison squinted into the afternoon sun as he stepped out onto the main street of Hideaway Cove. Behind him, the front door of Sweet Dreams Ice Cream Parlor swung shut on a cacophony of children's excited screams. He ran a hand through his hair, grinning at the scene he'd just left.

As he stood on the sidewalk, enjoying the afternoon sun on his face, the door swung open and shut again behind him, jingling merrily.

"How does it feel being the hero of the day, Sparky?" he said, looking sideways at the man who'd just followed him out.

Apollo Jenkins—Pol to his friends, and Sparky to his boss, at least when his boss was deliberately teasing him—was tall and lanky, with blond hair that flopped over his face when he didn't keep it tied back.

Harrison always felt strangely land-bound when he hung out with him. His human form was heavy and sturdy beside Pol's loose-limbed frame. He supposed they looked an odd pair, though oddness was nothing strange here in Hideaway.

Pol's human body sometimes looked almost as ethereal as his shifter form, with his Legolas-like hair and pale golden eyes. Next to him, Harrison couldn't look more ordinary. Brown hair, crooked nose, tanned skin. His work often left him a bit grimy, with wood shavings curled into his hair or oil rubbed into the lines of his hands.

Harrison wasn't sure whether Pol had ever actually worked with his hands in his life. He certainly didn't now. His particular talents meant he didn't need to touch so much as a circuit breaker to look after Hideaway's electrics. Which was why, while Harrison had been re-hanging the sign over the door that had come loose in the last storm, Pol hadn't even taken a toolbox in with him to fix the broken ice cream freezer.

But for some reason, right now Pol didn't seem to be properly appreciating the fact that all he had to do was wave his hand over broken electronics to fix them.

Pol groaned dramatically and glared at Harrison over the top of a triple-decker cone piled high with sprinkles.

"I think that just took ten years off my life. One per ear-shattering screech. Why didn't we leave that job until tomorrow, again?"

Harrison laughed. "If we'd left the job any later, Tessa Sweets would have taken *twenty* years off your life. The first real sunny day we've had in weeks, and the parlor's ice cream freezers break down? Every kid in the town must've been breaking down her door since school let out. Imagine the chaos if the ice cream ran out."

Pol shivered elaborately and took a long lick of ice cream. "Well, frankly, I don't know what their hurry is. It might be sunny, but have you noticed how the sun isn't actually *warm* yet? Tessa had better gird her loins for public complaints if any of the little tykes get too cold and go crying home—oh, *hello*." His expression of put-upon misery evaporated and was replaced by a keen grin. "There's fresh meat around. *Ooh.* Apollo likes."

"What are you on about?" Harrison raised an eyebrow at Pol, whose eyes were narrowed in concentration.

"Oh, just a little exotic interloper. Weren't you expecting an out-of-towner this weekend?"

"Not until tomorrow. This must be someone else." Harrison frowned. If an outsider was arriving in Hideaway, the residents had to be warned.

Not least the excited kids in the ice cream parlor behind them. "What've you got?"

Pol closed his eyes. For a moment, his expressive face was still as he concentrated.

"Hmm… oh *nice.* Sleek little body, small but punchy once you get going. A real smooth ride. And All-American, too." He sighed and opened his eyes. "Only two-wheel drive, though. Whoever's in the driver's seat had a bit of trouble getting her over the ridge."

Harrison snorted. "What, at the town boundary? Was that your work, or the car's?"

Pol's affinity with electrics was good for more than just fixing broken freezers. The summer before, he had set up a magical blockade around the small shifter settlement of Hideaway Cove, to make sure no newcomers could arrive and catch the locals unawares. A drained battery or misfiring engine in the newcomer's car gave the townsfolk time to shift back into human form, or swim out beyond the waves and out of view.

It also gave Hideaway Cove a reputation for being a pain in the ass as a tourist destination. Who wanted to vacation somewhere where your phone (and only *your* phone) gets no reception, the WiFi keeps turning off, and your electronics kept dying on you?

"A little from column A, a little from column B," Pol replied absently. "As for whether our visitor is human or not, we'll have to wait until she's in sniffing distance, same as everyone else. But better safe than sorry, right?" He pulled out his cell phone, gave it a stern look, kissed it, and stuffed it back in his pocket. "There. The news is out: *Beware, incoming potential human!*"

He repeated the warning telepathically, for the benefit of anyone not permanently attached to their phone: *Human visitor in town! Bewaaaare!*

Harrison snorted. His own phone chirped in his pocket, and he knew everyone in the town would be receiving the same alert. "That's the official wording, is it?"

"Signed off by the town council and everything." Pol flashed him an angelic smile. "At least, that's what the electronic version says."

"Don't let the Sweets hear you say that," Harrison said, grinning. "Interfering with town records—tsk, tsk."

Mr. and Mrs. Sweets held court over Hideaway Cove's town council. Mr. Sweets was acting mayor, following the previous mayor's retirement, and most people assumed he'd keep the position after the elections in a few months' time. That was fine with Harrison. The old guy wasn't the sort to cause trouble. In fact, he was so relaxed he seemed comatose most of the time.

His wife, on the other hand, was always into everyone's business.

Harrison groaned. He'd managed to keep out of Mrs. Sweets' sights for the past few weeks, ever since he'd finally convinced her he wasn't interested in her granddaughter, Tessa. But he could already tell she was going to give him a headache over his work with the out-of-towner.

Pol shrugged and licked up a glob of melted ice cream and sprinkles before it fell off the cone. "Well, I'm not worried about the Sweets. After all, I'm working for the next mayor of Hideaway, aren't I? Even the terrifying Mrs. Sweets won't be able to rag me about paperwork when you're stomping around in the chain and robe."

"I've already told you, I'm not going to run for mayor," Harrison said, sighing. He stuck his hands in his pockets. "The workshop's enough for me. Besides, I would've thought the gold chain would be more your thing."

Pol shrugged. "Oh, sure. If I ever decide I want to live the cliché, the mayoral bling will be my first stop. Here's our guest, by the way," he added, nodding at the road behind Harrison.

Harrison turned and raised one hand to block the late afternoon sun. A silver Ford Focus was making its way down the road, with the careful slowness of a driver unfamiliar with the local streets.

Behind him, the ice cream parlor door opened again, and he caught Tessa Sweets' voice as she warned the kids to stay inside. All the children in Hideaway Cove knew how important it was they didn't give away the town's secret to visitors, but their excitement over possibly seeing a human visitor might be too much for them, and they might lose control over their shifter powers.

Harrison nodded in absent approval as the door swung shut again. Tessa was a good, responsible woman—so good, in fact, that he frequently had difficulty believing she was related to the awful Mrs. Sweets.

He waved a greeting to the newcomer as the silver car drew closer and caught a glimpse of the driver as she passed them.

He saw her for less than a second. A flash of glossy blonde hair, and a round face mostly hidden by sunglasses. A Cupid's bow mouth set in firm concentration.

That one glimpse struck him like a thunderbolt.

Harrison staggered backwards, leaning against the outside wall of Sweet's Ice Cream Parlor.

"Oh, hell," he breathed.

"What's the matter? Stub your toe on the curb, big guy?" Pol elbowed him in the side as he finished off the massive ice cream cone. "Oh, geez, it looks like those kids are about to vomit themselves out of the shop. I'm off—see you at Caro's tonight?"

"What? Yeah. Sure." Harrison had no idea what Pol had said. He was still staring after the woman in the car. His heart was pounding. *She's the one. She's the one,* it seemed to be saying, thudding in his chest and his ears.

His feet started moving without any input from his brain, following the car, then stopped short.

He watched as she turned up one of the few side streets off Hideaway's main road. He knew exactly where she was going. The road led to Hideaway's sole visitor accommodation: the Innlet.

If she was staying there, she couldn't be a relative come to visit family in Hideaway Cove. And Harrison hadn't heard of any new shifters coming to town. So she was probably human, a random tourist who'd stumbled on their coastal sanctuary.

Harrison imagined barging in there and asking the inn's owner, little old Marjorie Hanson, if he could speak to her guest, and groaned. Even if he didn't freak the hell out of the blonde woman by demanding to be introduced to her, that was a bad idea. It would be a one-way ticket to being the talk of the town. And making the woman the talk of the town, too.

As much as he loved his home, he couldn't think of any worse fate for a visitor to Hideaway. Telepathic gossip moved faster than light; everywhere she went, she'd be the subject of whispers she couldn't even hear.

No. He couldn't do that to her.

Not to his mate.

# 3

# LAINIE

"No. Yes. No, I—" Lainie broke off with an exasperated sigh. "I've arranged to meet with a local builder tomorrow, to look at the house while I see what needs to be done to complete a survey of the land. No, this isn't *work* work, this is a personal project, I won't be billing it—yes, I know the report for the Morrison account is due on Monday. The report's on your desk. In the yellow folder. Yes, that one."

Lainie rubbed her forehead as her manager launched into another bullet-pointed lecture on the other end of the phone.

It was times like this that Lainie really, truly wished for one of those old-fashioned landline phones. One of the ones you could slam down. Throwing her cell phone down just didn't have the same cathartic effect, especially since she had to be careful not to break the screen. There was no way she could deal with a phone repair bill on top of everything else right now… though she might have to anyway, given how patchy the reception had been. It was as though her phone had started dying the moment she set foot in Hideaway Cove.

She waited until her boss hung up and settled for throwing herself down on the bed instead. The thick down coverlet enveloped her like a cloud, muffling her frustrated scream.

She'd taken a day of paid leave for the drive to Hideaway, damn it. Maybe she should have "accidentally" left her phone in her apartment, as well. This trip was going to be hard enough without her needy boss calling every half-hour.

Then again, reassuring her manager that the world wasn't going to fall down if Lainie spent one day away from her desk was a *great* distraction from actually dealing with her feelings about returning to Hideaway Cove.

Her grandmother was dead. Lainie's last relative on her father's side. And Lainie still hadn't figured out how she felt about it.

Oh, she knew how she felt about all the stuff *surrounding* her grandmother's death. The inheritance. The bureaucracy. The endless, maddening meetings with lawyers. It all made her so angry, she could scream.

The thing that made her stomach twist was that she didn't know what she felt behind the anger. Once all the legal headaches were over, how would she feel about her grandmother's death?

Lainie knew she should be grieving, but Iris Eaves hadn't been a part of Lainie's life for fifteen years. Lainie had tried to reach out to her again after she graduated high school, but that hadn't ended well.

She might as well have been dead the whole time. And now that she actually was…

Lainie groaned and closed her eyes. Now that she was dead… it was kind of a relief.

She swore quietly. *Wow. Some loving granddaughter you are.*

Maybe she would be able to mourn for her later. Maybe when the creditors had been appeased, Lainie would have time to grieve her grandmother's death, and the wasted relationship they never had.

Or maybe by the time everything was settled, the whole ordeal would have soured any good feelings she had left for that half of her family.

Lainie sighed and turned her phone off. Not just screen-locked, but *off*. She'd spent what was left of the afternoon catching up on work calls and emails and playing phone chicken with her grandmother's lawyer. She knew she should call the storage company where her grandmother's furniture was being held, but she couldn't face that right now. She deserved a few hours off. She *needed* it.

And she needed dinner.

Lainie rolled over and grabbed a pile of glossy leaflets from the bedside table. It was only a small pile—Hideaway Cove was one of those places that had just one of everything. One guesthouse, one gastropub, one corner shop.

*Cute, but surely it gets boring after a while? What if you didn't like what the restaurant served—or what if the people who ran it didn't like you?*

She leafed through ads for an ice cream parlor, boat hire and one of those crystals-and-candles wellness center before she found what she was looking for. Caro's Hook and Sinker, Hideaway Cove's famous, local, and *only* restaurant.

Her stomach growled at the plates of food pictured on the front of the leaflet.

*Well, if it's the only restaurant to survive in the town, it must be good,* Lainie told herself, and grabbed her purse.

The salt air struck her as she stepped outside. She waved goodbye to Mrs. Hanson through the big bay windows at the front of the B&B. The old woman smiled cheerfully back at her.

Mrs. Hanson looked like she was in her eighties, but had wrestled Lainie's bag up the stairs to her room as though she was half that, ignoring Lainie's protests that she could carry her own luggage.

*It must be the sea air,* Lainie thought, breathing it in. *Isn't sea air meant to be good for you? Or is it just that all this salt acts as a preservative…*

Lainie let her mind wander as she walked along the main street to Caro's Hook and Sinker. She had the leaflet with her, in case she needed to check the little map on the back, but soon realized she wouldn't need it. Hideaway Cove was almost ridiculously tiny: one main street along the waterfront, with a few roads leading back toward the hill that edged the inlet. Mrs. Hanson's B&B was right at the end of one of these, practically wedged into the side of the hill. The Hook and Sinker was on the main road. Lainie just had to keep walking until she hit it.

It was a calm evening, and Lainie wasn't the only person out walking. She exchanged smiles and greetings with a young family and an old couple.

*This isn't so bad,* she told herself. *Probably no one here even remembers me. And so what if they did?*

Lainie tried to ignore the flutter of anxiety that twisted her stomach every time she caught sight of someone new. Ever since she'd realized she would have to go back to Hideaway Cove to look after her grandmother's belongings, she had been haunted by the ridiculous fear that everyone in the town would remember her. The girl whose grandparents threw her out of town.

*Stupid.* She shouldn't let what happened fifteen years ago affect her so much. Even if her family had been the subject of town gossip once, surely that was all water under the bridge by now.

A burst of music interrupted Lainie's moody thoughts, and she looked up to see the sign for the Hook and Sinker right in front of her.

The pub was an old wood and stone building, with heavy-duty storm shutters around all the windows. Golden light poured through the windows and the open door, and Lainie stepped through into a warm cacophony of music, laughter, and the smell of food cooking.

There was a momentary hush as people turned to look at her but, to her relief, they just glanced at her and then returned to their meals and conversation.

The place was busy, but not crowded. Lainie looked around for a table, and then paused—was this a sit-down-then-order sort of place, or order-at-the-bar?

She glanced across at the bar and caught the eye of the woman working behind it.

"Grab a seat!" the woman hollered, waving a dishtowel at an empty table in a far corner. She was stocky and deeply tanned, in her forties, with a shocking scar across one cheek. "Be with you in a tick!"

Lainie made her way through the room to the empty table, surreptitiously looking around at the other diners as she did so. There were maybe twenty people scattered around the comfortable chairs and tables, tucking into plates piled high with seafood and crusty bread rolls.

*And I don't recognize any of them.* Lainie let out a quick sigh of relief as she sat down. Old memories flickered up from those long-ago summers she had spent in Hideaway. She had spent most of her time with her grandparents in their house up on the hill, and swimming in the small beach below their house, rather than exploring the town itself. As a result, she didn't actually remember much of the townspeople.

*Let me think…* There had been the ice cream shop, and the awful old woman who ran it. Would it still be here? Lainie could only hope the old woman wasn't still working there. The sour look on her face as she served eleven-year-old Lainie had almost curdled her ice cream.

"There you are!"

Lainie blinked as the woman from behind the bar plonked a jug of water and a folded menu in front of her. She leaned her hip against Lainie's table, looking down at her with a friendly smile that made her scar twist.

"Hi, I'm Caro. It's not often we get visitors… I mean at this time of year. I hope you like seafood, because that's most of what we do here. Regular fish, shellfish, chowders…"

"I'll have the chowder, thanks," Lainie said quickly. She hoped Caro couldn't hear her stomach gurgling.

"Great choice. And anything to drink? I recommend the Blueskin Bay Chardonnay with the clam chowder."

"That sounds lovely, thanks."

"Not a problem." The woman grinned, hollered Lainie's order over her shoulder to the kitchen behind the bar, and didn't move from her perch on the edge of Lainie's table. "Have I seen you here before? There's something about you that looks familiar. You have family around here, or something? How long are you in town for?"

"Just overnight," Lainie said, returning Caro's smile with a nervous one of her own. "I've got some business to look after, and then I'm headed back to the city." She hoped Caro wouldn't notice that she hadn't answered the question about her family.

Caro raised her eyebrows. "That's a long way to drive just to stay overnight!"

"I have to get back for work," Lainie explained with a tight shrug. "You know how it is…"

*Or maybe not,* she thought, glancing around the room. Most of the people in here probably worked in the town, or on the boats moored out in the small marina. They were eating heartily, but without the furtive, stressed speed that Lainie was familiar with from back home. *If any of them are stressing with one ear out to hear the phone ring and deal with a new client, I'll eat my hat.*

"Well, ain't that a shame," said Caro with another grin. "I hope you have a chance to check out the ice cream parlor down by the water before you go. It's Hideaway's best-kept secret."

That seemed to be all Caro wanted to know; after the smallest amount of more small talk, she swaggered back behind her bar.

Lainie's meal arrived a few minutes later, brought out by one of a pair of waitresses she'd seen flitting around the room. They both looked as though they were in their late teens, probably working at the restaurant as a part-time job after school.

The one who sauntered up with Lainie's chowder and glass of wine was wearing long feather earrings that looked as though they came from some sort of gull. They flipped back and forth over her shoulders as she walked.

"I hope you enjoy it," the waitress said with a smile as she put down the bowl of chowder in front of Lainie. "Jess 'n' me brought in the clams yesterday—nice, eh?"

"It looks delicious," Lainie said truthfully. The steam wafting off the bowl of chowder made her mouth water. The waitress beamed, and Lainie added on a sudden friendly impulse, "I like your earrings."

"Thanks, they're mine," the girl said breezily, and then froze. She clapped one hand over her mouth, eyes wide, and fled.

Lainie stared after her, flabbergasted. *Was it something I said?* she thought. *No, don't be silly. The poor girl is probably just mortified about sounding silly in front of a new customer. "They're mine"—who else's would they be?*

Biting her lip to keep herself from giggling—she didn't want to embarrass the girl even more—Lainie picked up her spoon. It had been a long day, and she was more than ready for dinner.

As she looked down at her bowl, the back of her neck prickled.

A lifetime of being the chubby girl at school had given Lainie a sixth sense for when she was being watched. Particularly during meals. These days she knew how to dress to flatter her figure, and how to do her hair so that it fell in straight waves rather than a flyaway cloud, but she still got twitchy when she felt people watching her eat. Like now.

*Well, screw them. As long as no one tips creamed corn in my hair, they can stare all they like.*

Lainie dipped her spoon in the creamy chowder and glanced sideways. She didn't look at the other diners directly, but at the window beside her table, which reflected the room like a mirror.

The reflection in the window wasn't the clearest, but she could still see half-a-dozen pairs of eyes gleaming at her from the glass.

Lainie's stomach clenched.

*Stop it,* she told herself. *They're just nosy because you're new in town. It doesn't mean anything.*

Behind her, the restaurant door opened, letting in a gust of wind. Luckily, whoever was walking in also distracted Lainie's audience. With the pressure of their eyes gone, Lainie breathed a sigh of relief and put the spoonful of chowder in her mouth at last.

It was as delicious as it smelled, rich and creamy and thick. Lainie closed her eyes, savoring the flavor. That was one downside of living away from the coast: nothing beat really fresh seafood.

She dug in, only vaguely paying attention to the rest of the room. Behind her, whoever had just come in was holding what sounded like at least three conversations, occasionally punctuated by cheerful greetings as he saw people he knew around the restaurant.

"You can't tell me that—hey, Carter, how's things?—this sort of thing hasn't happened before. And maybe she's got some connection with this place, or—evening, Guts, great to see you on your feet again—I mean, sure, maybe it's just chance that brought her here, but…"

His voice trailed off. Lainie, still intent on her dinner, felt a strange regret. The man's voice was deep and rich, and just… nice to listen to. Like smooth, warm chocolate.

She thought, briefly, that she would have liked to be one of the people he was talking to with such casual friendliness.

She glanced back over her shoulder, hoping to catch a glimpse of the man with the gorgeous voice. He was facing away from her, leaning over another table and talking with the family seated around it in a low voice, too quiet for her to eavesdrop.

He was tall, with broad shoulders that stretched the back of his faded flannel shirt. He wore it with the sleeves rolled up over his tanned forearms, which Lainie had a great view of as he leaned one hand on the back of a chair.

And so far as Lainie could tell, the person he'd been talking to when he came in… was a dog.

A big dog, with thick black hair, a sharp muzzle, and inquisitive blue eyes. Man's best friend, sure, but not the type of friend you'd expect to hold an in-depth conversation with.

Lainie blinked. The dog stared back at her with its wet dark eyes and whuffed quietly.

Its owner turned around. Lainie jerked, intending to return to her meal and pretend she'd never been sneaking a look at anyone, certainly not him—but he caught her eye before she managed to move.

His eyes were a warm hazel, with deep smile lines at the corners. He was tanned and clean-shaven, with no beard or stubble to hide his strong jaw and sensitive mouth. As he caught Lainie's eye, a surprised smile spread across his face.

She mustered a weak grin in return and turned back to her chowder.

He was still looking at her. She didn't need to look in the window to know that.

*I can't believe he caught me staring at him,* she thought, her cheeks getting hot. *I hope the waitress saw that. At least it would let her know she's not the only one to embarrass herself tonight.*

There were footsteps behind her, the clink of workman's boots on wooden floorboards. Then the scrape of a chair. Lainie looked up.

The man who'd caught her staring was standing beside her table, the surprised smile still playing on his lips.

"Mind if I join you?" he asked, in that gorgeous voice.

# 4

# HARRISON

Her eyes were a dark brown, almost black. They stood out like coals against her blonde hair and pale skin. As she looked up at him, they widened with shock—narrowed with suspicion—and, finally, flicked away from him.

"Sure, go ahead," she said, her cheeks going pink. She put her spoon down and rested her hands on the edge of the table, watching him out of the corner of her eye.

Harrison slid into a chair opposite her. His heart was pounding. This was the woman he'd seen earlier, in the car. She'd sent him reeling then, and that had been from ten feet away, through the windshield. Right here, right now, she was close enough that he could reach out and touch her. His head was spinning.

"I'm Harrison," he said, forcing back the impulse to hold her hand and kiss it instead of shaking it like a normal person. *And you're the most beautiful woman I've ever seen.*

"Lainie. Lainie Eaves."

Lainie Eaves. Harrison reached out to shake her hand, focusing with his shifter senses at the same time. Lainie Eaves: beautiful eyes, soft hands, and not a hint of shifter about her. She was human.

Harrison released her hand and settled back into his chair. Lainie being human didn't matter to him. He already knew she was perfect just the way she was.

He nodded to her bowl. "I guess Caro's already given you the welcome speech?"

Lainie bit her lip, but the hint of a smile edged its way through. "Chowder and ice cream? Oh, and it's a shame I'm only staying overnight. Does that cover it?"

"You're only staying overnight? Caro's right, that is a shame." Harrison spoke without thinking, and with too much undisguised passion in his voice. Lainie glanced up at him, her eyes questioning. "I mean there's more to Hideaway Cove than just chowder and ice cream. If you were here longer—"

"I really won't be." Lainie spoke so quickly, she almost tripped over her words. Harrison frowned slightly as she took a sip of wine, giving herself time to recover.

*That's strange. There's something more going on there, I'm sure of it.*

*Then again, there's more to Hideaway Cove than chowder and ice cream, too. Much more.*

Harrison glanced down at where Arlo was sitting patiently on the floor beside the table. The wolf shifter stared back at him. Harrison didn't need to use his shifter telepathy to understand the message behind *that* look.

"Caro," he called, waving over the heads of the restaurant's other patrons to get her attention. "My usual? And, uhh, the mutt's usual, too…"

He could see Caro rolling her eyes even from across the room. When he leaned back in his chair, Lainie was hiding another smile.

"Your dog has a usual?"

"Oh, sure," Harrison said, inventing wildly. "Usually everyone else's leftovers, mashed up and stuck in a washing-up tub. You wouldn't believe how much the old mongrel eats."

He grinned down at Arlo, who gave him the most disgusted look his wolf form was capable of.

**You owe me, Harrison,** the wolf shifter grumbled silently.

"What is he? He looks kinda…" Lainie frowned. Harrison didn't blame her. Arlo looked like what he was: a giant, black-gray wolf. At the moment, after a full day out on his fishing boat, a giant, black-gray, salt-encrusted wolf.

"Oh, he's a bit of everything, aren't you, old boy? Husky, German Shepherd, a bit of Pomeranian…"

*Asshole.*

"He's very well behaved."

Harrison leaned down and ruffled Arlo's ears with a wicked grin. "Isn't he? Good boy, waiting for your din-dins." He nodded at Lainie's plate. "Don't let me keep you from your dinner. I'm happy to yammer on while you eat."

"No, I'm fine," Lainie demurred. She was only halfway through her bowl of chowder, which Harrison knew by long experience was mouth-wateringly good, but she pushed it away firmly. "So… you live here in Hideaway Cove?"

"I've got a place on the water, around the other side of the bay. Lived here for ten years, more or less." Harrison settled into telling the story, which was as familiar as an old sweater. "I grew up out of state and left home after my parents passed away suddenly. I had all these grand ideas about living on the road—the Lone Ranger in a mustang. That lasted until I drove in here, and somehow I never got around to leaving. I did an apprenticeship with the local builder and handyman and took over his business when he passed."

"It sounds like you're here to stay." Lainie played with the stem of her wine-glass, not meeting Harrison's eyes. "I'm sorry to hear about your parents. You didn't have any trouble fitting in here? I mean, you hear about small towns being…"

"…Welcoming, friendly and caring?" Harrison interjected with a laugh. "No, I know some places do have a reputation. But I fitted in to Hideaway Cove like I belonged here. And now, I do."

*It's not like there's anywhere else I can live openly as a shifter.*

After his parents died, Harrison had thought he would have to live constantly on the move, in case someone got too close and he let slip what he was. Instead, he found a place that welcomed him like a lost son.

The arrival of the waitress with Harrison and Arlo's meals interrupted their conversation briefly. Harrison winked at Jools, who grimaced back at him. He'd already heard from Guts about Jools' slip earlier, about her feather earrings. Made from her feathers, of course. Jools was one of four gull shifter sisters, Guts' nieces, all of whom seemed to enjoy making crafts out of their shed feathers.

Harrison raised his pint in a toast. "Here's to your first visit to Hideaway Cove," he said.

Lainie's mouth quirked, as though she was about to say something, but she just smiled and clinked her wine glass against Harrison's.

He tucked into his meal, a triple serving of chowder with a side of pan-fried bass and a sprinkling of salad. Lainie began to pick at her own food, apparently encouraged by his appetite.

The break gave Harrison a chance to think, though thinking in the face of so much of Caro's delicious food was a difficulty at the best of times. With food and his mate in front of him? It was almost impossible.

He glanced down at Arlo, who was making short work of his meal with resigned determination. If Lainie had noticed that the waitress had placed a bowl of prime beef in front of the "dog," she didn't say anything.

In the ten years Harrison had lived in Hideaway, he'd seen maybe a couple of dozen human visitors to the town, not including the regular visits from county officials. Everyone in Hideaway knew to keep the town's secret safe from outsiders. But so far as Harrison knew, no one had ever recognized an outsider as their mate.

If old Mr. Mackaby had still been around, Harrison could have talked to him about it. Arlo thought he should bring it up with Caro, which seemed like a good idea. Until he'd stepped into the restaurant and seen his mate sitting at the window table.

*Lainie.* Lainie Eaves. A beautiful name for a beautiful woman.

Well, so much for Plan A. Plan B—wine and dine a beautiful woman, in the best restaurant in the best town on the coast—was going perfectly.

He didn't want Lainie to think he was staring at her, but he couldn't help shooting quick glances her way. She ate quietly and neatly, with small bites, and Harrison was struck by a sudden vision of them both together, in front of a roaring fire, eating together in the quiet comfort of long familiarity.

His pulse quickened. Beneath his skin, his griffin chirruped with contentment.

For the last ten years, Harrison had felt a hole in his heart. He'd lost both his parents suddenly when he was in his teens, and with them dead, his home—their nest—had lost its soul. He'd left the empty home in the hopes of finding someone to fill that hole.

His parents, both griffin shifters, had had the perfect marriage, and all Harrison wanted out of his life was a mate he could love as his parents had loved one another. To have his mate at his side, in a warm, cozy home he had built with his own hands. Every plank, every nail, every stick of furniture lovingly crafted by him, for her.

A nest, warm, safe and secure.

And this was it. This was *her.*

Maybe it was a good thing he'd met Lainie in person for the first time here, around so many other people. If they'd been on their own, he might have blurted out what he was imagining, and left her thinking he was drunk, insane, or both.

Harrison took a deep breath, bracing himself. He was lucky his griffin had always been a placid creature, content for him to spend most of his time in human form, even here where people were free to take their animal forms whenever they pleased. Even now, meeting his mate, it was happy for him to take the lead.

Given what he'd heard about other shifters' reactions when they met their mates, he was glad. There were so many curious eyes on the two of them as they ate. A more aggressive shifter might have taken offense. He didn't want Lainie's first impression of him to be 'that guy who picked me up in his talons and spirited me away to his lair'.

Not that he had a lair, unless the rooms above his workshop counted.

Lainie cleared her throat, instantly getting Harrison's attention.

"So, I guess you don't get many visitors here?" Lainie's expression was neutral, but her gaze flicked to the window, which reflected the room. Harrison didn't need to look around to see his friends and neighbors sneaking glances at the two of them. He didn't blame Lainie for feeling unsettled.

"Not a lot," he said. It was only a small white lie. Hideaway Cove did see some tourists, hence the existence of the solitary B&B. But they were all shifters, friends or family of the people who lived here already. A human visitor was as rare as hen's teeth. Or as rare as a griffin shifter, maybe.

Lainie slumped almost imperceptibly. Harrison noticed her eyes darken, as though she was resigning herself to her status as the object of the other townspeople's keen interest.

Harrison leaned forward, smiling conspiratorially. "Want to get out of the spotlight? I can give you a private tour of the town, if you like. You won't be able to see much in the dark, but the lights on the water are worth a look."

This time, Lainie was too slow to catch the smile that darted across her lips. "Are you sure? I don't want to intrude."

"Accepting an invitation is hardly intruding," Harrison argued gently. His heart glowed as Lainie smiled, the last traces of her reluctance melting away like sea-mist in the sunlight.

"All right," she said. "If you insist! I'll just settle my bill."

"No need. I'll let Caro know to add it to my tab." Lainie looked like she was about to protest, so Harrison raised his hands in a gesture of surrender—and refused to back down. "You're my guest! Please, let me make up for my dog stinking up your dinner."

*Hey, man, that's not fair!*

"Oh, your dog isn't…" Lainie shook herself, and held up her hands in mock defeat. "Okay. Thank you. That's very kind of you, even though we both know your dog isn't stinking up anything."

Her dark eyes flashed at Harrison as she gathered up her purse and coat, sending shivers down his spine. He caught Caro's eye across the room.

*Add her bill to mine, will you, Caro?*

He didn't wait for Caro's response. Lainie was struggling with her coat and he leaped up to help her into it.

By the time he realized his mistake, it was too late. He was already standing behind her, the soft wool of her coat in his hands and the scent of her body in his nostrils. She was wearing a floral perfume, but he could just smell the real her underneath the artificial scent.

Harrison closed his eyes, biting back a groan. Steeling himself, he quickly slipped the coat over Lainie's shoulders and stepped back.

"Thanks," said Lainie.

Was it his imagination, or did she sound slightly breathless?

# 5

# LAINIE

Lainie caught her breath. She could still feel the memory of Harrison's hands on her shoulders. They had only rested there for a split second, but that had been enough to set her heart pounding. She looked back at him over her shoulder as she did up the buttons of her coat.

"Thanks," she said. Harrison gave her a brief smile, pushing his hands into his pockets. "Do you have a coat?"

He laughed softly. "I don't feel the cold. Shirtsleeves unless it's snowing, that's me."

Lainie shivered at the thought. "Does it snow here?" she asked as they walked to the door. She could still feel eyes on her back, and a knot of worry formed in her stomach. *Is walking out of here with a guy I just met really the best way to prevent people gossiping about me?*

Well, it was too late to back out now. And besides, she didn't *want* to back out. She couldn't remember the last time a guy had shown any interest in her, let alone been so obvious about it. And gentlemanly.

*Maybe I don't have to make* every *decision based on what I think other people think I should do,* she thought firmly.

Another thought struck her as Harrison held the door open.

"Oh—what about your dog?"

Harrison slapped his hand to his forehead and looked back to where his dog was sitting patiently by their table. The dog stared back.

"Uh, he'll be fine here. Caro will look after him."

"Oh." The knot in Lainie's stomach grew a few extra tangles. "Are you and Caro…?" *And if you are, have I just totally got the wrong signals off you right now?*

"Me and—? Oh, no. I mean, the dog isn't really my dog. He's sort of the town stray. We all look after him. And I know he'd prefer snoozing in front of the fire in here tonight over curling up under my workbench back home."

*Well, that sounds at least somewhat believable.* She took one last look at the dog sitting forlornly by their table. Except he wasn't sitting forlornly anymore. He'd made his way to the next table and was enduring a head-scratch from a screeching toddler in exchange for the kid's leftovers.

Beside her, Harrison snorted. "Scrounger."

Lainie laughed. She hadn't noticed before, but the dog wasn't wearing a collar. That, along with its generally bedraggled appearance, and the way it didn't seem to even notice Harrison was leaving, were enough proof for her that Harrison wasn't trying to pull the wool over her eyes.

"So, where to first?" she asked, stepping out into the brisk night air.

Dusk had been falling when Lainie arrived at the restaurant, and by now, night had truly fallen. The streets were empty.

*Everyone must be either at home, or behind us in the restaurant,* Lainie thought.

Lainie pushed her hands into her coat pockets. The breeze coming off the water was chillier than she had expected when she packed for her overnight trip.

*But it wasn't like I was expecting to go on a moonlit walk along the waterfront when I was picking out clothes,* she thought, suddenly giddy. She looked up at the night sky. No moon stared back. *Well. A starlit walk, at least.*

"Beautiful, isn't it?" Harrison stepped up beside her on the sidewalk. "You wouldn't believe we had a massive storm only a few days ago."

"Really?" Lainie asked. "I haven't seen a cloud in the sky all day."

"Sure. They come down quickly at this time of year. That one dumped so much water on us, I was worried the whole town would float out to sea."

Lainie looked around. The sky was clear, and bright with stars; around her, what she could see of the surrounding buildings by the light of the streetlamps looked undamaged. "There wasn't any damage, I hope?"

"Oh, we have enough storms this time of year that any buildings that were going to slip off their foundations would have done it years ago. The worst that happened was a fuse blew in the ice cream parlor."

"Sounds tragic!"

"It very nearly was," Harrison agreed solemnly. "Luckily, my team was ready to spring into action."

"Your team?"

"I run a—well, I guess you'd call it a Jack-of-all-trades workshop. I told you I took over the local building company? Well, apart from me, there's Pol, our local electrician, and Arlo, who you—uh, who looks after any boat work that needs doing. He runs the storage facility you must've driven past on your way into town, too."

"Sounds like between you, you keep this town running," Lainie said.

"Oh, I wouldn't go that far. There are more important town institutions. Caro's chowder, for one."

"A town that runs on chowder? I can believe that, it was probably the best I've ever tasted. And thanks for reminding me, I'll need to make time to see your friend Arlo tomorrow, about a storage container." Lainie swept her hair back behind one ear. "So—what's the first stop on this tour?"

"A storage container?" Harrison's eyes lit up. "I've gotta say, the words 'storage container' and 'only staying one night' don't sound like they go together. Are you sure you're not planning on staying around?"

Lainie twisted her automatic grimace into a smile. *Stay in Hideaway? Never.* "Well, I wasn't planning on it," she said lightly.

Harrison winked at her. "All right. Anyway, I thought we'd start on the northern end of the bay, seeing as we're almost there already, and head south. That way we'll end up close to Mrs. Hanson's B&B. That's where you're staying, isn't it?"

"You know, some people might call that a bit creepy," Lainie said, laughing. "Have you been stalking me?"

Harrison grimaced. "Sorry, I didn't even think about that. I'm so used to Mrs. Hanson's being the only place anyone stays."

"It's a lovely little place," Lainie said, thinking of the airy room Mrs. Hanson had put her in, with the picture-window overlooking the town and, beyond, the water. "And reasonable rates, too, given she's got the monopoly on tourist accommodation in the town."

"Don't let her hear that—she'll get ideas." Harrison laughed.

They walked together for a while in silence. Harrison led Lainie along the broad sidewalk at the seaward side of the main road. A low stone rail separated the path from the water, which splashed against the retaining wall. Occasional stone steps led down to the water, and as they walked, the water retreated, pushed back by a pebbly beach.

Lainie kept her eyes on the ocean. After the beach, she knew, the hill on which her grandparents' house stood rose up like a knuckle from the protected bay.

"Here we are," said Harrison suddenly, and for one moment Lainie thought he was talking about the road up to her grandparents' house. Her heart hammered in her chest, even after she saw that he was waving his hand at a small building nestled against the sea wall.

"What—oh!" Lainie chuckled. "The famous ice cream parlor?"

"The one and only."

Lainie looked at the small shop. It was just as she remembered it: wooden walls, tile roof, and wooden fretwork around the eaves and under the windowsills. Like it had jumped off the pages of a storybook.

It was closed, of course, the windows shuttered and a curtain drawn across the inside of the front door.

"I'll have to see if I can make room in my schedule for it," Lainie lied. If there was any chance the place was still run by the old lady she remembered from her childhood, there was no way she was coming back here when it was open.

Harrison stuck his hands into his trouser pockets, staring out onto the water.

"What did you say it was brought you out here, again? I don't mean to pry, but although we might not get many visitors, they do usually stay longer than overnight. And they don't usually prioritize storage containers over ice cream."

"It's a long drive for a short visit," Lainie agreed. Her mind raced. Should she tell him? "It's… family business," she said in the end. "Just some loose ends I have to tie up."

"You've got family here?" Harrison sounded surprised, but more than that—excited, as well.

"Sort of. Not anymore." Lainie shrugged. "My grandparents, on my father's side, used to live here. They've both passed now."

"I'm sorry," Harrison said. Lainie just shrugged again.

"It's okay. We were never—we weren't close. My mom brought me up."

Lainie couldn't help glancing up the hill at the old house. From here, it was practically invisible against the dark shadows of the hill, and the black sky. Only a few straight lines in the shadows hinted at something man-made up there.

Lainie turned her back on it and started walking back along the sidewalk. She made herself walk slowly. *Not like you're running away. Which you're not. The whole point of coming here was to return to the house. Just… not right now. Tomorrow.*

Harrison kept pace with her. "I'm sorry," he said again, his voice low. "I didn't mean to pry."

"Don't worry about it." Lainie flashed a grin at him. "It's old news, really. Water under the bridge."

For a few minutes, there was nothing but the sound of waves lapping against the shoreline, and the distant murmur of voices spilling out of the restaurant. Lainie relaxed. She was aware of Harrison's presence beside her, but it wasn't a prickly, uncomfortable awareness, like all those eyes back at the restaurant. Even his silence was comforting.

"You were right," she said after a while.

"I was? About what?" Harrison sounded genuinely confused, and Lainie pinched back a giggle.

"About the lights."

The bay stretched out ahead of them. The land curved around the water like a sleeping cat, a patchwork of gold and yellow lights gleaming out through house windows and from streetlights. The light reflected on the constantly moving water, shimmering in the darkness. The water was black, blending into the sky in the distance. The lights moved on its surface, glimmering as though they were coming from deep below the waves, instead of from the houses nestled around it.

"It looks beautiful."

"I'll let Pol know you said so," Harrison said. Lainie frowned before she remembered: Pol, the electrician who worked for Harrison.

Was it her imagination, or was there a hint of jealousy in Harrison's voice?

She glanced sidelong at him in time to catch a fleeting self-deprecatory grimace flit across his face. She *hadn't* imagined it.

"You can't tell me one man is responsible for *all* the lighting in the town," she said, needling him. "Doesn't the municipal council have any-thing to do with that? Anyway, what about you? You said you're the builder around here—does that mean all the buildings in town are your handiwork?"

She watched Harrison as she spoke, still out of the corners of her eyes. He smiled to himself, deep creases forming along his cheeks.

"I wish I could say yes," he admitted. "But there isn't much call for new builds here. Mainly just keeping the old buildings from falling apart."

"And floating into the sea, right?"

"Funny you should say that right now," he said. He stopped and took her arm. "See that house over there?"

Lainie forced herself to look where he was pointing. She was acutely aware of his hand on her arm—and the rest of him, so close to her. His bare, tanned arms, and the movement of hard muscles under the worn fabric of his shirt.

The top button of his shirt was half-undone. It must have been working its way loose as they walked. A curl of brown hair poked out from under it. It was hard to tell in the light of the streetlamps, but Lainie thought it might be a shade darker than the hair on his head. Like his tanned skin, his hair must have been lightened by a summer spent working outdoors…

Lainie shook herself, trying to escape the vision her imagination had called up. Harrison, working on a construction site under the blazing sun. Shirtless. Sweat running down his forehead, and along the hard curves of his chest.

"Um," she said, her mouth dry. *Get a grip!*

She frowned, and squinted along Harrison's arm—*Don't look* at *his arm, come on, keep it together*—to try and make out the house he was pointing at. The houses along here were set down and back from the road, at the edge of what looked in the darkness like a shared yard.

"Which house, sorry?"

"Next along from the colonial with the French doors. With the cat parked out front."

Lainie's frown grew deeper. *The cat…?* All she could see was a single-level weatherboard house with a small boat tethered to the front porch.

Oh. Cat. *Catamaran.*

"I see it," she said, blushing.

"Notice anything strange about it?" Harrison was practically glowing with smug anticipation.

Lainie stared. She'd assumed the small boat—the catamaran—was grounded on the front yard, but now that she really looked at it, it seemed to be rocking up and down. She followed the black patch of "yard" towards the road and saw the light from the streetlamp playing on it.

"That's all water! So, what, the house is on stilts?"

"And here I thought I'd get the fun of explaining it to you," Harrison said, groaning. He walked ahead, beckoning to her. "See—there's a small lagoon here that goes back from the road. Easy to see in the daylight, but not so much at night."

"Can the catamaran—uh, the cat fit under the road? I mean, the bridge?"

"With the mast down, sure."

"And the house doesn't float away on the tide?"

"Not recently." Harrison's teeth caught the light as he smiled at her. "This was my first build after I finished my apprenticeship. The house had come off its foundations in a big storm, so my boss, Mr. Mackaby, tasked me with getting it fixed up to the owner's satisfaction."

Harrison leaned on the stone wall at the edge of the road above the lagoon. It was clear he was proud of what he'd achieved. Lainie slipped in beside him, standing just close enough that the hem of her coat brushed against him.

"I imagine if you owned a boat, being able to moor it right at the front door would be pretty ideal," she said.

Harrison's face was in shadows, but his hazel eyes caught the light, gleaming gold. "My boss agreed. Which is a good thing, because that was his house." He paused. "His daughter lives there now, with her husband and the kids. So I better hope I did a good job, or he'll come back and haunt me."

"Still getting annual work reviews from beyond the grave? Ouch."

"Well, if it does happen, I'll just have to make sure to keep his ghostly attention on Marcie's house, and not his old workshop. He'd really blow a gasket if he saw what I've done to the place."

"Oh?" Lainie was intrigued. Harrison spoke about his old boss with such fond respect, she was surprised to hear he had gone against his wishes.

"Yeah." Harrison looked sheepish. "It's meant to just be a workplace, but I spent so much time there the first few years after I took over, I ended up moving in. Boss always liked to keep work and home separate, but..." He shrugged.

"I know how you feel. I can't count the nights I would have rather pulled out a cot bed and slept under my desk than hauled myself all the way home," Lainie said. "Mind you, I expect you're less likely to get stuck in the middle of a subway breakdown here than back home."

"We have very few subway breakdowns here, true," Harrison said solemnly. "Not having any public transport helps, of course." He paused. "Would you like to see it?"

"Your workshop?" Lainie bit her lip. *Is he saying what I think he's saying?* "...Now?"

Lainie glanced sideways at Harrison. He was staring wide-eyed out at the lagoon. A look of faint horror spread across his face, as though he'd just realized what he'd said and was desperate to reel the words back in.

"I mean... Oh, God. That came out all wrong," he said, sounding mortified.

"It came out wrong, but you did mean to say it?" The words came out before Lainie could stop them. Now they were *both* blushing.

A warm glow kindled inside Lainie, overriding the hot blush of embarrassment on her cheeks. She turned so she was looking at Harrison straight on. No more sidelong glances.

The streetlamp was behind him, lighting up the stretched fabric of his shirt and his broad, powerful shoulders. Somehow, the knowledge that he'd built those muscles from manual labor, not hitting the gym, made them all the more attractive to Lainie. He seemed solid, strong and reliable. His slight self-consciousness only made him more attractive, like he didn't realize how good-looking he really was.

The light back-lit his brown hair, and the strip of tanned skin between his hairline and collar. That top button was still holding out. Lainie itched to pull it free.

*And why not?*

Hadn't he basically just asked her back to his place?

Harrison turned toward her, and the light hit his face. His eyes were bright and searching, staring deep into her own. Had he been watching her watch him, when his face was in the shadows?

"Yes. I did mean what I said, even if I didn't mean to say it quite like that," he said softly. Hesitantly, he raised one hand and brushed a loose strand of hair behind Lainie's ear.

"I thought small-towners were meant to be conservative about this sort of thing," she teased, her light tone masking the buzz of anticipation racing through her veins.

"Well." Harrison drew out the word, his hand lingering at the side of Lainie's face. "I'm not from around here, after all."

Lainie sank into his eyes, bewitched by the flickers of green, brown and gold. *Like fall,* she thought, *and I'm falling right in.*

She stepped forward and found herself in his arms, cocooned in warmth. Harrison spread his hands out across her back, holding her close, and tipped her head up to meet his lips with her own.

Harrison kissed her, gently at first and then with a controlled passion that told her how much he was still holding back. Lainie's whole body tingled, from the soles of her feet to her scalp.

She raised her hands, meaning to sweep them up his chest and over his shoulders, but stopped just short of his collarbones. Her finger snagged on the half-undone button, pulling it free.

Lainie let her hand slip down, hooking her finger over the next button. Harrison mumbled something against her lips and she broke the kiss to find him looking down at her, his eyes dark with desire.

His eyes flickered down to his shirt, and back to Lainie's. "Planning to drag me away?"

"You have to tell me where to drag you, first. Honestly, this tour isn't very good, is it?"

Harrison slapped his hand to his forehead. "You're right!" he said, feigning shock. "I guess I'll have to do the dragging away, huh?"

Lainie burst out laughing, and to her delight, Harrison laughed, too. Her whole body was tingling, her skin sensitized and desperate to be touched. She'd never felt like this with anyone before. Oh, attraction, that was one thing, but she'd never felt so comfortable around someone she'd only just met. So willing to let her attraction blossom into something more.

They were joking together. He'd made her laugh, a lot, when she'd expected to spend the whole trip miserable. This was crazy—but she was actually enjoying herself. A lot.

And she anticipated enjoying herself a lot more in the near future.

Harrison held out his hand to her and—only slightly regretfully—Lainie unhooked her finger from his shirt and took it.

"Shall we?"

Lainie didn't answer. She just squeezed his hand, unable to wipe the smile off her face, and followed him along the path.

Harrison's hand was much bigger than hers, and callused from his work. As they walked toward his house, their hands were the only parts of them that touched. Lainie's lips were still burning from the kiss, and electricity seemed to zap from them, to her hand, and back, until she wanted nothing more than to pull Harrison into a quiet corner and drag his mouth to hers again.

No. There was *one* thing she wanted more. And it wasn't something she wanted to do in the middle of the main road.

They came to a stop outside a two-storied building. A sign hung above the door, but it was too dark for Lainie to read it. By now it was cold enough that she could see her breath.

But, oh, she was so warm inside.

"This is it," Harrison said. He sounded more nervous than Lainie had expected.

She raised one eyebrow. "*This is it?* Because I was kind of expecting we'd make our way indoors…"

Nerves apparently defused, Harrison grinned at her as he unlocked the door and held it open. She stepped across the threshold, her pulse quickening.

The first thing she noticed about Harrison's house was the smell. It wasn't a bad smell—quite the opposite. Lainie inhaled deeply, trying to place the scent.

Of course—he was a builder, wasn't he? And this was his workshop. Wood shavings, a hint of old smoke, and the faintest, lingering chemical tang of turpentine and paint. The same smells as any of a dozen worksites she'd been on during her work as a planner. Familiar. Comforting.

And without the inevitable thick mud tracked over every surface, which was her least favorite part of site visits.

"May I take your coat?"

Lainie looked over her shoulder to see Harrison closing the door. She nodded, and a few moments later, his polite gesture somehow found the two of them in each other's arms, her coat forgotten on the floor.

Lainie let out a soft cry as Harrison wound his fingers through her hair, clutching her to him. Her skin was on fire. The silk of her blouse was so thin she could feel every touch of Harrison's body through it, but at the same time it was still a frustrating barrier between her skin and his.

She grabbed the bottom of Harrison's shirt and pulled it up, revealing his flat stomach and hard abs. His hip-bones made a V that disappeared under his belt, inviting further investigation.

Lainie ran her hands over Harrison's abs, and he drew his breath in with a hiss. He let her go long enough to pull his shirt over his head and throw it to the side, then pulled her to him again.

Lainie batted his hands away. He looked at her, momentarily confused, but his face cleared as she stripped off her blouse. She stood in front of him, chest heaving, in nothing but her pants and bra.

"God, you're so beautiful," he breathed. His eyes swept up and down her body, as though he couldn't get enough of looking at her. She took the opportunity to return the compliment.

Harrison was toned all over. Hard pecs, six-pack—and that tantalizing V. He wore his jeans low on his hips. Back in the restaurant, Lainie had admired how his ass looked in them. Now she was looking forward to seeing them on the floor.

The air between them seemed to hum with electricity. Lainie reached out, half expecting to see sparks flash from her fingertips to Harrison's chest. She threw herself into his arms, pulling him down into a long kiss that left her dizzy.

Harrison's skin was hot against hers. Pressed against him, she could feel his erection pushing against the crotch of his pants. Pressing against *her*. Her desire throbbed inside her in response. She was ready for him.

Harrison buried his face in her hair, his hands exploring up from her waist to her hips. She moaned as he moved up to her breasts, squeezing them gently.

"You don't want to see the rest of the house?" he murmured wickedly in her ear.

She growled, but she couldn't let him get away with teasing her. "Maybe your workshop? I'm assuming it doubles as the bedroom—rollaway bed under the workbench, is it?"

"How did you guess?"

"I bet you built it yourself, too." Lainie gasped as Harrison nibbled on her neck. "Um. Show me now?"

"If you insist…"

Lainie squealed as Harrison put his arms around her waist and slung her over his shoulder. He strode down the hallway, careful to duck through doorways so Lainie didn't hit her head. She was too busy giggling to keep out of their way herself. She got a glimpse of other rooms as Harrison carried her through to the back of the house: a front room with a few sofas and a coffee table stacked with papers; a home office, with a desk also stacked with papers; and finally, his workshop.

"Really?" Lainie blurted out. The workshop was scrupulously tidy, unlike all the other rooms she'd seen, but—still! Besides, there was no sign of a bed, roll-away or otherwise. "I was sort of joking…"

"Is that so?" Harrison kissed her, pushing her backward until she bumped up against a workbench. The bench was high, tailored for Harrison's tall frame. When he picked her up and sat her on it, Lainie's feet dangled in the air.

Harrison ran his hands up her thighs, stopping with his fingertips just short of her crotch. He ran one thumb between her legs, brushing her clit through her pants. Lainie groaned.

"Damn it," she muttered, and wriggled so she could pull her pants down. Harrison helped, sort of, but seemed mainly distracted by the effect all that wriggling had on her cleavage.

"Like what you see?" she said brazenly. The look of amazement in his eyes made her glow inside.

*There are* some *benefits to being curvy,* she thought smugly.

"I like all of you," Harrison said. He grabbed her hand and kissed the palm, then her wrist, moving up her arm to her neck. "Every—part—of—you," he murmured, the words punctuated by kisses.

Lainie caught her breath as he nuzzled her neck, his hands reaching behind her to unlatch her bra. He pulled it off her slowly, stroking the sensitive skin of her breasts as he uncovered them. Lainie arched her back.

"Yes—" she gasped as he brushed one nipple with his thumb. "Oh, yes."

He teased her nipples until they were both hard, and Lainie was almost crazy with desire. She grabbed his belt-buckle and pulled him closer, looking up at him from under her eyelashes.

Harrison's pupils were so wide with desire, his eyes looked black, not hazel. There was only the slightest ring of green-gold around the outside. He let her pull him in, moving his hands to her hips.

Harrison's fingers tightened on her hips as she wrestled with his belt buckle. Once she'd undone it she moved on to his fly. For the first time she got a good look at the bulge between his legs.

She bit her lip. *Damn.*

Harrison must have misinterpreted her hesitation. "We can stop. If you think we're going too fast—"

"No, it's not that." Lainie gave him a shy smile. "It's just... it's been a while." *And you look bigger than any guy I've ever been with before.*

Harrison cupped her face in his hands. "I'll be gentle."

He kissed her as she slowly undid his pants, pushing them and his boxers down over his toned ass. With her eyes closed, still caught up in the kiss, Lainie didn't see his cock—but she could feel it.

She felt Harrison tense as she ran her hands along his shaft. *Oh my God. He is huge.*

His cock was hot in her hands, hard and thick and long. She ran her fingers over its head and Harrison moaned into her mouth.

"Take me," Lainie whispered back.

Her slacks were still half-up her legs. Harrison pulled them down and she kicked them off, along with her ankle boots. She was completely naked, exposed, with a man she had only met a few hours before.

And she wanted it. Wanted *him*, so badly she couldn't find the words for it.

"Now?" Harrison asked, his voice rough with lust, and Lainie nodded.

He positioned himself at her entrance. Lainie shivered with anticipation as she felt the head of his cock press against her folds. She was already wet, and incredibly aroused, but even so he was so big that she wasn't sure she could take all of him.

Harrison had his hands on her hips again, and she flung her arms up over his shoulders. As he pushed himself into her, Lainie's hands clenched.

"Oh my God," she moaned, breathless.

She felt every inch of his as he entered her. Her body stretched to fit him. She would have expected it to hurt. Instead, the stretching sensation aroused her even more.

"Is this all right?" Harrison murmured into her ear.

"Y-yes," Lainie stuttered. "Oh God, yes."

She let herself fall forward, resting her cheek against Harrison's chest as he pushed into her. His cock brushed against a sensitive spot inside her, making her gasp. In response he sped up, burying himself to the hilt in one smooth movement.

Lainie moaned deeply, winding her legs around Harrison's waist, holding him fully inside her. Her heartbeat seemed to fill her whole body, and all at once, she didn't want to go slow anymore.

"Fuck me," she said, raising her head. Harrison's eyes burned into hers.

He grasped her hips, adjusting his grip as he pulled out. Lainie sighed. Being filled by him had felt amazing, but almost overwhelming—without him, she felt emptier than ever before.

She wanted him again, *now*, harder than before, and he thrust into her as though he'd read her mind. Lainie gasped as he filled her. Her body adjusted, again, faster, but not fast enough. She moaned as he pounded into her, relishing the overwhelming feeling of being stretched by his massive cock.

She'd never experienced anything like this before. Never *done* anything like this before. But it felt so right.

Harrison's cock slid against that sensitive spot inside her, over and over as his thrusts grew stronger. Lainie's toes curled. Each thrust set off sparks inside her, coiling out from her center to dance across her skin.

Her head fell back as she felt her orgasm approaching like a cresting wave. She crashed over it, crying out, and felt Harrison's cock twitch inside her as he came.

They clung together, panting, Lainie's head still spinning with the last waves of her orgasm.

Harrison's arms tightened around Lainie. "Shit," he muttered. "Birth control, we didn't—"

"Don't worry," Lainie said quickly. "I'm on the Pill."

It seemed ridiculous to be having this conversation with him still inside her. She wriggled, enjoying the feeling.

Harrison leaned his forehead against hers. He sighed with pleasure, so deeply Lainie felt his whole body tremor.

"Hey," she said.

He smiled. "Hey."

"So…" Lainie traced patterns on his chest. "That was nice."

Harrison slid his hands down to rest on her ass. "Lainie, I…" He paused. "I don't want you to think I'm the type of person who does this a lot."

Lainie raised her eyebrows, and looked down, to where their bodies joined. "No?" she said innocently. Harrison smiled, shame-faced.

"No."

Lainie giggled. *This is so ridiculous.* "I guess that makes me one special lady, then," she drawled.

"It does." Harrison sounded entirely serious.

Lainie smiled and unwound her legs from his waist. He stepped back and she felt that strange emptiness again as he pulled out of her.

"Well, good," she said facetiously. "I'd hope not all of your round-the-town tours end this way."

"Only yours."

Lainie touched his cheek. She'd noticed the laughter lines around his eyes and mouth earlier. They seemed softer, now. Relaxed and content.

She felt the same way. For the first time in… *A very long time,* she thought with a pang.

*Sheesh. If I'd known all I needed to get over my stress about this trip was a decent orgasm, I could have taken care of that weeks ago!* For the first time, she regretted the fact that she was only staying in Hideaway Cove overnight. But maybe, if things went okay tomorrow, she could come back.

Yeah. That could work.

Harrison showed her to the shower and helped her wash.

Well. "Helped."

It was past midnight by the time Lainie pulled her pants and blouse back on. The game of hunt-the-discarded-clothes had brought her back to the front door, past the public area of the workshop.

*Good thing none of Harrison's colleagues are working overtime tonight,* Lainie thought as she wound her wet hair into a knot at the back of her head to keep it off her neck. She would tidy it up properly when she got back to the B&B.

Harrison had put his jeans back on. The ones that accentuated his V, and hung low on his hips. Even though she already knew what was under them, Lainie found the sight tantalizing.

"So… should I call you?" she said.

Harrison looked startled. "Call me? You're not going to stay?"

"I would love to." Lainie was surprised at how true the clichéd words were. "Really. But I have an early start in the morning. There's some things I need to sort out beforehand, and…"

She trailed off and shrugged, hoping he would understand. She really did wish she could stay. The idea was tempting—too tempting. She could all too easily see how waking up next to Harrison would lead to a late start.

Harrison met her eyes, his lips quirking into a small smile. "I understand," he said. "Here—just a sec…"

He raced into the next room. Lainie followed him, watching him tip over the stacks of paper that covered the coffee table, and hunt under the sofa cushions. At last he found what he was looking for. He snatched it up with a shout of victory.

"Your business card?" Lainie raised an eyebrow as he passed it to her. Harrison grinned sheepishly.

"I don't have much call for them usually. Everyone who wants to hire me already knows my number. Or just comes and knocks on the door."

"Well, now I feel *extra* special." Lainie laughed. "Where did my purse end up—oh, thanks." She slung it under her arm and kicked her feet back into her ankle boots.

Now that it was time for her to leave, she definitely didn't want to. She lingered in front of the door.

"You know, you could stay," Harrison said. He walked up to her, filthy promises in his eyes.

"Mmm." Lainie closed her eyes. "That's tempting. *Too* tempting."
She felt Harrison's breath on her lips, and then he kissed her.

"Tomorrow?" he whispered.

"Tomorrow," she agreed. *I'm sure I can find some way to—don't think "fit him in". Too late. Ugh. Some way to make it work.*

It would mean leaving Hideaway Cove late and arriving home even later, but she was sure it would be worth it.

"I'll call you," she said, and slipped out the door before Harrison could convince her to stay. Or before she convinced herself.

# 6

# HARRISON

Harrison woke up with the morning birdsong. He groaned. The birds were gulls, so their style was more drunken karaoke than Church choir.

*Keep it down out there!* he hollered, and heard their answering laughter in his head.

*What's the matter Mr. Galway? Late night?*

Jools. Of course she'd seen him and Lainie leave the restaurant the night before. She must have told her siblings. Hell, half the town probably knew about it by now.

Harrison rolled over, stretching out as the sun warmed his skin. He hadn't bothered to pull the curtains when he finally made it to bed last night. He liked to watch the stars as he fell asleep, and wake with the sun. Except from the angle of the light pouring in his window, he'd slept right through sunrise and for several hours longer.

This morning, it wasn't only the sun that warmed him. Maybe that was why he'd slept in so long. He felt deeply content, in a way he'd never thought possible.

His boss, old Mr. Mackaby, had told him it would be like this when he finally met his mate. Depending on their animal type, different shifters reacted in different ways. No one in town had ever heard of a griffin shifter before Harrison came along, but Mr. Mackaby said that one thing all shifters shared when they finally met their mate was a feeling of great peace. Like everything was right in the world.

Well, Harrison certainly felt that.

*What else did the old man say?* Harrison thought back. Peace, and protectiveness. That was it.

He thought about Lainie. She'd been happy when she left in the early hours of the morning, he knew that. She'd smiled and laughed. A complete contrast to how she'd been when he first saw her in the restaurant, closed-off and tense.

Well, she wouldn't have to be like that again. She deserved to feel safe, and welcome, wherever she went. And she would. He'd make sure of that.

Somehow.

First, he had to convince her that last night wasn't a one-time thing. If only he wasn't expecting that other out-of-towner today. The job was meant to take the whole day, which didn't leave him much time to catch up with Lainie.

Maybe if she stayed in Hideaway a little longer than planned, they could get to know each other better…

His thoughts strayed to Pol, with his abilities to manipulate electronics. *No.* He wouldn't ask the other shifter to break Lainie's car to keep her in town. That would be wrong.

Hadn't she said she had family in Hideaway? Her grandparents—that was it.

If they'd lived in Hideaway, they must have been shifters. There wasn't a single human living in the town, after all. And if they were shifters… maybe the conversation ahead of him wouldn't be so difficult. If Lainie already knew about shifters, she must know about mates, as well.

Harrison racked his brains, trying to remember if he had known any Eaves in the time he'd lived in Hideaway.

Eaves. Why was that name so familiar? He stared out the window. His house was on the south end of the bay, where the land curved around. The view out his window took in a slice of the ocean, as well as the town, and beyond it, Lighthouse Hill. His eyes traced the winding road that climbed up the side of the hill, up to the rambling, half-derelict old house…

His eyes widened. *The old Eaves house?* How had he not made the connection before?

But if she was here about her grandparents, and her grandparents were old Mrs. and Mr. Eaves, then that meant…

His thoughts were interrupted by a knock on the door. Harrison got out of bed and pulled on some clothes, still berating himself for being so thick. He'd been so blown away by Lainie, his brain hadn't been able to put two and two together.

He took the stairs three at a time. Who was knocking on his door at this hour? Pol and Arlo had their own keys. The only job he had scheduled for today was…

He opened the door, already sure who was behind it.

"Lainie."

"Hi, again." Lainie blushed. She held up his business card and flicked it with her fingers. "I probably should have read this last night, huh? Harrison Galway, of Mackaby's Workshop. It's named after your old boss, right? That's why I didn't recognize the name. I was up at the storage unit just now, and your friend Arlo looked at me as though I'd grown two heads when I said I was looking forward to meeting you." She groaned and blushed.

Harrison ran his hand through his hair, grinning. He could just imagine Arlo's reaction. "Damn. I wish I had an excuse like that," he said wistfully. She raised one eyebrow, and he explained: "I should have recognized your surname."

The corner of Lainie's mouth twitched down. "Oh. Of course." She played with her purse for a moment, not meeting his eye. "Well, awkward as this is… shall we head up there now? Your car, or mine?"

"We'll take mine. If you don't mind?" He waited for her to shake her head. "My gear's in the back already, in case there's anything you want me to get onto right away."

"Oh." Lainie frowned. "Yes. I hadn't thought—no, that makes sense." She shook her head, her mouth tight.

Inside him, Harrison's griffin became alert. Something was wrong here.

*Whatever it is, does it have something to do with her only planning to stay here overnight? For a job that might take days?*

He walked her to his truck and opened the door for her. She stepped up with a smile, brushing past him too close for it to be an accident. Warmth blossomed inside Harrison. *That* hadn't changed, at least.

Determination stiffened his spine. She was his mate, and if she was unhappy, it was his duty to help her. Whatever was troubling her, he would do whatever she needed to help make it right.

"Okay," he said, getting in the driver's side and starting the engine. "So, you've already been to see Arlo about the stuff in the storage unit? He's the one who—uh, who took down the info when you called last week."

Harrison winced. Until he had determined whether or not Lainie knew about shifters, he couldn't go around saying things like *He's the guy who was in dog form last night. Remember, my German Shepherd-Pom cross?*

He shook his head. "He said you wanted an evaluation of the house?"

"Yeah… something along those lines." She pulled a keyring out of her pocket and started to play with it.

Most of the keys on it looked modern, except for two. One was a large house key, but it was the smaller one she paid the most attention to. It was a silver key half the length of her pinky finger, decorated with a complicated filigree. The sort of thing you'd imagine fitting the lock of a jewelry box. She turned it over and over.

"I was hoping to find something in the storage unit, but… oh, it doesn't matter. So, the house. I don't know what state it's in these days, but Arlo said you're certified to do a safety check, and see how much work needs to be done on it?"

"I can do that, sure. Not a problem."

Lainie tucked her hair back behind her ears. Harrison watched the road as he drove through town, but he couldn't help sneaking glances at her. Her eyes flickered across to him, as well. When their eyes met, she blushed.

"Did you sleep well?" Harrison teased.

That made her smile. "Like a log," she said, relaxing into her seat. "For some reason, I was all worn out."

"Well. You had a long drive earlier in the day, after all."

Lainie snorted, and Harrison grinned. He swung off onto the road up Lighthouse Hill, keeping his mate in the corner of his eye.

Her smile faded. *Damn it. Whatever's wrong, her grandparents' house is right at the middle of it, isn't it?*

The whole truck lurched as he hit a pothole. "Sorry about that! This road isn't used much anymore."

"I guess there wouldn't be any need for people to use it since my Gran went into the home," Lainie said. She sighed. "That was, what, eight years ago? Time flies."

Harrison couldn't miss the hint of bitterness in her voice. "That'd be why I haven't seen you in town before now. I only moved here around then."

Lainie shook her head. "You wouldn't have seen me before then, either. Like I said, I wasn't close with this side of the family." She sighed. "And now I'm the only one left, and I get to deal with the rest of the leftovers. Hooray."

Harrison's heart sank. If Lainie had never been close to the Eaves, then she might not even know about shifters.

Then again, if she'd inherited her grandparents' house… well, real estate was a very real connection to a place. Maybe she would end up spending more time in Hideaway after all.

They rounded the final bend, and the old Eaves house came into view.

From what Harrison had heard from people who'd lived in Hideaway longer, the house used to be a lighthouse. Hideaway didn't need or have a lighthouse these days, and the house had been converted into a family home. The old structure was barely visible under new additions to the building.

He parked in front. The drive had once been gravel, but most of that had been swept away by wind and rain, leaving a surface of dirt and potholes.

A strange sense of foreboding settled in his stomach. Up close, the old house looked even more ramshackle than it did from down in town. At some point in the past, the windows had been shuttered tight against the elements. More recently, most of those shutters had come loose, either hanging from their hinges or disappeared entirely. Harrison could see at least one broken window.

The house had once been painted a bright straw yellow, but after years of neglect almost all the paint had peeled off, revealing weather-stained wooden siding. Some of the boards were sagging. Harrison's heart sank.

Lainie swore softly as she got out of the truck. "The place looks like it's ready to crumble off the edge of the cliff," she said. She turned to Harrison. "Any idea if your friend the electrician serviced up here recently?"

"I don't think so," Harrison said, his heart sinking further. "I'll get a flashlight."

When he caught up with Lainie, flashlight in hand, she already had her keys out. She picked out the large, old-fashioned one and turned it in the lock. The mechanism grated, but it opened.

"Here we go." Lainie's voice was so soft Harrison could barely hear it.

She stepped inside, and Harrison heard the click-click of a light switch. "Power's off," she said, and turned on a flashlight app on her phone. Harrison followed her in with his own flashlight.

They were standing in a large front hall. The two beams of light illuminated clouds of dust that whirled up every time he or Lainie took a step. Inch-thick dust covered the wooden floorboards, and a layer almost as thick seemed to have settled on the walls and windowsills.

Lainie sneezed and covered her mouth. "Well, that's one creditor the lawyer can dispute, at least," she muttered. "There's no way in hell this place has seen a housekeeper in the last decade."

They explored further, passing by a sweeping wooden staircase that disappeared up into the gloom. A white concrete wall curved up one side of the stairs, looming like the ghost of some other, older structure. As he stared, Harrison realized that was exactly what it was: the outside of the old lighthouse, now standing in the center of the Eaves family home.

The empty, broken-down Eaves family home.

Harrison glanced at Lainie. What had this place been like when she was young? And what had happened that it had been left to fall to pieces like this?

He bit his tongue on his questions and followed her into what looked like a sitting room.

*If those windows were open, the room would be flooded with light in the mornings,* Harrison thought. Instead, it was pitch black outside the thin beams of their flashlights.

"I'll see if I can open any of those windows," he said, and made his way over to them. The floor creaked under him, and he jumped back at one point when the floorboards sagged worryingly under his weight.

He carefully tested the window. The sash had almost rotted through. If he tried to open it, it would only fall shut again—unless the frame had rotted as well, in which case the whole thing might come tumbling down.

He turned to explain to Lainie and saw her staring back the way they had come. Not at the door they'd come through, but the fireplace beside it.

Her posture changed. She'd looked uncertain when they reached the house, but now, she strode forward angrily, her flashlight pointed above the fireplace.

"That—that should have been in the storage unit!" she cried out.

Her flashlight illuminated a large oil painting. The dust on it was so thick, Harrison could hardly make out what it was. As he walked closer, aiming his own light at it, the image became clear.

It was a portrait of a couple in their early thirties. Harrison saw their resemblance to Lainie immediately: the woman had her blonde hair, pulled back in a fancy roll at the back of her head, and the man had Lainie's piercing dark eyes. The woman was seated, the man standing behind her with his hand on her shoulder. He was wearing a military uniform; she was all in white, with colorful jewels sparkling at her neck and on her fingers.

"Are they your grandparents?" he asked.

"Yes," replied Lainie shortly. "And those are the famous Eaves jewels. The ones no one seems to have set eyes on since... ugh. Why didn't the movers take it away when they stripped the house? They were meant to take everything."

She strode forward and tried to hook her fingers under the frame. It didn't move. Lainie stepped back, frowning.

"It's attached to the wall. Damn it! This stupid, *stupid* house!"

She opened her mouth to say more, wheezed, and broke into a coughing fit. Harrison rushed to her, putting his hand around her shoulders.

"I'm fine. I'm fine," she muttered, but she leaned into his embrace, her shoulders shaking. She fumbled for her purse and her light blinked out as she rummaged through it and found a packet of tissues.

"It's all this dust…" she croaked, and burst into tears.

# 7

# LAINIE

*Oh, God. What are you doing? Stop crying! Of all the stupid things…*

Harrison had noticed. Of course he had. She could tell the moment he realized her sniffs had changed from dust allergies to sobs: his arms went stiff, and he pulled away from her, almost imperceptibly.

He tried to gather her in his arms a moment later, but the damage was done.

Lainie pulled away from him. "Don't. Please. I'm fine. It's just the dust, really."

*Which is a lie, but I'm not going to admit that to my one-night stand. Even if he did turn out to be the guy I hired to evaluate my grandparents' house. Especially because of that.*

She took a deep breath. "Okay. I'm fine. Can we look at the rest of the house? Just quickly?"

She didn't meet Harrison's eyes. She wasn't sure what she would do if she saw concern in them.

*Probably cry some more*, she thought bitterly. *God, this is so pathetic. I hate it so much. Crying doesn't help anything, so why does my stupid body keep doing it?*

"Of course," Harrison said softly. He aimed his flashlight at the door and offered her his arm. She took it, telling herself it was just because she didn't want to trip and fall on anything in the dark.

He didn't mention her outburst as they ventured around the rest of the house. Lainie was glad. Despite all her preparation, looking around the old rooms was harder than she had expected.

*It wasn't all bad, after all,* she thought. *Most of the time I spend here was wonderful. It was just those last few days that it hurts to remember. Before that…*

It was easy to fall into memories, walking around the familiar rooms. Here was the kitchen where she'd shared meals with her parents and grandparents, or bothered her Gran while she was baking. The front hall—those wooden floorboards had once been polished so smooth she could slide around on them in her socks. After riding down the banister of the main staircase, for instance.

Then there was the old lighthouse. Lainie remembered thinking it looked like a wizard had teleported it into the middle of her grandparents' wooden house. No one had ever painted or papered over its white walls to make them match the rest of the house.

And climbing up the staircase inside it was like stepping into another world, Lainie remembered. The thick walls insulated the old lighthouse from the creaks and groans of the wooden house.

And the shouting. Lainie remembered that.

Harrison stopped her as she made for the stairs. "I don't think that would be safe," he said. "The boards down here are bad enough. I don't want either of us falling through the floor. You, especially." He moved his hand to the small of her back and whispered conspiratorially, "I haven't even had my breakfast yet. I'm afraid I'm not up for any heroics on an empty stomach."

Lainie smiled. She couldn't help it. "All right," she said. "Let's leave all this behind us and get back to your office to figure out the next step."

She hadn't noticed the floor creaking before—just the dust carpeting it—but she did now. By the time they made it to the front door, she was more than happy to see the back of the crumbling house.

Outside, the sun was shining, but the air was still crisp. Lainie breathed in deep, imagining she was cleansing the dust out of her lungs with the fresh salt air.

*Well, that was useless. The storage unit, the house—I haven't found anything that could help.*

*I just have to face up to it. There's only one way for me to get out of this mess.*

"Right," she said once they'd both dusted themselves off. "I think it's pretty clear we'll have to knock the whole thing down."

"Knock it down?" Harrison looked genuinely shocked, and Lainie frowned at him, puzzled.

"Yes, knock it down." She stared at him. "Look, I work in planning, so I know how this is going to go. There's no way I'll be able to pay you to fix up the building to sell and make any profit on it at all. The renovation costs would suck up any revenue." She sighed and wiped her face with a fresh tissue. It came away gray with dust. "Ugh. The land is probably worth more without the building on it, anyway. I'll have to check a couple of databases—I couldn't find any recent sales data for this region, it's like no one has moved here in years."

She stopped. Harrison wasn't looking reassured by her explanation. She knew she was rambling, but she was making sense, wasn't she? So why did he look like he was going to be sick?

"What's wrong?" she said, her voice faltering.

Harrison's face cleared—or maybe he just got control of it. He gave her a weak smile, but she couldn't miss the line that formed between his eyebrows. He was acting like everything was okay, but clearly she'd done something wrong.

"It's nothing," he said, as though that was the truth. "I didn't realize you were wanting to sell, is all."

Lainie shrugged tightly. "*Wanting* has nothing to do with it. I just have to do the best I can with a bad situation."

She clamped her mouth shut. *And that's all you need to know about that,* she thought fiercely. *I'm not having my sob story make its way around town.*

She knew she wasn't being fair, assuming Harrison would gossip about her situation. But she knew how easy it was for one person to let slip a few details to someone who passed them on, in confidence, to someone else… and then somehow everyone knew what was going on.

"You can give me a quote for demolition, right?" she said, her voice sharper than she'd intended.

Harrison's shoulders stiffened. "Yes. But not based on just what we saw today. I'll need the plans for the house, if they exist, and info on any recent renovations. Asbestos, any supporting walls removed, that kind of thing. I can do the tests myself if you don't have the paperwork." His voice was flat.

"I'll email you copies of everything I've got," Lainie said. Her mind felt full of cotton wool. She thought she had some of the things she'd mentioned—but all of them? She needed to get back to her files and check. "If you can't give me the quote now, can you drop me back at by B&B? I need to… there's some things I need to look after," she finished lamely.

So much for her plans to leave late today. Harrison looked like the last thing in the world he wanted was to spend more time with her.

# 8

# HARRISON

Harrison spent the entire drive back down the town trying to find the right thing to say, and terrified he'd say the *wrong* thing, and mess things up even more.

So he said nothing. He concentrated on the bumpy road, trying to avoid as many potholes as possible. He kept an eye on the horizon, where dark clouds were brewing, and made a mental note to check that Arlo's boat was in the marina. All the while, a bitter premonition boiled inside him.

He didn't know what Lainie's situation was, but whatever it was, she was about to discover it was a whole lot worse. Sell the land? If that was what she was planning, things were going to get tricky.

Harrison sighed. He couldn't keep this from her. His feelings for her, the fact that she was his mate—that could wait. What was important was keeping her safe.

"Lainie, there's something you need to know about Hideaway—"

Harrison was so busy trying to make sure his words came out right, that he almost missed the man who stepped out in front of his truck, waving. He stomped on the break, swearing in surprise.

"Jesus, Guts, what are you playing at—roadkill?"

Guts was a permanently sunburned man in his mid-fifties. Harrison had always found it hard to believe he was related to fashion-plate Jools and her siblings, but he was their uncle. Even his gull form looked like it'd had one too many.

Guts came around Harrison's side of the car. He gave Lainie a polite nod, then beckoned Harrison to lean down. Harrison wound down his window and stuck his head out.

"What's got your tail feathers in a twist, Guts?"

Guts' eyes darted to either side. "Everyone's down at Caro's. They want to talk to your girlfriend. Er, Ms. Eaves." He leaned in closer and whispered, "She *is* your… right?"

Harrison glared at him. "What do you mean, everyone wants to talk to Ms. Eaves?" The hairs on his arms prickled, the only visible sign that inside him, his griffin was puffing out its feathers defensively.

He'd warned everyone ahead of time that they should expect a human visitor, of course, but no one had said anything about wanting to meet Lainie when she was here.

Guts ducked his head guiltily. "It's the Sweets, and their lot," he muttered.

"Can we go, please?" said Lainie from behind him, her voice tense. "I still need to get those files to you."

Her voice was steady, but sounded brittle. Harrison remembered how quickly she'd gone to pieces before, and how annoyed she'd seemed by her own distress. His heart twisted as he realized how scared she must be that anyone would see how distressed the old house had made her.

All those years away from Hideaway must have hurt so much, her only defense had been to build walls around her feelings. Alone.

Well, not any more. She was his mate, and Harrison would do everything in his power to protect Lainie from whatever it was that was causing her pain.

"Guts here says some people from the town council want to talk to you," he explained. "I don't know what they're after—"

"They want to talk about the old Eaves place," Guts interjected helpfully.

"Thanks, Guts," said Harrison, not looking away from Lainie. He cursed silently. *Of course they do. Just what she needs.*

He glanced up the road. Caro's was only ten or twenty feet away. Guts had left his warning a bit late—if he meant it as a warning.

"You don't have to see them if you don't want to, Lainie."

Lainie's face went tense. She kept her eyes on the dashboard, but Harrison still saw how the corner of her mouth folded under. She took a deep breath.

"Fine. I'll talk to them." She rubbed her face, then hesitated. "Just give me a few minutes to do my face before we go in?"

Harrison waited outside the truck as Lainie tidied herself up. When she was ready, he opened the door for her. Her mouth was still stuck in that unhappy line.

He offered her his arm, and she stared at him. "You don't have to—look, I know you're not happy about the property being sold. You don't have to look after me."

Her voice was firm, but her eyes begged him to stay. Harrison squeezed her arm.

"I want to," he said simply. "You're one mysterious lady, Lainie Eaves. I might not know what's going on with you, but I know I'm not going to let you go in there and get the Sweets once-over without backup."

"Thanks, Harrison. That—that means a lot to me," she muttered. She took a deep breath and blew her cheeks out. "Okay. Let's do this. And afterwards, do you want to come back to the B&B and finish what you were saying before your friend stopped us?"

She said that last bit all in a rush, her eyes darting nervously up to meet Harrison's. He smiled and touched her hand.

"Of course. I'd love that," Harrison reassured her. *And I'm sure you'll have a hell of a lot of questions, after even a quick conversation with Mrs. Sweets.*

Caro's was strangely empty. Normally at this time of day it would be packed, as the fishing boats all came back in and spilled their crews onto the marina in search of a hot lunch. But today, only one table had people sitting at it.

Mr. and Mrs. Sweets and their cronies looked out of place in the homey pub, though Harrison had seen them all here before. Maybe it was the way they were holding themselves: on edge, like they were all waiting for something to happen. Mrs. Sweets' eyes widened with genteel excitement as Harrison and Lainie walked in.

To Harrison's surprise, Arlo was there, too. Among the clean-cut councilors and business-owners he stuck out like a sore thumb, with his unruly black hair and thick dark stubble. His piercing blue eyes met Harrison's.

*Watch out. I don't know what they're planning, but Mrs. Sweets has that look in her eye.*

*Like she's just seen a canoe of tasty tourists floating down the river?*

*That's the one.*

Harrison drew Lainie closer to his side. She glanced up at him, questioning, but he didn't have time to say anything.

"You must be Lainie Eaves." Mrs. Sweets rose from her chair like a leviathan from the depths. "My, you've grown! I can't tell you how happy we all are to see you again."

Mrs. Sweets was five-foot-nothing, on the far side of sixty, and no one ever saw her human form in anything but a twinset and pearls. She bared her set of even, pearly white teeth in a welcoming smile as she approached Lainie and Harrison.

Harrison wondered if Lainie would notice the one strange thing about the councilwoman's expression: she was smiling, but her teeth didn't quite meet.

*Ready to bite*, he thought uncharitably.

"Mrs. Sweets," Lainie said steadily. "Yes. I think I remember you." She leaned almost imperceptibly toward Harrison, and he put his arm around her waist.

"And young Harrison! Imagine seeing you here," Mrs. Sweets said, her bright eyes wide and innocent. "Well, I'm sure Caro can find you a bite to eat, if you'll just wait on the terrace for us to finish…"

"I'll stay with Lainie, if it's all the same," Harrison replied flatly. There was only one spare seat, at the foot of the table. He ushered Lainie into it and stood behind her, one hand placed on her shoulder. On guard.

Mrs. Sweets tutted at him, but her eyes narrowed suspiciously. She sniffed and sat down at the head of the table, folding her hands in front of herself.

"Now, I'm sure you realize why we all wanted to talk to you, dear," Mrs. Sweets began.

"I'm afraid not," said Lainie hesitantly. "I'm not even sure who most of you are, actually…?"

Mrs. Sweets gave her tinkly laugh. "Oh, dear, I don't expect you to remember us!" She went on, breezily failing to introduce anyone. "*Now*, dear. We were all *so* distressed to hear of your grandmother's passing. She and your grandfather were such good people. Truly pillars of the community here in little Hideaway Cove. He was Mayor, once, you know, *such* a good man. We are all simply dying to know—what are you planning to do with your inheritance?"

She slipped the question in like a needle. Harrison squeezed Lainie's shoulder reassuringly.

"My inheritance?" Lainie's voice was flat.

"The house, dear, on Lighthouse Hill. I understand you went up there this morning with our dear Harrison?"

*What would she say if Lainie announced she was going to move in?* Harrison thought suddenly. He felt uneasy. Lainie was human. No one knew she was his mate yet—or not for sure, anyway. He was sure there were rumors. But nothing confirmed.

He hadn't even told *her*.

What would the town council say to a human wanting to move to the shifter sanctuary of Hideaway Cove, even if she was related to an ex-inhabitant of the town?

"Yes, we did a brief inspection. There's not much left to see," Lainie said. "It's strange; I know my grandmother hired someone local to maintain the house after she moved into assisted living, but the place doesn't appear to have been looked after at all. Despite the number of housekeeping invoices that have landed in my lap since the will was read."

Harrison glanced around the table. One of Mrs. Sweets' cronies, a plover shifter called Sharon Walbol, flushed red.

He looked down at Lainie. She sounded cool, but her smile was half-frozen on her face. He realized just how much of a strain this gauntlet was for her.

"What is it you wanted to say to Lainie, exactly?" he demanded.

Mrs. Sweets raised her perfectly plucked eyebrows at him.

"All in good time, dear."

Beside her, Mr. Sweets roused himself at last. He was of the same vintage as his wife, but whereas she held herself ramrod-straight and kept her eyes on everyone in the room, Mr. Sweets' bones seemed loose within his skin. And he never looked at anyone, even when he was speaking to them. As acting mayor of Hideaway Cove, he mostly played possum.

"Seventy-five thou," he huffed, and apparently went back to sleep.

Beside Harrison, Lainie almost jumped out of her chair. "What?" she yelped.

Mrs. Sweets kept her cool, and her prehistoric smile. "My dear, surely you understand? A… city girl like you can't possibly want to relocate to a small town like ours. And as you've no doubt already discovered, our town doesn't have any real estate services. We thought it would be much easier to arrange a private sale."

"A private sale?" Lainie relaxed back in her chair, but her eyes were still flicking suspiciously around the table. "With half the town here?" she added in an undertone to Harrison.

Harrison took in the tense angle of her shoulders. "I know it's a bit weird, but you were planning to sell anyway, weren't you?"

A murmur went around the table, and Harrison cursed silently. He'd barely whispered the words—but in a room full of shifters with acute hearing, he might as well have shouted.

Mrs. Sweets' smile became, if possible, even toothier. Hairs went up on the back of Harrison's neck.

"You're planning on selling the property? Well, that does seem to solve all our problems. If you will have your lawyer send the paperwork to me directly—"

"No." Lainie's voice was quiet, but firm. "No, that isn't going to work. I'm sorry."

"Ex*cuse* me?" Mrs. Sweets' hand flew to her pearls. Her smile disappeared, and the change in the old lady's appearance was chilling. Her smile might have been predatory, but at least it was a smile; without it, she looked like a death's head.

"Perhaps I wasn't clear, my dear," she purred. "I realize you have family connections in Hideaway Cove, but it is impossible that you should move here. It will not be tolerated. Really, girl, not even your grandparents wanted you here after you proved such a disappointment—why would you think things would be any different now?"

"How dare you speak to her like that," Harrison growled, his free hand forming a fist at his side. Inside him, his griffin screeched in anger. He and it were in perfect accord: eagle, lion and human, all united in protective rage. "Lainie Eaves is my—"

"Don't worry." Lainie's voice cut in under his, dripping with bitterness. "Nothing in the world could entice me to move into that broken-down old house. I'm going to sell, and leave this place behind me—but I'm sure as hell not going to part with the property for such a low sum. Seventy-five thousand dollars? That's *insulting*. It wouldn't buy the lighthouse, let alone the rest of the land!"

She stood up, shrugging off Harrison's hand. This close, Harrison could see she was trembling. Would anybody else be able to tell? Or would they just see her anger, and not her tears?

"Lainie, I—"

She turned to him, her eyes full of angry tears. "Oh, don't you start. You don't want me to sell—would you prefer me to stay? After hearing *that?*" Her whole body was shaking with anger. "This whole thing was a mistake. I never should have come here in the first place. I'm leaving, now. You'll hear from my lawyer about the demolition work, and *you—*" She turned back to Mrs. Sweets. "*You* will hear *nothing*, not from me or anyone who has anything to do with the estate."

Without another word, she stormed out, slamming the door behind her.

Harrison stared after her, a hole forming in his chest.

"Well," said Mrs. Sweets behind him, sniffing. "What a catastrophe. And what a conniving, thoughtless—"

Harrison rounded on her. "Lainie Eaves is. My. Mate," he growled. "Whatever you were about to say—*don't.*"

"Ah. I had heart some disturbing whispers about that, but… you're sure? That is unfortunate." Mrs. Sweets was two feet shorter than Harrison and still managed to look down her nose at him. "You have a difficult decision ahead of you, Mr. Galway. I hope you make the right choice."

"What are you talking about?" Harrison snarled.

Mrs. Sweets brushed an invisible speck of dust from her skirt. "Dear little Lainie's nonsense about selling off her grandparents' property will come to nothing. It will be a nuisance, but that's nothing new when it comes to her family!" She sniffed. "I mean, Mr. Galway, that you will have to decide between remaining in the sanctuary of Hideaway Cove—or leaving with your *human*."

"I'm not going to leave Hideaway," Harrison said automatically. Mrs. Sweets smiled.

"Then no more talk of Ms. Eaves being your *mate*, please. It will be better in the long run if you forget all about her."

She swept away, gathering up her husband and cronies as she left the restaurant. None of them met Harrison's eye.

The place was almost empty now. The only people left were Caro, wiping down the bar with a stony look on her face, and Arlo. The wolf shifter was still sitting at the table, a stricken look on his face.

"Jesus, Harrison," he muttered.

"And what the hell are you doing here, again?" Harrison snapped at him. "Since when are you on the town council?"

Arlo glared at the table, not meeting Harrison's eyes. "It's not like that, Harrison. Ma Sweets asked me to talk to you…"

"And what? Convince me to leave Lainie—or just to roll over and listen to Mrs. Sweets insult her? Exactly whose side are you on?"

Arlo's shoulders went up around his ears, and Harrison tried to reel in his rage. Arlo might look rough, but Harrison knew his gruff exterior hid some ancient hurt. He was a loner, always had been. Intelligent, and savvy, but not comfortable around people. Even the Sweets—who, Harrison remembered belatedly, had taken the wolf shifter in when he first washed up in Hideaway Cove.

"Just… think about it, Harrison," Arlo muttered now. "Ignore that it's Mrs. Sweets who said it. Hideaway Cove is the only place most of us have ever lived where we feel safe, and Lainie Eaves is endangering that. If she sells the property…"

"If Mrs. Sweets doesn't sabotage the sale, you mean."

Arlo lifted his eyes to meet Harrison's. "Harrison, what happens to Hideaway Cove if Lighthouse Hill fills up with humans? We'll lose everything we have here. Our safety. Our *home*."

Harrison sagged. He sat down opposite Arlo and leaned his forehead on his knuckles, rolling his head back and forth to massage out a growing headache.

"No. Lainie's a good person. If she knew what was at stake…"

"Does she even know you're a shifter?"

The answer must have been clear on Harrison's face. Arlo groaned. "You haven't told her, have you?"

Harrison rubbed his face. "I need to talk to her. I have to explain everything. Damn it all, I thought I'd have time…" He stood up.

"Be careful."

"Don't worry. I'm not going to do anything stupid."

"I mean—think about what you're doing. The Sweets don't want her around because they don't want any humans to know about Hideaway Cove. If you tell her…"

"Then they'll have no reason to make her leave, will they?"

Arlo shook his head. "You don't really think it will be that simple, do you?"

"I know." Harrison started out the door, following the path Lainie had fled. "But I have to do something."

"She doesn't want to see you." Mrs. Hanson barred the front door to her B&B with her small, bird-like frame. "She doesn't want to see *anyone*. I don't know what you did—"

"It was Mrs. Sweets and her lot," Harrison explained. "They jumped her with this harebrained plan to buy the Eaves property off her and said they would run her out of town if she didn't sell to them." He tried to duck around Mrs. Hanson, but she stood firm.

"Oh dear, oh dear," she murmured. "I hoped it wouldn't come to that. Did she accept their offer, at least?"

Harrison stared at her. "You knew about this?" Mrs. Hanson hadn't been at the meeting. Harrison was starting to get the unpleasant feeling he was being kept in the dark, and Mrs. Hanson's next words only confirmed his fears.

"I'm so sorry, love, but no one wanted to involve you, given the circumstances."

"You mean because she's my mate."

Mrs. Hanson looked pained. "That, and... well, because of the history there. It all happened long before your time, of course."

Harrison was growing impatient. "If you want to make excuses about hurting Lainie *now* because of something that happened years ago, that's your problem," he growled. "I want to talk to her."

Mrs. Hanson sighed. "Go ahead, Romeo. She's in the front room, first floor."

Before Harrison could react, she'd nipped back behind the door and slammed it shut. He raised his hand to knock and heard the lock turn.

Harrison rested his open palm on the closed door. There was no point yelling to Mrs. Hanson to open up. Instead, he stepped back, looking up at the house.

*Front room, first floor…*

A flicker of movement in the large first-floor window caught his attention.

"Lainie?" he called, shading his eyes. "Is that you?"

There was no answer. Harrison concentrated. Lainie *was* there, he was sure of it. The curtain moved slightly—was that her?

"Lainie, please talk to me. There's something you have to know. If you just let me up there, I'll explain—"

The curtain was flicked aside and Lainie appeared, glaring down at him. Harrison's heart wrenched. Her eyes were red and puffy, but her mouth was set in a firm line as she tugged the window open.

"I don't want to talk to you! Just go away!" she yelled, her voice catching on a sob.

"Lainie, please—"

"Just leave me alone! Can't you see you've just made this all worse?"

She slid the window shut and pulled the curtains across. Harrison stared up, still trying to find the words, any words, to convince her to listen to him.

There was no point. She didn't come back to the window.

Harrison stood there, waiting. The curtains didn't flicker. She wasn't standing on the other side, waiting and wondering whether he was still there.

But her words still echoed through his head. *Can't you see you've just made this all worse?*

It was true. He could see that. Whatever was happening here, whatever the reasons behind Mrs. Sweets' cruel treatment of Lainie, his actions in drawing her into his life had only made things more difficult for her.

He'd swept her off her feet, when he should have been finding out the best way to protect her.

# 9

# LAINIE

L ainie lay on the bed, staring at the ceiling but not seeing it. She
had thought she would cry herself to sleep, exhausted by pain and
anger. Instead, ever since she'd slammed the window in Harrison's face, she
hadn't cried at all. She was angry, and confused—and implacably, horribly
awake.

Why had she come here in the first place? Hope. Stupid, foolish hope.
She had told herself that she had to oversee the property valuation herself,
after seeing enough clients swindled by unscrupulous contractors. But she
could have hired someone to do that. Even seconded one of her colleagues
from the realtor's office to deal with the whole bloody project.

She could have let someone else sort the whole thing out, and never
even set foot in Hideaway Cove again.

*So why didn't I? Why did I set myself up for all this misery?*
Because of hope. The same thing that always tripped her up.

Hope that a stupid family story would turn out to be true and solve all
her problems. Hope that coming back to Hideaway might, in some way,
help her untangle the ugly mass of knots inside her.

Lainie groaned and closed her eyes. *Instead, you've just made everything
worse.*

Another knot formed inside her as she remembered yelling the same
words at Harrison. Poor guy. He'd only wanted a night of fun, and here
she was, dragging him into the house of horrors that was her life.

That was her fault. She'd seen the chance for a fun distraction from the work that brought her here and grabbed it with both hands. She hadn't thought about the consequences. Her fault.

*Just like it's all your fault,* she thought, suddenly feeling very tired. *Dad leaving. Never seeing Gran and Grampa again. You should have learned eight years ago that trying to fix things only makes them worse…*

She buried her face in the pillow, as though that would help her hide from the memory of her eighteen-year-old self, so hopeful and wanting to help.

*Well, that all sure backfired, didn't it? If you'd just been a bitch back then instead of trying to fix things, you wouldn't be in this mess.*

Seventy-five thousand dollars. That sort of money should have made all her problems go away. Unfortunately, that hopeful, helpful eighteen-year-old Lainie had gotten herself into far more than seventy-five thousand problems.

A sudden clatter made her sit bolt upright. For one insane second, she thought Harrison had come back, and was rattling at her door. Then the noise came again, and this time she placed it. Heavy rain was falling in bursts against the picture window. As the wind picked up, so did the sound of the rain gusting against the walls.

Lainie shivered. *When did it get so dark?* she thought, wrapping her arms around herself. She checked the cutesy maritime-styled clock on the wall: it wasn't even late afternoon yet, but it looked like early evening. She walked over and looked out the window. The sky was a forbidding dark gray, and the cove, which had been so calm before, was a boiling mass of whitecap waves.

*This must be one of those storms Harrison talked about.* Guiltily, Lainie looked down to the path in front of the B&B, where Harrison had been standing earlier. He was long gone, of course.

*Shit. So much for my plans to drive home today.* Even if she left now, it would be well after midnight by the time she made it back, and that was assuming she didn't run into trouble with the bad weather.

Another squall of rain battered the window and Lainie winced, letting the curtain fall back over it.

At least the rain had achieved something. The miserable exhaustion that had plagued her since she came back from that godawful interrogation had lifted. She felt energized.

She had to *do* something. Lying around in a fog of unhappiness wasn't going to help her.

She shivered as she remembered Mrs. Sweets' look of disgust. It was the same expression the old woman used to have on her face when she handed eleven-year-old Lainie her ice cream.

*I could actually do some work,* she thought, imagining the stacks of projects waiting for her at her desk in the city. *Or…*
*Maybe I should call Mom.*
Her automatic reaction to the thought was reluctance. She'd tried talking to her Mom about this before, with no success. When it came to Hideaway Cove and her divorce, Lainie's mother was a closed book.

*But this is different. I'm actually* here, *now. And after I tell her what happened this afternoon, surely she will have to explain something. The whole situation is just… crazy.*

*If nothing else, if I burst into tears over the phone, maybe that will convince her.*

Lainie grabbed her purse, hurrying to make the call before she changed her mind. Her phone wasn't in its usual pocket. She checked again and then rummaged through the rest of the bag. Nothing.

Frowning, she checked her laptop bag, and then her suitcase. No phone.

*This is getting stupid. Where is it?*

Lainie thought back to the last time she'd used it. *On the way here, to make sure I was on the right road… checking my work email after I arrived… Calling my manager… Oh, no.*

The last time she remembered using her phone was that morning. It seemed so long ago now. She'd used it as a flashlight to light up the dingy interior of her grandparents' house.

*I must have used it since then. Surely. I—oh, shit. I must have dropped it after I saw the painting. We went around the rest of the house with just Harrison's flashlight, didn't we?*

*Shit.*

She would have to go back for it. She couldn't leave it there, not in this rain—with her luck, the old wreck of a house would spring a leak and she'd turn up in the morning to find her phone had drowned to death.

*Damn Hideaway Cove.* Lainie flung her suitcase open and grabbed the raincoat she had packed in the hopes of not having to use it. At least she still had the rental car. *Please tell me I didn't drop the keys as well—oh, thank God, there they are.*

Lainie poked her head into reception on the way past, but there was no sign of Mrs. Hanson, the B&B's owner. She called out, but heard no response. Fighting back the uncharitable thought that the old lady had probably gone to join the rest of them in planning the best way to kick Lainie out, she wrote a short note on a pad at the reception desk:

*Dear Mrs. Hanson. Change of plans. Need to stay one more night due to storm, hope this is OK. Thanks, Lainie.*

The storm was raging by the time Lainie pulled up in front of her grandparents' old house. The drive up the hill had been hairy, and she took a few minutes to pull herself together. Her little Ford hadn't coped with the potholes as well as Harrison's truck had.

Rain lashed at the windscreen. It was so heavy the windscreen wipers hadn't been any use on the way up. Now, she turned the engine off, and the outside world blurred and dripped on the outside of the glass.

Lainie zipped up her raincoat and pulled the hood as far over her forehead as it would reach. "Here goes…"

She gritted her teeth and launched herself into the rain.

The wind was stronger than she'd expected, buffeting her from side to side as she raced to the front door. She wrestled with the lock for a moment—long enough for every part of her not covered by the coat to become soaked—and tumbled inside. The chill of the wind and rain left her gasping as she wrenched the door shut.

That morning, she had thought the shuttered, dust-caked windows hadn't let any light in. So why did it look even darker now?

It was like she was wearing a blindfold. Lainie swore as she realized she hadn't brought a light. Well, of course she hadn't. She was going to *find* her light, e.g., her phone. She would have to find her way around by touch, that was all.

At least she was fairly certain where her phone was. In the sitting room, on the other side of the house.

Lainie stepped forward, her hands stretched in front of her. So far, so good. She edged forward until she found the far wall. So far… still good.

Navigating by memory, Lainie made her way slowly towards the sitting room. *Thank goodness all the furniture was cleared out years ago*, she thought.

Around her, the house creaked and groaned as the storm raged outside. Lainie flinched as an extra strong gust of wind made the whole building shudder. She didn't even want to think of what her pants would look like after this. Soaked by the rain and then marinated in all the dust she was kicking up—bleugh.

At last she found the door to the sitting room. The room overlooked the open sea, and even through the shutters the noise of the surf was deafening. It almost sounded as though it was coming up from under the floorboards. Lainie shivered.

She edged sideways until she found the old brick fireplace. *God, my hands must be filthy. Right—here I am. Now, where was I when I dropped the phone?*

Lainie imagined herself looking up at the painting, and stepped slowly backward, sliding her feet across the floorboards. Another squall hit the house, making her jump. Her heel hit something.

Trying to ignore the deafening sounds of the storm and surf outside Lainie bent down and, after a moment's scrambling, picked up her phone.

"Finally! Time to get out of here."

Lainie turned the phone on and, miraculously, it still had some battery left. She used the light to look around. The room was just as she remembered it—from the day before, not from her childhood. The overstuffed sofas and colorful rugs were long gone, replaced by thick sheets of dust and muck.

She squinted into the shadows. Was that a trick of the light, or did something just move out there?

Lainie lifted her phone-light higher, peering into the darkness. Was there an animal or something stuck in here, hiding from the storm? Oh, hell, it couldn't be a kid, could it? This place was probably the coolest hang-out spot for Hideaway Cove teens. The haunted Eaves house.

"Hello?"

The house groaned, a long, drawn-out crackling creak that seemed to go on forever. There was definitely something moving out there. Lainie was halfway across the room before she realized that the thing that was moving *was* the room.

She swore and jumped backwards, but it was too late. With a roar, the far wall peeled off the house. Lainie watched in horror as the floor seemed to sink away with it. Rain flooded in, as heavy as the tides.

Lainie jumped backwards as the boards beneath her feet began to move. Her feet skidded on the wet dust, and she fell onto her hands and knees, swearing. Behind her, the house groaned again. She turned around just in time to see half of the room disappear.

*What—where the hell did it go? We're not that close to the cliff!*

"The hell with this." She gritted her teeth, pushing herself up. Her left wrist buckled, and Lainie whimpered as pain shot up her arm. *No time to think about that.* Her phone light was still on, at least. She held her injured arm against her chest and pushed forward, heading for the door.

Under her feet, rotten floorboards creaked. Lainie froze.

*Oh, no. No, no, no.*

Lainie slid one foot forward slowly, and the floorboards sank even more. *Every time I move, I'm damaging them more.*

She risked a quick glance back over her shoulder. Rain lashed her face. She couldn't tell how far a drop to the ground would be—or even where the ground was. What if the edge of the cliff had crumbled from under the house, and that was why the room had fallen away?

She was stuck. If she moved, her the floorboards might crumble underneath her. But if she stayed where she was…

*The same thing will happen, only more slowly.* She gritted her teeth. *I can't just cower here and wait for that to happen.*

# 10

# HARRISON

Harrison stared at his hands.

When he'd first come to Hideaway Cove, he had thought it was paradise. A whole town of shifters? He'd never even dreamed such a place could exist.

He'd been so content here, he'd never wondered why *everyone* in Hideaway was a shifter.

Well, that was clear now. The Sweets and their cronies must have driven off any humans who wanted to move in. Regardless of whether they were related to shifters, or not.

*Not any more*, he thought grimly. He couldn't go back in time and prevent Lainie from ever being hurt, but he could keep her safe now.

If she ever wanted to speak to him again.

There was a knock on the door, barely audible over the sound of the storm outside.

"What?" Harrison growled. He reined in his frustration as Arlo poked his head around the door. "What do you want?"

"It's about Lainie."

Harrison dropped his tools. "Did she call?" He could hear someone in the corridor behind Arlo. Was she here? "I have to talk to her." He started for the door, but Arlo put up a hand, holding him back.

If it had been anyone but Arlo, Harrison would have pushed past him. But he knew Arlo.

He took a deep breath. *Be patient. Rushing into things is what went wrong in the first place.*

"What is it?" he asked, trying to get a sense of whoever it was behind Arlo. It was a woman, but now that he was closer, he could tell it wasn't Lainie. He would have recognized her scent at once.

Arlo sighed and beckoned to the woman lurking behind him. "Tell him what you told me."

To Harrison's surprise, the person who stepped forward was Tessa Sweets, the current manager of the ice cream parlor.

Tessa was in her early twenties, a plump brunette with runaway curls and chocolate-brown eyes. Like her grandmother, she was a gator shifter.

Her grandmother, who was trying to run Lainie out of town.

"What do you want?" Harrison said harshly. What was Arlo playing at? What could he possibly have to say to the granddaughter of the woman who'd just insulted his mate? "If your freezers are playing up again, I think that can wait until after the storm."

"It's not the shop. There's something you need to know," Tessa blurted out. Her eyes darted from side to side. "About… about what happened this afternoon."

"It's all right," Arlo said softly. "There's no way your grandmother or any of her lot will hear you in here."

Tessa's mouth jerked downward. "Oh, I know. They're all holed up at the parlor, cackling." She took a deep breath and looked Harrison in the eye. "I shouldn't be telling you this, but I can't keep it to myself. I heard Gran and Grandpop talking last night. According to Gran, she's the reason Lainie was kicked out of Hideaway in the first place."

"Kicked out?" Harrison was stunned. "I didn't know she used to live here. That explains…"

He stopped. *That explains why being here makes her so upset.* "She told me she wasn't close with her grandparents," he said slowly.

"Yeah, Gran was really proud of that one," Tessa said, her mouth twisting. "She was practically crowing about it last night."

"When did this happen?"

"Before you moved here. Either of you." Tessa nodded her head to include Arlo. "Honestly, I don't know how many people here would know about it, though, even people who've lived here forever. Gran seems to have hushed it up really well… except when the temptation to brag becomes too much, I guess."

Arlo cut in. "What Tessa's saying is, fifteen years ago, Lainie and her mother were made to leave Hideaway Cove. Because her father had married a human, and Lainie wasn't born a shifter."

"That's *it*? Just because they were human?"

Tessa snorted. "That's enough, apparently. Gran says this town is a sanctuary for shifters, and that means no humans allowed."

"That's crazy."

"Is it?" Arlo asked. "Think about it. The outside world isn't exactly a friendly place for shifters."

Harrison exchanged a look with him. True, neither of them had exactly had a happy life before they found Hideaway. The stress of constantly hiding who—well, *what*—you were was a constant tension in the outside world.

"But Lainie's related to shifters," he argued. "They broke up her family, for what? Did they think she would betray her own grandparents to the outside world?"

Arlo shrugged, looking miserable. Tessa didn't meet his eyes.

Harrison groaned and ran his fingers through his hair. "Fine. I'm going to go ahead and assume their reasons were ass-stupid, then. And I'm going to talk to Lainie."

He stalked past Arlo and Tessa, who was still looking miserable. He grabbed his coat and keys and was about to leave when he banged into Pol.

Pol was pale, almost green under his golden tan. Harrison paused. "Are you all right?"

Pol shrugged, flashing a weak grin at Harrison. "Power surge. Everyone's gone home and turned on the heating. I'm fine, I just need to carb-load and crash."

"Look after yourself, all right?" Harrison frowned as Pol staggered through to the waiting room and flopped down on one of the sofas. But he didn't have time to deal with Pol's problems right now.

He drove to the B&B, rain pummeling the roof of his truck. The noise was like a jackhammer driving straight to his brain.

*I have to get this right. I have to explain—everything. Shifters. The mate bond. That her grandparents didn't want to send her away, they just didn't have a choice.*

*And I'm going to make sure she knows there is no way in hell I'm going to let the Sweets get away with this.*

He just had to find the words to say it.

He parked in the empty space in front of the B&B, and splashed up to the front door. It opened almost before he started knocking, and Mrs. Hanson stared up at him. Her face fell.

"She's not with you?" she said.

"Who's not with me?" Rain was trickling down Harrison's neck. "You mean Lainie? Isn't she here?"

"You'd better come inside." Mrs. Hanson tottered back into the B&B and Harrison followed, rain streaming off him. Mrs. Hanson disappeared behind her desk briefly and came back waving a piece of paper.

"I just left for a minute to check the shed roof was holding up in the rain, and she must have gone then. She left this. I thought she'd gone to see you—well, I hoped she had, after everything that happened."

She handed Harrison the note. He scanned it.

"Her car's gone. If she hadn't left the note, I would have thought she'd left town. Her luggage is still here, too." Mrs. Hanson wrung her hands. "Where could she have gone? It's not safe, driving around in weather like this."

*Where would she have gone?* Harrison couldn't imagine Lainie going back to Caro's, not after this afternoon.

How well did she remember Hideaway Cove from her childhood? Maybe she had some private bolt-hole where she used to run away…

…Or maybe he was missing the most obvious answer. "The old Eaves place."

"Oh, no! In this weather?" Mrs. Hanson flapped her hands unhappily. "Are you sure?"

"Where else would she have gone? It's not like people here have gone out of their way to make her welcome." Harrison stormed outside, not waiting for Mrs. Hanson's response.

He stared up at Lighthouse Hill through the rain. Was that glimmer of silver Lainie's car? He had to know for sure. Harrison swung himself back into his truck. Despite the thumping of his heart, he drove carefully. He'd seen too many cars end up in the lagoon to risk driving fast in a storm.

The road up to the old Eaves place was more like a river. The potholes were invisible under the rush of water and Harrison gritted his teeth as he bumped and bunny-hopped up the hill. At last he crested the top of the hill and saw Lainie's car, parked in front of the house.

He didn't know whether he was relieved or horrified. *What the hell is she doing in there, in this weather?*

"Lainie!" he called, but the wind whipped his voice away. The front door was unlocked, and he pulled it open, shaking the rain out of his hair. "Lainie, are you here?"

He'd thought being inside would mute the sound of the storm, but it was as loud as ever. The whole house was groaning under the onslaught. "Lainie?"

"Harrison?!"

Harrison followed her voice to the back of the house. A cold wind whipped at his clothes, but he paid no attention to it until he reached the door to the sitting room.

Lainie was standing stiffly a few feet from the door, hunched over against the rain and wind. She was completely drenched, her blonde hair plastered to her pale cheeks. Behind her, was… nothing.

"Oh my God." Harrison started forward and Lainie's eyes widened.

"No, don't—!" she cried out, but it was too late. The floorboards creaked under Harrison's feet, and with a crackle of splintering wood, they were both falling.

Harrison didn't think. There was no time. He reached inside himself and found his griffin form, shifting faster than he ever had before.

# II

# LAINIE

Lainie screamed as she fell. Something huge slammed into her mid-air. Heavy limbs wrapped around her. *Harrison?*

She hit the ground, winded, landing on top of Harrison. Or what she thought was Harrison. She felt around with her chilled hands. Whoever—whatever—she had landed on, it was huge. And… feathered?

Lainie shoved herself backwards. Her feet found solid ground and then slipped again. The thing she had landed on grunted and started to get up. There was just enough light for Lainie to get a glimpse of its huge bulk. A flash of lightning lit up rain-drenched feathers and a huge, sharp beak. Predatory eyes gleamed black as it turned to look at her.

"Oh *shit*," she gasped, and stepped backward. Another flash of lightning filled the sky, confirming what she thought she'd seen.

The creature had an eagle's head, but it was bigger than any bird Lainie had ever heard of. It had two huge, clawed front legs, and dark-striped wings. But that wasn't all. Its rear half looked like a giant cat, not a bird. Fur. Huge paws. And a tufted tail whipping back and forth in the rain.

A griffin. There was a fucking *griffin* in her grandparents' house.

*No,* Lainie thought, frozen. *That's impossible. You must have hit your head. It's impossible.*

The griffin raised its beak, sniffing the air. Behind it, the house groaned. Lainie skidded backward as the griffin hauled itself to its feet. It was as tall as she was.

*I've got to get out of here.* Lainie looked around desperately. She'd fallen into what must be the old foundations of the house. A long enough drop to wind herself, but not to break anything. If she could just make her way through the rubble without disturbing the—she could barely make herself think it. The griffin. The griffin that had to be some sort of trauma-induced hallucination.

*…And where's Harrison?*

Lainie wiped her wet hair off her face. The rain was still sheeting down, but at least out here in the open it was still just light enough to see by. There was no sign of Harrison.

*Which means he's probably trapped under* something, she thought, her throat going tight. *God, I hope he's all right.*

She had to get help. She had to believe that Harrison was still alive in there somewhere, and get help from Hideaway Cove to chase off the griffin and save him.

*Chase off the griffin? Have you decided it's real now? Is that what's going on?*

Lainie took a careful step backward, making sure her footing was secure before she shifted her weight. She'd already sprained one wrist. There was no way she'd be able to get out of here if she got her foot caught under a beam, or trapped herself in falling rubble.

The griffin was definitely looking at her. Lainie held her breath. *It's not real,* she told herself.

*But it sure as hell* looks *real.*

Another crash from the house distracted her. She looked up behind the griffin to see another wall crumbling down toward her. There was no time for her to get out of the way.

The griffin moved faster than she would have thought possible, leaping between her and the falling masonry. Lainie screamed as the wall hit the creature, pushing it into her. They both tumbled backward. Floorboards shattered under their combined weight and Lainie shrieked as the ground disappeared beneath her. *Again.*

This time, she opened her eyes to pitch darkness. Her back was pressed up against cold stone, and her whole body felt battered.

Hot breath hit her face and she lashed out with her fist. Whatever she'd hit fell back with a strange noise like someone cracking all their knuckles at once.

"Ow!"

"Harrison?" Lainie couldn't believe her ears.

"Lainie? Where are you? And… where are we?"

Lainie could have cried with relief. She felt the wall behind her. It was solid granite, too smooth to be natural. "In the basement, I think. Are you hurt?"

"Apart from my nose?"

Lainie reached out. Her fingers brushed against Harrison's jaw. "I'm sorry. There was a—some sort of animal, or something…"

Harrison took her hands and held them between his. His hands were warm, and Lainie shivered, suddenly aware of how cold she was.

"I think it's gone," Harrison said after a moment. "At least…it's not down here with us."

"Well, that's something." Lainie shuddered. She didn't resist as Harrison pulled her to him and wrapped his arms around her. "I thought—I didn't see you, after the floor collapsed, and I thought…"

"Shh. I'm fine," Harrison reassured her. "I came here to find you, and I'm just glad I got here in time."

She let her head fall onto his shoulder. His skin was slick with rain, but he radiated heat. She snuggled into him. *Hang on…*

"What happened to your shirt?"

Harrison's jaw tensed against the top of her head. "It, er—"

"You'll freeze," she said. "We've got to get out of here."

She felt Harrison look up. "I think we smashed through the staircase on the way down," he said with a groan.

Lainie rubbed her face. "I guess it's too far out to climb? Damn. Well…" She thought hard. "I think there's a way out through the basement. An old tunnel that leads down to the beach. I don't remember it very well. I was never allowed down there on my own."

"Let's see if we can find it," Harrison said. He stood up, pulling Lainie with him. She hissed as he bumped her injured arm.

"What's wrong?"

"My wrist… I think I sprained it earlier. Don't worry about it. The important thing is finding a way out of here." She reached out to find the wall and started to feel her way along it. "There should be a door…"

Harrison put his hand on her chest, holding her gently in place. "You're hurt," he said, his voice firm. "Stay here, and I'll find the door."

Lainie did as he said, holding her hands to her chest where she could still feel the memory of his touch, warm and comforting. She listened to his steps as he walked carefully along the wall, and into something solid.

"Ow! I thought all the furniture had been taken out of here?"

"What is it?" Lainie hurried forward.

She could feel the heat of Harrison's body as she came up beside him. The rain was so cold, she couldn't help leaning against him, just a bit.

*Just because I'm cold. And sore. And… have his pants disappeared, too?* Lainie straightened up again quickly.

"It's a cupboard of some sort," Harrison said, his voice muffled. "It must have been tipped over when I—uh, when we fell down here. Hang on, there's something behind it. It feels like a door."

"Behind a cupboard?" Lainie rubbed her aching wrist. "That doesn't make any sense."

"Well, that's where it was… shall we have a look? Er, a blind grope around? Er, I meant—"

Lainie snorted. "Let's go."

She stepped back as Harrison hauled the cupboard out of the way. The door had been broken half-off its hinges when the cupboard fell, and they made their way through it carefully. Lainie didn't want to add a black eye to her list of injuries.

"Does this look—uh, feel—familiar?"

They were still poking around in the pitch dark. "Well, it's a stone tunnel, with—oops—steps going down. Unless the hill is riddled with secret passages, I'd say this is it." Lainie took a few careful steps. "I guess my grandmother must have had someone hide the door when she moved into the home. Keeping the secret passage secret even after she left."

The tunnel was narrow enough that Lainie's shoulders sometimes brushed up against both walls at once. She heard Harrison grunt once or twice as he twisted himself sideways to get through.

"I hope you're not claustrophobic," he said at one point. Lainie laughed with surprise.

"Me? You're the one who sounds like he's twisting himself into pretzels to get through. What happens to me if you get stuck?"

She had meant it as a joke, but Harrison took it seriously. "That's a good point. Here, the passage opens out a bit where I am now—can you fit past me, and go in front?" He paused. "Given how my first rescue attempt this evening went, it'll be just my luck if I do get stuck, and trap you in here."

Lainie reached forward until she was touching Harrison's shoulder. The tunnel had widened out, yes, but it was still narrow enough that she had to press her body against his to get past him. She slid her hand from his shoulder to his chest as she edged past. His heart was hammering.

"Don't beat yourself up over what happened up there," she muttered. "It wasn't like I was up to much before you got here. I didn't even dare to move in case I sent the whole floor crashing down, and me with it."

"Which was smart, seeing as the moment *I* moved near you, the whole house fell down on us," Harrison grumbled into her hair. She'd stopped moving, wedged between him and the wall.

"Thank you for coming to find me." She tipped her head up, even though she knew there was no way she'd be able to see his face in the darkness. "How did you know where I was?"

"I guessed." Harrison slid his arms around her. "Mrs. Hanson showed me your note, and, well, I couldn't think of anywhere else in town you would be."

"I was looking for my phone," Lainie admitted. "God, that sounds stupid. It's probably smashed to bits by now." She sighed. "Sorry for yelling at you, before."

One of Harrison's hands stroked up her body to cradle her head against his chest. "Sorry my neighbors are such a pack of assholes," he replied. "If I'd known how they were going to treat you, we never would have gone in there."

She shrugged. "Let the crazies be crazies. It won't make any difference." Her heart ached at the reminder that even once they got out of this ridiculous situation, she would still have to face up to Mrs. Sweets and the other townspeople until this project was over.

Reluctantly, Lainie pulled away from Harrison. The tunnel was cold, and he was wonderfully warm, but she knew that the longer they stayed here, the more likely both of them were to develop hypothermia.

"I can't tell how far we've come already," she said, one hand still trailing down his arm as she stepped forward. "But don't you think the sea is sounding close—aah!"

Lainie's feet shot out from under her. Harrison was already grabbing her arm, but she windmilled the other one, trying to regain her balance. Her flailing arm caught something on the wall and sent it crashing down onto her legs.

"Ow!" she groaned. "What the hell was that?"

She clutched her arm to her chest. Just her luck that her injured arm was the one she flailed out madly with to keep her balance. And what had she hit, anyway?

Harrison put his hands around her waist and pulled her upright. "What happened? Are you all right?"

"I hit something off the wall…" With Harrison still holding her, Lainie groped around the wall. There was a shallow alcove cut into the stone at waist height. "I must have knocked something off this shelf when I fell—ouch. And I've got something in my shoe now, too."

She wriggled her foot around, trying to encourage the bit of gravel into a more comfortable spot. "On the upside, I'm pretty sure I slipped on a patch of seaweed, so I guess that means we're near the end of the tunnel."

The sound of waves had been growing louder, and as they rounded the next corner—Lainie limping slightly—a glimmer of light appeared ahead. Dim light, but compared to the solid darkness inside the tunnel, it might as well have been the midday sun.

The stone steps under Lainie's feet became gritty with sand and then disappeared completely. Salt spray hit her face, and she stopped.

"Oh, no," she said, her heart sinking. "If the water's already coming into the cave—" *Then we're stuck. Even wading around the bay in this weather would be suicide.*

"I'll go check. Wait here." Harrison squeezed her hand, and she watched him as he walked slowly towards the mouth of the cave. He was barely more than a silhouette, his footsteps darker shadows in the wet sand.

*I still can't believe this is happening,* Lainie thought, steadying herself against the cave wall. *The house, the* griffin-hallucination—*God, I probably have a concussion, it seemed so* real—*and Harrison coming to find me. I can't believe he did that for me.*

"Lainie!" Harrison was beckoning her over. She hurried over to him, wincing as the bit of gravel in her shoe cut into her ankle. *Oh, don't be such a baby,* she told herself. *Think of Harrison, squishing through that tunnel without a stitch of clothing on.*

Harrison put his arm around her and pointed along the bottom of the cliff.

There was a small sandy beach at the mouth of the cave. On sunny days, it was a pleasant spot between the piled rocks that lay at the bottom of the cliff. Tonight, the flat beach made a funnel for the incoming storm tide.

Lainie raised a hand to keep the sea spray off her face, squinting in the direction Harrison was pointing.

"There—see? There's a path in the rock."

Lainie wiped her eyes. Yes—she could just make it out. A narrow path cut into the side of the cliff.

As she watched, a wave smashed over part of the path, then sucked back into the sea. "You're not seriously suggesting we go for it?"

"I know it doesn't look like it, but it's low tide right now," Harrison explained, his voice urgent. "The longer we wait, the further the tide will come up into the cave. We can't wait out the storm in there. You're already too cold. You're not even shivering anymore."

Lainie opened her mouth to protest, but it was true. She shut her mouth again. "How are we going to get across there?"

"I've been watching the waves. They're going in series, starting small and getting bigger. After the biggest wave crashes, they start off small again." He put his arms around Lainie, and she leaned in to his warmth. "The smaller waves don't get anywhere near the path, and the path gets higher further along. We'll wait for the series to start again, and I'll carry you."

"Okay."

"Really?" Harrison raised his eyebrows. "I expected you to—well, not argue, but I thought I'd have to convince you."

Lainie wrapped her arms around herself. "No. You're right. I'm cold, and wet, and we don't know how long the storm is going to take to blow over." *And there's a goddamn… something back at the other end of that tunnel, although right now I'm honestly not sure if I didn't hallucinate it.*

"All right." Harrison leaned down and kissed her, so quickly she didn't have the chance to kiss him back, and then swung her up in his arms.

He stood still for a moment, judging the waves. Lainie flinched as another massive wave crashed down on the beach, swirling around Harrison's ankles.

As the water retreated he launched himself forward, sprinting across the thin stretch of sand to where rocks rose out of the surf. Lainie held on tight to his shoulders as he leaped up the piled rocks and onto the stone path.

She could feel his heartbeat thundering against her chest as he ran. Her own heart was in her throat. If this didn't work—she couldn't think about it.

If she looked straight ahead, all she could see was the ocean, waiting to drag her away. If she turned her head, it was the sheer cliff whipping past her face as Harrison ran to beat the waves. She squeezed her eyes shut.

It felt like years later that Harrison's pace slowed. He squeezed Lainie gently. "We're safe."

She opened her eyes, and the first thing she saw was Harrison, staring back at her. His hazel eyes were warm, and looking into them, she felt safe.

"Let's get you home," he murmured softly.

# 12

# HARRISON

Harrison barged through the front door of Mackaby Workshops, ignoring Pol's shout of surprise as he rushed past the waiting room. He had something more important to look after: his mate, who was still shivering in his arms.

He took the stairs to his second-floor apartment three at a time, not stopping until he reached the bathroom. He lowered Lainie to the ground and held her to his chest as he turned on the shower.

Lainie didn't bother stripping off before stepping into the shower.

"Oh, this is wonderful," she breathed, putting her face under the water. She wiped her hair off her face and looked up at Harrison. Her black eyes were ringed with dark circles, but she was smiling. "I can't believe we made it out of there. You saved me, Harrison."

Lainie grabbed his hand and pulled him into the shower with her. Harrison put his arms around her. Even in the hot shower, she was shaking.

She leaned her forehead against his chest. "I can't believe any of this is really happening," she whispered.

Harrison's heart wrenched. He wished he could believe she meant that in a good way—but there was no way that was possible. She'd been insulted, humiliated, and almost killed. She was probably just amazed to be alive, and desperate to leave Hideaway behind forever.

For now, though, she seemed happy to stand encircled in his arms.

Eventually, she shook herself. "God. What am I doing? Wearing a raincoat in the shower?" She wriggled free of Harrison's arms. "Help me out of this, will you?"

Harrison gladly complied. Lainie's coat was as wet inside as it was outside, the same as his had been. Under it, her silk blouse was transparent. Harrison would have found the sight enticing, if it wasn't for the shaky way Lainie was moving.

"When did you last eat?" he asked, frowning.

"What? Oh…" Lainie grimaced. "Breakfast?"

"You—" Harrison began, and bit his tongue. *You had a lot else on your mind today*, he thought, kissing the top of her head. "Never mind. I'll put something together."

Harrison dried off and wrapped the towel around his waist. Before he went through to the kitchen, he paused, and looked back at Lainie. She was standing under the water, head tilted back, eyes closed. Safe.

*No, she's not*, he realized. *Not safe from her own memories and pain. And she won't be, until she knows the full story.*

He knew what he had to do.

*Harrison! What the hell is going on?*

Pol. Harrison closed the bathroom door behind himself. It didn't seem right to talk to Pol while he was looking at Lainie.

*There was a situation up at the old Eaves house,* he said simply.

*I'll say! We heard the crash from here. It looks like half the house fell into the sea. Christ—don't tell me you and Lainie were up there?*

*We made it out.*

*Jesus, Harrison. Enough with the hero act. What the hell were you doing up there?*

*Pol, listen.* Harrison's mind was racing. *I need you to do something for me.*

*Shoot, boss.*

Harrison explained his plan. He could almost feel Pol shaking his head. *You sure I'm the right person to do this? People like me, sure, but let's be honest, I'm not great at the serious stuff.*

*Sorry, Sparky. You're the best I've got right now. Good luck.* He paused. *Talk to Tessa, if you can. If there's anything else she knows that could help…*

*You got it, boss.*

Harrison waited until he heard the front door close downstairs and then sagged against the door.

*If only this was the end of it. Save the girl and win the day. I wish it were that simple.*

Half an hour later, Lainie was sitting at the kitchen table, wrapped in Harrison's warmest robe and with a half-eaten plate of grilled cheese in front of her. Harrison was keeping his hands busy making them both mugs of hot lemon and honey, but he couldn't help the way his gaze kept landing on her.

His whole body ached to hold her. His griffin was complaining. Its aggravation was so strong, it was making Harrison's skin itch: *What are you waiting for? Take her to your bed. Surround her with pillows, and blankets, and keep her warm with your body. Why are we still here in the kitchen?*

He couldn't put it off any longer.

"Lainie, there's something I have to tell you." Harrison closed his eyes. There. He'd done it. Step one—and no turning back now. "I wanted to wait until I had the perfect way to tell you, the right words, the right moment—but now I know that moment's never going to come, and the longer I put it off, the worse things will be."

Lainie looked up at him. Out of the rain, warm from the shower and with a hot meal inside her, she no longer looked on the verge of collapse. But there was still a careful wariness in her eyes as she said quietly, "Things are pretty shit already, to be honest. But go on. What is it?"

"It's to do with what happened at Caro's earlier. And—"

Harrison stopped just short of saying *It's about us*. Lainie's mouth had gotten that pinched look the moment he mentioned the meeting. *Damn it.*

"You know, I'd really rather not talk about that," she said quietly, staring at the table.

"I understand. God knows if I was in your position I'd feel the same way." Harrison sat down opposite her. "But I think this will help you to make some sense of why Mrs. Sweets and the others are behaving the way they are. And…why your grandparents were forced to make you leave."

That got her attention. Lainie's eyes flicked up. She stared hard at him for a few breaths, as though trying to find something in his gaze. At last she took a slow breath. "Okay," she said. "Go on. I'm listening."

*This is it. If you do this, you're setting yourself up to be kicked out of town, too.*

Harrison thrust the treacherous thoughts aside. *Better to leave Hideaway, and have a chance of staying with Lainie, than stay here, knowing that I took part in the lie that drove her away.*

Harrison pushed his chair back from the table. He hadn't bothered to get dressed. Despite wrapping Lainie in his thickest robe and pushing as many blankets at her as he could find, Harrison himself was still only wearing a towel wrapped around his waist. That would make this easier.

"The only way you're going to believe this is if I show you," he said, and reached deep inside himself for his griffin form.

Heat rushed through him, a fire that started in his heart and flared out. It filled his chest, his limbs, and then there was that heart-stopping moment where, just for a heartbeat, he felt as though the fire would burst out of him. Instead, his body changed to fit it.

His bones creaked, changing shape and size. Claws stretched from the end of his fingers, and he dropped to all fours. Two sets of razor-sharp talons, and two heavy paws. Thick, dark-gold hair covered the back half of his body, transitioning to sleek feathers from his chest forwards.

The only part of his body that did not change were his eyes. They stayed the same bright hazel as they were in his human form.

It took Harrison a moment to focus on the room. Things were always a bit hazy for a few seconds after he shifted. When his vision cleared, he immediately looked around for Lainie.

She was standing half-out of her chair, frozen mid-action. Her eyes were wide—but there was no trace of the horror Harrison had been afraid he would see in them.

# 13

# LAINIE

*Am I dreaming?*

Lainie felt dizzy. For a moment, she wondered if she was still up on the hill in the ruins of her grandparents' home, delirious from the cold.

What she was seeing couldn't be real. Harrison had stood up in front of her and, as casually as if he was buttoning a shirt, transformed into a massive griffin.

*This is just like what I thought I saw in the house. I must still be hallucinating.*

But she couldn't be. That terrifying sprint across the cliff-side path, the feeling of warmth seeping back into her body under the hot shower, the grilled cheese she could still taste in her mouth—she couldn't have imagined all that.

Which left only one explanation.

"Is this real?" she breathed.

The griffin took up half the kitchen. It looked at her with Harrison's hazel eyes and nodded.

"Oh, my God." Lainie staggered, bracing herself against the table. She hadn't even realized she was standing up. She made her way around the table, with one hand on it for balance, until she was standing in front of the griffin. In front of Harrison. In front of Harrison, the griffin.

She reached out and stopped with her fingertips inches away from the griffin's beak. From Harrison's beak.

Some prehistoric part of her brain was screaming at her that this was a dangerous animal. That she should run, now, as fast as she could.

But a bigger part of her, a far bigger part, was caught by a sense of dizzying wonder. What she'd just seen—it was amazing. And the longer she looked at this griffin, the more she could see Harrison in it. The way he held his head. His stance, even on four legs, was strangely reminiscent of how Harrison would stand.

As was the watchful look in his eyes, as he waited for her to react.

"This is crazy," she said. "This is just… oh." She sank to her knees. The griffin dropped its head, to keep it level with hers. *Just like Harrison, keeping an eye on me*, she thought distractedly.

A new, horrifying realization had struck her. "This is why I had to leave Hideaway Cove, isn't it? You're all… like this?"

Harrison nodded.

It all made sense now. Her parents' fights, which always stopped the moment she entered the room, as though there was more than just their marital problems in the air. Mrs. Sweets' determination that Lainie not move to Hideaway Cove. Even the strange, curious looks she got from the other people who lived here. If they were all keeping a secret like this…

*Then it's no wonder they all wanted to get rid of me*, she thought. *Even my grandparents. Even my father. Because I don't belong here.*

"I always thought my parents split up because of me," she said, her voice wavering. "Because of something I did. But it wasn't that, was it? It was because of what I *am*."

Her heart felt heavy, and her chest went so tight it was difficult to breathe. There was that knuckle-cracking noise in front of her again, the one she remembered from the house, and then Harrison's arms were around her. She collapsed against him, letting him hold her to his chest.

"Why didn't they tell me?" she cried out. "Oh, hell. I can't—the estate, the money—what am I going to do?"

Harrison's arms tightened around her, warm and secure. "I'm so sorry," he said, his own voice catching.

Lainie took a deep breath. Somehow, being in Harrison's arms made the knot in her heart hurt less. "So—what? Everyone in this town can turn into a griffin?"

"No. I'm the only griffin." Harrison sighed. "I shouldn't be telling you this, but I can't keep you in the dark any longer. I won't. We're called shifters. Each of us has an animal side, a creature we can transform into. Like a griffin. Or a bird, or a fish…"

Lainie was listening to his explanation, eyes wide. But at that, she couldn't help interrupting. "A *fish*? What if they shifted when they weren't around water?"

Harrison smiled. "Well, we're a coastal town, aren't we? Anyway, shifters can control when they transform. It's not like—oh, stories about werewolves, where the full moon forces them to transform."

"I can't believe I'm asking about the technicalities of how people handle turning into other animals," Lainie grumbled. She lay her head against Harrison's shoulder. "How do you know if you're a shifter?"

"Well, for me, I grew up with it. My parents were both griffin shifters, too, so they taught me all about it. I could shift from when I was a baby, but it's not like that for everyone. Which is a good thing, I guess? I can't imagine any human parents wants to look down into the cradle and see their newborn has transformed into a baby weasel." He paused. "Not much fun for a parent no matter what age their kid is, really. Some of my friends here are like that, shifters whose parents were human."

"When did it first happen for them?" Lainie asked. Her mind was racing as she pieced together her memories of childhood with this new information. "When did they first find out they were shifters?"

Harrison's hand stilled on her hair. She wondered if he guessed why she was asking. "From what I've learned from the people here, it's normal for shifters who don't grow up around their own kind to change when they're ten or eleven. Shifter kids from shifter families tend to start shifting in the cradle, but I've never heard of a shifter who hasn't found their animal before puberty."

"That explains a lot." Lainie swallowed down a lump in her throat.

"I thought it might," Harrison said hesitantly. She pushed herself off his lap and looked at him. He grimaced and explained: "Tessa Sweets came around earlier and told me what happened with your family. She says her grandmother and the rest of the town council made your grandparents send you away after it became clear you were never going to shift."

Lainie let out a slow breath. "They *forced* them to? I thought…"

"That they rejected you?" Harrison dropped his head to rest on hers. "I don't know the full story, and I can't tell you what your grandparents were thinking. But I do know that the Sweets were behind the decision."

"I thought they hated me," Lainie whispered. "All this time…"

She stopped. She'd never told anyone about this, not even her closest friends.

But Harrison was different. He'd saved her life. And he'd just trusted her with his secret.

"I was eleven," she said at last. "Mom and Dad used to take me to visit my grandparents every other weekend, when I was younger, but that last trip… something was different. I guess I was older, so I was starting to want to do more on my vacations than just hang around at the house. I wanted to explore more of the town. But they never let me go down by myself. Even just going to get ice cream was always a huge mission." She sighed. "Which makes more sense, now. I guess they had to warn everyone down in the town that a *human* was coming."

Harrison nodded. "We don't have many human visitors. Everyone has to be careful when one does visit."

"Like me, now?" Lainie grimaced. "I wondered why everyone seemed so on edge last night. I guess it would have been easier on you all if I just had dinner in my room at the B&B."

"I'm glad you didn't." Harrison reached out and took her hand. He turned it over, stroking her palm with his callused thumb, and she was suddenly very aware that he wasn't wearing so much as a strip of clothing. A tingle went up her arm.

"I—um—oh," she mumbled. *I'm glad I didn't, too,* she thought. *I can't imagine going through this all without* someone *on my side, at least.* "Why are you telling me all this?"

Harrison smiled sadly. "Because you deserve to know."

"I wish you weren't the only person to think that." She sighed. "Things would have been so much easier if I'd known years ago… well, there's nothing I can do about it now."

She looked across at Harrison from under lowered eyes. He was still holding her hand. His touch warmed more than just her skin; just being with him made her feel calmer, more in control of herself.

She usually coped with unhappiness by distancing herself from people, pushing them away, but with Harrison, she felt… safe. That was it. Safe to show her emotions. To be herself.

She reached out and spread her fingers across his chest, feeling his heartbeat thud under his warm skin. Harrison had revealed the town's secret to her. He'd shown her a level of trust no one else in her life had done.

There was something she needed to explain, too.

"You've been amazing through all of this," she began, her voice wavering. "Knowing why I had to leave Hideaway Cove when I was a kid… well, I'm glad I know the story behind it, now. But it doesn't solve everything." She nodded at the kitchen table. "Can we sit up there while I explain? It's complicated."

Harrison picked up his towel as he stood up. Lainie smiled. He'd seemed comfortable enough being naked before—and, hell, even earlier, when they were making their way through the tunnel—but *complicated* required some coverage, apparently.

Lainie picked briefly at the remains of the grilled cheese, then rested her elbows on the table. "Okay," she said, then grimaced. *You're already stalling. Stop it.*

Lainie groaned. "I'd better just say it…" She rubbed her face. "When I was eighteen, my grandmother went into care. My grandfather had died a few years earlier, I think. Well, the assisted living place she went to needed someone to co-sign for the fees. She needed specialist care—because of her being a shifter, I guess." She shrugged tightly, staring at the table. "I hadn't seen her for six or seven years at that stage. The care place addressed the papers to my dad, but he was long gone. So I signed them under my own name."

Harrison made a small noise of understanding. "And now that your grandmother is dead…"

"…Her debts have come home to roost with me." Lainie frowned and rubbed her forehead. "Mom seemed to think that Dad's family were really wealthy, but there's no sign of it. My grandmother didn't have anything but the house, and everything in it, which to be honest wasn't a lot. Just old furniture and kitchen stuff. No bank accounts straining under the weight of her hidden millions."

"Hell," Harrison murmured. "That's why you need to sell up."

Lainie nodded miserably. "Mr. Sweets said they'd raised seventy-five thousand dollars to buy the house. Well, that's not going to cover it. Subdividing the section will cost, but the returns from selling off the separate bits of land… it might work. It's my only option at this stage." She looked at her hands. "No, that's a lie. My other option is to eat the debt, on top of my student loans."

"No one could ask you to do that." Harrison sounded certain.

"Are you sure about that? What about this afternoon? I can't see Mrs. Sweets valuing my future over keeping Hideaway Cove safe from newcomers."

"Dorothy Sweets isn't in charge of what happens in this town."

"Really? Because it sure seems like it from where I'm sitting," Lainie snapped. She held up her hands. "Sorry. I keep yelling at you, and that's not fair. None of this is your fault. You've been nothing but kind to me since I arrived."

She tentatively looked up and met Harrison's eyes. He smiled back.

"I couldn't do anything else, Lainie. I can't stand by and watch you suffer while there's anything I could do to help. It's… a shifter thing."

Lainie's stomach flipped over. "What do you mean?"

Harrison licked his lips. *Does he look nervous?* Lainie thought, taking in the lines between his eyebrows and at the edges of his mouth.

"I would do anything for you, Lainie. I hate to say I'm glad you came here, because being here has been so painful for you, but meeting you is the best thing that ever happened to me."

"I don't understand." Lainie reached out for him, and he took her hand. "I only met you *yesterday*. I know we—well, we took things pretty fast, but…" She trailed off. Harrison was looking even *more* nervous now. He was so big and strong, and had so many friends here—what could possibly make him nervous?

He cleared his throat. "Every shifter has one person who they're meant to be with. Their soulmate. Some shifters go all their lives without meeting their mate, but when you do meet them, you know immediately. That you've just met the one person in the world who will make your life complete." He leaned forward. "Lainie, you're that person to me. The moment I met you, I knew. It was like the sun coming out from behind a cloud I'd been living under my whole life. You're my mate."

For a moment, Lainie didn't react. She felt as though she was floating outside of herself. Harrison's words made sense individually, but put them together…

It was crazy. *Impossible*. It didn't make any sense.

Lainie stared into Harrison's eyes. The gold in his hazel irises flashed as she looked into them, reminding her of his griffin form.

Impossible? Men turning into mythical creatures should be *impossible*, but she'd just seen it happen. The world was more complicated than she ever thought possible. Who was she to say what was possible or not?

"If that's true," she said carefully, worried if she put words to her thoughts then everything around her would melt away like a dream. "If that's true…"

"It is true," Harrison insisted. "I know it's hard to believe, and I don't expect anything from you, just because you're my mate. It seems to me that people have made too many decisions about your life without your input already. I just want you to know… this means I'm on your side. Whatever happens."

# 14

# HARRISON

Harrison woke up, for the second day in a row, to the sun streaming through the window and onto his face. But this time he wasn't alone.

He rolled over and sat up on his elbow, looking down at Lainie. She slept curled up on her side, wisps of blonde hair spread out across the pillow. One of her hands was resting beside her face. The other stretched out toward him.

He stroked her outstretched hand gently, not wanting to wake her. She looked so peaceful, and it made his griffin's heart glow to see her sleeping in his bed. This room was the closest thing he had to a nest to bring his mate to… and here she was.

The storm had still been raging when they went to bed last night, both of them too exhausted from their escape from the collapsing house, and the revelations about Hideaway Cove and Lainie's past, to do anything but hold each other.

Lainie's breathing changed, and Harrison stopped stroking her hand, worried he had disturbed her. But she was already waking up, her eyes flickering beneath her eyelids, her fingers flexing as she stretched.

"Good morning, sleepyhead," Harrison whispered as Lainie's eyes opened.

She frowned up at him, her eyes still bleary with sleep. "You're the sleepyhead," she muttered grumpily. "I woke up hours ago, and you…"

she broke off and yawned hugely. "… *You* were out like a light. I just closed my eyes again to wait for you to wake up."

"Hmm? You just closed your eyes? How many hours ago?" Harrison leaned over Lainie, tracing her jawline with his finger. Her lips were plump and pink and begging to be kissed. So he did.

Lainie stretched underneath him, wriggling to press her body against his through layers of blankets. He was naked. So was she. The only thing separating them was the cocoon of comforters he'd wrapped around her before they went to sleep.

*A nest for our mate*, his griffin purred. A nest she was now sleepily trying to fight her way out of.

Harrison kept kissing her, pretending he didn't notice her clumsy attempts to pry her way out of the blankets. Her lips were soft, and warm, and she kissed him back as though she really *had* been sitting up for hours waiting for him to wake up.

"Mmf," she murmured grumpily. "These damned blankets…"

Laughing, Harrison helped her unravel herself. He couldn't help the hum of appreciation that escaped him as Lainie's body emerged from the pile of blankets. Her soft, creamy skin and generous curves made his heart race. Kiss her? He wanted more than just to kiss her. He wanted all of her.

"Oh… good morning," said Lainie with a wicked giggle, looking down between his legs. Harrison smirked. He was hard already, and Lainie's reaction only aroused him more.

He stroked her cheek with the back of one hand, then ran it down her neck and shoulder. Lainie trembled as he caressed her breast, and he felt her nipple go hard under his palm.

Lainie moaned and pulled the last of the blankets away. She slid against him, and every touch of her soft body sent thrills across Harrison's skin. He kissed her breasts, moving his hands to her waist, her hips, her thick thighs…

Encouraged by the way Lainie was writhing against him, Harrison dipped his hand between her legs. She was already wet and gasped as he stroked her.

"Yes…" she whispered, and he rolled on top of her. Lainie's black eyes shone up at him, heavy-lidded with need.

"You don't know how much it means to me, having you here," Harrison found himself whispering back. "You mean everything to me."

Lainie's lips parted, red and wet. "Harrison," she murmured. "My Harrison. My protector."

He couldn't hold back any longer. Not after that. Lainie opened her legs beneath him and he positioned himself at her entrance, watching her eyelashes flutter as she felt him press against her.

He thrust into her in one smooth motion. A deep moan escaped his throat at how hot and wet she was. How easily he filled her and how perfect it felt.

Lainie had closed her eyes as he entered her. Now she opened them and took Harrison's face between her hands. "I've never wanted anyone as much as I want you," she admitted. Her whole face was flushed, her black eyes shining. "Is this… is this part of the mate bond? Everything feeling so *right*?"

Harrison rocked against her, making her arch her back with pleasure. "Yes. Because it's right. It's perfect. *You're* perfect," he said, increasing his speed. "My Lainie. My mate."

Lainie's whole body tensed beneath him and she cried out, digging her fingernails into his back as she came. Harrison rode her through her orgasm as long as he could before the sight of her pleasure became too much for him.

He groaned, burying his face in Lainie's shoulder as he came deep inside her. He caught his breath, still nuzzling her neck, and then started to pull himself off her.

Lainie held on to him, keeping him on top of her. For a moment they lay together in silence, the only noise the sound of their intermingled breathing, and Harrison's heartbeat thumping in his ears. His heartbeat slowed, his breath keeping pace with Lainie's.

"I wish we could stay here forever," she said quietly. "But we can't, can we? I have to figure out what I'm going to do. Somehow."

Harrison rested his forehead against hers. "We'll figure it out. Together. Remember, I'm on your side."

Lainie smiled up at him. "I remember."

Harrison made a pile of scrambled eggs for breakfast, flavoring them with fresh herbs and serving them alongside a loaf of crusty bread from Pol's shelf on the shared work pantry downstairs. His own kitchen supplies didn't extend much far past grilled cheese. He'd even snaffled the lemon and honey for the drinks last night from Pol's shelf.

*I'll need to step up my game now Lainie's here*, he thought, sliding the eggs onto two plates. *…And head to the store before Pol notices his depleted supplies*, he added.

"That smells delicious," Lainie said, coming in from the shower. She buttoned her blouse and sat down, dropping her shoes under the table. "Mmm."

"I'm better with a hammer and nails than in the kitchen, but I can manage some things," Harrison said, grinning as he placed Lainie's plate in front of her. "Simple, hearty meals."

"After the storm yesterday, *simple, hearty meals* sounds perfect." Her eyes widened as Harrison put a cup of coffee down by her plate. "And you just made it perfect *plus*."

Harrison checked in with Arlo and Pol while they ate. *Is there much damage from the storm?*

*Not a lot. A couple of windows smashed by falling branches. The old Eaves place is gone, though.* Arlo's telepathic voice grew outraged. *Pol says you were out there?*

*Lainie was in trouble. Hey, Pol—how did that job I gave you last night go?*

Pol gave a telepathic groan. *I've had to auction myself off for Christmas lights this year… but everyone's on board. They're willing to listen, at least.*

Harrison shoveled egg into his mouth, struggling to keep his feelings off his face. He didn't want Lainie to ask what was going on before he had all the details sorted. He didn't want to get her hopes up for no reason.

Harrison could feel the embarrassed wriggle in Pol's voice when he spoke again. *Look, boss… this whole thing is bringing out a lot of feelings in people, not all of them good. You do what you need to do, Harrison. I'm on your side, whatever happens.*

A moment later, Arlo chimed in. *Me too.*

*Thanks, guys.* Harrison didn't know what else to say. He didn't know how today was going to turn out. None of them did—and yet they were willing to back him up. And not because of any mate bond. Because they were his friends, and they trusted his judgement.

All of them were outsiders of one sort or another, here in Hideaway. None of them had been born here, and some of them had blended in with the community better than others. Pol, with his casual friendliness and special talents, had made himself at home in Hideaway within weeks of arriving. Harrison knew he'd be able to charm his way back into their good books, even if he did back Harrison and Lainie in the face of the town's judgement.

Arlo was risking more by going against the Sweets and the rest of the town. He was a loner, and only had a few real friends in Hideaway. How many would decide he wasn't worth keeping around if he caused trouble?

Harrison blinked, and muttered "Damn it." His vision was swimming. He tried to shake the tears away, but it was too late. Lainie was looking across at him, her dark eyes full of concern.

"What's wrong?"

"It's nothing. I was just—" Harrison waved his fork and paused. *Ah.* "I was just, uh, talking to the guys, using… my shifter telepathic powers…"

"Your *what?*" Lainie dropped her cutlery and covered her eyes. "You know what—okay. On top of everything else, telepathy doesn't seem that weird. What were your friends saying?"

"Pol and Arlo. I don't know if you've met Pol—tall, blond?" Lainie shook her head. "Well, you'll see him today, anyway. Arlo you met yesterday morning, of course. And, uh. The night before. My, uh. The dog."

"The dog?" Lainie groaned, then chuckled. "Oh, the poor guy. And he had to pretend to be a real dog, because you weren't expecting me to be at the restaurant… jeez."

"Yeah. He's not going to let me live that down for a *long* time." Harrison laughed, then grew serious. "They were saying that they've got our backs, whatever happens today."

Lainie visibly shuddered. "That's really nice of them," she said quietly. "But I still don't know what I'm going to do. I don't know if there's anything I *can* do, except try to make everyone understand my side of the story."

Harrison reached across the table and took her hand. "We'll do it together," he reassured her.

She sighed and grabbed her shoes. "Well, there's no point putting it off," she said. She smiled across at Harrison, but even from across the table he could tell it was wavering.

He watched while she pulled on one ankle-boot, and then the other.

"Ugh, these are still wet—ouch!" She kicked off her right boot and grabbed her foot. Harrison swooped over and kneeled by her chair. "Damn it, I forgot. There was a bit of gravel in there yesterday, cutting into my foot. I forgot to knock it out. It's *really* sharp."

Harrison picked up her shoe and turned it over. A small, grime-covered object fell out. He frowned. Some of the grime had been rubbed off by Lainie's sock, but what was underneath it didn't look like gravel. It *gleamed.*

Harrison rubbed the object against his pant leg. "This isn't a stone," he said, wonderingly. "Look."

He held it up to her. Lainie's eyes widened. "A ring!" she gasped. "But that looks like—"

"—The ring from your grandparents' portrait." Harrison finished her sentence.

The ring twinkled in the light pouring in the kitchen window. It had a slender gold band, and was topped by a diamond the size of Harrison's thumbnail. Smaller stones were set on each side, catching the light and sending it back broken into glittering shards.

"But where—oh, my God," Lainie breathed. "When I fell over, I knocked something out of that alcove, do you remember? The ring got lodged in my shoe after that." She met Harrison's eyes. "Harrison… how much would a ring like this be worth? And what if the rest of the Eaves treasure is there, too? What if it really exists?"

Her eyes were lit up with hope. Harrison slid the ring into her hand.

"I asked Pol to gather my friends together so we could talk to them this morning. Figure out some way that we can stay together, and solve your debt problem," he told her. "But I just thought of another thing they can help us with.

"Let's go," he said, and pulled her to her feet.

# 15

# LAINIE

Lainie wriggled her toes in the sand. She'd been holding her grandmother's ring ever since Harrison handed it to her. It felt warm in her hand.

*That's just because you've been holding it for so long*, she reasoned with herself. But it still felt like something more. So many magical things had been revealed to her in the last twenty-four hours. *Who's to say it wasn't an accident that this ring fell into my boot?*

She blushed and looked around. Harrison had reassured her that shifters' telepathy didn't mean they could read her mind, but she didn't want anyone overhearing her thinking that her grandmother's spirit might have sent the ring to her.

How else could she explain what was happening?

She was standing on the same beach she and Harrison had fled from the day before. Today, at low tide and with only the lightest breeze coming off the sea, it was idyllic. The sun shone on the small waves, glittering as they broke on the tiny beach and the rocks to either side of it. The sand was warmed by the sun. Even the cave looked welcoming.

Lainie could hardly believe that this was the same place where she'd stood, shivering, trying to decide whether to risk racing over the cliff path and being swept off, or hiding in the cave and succumbing to hypothermia.

She and Harrison had walked along that path just half an hour ago. It was lovely. At no point had she been terrified that a wave would pick her up and slam her to bits on the rocks.

They'd searched the cave first, of course. They hadn't found anything, not even the remains of whatever box or crate Lainie had knocked off its secret shelf. The waves had washed everything away.

Lainie had been ready to give up hope, but then Harrison had paused, a distant look on his face. And he'd smiled.

He'd told her that Jools, the girl who'd been her waitress the first night she spent in Hideaway, had found something. She'd been flying—oh, had he mentioned she was a gull shifter?—and seen something glittering in the water. A necklace.

Now, less than an hour later, the water was full of animals. No, not animals—*shifters*. She tried to count them through the waves, but couldn't. She knew there was a sea-lion shifter somewhere out there, and Jools and her brothers and sisters were alternatively flying above the water and diving into it. She was pretty sure there was a ray on the team, as well. A ray! She'd never even *seen* one of those before, not outside of *Finding Nemo*.

And there was Harrison. She had thought he would join the gulls in the sky, and he had—and then, like them, he'd dived beneath the waves.

*Why are you surprised?* She'd asked herself. *A griffin is, what—part eagle, part big cat? Both of those species go in the water sometimes. Well, some species of eagle, at least. And some cats.*

*Besides. Until yesterday, you didn't know that griffins existed. Now that you know they do, why is anything about them surprising?*

A black-striped gull swooped down from the sky and landed beside Lainie, transforming into a young woman.

"Jools!" Lainie cried. "I—oh, you're naked." She blushed and covered her eyes.

"Jeez, don't worry about that," Jools said breezily. "Harrison sent me over to pass on a message. He says they've found something!"

Hope filled Lainie's chest. "Did he say what it was?"

"He says…" Jools' eyes went unfocused, as though she was listening to something far away. "He says it's the box, or, most of it. Maybe. He's bringing it up now."

Lainie turned wide-eyed to look at the water. A dark shape formed under the waves, growing larger as she watched. At last it broke through the waves.

Harrison was in his griffin form. Saltwater sheeted off the feathers of his head and fore-legs, and then off his wings as he spread them above the waves. His eyes were more gold than hazel, burning with pride.

He was holding a small, brass-bound wooden chest in one massive claw.

"Harrison!" Lainie cried out, racing down the beach towards him. Her feet sank into the sand, slowing her down. By the time she reached Harrison, he had transformed, and had arms for her to fall into.

"Lainie," he breathed into her hair, dripping saltwater all over her. "I haven't looked inside it yet. And it's broken. I don't want you to get your hopes up…"

"It's too late for that." Lainie took the chest as he offered it to her. It was heavier than she expected. *Please let that mean it's full, and not just water-logged,* she begged silently.

She staggered back up to dry sand and dropped to her knees with the chest. Harrison jogged up the beach to where a pile of clothes marked where he and the rest of the search-party had shifted earlier and pulled on a pair of pants. Then he joined her, his hand on her back. She looked up at him. "Ready?"

He smiled back. "Ready."

The chest had a heavy lock on it. The lock was still intact, but the wood was mostly rotten. At one corner, it was completely rotted through.

"That must be where the ring fell out," Lainie said.

"And the necklace Jools found," Harrison added.

"Well, I don't think there's much point calling for a locksmith," Lainie joked. She traced the design on the face of the lock. "Wait a minute…"

She rummaged in her pocket and pulled out her keys. There it was: the small silver key that had been folded into her grandmother's will, according to the lawyer who'd given it to Lainie. She'd wondered what it was for. The will hadn't mentioned it at all.

Lainie inserted the key into the lock and held her breath as the twisted it. *Click.*

"Oh, my God…" Lainie breathed as she opened the lid of the chest.

Lainie's mouth hung open. The old wooden chest had hidden treasure. Not just any treasure: the legendary Eaves jewels.

Lainie sifted through rotten velvet bags and cases, pulling out glittering handfuls of gemstones. Some were set into necklaces, and earrings, and even a tiara, but many were just loose stones: clear diamonds, sapphires, emeralds, and rubies.

Harrison's arm tightened around her. She looked up at him, speechless.

"This is incredible," she breathed at last.

"It's yours."

"It—but…" Lainie shook her head. "Grandmother's will mentioned jewels, but I never thought… this is way more than in any of the records the lawyers found. Some of these I recognize from the portrait, but most of them…"

Harrison chuckled. "Magpies."

"What?"

He laughed and kissed her. "Magpies," he said again. "I never met your grandparents, but Tessa said they were magpies. Collectors of shiny baubles."

Lainie stared at him. "Really? I had no idea..." She ran her hands through the sparkling jewels again. "Someone from the town emptied my grandparents' house after my Gran went into care and put everything in storage. The jewels were never found. And that cupboard was in front of the passage down to the beach, but I don't remember it being there when I was a kid." She frowned. "I wonder..."

"What is going on here?"

Lainie felt Harrison's arms tighten protectively around her as Mrs. Sweets' voice cut through the air. Lainie frowned.

*I wonder if my grandmother wanted to keep the jewels safe from someone in particular.*

The old woman was stalking along the cliff path, looking completely out of place in her twinset and pearls. Her husband was following her, and behind him were a few other faces Lainie recognized from the surprise meeting.

"Do they always walk in a crocodile behind her?" Lainie muttered to Harrison. He laughed, but didn't move from where he was kneeling protectively beside her.

Lainie was glad. She was angry at Mrs. Sweets for the way she'd treated her, but anger alone wouldn't get her through this. She needed support, as well. The knowledge that someone was on her side.

She grabbed Harrison's hand and squeezed it as Mrs. Sweets walked up to them. She had to clench her other hand in her lap to stop herself from sweeping up the jewels to keep them out of the old woman's sight. *They're yours*, she reminded herself. *There's nothing she can do to take them away from you. Even if she's already taken so much.*

*And who are her cronies, anyway?* Lainie looked behind Mrs. Sweets, for the first time getting a really good look at the men and women who tagged along behind her like ducklings.

There was Mr. Sweets, of course, somehow looking like he was asleep even when he was standing up. Two older women, one thin and one chubby, with matching lavender rinses, peered down at Lainie and Harrison through matching spectacles.

And behind them, to Lainie's surprise, was another woman, who must have been at least fifty years younger than anyone else in the group. Unlike the others, whose faces all held expressions of mingled glee and curiosity, she looked miserable.

"Did you not hear me, Ms. Eaves? I asked what you were doing." Mrs. Sweets' smile had too many teeth in it for Lainie's liking.

"I heard you," Lainie replied, her voice cool. She swept her hair back off her face as she looked up at the old woman. "I was just too busy wondering what you were doing on my land to answer straight away."

Two red spots appeared on Mrs. Sweets' cheeks. "Young lady—" she began, and then stopped. Her eyes narrowed, and she let her breath out slowly through her nose. By the time she opened her mouth again, there was no trace of rage on her face. "I came to offer my condolences about your family home. How terrible, for you to see it destroyed only one day into your visit."

Lainie's confidence wavered. Something about Mrs. Sweets' swift mood change unnerved her. "That place hasn't been my family home in a long time," she said quietly.

"But you know all about that, don't you?" Harrison curled his hand protectively over Lainie's shoulder, his gentle touch in stark contrast to the growl in his voice.

Mrs. Sweets' lips narrowed. "I'm sure I don't know what you mean," she sniffed.

"You destroyed my family!" Lainie cried out. Murmurs broke out around her, and her breath caught in her throat. *Don't listen to them. Don't pay any attention to what they're saying.* "You forced my grandparents to send my mother and me away from Hideaway, because I didn't turn out to be a shifter. I'm surprised you didn't come down on my father when he married Mom in the first place!"

Mrs. Sweets looked down her nose at Lainie. "You really don't know much of your family history, do you? Your father was always flighty. He met your mother while he was traveling. By the time he introduced her to his parents, it was too late. If it had happened here, the town would have had something to say about it, believe me."

"You mean *you* would have had something to say about it," Harrison growled. "I used to think this place was paradise, a place of safety. But the way you've treated Lainie is far worse than any human ever treated any shifter I've known."

Lainie held on tight to Harrison's hand as he stood beside her, feeling as though he was the only thing anchoring her.

"I stayed with my grandparents most weekends when I was young. I might not know much, but I do remember that," she said firmly. "They welcomed me in their home."

"Only while there was some hope you would turn out to be one of us," Mrs. Sweets hissed. "Don't you see, dear, you're exactly the reason why we have this rule in the first place? If shifters mate with humans, *you* are the risk they're taking. A human child."

"That's *it*? That's all? Just that I was born human?" Lainie choked back something that was half-laugh, half-sob. She was holding onto Harrison's hand so hard, pins and needles were starting to dance up her arm.

"Does there need to be anything else, dear?" Mrs. Sweets' eyes swept up and down Lainie's body. "I'm sure we can come up with something, if you insist."

"Don't you dare talk to Lainie like that," Harrison growled.

"And you. Harrison Galway." Mrs. Sweets sniffed. "We had such high hopes for you. What a pity your griffin was fated to ally you with... *her*."

Lainie's chest hurt. *He didn't choose, did he? The mate bond just happened.*

But Harrison shook his head. "I *choose* to be with Lainie. Even without the mate bond, she's the most wonderful woman I've ever met. And I think it's disgusting, what you've done here. How many other families have you done this to? How many people have left Hideaway because you wouldn't let them stay here with their mates?"

"Enough to keep Hideaway safe," Mrs. Sweets snapped.

To everyone's surprise, including her own, Lainie burst out laughing.

"Safe?" she exclaimed, tears running down her cheeks. "Is that what you think?"

She was aware of a dozen pairs of eyes staring at her. Even Harrison was watching her, his hazel eyes confused. She didn't blame him. Her brain had spent the entire conversation leaping in a panic from idea to idea—and had finally landed on one that made sense. Horrible, cruel sense.

Mrs. Sweets looked smug. "Even you must see what a success our policy has been."

*You think you've won*, Lainie thought, looking at Mrs. Sweets' calm face. *You can't even see that in your mad rush to keep me out of Hideaway Cove, you've put the whole town at risk.*

Lainie spread her arms wide. "Exactly what *success* do you think you've achieved here? Thanks to you, I haven't set foot in Hideaway in fifteen years. I don't have any connections to the place. No loyalties to the people who live here, especially now my Gran has died. Even my father never moved back here. And you never thought about what that would mean? That one day, I'd come back, and not have any reason to protect your secret?"

Mrs. Sweets' mouth fell open slightly. Behind her, murmurs sprang up from the other onlookers. Lainie barreled on, anger pouring through her.

"Even if I hadn't co-signed for my grandmother's medical debts, her executor would have had to sell her entire estate to pay her creditors.

You don't have any real estate agents here, so someone would have been brought in from out of town. You wouldn't have any way of controlling whether the land went to shifters, or humans."

Mrs. Sweets sniffed. "We have certain *unique* ways of convincing people to change their minds—"

Lainie didn't let her finish. "Really? How? Bite-marks in their tires? Strange noises in the night? Or are you talking about good old-fashioned harassment? You don't think that would be *investigated*? That someone would lay a complaint? And what then?"

Someone murmured in the crowd. Lainie shot her head around and saw the pot-bellied man—Guts?—looking uncomfortable. "She's right," he muttered. "No law enforcement here. If anything happened, the county'd send in from the city."

Mrs. Sweets flashed him an irritated glare. "Thank you for your input, Mr. White." She turned back to Lainie. "I note that nothing you've just been describing has *actually* come to pass."

"No." Lainie grinned fiercely. "Instead, you've got *me*. And what do you think I'm going to do? Roll over and let you walk all over me? You—you *idiots*! Don't you see how easy it would be for me to destroy everything you've made here? Harrison is the only reason I have to be loyal to Hideaway, and you've just told him to leave!"

The words tore out of her throat and left nothing behind. Not victory. Not even vicious glee. Just a hollow feeling that ached under her breastbone.

"Oh, God—I've got to get out of here," she muttered. "Harrison—"

"Back up the tunnel," he said at once. "Pol and Arlo have been clearing the site—Pol, look after this, will you?" He gestured with his free hand at the piles of glittering jewels that had been lying forgotten on the beach. His other hand was still firmly grasping Lainie's. Her anchor.

But it hadn't been enough to stop her from putting her foot in her mouth. God, she needed air. Space. Needed time to think, without Mrs. Sweets' eyes boring into her brain.

"Let's go," she said, and stalked towards the cave entrance, dragging Harrison after her.

*Please understand,* she begged him as she raced through the tunnel, her chest so tight it felt as if it would burst. *I want everything to work out—but how can it, if everyone here hates me?*

# 16

# HARRISON

"Will any of them be able to hear us from up here?" Lainie turned to him, beseeching, her arms wrapped tightly around herself. Harrison touched her briefly on the shoulder and then concentrated:

*Arlo? Pol? Did you hear her just then?*

*Not a peep,* came Pol's reply. *And don't worry, we're making sure no one sneaks up the tunnel after you.*

"No. Shifters have better hearing than most people, but there's enough noise from the waves and everything else to blot us out up here," he reassured her. At her questioning look, he added, "I just checked with Pol and Arlo."

Some of the tension drained from Lainie's shoulders. "All right," she said to herself. "That's something, at least."

Harrison held his tongue as she stalked around the ruins of her grandparents' house. *She's not going to fall off the side of the cliff,* he told himself as his muscles jumped, ready to swoop in and grab her. *And look around. Someone, Pol or Arlo probably, has already been up here and started tidying up the site. They won't have left anything dangerous around.*

He waited as Lainie glared at the wreck of the house. Most of the structure had collapsed in the storm; Harrison's professional side was horrified that the old place had been so woefully below the building code. But most of him was too busy worrying what Lainie was making of it all.

At last she made an impatient noise and stared up at the sky. For a moment, neither of them spoke. The abandoned lighthouse stretched up beside them, washed white by the rain, and broken planks and bricks crunched under their feet.

Harrison watched Lainie carefully. He didn't like the way she'd shut down back on the beach, her face and body shuttering like she'd closed a door on her emotions. It reminded him too much of how she'd been at the restaurant the first time he'd seen her. Defensive and uncertain, and with no one to defend her.

Lainie kicked a broken slat into a pile of rubble, looking back at Harrison out of the corner of her eye.

"You don't need to say it," she said, her voice tight. "I know I was being a bitch back there."

"What? Lainie, no. You didn't say anything out of line, not a thing." Harrison laughed, but stopped the moment he saw Lainie's shoulders tighten again. "Lainie, no one could blame you for what you said."

"I hate it," she said quietly. "I hate the way being around her makes me feel. Being *here*. I get so, so wound up, and scared, and then I lash out—I don't want to be that person." She turned to Harrison. "I don't want to sneer and make threats to try and get the upper hand. I don't want to be like *her*."

Harrison picked his way through the rubble to her side. "You're nothing like her," he reassured her, rubbing her shoulders. She leaned against him, resting her head against his chest. "You were hurting, and scared, and she was attacking you."

"I don't want to sink to her level. I bet *she's* scared, somewhere under that Teflon grin. This whole thing started because she thought any human who found out about Hideaway Cove would start twirling their mustache and destroy the place—and I just threatened to do that, Harrison! I'm the gold-digging monster who wants to sell off half the town to intruders!"

"No, you're not." Harrison tipped her chin up, smiling down into her eyes. "A real monstrous gold-digger wouldn't be so upset about everything going her way."

Lainie smiled back weakly. "I know," she said, closing her eyes. "But it's so *tempting*. And part of me does want to be that person. To show Mrs. Sweets and all the rest of them that I'm not some scared little girl they can bully."

"What do you want? The real you, not the mustache-twirling gold-digger." Despite the joke, Harrison felt as though he was walking on a knife-edge.

Lainie rubbed her face. She turned around and placed her hands on Harrison's chest. "Truthfully? It would be so easy, now, to leave this place behind. If those jewels are real—well, I don't know what they're worth, but it must be close to what I need. I could pay off all my debts, leave Hideaway, and never think about this place again."

She sighed. "I could... if it wasn't for you."

Harrison frowned. "Why not? It sounds like the perfect solution." He gulped back the heavy feeling that settled in his heart. *Leave Hideaway?* Leave the only place that had felt like home to him since he lost his parents? "I could come with you."

Lainie shook her head. "No. If this thing we have is going to go anywhere, it can't start with me forcing you to choose between this town and me."

"You wouldn't be forcing me to do anything," Harrison insisted. "I want to be with you, Lainie. More than anything else in the world."

Lainie tapped him on the chest and smiled. "You know, you're not any good at hiding your emotions. I don't know if it's this magical bond, or what, but it's like I can tell exactly what you're feeling."

Harrison's griffin stirred with wonder inside him. This was what it meant, to have a mate who loved you. They understood you completely, loved you and accepted you for who you were.

Lainie's face grew serious. "Harrison, my parents broke up less than a year after my mother and I were kicked out of Hideaway Cove. This whole mate-bond thing is like something from a fairytale, but… Their marriage broke up because Dad had to choose between his parents, and us. Between his shifter community, and his human family. And in the end, he chose neither of them. He just… disappeared. I have no idea where he is, but I know wherever it is, it isn't his home. I don't want you to lose your home, too. I don't want to start our relationship with that sort of sacrifice."

"Our relationship?" Warmth filled Harrison, warmer and more comforting than the sun.

Lainie laughed awkwardly. "I mean, it sounds silly to be making decisions based on a potential relationship so early, but… it feels right. And there's so little in my life that *does* feel right, I don't want to muck it up." She shrugged. "So… that's it, I guess. Stay here with you, and deal with Mrs. Sweets and the rest of the town hating me. Or leave, and drag you with me."

"There is another option," Harrison said, tipping her head back and planting a tender kiss on her forehead. "Why do you think I told Pol to bring everyone together this morning?"

"To look for—no, that's not right. You asked him before we found the ring, didn't you?"

"Because I wanted to talk to them." Harrison smoothed Lainie's hair down and rested his hand on her back of her neck. "When I first came to Hideaway Cove, I thought I'd found paradise. Now I know that this place isn't the sanctuary I thought it was. We shouldn't be breaking families apart. And I won't sit back and let it happen." He took a deep breath.

"Lainie, I love you. I love you so much I feel like my heart could explode. I won't ask you yet if you love me too, but… Do you trust me?"

"I—" Lainie paused, and an expression of wonder crossed her face. "Yes. Yes, I do trust you, Harrison."

"Then come down with me now. It's my duty to protect you, Lainie. And that's what I'm going to do."

He looked into Lainie's eyes and felt the fire grow within him. *This is for you. All for you, my love. Anything for you.* He stretched, and felt his wings crackle out of his shoulder-blades, and the strange feeling of vertigo as he fell onto all four legs.

The first thing he felt after he finished shifting was Lainie's touch. She rested her hand on his feathered head, and the feeling of it lit a bonfire of fierce, proud joy within him.

"I don't think I'm ever going to get used to that," she admitted, eyes wide. Harrison preened, and then thought:

*Shit. I should have explained to her before I shifted.*

*Hmm.*

Harrison turned side-on to Lainie, twisting his head over his massive winged shoulders and tapping his beak on his back. Then he tilted his head at her.

# 17

# LAINIE

Harrison motioned to his back again and then looked at Lainie, making a small, inquisitive trilling noise. Lainie's heart jumped.

*Wow,* she thought. *Does he really mean…?*

She reached out and touched Harrison's back, where his feathers faded into thick fur. She could feel his muscles moving under them, strong and firm.

"Do you want me to… ride you?" she asked, stumbling over the words. Harrison nodded his huge feathered head.

Lainie gulped and slid her hand further across the griffin's broad back, resting it at the base of one of Harrison's wings. If she sat up there, behind his wings…

Her mind was still blanking at the thought of Harrison *flying*. Now it stuttered to a halt on an unpleasant thought.

*He's going to fly with me on top of him? All that extra weight?*

Lainie's free hand drifted unconsciously to her hips. *Harrison likes your curves,* she told herself, but the brittle, scared part of her added: *That doesn't make you any lighter.*

Harrison turned to look at her over his shoulder. *Probably wondering what's taking you so long,* she thought. She gave him a tight smile.

"Um," she said out loud. "Are you sure about this?"

Harrison nodded. She couldn't see any expression on his hawk-like face, but she *felt* reassurance pouring off him.

"All right," she said, hearing the doubt in her own voice. She looked down and something caught her eye. "Oh, we'd better take these down, right?" she said, bundling Harrison's pants into her arms. *Not that the folks on the beach seemed bothered about chilling in the altogether.*

Harrison's griffin form really was massive. His shoulder was level with her chest when he was standing, but he kneeled down now, folding his claws neatly in front of himself. This brought his back closer to waist-height. Lainie took a deep breath, wedged the rolled-up pants under one elbow, and reached out.

Before she could change her mind, she grabbed the base of Harrison's wing and swung one leg over his back. He wriggled underneath her and suddenly she was sitting astride him, gripping onto handfuls of feathers.

"Oh my goodness. Oh. Wow."

Lainie had never been horse-riding. It had been years since she got on a bike. And neither of those compared even remotely to this.

Harrison glanced back over his shoulder again. *Ready?* he seemed to be asking.

Lainie fixed her grip on Harrison's back. "Ready," she said.

Harrison crouched, his muscles bunching, and then launched himself into the air. Lainie whooped, the wind whipping her hair back. Massive brown-and-cream-banded wings spread out to either side of her, blocking her view of the rubble—and then they were airborne, soaring out over the edge of the cliff.

Lainie dug her fingers into Harrison's thickly feathered shoulders. She was flying. She was *flying*, riding on the back of a mythical creature. A mythical creature that wanted to be her boyfriend.

She wasn't sure which of those statements was the most impossible.

*Today is a day for the impossible,* she thought suddenly, glee bubbling up inside her. *Impossible griffins. Impossible treasure. Impossible possibility that all of this might turn out all right…*

Harrison glided out over the water, and Lainie narrowed her eyes to see through the glare of sunlight glittering on the waves. Another soaring turn, and she saw the lighthouse, still holding on to the top of the hill even when the rest of the house had crumbled.

Harrison was holding his wings out stiffly, drifting with the air currents. He swung around again, and this time Lainie caught a glimpse of the small beach at the base of the cliff. From up here, the people standing on the beach were as small as peg dolls. She could just make out Mrs. Sweets in her distinctive lavender twinset. And a few other figures wearing nothing at all.

*They must be the shifters who were helping search for the treasure. I don't even know most of their names. I can't just refer to them as… my naked, mystery helpers?* A giggle escaped her lips and was whipped away by the wind.

She didn't even know these people, but after Harrison had called them together, they hadn't hesitated to help her.

Harrison wheeled back out over the waves. Lainie leaned forward until she could rest her cheek against his neck. His feathers tickled her nose.

From here, she could just see the beach again. What would happen when they landed? She was still sure something was going to go wrong. Or *everything*. Would she lose everything she'd found in the last two days?

Even the shifters who'd helped her find the jewels—they'd agreed to help before they heard what Mrs. Sweets said about her. Now that they knew she'd already been thrown out of Hideaway Cove once, would they still welcome her… or reject her?

Would she be the reason Harrison left his home?

Lainie held her breath, heart aching, as Harrison swooped down towards the beach. The sand and waves approached alarmingly fast, but ten feet above the ground Harrison flared his wings out and landed lightly on all four feet.

Lainie slid off his back, keeping one hand on him even once her own feet were safely sinking into the damp sand. The feathers under her palm rippled, and then disappeared, replaced with soft skin. Lainie smoothed her hand over Harrison's human shoulder, then passed him the pants.

*I'm never going to get used to seeing him transform like that,* she thought with a pang. *But oh, I really want to try. I want the chance. I don't want to lose all of this, all of him, when I've only just found him.*

She stepped forward, ready to speak, with Harrison at her side.

Harrison squeezed her hand "No more secrets," he announced, staring coolly at Mrs. Sweets. "I've heard some things these last few days that have shaken my faith in the people of Hideaway Cove. Decisions made about our home that we had no part in making—that we weren't even *told* had been made. It can't continue."

"You naïve fool!" Mrs. Sweets hissed. "Our rules have kept Hideaway Cove safe for decades. Security is even more important these days, when one phone video could reveal us to the world. And this woman has just threatened to sell off half the town to outsiders!"

"As a last resort," Lainie cried out. "And that was before I knew about shifters!"

She bit her lip, acutely aware of all the eyes focused on her.

*Which idiot said to envision your audience in their undies if you have trouble with public speaking?* she thought, gathering her courage. *Half these people are completely nude, and it is* not *helping.*

She stepped forward, planting her feet with a confidence she didn't feel.

"I didn't come here planning to sell off Lighthouse Hill, but I knew it was an option," she admitted in front of everyone. "I don't know how many of you knew my grandmother, but she was very ill in her last years. Payment for her care had to come from somewhere, and the land is the only part of her estate that was worth anything."

"Then what do you call *that?*" one of the lavender-rinsed women asked, her mouth pinched into an unpleasant knot. She pointed an accusing finger at the jewels lying in piles at Lainie's feet.

Lainie stared at her. "I'm getting to that, ma'am," she said as politely as she could. "You're right. Selling the land is clearly no longer my only option."

"So you're choosing blackmail?" Mrs. Sweets sniffed. "What next—'*Play nice, or I'll sell to a consortium of big-game hunters?*'"

Mrs. Sweets' eyes were acid with disgust as she accused Lainie. Lainie stared back. Understanding dawned inside her, and with it, a strange sort of peace.

Mrs. Sweets and her friends might never change their mind about her. Regardless of what she said, they would twist it, putting it in the worst light possible.

But that didn't mean Lainie needed to match her blow for blow. If she played Mrs. Sweets at her own game, the only people that would be hurt were the innocent citizens of Hideaway Cove.

"No," she said quietly. "No, I've made my decision. If those jewels will cover the debts, then that's what I'll use them for. If they don't quite make it—well, I hope your very generous offer still stands. I have no intention of selling off the estate to anyone who would destroy this place. You have Harrison to thank for that."

She stepped closer to Harrison and wrapped her arm around his waist. He put his arm around her shoulders in return, smiling down at her.

And he wasn't the only one. All around her, people were smiling and nodding at her. Except for the Sweets.

"Well," Mrs. Sweets snarled. "That's all very well, but—"

"That's not all," Harrison interrupted her. "Lainie is my mate. I knew it the moment I met her. And it horrifies me, what you've done to her. Taken away her family. Left her wondering for all these years why her grandparents abandoned her." He turned on Mrs. Sweets and her husband, furious. "How many years ago would we have met if you hadn't done that to her? How many years could we have already been together? And how many other families have you done this to, and kept it a secret from the rest of us?"

In the crowd, someone choked back a gasp. Lainie looked across to see Caro from the restaurant, her face pale.

Harrison followed her gaze, and his eyes widened as he looked at Caro. He looked around, pausing to look into the eyes of every shifter in the crowd.

"A lot of you have been teasing me about running for mayor this year, well, if I *was* running, this would be my platform. If Hideaway is meant to be a sanctuary for shifter families, we need to accept *all* members of those families. No one should live here in fear that they're going to be thrown out of town for falling in love with the wrong person or, God forbid, having a child who can't shift.

"What's been done here is shameful. We can keep ourselves safe without tearing apart innocent families, families built on the mate bond, the most powerful force in any shifter's life." He took both of Lainie's hands in his own and looked deep into her eyes. "Lainie isn't some gold-digging monster. Even after everything that's been done to her, she doesn't want to put Hideaway Cove at risk.

"If you all want her to leave, then I'm going with her. But it's up to you—Caro, Guts, Jools, everyone here. Not just Mrs. Sweets and her friends. Do you want us both to stay?"

"Yes!"

Lainie looked across the sand to see Jools, the gull shifter, standing with her arms crossed defiantly across her chest. "Of course we want you to stay!" the teenager yelled.

Mrs. Sweets hissed. "Bird shifters! You're all the same—"

"I want you both to stay, too!" another voice cried out from the crowd. "And that's from a stumpy old land-based predator, Mrs. S!"

"Harrison's worked through the night more times than I can count to help the people of this town," a woman called out. "What have you done? Worked through the night to take people's children away from them?"

More voices joined in. Lainie strained her ears, but she couldn't hear anyone calling out *No, no, make them leave!* Even Mrs. Sweets' backup band were keeping quiet in the face of so much support for Harrison and Lainie.

Lainie looked around in amazement. In exactly none of her wildest dreams had she imagined being welcomed back to Hideaway Cove by a cheering crowd of mostly naked men and women.

Harrison stepped in close to her, cupping her cheek in one hand. "What do you say, Lainie?" he asked, his voice low. "Will you give us a chance? Will you give me a chance?"

There was only one thing left to say. "Yes, Harrison. Yes, of course I will."

# EPILOGUE

## LAINIE

Lainie pulled up at the end of the drive. The evening sun lit up the new house like a spotlight, turning its painted walls gold.

Today was the day. After six months of planning, and getting permits, let alone actual construction work, the new Eaves house was complete.

Six months since she'd set foot in Hideaway for the first time in fifteen years. Six months since she'd met Harrison, discovered the secret existence of shifters, and felt the knot of unhappiness that had plagued her for so many years finally start to unravel.

She'd sold the jewels through one of Pol's contacts, for a price that made all her financial problems disappear. After paying off her grandmother's debts and setting aside enough for taxes, there had still been enough left for a new project. The house.

Lainie still owned the land her grandparents' house had stood on, after all, even if the old house was gone. The property she'd inherited made up most of the hill, from the coast up to the lighthouse. With Harrison's help, she'd selected a new site to build on, a little further down from the lighthouse. After that storm, she didn't want the new house to be *right* on the edge of the cliff like her grandparents' had been.

Bit by bit, the house had transformed from an idea into something real. Lainie kept her job in the city, driving out on weekends to see Harrison and check on the build. And something else had happened. Instead of living at home during the week, and visiting on weekends, Lainie had started to feel like she was coming home on the weekends. Home to Harrison, and Hideaway Cove.

And this was it. The last weekend.

Lainie the guys had been around earlier in the day, helping Harrison with the finishing touches. For some reason, he'd asked her to stay away. Lainie wouldn't have minded lending a hand, but she had been more than happy to spend the sunny day down in the town.

She'd caught up with Tessa at the ice cream parlor, and they'd bonded over raspberry sorbet and the knowledge that their new friendship was probably giving old Mrs. Sweets an ulcer. After that, she'd gone to the store to pick up things for an easy dinner—plus a bottle of bubbly to celebrate the new house. And after *that*, the squirrel shifter from the post office had sent her a message to say that her latest shipment of homewares had arrived and was filling up his back room. Everywhere Lainie went, people seemed to go out of their way to make sure she knew she was welcome here now.

By the time Lainie had packed her mail Tetris-style into her trunk, the day was almost over. Now, looking at the house bathed in the golden evening light, a sense of peace washed over her.

She'd watched this building transform from lines on paper, to a skeleton frame surrounded by building materials, to what it was today: a finished house, ready for someone to move in. And each step of the way Harrison had been there, poring over the plans, overseeing deliveries, building the structure with his own two hands. There wasn't a room in the house that wasn't his handiwork.

Maybe that was why Lainie was already starting to think of it as a home, not just a house.

Just as she was thinking about that, Harrison appeared around the corner of the house. A smile blossomed on his face, and he waved at her.

"Lainie!"

Lainie got out of the car, dragging the groceries behind her. "Every time I see this place, I can't believe how amazing it looks," she said as Harrison strode up to her. "I—"

Before she could say another word, Harrison took her in his arms and kissed her. Lainie let herself melt into his embrace. He smelled of wood-shavings and sweat, and the musky scent she'd come to recognize as his griffin.

He took his time with the kiss, nibbling and nuzzling at her lips until Lainie thought her whole body was going to dissolve from happiness. She sighed as he pulled away.

"What was that you were saying?" he murmured, his hazel eyes hooded and dark.

"I… have completely forgotten," Lainie admitted happily. She tugged the top button of his work shirt open and pressed her face into the triangle of hair underneath. "Mmm."

"How about I grab these before our dinner goes flying back down the hill?" Harrison nibbled her ear briefly, slipping the bags of groceries out of her hand.

"Oh, I see. All this romance business is just a cover for you to get some food, is it?" Lainie teased. She grabbed his free hand and started walking up the path to the house. "Why so hush-hush today? Is everything okay with the build?"

"Everything's perfect." Harrison looked sideways at her, his eyes gleaming. "It's almost finished, in fact."

"Almost?" Lainie pretended to look shocked. "Frankly, Mr. Galway, that's not good enough. I didn't sell the family jewels to *almost* have a house."

Harrison glanced over his shoulder at the sun. "Oh, I don't know about that. I'd say I've got at least three hours before the job is officially behind schedule," he drawled.

They approached the front door and Harrison grabbed Lainie by the waist, squeezing her. "Notice anything missing?"

Lainie looked. "Let's see. There's a hole in the door instead of a handle… I'll have to dock your wages for that one." She giggled as Harrison carefully set down the groceries on the step and produced a door handle from his pocket. "Oh, no. You know I'm not handy, I can't…"

"All you need to do is screw it in," Harrison said. "I'll show you how. And then your house will be one-hundred-percent finished."

*With a massive gouge out of the faceplate where I slip and jam the screwdriver, I bet,* Lainie thought. Harrison held the handle out to her, his eyes beseeching.

"Oh, all right. I'll probably just stuff it up, though." She relented, only half grudgingly, and took the heavy brass handle off him.

Harrison kneeled down, and Lainie crouched beside him. "Here, see—I've already put the latch in. All you need to do is attach the handle." He put his hands over Lainie's and lifted them, directing her where to hold the handle in place. His hands almost completely engulfed hers. He showed her where to put the screws in and waited patiently while she laboriously screwed them in.

At last Lainie pushed down on the handle and heard the latch open with a click.

"It works!" Lainie couldn't help squealing with glee. For all her experience with architectural planning, she had always had a black thumb when it came to home maintenance. Or whatever you called a black thumb when it applied to window latches and lightbulbs instead of plants.

She pushed the door open. It swung smoothly, of course—perfectly hung by Harrison. The late-afternoon light poured in, illuminating warm polished floors and cream-painted walls.

Behind her, Harrison cleared his throat. Lainie looked around, and then down. He was still kneeling on his knees on the front step, but this time, he was holding something else up to her.

Harrison cleared his throat again. For the first time in months, Lainie saw he looked nervous. "Lainie," he began, and stopped, choking up. "Lainie. My love. The last six months, since I met you, have been the happiest of my life. Building this house for you has been the best thing I've ever done. Will you take this ring, and together we can turn this house into a home?"

Lainie fell to her knees. The box Harrison was holding out to her was black velvet, and there was a glittering ring nestled inside it. A cushion-cut diamond, ridiculously large, was set in warm rose-gold in the middle of the ring, surrounded by smaller yellow stones. Her grandmother's ring.

"But I sold this," she breathed. "How did you…?"

The laughter lines at the edges of Harrison's eyes crinkled. "You sold it to me," he said. "Well, through one of Pol's contacts, at least. He's going to use it as an excuse to turn up late to work for the next ten years, but that's worth it, if…"

He trailed off expectantly. Lainie reached forward and grabbed, not the ring, but the hand holding it.

"Of course I do," she said. "I mean, yes. I do. Of course," she cried, laughing with joy.

Harrison slipped the ring out of the box and onto her finger, where it fit perfectly. The sight of it filled Lainie's heart. She had lost the chance at a relationship with her grandmother, but this ring was a connection between the generations. A promise that things would be different for her own children, when she had them.

Harrison covered her small hand with his own and then pulled her into a kiss that made her heart sing.

"My love," Harrison murmured against her lips. "My Lainie. My mate. My darling, sweetest, most beautiful…"

His kisses began to drift down her neck, and Lainie giggled. "Do we want to take this inside?" she said. "Into the nest?"

She didn't know what made her call the house a *nest,* but whatever instinct it was, it was a good one. Harrison's eyes burned into hers, gold flaring around pupils as black as coals.

"There isn't any furniture in there yet," he said, his hands slipping under Lainie's shirt. "Are you sure you don't want to go back to the workshop?"

"We can improvise," Lainie said, waving away his half-hearted argument. "Come on. Let's make this place our home."

# THE SEA WOLF'S MATE

# I

# JACQUELINE

"**I**'m sorry, you have the wrong number. Yes—no, I realize you dialed the number listed for the pizza parlor, but something's wrong with the interchange and I'm afraid… This is the sheriff's office, ma'am, I'm afraid I really can't take your pizza order."

Jacqueline rubbed her forehead as the caller let her know just how unacceptable that was. *This is what I get for taking the evening shift,* she thought. *That storm must have seriously messed with the phone lines. I knew I shouldn't have trusted the boss when he said it was all sorted…*

She bit back a sigh, careful not to let even a hiss of breath escape. The last thing she wanted was the woman on the other end of the line thinking she was sighing at *her.* Even if it was kind of the truth.

If the pizza-woman had been the first wrong number to call her today, that would be one thing. But no. The storm a few days back had come up from Hideaway Cove to the south, and like all bad weather that came from that direction, it had left havoc in its wake. Not only broken shutters and saltwater-whipped gardens, but electrical mix-ups. Computers went haywire, lights flickered… and phone lines got crossed.

The sheriff's office landline had somehow become mixed up with that of a pizza joint on the other end of town—and an auto shop, and the local kindergarten, and what felt like half the businesses within ten miles—and as if that wasn't enough, the connection was bad.

At least, Jacqueline assumed it was the bad connection that was making this caller squawk like a seagull descending on a garbage bin.

She rubbed her forehead, waiting for the woman's rant to come to an end.

"I—oh. You'd like to make a formal complaint? About me not providing you with an appropriate level of service? Well, you go right ahead, ma'am. We have a contact form on our website, or… you'd like me to type it out for you? Of course. That will be no problem *at all.*"

Jacqueline gritted her teeth as the woman on the other end of the line dictated a list of Jacqueline's many sins. Including not taking her damned pizza order. *Why don't you blame me for the weather, as well?*

"Thank you, ma'am, I'll make sure the sheriff receives this when he's next in. Excuse me?" Jacqueline blinked. "Well, he's…"

*At the Spring Fling, celebrating the fact that winter's finally over. With the rest of the office, and most of the town… and my ex.*

Jacqueline swallowed. "…He's out on another call at the moment, ma'am. But I'll put your note on his desk for his priority attention."

There was a dangerous silence at the other end of the phone. Jacqueline thought the woman was rallying her strength for another attack—and then the other phone clattered against something, and the noise of excited shouts clamored down the line. Jacqueline closed her eyes. *A teenagers' party. Something the town put on to keep them out of trouble while everyone's at the Spring Fling getting respectably tipsy… and this woman's stuck babysitting. No wonder she's annoyed.*

"Ma'am—"

"Forget about it. My neighbor has brought over snacks. No thanks to *you.*"

Jacqueline's breath caught in her throat as the woman slammed the phone down. Pinching the bridge of her nose, she set down her own receiver. Gently.

*It doesn't matter how good it would feel to slam it down. You know Reg would take any breakages out of your pay.*

And she couldn't afford that. She was *done*. All the scrimping and saving, all the extra hours and odd jobs and humiliation—she just had to wait for her final check to clear, and it would all be over. She'd have finally paid down her home loan.

She'd be free. Free to reclaim her life. Leave this crushingly small town and do all the things that had passed her by.

And no way was her first home-loan-free paycheck going to go towards replacing broken office equipment. She was going to cut loose. Stay out late at clubs, wear short skirts and too much make-up, all the fun things she'd spent the last decade and a half missing out on. No ball and chain, no mortgage, no responsibilities—

She flung herself back in her chair and spun around. When she stopped, she was looking straight at the oversized, framed family photograph that took pride of place on her boss' desk.

Five pairs of eyes stared back at her. Reg, his wife Susie, and their three beautiful children.

A lump formed in her throat. She looked down, but all that did was draw attention to her outfit. She'd fretted over it all week, because the Spring Fling was going to be *it* for her. The mortgage was the last remnant of her old married life she'd been dragging behind her and now it was finally meant to be time for her fresh start.

She was wearing a bra that the shop assistant had promised would give her "like, amazing self esteem", a silky dress that shimmered when she walked—heck, she was even wearing *heels*…

And then Reg had sauntered in just as she was putting the finishing touches on her make-up and said *Oh, by the way, you know Deirdre can't do the evening shift tonight because of her thing on the weekend, and I was wondering* and he'd hmm'd and haww'd and gone on about *and it's Jonesy's first Spring Fling since he made deputy and you know his Ma's going to be so proud* and *Now young Marsha, it would just be a shame for her to miss out, what with her not making it to her prom last year* and he'd made it the whole way around the office twice before getting to the meat of the matter:

Jacqueline's ex-husband would be at the party. And his new wife. And their kid.

So Jacqueline took the night shift.

She swallowed angrily, spinning back to face her computer.

*I'm done. Free. So what if I don't make it to the Spring Fling? I don't need it. I could move out, today—well, not today, maybe tomorrow—or next week—and start my super amazing, dirty thirties lifestyle in the city. I'll live in an apartment, and drink cocktails with stupid names, and* date, *and—*

The phone rang again and all the anger Jacqueline had held back while she was talking to the pizza woman exploded. She snatched up the phone.

"This had better not be another—"

The line crackled so loudly Jacqueline pulled the phone away from her ear. She squeezed her eyes shut. *Stay calm. Stay professional. Even that angry pizza lady is probably just pissed because she has to babysit while everyone else is at the Fling.*

The phone hissed and popped, and then a male voice quavered:

"Hello?… calling… Hideaway…"

Jacqueline's heart sank. *Is someone seriously calling to complain about the curse?* Complaining about the weather was one thing, but…

She sighed. Most people she knew joked about their neighboring town being responsible for any problems they faced—everything from late buses to, yep, electrical problems after storms—but calling to lodge a complaint with the sheriff was going too far, surely?

"Sorry, sir, can you repeat that please?"

"Trying to call—is this Hideaway? Got the number from…" His voice crackled and faded out.

Jacqueline rubbed her forehead. Not a curse complaint, then; just another crossed wire. "I'm sorry, sir, this is the Dunston sheriff's office. I can try to transfer you…" *And it'll probably go through to the pizza place, knowing my luck.*

"No, I… trying to get to… left them… storm…"

Jacqueline frowned. The voice on the other end of the line was male. His voice was deep, but it kept cracking, going up and down and wobbling with tension. Either she was imagining it, or the phone line was so bad it was making her hear things… or this guy was scared.

Alarm bells started going off in her head, but she forced her voice to remain calm.

"Sorry, sir, could you please repeat that?"

There was another burst of static, and then: "I'm sorry. I'm sorry, I didn't know what to do, but I left them there and now I can't get back, the road's closed and none of the buses are running and my car won't start and I can't get back to them—"

"To who?"

"I thought they'd be safe there, they're only… too small… left them… marine reserve. Trying… get to Hideaway but I couldn't call and now…"

Jacqueline's heart dropped. *Too small? Is he talking about children?* "I—you're saying you left someone at a marine reserve? During the *storm?*"

She could have hit herself. *Stupid.* Her job was to get the details and keep the caller on the line until she could get hold of someone to take action—not to berate them for whatever had made them call.

Especially not if there were children involved. Jacqueline's stomach clenched. She knew better than this. She couldn't let her own situation affect her professionalism.

"Sir, I understand if you don't want to leave a name, but if you could let me know where you are—we'll do whatever we can to help—"

She thought he started to say something else, but then there was a roar like a huge engine—*Or a storm*—and the call cut out.

Jacqueline stared at her computer screen.

*The call logger will have the details of the call*, the organized, sober part of her brain reminded her, but she couldn't focus on it. Her mind was miles away, in the open, exposed marine reserve that must have borne the brunt of the last week's storms.

She took a deep breath and glanced out the station's front window. The massive storms had broken windows and torn down tree branches here. What might they have done out on the wild coast?

Her hands moved automatically, probably because they had noticed her brain wasn't capable at the moment. They picked up her mobile and called her boss.

The call rang. And rang.

"Hi, this is Reg—"

"Boss, thank God. I've just had a distress call, I think, and it sounds like—"

"—probably a bit busy at the moment, so leave a message and I'll get back to you. Brent out."

*Shit.* Jacqueline grimaced. Answerphone. Of course. Because God forbid Reg actually take the "on call" part of his job seriously when there was punch and a live band on offer.

She took a deep breath and waited for the beep.

"Hi. Boss. This is Jacqueline. We've had a call reporting possible child abandonment at the marine reserve, up the coast. I'm going to go check it out. I'll have my mobile with me if you need me."

The office seemed to ring with silence as she ended the call.

*I'm going up the coast.*

Of course she was. There was no way she could take that call, hear the panic in the guy's voice, and not follow up. If it wasn't a prank, and he'd actually for whatever reason left some kids at the marine reserve...

She got up quickly, sending her office chair spinning away.

"It's probably just some teenagers having a joke," she told herself out loud. Her voice echoed around the empty office.

*Good job, Jacqueline. You can't even convince yourself.*

# 2

# ARLO

Arlo furled the sails, letting the *Hometide* slip gently through the swell as the wind whipped through his hair. The sun had set, and soon the night would be so dark that the water turned black, nothing to separate it from the heavy canopy of sky. It was too cloudy for the moon to show, let alone any stars. The sailboat would seem to be drifting in space, only the distant lights on the coastline a reminder that the rest of the world existed.

Even those few lights grated against Arlo's skin. Later in the season, when the weather was more reliable, he'd sail further, away from the towns, away from streetlights and the glowing windows of people's homes. Until it was just the sea, and the sky, and him. Maybe then he'd be able to get his head right.

Arlo cursed and tied off the sail. The storms that had kept him landed for the last week had disappeared like smoke overnight, and he'd left Hideaway before first light, sliding out of the bay on still waters with his tail between his legs.

And he didn't even know *why*.

Everything had been going fine. Work was good, and Arlo's best friend Harrison had been preening like a peacock ever since he put a rock on his mate Lainie's finger.

Even Lainie's plan to build more houses in Hideaway Cove was going well. Arlo was proud to be a part of the project. More houses meant more homes for shifters, and that was what Hideaway Cove was all about. Shifters always looked after their own.

He, Harrison and the other builder on their crew, Pol, had celebrated the completion of the first house in the project the night before the storm hit. They'd broken out a few beers. Lainie had abstained, with a meaningful look at Harrison, and Pol had ribbed them both about how at least they'd finished their own house first, and then turned to Arlo and made a joke about which one of them would be next, and Arlo had been in a foul mood ever since.

*Hrngg?* his wolf whined, and Arlo sighed.

"Yeah, I know, buddy. It doesn't make any sense. Blame it on the weather."

The storm had hit that night—a first strength-test for the new build and a trial and a half for the headache that started pounding at Arlo's skull the moment Pol suggested he might be the next to find his mate. On a whim that he didn't understand, Arlo had asked Lainie how sales of the new sections on Lighthouse Hill were going. The build they'd just finished was spoken for, but he'd thought—he didn't know what he'd thought. His head had felt like someone was scraping it out with a rusty spatula, and when Lainie had reassured him that there were still sections available, he'd felt even worse.

*I don't need a new house, anyway. I have the* Hometide, *and a room above the workshop. Why do I need anything else?*

*And why would that give me a headache, anyway? Or the idea of finding a mate? Hideaway's my home. Creating a family here, bringing them into the Sweets' pack, would be the best thing to ever happen.*

His head throbbed.

*No, that can't be it. It must have been the weather change coming in.* It was ludicrous to think that the unease coiling in Arlo's stomach and pounding at his skull might be because he was worried about finding his mate.

A spray of salt water burst over the port side of the boat and Arlo jerked, automatically scanning the water for what could have caused the disturbance.

He couldn't see anything; even the distant lights from the nearest human town were barely a glow on the horizon, and he was far enough from Hideaway that he couldn't sense any of his shifter friends or neighbors.

But, just in case…

He sent out a cautious telepathic signal. *Hello?*

There was no reply. Arlo relaxed. Just a stray wave. He was alone out here. Just him and his migraine.

*God knows what I'd do if someone did pop by and want a chat*, he thought glumly. *Bite their head off, probably.*

He released the anchor, trying to transform the relief he'd felt at realizing he was still alone into real relaxation. It didn't work. The headache was like a hammer, beating hot, sharp knocks on the back of his head. Constant. Frustrating. It was like…

*It's like someone's trying to get my attention.*

Arlo's shoulders tensed. He tentatively extended his shifter powers, checking for any telltale echoes of other shifters in the area. Nothing.

He shook his head and winced as it throbbed.

Nothing. Nothing certain, at least. Just a hint, a suggestion, of someone at the other end of the constant thudding in his head.

Arlo growled. *This had better not be one of Jools' pranks…* But, no, that wouldn't be like her. Jools' jokes were stupid, but they never hurt anyone.

This was something new. Or some*one* new.

Arlo groaned. He'd slipped out of Hideaway before dawn to avoid having to talk to anyone, not to trip over a new arrival and play welcoming committee.

A *lost* new arrival, apparently. Hideaway Cove was miles away, and that would explain why they were knocking on his skull like it was a door and they were after directions.

He'd dropped anchor as he debated with himself, and the boat swung towards the coast with the movement of water. It wasn't much, a few yards closer to land, but it was enough.

The psychic attack hit him like a sledgehammer. He sprawled over the deck, gasping.

*Shit. Shit, shit, shit.* Ignoring this wasn't a possibility.

He threw himself back at the anchor and began to raise it. Sails—he needed to let the sails down. Set a course for land. The clamor in his head almost blinded him and he squinted through streaming eyes.

It hurt. God, it hurt. Almost beyond bearing.

He should turn back. Find Harrison. Harrison would deal with this better than he could. Arlo was sure to fuck it up—if he even got there in time and didn't pass out from the pain.

But he couldn't. There might not be time. He couldn't even look at the point on the coast he was aiming at. It seemed to shimmer, crackling with the weight of the psychic force coming from it.

He couldn't have done anything else. He knew the emotions roaring like wildfire out across the water. It wasn't an attack—not a deliberate one, at least.

It was fear, and sorrow, and confusion. And loneliness so sharp it felt like a knife twisting in his gut. He'd been there before. It was too familiar.

But that wasn't what made him urge his boat faster toward the shore. That sheer force of telepathic power, the solid weight of emotion carried with it… he couldn't imagine any adult shifter being so open.

The headache that had been plaguing him all day, the wall of pain and fear—it was a shifter child, crying out for help.

3

# JACQUELINE

acqueline hissed through her teeth as the car's back wheels slid on slick black mud. The coastal road out to the marine reserve was a twisting, broken-up mess at the best of times, but it had taken an extra beating in the latest storms—and the town hadn't sent anyone out to fix things up yet.

*Or ever,* Jacqueline thought, narrowing her eyes at the road ahead. *That—oh, come on. I remember that slip from last time I was out here… how many years ago?*

Jacqueline shook her head as she counted back. Not since she'd started working at the sheriff's office, at least. A few years into her marriage.

*Too long.*

The marine reserve was quiet and peaceful, but Jacqueline was in no mood to appreciate it today. It had taken her over an hour to get this far, but she had slowed down to a crawl the last half-mile as the condition of the road got worse and worse. And what she could see in her headlights didn't exactly encourage her.

She eased around a slippery bend and groaned. A landslide covered the road.

*And here I am in a two-wheel drive like some useless townie. If Reg hadn't taken the truck to cart everyone to the party…*

Jacqueline tightened her grip on the steering wheel. *No turning back now.*

157

Reg hadn't returned her call. She didn't know if he'd even got her message. Either way, this was up to her.

Wincing, she trundled closer to the rocky, silty landslide. The car's front wheels spun and spun—and gripped.

"Yes!" she shouted. "Let's do this!"

She made it another ten feet.

The car's efforts didn't end with a bang, or a crunch. It just sank slowly into the sodden dirt, wheels whining as they spun.

"Drat!" Jacqueline snapped, smacking the steering wheel. "Useless—freaking—ugh!"

She wrestled the door open and took stock. The car was sunk halfway up the wheels.

*So I'll have to call a tow truck. What'll that set me back? A few nights of cocktails?*

Jacqueline squelched around the car and grabbed her handbag from the trunk, slinging it over her shoulder and stomping awkwardly over the last of the slip. Her flashlight made a sad, small circle of light on the mud.

The caller's panicked voice echoed through her mind. She pulled her phone out of her bag and slipped it into her bra. *Just in case Reg gets back to me. Or a call comes through from the office.* She'd set up an auto-forward before she left, although she wasn't sure how much she trusted it what with all the electrical weirdnesses lately.

A light breeze made her shiver. It was almost pitch black by the time she made it to the parking area at the entrance to the reserve. Jacqueline swung her flashlight around.

There wasn't much to see. Just an empty parking lot and a concrete building with its doors and windows boarded up. The lights of a boat blinked out on the water. She couldn't tell in the darkness what type of boat it was, or how far away.

*Whoever they are, I hope they're having a better night than me.*

Jacqueline frowned at the concrete building. When she'd been at school, her parents had told her that when *they* were at school, the old building had been used for field trips. Jacqueline couldn't remember ever seeing it without its doors and windows boarded up.

She let her flashlight linger over one of the boarded-up windows. Some of the wooden slats had been broken away.

*Was that the storm, or…?*

Hairs prickled on the back of Jacqueline's neck. She told herself it was just the cold.

Beyond the abandoned building was a boardwalk, leading out over the shallows and rockpools.

*Given the state of everything else out here, that's probably rotten, too.* Jacqueline looked around. There was no sign of anyone, but—she ran her flashlight over the broken boards on the window again.

Just in case…

"Hello?" she called out. Her voice carried on the chill air. "Is there anyone there? It's okay, you can come out. Your friend called me, he wanted me to come check up on you."

There was no reply.

A gull cried in the distance. Jacqueline shivered. The sea breeze was growing stronger, filling her lungs with the taste of brine, and now that the sun had set, the already brisk air was becoming chilly. It wasn't raining, but… Jacqueline looked up. Clouds. Which meant rain might still be on the agenda.

Wrapping her arms around herself, she walked out into the middle of the parking area.

"If there's anyone out there… your friend asked me to come look for you. I've got food, and blankets back in the car—I work for the sheriff, I'm here to help you."

She bit her tongue. Come to think of it, that might not be the best tactic to take with a group of runaway-or-lost kids. *Hey, kids! I'm with the sheriff! You're all sure in trouble now!*

Again, there was no reply. Jacqueline looked around, uncertain. There was no sign of any children.

*Maybe it was a prank after all,* she thought. *Ha, ha. Very funny. Thank God.*

She tipped her head back and closed her eyes. Her car was stuck in a muddy ditch, she'd ruined her shoes, and the news that she'd got herself into a tizz over some prank caller was going to be headline news in the office come Monday… but just for a moment, she stood and enjoyed the cool, fresh air on her face.

What with the storm, she'd been cooped up inside all week. And even if she hadn't been—when was the last time she'd been up the coast?

*I used to love the water,* she thought with a sigh. *Swimming, fishing, going out on a boat or body board, even if I had to wear a head-to-toe wetsuit to keep from freezing. What happened?*

She absently rubbed the empty spot on her ring finger.

It was beautiful. Peaceful. The clouds above made the night sky look soft and endless, like a huge ink-blue blanket over the world. There was the soft shush of the waves in the distance, and—

A shout echoed through the air and was suddenly cut off.

Jacqueline's eyes shot open. She spun on the spot, ears straining as she faced the direction she thought the shout had come from.

The boardwalk.

She broke into a sprint, the light from her flashlight zig-zagging madly ahead of her as she ran. The boardwalk was slick with seawater and she almost skidded over, grabbing the railing just in time. Panting, she swung the flashlight around, trying desperately to find the source of whoever had shouted.

*Or whatever.* No. The voice had been human. High-pitched, almost a yelp—but human.

She was sure of it.

Jacqueline squinted, forcing herself to search the area thoroughly, and not just whip the flashlight randomly around. Light glittered off the waves and the water swirling through the rockpools at the edge of the coast, and off a pair of dark eyes half-hidden in a pile of boulders.

Jacqueline froze. Then she blinked, and the dark shadow around the gleaming eyes solidified into a small seal, hiding in the rocks.

"Oh, shoot. I am such an idiot," she muttered.

That short, cut-off yelp—it could have been a seal, couldn't it?

She let the flashlight swing sideways, not wanting to disturb the seal any more than she already had. Just a seal. The call had been a prank after all, just as she—

"Oh no," she gasped, the blood in her veins turning to ice.

The beam of her flashlight was illuminating the rocks right at the edge of the water, where the rockpools turned into open water. Perched on the top of one of the rocks, with waves breaking over her head, was a little girl.

Jacqueline gaped. The girl was butt naked, with a tangle of curly hair that looked white-blonde in the light from her flashlight.

The girl waved and grinned when she saw Jacqueline staring at her. Then she yelped as another wave broke behind her, swamping her with salt spray.

"Oh sh—hey, hey kid!" Jacqueline was moving before the words left her mouth. "Just stay there, I'll come and get you! Don't move!"

*If she falls in the water—*

Jacqueline cut the thought off sharp. *Not going to happen.*

She ran further along the boardwalk. A plank gave way under her foot and she stumbled, losing one of her shoes. Behind her, the seal barked again.

Jacqueline wobbled to her feet and kicked off her other shoe. She was as close to the little girl as she could get on the boardwalk, but there was still twenty feet of broken rock and treacherous water between them. She glanced further out to sea; the boat was still out there, but too far away to help, even if they heard her shouting. She was on her own.

Jacqueline steadied her flashlight and gulped.

"Hey, honey!" she called out, holding the flashlight so she could see the girl without blinding her. The girl was still crouched on the same rock, but the waves were crashing too close behind her for comfort. "I'll be with you in a sec, okay? Just sit tight."

Jacqueline stepped gingerly out onto the rocks. They were jagged, but not slippery. She took a few tentative steps and then became more confident.

"Okay, Jacqueline. You can do this," she muttered to herself as the seal started barking more loudly. "Save the girl. Leave the local wildlife in peace. Attagirl."

She was less than six feet away from the girl when she stepped on what she thought was a rock and found herself hip-deep in icy, sucking water, surrounded by ropes of clinging seaweed. Pain shot through her foot as it landed on something sharp.

"Ah-h," she gasped, and grappled for a hold on the rocks before the water swept her off her feet.

A wordless shout echoed across the rocks. Jacqueline glanced over her shoulder to see—*You've got to be kidding me*—another curly-haired kid following her. A boy, maybe nine or ten, and just as naked as the little girl.

"Stop!" she called out. "Go back to shore!" *And—put some pants on! What the hell? Have I stumbled on some sort of hippie commune?*

Jacqueline turned back to the little girl, trusting the boy would listen to her. *The last thing I need is* two *kids falling in—*

Panting, she tried to haul herself up and slipped back again. The tide sucked at her legs.

Shaking sea spray out of her eyes, Jacqueline raised her flashlight and checked on the girl. She was still there, and only a few feet away—but there was a deep pool between them. Dark water rushed through a gap in the rocks, treacherously fast.

*If I can hardly hold myself up in* this *current… then that one's gotta be bad. Really bad.*

Jacqueline looked across at the girl, whose face was creasing unhappily. "Hey, hey. It's okay, sweetheart. You just stay there and I'll come get you, okay? We can get you home—"

A decisive bark echoed across the rocks from back near the boardwalk. Jacqueline yanked herself up, managing to pull herself out of the water this time. She was measuring the gap—could she risk jumping across, or did she have time to find another way across?—when the girl stood up.

"No, no, honey, stay sitting down, the waves are—" Jacqueline began, and then her voice cut off.

*I can't be seeing this. It's… no way. No way this is happening.*

At first she thought the shimmering around the little girl was sea spray catching the light from her flashlight. Then the girl stretched out her arms, laughed, and *changed.*

Her tangled blonde hair disappeared, dark fur sprouted from her face and body, and a moment later there wasn't a little girl standing on the rocks. There was a seal pup.

Jacqueline swayed, dazed. A seal pup. That little girl had just changed… into a baby seal.

Part of her brain remembered the seal she'd seen hiding behind the rocks near the boardwalk… and the boy who'd appeared as though out of nowhere.

*This isn't a prank,* she thought wildly. *This is—this is—*

She blinked hard, as though it would change what she saw in front of her.

*Why did the guy on the phone want to call* Hideaway *about this?*

She opened her mouth, with no idea of what she was about to say—and then the pup overbalanced, yelped, and slid headfirst into the water.

Jacqueline didn't stop to think. She jumped.

Icy water closed over her head. The ocean was like a hand, wrapping around her and dragging her down. She dropped her flashlight and it spun around in the water, blinding her—but there, a darker shadow, seal-pup-sized. Jacqueline kicked wildly towards it.

The flashlight flickered out and she couldn't see anything, not even her own hands in front of her, but her fingers brushed something soft and she pulled the tiny creature into her arms and her knee hit something hard and she hoped it was the bottom, she hoped she was kicking off in the right direction because she had no way of telling what way was up or down and—

Air. Jacqueline gasped and flailed one hand until she hit rock. She grabbed it and pulled herself up, twisting her body so she wouldn't squash the seal pup—the little girl—the seal pup—*What is going on—*

A wave crashed over her head. Jacqueline pulled herself further up the rock.

"Hey kid," she gasped, then coughed out a mouthful of saltwater. The seal pup wriggled against her chest. "It's going to be—"

Someone shouted. It sounded close. Jacqueline raised her head. If that boy had come out after her—

Another wave hit, and she lost her grip on the rock. The water pulled her away and under.

# 4

# ARLO

"**N**o!"

The young shifters' shouts echoed in Arlo's mind as he threw himself into the water.

*His fault.* He'd shouted when he was close enough to see what was happening, and the woman had lifted her head to look around. And the next wave had taken her.

She and the child had disappeared under the surface as though they had never existed.

*I should have been faster. I shouldn't have distracted her. I should have—*
Arlo forced the thought from his mind.

The water was cruelly cold. His wolf reveled in it, staking its strength and agility against the power of the sea.

Arlo strained his eyes and ears, ignoring the salt burn as he searched the water. It was pitch black, but the tiny shifter's telepathic shrieks were more than enough for Arlo to locate her.

There—the sea had pulled them away, but the next swelling wave might dash them against the rocks again. He swam towards them, his strong strokes cutting through the water like a hot knife through ice.

The woman jerked as he grabbed hold of her. A bubble of surprise burst against his chest and then she clutched at him. He pulled them both to himself, his arm around the woman, the pup sandwiched between them.

His feet slammed against the rocks at the bottom and he kicked, launching himself upwards. Sea spray battered his face as he broke the surface and the woman in his arms sucked in breaths, so hard it sounded like she was sobbing.

Their mouths were inches apart. Their breaths mingled, and something in the back of Arlo's mind went *ping.*

His wolf bristled with urgency. *Get her safe! Now!*

The seal's heart beat like a tiny drum against his chest and without thinking about it he sent out a telepathic burst of emotion. No words, just feelings, as instinctive as the young shifters' cries. Comfort. Safety. Protection.

He hadn't communicated with anyone like that in decades, with primal, instinctual emotion. Not since… a long time ago.

There was no time to think about that now. His rowboat was bobbing in the waves a few feet away; he swam towards it and grabbed hold of the side.

The woman coughed out a mouthful of seawater. "We'll tip it—"

"I'll hold the other side while you climb in," he told her. His wolf whined, impressed. She'd almost drowned, but she'd still kept her head enough not to try to clamber on board the rowboat and flip it over in the process.

"Wait! The girl first," the woman gasped. Then her eyes widened and she twisted to look back at the rocks. "There was another kid—oh, God, if he's—"

Arlo swept the shoreline. He could hardly sense anything past the tiny seal's psychic shrieks of excitement, but whoever was on shore, they weren't hurt or panicked. Just confused. Worried.

"He's fine," he reassured the woman, and made a silent promise to make sure that was true. He sent out a psychic warning to whoever else was out there to stay safe while they got ashore.

"Oh. Good."

The child shifter's confusion popped against Arlo's mind as the woman lifted her up over the side of the rowboat. She flailed against the woman's attempts to put her on board. Arlo trod water, keeping the woman and boat steady and sending reassurance to the little girl until she let herself be safely deposited inside the boat.

"Now you," he said firmly.

"Right…"

Arlo hauled himself hand-over-hand to the other side of the rowboat and called that he was ready. The woman took a deep, shaking breath and Arlo's heart froze.

Then she muttered something under her breath, kicked up and pulled herself over the side. She rolled into the boat with a clatter and a bitten-off curse.

The seal pup wobbled over her and was trying to clamber into her lap before she was even sitting upright.

"Okay. Okay, this is all… hey, honey, hey, there you are. Don't worry. It's all right. Everything's going to be all right."

Happiness bubbled across Arlo's mind as the woman picked the seal pup up and cuddled her. Despite himself, he smiled. Shifter kids that young shared their emotions with everyone nearby. The little girl's joy was infectious.

"There has to be a light here somewhere," the woman muttered. "What do you think, sweetheart? Are we going to find a light?"

"Should be under the seat," Arlo called.

"Got it. Watch your eyes." Arlo looked away and heard a *click* as she turned on the lantern. White light turned the water around the boat into a cauldron of stars. "Oh, that's better."

Her voice was clearer, no longer shaking with shock—but she had to be freezing.

Arlo looked up, but her face was hidden in shadows cast by the harsh light.

"Ready for me to come up?" he called, and the woman shifted her weight to the opposite side of the boat.

"Go on," she said, and Arlo pulled himself aboard.

Even though she was balancing the boat, Arlo weighed more than her and the scrap of a seal pup combined, so the boat rocked as he climbed aboard. The woman reached out to steady him, one arm still safely around the pup.

Arlo got his footing and looked up, about to tell her he was fine, he spent more time on the water than on land—and then their eyes met, and his mind went blank.

She was—she was…

She was leaning too far forward, her hand on his shoulder, and the boat was rocking. Her foot slipped and she fell toward him.

Arlo grabbed her and pulled her onto the seat next to him. There was hardly enough space; she was pressed in tight against him. No, not just pressed in. She was leaning against him, gasping with the cold.

Arlo wrapped one arm around her shoulder, the other over her hands. Her fingers were cold. He knew he should say something, but his throat was too tight.

His eyes strained like a drowning man reaching for the surface, calling on his shifter abilities to improve his sight. He felt like a man on the edge of a precipice. He felt like he was going to jump. Then the lantern rolled in the bottom of the rowboat, illuminating them both.

Her hair was flattened against her head, dark red made darker by the water. Her face was pale with cold and shock, her lips parted as she caught her breath, dark circles around her eyes where her make-up had smeared. And her hazel eyes caught Arlo like a fish in a net.

Warmth blossomed inside Arlo despite the cold air and colder water. For half a heartbeat, he thought the feelings of love and homecoming were coming from the little bundle in the woman's arms. A young shifter, reacting instinctively to a kind touch.

That lasted until he breathed in, and the woman's scent filled his senses.

The emotions he was feeling weren't the seal shifter's.

They were his.

He wasn't in the water anymore, he told himself. He had all the air he needed, even if his chest felt like there were iron bands around it.

His wolf was trembling with excitement inside him, but his human side…

It should have been wonderful, it should have been the best thing that ever happened to him, but instead the same nausea that had hit him back at the building site struck him like lightning: *This can't be happening. Not now.*

This woman was his mate.

He tightened his grip on the woman's hand. "You're—"

*Human.*

*Oh, hell.*

# 5

## JACQUELINE

"Are you all right?" The man's voice was strange, almost choked. Jacqueline looked up quickly. Christ, if he'd inhaled half the ocean saving her and was about to fall over with secondary drowning…

"I," she began, and then she was the one swallowing her words. "I, um, yes. Fine. Thank you."

The seal pup snuffled and dove into her elbow. She repositioned her arms around it absently, still staring at the man who'd saved her life.

Mary mother of God, he was the hottest man she'd ever laid eyes on.

Not just literally, although heat poured from his body, as though he was hiding a furnace under—Jacqueline gulped. Not under his clothes, because he was barely wearing any. A worn shirt clung to his shoulders and biceps like it had been painted on, and hung open in front to reveal a muscular chest that gleamed and glittered in the light from the small lantern. His pants were low-slung enough that…

Jacqueline raised her eyes quickly.

Water streamed from his dark, curly hair, too, dripping over his forehead. He blinked a droplet away and suddenly Jacqueline couldn't look away from his eyes.

His eyelashes were dark and thick, surrounding eyes the color of the night sky, and he was staring at her with an intensity she hadn't experienced since… since…

"I'm f-fine," she repeated. The bench seat they were sitting on was very small, she realized. Too small for both of them really. Her hip and thigh were pressed tight up against his.

The man's eyes flicked down her body and darkened. "You'll freeze, wearing that."

"Really, I don't feel cold at all," Jacqueline replied automatically.

She glanced down at herself and bit back a grimace. The nice dress she'd picked out for the Spring Fling hadn't exactly fared well against the might of the Pacific Ocean. It was flattened against her body, rucked up and twisted from when she'd clambered into the boat. And—oh, God, how could she not have noticed it riding up *that* far?

Jacqueline tugged at the hem and managed to at least cover the tops of her thighs before the little seal pup started wriggling enough that she had to turn her attention back to it.

"Hey, hey, it's all right. I bet you're not cold, huh, with that lovely fur coat." she cooed to it. It snuffled at her, gazed at her with its big wet eyes, and then dove back into her elbow.

The man made a stifled sound like a groan. When she looked up, he was grimacing.

He caught her eye and looked away. "Let's get in to shore," he muttered. Without looking at her, he gestured at the oars. "I'll need to…"

"Oh. Yes. Sorry." Jacqueline moved to the bench opposite. It was still a close fit, their knees almost touching across the gap—but it was an *almost* touch, not a squeezed-so-close-I-can-feel-you-breathe touch.

Jacqueline let out a slow breath.

She had been telling the truth. She *didn't* feel cold. But she'd just dived headfirst into the ocean. It might technically be spring but no one had told the water that. She should be freezing, and the fact that she wasn't feeling it now wasn't a good sign.

"Mrrf!" The seal pup squeaked into her elbow. "Mrrf!"

"We'll be there in a minute," the man said, "and you can tell me all about it."

"I didn't say anything," Jacqueline replied, and he gave her a guarded look.

"Well. Yes," he muttered, and hauled on the oars. The sight of his muscles working in the lantern light was almost enough to distract Jacqueline from wondering who he'd been talking to, then.

She looked down at the warm bundle in her arms.

*I did see what I saw, didn't I?*

Except it was… just a seal pup. And people didn't turn into animals, that was crazy talk.

Doubt began to wriggle at the edge of her mind.

The rowboat crunched against gravel, and the man was already halfway out of the boat by the time Jacqueline looked up. He reached out a hand and, after a brief wrangle with her own mind over whether he could possibly have any other reason for doing so, Jacqueline took it.

His hand was calloused, but gentle. A rush of warmth found its way to Jacqueline's cheeks. In the water, his arms around her hadn't been noticeably gentle—but they'd been strong. The moment he'd touched her she'd grabbed on to him. Even before they'd broken the surface she'd felt safe in his arms.

*You mean you grabbed on to him as a drowning reflex,* she corrected herself. *And then stayed so clingy he had to literally tell you to back off so he could reach the oars.*

She sighed, then winced as she stepped out of the boat. The man's grip might be gentle, but the stony shoreline was anything but. She grimaced and tiptoed up to the relatively foot-safe concrete by the old building.

"Ow," she muttered, shaking off a piece of gravel that had gotten lodged—yes, in the tattered remains of her pantyhose.

There was a shout behind her, and a low bark. Jacqueline spun around to see…

Nothing.

She narrowed her eyes. The lantern was still on the boat, and only a little of its light filtered this far up the beach. But she was sure she'd seen *something*. A flash of movement.

"Who's out there?" she called. There was no sign of the boy she'd seen on the rocks earlier. "Kid? You don't need to hide. I already saw you, remember?"

A clatter of falling rocks closer to the boardwalk caught her attention, and she turned just in time to see another big fat nothing in the shadows.

"I just want to know for sure you're all right," she said, pitching her voice to carry into the shadows. "Your friend who called me, he was really worried about you."

"Why would Eric call you? You're human."

Jacqueline spun around. The boy she'd seen earlier was standing just a few feet away. He'd found some clothes, thank goodness, and was wearing a pair of stained sweatpants and a thick sweater, with a ragged backpack slung over his shoulders.

"You say 'human' like there's another option," she said carefully, and the seal pup in her arms gave an impatient wriggle.

The boy's eyes went wide. "There isn't!" he exclaimed. "Um, but, do you want me to take her? It? The seal. I'm… studying them? For school?"

"Uh-huh." Jacqueline was unconvinced, but the seal pup started wriggling more as the boy reached out and she decided to hand it over. The boy got a football grip on the pup and hunched over it, whispering.

"What's your name?" Jacqueline asked.

"Dylan," he replied absently, and then: "No, don't! Not now!"

"Let me take her!" Another figure darted out of the shadows. This one was a young woman with her hair in a messy braid. Jacqueline guessed she was in her early teens.

The girl gave Jacqueline a suspicious glare and took the seal pup.

Jacqueline crossed her arms. "So you're studying the local seal population too, huh?"

"I'm—" The girl glared at Jacqueline and closed her mouth with a scowl.

"We making introductions?" Jacqueline's mystery rescuer strode up from where he'd been pulling the rowboat above the waterline. "I'm Arlo." His eyes flicked to Jacqueline's, and away again. "Arlo Hammond."

His voice was a low rumble that seemed to reverberate through Jacqueline's bones. She shivered. "Jacqueline March."

Was she imagining it, or did his cheeks go slightly pink? No. She was making things up. *Crazy.*

"I'm Kenna," the teenaged girl admitted reluctantly. "Kenna Weaver. This is Dylan, and—"

She closed her mouth so quickly her teeth clacked together.

"All right. Kenna, Dylan, and Tally—uh, Jacqueline. Why don't you tell us what you're doing here?" Arlo cleared his throat and flashed Jacqueline a wary look.

An electric charge raced up her spine. *Okay, now I'm definitely suspicious. Tally? Who's Tally?*

She looked around the small group. Kenna and Dylan had to be brother and sister; they had the same wriggly blond hair and snub noses.

And then there was the seal.

And Arlo.

"I see," Arlo said, even though no one else had said anything. He took a heavy breath and ran one hand over his jaw.

"Wait, what's going on here?" Jacqueline demanded. "Dylan, you thought your friend—Eric—wouldn't call me because I'm human? And you both—" She flung up her hands. "What am I saying? Both of you? All *three* of you. That little seal was a little *girl* when I first saw her, I'm—I'm sure of it."

*Are you?* Doubt wormed at her. *Maybe you just* thought *you saw...*

She shook her head. "Either way, we need to get you back into town. I can organize a place for you to stay until we get everything sorted out."

"Get what all sorted out?" Kenna scowled. "You don't know anything about—no, not now!" Kenna made a frustrated noise as the seal pup wriggled around in her arms.

Jacqueline crossed her arms. "I know you've been staying out here for who knows how long, waiting for Eric to come get you. But he's not coming."

Kenna flinched, and Jacqueline immediately regretted being so blunt.

"He's really upset about that, but he wants you to be safe. And so do I, and that means not leaving you out here in the middle of nowhere. I can take you back to Dunston—"

"We're not going!" Kenna was scowling so fiercely Jacqueline was worried she was about to burst into tears.

Dylan was wincing, too. Even Arlo looked uncomfortable.

"What's going on?" she asked. "What am I missing?" Jacqueline's head was spinning. Maybe she was going into shock, after all. It was as though there was a conversation going on that she couldn't hear half of.

"Ms. March," Arlo began, and rubbed his jaw again with a wince. "I can explain."

He sounded so *reasonable*.

Jacqueline had met so many reasonable men. Especially these last few years. Derek had been perfectly reasonable when he told her there was nothing going on. Then he'd been just as reasonable when he told her he had a secret two-year-old, and that she didn't need to hire her own divorce lawyer, because didn't she trust him to do the right thing?

Arlo exchanged a glance with Kenna and Dylan and something inside Jacqueline snapped.

"Don't you dare lie to me." Jacqueline met Arlo's gaze, her heart in her throat. "I am so *sick* of people lying to me."

*Please,* she added silently. *Please, please don't lie. Don't tell me I'm crazy. Don't tell me I'm imagining things.*

She'd had more than enough years of that already.

# 6

# ARLO

A shock of horror jolted down Arlo's spine.

She was right. He couldn't lie to her.

"Ms. March," he said, and her eyes narrowed suspiciously. "I won't lie to you. You deserve to know the truth, but—"

"But what?" Jacqueline had her arms folded tightly in front of her. Her shoulders hunched and Arlo saw a flicker of uncertainty pass across her face. "I saw—I *know* what I saw…"

*I could use this*, Arlo thought miserably. *It's what I'm meant to do in this situation, isn't it? What all Hideaway shifters are meant to do if a human suspects what we are. Use her uncertainty and confusion. Tell her she didn't see what she thought she saw. Keep our secret safe.*

But she'd sounded so desperate when she told him not to lie to her. And she was his mate. He had to trust her.

His head was pounding with the three shifter children's voices.

**He can't tell her. Humans aren't meant to know about us!**

**But Eric called her—**

**Did he? Really? How do we know that? She said she works for the sheriff, she just wants to take us back to that stupid home and take Tally away again!**

Tally whined and a buffet of an emotion that could only be described as "togetherness" hit Arlo like a sack of bricks. He swayed back.

**No, Tally, that can't be—she can't be right, can she?**

*But you feel it too, right?*

*Hang on… no way…*

Arlo shook his head as though he could shake their voices off. Hadn't anyone taught these kids to keep their private conversations private and not broadcast them for everyone to hear? At least Tally was young enough for that to be an excuse.

*Kids, can you give it a rest? I can hardly hear myself think.*

Kenna and Dylan both gasped, eyes wide. *You can hear us? He can hear us!*

Their voices suddenly fell silent, except for the constant waves crashing from Tally's mind. Arlo's shoulders sagged. *That's something, at least.*

He looked back at Jacqueline—his *mate*—who was glaring at him suspiciously.

His heart sank. *My mate is looking at me like she's ready for a fight. My mate. She just threw herself into danger to save this shifter child, and she's looking at me like I'm the last person in the world she would trust.*

"You're right," he said, his voice rougher than the rocks that stood hard against the crashing waves. "I won't lie to you. We're—"

"Tally *don't*—" Kenna yelped, but it was too late. Tally wriggled and shifted back into her human form.

Jacqueline's eyes went wide and she swayed back. Arlo froze, watching her. Waiting for her reaction.

"Oh," she breathed. "Oh, you—you *will* get cold like that, honey. Does one of you have another sweater for her?"

*She's not scared, or disgusted.* Arlo's heart lightened, and for some reason it hurt as well as felt good. *She just wants to look after her.*

Dylan pulled some more clothes from his bag with a flourish. While he and Kenna wrestled Tally into them, Jacqueline glanced up at Arlo, her eyes wide with wonder.

"I wasn't imagining it," she whispered. She took a step closer to him. "And you're not surprised by any of this. Are you?"

The air between them seemed to shiver with possibility. Arlo was vaguely aware of the kids clustering together and whispering between themselves, but he couldn't tear his attention away from Jacqueline.

"No," Arlo admitted before he could stop himself. "I'm like them."

A complicated, closed-off expression took hold of Jacqueline's face. Arlo's wolf whined: it didn't want closed-off. It wanted everything to be open and clear between them, and it wanted to be able to *help*. To drive away whatever was hurting her.

Arlo almost groaned at the effort it took to not simply throw himself at Jacqueline's feet and beg her to let him in.

"You can turn into a… seal?" Jacqueline asked.

"Not exactly." Arlo gazed into Jacqueline's eyes. His mind had this all twisted up, but his heart? His heart, and his wolf, knew what he needed to do. "I—"

*Kenna Dylan wanna fish!*

"I—"

*Wanna fish fish FISH!*

Arlo paused. Dylan had told him the toddler's name before using his megaphone-like telepathy.

*Tally…* he began—and then realized his mistake.

Tally stared at him. He felt her look at him, and then look deeper, into what he really was.

"I—" he tried again.

*WANNA FISH WANNA PLAY WITH DOGGY—*

*No no no!* Kenna's telepathic voice was much more on edge than her spoken voice. *No, she was like this just before she slipped away before. Dylan, make her stop!*

*She already ate all the chocolate!* Dylan yelled back. He looked like he might cry.

"Hey, it's not that bad," Jacqueline said. She put her arm around Dylan's shoulder and squeezed. "Everything's going to be fine, okay?"

"But she already ate *everything*," he whined, sagging against her.

Arlo shook his head. His temples were pounding. He shot an apologetic look at Jacqueline.

"I think these kids need their dinner, and I've got food on the *Hometide*."

Jacqueline's eyes slid past him, to his boat, moored out in the darkness. "Oh," she said, her voice listless. Arlo opened his mouth to speak, but then her whole body stiffened, as though she'd stepped on a live wire.

"I'm coming with you," she declared, her eyes blazing.

"Of c—" Arlo began.

"I'm not going to go home and pretend I never saw any of this. I *can't*." Her voice broke on the last word, letting through a sliver of desperation. She caught her breath and Arlo felt like his heart had stopped as he waited for her to speak again.

She stared into his eyes as though she was searching for something. Arlo's chest tightened.

*What does she see when she looks at me?*

He knew the face that had looked out at him from the mirror that morning: hair a tangled mass of knots, stubble like he'd dipped the lower half of his face in a pile of iron filings, eyebrows that you could hide half a football team in.

She was beautiful, and he was… a mess. In more ways than one.

Jacqueline narrowed her eyes. "I'm not going *anywhere* until I know Kenna, Dylan and Tally are safe."

*Good*, Arlo's wolf huffed, satisfied. Arlo was bewildered at its reaction—and relieved.

Jacqueline took another deep breath. "If you're going to tell me this is none of my business—"

"I'm not." Arlo raised his hands in surrender. "I was going to say thank you. *Am* going to say thank you. I appreciate the help."

"Oh." The fight went out of her. "Um. Good. Because my car is stuck in a ditch about a half-mile back, and I don't expect my phone will have agreed with that little dip I took in the sea back there, so going with you is basically my only option here, anyway." Her shoulders dropped and the wan smile she gave him made his heart break.

*If I'd lied and tried to get the kids away from her, I would have abandoned her here with no way to get home.* Arlo's gut clenched. *There's no coming back from that.*

"We'd better get moving," he said. "No chance of sailing tonight, but there's warm clothes, and food."

"What else could we need?" Jacqueline said brightly.

Arlo's eyes trailed after her as they gathered up the kids' belongings and squeezed everyone into the rowboat.

*What else? So much more. But I'm beginning to think I'm not the man who can give it to you.*

7

# JACQUELINE

Arlo's boat was not what she'd expected. He was so salt-crusted and rough-looking, Jacqueline had thought he must have come off a working fishing boat, covered in shed scales and chased by seagulls.

Which only went to show she shouldn't make assumptions.

The *Hometide* was a sleek cutter, all oiled wooden boards and crisp sails. The water slapped against its sides as Arlo secured the rowboat and helped them all climb aboard. Jacqueline went up last, and his touch burned against her skin.

*I really am cold*, she thought, biting her lip. She flexed her fingers, testing them. How many times was it you were meant to be able to clench and unclench your fists, before it was time to be worrying about hypothermia? She was sure she'd known, once. Back when she spent more time outdoors than doing vacuuming in that huge empty house.

"There's clothes downstairs," Arlo said, appearing at her shoulder.

"What?" Jacqueline jumped, and he seemed to curl in on himself.

"Dry clothes. In the cabin downstairs. You look…" He looked away. "Cold."

"And soaking wet," Jacqueline agreed, shaking out her arms. Arlo made a strange noise in the back of his throat.

"I'll show you."

The *Hometide* had a comfortable cockpit in the stern, fitted out with cushions on the seats and cup holders stuffed with sunscreen and water bottles. A wooden hatch with a round window led down into the cabin. Jacqueline climbed down the ladder after Arlo and he pointed behind it to a low-roofed alcove.

"Clothes in the cupboard. There should be a towel… I'll get dinner on."

His voice was rough, and Jacqueline bit back a sigh. He might have saved her life, but it was obvious he resented her presence here.

Too bad. She was going to see this through. She'd spent the last three years paralyzed by life. She'd almost frozen again, back there on the beach.

But she couldn't do that anymore. She had no excuses left for not *doing* anything with her life. And making sure this little family made their way to Hideaway to wait for the man she'd spoken to on the phone might not be the same thing as partying it up in a club, but at least it was something. It wasn't another Friday night at work or at home, terrified that she'd do something wrong and the rest of her world would come crashing down.

She waited until Arlo had gathered everything he needed from the small kitchen and then clambered into the alcove. Her knees sank into a mattress and she realized, too late, that the entire space was a bed.

Arlo's bed.

Jacqueline's face blazed. *I'm climbing into another man's bed*, she thought, stupidly, and even more stupidly felt a rush of guilt. She pushed it away, frowning.

*What do I have to feel guilty about? Even if Arlo was interested in me—Derek left me. I don't have to feel bad about noticing other men exist.*

She crawled over the bed to the cupboard set into the very stern of the cabin. There was something in the wall above the cupboard that looked like it should have been a window, but it was boarded over.

*Another victim of the storm?* Jacqueline wondered, and opened the cupboard.

Jacqueline pulled a shirt, sweater and pants from the cupboard and wriggled back into the main cabin. She glanced back at the bed—she'd left the covers a mess and that made her blush, too.

*Oh, no. I have it bad, don't I? What timing, my first crush since…*

She winced and pulled off her sodden dress. *Trust me to lose my head over another guy who couldn't care less.*

She scrubbed herself as dry as she could and pulled on fresh clothes. Arlo was so much bigger than her that she was sure she looked ridiculous—but at least she was warm. His woolen sweater enveloped her like a hug, warming her inside and out—

*Oh, stop it*, she told herself, and climbed back onto deck.

She was greeted by the smell of frying butter, and three pairs of nervous eyes. Kenna and Dylan both looked like they'd had a rug pulled out from under their feet, but Tally's main concern seemed to be whatever was happening over the small gas cooker.

Arlo was turned away, his attention all on the stove.

"I brought you up a sweater," Jacqueline said awkwardly, holding it out. "You're only in your shirt—I thought you might be cold…"

He paused before he took it. "Thanks."

Then he stripped off his wet shirt. Jacqueline closed her eyes. *Oh lord.* "Shifters don't feel the cold, actually. We're really really tough."

Jacqueline opened her eyes to find Dylan grinning at her. His older sister, not so much. When Kenna saw her looking, she scowled and looked away.

"That's very interesting." Jacqueline sat down opposite them.

Despite what Dylan had just told her, she was pleased to see that all the children were in shoes and warm coats. She wriggled her bare toes and tucked them into the bottom of her over-long borrowed pants.

"Is that what you are? Shifters?"

"Yeah." Dylan sighed dramatically and leaned against his sister, who hunched down into her collar. "Don't be like that, Kenna, Mr. Hammond said we could tell her!"

"Not everything!" Kenna met Jacqueline's eye and then glared and stared at her hands.

*She can't be more than twelve or thirteen,* Jaqueline thought. *What is going on here? Where are their parents?*

*And why do I keep feeling like I'm missing half the conversation?*

Butter hissed as Arlo laid fish fillets in the pan. "There's bread and butter," he said over his shoulder. "Any of you want to—"

"Dylan will," Kenna said quickly, elbowing her brother.

"Hey!"

*They certainly act like normal kids,* Jacqueline thought as the two squabbled over who would cut and butter the bread. Her heart ached a little, but she ignored it. *Not the most important issue here, Jacqueline.*

By the time the fish was cooked, Jacqueline's stomach was rumbling. She'd planned to eat at the Spring Fling, but that hadn't happened—and she *hadn't* planned to jump headfirst into the ocean. Almost dying had an invigorating effect on the appetite, apparently.

Dylan and Arlo got a system going: Dylan handed Arlo a plate of bread and butter, Arlo put fish on top, and Dylan passed them out.

Tally's eyes were as big as saucers as she watched the plates go around. When Dylan put one in front of her, she leaped in with both hands.

"This looks delicious. Thank you," Jacqueline said to Dylan as he passed her a steaming plate.

The fish was melt-in-your-mouth delicate. Jacqueline closed her eyes as she took her first bite. The salted butter and fresh bread were better than any restaurant meal she'd ever had.

"Oh, man," she murmured, and wiped a smear of butter off her chin. "This is…"

"It's not much." Arlo's voice was rough. "I wasn't expecting guests."

"I think this is the best thing I've ever eaten," Jacqueline said honestly, and took another bite.

Arlo's eyes burned into hers, and when he looked away, she was sure his cheeks were pink. "Good," he muttered.

Warmth bloomed inside her chest. Maybe he didn't resent her being here so much, after all. Except he kept wincing like he was in pain.

"Are you okay?" she asked tentatively. "You didn't get hurt back there in the water, did you?"

*Oh geez. If I kicked him in the ribs or something while he was saving my life…*

"It's nothing," Arlo said quickly, and winced again. He sighed and rubbed his forehead. "That is, it's a…"

He trailed off, and Jacqueline felt a tug on her sweater.

Tally had already finished her dinner and had wriggled down off her seat. When she saw Jacqueline looking at her, she raised her arms to be picked up.

"Come on then. You're not a big talker, are you?"

Jacqueline picked Tally up and arranged her on her lap. She looked up. Arlo, Kenna and Dylan were all wincing, now.

"What's wrong?"

"*Ugh*," Kenna said, and turned side-on in her seat so she wasn't facing Jacqueline and Tally.

Arlo tapped his forehead. "She's loud in here," he explained in response to what was probably an expression of utter confusion on Jacqueline's face. "Telepathy. Or mindspeaking, some call it. Shifters use it to talk when we're shifted, or…"

"When your mouth is otherwise occupied?" Jacqueline suggested. While her attention had been distracted, Tally had started to help herself to Jacqueline's plate, and now she was busily gnawing on a crust of bread.

*Did she eat that whole slice while I wasn't looking?* Jacqueline marveled. "Um… what's she saying?"

The corner of Arlo's mouth hooked up. Like a smile. Was he smiling at her?

"Before or now?"

"Now?"

He cleared his throat. "That would be something along the lines of: *Bready bready bread, yum yum bread, mmm bread I love you.*"

Jacqueline burst out laughing. "No. Seriously? And before?"

Dylan piped up. "Before she was saying *fish fish yum fish yum.* Over and over. She *really* likes fish."

"You're not kidding." Jacqueline's second fish sandwich was disappearing as fast as the first. First, Tally hoovered up the fillet, then she chomped through the soft bread until she was left with another crescent-moon crust. "Should I be sorry or glad that I can't hear her?"

"You're lucky," Kenna grumbled. "She *never* shuts up. She even sings in her sleep sometimes."

*If this was a cartoon, I'd have hearts in my eyes right now.* "Really?"

"I wish—" Kenna continued, and then frowned at her plate and fell silent. "Never mind."

Kenna and Dylan had both cleared their plates, which was lucky, because as soon as the last of the crust disappeared into Tally's mouth, she started looking around in interest. When she saw the others had already finished, she sighed, lay back, and promptly fell asleep in Jacqueline's lap.

*One million heart-eyes,* Jacqueline thought.

"You haven't eaten." Arlo's voice was gruff. Jacqueline gestured to the slumbering toddler in her lap.

"I didn't get much of a chance," she replied.

He frowned. "I'll get you—damn. That was the last of the bread."

Kenna frowned. "Tally…" she groaned.

"I'm okay, really. Don't worry about me." The last thing Jacqueline wanted was to make a fuss and have Arlo regret letting her on board.

"You're sure?"

"I'm not even hungry," Jacqueline lied. Her stomach gave a slight gurgle as she breathed in the remnant smell of buttered bread and hot fried fish, but luckily Tally gave a tiny snore at the same time, so she was almost certain no one would notice. "What about you two? Neither of you had as much to eat as your sister."

"That's because we have manners, actually," Dylan announced, kicking his legs. "But also she's growing a lot and she has to grow for her *and* her seal."

"And you two don't?"

"You're probably past that first growth spurt." Arlo raised an eyebrow at the two of them and got a vigorous nod from Dylan and a grunt and a shrug from Kenna.

"First growth spurt?" Jacqueline hadn't meant to look at Kenna, but she did, and the girl jumped like she'd sat on a bee.

"Shifters have our first growth spurt when we're, like, um, however old we are when we first shift, which for Tally is *really* early, because the seal needs a lot of energy to even exist that first time. And then we have normal human growth spurts or whatever and then it all settles down and we can pretend to be normal humans, if we're old enough."

Arlo wiped the cooking pan clean and added, "Not completely. We still have to eat more than normal humans do." He nodded at Jacqueline. "Our animal sides still need extra energy."

*And I bet it takes a lot of energy to keep your body looking like that,* Jacqueline thought. Her cheeks heated up and she looked down at Tally dozing in her lap. When she looked up again, Kenna was staring at her.

"You really don't know anything about shifters?" she asked. "But..." Her eyes flicked between Jacqueline and Arlo.

Arlo held up a reassuring hand. "Don't worry. She'll keep your secret. Won't you?"

"I won't tell anyone," Jacqueline said. "Promise."

"That wasn't what I meant," Kenna protested.

"Yeah, if you don't know about shifters, then how can you be—"

"Not that, Dylan!" Kenna hissed. She caught Jacqueline's look of confusion and bit her lip. "I mean, how did Eric know to call you if you're human?"

Jacqueline tugged on her sleeves to buy time. "I, er, I think he was just looking for anyone who could help you."

Kenna pursed her lips as though she didn't quite believe her. Jacqueline didn't blame her—but she wasn't ready to tell the truth just yet. Maybe it was selfish, but she didn't want this crazy adventure to end just yet.

Not before the kids were safe, at least.

Dylan was tugging on Kenna's shirt. "But what about…"

"We'll talk about that later!" Kenna shout-whispered back.

*What's that about?* Jacqueline exchanged a questioning look with Arlo, and he shrugged. Somehow, that helped. It couldn't be a mysterious shifter thing if Arlo didn't know what was going on, either. Just a mysterious kid-sibling thing.

"Do you have a phone out here?" she asked Arlo. "I should check in with my work. Let them know I'm okay and that I found the kids. And…" she added cautiously, "if there's anyone you need to call, Kenna, Dylan…"

"Like who?" Kenna was back to being surly.

"Any relatives, or…"

"There's just Eric," Kenna said sharply. "He's looking after us. I guess he's, like, our uncle."

"He's the one who left you on the beach?" Arlo growled.

Kenna's eyes flashed. "He's taking us to Hideaway Cove! Where we'll be safe! No one else—"

"Our parents died," Dylan said quietly.

"I'm so sorry." Jacqueline reached out for Dylan automatically and he wriggled over to her. Arlo put a hand on Kenna's shoulder and she sort of sagged into it.

"They were in a car crash," Dylan whispered.

"So it's just us." Kenna was scowling again and this time Jacqueline was convinced it was to stop herself from bursting into tears. "And we got put in a home, which was fine, except Tally started shifting early and they were going to find out."

"You have to keep yourself safe from humans." Jacqueline's heart dropped.

Kenna nodded angrily. "Eric told us about Hideaway Cove, he said we'd be safe there—"

"And you will be," Arlo rumbled. Jacqueline was struck by the certainty in his voice. "Hideaway Cove is a sanctuary for all shifters. You'll be safe there, and welcome, and cared for. Your whole pack." He paused and frowned. "Eric, too."

Dylan and Kenna exchanged a look. "Really? That's actually true?"

"One hundred percent." Arlo hesitated again, his eyes flicking to Jacqueline. She couldn't read the expression in them. "They took me in when I was just a bit older than you. I lost my family, too. Hideaway Cove gave me a new one."

Jacqueline let out a short breath. *So many broken pasts,* she thought, her heart aching.

"Anyway," Arlo muttered. "We've got an early start if we want to make it to Hideaway and call your work, Ms. March. There's no phone on board, I'm sorry. I'll just get this cleaned up—"

"I'll help!" Kenna said quickly.

"—and then we'd better pack in for the night. You kids can take the bed. Ms. March…" His voice went gravely, and Jacqueline felt another blush start to prickle across her skin. "The seat in the kitchen booth isn't much, but I can pull some extra blankets out."

"That'll suit me fine. But what about you?"

Jacqueline regretted asking the moment the words were out, because as soon as she'd spoken them, she was imagining Arlo in bed. His long body stretched out across the blankets. His head resting on one arm, his chest the perfect pillow just begging for her to...

Jacqueline squeezed her eyes tight. *What is wrong with me? He's made it clear he's not interested, anyway.*

*...Which maybe makes this all right? There's nothing wrong with* imagining, *right? And if it's not going to go anywhere...*

"I'll sleep up here," Arlo said, and Jacqueline's mind immediately filled in the dots.

"Er, won't you be cold?" she asked, mentally dodging the images her brain was throwing at her.

Arlo half-smiled. "I've got my own fur coat. I'll be fine."

"Oh. Yes. Of course." Jacqueline felt like she'd just stuffed her entire foot in her mouth. Her cheeks might as well have been on fire.

Tally was still asleep, so she stayed up on deck with Dylan while Arlo and Kenna dealt with the dishes. Dylan was full of questions about Hideaway Cove, most of which Jacqueline couldn't answer. Everything she knew about the town could have fit on the front of an envelope.

Everything true, at least. The rumors could have filled a phone book, but she wasn't about to tell Dylan that people back home thought Hideaway Cove was full of telephone-cursing witches.

Suddenly, Dylan sat up straight. "They're all done!" he chirped, and hopped over to the hatch.

"Be careful with that—and how do you know?" Jacqueline balanced Tally over her shoulder and got to the hatch just before Dylan hauled it open and, she suspected, threw himself headfirst down the steps.

"Arlo said." Dylan tapped the side of his head. "In here."

"Right. Well, go down backwards, okay? I don't want you to slip."

"Shifters don't *slip*," he said, and Jacqueline raised her eyebrows at him.

"Someone needs to tell Tally that, then," she said. "Before she *slips* off any more rocks."

"She's a baby! She doesn't count."

Jacqueline's eyebrows shot up. "Don't listen to him, honey," she said facetiously to the slumbering Tally, and Dylan cackled.

She held the hatch open as he clambered down, then climbed after him and found herself back-to-chest with Arlo.

"Oh," she said, stupidly, and turned around, also stupidly, because now she was still pressed against him, but in a way more awkward position.

Why, why, why hadn't she put her bra back on when she got changed?

She climbed a step back up the stairs, but that only put her boobs level with his eyes.

Arlo's eyes darted either side of her. "Excuse me," he muttered in his gravelly voice, and dodged around the ladder.

"It's small with us all down here, huh?" Jacqueline said, trying to ignore her blazing cheeks. "Cozy."

"Uh-huh." Kenna had scooted into the booth to get out of the way. "Um, you can have the bed, if you want. We've got fur coats, too, so we don't need—"

Jacqueline fixed her with a mock glare. "How long have you been camping out in that ancient concrete block?" she demanded.

"Um, a few weeks, I guess…"

"Then it's definitely your turn to sleep in a bed. I'll be fine on the bench."

"Here you go." Arlo grabbed an armful of extra blankets from the cupboard at the end of the bed. He handed a few to Jacqueline, and spread the others on the mattress, making a sort of nest on top of it. "It's a few hours down the coast to Hideaway. By lunchtime tomorrow, you'll be in your new home."

"Isn't that a bit—" *optimistic*, Jacqueline had been about to say, but managed to stop herself at the last minute. "Quick? I mean, I don't know how shifters do things, but they're just kids. Won't you have to wait until Eric is here to decide a place for them to live?"

Arlo shook his head. "This isn't the first time the town's taken in strays. There'll be more than enough houses open to them until this *Eric* gets here. And anyway…"

He pressed his lips together, his eyes shadowing. Whatever he'd stopped himself from saying, it looked like an old hurt.

Dylan raised his head quizzically and Jacqueline decided to interrupt.

"And anyway, now that they're here there's no way you're letting them get away, right? No more camp-outs in derelict buildings."

"Exactly." Arlo flashed her a relieved smile and her heart lifted. Maybe this all was going to be all right after all. It wasn't the fling she'd been hoping for this weekend, but it was something. A tiny sliver of magic, and helping people, before she headed back to her own life.

Or whatever it was she was going to make of her life.

"No more baths in a sink," Kenna muttered. She caught Jacqueline's eye and blushed, her hand going to her tangled mop of hair.

"What's your house like?" Dylan piped up.

Arlo frowned. "My house?"

"Yeah, where we're going."

Arlo straightened. "Well, it's…" He ran his fingers through his hair and closed his eyes in a silent groan. Jacqueline thought she saw his lips moving as though he was saying something under his breath. "You know I'm not taking you to stay with me, right?"

Kenna folded her arms, her face settling into mutinous lines. "Then where are you taking us?"

"Well, maybe my parents—my foster parents. Dorothy and Alan Sweets. They're all set up with the county to take in kids that need a home. They'll look after you until Eric gets a place set up for you."

"But—" Dylan began, and Kenna shushed him. He stared at her, bewildered, and then turned to Jacqueline. "But what about…"

Jacqueline was confused. "Me?"

Dylan nodded, his eyes huge. Kenna growled something and Dylan swatted the air as though he was trying to bat away an invisible fly.

"I live in Dunston, not Hideaway Cove. I doubt you want to live there after everything you've been through to get to Hideaway," Jacqueline said, smiling, and Dylan's face fell.

"You're going back to Dunston? But I thought you and A—"

"Shut *up*, Dylan!" Kenna screamed, jumping to her feet. "Just *shut up* for once, will you?"

"Hey, now—" Arlo began, as Tally stirred in Jacqueline's arms and began to grizzle.

"But I thought we were going to—" Dylan's face creased with confusion.

"*Stop talking!*" Kenna bawled at him, pink spots spreading like a fever across her cheeks. "Stop—they—you can't just—and we—you're going to *ruin it*!"

Tally's grizzle blew into a full-out wail, and she kicked her legs like she was trying to swim out of Jacqueline's grip. Jacqueline got a better hold on her and just managed to fling her other arm in front of Kenna as she threw herself down the cabin towards Dylan.

Dylan's look of confusion morphed into mulish anger. "No, *you're* going to ruin it all, because *you're* yelling and you said humans couldn't—"

"*Shut up!*"

"So it'll be *your* fault anyway if—"

Jacqueline hadn't been able to hear what humans "couldn't" do over Kenna's shriek, but her heart was breaking for both of them.

There were so many times she'd wanted to scream her heart out over the last few years. She knew how much they were hurting, and how much more it would hurt when they'd all calmed down and remembered what they'd said.

Arlo was still bent over double in the bed nook. He raised his head and clonked it on the ceiling. "Ah, blast—Hey, kids, that's enough of that. Calm down."

Kenna's head snapped back like she'd been slapped, and her eyes filled with tears. She stared at Arlo, then Jacqueline, her mouth opening and closing like a goldfish. "I didn't mean—you can't—oh *no*..."

Behind her, Dylan's face creased. Arlo rubbed his forehead and groaned.

"Damn it, kids, it's not like that. You'll be fine," he growled.

"But—"

The kids' distress whiplashed through the air. Jacqueline let her hand drop on Kenna's shoulder as the tears in the girl's eyes threatened to spill over.

"I'm sorry!" Kenna gasped. Her face twisted. "I wanted everything to go perfect and now..."

"Everything's still fine," Jacqueline reassured her, and Kenna's face pinched shut in a way Jacqueline knew too well.

*She's not going to believe me that easy*, Jacqueline thought. *And Tally's still screaming, and Dylan's on a knife's edge to start crying, too. How am I meant to fix this?*

*Oh God. Arlo was right. I can't help them. I'm completely out of my depth. I don't belong here at all.*

She met Arlo's eyes across the cabin. She wanted to yell "Help! Do something!" but what could he do?

Arlo climbed out from the bed nook. Standing straight, his head almost brushed the ceiling. "Kids," he began, and when that had no effect on the thunderstorm-heavy atmosphere: "Kenna, Dylan, Tally—"

Tally stopped screaming. The look of relief on Arlo's face was almost comical—and then he realized she'd only been sucking in another breath to scream even louder.

He ran his hands over his face and gave Jacqueline a look that was half-bashful, half-determined.

*What's he doing?* she wondered, and then watched amazed as he grimaced and shook himself. The shaking rippled down his body and he transformed into a huge black and gray wolf.

Kenna squeaked with surprise and transformed, flopping to the cabin floor as a spotted seal. Dylan changed shape, too, slipping awkwardly down the ladder. It was as though their transformations had caught them by surprise.

In Jacqueline's arms, Tally's kicking legs were suddenly kicking flippers. She wriggled through her sweater and Jacqueline kneeled to catch her before she hit the floor. She eased the tiny seal pup to the ground and bundled the abandoned sweater against her chest.

It was only when she started feeling light-headed that she remembered to start breathing again.

The three seal shifter siblings were gorgeous. They all had the same thick, glossy coats with mottled brown, gray and white coloration. And Arlo…

Jacqueline gulped. She was still kneeling down, and her eyes were level with Arlo's. He was a *wolf*, a *huge* wolf, with pointed ears and long legs tipped with heavy claws.

He should have looked like something out of a bad dream. The big bad wolf from a fairy tale. But…

Even in wolf form, his eyes were so… human. They were the same midnight-blue as before. But they weren't as closed-off and wary as his human eyes had been. His wolf's eyes practically overflowed with emotion.

Jacqueline's heart was in her throat. She felt as though the wolf-Arlo was trying to communicate something with her, but what?

He broke eye contact first. Jacqueline watched, frozen, as he sniffed at each of the seal pups in turn and barked softly. He shook his coat and flicked his ears towards the bed.

The seals *whined*. Jacqueline blinked. There wasn't any other word for it. Kenna made a grumbling noise that sounded so, so… *teenaged*. Even coming out of a seal's mouth.

Regardless of how much they grumbled and whined, all three seals followed what were obviously the wolf's instructions, and clambered up onto the bed. Tally was too small to make it by herself, so Arlo helped her, pushing his snout under her sausage-like body and boosting her up.

The kids cuddled together in a heap, their fat bodies making a cozy dent in the middle of the mattress. Jacqueline's breath caught as Arlo leaped up on the bed and trotted around them, gently pressing his nose to each of their snouts in turn. Tally gave a whuffly bark, and he licked her forehead. Then he picked up a corner of the blanket between his teeth, dragged it up over the seal pups, and lay down curled around them.

It was the strangest, sweetest picture of family love that Jacqueline could have imagined. And it hurt more than she could have imagined.

*I have to get out of here.*
She stood up so quickly her head spun.

"I, er," she muttered brokenly as Arlo raised his head and pinned her with those too-human eyes. "I just need to…"

Jacqueline gave a stupid smile and climbed, practically flew, up the stairs to the hatch. She wrenched it open and barely managed to stop herself from slamming the door shut behind her.

Up on deck, all her breath rushed out of her at once. She closed the hatch—slowly, carefully, not wanting to interrupt—made it to the side of the boat, and folded over the railing like a wet towel.

"What the heck was that about?" she asked herself when the world stopped spinning around her. As though she didn't know.

She stared out across the water for she didn't know how long. Darkness had properly fallen now, coating the world in inky black. The boat lights made rippling golden lines on the water. Far away, past the darker texture of black on the horizon that she assumed was the coastline, the sky glowed faintly.

*Dunston*, she thought. Home.

Her whole life was there, somewhere under that faint yellow glow.

And here on this boat, in the dark, gently rocking ocean…

"Jacqueline?"

# 8

# ARLO

Jacqueline wiped her eyes before she turned around. Arlo's chest clenched.

"Are you all right?"

Jacqueline smiled and shook her head slightly. "I'm fine."

Arlo frowned. His wolf was confused—the smile was an obvious lie. It didn't go to her eyes. It looked like it *hurt*, and that was wrong. His wolf wanted to go to her, to give her the same simple comfort it had offered the pups. They were asleep now, after all. And his mate needed him. Why wasn't he already at her side?

*Humans are more complicated than that*, he told it, and cleared his throat. "You moved pretty quick back there, I was worried—"

"Are the kids okay? They got to sleep?" Jacqueline's voice teetered on the edge of brittle. Arlo took the hint.

"They're out like lights. It's—" he paused, and then added: "Things are simpler, when we're in our animal forms. Human worries don't seem so important. It's easier to let them go for a while."

Jacqueline's eyebrows pulled together. "That's good. But—what about their animal worries, are they—" She stopped, grimacing. "Sorry. This is none of my business. I shouldn't have—have forced you to bring me along."

*You screwed it up. Now she thinks you hate her.* Arlo's mouth was dry. He had to fix this. He'd panicked, before, but everything was under control now. The kids were going to Hideaway, and he could… try to make this work.

God, she was so—so—he bit back a groan. The sweater and pants she was wearing didn't cling to her body like her soaking wet dress had. What they did was a thousand times worse.

He knew what her body looked like. He knew what she *felt* like, those warm curves pressed against his side.

And now she was wrapped in *his* clothes. He knew that sweater like the back of his hand. Its fabric was softened by years of wear, but still warm and cozy. There were a few loose threads that he'd meant to darn but not gotten around to yet, because he only remembered them when they tickled.

As though the universe had heard his thoughts, Jacqueline wriggled slightly and slipped one hand under her—*his*—sweater. It was too easy to imagine his own hand sliding under the soft fabric to brush away the stray thread and resting, just for a moment, against her even softer skin…

She was gorgeous. Gorgeous and inquisitive and so brave.

His heart sank. She was perfect. She clearly had her life together. He'd have to be arrogant beyond belief to imagine there was any room for him in it.

He cleared his throat. "Is there anyone waiting for you back home? Like I said, I don't have a phone on the boat, but I can radio in and ask for a message to be sent through."

Jacqueline's face went carefully blank. "No," she said quietly. "I'd better call in to work about the kids' missing friend, and there's my work, but… I don't think they're likely to check in on me until morning at the earliest. I'm free as a bird."

She didn't sound happy about it. Her hands were twisting together; no, Arlo saw as he looked closer, she was rubbing her ring finger. Her empty ring finger.

He'd thought he was an arrogant dick. Now he knew he was an asshole. Only an asshole would be as relieved as he was by something that clearly made her miserable.

"I'm sorry," he said. His voice was rougher than he'd intended, and he braced himself for her to flinch away, like people usually did when he started growling. It was all he deserved, after all. "I shouldn't have said anything."

"No, don't be." She didn't even seem to have noticed the roughness in his voice. She tucked her hands into the too-long sleeves of her sweater. "It's a sensible question. If there was anyone waiting up at home for me, I'm sure they'd be glad to know I wasn't lying dead in a ditch somewhere."

Her voice grated and Arlo was walking towards her before he could stop himself. He just managed to veer off at the last second and stand beside her, staring across the dark water towards the coastline, instead of wrapping his arms around her.

Jacqueline sighed and stopped rubbing her ring finger. "Not that it's really home anymore, anyway." She stared out over the water, her eyes squinting as though she was staring into the sun.

Before Arlo could say anything, she shook her head. "God, listen to me rabbiting on. You'd think I'd be happy to meet someone who doesn't already know everything about my life."

She glanced at Arlo nervously. He hoped his expression was reassuring. He wasn't a good judge of what other people thought of his face, for the most part.

"That must be one thing small towns all have in common, shifter or human," he said.

"Hah!" Jacqueline looked as though she was smiling despite herself. "We don't have telepathy, though. God. I can't even imagine how much worse that would be. Or maybe it would be better, maybe I would have—"

She took a deep breath and ran one hand over her eyes in a gesture that Arlo suspected was meant to look like she was pushing her hair off her forehead, not buying time as she got her feelings under control. "Forget it. I was meant to be somewhere else tonight, celebrating a, a fresh start. That's going to have to wait until the kids are safe."

Arlo's wolf whuffled its approval. Of course she was going to stay with the kids. And with him.

Arlo frowned. *We don't know that. We can't just assume everything's going to be all right. Not with—*he sighed. *Not with me involved.*

"You can always celebrate in Hideaway Cove," he suggested.

She actually smiled. Which he didn't understand, but hell, it was a win anyway.

"You know, that sounds even better than my original plan," she said. "What do you recommend?"

*Dinner. With me. Here on the boat, under the stars, with all the time in the world to get to know each other.*

Arlo swallowed. "There's a good restaurant in town—Caro's Hook and Sinker. Best chowder you'll ever eat."

"Celebrating a fresh start in Hideaway Cove. The town where people can turn into animals." Her voice echoed with wonder. "You're right, that does sound better than the Spring Fling, and being pawed at by the same guys who've been trying it on since I got single. Why did I ever think having a fresh start in my home town was a good idea?"

Longing flooded Arlo's veins, along with a protective anger at these men who'd bothered her. He should have said he would take her to Caro's. Invited her.

Or would she think he was as irritating as those men in her home town?

Jacqueline's eyes slid towards his and her cheeks went slightly pink. "I just want to be clear, what happened before, it's nothing to do with—well, what you can do. The wolf thing. Or the kids, of course."

Her cheeks went even more pink and she looked down at her hands.

"This is the first time you've ever met shifters." Arlo said. "You're taking it well."

"Have I ever met people who can turn into animals before? I think I'd remember that." Jacqueline shook her head. "But it's… I don't know. I feel like I *should* be more surprised than I am, but I'm not, and anyway the important thing here is making sure the kids are safe. So I'm not complaining. In fact…"

Her cheeks darkened again and she made a small strangled sound. Arlo jerked towards her, and just stopped himself from placing his hand over hers. "What?"

Jacqueline was still shaking her head. "I just figured out why I'm so fine with it all," she explained, laughing ruefully. "It's because you're all from Hideaway Cove."

Arlo sat back. "Hang on." He couldn't help the alarm bells going off in his head. "How so?"

"Don't worry." Jacqueline raised her hands. "No one in Dunston has a clue about shifters. Your secret's safe." She pushed a stray curl off her forehead and leaned against the railing again. "Hideaway Cove is our closest neighbor but no one really knows anyone from there. Which makes sense, since you're trying to keep yourselves secret. But it also means you're sort of like the creepy empty house at the end of the street that everyone says is haunted."

Arlo laughed. "Ghost stories?" *I'll have to tell Harrison. He'll be thrilled.*

Jacqueline grimaced. "More like you're the boogeyman to blame for everything that goes wrong. Silly stuff, like—oh, you know. The mail's late, must be Hideaway's fault! The wind's coming from Hideaway way, watch out for electrics playing up!"

"Wait." If he'd just heard what he thought—that was even better than ghost stories. "Electrics?" Arlo asked carefully.

"Oh, like… after this last storm. It came up the coast from Hideaway, and ever since then phone lines have been getting crossed, the mayor's electric car keeps doing wheelies down main street by itself…" Jacqueline trailed off. "What? You look like the cat who got the cream. I'm missing something. And—" Her expression changed, back to that almost-panicked wariness when she'd said she didn't belong here. With him. Arlo's chest tightened. "It's okay if it's a shifter thing, you don't have to tell me."

*The more secrets you keep, the longer she'll feel like you're pushing her away.* Arlo's stomach twisted. Is this what Harrison had felt, when he met Lainie?

"It is," he said out loud, "but mostly it's a work thing."

"Now I'm even more confused."

"I've been having a long argument with a friend of mine about… certain things. I'd like to be there when you tell him that story about the electric car doing wheelies."

Jacqueline raised her eyebrows. "He's going to lose a bet?"

"I'm going to win the I-told-you-so of the century." Arlo grinned.

"And…" Jacqueline licked her lips and Arlo's eyes tracked the movement. He met her gaze again to see it bright with curiosity and… excitement? Anticipation?

Damn it, he wasn't good enough at this. Telling people's feelings just from what they looked like. It was easy with the kids, but Jacqueline? She was a closed book.

He took a deep breath, but Jacqueline got in first.

"You're going to introduce me to this friend of yours?"

She still had that look in her eye. Arlo cleared his throat.

*Please let this be the right answer.* "Yes? There won't be any avoiding it, sorry. Hideaway Cove's pretty small. As soon as we dock, it'll be all questions."

Jacqueline was quiet for a moment. Her eyes searched his. Whatever she found there seemed to reassure her.

"Then maybe I'm meant to be here, after all," she said quietly.

Arlo's hand was less than six inches away from Jacqueline's. A shiver of wolfish anticipation went through him and he tightened his grip on the railing. Like he'd told her only a few minutes before, his wolf didn't understand human worries.

"I think you're exactly where you need to be," he murmured, his voice as gentle as he could manage. He wanted to say more, but his wolf was too bristling-high inside him, every nerve on edge, for him to make human words.

He stared pleadingly at Jacqueline and slowly, like the sun rising over still waters, her face lit up. Her smile was tentative, only half-believing, and God, he needed to say something, anything, to push that smile from a half-believing sunrise to full midday heat.

"Would you," he began, and stopped to clear his throat. "Would you like…"

# 9

## JACQUELINE

Jacqueline didn't breathe as she waited for Arlo to finish the sentence. Even her heart seemed to have stopped, as though her body didn't want to risk the thud of her pulse in her ears blocking out whatever he was about to say.

"…Dinner," he said eventually, and Jacqueline would have been disappointed if it wasn't for the sudden flash of regret in his eyes.

He hadn't meant to say dinner. At least, she thought not. Hoped not. God, she was practically dizzy. She wasn't even making sense inside her own head.

But—he said she was meant to be here. And that she was going to meet other people from Hideaway Cove. Those didn't sound like the words of someone who was going to tip her overboard the moment they were close enough to shore. They sounded like someone who wanted to spend time with her.

*Oh lord,* she thought, and swallowed down a sudden bubble of giggles. He was still looking at her, an expression of mild panic in his eyes. Something inside her melted.

"Dinner?" she said, and leaned the tiniest bit closer to him.

"The kids cleaned me out of fresh food, but…" Arlo shrugged tightly.

Was he nervous? How did a man who looked like that get nervous? Oh God. *She* should be nervous, but instead, she was edging closer to him, like he was some sort of giant mouse and she was a hungry cat.

"Cornbread isn't hard to throw together, and there's… tins of, uh… it's bachelor rations, but better than nothing. Since Tally ate most of your meal earlier."

*Dinner.* A shiver of anticipation went down Jacqueline's spine. She might be reading this whole thing wrong but until she had proof either way, couldn't she just enjoy pretending?

And if she wasn't reading Arlo wrong…

The shiver of anticipation turned into electric delight.

Jacqueline took a deep breath. "Dinner sounds lovely," she said.

"Right." Arlo's lips hooked into a bashful smile. "Good."

Jacqueline couldn't help smiling back.

Arlo crept below decks and returned with a box from the pantry. Jacqueline joined him next to the cooker.

"Can I help?"

"Sure. Could you oil the pan? It'll need a few minutes to warm up."

Jacqueline sat down beside Arlo and took the frying pan he handed her. They worked together in silence for a few minutes, Jacqueline lighting the cooker and Arlo mixing ingredients. By the time the pan was hot enough and the mix was ready, Jacqueline's mouth was watering.

Her stomach gurgled as Arlo tipped the dough in to cook. "Sorry. I'm starving, and that already smells delicious."

"Wait until you try it before you make any judgements. I'm only used to cooking for myself." Arlo fixed the lid on the skillet.

"The fish earlier was amazing. The bite of it I had, at least."

"You have to be a worse cook than me to ruin fresh fish and bread someone else baked," Arlo demurred. "This could burn, or not cook through, or…" He waved his hand as though encompassing a world of terrible cooking disasters.

"I see a fresh stick of butter in here," Jacqueline announced, digging in the box. "That's enough to fix anything, in my books." Her stomach growled again and Arlo gave her an apologetic look.

"I should have noticed Tally was staking a claim on your plate."

"I didn't want to stop her. God knows when those kids last had a hot meal."

"They won't have to worry about that anymore." There was a strange growly undertone to Arlo's voice. It wasn't threatening, though. If anything, it reminded Jacqueline of watching him curl around the kids downstairs. Warm and protective.

"It's amazing they've made it this far. Impressive, I should say. But I bet they're more than ready to stop being tough adventurers and just be kids again." Jacqueline's heart fluttered. "They're lucky you were nearby."

"They're lucky you were."

Jacqueline snorted. "What, so I could almost get myself drowned in front of them? Add some trauma to everything they've been through?"

"I would never have let that happen."

Jacqueline swallowed. The protective growl in Arlo's voice was so deep it rumbled in her bones, somehow grounding her and making her feel like she was flying all at once.

She met his eyes and let herself sink into them.

"I guess I'm lucky too, then," she breathed.

Arlo's gaze was warm and intense. The way he was looking at her, hopeful and bashful, pupils so dark they made the night seem bright... No one had looked at her like that in years. If ever.

"I'm the lucky one," he murmured.

He turned back to the pan. Jacqueline tucked her hands into her sleeves, even though she wasn't feeling the cold anymore. Her damp hair was catching the breeze, but the warmth bubbling inside her swept away all the night's chill.

Maybe she would get her spring fling, after all.

# IO

# ARLO

*They will be safe here. Won't they?*

Doubt had started prickling at the back of his neck when Jacqueline went to bed the night before and now, even the blazing mid-morning sun wasn't enough to burn it away.

There was no reason the three shifter children wouldn't be safe in Hideaway. The small town was a sanctuary for all shifters. They'd even taken Arlo in after he turned up in town, all snarled coat and teenaged surliness. Arlo wasn't sure even his closest friends, Harrison and Pol, knew how much the Sweets meant to him. Neither of their shifters were pack animals. Well, sure, maybe the Sweets weren't either—he didn't know how gators lived in the wild—but Ma and Pa Sweets had been better parents to him than his own pack had been after his mother's death, and now, assuming this Eric didn't show, they'd do the same for—

He shivered. *Why does that feel so wrong?*

"Cannonball!"

Dylan whooped and raced along the deck.

*Don't—* Arlo shouted, but it was too late. Dylan leaped off the side of the boat and landed in the water with a splash, his laughter echoing in Arlo's mind. Tally, who was sitting beside Arlo and "helping" him steer the rudder, chortled. *We're not anchored anymore. Don't make me turn this boat around!*

"He's okay!" Jacqueline called over from the bows. "Gosh, they're fast in the water, aren't they?"

There was a clatter as Dylan launched himself at the boat, shifted back into human shape midair, and scrambled aboard. "That was fun!" he gasped. "I'm going to do it again!"

His excitement fluttered against Arlo's mind and Arlo laughed despite himself. There was no point trying to reason the kid into behaving, that was for sure. After what the three of them had been through during the storm, this was probably the first chance Dylan had had to cut loose in ages.

Arlo decided to take a different tack.

"Don't you want to see Hideaway Cove when we come around the bluff?" he asked.

Dylan's eyebrows shot up. "Are we almost there?"

"You tell me. Can you sense we're close to other people like you?" The older shifters in Hideaway Cove kept their telepathic presences hidden, but the kids wouldn't be so careful, especially on a sunny weekend morning. The waves would be singing with excitement.

Dylan scrunched up his face. "Umm…"

*Reach out like you're trying to talk to someone who's too far away for you to see,* Arlo advised him.

*Reach out? What do you mean? We're just talking.*

Arlo laughed. *And that's why every other shifter around can hear you when you do. Don't think about it like you're just plain talking. Go look for someone to tap on the shoulder and whisper in their ear.*

*Okay…* Dylan screwed up his face until his eyes almost disappeared. *Um…*

His telepathic voice faded out. He gasped.

*You got it?*

Dylan's eyes were shining. "There's heaps of people there!"

"Maybe a few hundred." Arlo leaned back and grinned, not hiding how pleased he was.

"A few hundred?" Kenna emerged from below decks, her eyes wide. She stared at Arlo in dismay and then looked out towards land. "And they're all waiting for us?"

"They don't know you're coming, yet," Arlo reassured her. Kenna had been below deck all morning, "getting ready". She'd been completely silent except for the occasional bolt of anxiety, but Jacqueline had reassured him that that was completely normal, and had loaned Kenna the contents of her handbag.

Her forehead wrinkled. "But—you told us yesterday we're really loud…" She bit her lip. *Dylan we've got to be careful, we don't want to be annoy—oh no…*

Kenna's face fell and Arlo held up his hands. "Don't worry. You won't annoy anyone. Day like this, half the kids will be on the beach, shouting about how much fun they're having to anyone in telepathic distance. You'll fit right in."

Kenna didn't look entirely reassured.

Jacqueline walked over and Arlo's wolf perked up. *She's—*

*Yeah, yeah, I know.* Happiness shivered across Arlo's skin as Jacqueline stepped down beside him.

He ran a careful eye over her. She didn't look any the worse for wear after her time in the water. Her eyes were bright, and her cheeks slightly flushed from the wind. Her red curls danced in the breeze.

"Morning, Kenna," she said. "Your hair looks nice. Did you find everything you needed in my bag?"

Kenna ducked her head and mumbled something. To Arlo's secret amusement, she mumbled telepathically at the same time. But her mind glowed with pleasure as she went to sit in the bows.

"We must be getting close," Jacqueline said, staring out towards the coast. "Is that a lighthouse?"

"Hideaway's just around that next bluff. Dylan, want to give me a hand guiding us in?"

Dylan's eyebrows almost shot off his face with excitement. He sat down beside Arlo and listened carefully as Arlo explained how to control the ship's direction.

Arlo's heart lightened as the *Hometide* slipped around the bluff and Hideaway Cove came into view. The small town sparkled like a jewel in the morning sun.

He glanced towards Jacqueline. Her eyes were shining, too, as bright as the calm waters around his home.

*SWIM!* cackled a voice in his mind, and movement flashed at the corner of his attention—Tally, making a bid for the freedom of the water. Arlo half-rose, but Jacqueline was already scooping her up.

"Hey now," she said, hoisting Tally in her arms so the girl could see the shore, "We'll get there faster on the boat than with you jumping overboard, okay?"

Tally's impatience batted against Arlo's mind, and his wolf huffed with amusement.

Jacqueline waited for Tally to respond out loud. When she didn't re-ply—but also didn't wail or shift into her seal pup form—Jacqueline raised her eyebrows at Arlo.

"I guess that's an 'okay'?"

His chest tightened so fast that his "Yes" came out more like a grunt. The light in Jacqueline's eyes, the smile dancing around her lips, even the way she'd smoothly out-maneuvered Tally's leap for freedom—it was almost too much.

*I'm taking her home.*

His heart thudded. *I'm taking her home. I should feel happy, not terrified.*

Dylan tugged on his arm. "What's that?"

Arlo followed Dylan's pointing finger. "That's the marina. I've got a berth along a bit further, by our workshop."

"No, what's *that*? And what workshop? And should I try to talk to him?"

"Where I work when I'm not out on the water." Arlo squinted across the water. If Dylan wasn't pointing at the marina, then what was he looking at?

Talk to him? What was he on about?

The water was calm past the entrance to the cove, with just a few ripples catching the sunlight. The water glinted gold where the light touched it, and—

Arlo groaned. It wasn't just the water glinting gold.

"You have got to be kidding me," Arlo muttered. Jacqueline shot him a questioning look and Kenna leaned forward, curiosity getting the better of her teenagerliness.

"What *is* that? It looks like—"

*Damn it, Pol, this is* not *the time,* Arlo growled to the figure shimmering through the water towards them.

*What's not the time?* his most irritating coworker replied. *You'd better be done sulking, because—wait, who are they? You've brought visitors? Why didn't you say?*

Arlo groaned. Jacqueline moved up beside him.

"Anything I should be worried about?" she whispered.

Arlo shook his head. "No, he's—" He broke off as Pol got closer and began to surface. *Damn it, Pol, you can't just—*

*What? They're shifters, aren't they? I can hear them yelling in my head about what they think I am.* Pol's psychic voice was irritatingly smug. *Smart kids you've got there.*

*They're not mine, and it's not just them—*

Before he could say "There's a human on board, too," Pol surfaced.

And stayed shifted, because of course he did.

*Damned dragon,* Arlo grumbled silently as the others gasped in amazement.

"No way." Kenna stood up, her mouth hanging open. "No *way.*"

Dylan didn't say anything, but his eyes were wide as saucepans and he was so excited he was actually vibrating. Tally giggled and cooed happily, probably more from coasting the swell of her siblings' amazement than understanding how supernatural the sight in front of them was. And Jacqueline…

Arlo stopped himself from looking at her and glared at Pol instead. The last thing he wanted to see was Jacqueline speechless with wonder at the mythical beast that had burst through the waves in front of them.

Pol's dragon form was the length of a train car, slender and agile with gleaming scales and wings that looked like sails made from pure gold when they caught the light. When he was swimming, he kept them tucked close to his long, lizard-like body, so it was possible the kids just thought he was some sort of giant, malformed sea snake.

He glanced at their faces, lit up with wonder. Nope. No chance of that.

Pol poked his head out of the water as he dragon-paddled beside the boat. His neck was long enough that he could look onto deck and when he saw that Arlo wasn't alone, he did a dramatic double-take.

*Well, hello!* he said, broadcasting his voice to everyone on the *Hometide.* *Welcome to Hideaway Cove! My name's Apollo. What are your names?*

The kids replied—psychically and out loud.

Jacqueline swayed on her feet.

"They're… introducing themselves to the… dragon?" She took a small step closer to him and Arlo started finding it hard to breathe. "Am I supposed to as well?"

"Yes, he's a dragon, and right now he's being an asshole. Jacqueline, meet Pol. Pol—come up here and introduce yourself properly!"

He gritted his teeth. Pol was always annoying, but this was something else. Arlo didn't know why, but even his wolf was on edge as the dragon approached the *Hometide*.

Pol reared up and launched himself towards the boat. Arlo jumped up, grabbing Jacqueline around the waist to anchor her in place and calling to Kenna and Dylan to hold on.

*Right,* he thought, gritting his teeth. *This is why Pol turning up always gives me a sense of impending, exhausting doom.*

Pol managed to jump half-out of the water, landing with his front legs on the port side deck. The boat lurched to one side under his weight. Dylan hooted with laughter, Pol's claws scrabbled on the deck—Arlo was caught between irritation that he'd have to fix the wood, and satisfaction at seeing the dragon shifter less-than-graceful for once—and then there was a sparkle like goddamn fireworks and a moment later Pol was standing on the *Hometide's* deck.

Naked.

The younger kids didn't react; Kenna muttered "Gross" and went back to slouching over the bows.

"Wow," said Jacqueline, and Arlo's world froze solid.

Nope. His and his wolf's bad mood had nothing to do with Pol being a show-off, and everything to do with the fact that Pol was a shiny dragon shifter who looked like he stepped out of a movie screen, and Arlo still hadn't given Jacqueline any reason to think he was more than a salt-crusted sea hobo.

His gut twisted. If two shifters were mates, they knew immediately, bam, no questions asked and none needed. But when a shifter's mate was a human?

What if Jacqueline didn't feel the mate bond like he did? What if she didn't feel it at all?

What if she felt something for goddamned *Pol?*

"Wow," Jacqueline said again, and then, "O-kay."

She'd tipped her head back as though she was staring at the sky, but had her eyes closed, as though even looking away hadn't quite done the trick.

"You know, at first I thought maybe the kids were some sort of hippies, but I'm beginning to get the feeling that shifters have different feelings about clothes than the rest of us," she said to the sky.

"'Fraid so," Arlo replied gruffly. "Hey, Pol! Go find yourself some pants." He nodded sharply towards the cabin door.

To his relief, Jacqueline kept her eyes closed until the door clicked shut after Pol.

He glanced at her warily. She cracked one eye open and looked around until she met his gaze.

"Please tell me that's the weirdest thing I'm likely to see in Hideaway Cove," she whispered.

Arlo grimaced. *Let me count. Pol's the shiniest bastard in town, but then there's Harrison...* "Sorry."

Jacqueline groaned. "Then I hope you have a good bar in town, because I am going to need a stiff drink."

Arlo's heart leaped with hope. *That doesn't sound like a woman hopelessly in lust with a blond, godlike dragon shifter.*

He cleared his throat. "Anyway, that's Pol. He's another one who washed up in Hideaway a few years back."

"Washed up? So I don't need to worry about a whole family of dragons swimming over here after him?" Jacqueline asked faintly.

"Not—" Arlo began as the cabin door swung open.

"*Thankfully* not, is what he means to say," Pol announced, leaping through the door. He'd found some pants. Thank God. "I expect we'd have been driven out of town by now, if there was more than one of me. Arlo, what have you been up to? Who is this lovely woman?"

"Jacqueline March." Jacqueline held her hand out and Pol reached for it.

*Mine!* Arlo's wolf snarled. Pol's hand jerked back.

*Did he hear that?* Arlo was horrified. Usually shifters only heard their own animals. He'd never heard of someone's creature communicating psychically with another shifter, and certainly not when they were in human form.

Pol raised his eyebrows. *Everything all right, Arlo?*

Arlo desperately reined in his wolf, which was still snarling—*snarling!*—at how close Pol was. *Fine,* he muttered, and Pol's eyebrows shot up even further.

*I see.* His eyes slid sideways towards Jacqueline, who was looking at them both like they'd just gone mad, and Arlo's wolf raised its hackles. *That's how it is, is it?*

Arlo braced himself for Pol to say something embarrassing, but to his surprise, he simply withdrew his hand. Jacqueline made a short movement as though she was going to try to grab it to shake, which made Arlo's wolf whine.

Pol blinked, placed his hand on his chest, and bowed dramatically.

"My apologies. My name is Apollo Jenkins, but you can call me Pol."

"It's a pleasure to meet you." The faint hollowness was fading from Jacqueline's voice; Arlo's chest tightened as she visibly pulled herself together. "Arlo said you washed up here—does that mean you're a relative newcomer, too?"

"The most recent, not counting the prodigal daughter. Which I don't, personally. You don't count as a newcomer if you half-grew up in a place." He heaved a sigh. "I've been bracing myself to lose the crown, what with the new subdivision on the hill, but it looks like I'm going to have to hand it over earlier than expected."

He smiled at Tally, who promptly squealed with delight and shifted. Arlo dived forward to grab her before she wriggled out of Jacqueline's arms, and somehow he ended up with one hand on Jacqueline's waist, the other helping her hold Tally over one shoulder.

Pol's laughter echoed in his head. *I can't believe this. You sneaky bastard.*

"That's why I'm here," Jacqueline explained before Arlo could reply to Pol—or tell him to shut it. "These three—Kenna, Dylan, and Tally here—have been trying to make their way to Hideaway Cove. Arlo offered to bring them the rest of the way, and I…" Her cheeks glowed. "I, er, came along for the ride."

"You were traveling by yourselves?" Pol looked aghast. Kenna and Dylan had sloped up while the adults were talking, and at his words, Kenna scowled.

Pol exchanged an uncharacteristically serious look with Arlo and turned his attention back to Kenna. "Well you've fallen on your feet here, I'll tell you. Arlo Hammond might look like something he scraped off the bottom of his own boat, but—"

"I'm taking them to the Sweets. Until their actual guardian turns up." Arlo's chest twisted as he said the words, and that must have been why they came out as a half-growl. Three pairs of seal-shifter eyes snapped to his and the wave of disappointment crashing off the children almost made him rock backwards.

Arlo rubbed his temple as the emotions throbbed like the beginning of another headache. This was the right thing to do, he knew it—and what else could he do, anyway?

"I won't be far away," he reassured them. "No one will. Town's so small, everyone's in everyone else's pockets. Besides, the Sweets are my pack. Being with them is pretty much the same as staying with me, except you won't have to sleep on the floor of my workshop."

"I don't mind sleeping on the floor," Dylan said quietly. Arlo shook his head.

"Well, you don't have to," Arlo repeated. He smiled, but on the inside, his wolf was whining fretfully. Something about the situation was worrying it.

*I don't have time to mull it over now,* he thought. *Jacqueline and I have got to get these kids home.* His wolf calmed down a bit.

*About that,* Pol began, but was interrupted.

*What about Eric?* broadcast Dylan in a whisper that was probably meant just for Kenna.

Pol's eyes bulged. "There's another one?"

Jacqueline looked around the group. "Wait, did I just miss something again?"

A wave of guilt poured off Dylan. "We're talking about Eric," he explained. "We're going to find him, aren't we? He wants to live in Hideaway Cove too."

Arlo's stomach hollowed out. "Sure, kid," he said, trying to hide the surge of frustration that filled the suddenly empty space inside him.

*This* was what had his wolf so bothered. The kids needed help, and whoever this Eric guy was, their so-called uncle, he'd failed them. He didn't deserve to look after the pack—*kids*, he quickly corrected himself.

"I work at the council over in Dunston," Jacqueline said. "I can ask people there to keep an eye out and let him know where you are, if they see him."

"That covers the human side," Pol announced. "And Harrison will manage the shifter side. We'll round this Eric up before too long, you'll see. And then you can all play happy families in Hideaway." He shot Arlo a cheeky grin that he didn't even want to contemplate translating.

He had enough to worry him as it was. Once the kids were settled with Ma and Pa Sweets… maybe he and Jacqueline could go for that drink she'd mentioned.

# II

# JACQUELINE

*A freaking dragon.*

Jacqueline inspected Apollo—Pol—from under her eyelashes. In his human shape, dressed in a pair of Arlo's old pants—seriously, at this rate Arlo would be lucky if he had any clothes left—there was no sign that he was anything other than human.

But wasn't that the case with all of them? The kids just seemed like normal kids, if a bit strange—well, normal-for-kids strange. And Arlo…

Her heart fluttered as she glanced at him. He was showing Kenna and Dylan how to ease the boat into dock. The wind riffled through his hair and he looked up—to check their course, not to look at her, of course—but she blushed anyway.

"So, Jacqueline." Pol came over and leaned on the railing with her, though she noticed he kept a careful couple of feet of space between them. She blushed again, for a different reason. Everyone must have seen him avoiding shaking her hand earlier. Like she had cooties or something.

She suddenly realized she hadn't heard a word Pol had said. She shook her head.

"Sorry, what was that? I was distracted."

Pol chuckled. "Understandable! I was saying, so you're from Dunston? Did you get hit badly by the weather this last week?"

*At least shifters are the same as regular humans in one respect. The weather is always a safe topic of conversation.*

"Absolutely. The town's Spring festival starts this weekend, so everyone's glad things have cleared up."

"And you're missing the celebrations?"

"I was…" Jacqueline's brain swerved around the subject of *why* she hadn't been at the Spring Fling. "I work at the sheriff's office, and I was on phone duty last night. Not that that's usually much help to anyone after one of those storms…"

She told Pol about the urban legend of curses riding the breeze from Hideaway Cove. When she got to the bit about electronics going haywire, he went pale.

*Oh God. Have I said something incredibly rude? What have I done now?* She bit her lip.

"You're sure it was only after the storm?" Pol asked urgently.

"Ye-es." Jacqueline was still running over the last few minutes of conversation to make sure she hadn't accidentally said anything insulting. Joking about a tired urban legend wasn't insulting, was it? Or maybe it was for shifters. "I mean, it's probably just some crossed wires somewhere, or…"

"That wouldn't explain the car." Pol dropped his head into his hands and groaned. "I had no idea this was happening!"

His shoulders stiffened and he turned to Arlo. "Did you know about this?"

"Only since yesterday!" Arlo grinned. "Maybe it's time you got that electrician's certificate after all, eh sparky?"

"Haunted cars." Pol groaned. "This is humiliating."

"That's what makes it so great." Arlo's eyes sparkled mischievously as he caught Jacqueline's look of confusion. "If you hadn't guessed, Pol here is the friend I wanted to see hear that story. He's got some powers over electricity—some dragon thing that even he doesn't understand."

"Hey!" Pol objected.

Arlo snorted at him. "Half the places in town only run because he's poked his nose into them. I keep telling him he needs to learn how electricity is *meant* to work before he ends up wiring us all up backwards, but will he listen?"

"Haunted cars," Pol repeated.

Jacqueline laughed. She couldn't help it, it was too ridiculous. Pol looked so stricken, and Arlo so smug, and the kids were staring at the town like all of their dreams had come true.

Kenna and Dylan helped Arlo dock at the wharf next to his workshop. Pol, still looking vaguely shell-shocked, ducked inside muttering that he had to sort something out, and the remaining five of them headed for the main street.

"So you're telling me Pol just… magics up electricity for the town?" Jacqueline was still trying to get her head around it.

"Something like that, the idiot."

"What happens if he moves away?"

"That's why I call him an idiot." Arlo huffed out a breath and smiled. "Nah. He's an ass, but he's reliable. I doubt you'll have any more problems over in Dunston now he knows what was happening."

"Shame." Jacqueline caught Arlo's eye and grinned. "Watching the mayor chase after his car like it was a runaway dog was the highlight of my week. Until now, I mean."

"Now?" There was a strange light in Arlo's eyes.

"All of this." Jacqueline gestured to the street and the surrounding buildings.

Hideaway Cove looked like one of the touristy towns along the coast. The houses and shopfronts lining the main street were all old-fashioned, with painted shutters and carved curlicues on the eaves. It could have come straight off a postcard.

The main street—and it looked like there was only one—was wide, and a broad promenade stretched along its side, next to the water. Concrete steps led down to a sandy beach, and a small building partway down advertised ice cream.

Kenna and Dylan were walking slightly ahead of Jacqueline and Arlo. Every few steps one of them would rush forward to look at something and then dart back and exchange excited whispers with the other. Tally was human shaped again and had been convinced to wear an oversized t-shirt like a dress. She kept running between them and Jacqueline and Arlo, laughing to herself.

"All of this," Jacqueline repeated. "And all of you. Seals. Wolves. Dragons. I don't think anything's going to top this."

"Arlo!"

A tall man with golden-brown hair strode up to them. Arlo waved him over.

"Harrison! Jacqueline, meet Harrison. Hideaway's mayor. Harrison, this is Jacqueline March."

"Pleasure." Harrison held out a hand and Jacqueline shook it. "My fiancée, Lainie—oh. Well, she's the one over there, on her phone."

Jacqueline looked past him to a short, blonde woman whose attention was locked onto her phone. As she watched, the woman sighed and put it away.

Harrison cocked an eyebrow at the kids. "And who are all of you?"

Jacqueline stood back as Arlo made the rest of the introductions. Harrison frowned as Arlo told him they were looking for the Sweets.

"Aren't they out of town this weekend? Lainie—" He called the woman over. "Didn't a little bird tell you the Sweets were away this weekend?"

"Jools said they were off at a bridge tournament or something," Lainie said.

"Playing against humans?" Harrison seemed surprised. "Ahh. *Winning* against humans. Securing Hideaway's safety from the human scourge by beating them at cards. Cunning."

"Feeding into their gossip networks, more like. How else are they meant to keep up with everyone else's secrets?"

"It's just a game," Arlo protested. "You're acting like it's some sort of secret warfare."

"To hear my coworker talk about it, bridge *is* secret warfare," Jacqueline said. "She spends most of the workday trying to plot how to beat this one other couple who keep taking out the pairs championships."

Lainie and Harrison exchanged a look.

"Maybe they're coming around, if they're happy to play against humans," Lainie suggested. "Slowly."

"Or maybe they're looking for fresh territory to chew on, now that people in Hideaway are starting to see through them." Harrison's voice was dry.

Jacqueline frowned. Everyone was keeping a light tone, but there was an undercurrent of something she couldn't quite get hold of going on under the conversation.

Lainie caught her eye and grimaced. "Anyway. If anyone's got a spy network, it's me. I think Jools sees herself as my personal James Bond. Letting me know when the coast is clear."

She put one hand over her midsection, and Harrison bent to kiss the top of her head.

"What do you want them for, anyway?" Harrison put an arm around Lainie's waist and pulled her close. It was an oddly protective gesture, given they were only talking about Arlo's foster parents, Jacqueline thought.

"The kids need somewhere to live until their pack leader gets here," Arlo replied. "The Sweets—"

"—have that going for them at least," Lainie said as Harrison's face darkened. He looked at her in surprise and she shrugged. "You kids are shifters, aren't you?"

Kenna and Dylan nodded. Tally joined in a moment later, copying her older siblings.

"Then I'm sure the Sweets would move heaven and earth to look after you," Lainie said dryly. "Regardless of what they think of the rest of us."

"Right." Something in Arlo's tone made Jacqueline look at him. There was a strange expression on his face. Discomforted and lost.

"Well, they're not here, anyway," Harrison said. He raised his eyebrows at the kids. "What do you want to do? We can put you up in the bed-and-breakfast—wait."

He frowned, and so did Arlo. Jacqueline connected the dots. Someone must have telepathically said something—and from the tense expressions on Kenna and Dylan's faces, it was one of them, and they hadn't meant to be heard.

"You know, this whole telepathy things seems like more trouble than it's worth," she joked, trying to break the tension. Lainie raised her eyebrows at her.

"No argument there," she said, and Jacqueline shot her a grateful smile for picking up the end of the tension-breaking stick. "I had to practically re-teach Harrison here to use a phone after we got together. Speaking of which, hon, don't you need to send out the red alert that another—dramatic gasp—*human* is walking the streets?" She winked at Jacqueline.

*She must be human, too*, Jacqueline thought.

Harrison shook his head. "I think the cat's out of the bag already, sweetheart. I might be wrong, but I do get the feeling this woman might already know about shifters. But that doesn't solve the problem of the Sweets not being here the one weekend they could make themselves useful."

"Hey," said Arlo in a warning tone. "They're still my parents."

"Sure, but you have to admit…"

"We could stay with you on the boat," Dylan blurted out, and Kenna punched him. "Hey!"

Arlo paused. "That's…"

His eyes slid sideways to meet Jacqueline's. For some reason her cheeks felt hot.

"Why don't you set up camp with us for the night," Harrison interjected. Lainie's eyes lit up.

"Yes! That's a great idea. We've got all these rooms no one is using."

Jacqueline expected Kenna, at least, to protest, but both children agreed. Tally nodded happily, too, and Arlo and Harrison winced in the way she'd come to recognize as evidence that the smallest shifter in their little group had the largest telepathic voice.

Lainie clapped her hands together. "Well, why waste time? We've got the Land Rover, so let's all trundle up the hill now and get you three settled in. And some lunch. I don't know about the rest of you but all this early morning strolling has left me starving."

"Up the hill?" Dylan asked, and Lainie gave him a conspiratorial wink.

"That's right. Didn't I say? We live next to the lighthouse."

# I2

# ARLO

There wasn't room in the Land Rover for all of them; Arlo and Harrison decided to walk. Harrison didn't even wait for Lainie to start the engine before he started to interrogate Arlo.

*So. Jacqueline.*

*Yes.* Arlo gritted his teeth. *Did Pol tell you?*

*Pol? I haven't seen him all day. I just have eyes in my head, is all.*

Arlo groaned. *That obvious?*

*You might as well be singing and dancing.*

Arlo thrust his hands deep in his pockets and didn't reply.

Harrison frowned. *Why aren't you singing and dancing?*

*Do I have to tell you?*

*She's human. It shouldn't matter.* Harrison strode in front of Arlo and stopped, arms crossed. "It doesn't matter, does it?"

Arlo knew what he meant, and the knowledge tasted bitter. When Harrison first met his human mate, Lainie, Arlo had behaved like an ass. He'd fully bought the Sweets' line that Hideaway Cove could only be a sanctuary for shifters if they didn't let any humans settle there. He'd been afraid to lose the one place he'd been able to call home. And now?

Did he know better, now, or was he just afraid in a different way?

*Doesn't matter anyway,* he said. *Look at me. I'm not the sort of man a woman like that would want to date.*

"Huh! Is that what you think?" Harrison clapped him on the back and pulled his shirt off over his head. "Come on. A run'll clear your head."

He kicked his pants off and shifted. Harrison's griffin form was almost as magnificent as Pol's dragon, but the effect was slightly spoiled by him pecking around to pick up his discarded clothes.

Arlo shucked off his own clothes and shifted. His wolf stretched its legs, snapping its jaws as it shook off his human anxieties.

He nosed his clothes into a bundle and picked them up in his jaws.

*Race you,* Harrison laughed, and took off. His wings flashed in the sunlight and Arlo caught a swell of amazement from the Land Rover.

*Flying's cheating!* he called back. *Try running on those mismatched legs and see how far you get!*

By the time he got to the house at the top of the hill, Arlo was panting and, if not happy, then at least at some sort of equilibrium. He nosed through the front door and made his way to the guest shower.

"You need a change of clothes?" Harrison called from elsewhere in the house when he'd finished washing.

"These are—" *fine*, he'd about to say, then he actually looked at the clothes he'd brought up. His shirt was so faded even he couldn't remember what color it had once been, his pants had scuffs on the knees, and there were distinctly wolf-bite-shaped drool marks over everything. "Uh. Thanks."

"You know, you can't rely on a human to pick up on the mate bond straight away. You're going to have to rely on your good old-fashioned charm and good looks." Harrison tossed a bundle of clothes into the bathroom.

Arlo sighed. "That's what I'm worried about."

Showered, dressed, and full of dread, Arlo found Harrison on the deck outside. Harrison was laying out lunch on a picnic table overlooking the cove.

Arlo couldn't help but whistle. "This is just for lunch?"

"We do a lot of entertaining these days, what with me being the mayor and Lainie trying to steal allies off the Sweets," Harrison said frankly. "We count you among the already stolen, by the way."

"Sure." He wandered over to the table and reached for a bowl of brightly colored prawn crackers. An eagle-like screech stopped him.

"Sorry about that." Harrison cleared his throat. "Those are Lainie's. I won't kill you if you eat them, but she might. We have to order them in special."

"Message received." Arlo pulled his hand back as the Land Rover pulled up on the other side of the house. His wolf pricked its ears up. *She's here!*

Arlo smoothed down his shirt nervously and Harrison snorted at him. Footsteps clattered as the others entered the house.

"Showers are through there, lunch is—oh, God. Lunch. Harrison, can you show them around? I need to eat."

Lainie descended on the lunch table like a seagull who'd just discovered the world's biggest bowl of fries. She hugged the bowl of prawn crackers to her stomach and sat down with a sigh. "I should have invested in these instead of land…" She closed her eyes and popped a cracker in her mouth. "Mmm."

Arlo sat down awkwardly opposite her.

"How's that going?" he asked.

Lainie cracked an eye open. "Not fantastic," she said. "Are you *sure* there isn't a secret all-shifter newsletter for real estate?"

"Not that anyone's told me about," Arlo replied.

"Guh." Lainie groaned. "Well, we've sold enough sections and basic builds to make back our investment, at least. But I really want to branch out with shifter-y designs, you know? The architect I've got working on the subdivision has all these great ideas…"

Lainie had inherited half the hill they were sitting on from her grand-parents, who'd settled in Hideaway decades ago. Since she moved to town, she and Harrison had been developing the land, adding more—and more modern—houses to Hideaway's stock.

Arlo frowned. "If you can't find enough shifters to move in," he began, and Lainie froze.

"You too?" she asked.

"I didn't mean—"

Lainie sighed and popped another prawn cracker in her mouth. "I'm not selling to humans. Shifter and shifter-adjacent only. You can tell Dorothy that. Should make her happy."

"I wasn't—"

"It's okay, Arlo. I know. You're in a tough situation." She waved his protestations away. "Let's just eat lunch, and I want to hear more about these kids you picked up out of nowhere."

Arlo sighed. Lainie was the best person he could talk to about Jacque-line—but he still didn't know her well enough to know how to make the conversational leap.

"They're amazing," he said instead. "I wish I was half as smart at their ages. They made it all the way here without being picked up by human authorities—but they don't have to do that anymore. Shifters look after their own."

Again, that little twinge of wrongness. Lainie's lip twisted.

"They sure do," she murmured blandly. "Lemonade?"

The door opened, and Arlo was already leaping to his feet before Jacqueline's voice floated out over the patio.

"Is this the right place?"

She was standing in the doorway. He opened his mouth to usher her to the lunch table, but no words came out.

Yesterday, soaked through and out of her depth, she'd been stunning. This morning, salty tangled hair and all, she'd been the most beautiful person he could imagine. But now?

Her hair shone in a mass of curls. Her eyes seemed brighter, somehow, and the soft t-shirt and jeans she was wearing caressed her figure.

Her cheeks went pink as she met his gaze, and then her eyes slipped past him to Lainie.

"Harrison lent me some of your clothes, I hope you don't mind," she said.

Lainie quickly reassured her, and then the others all appeared behind her. Jacqueline rode a tide of hungry shifters to the picnic table and ended up sitting beside Arlo.

"Dig in, everyone," Harrison announced, and for a few minutes there was nothing but the sound of happy eating.

Arlo felt Lainie's eyes on him. Even knowing he was being watched, he couldn't help stealing glances at Jacqueline. When she reached for the salt, he handed it to her. When her lemonade ran low, he refilled it before she'd even noticed she needed more.

Lainie narrowed her eyes.

"So what's the next step?" Harrison said once everyone had eaten their fill and was caught up on how three orphan shifters had turned up on their doorstep.

Kenna and Dylan exchanged a glance, and then:

*We should tell them—*

*Shh! They'll hear!*

Dylan winced, and Arlo wondered what it was that he'd been about to tell Kenna they needed to say.

Kenna was fiddling with the edge of her napkin. "We still don't know where Eric is," she said, and Jacqueline nodded.

"If I can borrow a phone, I'll call in at work and ask my boss to put the word out," she said.

"Go ahead. And I'll put the word out here. Someone might have heard something. If your friend does find his way here, we'll get you all back together ASAP," Harrison said.

"But apart from that…" Kenna tore little pieces off the napkin.

"Well, waiting around here doesn't sound like much fun," Lainie declared. "Why don't we all go back into town? If you're going to be staying here you might as well get to know your way around."

Arlo remembered Kenna's hesitancy about meeting new shifters earlier. "Or we can stay here. It's up to you."

"No! I mean, you don't need to hang around with us," Kenna said. "You and Ms. March can—um, I mean…"

"I'd like to see more of the town, too," Jacqueline said. "Er—if that's okay?"

"Why wouldn't it be?" Lainie stared hard at Arlo. "We'll just clean up here—"

"We'll help!" chimed in Kenna and Dylan. Tally cooed and waved her fork around.

*There's something weird going on there,* Arlo thought, watching them file through to the kitchen. *One minute they're upset because I can't put them all up in the* Hometide, *the next they're telling us not to wait around?*

He sighed and shook his head. The most likely explanation was "they're kids", with a chaser of "and they've been through a hell of a lot, so cut them some slack". But his wolf was worrying over them like a dog who'd lost its bone.

*They just need some stability. And to be sure the rug isn't going to be ripped away from under their feet again. Ma and Pa Sweets will give them that, until Eric decides to show his face.*

His neck prickled again. Somehow, that still felt wrong. And not just because he doubted this Eric fellow was ever going to show up.

He gathered up a handful of dishes and followed after the kids. Lainie waited until the kids had gone back to get another load, then cornered him.

"You and Jacqueline?" she asked. He'd have had to pretend to be an idiot not to get her meaning.

He nodded.

"And you haven't actually told her yet, of course." Lainie blew her bangs out of her face. "Be nice."

"I am nice!"

"Sure. I know that. But it takes a while to get past the crusty exterior to your nice squishy insides." She folded her arms. "I'm serious, Arlo. It's better now than when I first got here, but I won't lie, it's hard. Hideaway Cove is a sanctuary but if you're her mate then your job is to be *her* sanctuary. And you're a bit too close to the sharks for that to be easy."

Arlo's heart sank. "You mean the alligators." Dorothy and Alan Sweets were alligator shifters.

"Bingo."

Kenna and Dylan came back in then and Arlo slipped out while Lainie was distracted.

Jacqueline called her office, and by the sound of it only managed to talk to the answering machine. She shrugged when Arlo gave her a questioning look.

"Either they'll check it or they won't. And frankly, if they end up thinking I've drowned myself because they forgot to check the freaking answering machine, it's no skin off my nose." She reassured Kenna and Dylan, "I made sure to ask about your uncle Eric. If they check the message, they'll know to send him this way if anyone sees him."

"And I've put the word out around my contacts out of town," Harrison added. "Now, who's ready for ice cream?"

Tally was almost snoozing by the time they started down the hill again. They all walked this time, after a short argument where Lainie reasoned with Harrison that, even if she was too tired to walk back up later, he could always carry her.

Arlo watched them bicker companionably.

*They've been together for—what, six months?*

Arlo counted back. Lainie had first arrived in town the previous autumn, and one winter of bad storms had cemented their bond. Arlo couldn't imagine either of them without the other now. Lainie might not be a shifter, but she was as much a part of Hideaway Cove as any of them, even if some locals—mainly the Sweets, he thought with a pang—still didn't totally accept her.

Six months, and the rest of Harrison's life stretched out in front of him, shining like the sun on still waters. Marriage. A baby. Maybe not in that order, depending on how quickly they managed to organize the wedding.

And Arlo…

Jacqueline was walking a little ahead, with Tally bundled sleepily over her shoulder. Lainie was walking with her.

"So, how long will you be in town, Jacqueline?" Lainie asked.

"Honestly? I wish I could stay forever." Jacqueline laughed, but softly, as though she was trying not to disturb Tally. "But I have work, and a house back in Dunston… Now that the kids are safely here, I should probably be heading back."

Arlo swallowed, and Lainie shot him an entirely too innocent look.

Arlo had less than a day, if he was going to have even a chance at six months, or longer.

They reached the promenade, the wide pedestrian area that stretched the length of the main street on the water side.

"Ice cream! Ice cream!" Dylan yelled, running towards the small shop halfway down the promenade. The sign, Sweet Dreams Ice Cream Parlor, used to make Arlo's stomach rumble just looking at it.

Arlo groaned. He wouldn't have minded going there earlier, but they'd run into Harrison and Lainie and bypassed it. Now, after what Lainie had said about his foster parents…

"Can we?" Dylan begged Kenna, who bit her lip.

"Eric has all our cash…"

Arlo straightened his shoulders. The parlor belonged to Tess Sweets, his foster parents' granddaughter. "My treat. Come on."

# I3

# JACQUELINE

Jacqueline didn't miss the way Arlo straightened his shoulders just outside the ice cream parlor door. Almost as though he was preparing himself for battle.

He stepped through—and then backed out as though a swarm of bees was after him.

Jacqueline caught his arm. He was wincing and clutching his head. "Are you okay? What happened?"

"Loud," he grunted, and Jacqueline looked past him to see the ice cream parlor full of… kids?

Dylan shrieked with excitement and ran in to join the throng.

"Ah." Jacqueline nodded and let the door swing shut. Arlo was still clutching his head, so she guided him carefully away, towards a seat overlooking the water. "A thousand happy screams, direct to the inside of your skull?"

"Yeah."

"Do you need some space?" Which she one hundred percent wasn't giving him right now, clinging to his arm like this. If he insisted, though…

"It'll pass." One side of his mouth hooked up. "Or I'll get used to it."

He didn't pull away from her, so she didn't let go. Her hand fit into the crook of his elbow like it was meant to be there.

"Headache?" Harrison dodged past them en route to the ice cream shop. The door swung open and Arlo winced again. Harrison looked bemused. "The kids? I know you've always been more sensitive to it than me, but—geez, Arlo. Are you all right?"

Arlo scowled at him and must have said something telepathically, because Harrison shrugged his shoulders and backed off.

"I'll grab you a cone," he said. "Caramel, right? What about you, Jacqueline?"

"Caramel sounds great."

"On it."

Arlo sighed heavily as Harrison went inside, and sat down on the seat. Jacqueline sat next to him. They weren't as close as they had been on the rowboat, not hip-to-hip… but close enough, with her hand still folded under his arm.

"Part of me is glad that didn't work," Arlo admitted ruefully. "Saved by the screams of a hundred happy children."

"There can't have been more than five people in there," Jacqueline protested.

"And Tally. She counts for at least fifty by herself." Arlo smiled, then his expression became serious. "My sister owns the ice cream parlor. With the kids, and my parents… maybe it's best I don't see her right now."

"But I thought your parents were going to look after them?"

"I…" Arlo raised his hands and dropped them in defeat. "I need to figure some stuff out." He frowned.

"Like how you're the only one who get migraines around the kids?" Jacqueline bit her lip. She still wasn't sure whether she should mention all these things she was noticing. She was probably reading things wrong, and even if she wasn't… she was only going to be here for a day. It was none of her business.

Arlo smiled weakly. "That. And some other things." He hesitated, and then wrapped his hand over hers. "I was wondering…"

Warmth spread across Jacqueline's skin. "Oh."

Arlo tensed. "Good oh, or bad oh?"

Jacqueline laughed out loud. Here she'd been, tying herself into knots over missing out on her spring fling, and Arlo was practically throwing himself in her lap. At least, as close to throwing himself as she imagined the quiet, stoic man ever got.

"Good oh," she reassured him. "Definitely. What were you wondering?"

"That, for a start." He looked down at their intertwined hands.

"Do you have your answer?" Jacqueline's skin was humming. God, this was incredible. She was just holding hands and felt like she was flying. She was sure it hadn't been like this with Derek, even at the start. Why had she waited so long to stop being a sad lump at home and get out and enjoy her new life as a single woman?

"I hope so." He cleared his throat. "I know you wanted to stay until the kids were settled in. With the Sweets not being here yet…"

"With what not what? Who are we talking about?"

"Dylan!" Kenna's groan was like a jet engine dying.

Dylan torpedoed around the seat, and Jacqueline had to whip her head back to avoid getting an ice cream cone to the face.

"With, er… is that for me? Thanks." Jacqueline inspected the ice cream carefully. "Caramel?"

Kenna slouched into view. "Apparently. The lady said she experiments with the flavors."

"Is that why it's green?"

Kenna handed Arlo his cone and Arlo gave it a suspicious look. "Tessa," he sighed, and then: "Cheers."

He bumped his cone against Jacqueline's.

It tasted like…

"Sort of caramel-y… seaweed?"

Dylan burst out laughing. "Yes! That's what it said on the board!"

"Seaweed caramel." Arlo shrugged and took another bite. "I swear, Tessa is wasted in this town."

"Tessa is your sister?" Jacqueline licked the cone again. It was strange, but it was kind of growing on her.

"Tess, I mean. That's what she prefers now, anyway, even if I keep forgetting." Arlo licked his ice cream again and frowned. "She's my foster parents' granddaughter. I guess technically that makes her my foster niece, but she says that makes her feel like she should be nine years old, so, sister it is."

"She said she wanted to talk to you," Kenna said. "She just needed to finish serving—oh, there she is."

Arlo's fingers tightened around Jacqueline's. She turned to look where Kenna was pointing, and caught a glimpse of a strange expression on Arlo's face. Almost as though he was scared.

When she glanced at him again, the expression was gone, so quickly she must have imagined it was there in the first place.

The woman walking over from the ice cream parlor looked a few years younger than Jacqueline. She had her hair pulled back under a retro-style hairnet, and huge dark eyes behind thick-framed glasses.

When she spotted Jacqueline and Arlo sitting together, those huge eyes got even bigger, and she spun around and darted back into the ice cream parlor.

"What—" Arlo began, and frowned. "One moment," he muttered to Jacqueline, and his eyes went vague.

"He's mindspeaking to her," Dylan explained.

Jacqueline raised her eyebrows. "Oh. You can hear?"

"No, because he's *really* good at it." Dylan heaved a sigh. "But it feels kind of buzzy against my brain. It's nice."

"How's your ice cream?" Jacqueline didn't want to guess at what flavor Dylan's bright pink cone was.

"Really good!" his eyes lit up. "It's like cotton candy."

"I got chocolate," Kenna said, ducking her head. "Not chocolate-and-anything, just chocolate."

"And what did—wait, where's Tally?" Jacqueline stood up. *Oh God. I lost one of them.*

Arlo snapped to attention. "What is it?"

"Tally's—"

"With Ms. Eaves and Mr. Galway," Kenna said quickly.

*Who?* Jacqueline thought. Arlo caught her confused look.

"Lainie and Harrison," he explained.

"Oh. Good." Jacqueline sat down. Her heart was racing, and everyone was staring at her. "I guess I'm more on edge after what happened yesterday than I thought."

Dylan was jumping on his heels and tugged at Kenna's sleeve. "Yeah, I *know*," she muttered, shaking him off. Despite her surly tone, her face was glowing.

Jacqueline sat back. Her ice cream was melting, so she ate a few bites while she gathered her thoughts.

Arlo still had that second question for her. And she had a pretty good idea what it might be.

She'd let go of his hand when she stood up, but even the memory of his fingers wrapped around hers made her skin go hot all over.

She knew what she wanted that second question to be and, damn it, she knew where she wanted the answer to land her. Not on a car back to Dunston that evening, that was for sure.

There was still one more day left to the weekend.

"I was saying that I've decided to stick around for the rest of the weekend," she said, and Arlo made a soft, strangled noise that made the heat on her skin blaze. "At least to see you kids settled."

*And spend more time with the hot guy who saved my life*, she added privately.

# 14

# ARLO

Harrison appeared a few moments later, surrounded by small children and with Tally on his shoulders and half of her ice cream running down the side of his head. He rounded up Kenna and Dylan and led the shrieking mob straight into the water.

Arlo watched them, his head still spinning. One minute he'd barely as good as hinted to Jacqueline that he'd like her to stick around—and the next she announced she was staying the night.

His wolf growled happily and he shushed it. *In town. Not with me. That's not…*

He shook his tangled thoughts away.

Jacqueline was watching the water, too, her face glowing.

"So, what was your second question?" she asked chirpily.

Arlo stiffened. "My—? Oh." His tongue felt thick. "I, er." Her hand was warm in his, small and soft but strong, too. "I was wondering if you'd like to join me for dinner."

Jacqueline's lips twitched, as though she was trying not to let a smile escape. "I'd like that. Very much. Dinner and a drink," she declared, "to make up for your shiny friend earlier."

Arlo's head was ringing. "Yes," he said, and tripped over his tongue again. "That sounds, yes. I'd like that."

"Before then..." Jacqueline seemed lit up from inside. "I'd love to know more about Hideaway Cove. Would that be okay? Since Harrison said the cat's out of the bag already..."

*She wants to find out more about Hideaway. She wants* me *to show her my town.*

"Of course," Arlo said. "Where do you want to go first?"

They sat and finished their ice creams, watching the kids play in the surf. Other Hideaway locals joined them and Arlo pointed them out—including the seagull sisters Jools and Jess, who soared over in their gull forms and then, when they saw the newcomers, flew off to get changed and dressed and raced back to the beach.

"I don't know if you saw the Rodríguez kids before." Arlo pointed to three dark shapes flitting through the water out past the breakers. "Diego, Aarón and their baby sister, Ana."

"A friend for Tally?"

"She's closer to Dylan's age. I think." Arlo frowned. "Never been good with kids' ages."

"I'm not sure how old Tally is. Not older than three, though, I think." Jacqueline sighed. "Those kids have had a rough few years. I'm glad they're here now."

She sounded sad—but determined, too. Then she sighed. "I'd like to say I'll stick around until I'm sure they're settled, but... work..." Her voice dropped. "You know, yesterday morning, I was half planning to quit?"

Arlo's heart leaped. "Why?"

If she didn't have her job keeping her in Dunston—he cut the thought off before it could overtake him.

Jacqueline shrugged. "I feel like I've been... stuck, these last few years. I've finally gotten rid of the last thing that's been holding me back, and I was ready to let everything else go, too. Except now, seeing the kids like this… knowing how quickly everything can fall apart… except I already *know* everything can fall apart…"

She shook her head, glared at the remains of her ice cream cone, and ate it in two bites. "Sorry. I'm not making sense. How about that town tour you mentioned?"

"Sure." Arlo stood up. "Let's start…"

His mouth went dry. *Let's start by introducing her to shifters whose first thought will be to realize she's my mate. And whose second thought will be…*

*What the hell is the Sweets' boy doing with a human?*

He gulped.

"What about your workshop?" Jacqueline suggested, and Arlo let out a huff of relief.

"Great idea."

"You still here, Pol?" Arlo pushed the workshop door open and ushered Jacqueline in before him. "Pol?"

The foyer was small. There was a low sofa against one wall, which Pol usually spent the working day lounging in, and a desk with an old computer and half-alive potted plant on it. The room was a bit dusty, a bit worn—but with Jacqueline in it, it lit up.

There was a strangled noise from further inside. Arlo raised his eyebrows and exchanged a look with Jacqueline. She snorted and covered her mouth.

"It feels like we're sneaking in," she whispered, tiptoeing into the foyer. "So this is where you work?"

"When I'm not on the water. The three of us—Harrison, Pol and me—went in on this place together a few years back."

"Isn't Harrison the mayor?"

"And our builder and handyman. Pol looks after electronics—well, you already know how well that goes—and I do boats. And other carpentry. It's not guaranteed work, but with the number of boats around here and the sea doing its best to beat the town underwater, it's as close as you'll get."

"So you work on buildings all around town? If I go out and look, I'll be looking at places you had a hand in making?"

"Or at least maintaining."

"That's wonderful." Her gaze went distant. "It must be great, knowing the work you do is so important to the town."

"Don't you work at the sheriff's office?"

"The sheriff's office in Dunston," she said, as though that said everything. She caught the expression on his face and waved her hands. "I worked as a tutor during high school, to save for college. Then after I got married I got the job at the sheriff's office, and… kind of kept up the tutoring?" Arlo must have still looked confused. "Dunston is a quiet town. There *is* a lockup at the sheriff's office, but mostly Reg just uses it to hold any teenagers he finds getting drunk or frisky where they shouldn't. And they tended not to have done their homework before they went out to get into trouble, so… I guess I'm still tutoring. Still doing the same high-school job anyone could do, and not particularly contributing to anything else."

Arlo frowned. "I bet the kids you taught would say different."

"I'm not a teacher. It's just… homework help. While they try not to vomit into buckets." She sighed. "Never finished that degree, after all. Anyway. We were talking about you. You like the boats best?"

"Of course." He wanted to ask her more about herself, but she'd made it clear that she'd prefer not to. And she seemed interested in his work, so he added: "I built the *Hometide* myself."

"No!"

"It took me the best part of five years." He led her through to the main workshop. The air was filled with the scents of wood dust and oil. Arlo breathed in deep. It smelled of long days of hard work.

Jacqueline grimaced. "I just spent the best part of five years… never mind. Is this for the boat?"

She walked over to Arlo's bench and, when he gestured it was okay, picked up a wooden frame.

"How did you guess?" *How* did *she guess?*

"It's the same size as the broken window above—" Her cheeks went pink. "Above, um, the bed."

"I'm trying to decide what to put in it." Arlo tried to keep the growl out of his voice, but his wolf was very interested by the way Jacqueline was blushing. "Plain glass, or…"

He stood next to her in front of the desk. She was so close he could smell her feminine scent under the wood, oil and smoke of the workshop.

Before the crowbar headache had hit him, he'd planned to spend the down-time after the house build working on a leadlight for the boat's bedroom window.

"I've been collecting these pieces of colored glass for a while," he said, sorting through a cardboard box of offcuts. "Watched a few videos online about how to do it. We've got all the tools here, I just need to decide what to make."

"You just watched a few videos and you can jump straight into making something?" Jacqueline sounded amazed. "You're not worried you'll ruin it?"

"If it goes wrong, I can always have another go. There's enough glass in here for a couple of bad tries."

"But what if…" Jacqueline twisted her hands together. "What if it goes wrong every time? Or there's one… design… that you really want to work, but it doesn't, and you can't try it again? Or… or maybe it's the first time you're having a go at it in a long, *long* time, and you don't want to mess it up?" Her cheeks blazed.

Arlo gazed at her, lost for words. He'd always been extra sensitive to other shifters' psychic signatures. He could feel emotions before he could see them, most of the time. Maybe that was why the kids had given him such a headache.

He'd never been good with humans, because he didn't have that cheat-sheet emotional background when he was talking with them.

But even an idiot like him could tell Jacqueline probably wasn't talking about stained glass windows anymore.

"It can be scary, trying something you haven't done in a long time… or ever," Arlo said carefully. "But I know that if something's meant to work out, it will." He paused. "And… I'm good with my hands."

Jacqueline blushed even harder. Her eyes flicked up to meet his. They were bright hazel, like intricately patterned heartwood, and the longer she kept his gaze, the warmer and more intense they became.

*Something you haven't done ever.* The words shivered down his back.

Arlo licked his lips. "Jacqueline," he said, her name like a prayer, "there's something I should tell you. Something about shifters."

"What is it?" Jacqueline's eyes filled his vision.

"I…"

"Aargh!" A heartfelt groan split the air.

Arlo jumped in front of Jacqueline. "Who—damn it, Pol!"

Pol was slumped in the door. He didn't even look up as Arlo swore at him. He was holding a battery in one hand and a lightbulb in the other, connected by wires.

"How does it *work?*" he groaned, hopelessly banging the two together. "It makes no sense!"

"Oh God," Jacqueline breathed from behind Arlo. "That's your friend with the electric powers. Did I break him?"

Arlo looked over his shoulder. Jacqueline looked stricken, but when she met his eyes, she stuffed her hand into her mouth to stop herself laughing out loud.

"Pol, read a book," Arlo told Pol as the dragon shifter slid down the doorframe in despair. "Jacqueline, I had a thought. Want to take the scenic route to the restaurant?"

*This is safer than parading her in front of all my parents' neighbors,* Arlo thought as they climbed the hill behind the workshop.

"This is like a goat path," Jacqueline said, panting slightly. "Or a…" She glanced at him and bit her lower lip.

"Wolf path?" Arlo suggested. He grinned. "If the weather's too bad for sailing, I'll come up here. Watching the water is almost as good as being on it."

Jacqueline put her hands on her hips and gazed out over the bay. The sea breeze tugged at her curls. "You come up here when the weather's bad?"

Arlo sighed. "Pol calls it my sulking perch."

Jacqueline laughed. "No!" Her grin turned wicked. "There's no way you could *perch* up here when it's windy. You'd need to cling on…"

"To this shrub," Arlo agreed, pointing at a nearby tree, twisted by the elements.

Jacqueline laughed again and the wind teased a hank of hair over her face. She pushed it back, giggling. "I guess this is the next best thing to being out on the water. It must be amazing, watching a storm from up here."

"That it is." He sat down and she settled in next to him, close enough that their arms brushed together and it seemed like the most natural thing in the world to take her hand. "I don't know why it is, but the sea always makes me feel at home. Tess says I should have been a fish shifter."

"Or a seal?"

Something jolted in Arlo's heart. "Or a seal," he repeated, slowly.

"I can't believe that Hideaway Cove exists, that you all live here openly as shifters, and none of us knew anything about it." Jacqueline gazed out over the water.

"Except about the curse?" Arlo joked, and was rewarded with an embarrassed smile.

"Except the curse, yeah." She sighed. "I've lived in Dunston all my life. I knew there was a whole big wonderful world out there, I just didn't know *how* wonderful. Or how close it was. I've spent all my life around people who know exactly who I am and what my story is, and all along..."

She hesitated. Arlo stayed silent, unable to take his eyes off her as the smile faded from her face.

"You must have all sorts of strategies in place to keep the fact that you're shifters secret from visitors, I'm sure. But when I think I could have driven a few hours out of town and been in a place where no one knew my husband left me five years ago, and no one's gonna corner me in the grocery store and tell me how his kid's in second grade now... I'm sure you all would have done your best to drive me out of town, but even that would have been a step up."

Arlo put one arm around her and she leaned into him.

"Sorry," she muttered. "You brought me up here for a romantic walk and here I am, grouching about my ex."

"It's the sea." Jacqueline stared at him, eyebrows furrowed, and he gestured out over the water. "That's why I come up here. And why I go out on the water. I know that whatever bad thing I'm feeling, the sea will pull it out of me."

Jacqueline took another deep breath, and under Arlo's arm, her shoulders relaxed.

"I think it's working," she said quietly. "I do feel better. Better than I have in a long time."

Arlo wasn't good at picking expressions, but even he could hear the weight behind her words. He frowned.

"You broke up with your husband five years ago, but he has a kid in second grade?"

Jacqueline groaned. "Damn it. I hoped you wouldn't pick that up."

"I shouldn't have mentioned it."

"No, it's fine." Jacqueline let her head rest against his shoulder. "That's why we split. This other woman, she gave him what he'd always wanted, which I… anyway. He got what he wanted, and I got the house, which I've just paid off. Next stop, Vegas!"

There was a hard edge to her voice, despite her toothy smile.

"Well I'm glad you've stopped by Hideaway Cove on your way to Vegas," Arlo said, his voice gravelly. Jacqueline's eyes flicked up to his.

"Me, too," she said. "Though I think I've had enough sea therapy for one night."

"In that case," Arlo said, helping her up, "I think it's time we had that drink."

He showed her the back route to Caro's restaurant, picking their way through low shrub along a path that existed mainly in the mental maps each citizen of Hideaway had of the land around their town.

He pointed out the ridge where Jools and Jess had dared each other into leaping from to learn to fly, the small cave where local kids invariably ended up when they were skiving off from the town's correspondence school classes, and the wild herbs Tess had used for her experimental ice cream flavors before she graduated to seaweed. All the small and secret places that hinted at the heart of the small town he called home.

By the time they clambered around to the path that led down to Caro's, Jacqueline's cheeks were red with exertion. Arlo took her hand to steady her as she jumped across a muddy creek. Her hand's warmth, and the way she puffed slightly as she blew a stray curl out of her eyes, made him want to smack himself. He cursed underneath his breath.

"Sorry," he said when Jacqueline raised her eyebrows at him. Even he could tell that was a questioning look. He hunched his shoulders. "It's just struck me that this might not have been what you meant when you said you wanted a tour of the town."

"What?" Jacqueline blew her hair out of her face again. "Are you kidding? The sea therapy I could probably have done without, but this? I haven't done anything like this since I was a kid."

She frowned as her hair bounced over her face again, and let go of his hand to grab it and braid it into a long rope.

"Which must be obvious, since I've apparently forgotten what the wind is like this close to the water," she added, sticking the end of the braid under her collar. "I hope this restaurant isn't too fancy. I bet I look like a mess."

Arlo swallowed. With her hair pulled back, Jacqueline's eyes seemed bigger and more full of light than ever.

"You're fine," he said gruffly. "Caro's isn't a shirt and shoes place. People eat there straight after coming off boats, or work sites, so you'll—I mean, shit, not that you look like you've—you look lovely. You…"

*Tell her.* The words thudded in his bones. *Look how she already seems to belong here. The wind in her hair and light in her eyes. She's the piece of your heart that's been missing all these years. Tell her you're hers, tell her she's part of your pack—*

*Take her to meet Ma and Pa.* Arlo's mind tripped over itself.

"…You're beautiful," he said instead, and the dazed delight in Jacqueline's eyes almost made his cowardice worth it.

"Well." Jacqueline folded her lips over a smile that looked like it was threatening to take over her whole face. "You know, you're not bad yourself." Her cheeks blazed as she tucked her arm into his.

*It can't be this easy,* Arlo thought as she smiled up at him. *And yet…*

Maybe it could be. A shifter's mate was meant to be the other half of their soul; why was he surprised that Jacqueline was slipping so easily and wonderfully into his life?

*She doesn't know what she is to me, but she's taking a chance on me anyway.* Arlo swallowed. *After almost drowning, babysitting three frightened shifter kids, and having to put up with me grumbling and growling all the time. Sure, she's taking a chance on me now, for one date, but I need to do better than this before I tell her.*

The path took them to the back of Caro's restaurant; Arlo led Jacqueline around piles of neatly stacked pallets and other delivery detritus, silently cursing himself for not thinking this plan through properly.

"Are you sure it's okay for us to be back here?" Jacqueline asked, picking her way around a stack of insulated buckets. Arlo recognized them from the Menzies' fishing boat.

"Sure," he said, biting the inside of his cheek. *Great job,* he snarled to himself. *Sneaking around the back with all the trash. Are you trying to put her off?*

His stomach twisted, but before he could berate himself any more, a door swung open in front of them.

"—out of the oven, and the chocs from Tess's are—what's this?"

Caro loomed in the door. She was in her late forties, with short-cropped brown hair and a deep scar running along one cheek. In Arlo's eyes she was the backbone of the Hideaway community. Forget Harrison and his mayor's chain, and the Sweets with their bridge-and-gossip group picking over the latest news: there wasn't a person in Hideaway who hadn't eaten to bursting in her restaurant, and dozed off their delicious gluttony in front of her blazing fireplace.

"Oh!" Jacqueline's hand flew over her mouth. "I'm sorry, we were just—we were, um—" She dissolved into giggles. "Oh, God, this is *just* like sneaking around as a teenager. I swear, if someone threatens to call my Mom…"

"It's me," Arlo called, putting one hand on Jacqueline's shoulder as he sent Caro a jumbled telepathic explanation: *This is Jacqueline—human—visiting from the next town over—shifter kids—pack—dinner?*

She frowned at him, which was no surprise given the pack of nonsense he'd just vomited at her, then shook her head. "I'm Caro," she said, holding out a floury hand. "Nice to meet you…"

"Jacqueline." Jacqueline shook Caro's hand, either not noticing or not caring that it was covered in flour.

Caro's eyes flicked to Arlo's. *She's human?*

*She's…*

*Ah.* Caro's jaw set and then she shrugged. *Figures.*

Arlo's stomach stopped twisting. If Caro was happy to welcome in a human with no connection to Hideaway Cove, then maybe…

Caro jerked her head over her shoulder. "Come on in." She snaked a grin at Arlo that made her scar pull. "Your usual spot's free, but I'm guessing you might be after a table tonight?"

*Damn it, Caro,* Arlo growled. *I'm trying to…*

His telepathic voice faded away. What was he trying to do? Put his best foot forward? Prove to Jacqueline there was more to him than just growliness and terrible ideas?

What if there wasn't?

Caro's expression softened. *You worry too much, sea dog.* "Through here," she said out loud, pointing to the door at the other end of the kitchen. "Take any table you like."

*You say that like there's nothing to worry about,* Arlo grumbled, and Caro snorted.

*You're taking her to dinner. Believe me, the way things work around here, that's better than a good start. It's more than—*

Her voice cut off suddenly and she grabbed a passing kitchen hand. "Guts, what the hell're you doing with those desserts? They're—they're melting already!"

Guts looked bewildered as Caro snatched the tray off him and marched off. *What? But those were...* He caught Arlo's eye. *Dumplings. Not desserts...*

Arlo had never seen Caro so off-kilter. *Everything all right?* he sent across the room to her.

She didn't look back. *Enjoy your date with your lady friend, sea dog.*

Arlo's eyebrows drew together as he held the door for Jacqueline. *That didn't sound convincing. I'll ask Tess to talk to her.*

The restaurant wasn't busy, this early in the evening. A few locals were nursing beers or coffees at the shared main table, and a ginger cat was lying stretched out on one of the windowsills. Arlo nodded to him and got a sharp-toothed yawn in reply.

"Is that...?" Jacqueline whispered.

"Tom Hanson. He's been lying there since before I left on the boat, days ago."

Tom's mouth snapped shut. *I'm on bed rest!* he replied, indignant but not so much that he moved any other muscles. *Doctor's orders.*

"He's Marjorie Hanson's grandson, here on break from college," Arlo explained. "Plenty of shifters come here for vacations, just to spend some time in their animal form without worrying about getting caught shift-ing."

"Oh." Jacqueline's mouth tightened. "I hope no one's worried about me being here. I don't want to make anyone feel as though they're not safe."

"Don't worry," one of the men at the beer-and-coffee table, Carlos, called over. Carlos was the father of the three dolphin shifters Arlo had pointed out to Jacqueline earlier. He was sitting with another local, Dave Oxley.

Arlo relaxed. Carlos was—he hesitated to say "one of the good ones", but he had only moved to Hideaway with his kids a decade or so back. He wasn't one of the old guard like Ma and Pa.

"Harrison already sent around the message," Carlos explained. He raised one hand and counted off his fingers, slightly slowly, as though he was hunting for each number through the bottom of his glass. "One. Lady from Dunston. Two. Came along with those three seal kids. Three…"

"Three, be nice," Dave said, thwacking him gently on the back of the head. "Though that last one was from Harrison's girl." He gave Jacqueline a friendly nod. "They seem like good kids. Be good to have someone who can give your lot a run for their money, eh, Carlos?"

"Pff. Ain't no one can beat my Ana." Carlos Ramirez raised his glass to Jacqueline. "Welcome to Hideaway, miss. And damn, Arlo! Can't wait for the Sweets to hear about this. Tell me you're going to sell tickets to—"

"That's enough of that." Caro swept in from the kitchen, armed with a picnic basket brimming with Tupperware containers. "Here's your order, Carlos. You'd better get it home before your kids start eating the furniture."

Dave gulped the rest of his coffee and bundled the basket under one arm. "I'll look after him, Caro," he said, and cuffed Carlos to his feet. "Come on, man, don't let your kids see you like this."

"It was one beer…" Carlos complained, and blinked. "*Half* of one beer."

"Yeah, and you've got the tolerance of an underweight bee," Dave grumbled good-naturedly, slinging Carlos' arm over his shoulder. "Come on…"

Beside Arlo, Jacqueline stiffened. He put one arm around her. "What's wrong?"

"Oh, it's just… that's something my ex used to say." Jacqueline shook herself. "Not in the same context, though. I'm sure if I'd gotten myself shamefully tipsy on half a glass of beer he'd have…"

She raised her hands. "You know what? I'm going to make a promise to myself right now. No talking about my ex while I'm on the first date in five years." Her hands dropped. "Or make that ten, because—no, I'm not doing this. I'm enjoying the moment." She took a deep breath. "Maybe I'm still not ready. Or I've left it too long. I should have done some practice… windows… before now."

Despite the anxious edge to her voice, she hadn't pulled away from Arlo's arm. And he didn't want her to.

"I'm glad you didn't," he said, and her hand slipped into his.

"Oh?"

"I'm out of practice, too," he said, his heart hammering. Out of practice? Christ. That was one way of putting it.

Jacqueline smiled. "Good," she said. "Then no teasing if I mess it up."

"Oh my God," she moaned some time later. Arlo's toes curled. "Oh. *God.* Mmmm."

Her eyes were closed. Shivers of ecstasy made her eyelashes flutter.

"This is incredible," she breathed. "*So much cheese.*"

She cracked one eye open and hunted out another crispy cheese dumpling from her bowl.

"I'm really sorry," she said as she lifted the dumpling to her mouth. "But after this, I'm wondering if I should—*mmm*—be asking Caro on a date instead."

Arlo's wolf whined. He cleared his throat to cover it, even though he knew there was no way Jacqueline would be able to hear it.

"Good luck," he said. "Caro's married to this place."

"Damn." Jacqueline sipped broth from her spoon. "No wonder this is the only restaurant in town. Anywhere else would go out of business in a second."

"You know, I worked here for a bit when I first arrived in Hideaway. The couple who took me in wanted to make sure I had a skill to build a career on."

"They sound like good people."

"They… are. They've done a lot for Hideaway. They're my pack," Arlo said, his voice becoming more confident.

"Your pack? Is that another—" Jacqueline cut herself off. "God, I must sound like the nosiest person in the world."

"What's wrong with that?"

"You live in a secret shifter town! Shouldn't you keep your secrets… secret?"

"Bit late for that."

Jacqueline bit her lips over a smile. "I guess."

Arlo put down his spoon and set his elbows on the table. "You saved Tally's life without thinking. You helped those kids get to a place they'll be safe for the rest of their lives. You've every right to ask questions about what their lives will be like." *Because you're my mate. Everything you want, I'll give you.*

Jacqueline bit her lower lip. "All right." She was silent for a moment, and then: "So. Pack. That's a shifter thing? Like a wolf pack?"

"For me, yeah. Since I'm a wolf." Arlo grinned, so fast and sharp he surprised himself, and then he realized it was his wolf grinning through him. *Thrilled to be part of the conversation, buddy?*

*Aroo!*

"A very handsome wolf," Jacqueline said, straight-faced, and Arlo's wolf spun around in delight as the back of his neck burned red-hot.

"Pack is family. The people you'd do anything for. Some shifters, those of us whose animals are meant to live in groups, aren't happy without pack around. Whether that's someone to look after, or be looked after by. Or a mate, which is both."

If his skin wasn't already burning, it would have caught fire at that. Jacqueline's eyebrows drew together.

Arlo's jaw tightened. *Oh God. I shouldn't have said anything. Now she'll—*

Arlo's senses went on high alert. The restaurant was busier now than it had been earlier in the evening. Most of the tables were full. Guts and Caro were constantly back and forth from the kitchen, and she'd even managed to prod Tom into taking people's orders.

It was busy, but noisy. Even shifters would find it hard to pick out a conversation from a neighboring table. And other shifters weren't as sensitive to emotions as he was, thank Christ.

He could tell her. A bit. And later, when they were somewhere a bit more private...

The restaurant door opened, letting in a burst of cool air from outside. Arlo shook himself. Why was this bothering him so much? He should want to tell her. *Need* to tell her. why was he so afraid?

Jacqueline leaned forward. "So... A mate?"

"Arlo?"

Too late, Arlo realized who had walked in the door.

# 15

## JACQUELINE

Jacqueline hadn't seen the woman come in, but it was impossible to miss her now that she was standing right behind Arlo. She was short and curvy, with dark hair tied back in a braided bun and thick-rimmed glasses.

She was staring at Arlo with an expression of grim determination.

"Tess?" Arlo said, turning in his seat. He muttered something under his breath and turned an apologetic look on Jacqueline. "I'm sorry about this. I said I'd talk to her later, but…"

Jacqueline recognized the woman now, although her hair wasn't hidden under a hairnet anymore. "She's your not-niece, right?"

"Foster sister, yeah." Arlo sighed and waved Tess over.

"Hi," Tess said, her determination fluttering slightly at the edges. "You're… Jacqueline?"

"That's me." Jacqueline shook Tess's hand.

"I'm sorry for running off earlier. I thought… I don't know." She wiped her hands on her pants and Jacqueline felt a pang of sympathy. Tess was clearly stressing about something—even if Jacqueline didn't know what.

"Tess, we're a bit busy," Arlo said in an undertone.

"I know, I know you said later, but I've been sitting in the shop worrying all afternoon!" She wrung her hands together. "How long have you known? Did you only bring her now because you knew Grandma and Grandpa would be away? Oh, God, Arlo, why didn't you *say* something?"

"Tess-I-met-her-*yesterday*," Arlo gritted out bullet-fast.

"Oh!" Tess said. And then: "Oh-h-h."

Her eyes skidded slowly across to meet Arlo's. Jacqueline could only guess what they said to each other, in that weird silent telepathy, or mindspeak or whatever it was, but Tess covered her mouth and groaned.

"I am so sorry. I am going to go home, and hide in the pantry, and never speak to anyone ever again," she whispered through her fingers. "Except..." Her eyes narrowed. "Maybe this isn't terrible after all. Maybe this is the kick in the pants I need to put my plan into action."

"Your plan...?" Arlo buried his head in his hands. "I don't want to know, do I." It wasn't a question.

"It was nice to meet you!" Tess said to Jacqueline. She grimaced at Arlo, waved, and hurried away, her horrified panic replaced by determination.

"She seems nice," Jacqueline said as the door slammed behind her. "But what did she mean about you waiting until your parents were away?"

Arlo looked abashed. "Tess thinks I've been hiding you away."

"Seriously? I know I joked about feeling like a teenager again, but..."

"My folks are..." Arlo lifted his head. She couldn't read the expression in his eyes. Half-amused, half-pained, half...

Her heart fluttered.

"Jacqueline, there's something I need to tell you." He paused and winced. "Several somethings. Can we walk outside?"

It was a cool, still night. The wind that had whipped her hair into a knotted frizz earlier had died down.

Jacqueline and Arlo walked arm-in-arm down the promenade.

Whatever Arlo had meant to say, he wasn't saying it.

"So," Jacqueline said, to break the silence. "Your folks?"

"They'd be… surprised I was with a non-shifter." Arlo's voice was gruff. "But they'll get over it."

He sounded strangely serious. "I guess opportunities to date humans are pretty thin on the ground here in Hideaway," Jacqueline said, lightly.

"I've never dated. A lot of shifters don't, unless…"

Jacqueline's heart thudded. *Unless what? This is just a fling, right? Just a crazy, weekend, casual…*

*…Meet his friends, see his workplace, personal tour of his hometown…*

*Fling?*

She swallowed. If this was something that *wasn't* a fling, then there were things she'd have to tell him. Awful things. Like the fact she couldn't have children.

The lump in her throat grew.

She already felt so comfortable around Arlo. Like they fit together. Even his weird date, taking her climbing around the hills behind the town, had unlocked a part of her she'd almost forgotten about, stuck in suburban Dunston. Standing there looking over the town and the sea, panting for breath with the wind in her hair, she'd felt… free.

*Because I am free. No more mortgage, no more Derek. I'm free to do whatever I want and what I want is—*

"Jacqueline? Is everything all right?"

Arlo's voice was concerned. Jacqueline pulled herself together.

"I…" She searched his eyes. *Is everything all right? It is, isn't it?* "This weekend's been so strange, and I…"

*Cocktails. Stupid dresses and high heels. The chance to be sexy again, to find out who I am now. That was the plan. That's what this weekend was about, wasn't it?*

She took a deep breath.

*I know what I want.*

She slid one hand up Arlo's chest, slowly, and the thud of his heartbeat against her palm seemed to echo in her ears. She leaned closer to him and stood on her toes. Arlo's eyes were like deep pools reflecting the night sky. His lips were an inch from hers—less—

Arlo pulled her close and kissed her. His lips were soft, gentle against hers and then harder as she clenched her fist in his shirt. She wound her other hand up over his shoulder, holding herself up against him. Not wanting to ever let him go.

She made a small noise of disappointment as Arlo's lips left hers, and his eyes went dark with lust.

*Oh God.*

Desire surged through her, so intense her knees went weak. And from the expression in Arlo's eyes…

She got the feeling that whatever he'd been about to say, it could wait.

Jacqueline licked her lips. "You know," she said, her voice hoarse, "I never booked that bed-and-breakfast. I don't have anywhere to stay tonight."

Arlo's fingers tightened around her waist. "That's where you're wrong," he growled.

Jacqueline felt so giddy as they walked back to the *Hometide*, she was half-worried she'd walk straight off the wharf into the sea. She wasn't entirely convinced that if she looked down, she'd see her feet touching the ground.

Arlo handed her onto the boat and slipped the tie rope off its mooring. The *Hometide* eased through the waves. Arlo sat by the rudder and Jacqueline curled into his side, winding her fingers through his.

When Hideaway Cove was a half-moon of lights lying on the horizon, he dropped the anchor and turned to her.

"Jacqueline," he murmured. "I want—ever since I first saw you…"

He pulled her close, kissing her with a growl that made her insides quiver. Jacqueline kissed her back, gasping as he slid one hand up towards her breast… and stopped.

"Hmm?" Jacqueline mumbled against his lips. "What's wrong?"

"Nothing's wrong." Arlo sounded out of breath. "I just…"

His hand smoothed down her side, slow and sensual.

"I don't want to rush," he said. "I want to know what feels good to you. I want to learn everything about your body, every…" He took a tense breath.

Jacqueline ran her fingers through his hair as his eyes dropped. "What is it?"

"I want to do this right. For you. I haven't…" A brief half-smile flickered across his features. "I haven't made a stained glass window before," he admitted.

*Does he mean what I think he means?*

"What? But…" *That's ridiculous,* Jacqueline stopped herself from saying, to this strong, careful man who'd let himself be so vulnerable in front of her. "I assumed… I mean, you built a *boat*… wait, this metaphor is getting out of control." She sucked in her breath.

"I did build a boat," Arlo agreed. "I built a whole life here. It didn't leave much time for… other arts and crafts."

His voice was still rough, almost ashamed, but the corner of his mouth curved in a tentative, hopeful smile. Jacqueline touched the dimple that formed in his cheek.

"I want to learn about your body," she whispered, trailing her fingertips down his cheek and over his jaw. "I don't care what you've done, or haven't done. It's been so long I feel like I've forgotten it all anyway."

She kissed him until his breathing hitched and then murmured against his lips: "I want to explore it all with you for the first time."

Arlo groaned. "God, yes."

He stood up, lifting her in his arms. Jacqueline wrapped her legs around his waist and heat raced through her. "Downstairs?" she gasped. He nodded.

It was a tight fit, but Arlo maneuvered them both down the ladder without so much as brushing her head against the ceiling. He put her down so gently Jacqueline still felt as though she was floating feet above the floor.

This wasn't her first time. She'd only ever been with Derek, but it wasn't as though they'd had a dead bedroom. They'd had clumsy figuring-it-out sex when they first got together, exhausted wedding-day sex and increasingly good honeymoon sex, lazy sleep-in sex and crazy late-night sex and…

…Rigorously scheduled sex, increasingly clinical sex, sex where she'd found herself thinking a turkey baster would be more efficient or at least more pleasant…

But that was then. And this was now, and now she was with Arlo, and sex could be something thrilling and wonderful again, and her skin was singing with the need to be touched.

And to touch.

Arlo was watching her, still tentative. She stepped forward and slid her hands under his shirt. His abs were smooth and hard under her fingertips, his skin so hot she gasped.

He shivered under her touch. "Too slow?" she asked.

"Don't stop."

Jacqueline looked up at him through her lashes. She smiled and kept exploring.

Arlo had a dark treasure trail that disappeared behind his belt. She ignored it—for now—and moved her hands further up. When she got to his chest, she couldn't hold back from pressing her whole palms against his pecs and sighing.

"God, Jacqueline," Arlo gasped. She pushed his shirt up further, pulling it off over his head and ran her hands over his shoulders, down his back, everywhere she could reach.

"You're incredible," she murmured, kissing his collarbone and dipping her head to lay more kisses down his chest. "I can't stop touching you."

He was so hot under her hands, firm and strong and unbelievably, inconceivably *real*. This was what she'd wanted for so long. What she'd been scrimping and saving for. Taking life by the horns.

*Or, in this case…*

The sight of Arlo's treasure trail had sparked an idea in her head. She let her hands drift down until they reached his belt buckle.

"I want to do something for you," she murmured, and got on her knees.

"You…" Arlo gasped and licked his lips. "I've never—you don't have to if you don't want…"

"I want to. So much. Do you?" If he'd never been with anyone before…

Jacqueline's skin warmed. She'd never thought *she* would be the one with more knowledge about, well, anything.

"Yes." Arlo's voice was hoarse.

Jacqueline undid his belt buckle slowly, then his flies, and eased his pants down over his hips. Then his boxers. *Like unwrapping a present,* she thought, *and…. Oh, lord…*

Arlo's treasure trail and deep V led down to a cock that made her suddenly ache inside. She wanted him inside her, filling her deep until she couldn't control herself any more. She wanted to touch it, touch *him*. She'd barely touched her wine at the restaurant but she was drunk with joy at finally escaping the paralyzed shell of her life and daring to want something more.

She stroked Arlo's cock, running her fingers along the thick shaft and brushing her lips against its head. He gasped and she turned the brush into a kiss, tasting him, glorying in every shivering breath her mouth and tongue ripped from his body.

She took him in deeper and Arlo moaned so deep she could feel it in her bones. He began to tremble and she pulled back, gazing up at him with her lips just touching his very tip.

He collapsed to his knees in front of her and kissed her, his teeth grazing her hot lips. "Let me do that to you," he begged.

Jacqueline lay back on the bed. There was hardly enough room for Arlo to hold himself above her. He kissed his way down her body, tentative, pausing after he kissed each new part of her to see her reaction. When she gasped out loud as his tongue flicked over her nipple he did it again, harder, until she felt as though he'd barely need to look at her clit for her to come.

He slowed down as he reached her stomach, tantalizingly gentle. He laid a trail of kisses down the crease of her hip and looked up at her.

Jacqueline could hardly breath. The sight of him between her thighs, eyes hot, mouth hotter, almost sent her over the edge.

"Yes," she whispered.

He lowered his head and kissed her.

Sensation flooded out from Jacqueline's clit to fill her whole body and then poured back, intensifying, until each kiss, each lap of his tongue, sent fire through her veins. Pleasure pooled inside her.

"W-wait," she gasped, and Arlo lifted his head. "I want you now. I want to come with you inside me."

He moved up on top of her, his body sliding against hers, his cock bumping against her thigh. His eyes were dark with desire.

"How do you want me to—" he began, and Jacqueline gently pushed him on his side, so they were lying together. She draped one leg over his hip and slowly guided him to her entrance.

"Like this," she whispered.

He pushed into her and she let out a shaking gasp. Arlo was gentle, careful, as though he was worried he might break her, and the expression on his face was unguarded wonder.

She rolled her hips, drawing him deeper and he moaned. Every movement, every sound, made her want him more.

He slid one hand down to her ass and used his grip to anchor her as he thrust in, making her gasp and moan as pleasure swamped her conscious thoughts. He went deeper and deeper, hitting her g-spot with each thrust.

"Oh God," Arlo gasped, and she couldn't stop her body from responding.

Her whole body clenched, ecstasy shuddering through her again and again. Arlo moaned and rolled on top of her. When he thrust again he went even deeper, filling her until she felt like she would explode. Her orgasm was still rolling through her. She cried out as he thrust into her again. Slowly. In control.

Her eyes fluttered open. Arlo gazed down at her, his expression enough to make her wrap her legs more tightly around him and pull him into her again. He groaned, meeting her intensity with her own need, and held her close against himself as he came.

He didn't let her go afterwards, and Jacqueline didn't want him to. She kept her arms around him, feeling the thud of his heartbeat, the ragged pants as he caught his breath. As they both did, their bodies still completely entwined.

"Are you all right?" Arlo asked.

Jacqueline was still panting. She laughed, breathless. "Am I—? Oh, God, Arlo. That was incredible." She pressed her cheek against him. "Am I all right. *Really.*"

He rolled off her, still holding her so they ended up tangled together side by side. "I wanted to be sure. I don't trust myself to pick things up, all the time."

His eyes were dancing. He was teasing her. Jacqueline tsk'ed.

"Well you don't need to worry about that." She snuggled close against him. "That was everything I've been wanting for a long, long time."

He was stroking her back; at her words, he paused. "It's all I've wanted," he murmured.

The first thing Jacqueline noticed as she woke up was warmth. Specifically, the solid, reassuring warmth of Arlo's body against her. It was so exactly what she wanted that for a moment she was sure she was in a dream.

She opened her eyes.

*Not a dream*, she thought, and it was the happiest thought she'd had in a long time.

Arlo was stretched out on his back and she was tucked against him, her head on his shoulder and one arm curled up on his chest. Her fingers twitched before the conscious thought that she wanted to stroke his golden skin even reached her brain, and she forced them to be still. Arlo was still asleep and she wanted to savor this moment as long as possible, before…

*Before he wakes up and this perfect moment falls to pieces.*

She swallowed a sigh. When she'd imagined her first post-divorce hookup, it sure as hell hadn't been with a ruggedly handsome sailor who could turn into a wolf. She'd envisaged nights on the town, ridiculous cocktails and short glitzy dresses, not a long evening sinking into his eyes over the best meal she'd ever eaten and a slow, sensuous seduction while the sea rocked under them.

Jacqueline shivered as she remembered the way he'd touched her. Tenderly, reverently, as though he was afraid she'd dissolve into mist.

A lump formed in her throat. No, it wasn't what she'd imagined at all. And now…

Arlo's breathing changed. His eyelids fluttered and Jacqueline blinked, driving back the sudden darkness at the edge of her mind.

"Good morning," she whispered.

Arlo's eyes opened. Jacqueline shivered again as he looked at her, the touch of his gaze like slipping into a warm bath.

"You're still here," he murmured, sliding one hand along her waist. Jacqueline laughed.

"What was I going to do, swim away?"

"I mean…" Arlo's eyebrows drew together. "You're here. You're real. The last two days weren't a dream."

Jacqueline's stomach lurched. Two days? Was that all? And she was already—

Arlo pushed himself up on his elbows. "Jacqueline? Are you all right?"

Damn it. Whatever she was feeling, and she wasn't even sure herself what that was, must have shown on her face. She reached for his shoulder and pulled herself to sit up beside him.

How could she explain how quickly she was falling for him, without sounding like a complete psycho?

"It's nothing. Just—"

Arlo suddenly doubled over. He clutched at his head with a strangled shout of pain.

"What's wrong?" Jacqueline wrapped one arm around his shoulder to support him. His muscles were so tense it was like holding onto a knotted tree trunk. "Arlo, what is it?"

"Head," he managed to grunt. "Voices."

"The kids?" Terror knotted in Jacqueline's stomach.

Arlo nodded and winced in pain again.

"We have to get to them." Jacqueline scrambled out of bed and grabbed her clothes from the floor. She pulled them on quickly.

Arlo was following suit, his face taut with pain. He swayed sideways, almost hitting his head on the ladder, and Jacqueline pulled him back to his feet. She wrapped both arms around his waist and held him steady, staring into his eyes.

He let his forehead rest against hers. This close she could tell he was actually trembling.

"Come on," she whispered, her breath shaking. "Let's go get them."

"I can't—" Arlo grimaced, squeezing his eyes tight. "It hurts too much. I can hardly see."

"I'll do the seeing for both of us. You make the boat move, and I'll tell you where to go." Jacqueline put her hands either side of his head. "Trust me. We can do this together."

"I trust you." The words came out on a breath so heavy Jacqueline was only half-sure what he'd said. She pressed her lips against his and felt him shiver.

"Then let's go."

The sun was still low, but Arlo swore under his breath as he climbed up on deck. He made his way to the skipper's seat with one arm up over his eyes. Jacqueline followed on his heels although it was clear he knew where he was going by memory alone.

Arlo collapsed on the seat. "Anchor," he growled, and started to stand up again. Jacqueline put a hand on his chest.

"I'll handle it," she said.

He grasped her hand and held it tight for a moment before letting go. "Thank you," he said, his voice ragged. "It's never been this bad before."

Their eyes met, and a jagged moment of shared realization thundered between them. Jacqueline gulped. *If it's never been this bad before—what's happened?*

Arlo unfurled the sails by feel and they were off the moment the anchor was out of the water. With Jacqueline directing him, Arlo sailed for the tiny beach at the base of the cliff with the lighthouse on top of it.

"I've got Harrison," he groaned, motioning to his temple. "Here. They'll meet us on the beach."

They didn't get that far.

Jacqueline had just dropped anchor. Arlo was hauling on the dinghy's tow rope to bring it close enough to board. An eagle's screech cut through the air and Jacqueline whipped her head up to see something that was definitely not an eagle leap off the top of the cliff.

"Is that a…" she began, grabbing Arlo's arm.

He didn't need to look up. "Harrison," he said. "And Tally. It's her voice."

"Is she hurt?" Jacqueline's throat went tight.

"She's—"

The not-an-eagle unfurled its wings mid-leap. Jacqueline gasped. It was a—she racked her memory for the word. Mandrake? Hippogriff?

*Griffin,* she thought as it—he—Harrison landed on the deck. The ship rocked under his weight, but Arlo and Jacqueline were already racing towards him.

"Do you have her?"

"What's wrong? What happened?"

"Is she—"

Harrison was holding Tally in his fore claws. She was in her seal shape, wriggling and making a howling, whining noise that made Jacqueline's heart rate rocket.

Jacqueline reached forward and swept her up at the same time Arlo did. They held her sandwiched between them, their arms tangled around her and each other.

"What is it, baby?" Jacqueline asked desperately. "What's wrong?" She looked up at Arlo, whose expression was stricken. "Can you talk to her? Hear her?"

"She…" Arlo's face relaxed and he leaned forward, resting his forehead against hers. Nestled between them, Tally fell silent. "She's fine. She was lonely, and scared. But she's all right now."

Tally snuffled against Jacqueline's neck. A second later, she turned back into a baby girl, her pale eyes damp with tears.

"Is everything okay now, honey?" Jacqueline ducked her head to look into Tally's face.

"Es," whispered Tally, wrapping her arms around Jacqueline's neck.

Jacqueline caught Arlo's eyes on her and smile. "Is your head feeling better?"

Arlo touched his temple gingerly. "Better. Still tender."

"I'm glad." She looked back down at Tally. "So much fuss just because you were lonely? Weren't your brother and sister here with you?"

Jacqueline looked towards shore. They were close enough that she could make out three figures on the beach: Kenna, Dylan and Lainie.

"Can you tell if they're all right? If Tally's this upset over something—"

Arlo cocked his head. "They're mostly worried about her. I'm telling them she's fine."

There was a whoosh of air as Harrison shifted. He marched over to them, frowning.

"What's wrong with your head, Arlo?"

"You didn't feel it?" Arlo looked at Harrison with an expression of surprise that turned into a wince as he swung his head around. "She was so loud, I could hardly hear myself think. And she was so lonely it… hurt. A lot."

"She was loud, sure. But you're the only one with a migraine." Harrison frowned. "Is everything all right, bud?"

Arlo rubbed his forehead. He glanced at Jacqueline, then away, then back at her, as though he couldn't keep his eyes away. "Better than all right," he said, his voice soft.

Warmth flooded through Jacqueline, turning into a smile as Tally chortled against her neck. Jacqueline squeezed her and kissed the top of her head.

"Well, I'm glad it wasn't anything serious. We'd better get back to shore and let the others know." Harrison rolled his shoulders back. "I could fly you over, or—"

"We'll row in," Arlo interrupted, then paused to check with Jacqueline.

She nodded happily. After the scare with Tally, she wasn't sure she could manage something as exciting as flying on a griffin's back—and a short trip in the rowboat might be the last chance she had to salvage a scrap of time with Arlo, before they got back into the bustle of real life.

Tally giggled and Arlo rocked back slightly, blinking.

"She wants to fly," he explained to Jacqueline as Tally shifted back into her seal form and started wriggling. "Harrison, you mind?"

"So long as she doesn't start yelling again," Harrison said gallantly, and tucked Tally under one arm. "Good practice, anyway, right?"

He shifted and leaped into the air in one smooth movement. Jacqueline leaned closer to Arlo.

"I'm assuming that noise she's making is happy?"

"Very." Arlo gazed into her eyes and for a moment, Jacqueline forgot what she'd been about to say. "Jacqueline…"

"Hmm?"

Somehow, their hands found each other's. Jacqueline tangled her fingers around his.

"There's something I want to talk to you about and this might be the only chance we have," he said. "I should have said it earlier, but last night—and now with Tally—I've let every chance slip me by. I won't let that happen again."

Jacqueline raised her eyebrows. "Sounds serious," she said as her heart started beating so hard she was worried Arlo might be able to hear it.

Arlo sighed. "I wanted to tell you this on the *Hometide*. At my workshop. Every minute since I met you. But I…" He shook his head. "I know you've been hurt before."

"I… yes," Jacqueline said slowly. "You could say that."

"You were betrayed by the man who pledged to care for you for the rest of both your lives."

*Only because I betrayed him first. Because I couldn't give him the one thing he wanted most from our marriage.*

She pushed the treacherous thought away but even with it gone, Jacqueline's chest tightened around her hammering heart. Another joke rose to her lips and she bit it back.

"I don't regret anything that happened last night," she said, instead of the jokey brush-off that had bubbled up at first. Her voice wobbled.

Arlo's eyes sharpened with concern. "That's not—I don't, either," he said, his voice gravelly. His hands tightened around hers. "I could never regret any time spent with you."

*Any time?* Jacqueline's treacherous mind took the words and spun them out into whole novels. *Any time—meaning more time than just now? More time than just this weekend? Does he want to see me again? Does he want—*

Jacqueline put a lid on her thoughts and pushed it down tight.

*Stop over thinking it. Just listen to him.*

Arlo took a deep breath. "Last night, you asked me about mates. I didn't answer you."

Jacqueline could see how much effort it was taking him to get the words out, and her heart was so full of sympathy that it took her another moment to realize what he was saying.

"Yes," she said slowly. "I remember."

The lid was coming off her pot of ridiculous thoughts and emotions. She held onto it, just for now, just in case this wasn't going where all those stupid thoughts thought it was going.

"You don't have to say anything now," Arlo said urgently. "I know it's different for humans. Don't feel like you need to answer, or say you feel the same, or—"

"It would help if I knew what it is I'm meant to be having these feelings about," Jacqueline said gently.

"Right." Arlo bowed his head. When he looked up, his expression was more vulnerable than Jacqueline had ever seen before. "Every shifter has a soulmate. One person, somewhere in the world, who's the other half of their heart. Shifters know who their mate is from the moment they first set eyes on them. And I knew from the moment I first set eyes on you. Every second since then has made me more sure. You're my mate."

Jacqueline swallowed. Suddenly, her eyes were swimming, and the only words she could find were a choked: "You're sure?"

"I am. God, Jacqueline, I am. But you don't have to be. I know it's too sudden, you have your own things going on." She saw Arlo grimace through the shimmer of tears. "I should have told you earlier. This is the wrong time, the wrong place, I—"

"Will you shut up for one second!" Jacqueline pulled her hands away from his and threw them around his shoulders. He was warm and solid and she buried her face in his chest, her lungs heaving. "These are happy tears."

"Oh." Arlo dropped his head to rest on hers and wrapped his arms around her.

Jacqueline smiled. "Is that a good oh?"

Arlo let out a sigh that seemed to shake his bones. "God, yes."

"Good." Jacqueline sniffled. "And don't worry. I always cry when I'm too happy and this is… so much, all at once."

"Too much?" Arlo stiffened. "I meant what I said. Anything you need, time, space, even if—" He took a sharp breath. "If you don't feel the same way…"

*If I don't feel like what? Like I knew I'd met my soulmate the moment he pulled me out of the sea?*

Jacqueline took a slow breath, her face still buried in Arlo's shirt. He smelled like salt and sweat, and she never wanted to breathe in anything else ever again.

"When I first saw you," she said, "don't laugh—I didn't see you at all. I was out of my mind with fear. I thought I'd gone. I'd just seen kids turn into animals and I jumped in the water, almost got myself killed, trying to save something I was sure shouldn't even exist."

"Why would I laugh at that?"

"Because as soon as you grabbed me, I wasn't scared anymore." She hadn't even thought about it at the time. But it was true. As soon as she'd felt Arlo's touch, some deep part of her had known she was safe. "I wasn't scared of drowning. I wasn't scared I'd gone mad and started seeing things. I wasn't even scared to harangue you until you let me go with you!"

"I didn't need much haranguing," Arlo pointed out.

"I didn't think there could be any reason you'd let me come with you. And I desperately wanted to. I wanted it more than anything I've ever wanted in my life." She swallowed. "*That* scared me. Wanting something that much."

*Wanting something, and knowing that wanting something with that much of my being is a surefire way to make sure the universe never gives it to me.*

"And now?"

Jacqueline stood on her tiptoes until she could kiss him. "Now I know why I want to stick around so badly."

*We're meant to be together. Soulmates.*

*He's been here all this time. Waiting for me.*

She blinked. Her eyelashes were still wet, and she tried to draw back enough to wipe her eyes, but Arlo held her close.

"If you're staying, then I'm not letting go of you just yet."

Jacqueline dropped down off her tiptoes and laughed into his shirt. "Fine. Have it your way."

She let herself melt against him, every curve of her body contouring to his muscular form. Arlo groaned deep in his throat.

"What happens next?" Jacqueline asked. "I mean, I can feel what *you* want to happen next…"

Arlo swore under his breath and maneuvered his lower half away from her. Jacqueline laughed and pressed herself up close to him again.

"I don't know," Arlo said, sounding honestly baffled. "I didn't think this would go so easy."

"With a human?"

"With anyone." Arlo's voice was rueful. "My life's been one wrong turn after another. Hideaway Cove was the first good decision I made, and part of me thought that was it, I'd used up my quota. But you… you're more than I ever dreamed of."

"Maybe we're both having a fresh start," Jacqueline suggested.

"I like that. As for what happens next, I'd suggest we sail off into the sunset," Arlo said, one hand stroking up Jacqueline's back to cup the back of her head, "but it's the wrong time of day for that."

Jacqueline bit her lip. A whole day of sailing with Arlo, watching the sun travel across the sky, the slow build of sensuous anticipation as they found a place to weigh anchor for the night and go to bed…

Arlo groaned. "We have an audience," he whispered in Jacqueline's ear.

"Oh." Jacqueline twisted to look past him, to the beach. "So much for sailing off into the sunset. Tally'd probably kick up another fuss if we were gone that long, anyway, and I don't want you struck down by another migraine just when you got over that one."

Jacqueline brushed the backs of her fingers over Arlo's temple. She'd meant it light-heartedly, but he frowned.

"I don't know what it is. Harrison isn't as badly affected."

"Maybe he just needs a longer exposure. You said you had her banging on your skull all day Friday."

"True…" His eyes caught hers, warm and tender. "You care about them."

"Of course I do! How could I not? I don't think I'll feel like I've done my job here until they're settled. And I'm glad the Sweets are going to look after them until we track Eric down." She slipped her arms around his waist. "You say they half-raised you and given how you turned out, they must know what they're doing."

"Right." Arlo's jaw tightened. "Yes."

He pulled her close again, his arms strong around her. Jacqueline sighed happily. Even just being held by Arlo made her feel safe. Grounded, somehow, even though they were on the water.

For the first time in a long time and despite all the magic, and dragons who messed with electricity, and seal shifters who gave people psychic headaches, Jacqueline felt as though she'd finally found a piece of the world where she fit perfectly into place.

# 16

# ARLO

Jacqueline was so obviously happy as Arlo rowed them both to the beach that he couldn't tell her what was weighing on his mind.

The Sweets.

Dorothy and Alan Sweets had taken care of him when he washed up in Hideaway a hopeless, helpless teenager, that was true. But their ironclad protectiveness for shifters was matched by an equal lack of trust for humans. He had to warn Jacqueline that things might get tense when she met them and he told them who she was.

*Later*, he promised. *When we're not around everyone. When she's had a chance to get to grips with… everything else.*

The Sweets were away for the weekend. He had time.

He helped Jacqueline out of the rowboat and shot Harrison an accusing glare over his shoulder. The kids' excited anticipation was so intense he could almost see it.

"Don't just stand there like you don't know what's up," he growled.

Lainie laughed and clapped her hands together. "No, you don't get off that easily! We want to hear you say it."

"You all already know?" Jacqueline leaned against Arlo as she got her footing on the soft sand.

Dylan was jumping on the spot. Tally was standing next to him, in human form, and every time he jumped she bobbed up and down in imitation. Even Kenna was failing to hide an ear-to-ear grin.

"How is anyone meant to keep any secrets around here?" Jacqueline asked, laughing.

Arlo's chest constricted. Luckily, Harrison answered for him.

"If you want to keep something like this a secret, you need to be a bit subtler about it than Arlo here. Even the kids picked it up. Right, Kenna?"

A prickle of uncertainty zipped off Kenna, but she caught it so quickly Arlo wasn't sure if he'd imagined it.

"Yeah," she said out loud, shrugging. "It was pretty obvious. He looked like he'd been smacked in the face with a fish."

"If that's not romantic, then what is," deadpanned Lainie. She nodded at Arlo. "Come on. No getting off the hook."

Arlo took a deep breath that felt like it aired out his entire soul.

"Lainie, Harrison—kids…" he began, and found himself grinning so wide he could barely get the words out. "This is my mate. Jacqueline March."

"And this," Jacqueline echoed him, wrapping one arm around his waist. "is mine. Arlo Hammond."

Her eyes sparkled brighter than the sun on the waves.

"Jacqueline March, from that little town across the hill? How lovely. I believe I know your colleague, Deirdre," announced a thin, educated voice from the shadows in the tunnel that led up to the top of Lighthouse Hill.

Arlo's shoulders tensed. He knew that voice better than the back of his hand.

"Well, Arlo? Do introduce us. I might have heard of Jacqueline but I don't believe we've actually met."

Ma Sweets stepped out of the shadows. She was wearing her driving outfit, a neat aubergine skirt suit with a lilac scarf over her perfectly coifed hair. Her husband, Alan, wandered out behind her, looking as usual one good yawn away from falling asleep on his feet.

Arlo cleared his throat. "Jacqueline," he said, trying not to show how much he was panicking, "these are my foster parents, Dorothy and Alan Sweets."

*She's human,* he added, speaking directly to the two alligator shifters, *and she's my mate. I won't have you say anything against her.*

*Dear, why would I say anything like that?* Ma Sweets replied, and the skin on the back of Arlo's neck prickled.

Lainie set the table. Rather, it looked as though she'd been halfway through setting the breakfast table when Tally woke up and started crying. She put out an extra two places, reluctance in every line of her body.

"So you know Deirdre?" Jacqueline said, sounding cheerful.

"Through bridge." Ma Sweets inclined her head. "Which is why we were absent this weekend. It is *such* a good way to keep abreast of what's happening in the neighborhood. But of course we left the tournament as soon as Sharon called us with the news."

Sharon Warbol was a plover shifter, and one of Ma Sweets' oldest friends.

"Why the rush?" Arlo asked.

Ma Sweets opened her eyes wide. "To meet the children, of course! And it will do Deirdre good to win a tournament for once, poor dear." She smiled at the kids and they shuffled their feet.

"Food's up," Lainie announced, sweeping between Ma Sweet and the kids. "Hope you all like pancakes."

The atmosphere lightened as they all dug into the food. Ma Sweets managed to maneuver herself into sitting next to Jacqueline, but refrained from saying anything rude about humans, even when Kenna retold the story about how they'd had to run away from their human foster home.

"Well." Ma Sweets winked at Kenna conspiratorially. "What a time you've all had! But never to worry. Pa and I are here now, and we'll make sure you never have to do anything like that again."

Kenna frowned. "But—"

"Sharon didn't tell you?" Arlo cut in smoothly. His wolf's coat was prickling with that sense of wrongness again. "They didn't do it all on their own. They don't need a foster home, just somewhere to rest up until their uncle Eric gets here."

Dylan wriggled in his seat and Arlo knew what was coming. He shot a warning at Kenna before she told Dylan to shut up and her mouth snapped shut in a surprised scowl.

"What's up, Dylan?"

"He's not *really* our uncle…"

Arlo rubbed his forehead. Jacqueline leaned forward. "Who is he, then?"

"He's just… another shifter… who found us, and said he'd look after us, and take us somewhere safe…"

*Until he abandoned you.* Arlo gritted his teeth.

"But he *is* responsible for you, isn't he, my dear? He's your pack leader," said Ma Sweets, nodding.

"Y-yes?" Dylan's answer sounded more like a question. This time, Arlo wasn't fast enough to stop Kenna from kicking him under the table. "I mean…"

"What do you mean, pack leader?" Jacqueline said, frowning. "If he's not related to you, I'm afraid I'm going to have some trouble explaining to my boss how you all ran away and ended up here."

Her eyes met Arlo's and he could imagine what she was stopping herself from saying: that it would be even more difficult to convince the county to let the kids stay.

"But that's no problem at all, my dear!" Ma Sweets trilled.

"But he'll need to be registered as a foster parent. And—" Jacqueline's expression tightened. "That's *hard*, there are a lot of hoops to jump through…"

"Oh, *paperwork*." Dorothy Sweets waved the idea away with a dismissive gesture. "Required to keep the county off our backs, yes, but we all know it's not *really* important." She tapped the back of Jacqueline's hand with one pointed fingertip. "*Pack*. That's all that really matters. The bonds that all shifters innately understand. Any shifter would move heaven and earth for their pack. And rest assured, we will make *absolutely certain* that this little pack receives all the help they need to settle here in Hideaway Cove."

She tapped Jacqueline's hand again. "Pack is the *one thing*, my dear, that we shifters value above all else. Don't you all agree?"

At the other end of the table, Harrison cleared his throat. "I don't know about that," he said, spearing a steak and exchanging a look with Lainie. "All sounds a bit wolfy to me. What do you think, Lainie? Are we pack?"

"Nest, maybe," Lainie suggested, wrinkling her nose. "Or—i-ree? Ee-rie? However you say that word. Eyrie." She turned to Dorothy and wrinkled her brow. "Would you say alligators have 'packs', Mrs. Sweets? Or is there a better term we should use for you?"

"The word isn't important," Dorothy snapped. "What is important is that, as shifters, we all look out for one another."

"That's right," Arlo interjected. He was starting to feel like the conversation was getting away from him. "And that includes our mates."

He took Jacqueline's hand and she smiled at him.

"Does that make me pack, then?" she asked.

*Yes,* Arlo's wolf yipped. *Pack!*

"Of course," Ma Sweets cooed. "We're all so looking forward to Arlo and you starting a little pack of your own. I know it's what he's wanted ever since he came here."

"That's true," Arlo admitted. He felt as though the sun was rising in his head. Of course. Of *course* that was what had been grating away at the inside of his skull.

Jacqueline dropped her fork.

The hairs on the back of Arlo's neck prickled. Ma Sweets was smiling, but Jacqueline had gone pale. Arlo bent to pick up Jacqueline's fork and brought his head close to hers.

"Are you all right?" he asked.

"Fine." Jacqueline's smile was tight. Arlo straightened, feeling uneasy.

"And when is it you're due?" Ma Sweets asked Lainie.

"A few months away still," Lainie replied, one hand on her bump.

"How lovely. It will be nice to have another griffin shifter around the place. Or a little human, of course." Dorothy shrugged delicately.

"Those aren't the only options," Lainie replied, her fingers white-knuckled on her cutlery.

"Excuse me," Jacqueline blurted out, and stood up so quickly she caught herself on the tablecloth. Arlo rose to help her, but she was already halfway out the door.

"Oh dear," said Dorothy. "I hope she didn't eat something that disagreed with her."

Arlo glanced at her over his shoulder as he headed for the door, and his wolf *snarled*. Ma Sweets' eyebrows shot up, and Pa actually woke up.

*What the hell was that?* Arlo asked his wolf as he raced after Jacqueline. It was still growling low in its throat, as though it expected Ma Sweets to jump out and ambush them.

*More importantly, what's wrong with Jacqueline?*

He found her in the bathroom, standing propped over the sink. Her eyes flew to his in the mirror.

"What's wrong?" Arlo asked, and she looked away. He touched her arm and she pulled away, folding her arms in front of herself.

"I should have known it was too good to be true," she whispered. She heaved a breath and straightened, turning to face him but still not looking him in the eye.

"Please tell me what's wrong. I'll do whatever you need to help." Arlo's heart was breaking. Just a few minutes before, Jacqueline had been laughing with Lainie, and now she looked as though her world was falling apart. "Anything. Just talk to me, please."

"All right." Even Jacqueline's voice was guarded. She squeezed her eyes shut and opened them again, almost but not quite meeting his eyes, as though she was trying to but couldn't quite force herself to. Her gaze settled somewhere over his shoulder. "Is what Dorothy said true? You want a family. A *whole* family. Kids."

*Pack,* Arlo's wolf barked, and before Arlo could stop himself or connect the dots, he said, "Of course. Wolves are pack animals. I *need* a pack."

*And I'd do a better job than this Eric bastard.*

"Oh. Well. Good," Jacqueline blurted, the words falling like bricks. "Good, that's, that's—that's good to know." She broke off suddenly and pressed her hands against her eyes. "*Shit.*"

"Jacqueline, for God's sake, tell me what's going on," Arlo pleaded. His instincts were screaming at him to help her, but he didn't know how. He reached out for her again and she flinched back.

Arlo stepped back and she raised her hands, palms out.

"I'm sorry," she said, her voice scratchy, "I'm sorry, I need to go."

"If you need time, you just need to say," Arlo reminded her. "I know this is a lot to take in—"

Jacqueline made a noise that was half laugh, half sob. "Time isn't going to help. This isn't anything new to take in. It's the same old—it doesn't matter." Her hands dropped. "It doesn't matter."

"Yes, it does." Hesitantly, Jacqueline's unhappiness like a scar twisting in his chest, Arlo stepped forward and put his arms around her. This time, she let him. Her head fell to rest against his chest.

Arlo held her gently. For a few seconds she didn't say anything, just breathed. He could feel her heart hammering through her back. Somewhere in the house, a phone rang.

Then she shook her head and pushed herself away from him. Her eyes were dry, and hard, like windows with the shutters closed over them.

"Arlo, I…"

Someone knocked on the door. "Jacqueline? Sorry to interrupt." It was Lainie, holding a cordless phone. "It's for you."

Arlo was about to say *Now isn't a good time* when Lainie caught his eye. Even he could see the steel in her gaze.

He'd told her he wouldn't hurt Jacqueline. And he had. Somehow. He'd failed at the most important thing a shifter needed to do: protecting his mate.

Shame twisted in his gut as Jacqueline ducked around him and took the phone.

"Hello? Oh, Reg… yes… Of course I've heard, I called you about them, remember? Oh…"

She listened to the phone for a few more minutes and then hung up. She took a deep breath that pulled at Arlo's heart—

—and turned to Lainie.

"That was the sheriff," she said, not even glancing at Arlo. "He's found Eric and has him at the station. Could we go and pick him up now, do you think? I know it's no notice at all but—"

"The kids need him." Lainie nodded.

"And…" Jacqueline's eyes did flick to Arlo now, but the pain in them made it hurt more than her ignoring him had. "I should go too. I think it would be best if I was there to vouch for him with the sheriff."

She held her arms straight at her sides, fists clenched.

Arlo's mouth was dry. "I can drive you—"

"No." Her voice was final. "Please. Let me go. You have to—this is for the best. I promise." Her shoulders slumped. "If you want to know more, ask your mom. I can't talk about it. Not now."

Everything moved too quickly after that. It was like looking underwater, with the light bending his perception of everything. Arlo felt constantly half a second behind everyone else.

Then the Land Rover's engine roared, and the world snapped back into focus.

# 17

# JACQUELINE

"**Y**ou might want to blink at some point."

She'd been listening to nothing but the sound of the Land Rover's tires on the road that it took Jacqueline a moment to notice Harrison was talking to her.

"Blink?"

Harrison was staring straight ahead at the road. "You've been staring into space ever since we got in the car, and that was a few hours ago. Your eyeballs must be dry as a bone."

*At least I'm not crying.* Jacqueline gnawed on the inside of her cheek. She didn't cry, though, not when she was sad. She got like this: eyes hot and dry, face and neck aching with tension. If she fell asleep without forcing herself to relax, she'd wake up with a three-day headache.

It was all so… familiar.

She made herself blink. Her eyes stung, but she still didn't cry.

*I'm still the same person I was before. I was stupid to think that any new life I had, any new relationship, would be any different to before.*

Jacqueline sighed and pressed her hands against her eyes. "Sorry. I haven't exactly been a thrilling conversationalist during this drive."

"Do you want to talk about it?"

"No." *Talking won't help.* She dropped her hands in her lap. "Oh—you'll want to turn here. If you go in on the main road, you'll get caught up going through all the rest of town before we make it to the sheriff's office."

"You know, sometimes I'm happy to live in a town with a single two-lane street, and some days I'm downright ecstatic." Harrison turned into the street Jacqueline had indicated. "It took Lainie a few weeks to really get her head around the idea that there's no 'next block over' in Hideaway. Things are either a ways down the street, or a few hours' drive to the next town."

Jacqueline closed her eyes briefly. *I can see where this is going.* "Next right," she said out loud.

"Thanks." Harrison was quiet for a moment. "You know, some things take time to…"

"Please don't. Whatever you're about to say."

Harrison sighed. "The Sweets are… well. Difficult. But not everyone in Hideaway Cove thinks the way they do. Whatever happens, Lainie and I will have your back. And Arlo will, that goes without saying."

Jacqueline didn't know what to say. Lainie and Harrison didn't know a thing about her, but they were on her side? There was no one in Dunston she could expect that of.

*Because they still think you and Arlo will end up together.* Jacqueline couldn't speak past the lump in her throat. Harrison thought Arlo would have her back?

She had his. That's why she was doing this. Better to cut it off now than leave things to fester.

"Th-thanks," she managed. "Sheriff's just up ahead."

Harrison pulled up outside and Jacqueline almost jumped out of the car, she was so glad to exit the conversation. Movement flickered behind one of the front windows and Jacqueline waved.

*Home again.*

Her whole body felt heavy, but it was easy to plaster on a smile. After all, this was no worse than coming back to work after Derek left, was it? At least no one here knew that she'd failed to make the grade for another man.

The office was quiet; just Deirdre at the desk, with the green reflection in her glasses giving away the fact that she was playing bridge on her computer, not doing work, and the sound of Reg somewhere in the back. Jacqueline interrupted Deirdre long enough to introduce her to Harrison and was about to ask after Eric when Reg burst through the door.

"There she is! You're here for the runaway?" Reg didn't wait for her to answer. He swept past her and pumped Harrison's hand. "And here's the man to complain to, I'm guessing. Harrison Galway? Pleased to meet you. Reg Hunt. So, you're mayor down there these days, eh? How you finding that in, ah…"

Talking to Reg was like having a train bearing down on you. A train that occasionally needed a nudge back onto the tracks.

"Hideaway Cove," Jacqueline muttered.

"Cove! Just the word I was after." Reg snapped his fingers. "And what brings you—ah, yes, of course. Sending the big man to give the truant a hard word, eh?"

He punched Harrison on the arm and then gestured for them both to follow him. Jacqueline almost lost her professional face as he pushed through the door to the cells.

"Boss, don't tell me you've been holding him back here all weekend?"

"Well, you asked us to keep an eye out for him," Reg replied, winking.

"Not to lock him up!"

"Is that really necessary?" Harrison asked Reg.

"Nowhere else for him," Reg announced cheerfully. "It'll do him good, anyway. Scare him back on the straight and narrow."

Anger pulsed in Jacqueline's temples. "Really."

*And now I get to explain to the poor guy why calling me for help got him put in the lockup for the weekend. If I'd only come back sooner, not spent the extra night in Hideaway. I could have gotten this one thing sorted out without hurting anyone.*

*Except then I'd still think I had a chance with Arlo. At least this way, I've gotten that over with.*

Reg was still talking. "You know kids—well, no, maybe you don't. If you had your own, you'd understand. Tough love, that's what they need."

*Hang on—kids?*

"Here we go. The Lost Boy himself. Say hi, kid."

Jacqueline's heart sank as she saw the figure sitting in the cell. "Eric?"

The man raised his head and Jacqueline's heart sank even further. Eric wasn't a grown man, no matter what the Weaver kids had said.

She rounded on Reg. "You've had him here all weekend? He can't be more than sixteen!"

Reg's eyebrows almost shot off his head.

*That must be the closest I've gotten to raising my voice at him all the years I've worked here,* Jacqueline thought. *Well, he deserves it!*

"Nineteen, it says on his license," he replied. "Which is somewhere about."

*And how real is that license?* Jacqueline wondered. From the expression on Harrison's face, he was thinking the same thing.

Harrison cleared his throat and walked over to the cell.

"Hey, Eric. My name's Harrison. I think you and Ms. March here have already spoken."

Eric looked confused. "On the phone," Jacqueline prompted, and relief and anxiety flooded across his face in equal measure. He stood up and hurried to the bars.

"Did you—" he began, and then anxiety won the battle. He fell silent, eyes huge.

"They're all waiting for you in Hideaway Cove," Jacqueline reassured him. "Tally, Dylan and Kenna."

"Oh, thank you. Thank you so much." Eric's head dropped against the bars. "I've been so worried. I only meant to be gone a few nights. I only meant to go for groceries but my car broke down after the storm, and I got a lift to just out of town but I—" His eyes slid sideways past Jacqueline, to where Reg was leaning against a desk. "I guess I didn't explain my problem very well," he muttered.

*God, the poor guy. He's the one who's been holding the kids together for the last few months? I thought he sounded young on the phone, but I thought that was just the panic making his voice squeaky.*

He wasn't another Weaver sibling, that was for sure, with his dark skin and eyes. His hair was cut close to his scalp, which was probably meant to be part of his looking-older-than-he-was act. He had huge, puppy-dog eyes that he kept squinted half-shut as he looked between Harrison and Jacqueline, probably for the same reason.

Eric was tall and loose-limbed, with the sort of lanky build that must have his parents worried how much more growing he had to do. Except he was here, locked up in Reg's drunk tank, and he'd spent the last how-many weeks on the run with three shifter kids.

*Parents probably not in the picture,* Jacqueline determined, wrapping her arms around herself. *There is far too much of that going around.*

"Let's get you out of here and back to Hideaway Cove," Harrison said garrulously.

"But I'm not from—"

"Back *home*," Harrison said, with emphasis, and Jacqueline got the feeling he backed it up with some mindspeak reassurances. Eric's eyes un-squinted again and he nodded vigorously.

"Now, Sheriff…" Harrison began, and within ten minutes had somehow managed to smooth everything over. Somehow even Reg not being able to find a pen or remember his computer password to log Eric in the system turned into him maybe letting the whole thing slide this time after all.

Jacqueline would have been seething—he'd had Eric in lockup overnight and hadn't even *booked* it?—but this was a good result. Eric was going back to Hideaway. All the kids would have a new life there. A fresh start, around people who knew how to look after them.

Gravel crunched under her shoes as she followed Harrison back out to the car. The kids would have a new start. But none of the plans Lainie, Harrison and Arlo had made to house them would work. Not with a sixteen-year-old Eric. Hideaway Cove was strange, but somehow Jacqueline knew it wouldn't be letting-kids-live-on-their-own strange.

No. They would need an adult guardian. Or guardians, plural. Mr. and Mrs. Sweets…

Jacqueline grimaced. The idea of the sweet, enthusiastic Weaver kids under the influence of Mrs. Sweets and her sweetly acidic tongue was enough to make her break out in hives. If only—

She shook her head. Hideaway looked after its own, that's what Arlo said. And Eric and the Wheelers were Hideaway's own, now. The Sweets might be sour assholes to anyone who wasn't a shifter, but Arlo didn't seem any the worse for wear for having the Sweets look after him when he was younger.

And she wasn't going back, anyway.

The house seemed bigger than ever.

It had grown like this once before. Right after Derek left. Jacqueline had left the lawyer's office in a daze, driven home, and found herself in a house that didn't fit properly. The rooms were too big and there were too many of them. There had always been too many of them, ever since she found out she couldn't have kids, but she hadn't been prepared for it to be just her, rattling around in the place she'd planned to build so many memories in.

And now it was just her again.

Jacqueline jumped as though she'd stood on a thumbtack. She started moving. She *had* to move, she knew, before the thread of regret she was tugging on like a loose thread unwound her entire life.

She had to move. And the house was empty, and there was nothing else to do, so she cleaned.

Jacqueline dusted. Scrubbed. Mopped. Swept the ceilings and light fixtures and then mopped again because of all the dust that fell down. Scrubbed more things until she realized she was scrubbing the outsides of her kitchen storage tins and rearranged them instead. Then the cutlery drawer. Then the china she only took out when her in-laws came over and why did she even still have it when she hadn't had in-laws in three years? Back in the cabinet.

Or she could throw it all out.

She paused, and that was a bad idea. *Moving good. Stopping bad.* She left the good china where it was and headed for the bathroom.

By the time she'd run out of house to clean, it was getting dark. She stood in the front hall, panting.

Moving good, stopping bad. Except when she was exhausted enough that stopping meant falling asleep, not just sitting gnawing over everything that she'd done wrong in her life.

She should shower. Eat something. Go to bed, wake up, go to work… oh, shit, she still needed to call a tow truck to pick up her poor car…

Jacqueline closed her eyes and leaned back against the front door. Her fresh start was going to have to wait a bit longer. She couldn't even bear to think about her old plans now. Parties. Cocktails. Sexy one-night stands…

She winced.

The first time she'd come home like this, to a suddenly too-big, too-empty house, she'd wanted to rage. To smash all the evidence of the way she'd hoped her life would go until it was all in as many pieces as her heart was.

She'd pushed the anger back, folded it small and tight and put it away where she couldn't feel it anymore.

But this time, there wasn't any anger. Damn it, she was ready for some anger now, some break-shit-now juvenile impulses, because she was done with this house, this town, all her *stuff*, she was going to throw it out anyway and repaint the walls realtor-friendly white and—

And she just felt small, and tired. And very, very alone.

She'd been so close to having, not everything she'd ever dreamed off, but things she'd never dreamed of at all.

Being with Arlo would have been… She didn't have the words to describe it. Magical wasn't enough, because magic made her think of flighty, floaty things, and Arlo was so real it took her breath away. If they stayed together, she could have seen the Weaver kids settle in Hideaway Cove and watched them grow up—making sure they had time to be kids, first.

Instead…

She groaned. "There you go," she murmured to herself. "Moping again. Shouldn't have stopped to think about it…"

She was about to step away from the door when someone knocked on the other side.

# 18

# ARLO

He knew before the car even came into view that Jacqueline wasn't in it.

The Sweets had left soon after Jacqueline and Harrison. Lainie had muttered something about them not having any reason to stay now they'd done their dirty work, and Arlo…

Arlo shook his head. There was some sort of misunderstanding. There had to be. Ma and Pa were the way they were because they wanted the best for Hideaway Cove. Because they wanted the best for *shifters.*

Didn't they?

He stood in front of Harrison and Lainie's house and watched the Land Rover crest the far hill and wind down the road towards town.

It was mid-afternoon and the streets were busy, at least, busy for Hideaway. People turned towards the car as it drove past. Arlo was too far away to see their faces, but their interest was obvious. A newcomer in Hideaway was always exciting news.

Arlo frowned. *Eric. No last name. Who is he? Some irresponsible oaf who left the kids to fend for themselves when they needed him most. And now he's going to get a hero's welcome in Hideaway, and Jacqueline…*

His heart ached. Jacqueline was gone, fleeing Hideaway as fast as she could, and he had no idea what had gone wrong or how to get her back.

"Arlo?" Kenna poked her head around the door. "What's going on? Where did Jacqueline go? Ms. Eaves wouldn't—"

299

Her eyes widened and excitement and relief rolled off her in waves. "Eric! That's Eric! Dylan, Tally, Eric's back!"

Arlo bit back a growl of frustration.

Dylan cannonballed out the front door, skidding on the path as he raced over to Arlo.

Lainie was right on his heels, Tally crowing in her arms. "Kenna, I told you not to bother Arlo right now," she began, but broke off when Tally abruptly shifted. "Oh, bother," she gasped, fumbling to keep from dropping the seal pup.

Arlo braced himself. Tally's psychic voice was louder when she was in seal form, and this close, any strong emotion would feel like he'd taken an anvil to the back of his head.

But Tally's joy didn't hit him like a ton of bricks. Instead, he felt buoyant, as though her happiness was lifting him up. Her human and seal emotions swirled together with a single thought at the center:

*Pack!*

He shut his eyes briefly. Of course Eric was the kids' pack.

He hung back as the Land Rover wove its way up Lighthouse hill. The air was thick with the Weaver kids' joy, and if he stayed too close to them, he thought he might choke on it. They deserved better than that. He wouldn't ruin their alpha's homecoming with his own bitterness. Eric might be a pathetic pack leader, but there would be others to make sure the kids had everything they wanted here in Hideaway without breaking those pack bonds.

Unless this Eric, whoever he was, wanted to start anything. Arlo's wolf bristled. If Eric wanted to have words about how Arlo had stepped into his place these last few days...

The Land Rover growled to a halt in front of the gathered kids. The passenger door burst open, and any thoughts Arlo had had about telling Eric exactly what he thought of a shifter who left his pack alone evaporated.

*He's just a kid!*

Eric half-stumbled getting out of the car. He was better at keeping his emotions private than the Weaver kids, but Arlo still caught the edge of his bone-crushing relief as they all screamed and leaped on him.

"Eric! Where have you *been*!"

"We went on a boat!"

"We found Hideaway Cove, it's really *real*, you were right—"

"Ahhhhhhh!" Tally screeched happily. *AHHHHH*HHHHH-HHHH!*

Eric hugged each of them in turn and straightened, his eyes shining. "I can't believe you're all here. Mr. Galway told me—"

Standing, he topped Kenna by more than a foot. He caught sight of Arlo over her head. Even ten feet away, Arlo could see him gulp.

A heavy weight settled over Arlo's shoulders as he watched the young man pull himself together.

*He's just a kid,* Arlo thought again. *Look at him now. Gathering his courage to come talk to me. Trying to do the right thing.*

He crossed his arms as Eric approached him, then thought better and put his hands in his pockets. Unthreatening and open.

*He's trying to do the right thing. The least I can do is not terrify the pants off him.*

"Mr. Hammond?" Eric asked, his voice cracking at the end. He stopped, looking horrified, and cleared his throat before he started again. "Mr. Hammond. Sir. I'm Eric Potts. Mr. Galway said you got the others from the marine reserve and brought them here."

"That's right. It's good to finally meet you."

Eric looked thrown by that. "I, um, thank you. For looking after them. You and Ms. March. I wasn't even sure we were in the right place…"

"You were close enough. We just stepped in to get you the rest of the way."

Arlo held out his hand and Eric shook it, eyes wide. His grip was firm, but the next breath he took was so heavy he rocked back on his feet.

"I've got experience working in shipyards, and on boats. I can fish and I can fix an engine, sometimes, if I know what's wrong with it. And nets. I'll do about anything, I don't mind—"

"Hang on, hang on. I don't need your whole resume." Arlo raised his hands and frowned. "Why are you telling me this?"

"I need a job." Eric looked as confused as Arlo felt. "I don't mind what it is. I don't even need pay, just somewhere for the kids to stay, and food. I'll do anything."

Arlo stared at him. There was something flickering behind his dark eyes. Arlo's wolf pricked its ears up and the flickering stopped, as though Eric's animal had noticed it was being watched.

His wolf barked softly and Eric blinked. "Uh, hello as well to your, um, to…"

"I'm a wolf shifter," Arlo explained.

"Woah."

"And you don't need to get a job. How old are you?"

"Ninet—Uh, eigh… seventeen?" He drew himself up. "You gotta understand. I said I'd look after them. I know we're not the same shifters, but I made a promise. We're in this together."

"They're your pack." Arlo nodded.

"I dunno? We're each other's pack. We don't…" Eric's shoulders slumped. "It's just us."

Arlo sighed. He looked up and caught Harrison's eye. *You hear all that?* he sent to him.

*Yep.*

"Right." Arlo looked Eric in the eye, then swept his gaze over the three Weaver kids as well, including them in the conversation. "I know we talked about getting you your own place, but that's out of the question. You've done a good job of looking after yourselves up until now, and it's time for the adults to take over."

"We're not going into some sort of home again!" Kenna blurted out, grabbing Dylan's hand.

"No, you're not," Arlo agreed. "Not some sort of home. Someone's home, and it'll be your home, too."

Kenna exchanged a look with Dylan and Eric. Arlo felt a whisper of their telepathic conversation against the edge of his own consciousness.

"Might have been easier if you told us all this earlier," Harrison pointed out calmly.

Arlo nodded. If they'd known when the Sweets were still here—

His ribs tightened, so hard and so quickly pain shot through his chest. *If I hadn't blown up over Eric, if I'd known that he was just a kid like the others, if I hadn't let my mouth run and driven Jacqueline off...*

Then the kids would be safe in their new home with the Sweets, and Jacqueline would still be here.

Arlo's wolf whined, and he frowned. Something about that picture still didn't fit.

"Harrison's right," he said, making sure to keep his own confusion out of his voice. "If we'd known sooner Eric wasn't old enough to be your guardian, we could have planned things a bit better."

"Well maybe we had our own plans!" Kenna blurted out. She slapped her hands over her mouth, eyes wide, and then let them from. Her head dropped. "Not that that matters, now..."

Arlo shook his head, confused, until he caught the edge of another silent conversation between Kenna and Eric.

*...him and Jacqueline...*

Arlo stepped away. He didn't want to hear any more, and he didn't want the kids to see his face.

He'd hurt the one woman he was meant to protect with his life. Hurt her so badly she couldn't bear the sight of him. And he didn't even know how.

He closed his eyes. Now that he wasn't worked up over the bogeyman failed-alpha Eric he'd built up in his head out of nothing, maybe he could see beyond his own frustration. Ma Sweets had been talking about pack. That was what had set him off, and—

God. That's what had set Jacqueline off, as well.

Snippets of images and conversations clicked together in his mind. The picture they formed made his heart ache.

Jacqueline's failed marriage. The sliver of ice in her voice when she said there was no one waiting at home for her. The way she'd talked around the fact her ex had gotten another woman pregnant, and what that meant.

And he'd told her the one thing he'd always wanted most in the world was a pack of his own.

*Christ. How could I be so blind?*

"I have to go," he announced. Everyone's attention was instantly on him. A flicker of satisfaction passed across Harrison's face.

"Keys?" Harrison tossed them over and Arlo caught them without looking. He had already turned to the kids.

He met each of their eyes in turn, and couldn't tell whether the anxious anticipation shivering across his skin was his, or theirs.

"Wait here," he told them. "I've got to fix something. And then I'll be back."

He swallowed. He could tell they wanted him to say more—but he couldn't. He wasn't going to make any promises he couldn't keep.

"Harrison, Lainie, can you look after them? I don't know how long—"

"As long as you need," Harrison said firmly, and Lainie nodded, taking his hand.

Arlo couldn't speak. His whole being was wound tight with the need to go, to fix what he'd broken. If he could. God, he hoped he could.

The Land Rover's engine roared and he drove off to find the other half of his heart.

# 19

# JACQUELINE

Jacqueline opened the door. Too quickly. She wasn't prepared for who was on the other side, and then there was no time to control her reaction.

"You!" she exclaimed. "What the hell are you doing here?"

Derek gave an easy smile. "Jacqueline."

Jacqueline froze. That smile, those crisp light-blue eyes and the equally un-crisp collars on his shirt—how many times had she asked him to hang his clothes up instead of throwing them on the floor after she'd ironed them…

She shook herself. "Why are you here?" she repeated.

"Can we talk? Inside?" He shot her that smile again and tried to get past her. She stepped in front of him. "Come on, Jacqueline. It's been years. You can't keep me out of my own house."

"It's not your house," she said automatically. "You gave it to me in the settlement. Remember?"

"Well, yeah…" He leaned back, hands on his hips as he looked up at the house. "It's just got so many memories, you know?"

*I know.*

"So, you gonna let me in?"

"Why were you at the Spring Fling?"

Derek eyeballed her. "Why weren't you? You always used to love that sort of rubbish."

Jacqueline's spine went wobbly. *He was looking for me?* She was instantly suspicious.

"Come on, Jackie," Derek said, smiling. "Let me inside. There's something I want to talk with you about."

"Oh, *now* you want to talk?" Jacqueline couldn't believe what she was hearing.

"Here we go again." Derek turned away, but not so quickly she missed him rolling his eyes.

"What do you mean, again?" The wobbliness in Jacqueline's spine grew prickles. "We've never talked about what happened. I never even got a chance to tell you how you made me feel! I—oh, shit, no."

Another car pulled up on the other side of the street. One she recognized. God, it would be too much to hope it was Harrison or Lainie, wouldn't it? It was their car after all—but—

Arlo stepped out of the driver's seat and the bottom fell out of Jacqueline's stomach.

*I can't believe this is happening. I'm going to face off with the man who divorced me because I can't have kids… and the man whose heart I'm going to break for the same reason.*

# 20

# ARLO

The hair on the back of Arlo's neck prickled. He sensed where Jacqueline was even before he saw her, a dark shape in the doorframe, silhouetted by the light inside.

There was a man on the step in front of her.

Arlo crossed the street in a few long strides. "Is this man bothering you, Jacqueline?"

Jacqueline's face was tense. Her hair was tied back, but she gestured as though she was pushing it off her face anyway. "Arlo, now's—"

"I'm not bothering her. I'm her ex-husband. Who the hell are you?"

"I'm—" *Her mate.* The word twisted on his tongue. He wanted it to be true, but he couldn't say it, and not just because the scowling man in front of him wasn't a shifter.

If Jacqueline rejected him, all the words in the world wouldn't make it true.

He stared at Jacqueline imploringly. Her eyes softened, just for a moment, and then went sharp with a pain that cut straight through his chest.

"Arlo's a—a friend," she said.

*Thank you,* Arlo thought. He knew some people might find being called a "friend" a slap in the face, but for him, it was a bright light of hope.

Maybe he still had a chance to make things right.

"Sure, fine, whatever." Jacqueline's ex—Derek, he remembered now—turned back to Jacqueline. "Look, this is getting ridiculous. Tell your friend to come back another time. What I've got to say is important."

Arlo's hackles rose. His wolf was growling, and it was all he could do to keep himself from growling, too.

Jacqueline made an exasperated noise. "Right. *This* is important."

"That's what I said." Derek jerked his chin towards the street. "Go on, you heard her. This isn't a good time for an impromptu visit."

"Oh, for—do you even hear yourself?"

Derek started forward and found Jacqueline standing in front of him, with her feet planted and her arms crossed.

"Get out of the way, Jackie," Derek said, his voice dripping patience.

Arlo stepped forward. If this man thought he could speak to Jacqueline that way in her own house—

"I'm not letting you in, Derek. I said that already. You just didn't listen. You never—" Jacqueline pressed the heels of her hands against her eyes. "I need to—to talk to Arlo. *That's* important. Whatever you're here for can wait."

Derek spluttered. Jacqueline ignored him and held the door for Arlo.

Arlo's nose wrinkled as he went inside. The house smelled strongly of disinfectant, but it wasn't just that.

He couldn't sense Jacqueline's touch anywhere.

It was a nice house, what he could see of it. Clean neutral carpets, walls papered with some sort of tiny flower pattern. Framed pictures with watercolors of other, bigger flowers. Halfway down the hall was an end-table covered in the sort of knick-knacks that Mrs. Hanson at the bed-and-breakfast loved to collect.

It was nice. But fussy. Which wasn't a word he associated with Jacqueline.

"Arlo."

The front door clicked shut, with Derek on the other side of it. Jacqueline sighed and Arlo heard the weight of years of unhappiness in it.

She was wearing the same borrowed shirt and jeans she'd left Hideaway Cove in, but they were dirty. The front of her shirt was patchy with sweat. Arlo ached to hold her.

"I'm sorry about Derek," she said. "He's… well. I don't know if it's tenacity or what it is, but odds are he'll have convinced himself in ten minutes that I don't know what I'm talking about and obviously I meant to let him in, not you."

She paused, clicked her fingers and turned back to the door. Arlo heard the lock turn.

"That should buy us some time," she muttered.

She didn't turn back. Arlo watched her shoulders rise and fall as she took a deep breath.

"Let me start," he said, and she raised her hands.

"No. I need to say this." She turned around and lifted her eyes to meet his. "You want a pack. A—a family. And I can't have kids."

"I know."

Her eyes widened and Arlo reached out to touch her shoulder. She leaned into his touch, so subtly he wondered if she knew she was doing it.

"I put it all together after you left. I'm so sorry for what I said, Jacqueline. God, I was so twisted up in my own past I didn't even think how that might sound." *Please believe me,* he added silently. "You're my pack. You're everything I need."

Jacqueline shook her head, her eyes closed. "We both know that's not true. You want a pack. A *real* family."

"I want *you.*"

She went on as though she couldn't hear him.

"And I can't give you any of that! I tried, Derek and I tried for so long, and it didn't work. There's something—"

She gestured painfully towards her midriff. Her mouth rounded.

Arlo grabbed her hand. He could see what word she was about to say, and he couldn't let her say it.

"There's nothing wrong with you."

Jacqueline grimaced. "Come on. That's obviously not—"

"Jacqueline." Arlo wrapped his hands around both of hers and held them to his heart. "You're perfect. You're *everything*. The only pack I need is you. Now or ever."

Jacqueline gulped. "You say that now. But I know how this works. You want a family, and I can't give it to you. You'll—you'll end up resenting me. I don't want to go through that again. I know it's selfish, but I can't. Not again."

Her voice was shaking. Arlo could see how every word hurt her to say.

And he understood.

"Part of that is true. I have always wanted a pack," he said. Jacqueline's eyes locked on to his, bone-dry and wary, as though she was bracing herself for him to give in and agree with her. Well, that wasn't going to happen. "A pack of my own. To cherish and care for. To dedicate my life to. Because the pack I was born into never did that for me."

"But you said—" Jacqueline hesitated, and he willed her to keep going. "Shifters always look after their own."

"Mine didn't." Arlo's voice dropped as he pulled up memories he'd kept hidden deep. How could he put into words things he'd never let himself think about? He felt like he was paddling over black water. Floundering. "My first pack abandoned me after my mother died."

"Oh, God, Arlo."

Jacqueline rushed forward and wrapped her arms around him. Arlo let out a ragged breath. She was a lifeline in the dark, holding him safe above the murky waters.

"I traveled around by myself for a while. I was a few years older than Kenna, and I could grow a beard by then, so people either thought I was older than I was, or they didn't care. I did odd jobs. Never stayed in one place long. I didn't fit anywhere, and I didn't know how to make myself fit. Losing my pack was like…"

His stomach lurched at the memory. Jacqueline shivered against him.

"I can't imagine," she whispered. "But the Weaver kids are their own pack, aren't they? And they went through so much to stick together. If they lost each other…"

"It would tear them to pieces."

Arlo's wolf whined. Another memory surfaced: Tally, screaming her head off until she saw Arlo and Jacqueline. The memory tugged at something inside him.

"But you found a place eventually, didn't you? Hideaway Cove. And the Sweets took you in."

"Right…" Arlo frowned. "I found a new pack. And they…"

He shook his head. "The point is, I've lost, too. I know how terrifying it can be to try and find something again that's been snatched away from you. But you *can* find it again. Jacqueline, I won't be like Derek. I won't resent you. I couldn't."

"But a pack—"

"A pack can be two people. Together. In love."

Jacqueline was still holding him close. She tipped her head back to look into his eyes and he lowered his until their foreheads just touched.

"I want that with you. Us. Together. Sailing off into the sunset."

# 21

# JACQUELINE

*I want to believe him. Oh, God, I do.*

Jacqueline felt as though her heart was going to rip itself in two. Arlo was saying everything she wanted to hear, everything she *needed* to hear, and she knew deep in her soul that he wouldn't lie to her.

So why was she still so hesitant?

*I'm afraid. I'm still so afraid of everything going wrong. I've been afraid all this time. All my plans to go wild, party hard… I never wanted any of that. I was just afraid to admit what I really wanted.*

*Someone who loves me just the way I am.*

"Sailing off into the sunset," she whispered.

"I know we missed tonight's," Arlo said, his words like kisses along the edges of her lips. "But there'll be more."

"Promise?" Jacqueline couldn't keep the hint of anxiety from her voice.

"I promise."

She drew a slow breath. "Derek wasn't the only one who wanted kids. I know it's hypocritical, after what I said about being afraid of you resenting me, but you have to know… I always dreamed of having a house full of kids. It's why we bought this place. But it never happened, and it's never going to happen. I'm sad about that. I'm likely to stay sad about it."

"I understand."

*Of course he does,* Jacqueline thought, staring up into his eyes. This strong mountain of a man, salt-crusted and callused and warm and caring. Of course he understood.

"I'm still scared," she admitted, "I…"

*I wanted a fresh start.*

*That's the one thing I told myself that was actually true. And now here it is.* Jacqueline raised her head. Arlo lifted his, his expression confused until he looked into her eyes.

"I'm scared," she said. "Because I don't want to lose you. But that isn't a good enough reason to run away. Just like it wasn't a good enough reason to lock myself up here in Dunston, barely living my life and not even admitting to myself what I wanted."

She took his hand, winding her fingers around his. His hand was so big and strong, practically dwarfing hers, and yet they fit together perfectly. How had she never noticed this before?

"Arlo," she said, and her voice wasn't shaking anymore. "You're my pack."

The noise he made was all she needed to know she'd made the right decision.

"And you're mine," he growled.

Jacqueline pulled him down for a kiss that made her whole body heat up. Their teeth clashed together and she pulled back at the same time he did, and the half-second they each spent checking the other was all right was too much. She kissed him again, hot and passionate, her fingers digging into his scalp.

The same throb of unexpected desire as she'd felt the night before hit her like a train. And this time, she had no desire to slow down. Jacqueline bit down on Arlo's lip and felt him groan, the reverberation coming through his chest and diving straight down between her legs. She was going to ride this need to exhaustion.

There was a knock at the door.

"No…" Jacqueline groaned. "Shoot. I forgot about Derek."

Arlo kissed her neck and then growled against it: "Keep forgetting him."

"What, just leave him out there listening in?" Jacqueline reluctantly unwound herself from Arlo. "I'll get rid of him. Quickly," she reassured him. "*Very* quickly."

She kept hold of Arlo's hand as she unlocked the door. He moved behind the door where he'd be out of sight when she opened it, and a thrill of excitement rippled through her.

"If you need me to make him back off…" Arlo said, and she shook her head.

"I can handle this. It's about time I did."

She opened the door.

"Finally," Derek sighed before she'd even let go of the door handle. "Come on. I've given you time to talk to whoever-he-is. I've got things to do this evening, I can't wait around after you forever."

"And yet here you are. Hanging on my doorstep." Jacqueline put her free hand on her hip. The other one was still holding Arlo's. "Besides. There's something I want to say to you, as well."

She closed her eyes and took a deep breath. This was her chance. For the first time, she felt strong enough to give Derek the tongue-lashing he deserved. To really make him *feel* what he'd done to her.

She tightened her grip on Arlo's hand—and the feeling went away.

Derek was never going to change. He was never going to admit that a version of the world in which he wasn't perfectly justified in everything he did existed. All the time and energy she spent thinking of ways to convince him otherwise were just… time and energy spent thinking about him. And he didn't deserve that.

She wanted a fresh start. Whatever that meant.

And he was holding her back.

Jacqueline opened her eyes.

"Here we go," Derek muttered. He glanced over his shoulder with a furtive look and Jacqueline bit back a groan. There was a car parked further down the street. She could just make out a figure in the passenger seat.

"You know what? I was wrong," she said, and his expression brightened. "I don't have anything to say to you. Have a good life. You and your family. Do a better job of it with them than we managed."

*And maybe don't leave them in the car while you go to chat to your ex-wife!* she added silently.

"I am," Derek said firmly. "That's why I want the house."

Jacqueline froze.

*God damn it.*

"Really."

Derek drove on. Jacqueline's ears were buzzing too loudly for her to hear him.

A breath whispered in her ear. "One of those odd jobs I did was guard dog. Just say the word."

Arlo's voice drove away the buzzing and the hollow feeling inside her was replaced by certainty.

"You know, that's handy," she said, grinning. "Because I'm thinking of selling."

"Great!" Derek's whole posture changed as his eyes lit up. "A private sale would be best, you know. I have some options here." He dug around in his coat pocket.

Jacqueline shook her head. "I don't believe it."

"What?"

"You're trying this again? You actually—" She pinched the bridge of her nose. *Being the bigger person is a lot easier when the smaller person doesn't keep trying to kick you in the face.* "Show me those." She snatched the papers from him. "Are you kidding me? This is what the house was worth when we *bought* it."

"The market—"

"Has gone up!" Jacqueline thrust the papers back at him. "Go away, Derek. If you're that desperate for this old place, you can bid at auction like everyone else. And—no, I'm not finished. I meant what I said. I hope you have a good life. But I'm done with you. Don't come back here again."

"Aw, come on, Jackie—"

"Good *bye*, Derek."

She shut the door on his face. Locked it. And threw the bolt, too, for good measure.

"Oh my *God*," she breathed. "I cannot believe I spent ten years of my life with him. No wonder I never want to make a fuss. He just slithers all over any argument like it doesn't exist."

"Jacqueline." Arlo's voice was a low rumble, tinged with an intensity that made her heart sing.

"I know. I'm going to stop talking about him, right now."

"No, I meant… you're going to sell the house?"

The sound of a car starting up and driving away filtered through the door. Jacqueline walked through to the kitchen, pulling Arlo with her.

"As soon as I can. I've put it off too long. I need to get out of Dunston, and I want…" She leaned against a countertop and met his eyes. "We're pack, aren't we? Pack should stick together and there's no way in hell I'm going to make you move to Dunston."

"You'd move to Hideaway?"

"Yes."

Arlo slipped his arms around her waist. His touch sent rivulets of desire through her veins, pooling deep inside her.

"But first…" she added and watched anticipation build in his dark eyes. "Let's finish what we started back there."

Arlo pushed her against the counter, his fingers digging into her waist as he kissed her. Jacqueline bit down gently on his lower lip, making him groan.

She let herself fall back over the counter, forcing Arlo to lean forward, covering her body. His hips were heavy against hers, his cock thick and hard against her stomach.

Need blazed inside her. "Arlo," she said urgently, "I don't think I'll be able to stand it if you take things slow this time."

Arlo growled something she couldn't make out and kissed down her neck to her collarbone. His stubble grazed her sensitive skin.

"Good," he rumbled, and Jacqueline's whole body clenched.

Arlo pushed her shirt up. The first touch of his fingers on her skin drove her mad. Jacqueline tugged it the rest of the way off and he buried his face between her breasts. One of his hands slid into her pants. Jacqueline jerked her hips, urging him further.

"Oh-h, God, yes," she gasped as his fingers slipped between her folds. She was so wet for him already.

"I need you." Arlo kneeled down, undoing her jeans. "When you left—"

His voice was raw. Jacqueline's heart ached, cooling the red-hot desire inside her. She was about to drop to her knees with him when he pulled her jeans and panties down and kissed between her legs.

The rush of pleasure was so intense it left Jacqueline dizzy. Then Arlo's tongue flicked out and it was all she could do not to scream.

Then he slid one finger inside her, and two, and she did scream.

"That's—" Jacqueline gasped, panting as her body shuddered around Arlo's fingers. His tongue flicked out again, teasing her already-sensitized clit, and she moaned. "That's... not fair..."

Arlo kissed his way back up her body. She swayed against him. Her orgasm was still sending aftershocks through her body, but one look at the expression in his eyes made her almost cry out with need again.

"I won't be able to go as slow this time," he said, cupping her face. "If I hurt you—"

"You won't," she gasped, and kissed him. "Please. Now."

He moaned deep in his throat, his breath hot against her neck. "I need you," he groaned.

She understood. He wanted the same thing she did. Hard and fast, burning away the misery that had separated them.

She tugged at his pants. He was already rock hard, and she ran her hands down his length, shivering in anticipation. Going slow had been intense enough—going fast…

She sat back up on the counter and kicked her jeans off. Arlo closed the space between them, his eyes dark as sin. He kissed her, claiming her mouth with a passion that left her breathless, and thrust inside her in one strong movement.

"Oh God!" Jacqueline cried out. "Please. More!"

She needed him with an intensity that made her whole body ache.

He filled her, hard and deep, each thrust driving more pleasure from her singing nerves until she felt like she was dissolving with ecstasy. It didn't hurt. It was just pleasure, her body yearning for his masculine power as he filled her again and again. His energy was almost animalistic, frenzied, but his eyes were full of the same warm, steady love as ever. He just needed her, as desperately as she needed him.

She wrapped her legs around his waist and pulled him closer, so every driving thrust brought him fully inside her. He groaned into her shoulder, his own body stiffening as he came closer to climax, and the knowledge that *she* was doing this to him, that her body was bringing him so much pleasure his eyes were ragged with it, sent her over the edge again.

"Oh, God! Oh, Arlo, I—"

Jacqueline's hand slipped, and something crashed to the floor.

"Oh, for the love of—" she panted. Arlo paused. "No, don't stop!"

He drove into her again, holding her close to his chest. She was dizzy with joy, and when Arlo came his climax was so intense it left them both breathless.

They clung together, panting. After a few minutes Arlo raised his head and looked over her shoulder.

"I'm sorry. That was a vase. Should have been more careful." Despite his words, his expression was utterly at peace.

"Don't be sorry. And don't be careful. I hate all this junk." She kissed him and grinned. "It's all rubbish the in-laws gifted us. Should have thrown it all out years ago."

"In that case…" Arlo hoisted her up again and made a slow circuit of the kitchen. Jacqueline cackled with laughter as her feet knocked knick-knacks off the counters. She made an especially dramatic swipe when she got to the rooster-shaped paper-towel-holder and couldn't help cackling at it crashed to the floor.

"Where to next?" Arlo asked, nuzzling her neck.

"The bathroom." Jacqueline nipped at his ear.

"You want to clean up?"

The light in his eyes made her skin thrill. *Again?* she thought silently. *Already?*

She narrowed her eyes. "After I've smashed one more thing."

When they got to the bathroom, she booted the be-doiley'd toilet roll doll off the vanity. It hit the mirror and bounced out the window, trailing toilet paper.

"Oops," she said unrepentantly, and swiped one foot across the decorative soaps. "Hah!"

"Why do you have all this stuff?" Arlo asked.

Jacqueline surveyed the mess. "You might as well ask, why have this house? I've been so *stuck*. I stuck here paying the mortgage because I thought it was the right thing to do, I stuck with all the furniture we got for wedding gifts because I thought it was more sensible than buying new… It's all leftovers. From another life." She grinned. "And now that I'm finally selling up, smashing it all now is the last chance I'll have to get any real use out of them."

Arlo's eyes shone. "Want me to carry you around any other rooms?"

"Maybe later. Right now, I want to soap you up."

She thought, as she watched hot water streaming over Arlo's chest, that maybe she'd found her equilibrium again and they'd go back to the slow, sensuous pace they'd had that night on the boat. A few minutes later, panting for breath as Arlo kneeled between her legs, she realized she was wrong. And started to wonder whether they'd ever be able to slow down again.

"Right," Arlo said after they'd each washed up a second time. His eyes were sparkling. "Which way to the bedroom?"

Jacqueline directed him down the hall, kicking figurines and paper flowers off end tables as she went. It took them a while to reach the bedroom, as now that she'd started violently dismantling her old life, she didn't want to stop.

Luckily Arlo didn't seem to see anything unusual about the fact that her route to the bedroom took them through the kitchen, the dining room, and the front hall again. She even managed to dislodge one of the miserable sad-kitten pictures someone had given her as a wedding present.

The house was a total mess behind them, and it was *great.*

"Ahh," she sighed as Arlo carefully put her down on the bed. "That feels good."

Arlo lay down beside her. She rolled on top of him automatically, planting her elbows either side of his head.

"Thank you," she said. "For chasing after me and making me see reason."

"Thank you for giving me another chance."

She stroked his cheek. "I spent so long chasing a dream I couldn't have. I forgot that sometimes dreams do come true."

She'd come so close to giving up, to letting her pain twist her up until she couldn't see how many wonderful things the universe had left in it.

Even if she would never have the home full of children she'd longed for…

A shadow of concern passed over Arlo's face.

"What is it?" she asked.

"Just a thought." Arlo pulled her down to kiss her. "About dreams."

"A good thought?"

"I think so." He rolled over until they were lying side by side and combed his fingers through her hair. "I have an idea…"

He whispered it to her and she covered her mouth, barely daring to believe what she'd just heard. "Really?"

"Really."

"You think it'll work?"

"If I know Hideaway Cove, it will."

Jacqueline kissed him, joy singing in her veins.

*Maybe dreams can come true, after all. All of them.*

# 22

# ARLO

Jacqueline woke up first; Arlo drifted into wakefulness with the same slight unease he always had waking up on solid land, and then heard her moving elsewhere in the house.

Something that sounded like china shattered, and Jacqueline's laughter drove away any trace of landsickness.

Arlo sat up. The bed creaked.

"Arlo?" There was the sound of footsteps, and then Jacqueline poked her head around the door. "I was going to make pancakes but, er, it just occurred to me that I smashed my only mixing bowl last night…"

Arlo frowned, going over her parade of destruction. "The one with the ducklings on it?"

"Ugh, yes." Jacqueline grinned and smoothed down her shirt. To Arlo's slight disappointment, she was wearing far more clothes than she'd gone to sleep in. "So I thought we could pick up something on the way."

Arlo's wolf stirred. He jumped up, its excitement firing up his body. "Great idea."

Harrison's truck was a stick shift, and the road to Hideaway wound up, down and around so many bends that Arlo was almost mad with not touching Jacqueline before they were halfway there.

*You just spent the night with her!* he reminded himself, but it didn't help.

He glanced sideways and caught Jacqueline looking at him. Her lips curved into a smile and she reached over to put a hand on his shoulder.

Arlo hadn't realized he'd been tense, but that simple touch relaxed him better than a whole week at anchor in a sunny bay full of fish. He sighed.

"Am I that obvious?"

"Maybe. Maybe I just want to keep hold of you so I know this is actually happening." Jacqueline whistled out a breath. "You're sure this is going to work?"

"You remember what Ma Sweets said." Arlo's voice became grim when he mentioned his foster mother. "Everyone at Hideaway works together to keep pack together."

"Shifters look after their own." Jacqueline's voice was soft, and sad. Arlo bent his head to kiss her hand where it lay on his shoulder.

"If she wants to keep saying that, then she'll need to play ball," he said.

*Or else admit that it's all a lie, and the only people the Sweets look after are themselves.*

He tightened his grip on the steering wheel.

"And what about the kids?"

Arlo blew out a long breath. "You already know I'm not good at connecting the dots," he said. "Well, I think I've just figured out one of the other things the kids were keeping on the down-low."

He'd called on Jacqueline's landline before he left, asking Harrison to make sure the kids all knew they were coming back, but Tally's lonely panic was still fresh in his mind. He didn't want to put any of them through that again.

He felt the Weaver kids a mile out from Hideaway and clenched his teeth. It wasn't the skull-busting agony he'd felt the night he sailed in to find Jacqueline diving into the waves, or the pure unhappiness of the morning before. The kids' packlessness throbbed like an old bruise.

*Don't worry,* he thought, wishing his telepathy reached further. *We're on our way.*

Jacqueline squeezed his shoulder as they crested the rise that swept down to Hideaway Cove. "Can you reach them yet?"

He hadn't said anything about mindspeaking to the kids. Jacqueline was just on the same wavelength as he was. He shook his head. *How did I end up with such a perfect mate?*

"Give it to the ice cream parlor," he said, nodding towards Tess's café. Its windows sparkled in the morning sun. "Wait a minute..."

"Hmm?"

*Tess?*

Tess's voice hit his mind like a splash of sea spray. *Arlo. Good. Come on down, everyone's here.*

"Strike that," Arlo said to Jacqueline. "They're all at the parlor."

She frowned. "Why? What's going on?"

"One sec." Arlo concentrated. *Kenna? Dylan? Tally?*

The seal shifters' minds sparked at his contact. There was another presence with them: Eric, he guessed. Harrison was there, too, which meant at least whatever else was going on, the kids probably hadn't tried to stage a midnight escape.

He reached further and groaned.

He parked outside the parlor and opened the passenger door for Jacqueline. "The Sweets are here," he warned her.

"Good to know." Jacqueline narrowed her eyes. "Don't worry. Now that I know what their deal is, I can handle them. Besides... I've been connecting some dots of my own. I may just have an ace up my sleeve."

He gave her a questioning look, but she just smiled.

The bell above the door jangled as he pushed it open.

Someone had pushed all the café tables into a square in the middle of the room, and everyone was seated around them. Harrison and Lainie on one side, with Ma and Pa Sweets opposite them. The Weaver kids and Eric were seated facing the door. Kenna had a familiar scowl on her face that melted away when she saw Arlo and Jacqueline, and Dylan jumped up.

"You're here!"

"That we are." Arlo sent them all a wave of support. Eric blinked, taken aback. *Of course. I've only been doing that with the younger kids.*

Then, to his surprise, he felt a tentative telepathic nudge from the teen.

**Thanks,** Eric said into his mind. **That means a lot. And... I guess Kenna was right about you. She said you'd come back.**

Tess was fussing behind the counter, which left the fourth side of the table free. Arlo pulled out a chair for Jacqueline, feeling Ma Sweets' eyes on him, as he sat down.

"Morning, everyone," Jacqueline said, bright and chirpy. "Did you four sleep okay?"

"Wee-e-e-e-ell—" Dylan began, stretching out the word.

"Did Tally have another nightmare?" Jacqueline reached across the Franken-table and Tally cooed and grabbed her finger.

"Not the *same* nightmare..." Kenna's expression was drifting back towards sullen. Her eyes flicked towards the Sweets.

"What's everyone doing here, anyway?"

Tess stormed out from behind the counter and plonked a tray of hot drinks on the table. "Coffee," she said, at the same moment Lainie muttered: "Neutral ground?"

Arlo met Tess's eyes. **All right, sis?**

She tugged on the cuffs of her long-sleeved shirt. **The usual.**

The problem was, Arlo didn't know what Tess's usual was anymore. Like him, she'd always been proud of Ma and Pa Sweets' strong line on keeping Hideaway Cove safe. But ever since they'd discovered exactly how the Sweets had gone about keeping Hideaway "safe", Tess's relationship with their parents had become strained.

And now Lainie was calling her parlor neutral ground?

He raised one eyebrow at Tess, thinking, but not mindspeaking, *Whose side are you on?* She glared at him and stalked back behind the counter.

"Waffles?" she called out, and everyone in the room under the age of twenty called out some variant of "Yes, please, I'm starving."

Tally's version was more of a high-pitched eagle-screech. Ma Sweets took advantage of the noise to pretend she was brushing a mote of dust off her sleeve, and speak telepathically with Arlo.

**I'm glad you're here. You know these children, and you of everyone knows what they need right now. Please, help me talk some sense into your poor friends.**

"Why don't you talk out loud, Ma?" Arlo kept his voice light. "There's two of us can't hear a word you're saying if you stick to telepathy."

Ma Sweets frowned. "That was *meant* only for you, Arlo," she said, pursing her lips.

"We're talking about the kids." Arlo nodded to them. "Seems rude to exclude them from the conversation, too."

"*Very well.*" Ma Sweets sniffed. "Dear?"

Pa Sweets shuffled slightly in his seat. "My thoughts exactly, dear," he mumbled, and appeared to fall back asleep. Ma Sweets frowned.

"What Dorothy is failing to say—sorry, Mrs. Sweets, I'm sure you were going to get to it in a minute—is that we caught them this morning convincing the kids they were being sent to live with them." Harrison sounded all good manners and one hundred percent pissed off at the same time.

Arlo exchanged a look with Jacqueline. "I'm glad we didn't leave any later," Jacqueline murmured. Arlo squeezed her hand.

Ma opened her eyes wide. "Well, I don't see what's so bad about—"

"Kidnapping?" Lainie suggested, quick as a whip.

"Now I'm confused." Ma Sweets tapped her pursed lips with one fingertip. "Surely you're not complaining that we're taking children in, now?

It's not like we're sending them away. Isn't that what you've had a bee in your bonnet about until now?"

"*Grandma!*"

Tess slammed down a plate on the counter. It cracked in two.

"You're not even pretending anymore?" There was only a hint of pleading in Tess's voice, but it was enough to make Ma Sweets' eyes sharpen.

"Pretend what? That our community isn't disintegrating around us?" She fixed Lainie with a knifelike stare.

Arlo tightened his grip on Jacqueline's hand. *How did it take me so long to see the Sweets for what they really are? I was so desperate for someone to take me in, I never questioned what being part of the Sweets' pack actually meant.*

Ma Sweets spoke slowly, as though she was explaining something to a child. "Seals are group animals. Seal shifters need a pack to thrive. These children have each other, but they're a pack without a leader. Arlo knows how difficult that is, don't you, dear?"

"I do."

"See—"

"But they already have a pack leader." Arlo raised his eyebrows at Jacqueline and she mock-glared at him.

"Two pack leaders," she corrected him, and grinned at the kids. "If they want us."

There was half a second of silence, and then the room exploded with noise.

It was something special, Arlo decided, that all four of the shifter kids met Jacqueline's suggestion with even more enthusiasm than they'd shown for the waffles.

"Yes! *Finally,*" Kenna cried out. Dylan threw his head back and whooped. Tally banged her fists on the table, and Eric gave a shy smile.

Arlo braced himself for the wave of unguarded emotion. There was no way he was going to let any of the kids see him wince with the migraine that would no doubt come along with it. But the only thing that hit him was the kids' joy.

His *pack's* joy.

Everything slotted into place. All his headaches had been his body's reaction to him rejecting the truth: that these kids filled a gap in his heart he hadn't let himself admit even existed.

Ma Sweets' eyes narrowed. "Have you really thought this through, Arlo? Where are you going to live? That boat of yours—"

"Lighthouse Hill." Lainie's eye gleamed. "I know the perfect section."

Ma scoffed. "And how do you intend to afford that?"

"I'm selling my house." Jacqueline sounded perfectly calm. "You can help me with that, can't you, Lainie? Arlo tells me you're a realtor."

"That's hardly instant money." Ma leaned back in her seat and sniffed. "What are you going to do until then? Set up camp beds in your workshop? I thought you were more sensible than that, Arlo."

*And I thought you actually had shifters' best interests at heart.* Arlo ran his fingers through his hair.

"This is Hideaway we're talking about. It's like you always said, Dorothy. Shifters look after their own. Whether that's other shifters, or the non-shifters we need to be whole."

The warmth and love in Jacqueline's face made his soul light up.

His own pack had let him down. The Sweets had let him down, too, tainting the true meaning of pack with their hatred.

But with Jacqueline at his side, that was going to change. Their pack would be what packs were meant to be.

Home.

# 23

# JACQUELINE

It worked. That was the strangest part. She and Arlo had marched into the tense confrontation between the Sweets and the other shifters, declared that, actually, *they* were going to look after the new kids, thank you very much, and everyone accepted it.

Even Mrs. Sweets had reluctantly agreed to support Arlo's new pack before she left in a huff. Of course, that might have had something to do with Jacqueline's ace up her sleeve. She'd put together the pieces and figured out how Mrs. Sweets knew so much about her that she could needle Jacqueline with barbs about her infertility.

Bridge. Deirdre must have told the Sweets everything about her. But Deirdre's gossip was a two-way street, and Jacqueline had spent enough work days listening to her grumble about the Dorothy and Alan who won every single bridge tournament they attended. All it had taken was for Jacqueline to whisper—*sweetly*—in Dorothy Sweets' ear that wouldn't it be awful if everyone here in Hideaway who thought she was such an upstanding member of the community—who would never do *anything* to risk their secret being found out by human outsiders—knew that she was using her shifter powers to cheat at cards, and she'd folded.

Jacqueline wasn't sure if she'd folded because she didn't want her neighbors to know about her cheating, or didn't want them to know she stooped so low as to cheat at a game against *humans*, but either way, the Sweets were going to support Arlo's pack.

*Except… it's not* Arlo's *new pack. It's mine, too. Ours.*

Tess had timed the waffles perfectly for her parents' exit. Across the table, Tally had wolfed hers down in a second flat. Jacqueline could guess what was coming next.

Tally slithered off her seat and ran under the table to hug Jacqueline's legs. She bit back a smile and then, thinking better of it, let herself laugh out loud.

*Perhaps that's the strangest part, actually. Over one weekend, I've gone from being single to finding the love of my life and four children. A family.*

She met Arlo's eyes. They were full of a deep, contented happiness that made warmth spread through her entire body.

It was strange, but it was a good strange. She wasn't scared; she was excited. Whatever came next, she was ready to greet it with open arms.

"Up you get," she said, lifting Tally onto her knee. Tally giggled and reached for her half-eaten waffle.

Jacqueline glanced at Arlo. She knew Tally's telepathic shrieks cut through his skull like a hot knife through butter. "Are you all right?" she whispered.

He kissed her hand. "Never better," he said, and slid his plate with an extra waffle along to her.

*Never better.* He was right. This wasn't the life Jacqueline had planned—it was so much more than that.

Forget two-point-five children and a house in the suburbs with a white picket fence. She had a pack of seals and a sea wolf to sail into the sunset with.

And whatever Eric was. She grinned at him across the table as he spooned ice cream onto his waffles.

"You're all right with all of this?" she asked. "The whole pack thing? We've hardly met yet, and it's a big decision."

He nodded fervently and Kenna answered for him. "Oh my God, yes. He's so sick of having to be in charge."

Eric gave an abashed smile. "Yeah. And it feels right, you know? Like Kenna said…"

"Hey!" Kenna smacked him on the arm. "I haven't told them about that yet!"

"About what?" Arlo asked.

"I think I can guess." Jacqueline put down her fork and carefully pushed the second plate Arlo had given her out of Tally's reach. "You knew from the start that you wanted Arlo to be your pack leader, didn't you?"

She remembered how the three of them had put their heads together and whispered conspiratorially back on the cold, windy beach that night. It felt like an eternity ago.

Kenna blushed. "Maybe."

"And you too!" Dylan burst out. He waved his knife and fork. "But Kenna said we couldn't just *say* that, because you're a human and we might scare you off and then nothing would work, so we had to wait until you fell in love and Eric got back!" He beamed at them and then dove back into his waffles.

"Wait." Jacqueline frowned. "Is that why you kept getting worried when you would argue, or when Tally stole my dinner?"

"I didn't want anything to go wrong!" Kenna blurted out. "I thought, if we didn't behave, you wouldn't want us."

A lump formed in Jacqueline's throat. "Well, stop worrying about that right now."

"That's right," Arlo rumbled. "Pack doesn't mean never fighting, or never disagreeing. It means we're there for you. Always."

Kenna dropped her eyes and stabbed her fork into her waffle. "Well, I know that *now*," she muttered.

"Good." Arlo said, and Jacqueline echoed him.

"Because in a few years we'll be a three-teenager household, and if that isn't a recipe for scrapping then I don't know what is," she added.

Arlo raised his eyebrows. "There's a thought." He flashed a grin at Harrison. "We'd better get started on that house."

"And selling mine. Good thing I have a buyer already lined up." Jacqueline narrowed her eyes. "But you have to promise me you'll squeeze him for everything he's worth, Lainie."

"It'll be my pleasure." Lainie pulled her phone out. "Now, about this house. What are you thinking? Open plan? How many bedrooms? The section closest to the water is still available. I'll need to talk to the architect but I had some ideas about over-water rooms…"

"What do you reckon?" Arlo asked the kids. "You'll be living there."

Their faces glowed and they all leaned forward, ideas spilling from their lips.

"Bunk beds—"

"A trapdoor to jump in the water—"

"A REALLY big den—"

"Their plan seems to have all worked out."

Jacqueline looked up to see Tess standing behind her. She smiled at her and Tess smiled back, crookedly.

"What about your plan?" Jacqueline asked, remembering what Tess had said before she ran away from the restaurant during her and Arlo's date.

Tess frowned. "It's… ongoing." Her face cleared. "But I have a good idea of what to do next." She nodded decisively.

"Okay, okay! That's enough ideas for now," Lainie laughed, putting away her phone. "Has everyone had enough to eat?"

There were nods all around. Arlo stood up and offered his arm to Jacqueline.

"I think we need to celebrate," he announced. "Who wants to go for a swim?"

Jacqueline took his arm. "Sounds great," she said.

The morning sun was high in the sky as they all picked their way down the concrete steps from the promenade onto the beach. Sunlight glittered in the waves. Jacqueline hesitated and then, seeing the kids tear their clothes off and run screaming into the water, she stripped down to her t-shirt and undies and tiptoed to the water's edge.

"Ooh, that's cold," she whispered as the waves lapped over her feet.

"As cold as it was on Friday night?" Arlo came up beside her and wrapped one arm around her waist.

"I had other things on my mind then…" Jacqueline shivered and checked on the kids. That bigger seal had to be Kenna, with the tiny seal pup Tally bobbing at her side. Dylan was still in human form, up to his ribcage in the water. As Jacqueline watched, a big gray bird landed on his head, honked, and flapped its wings until Dylan toppled over, laughing.

The goose honked again and dove under the waves as Dylan chased it.

"Is that Eric?" Jacqueline twisted to look back at where she'd last seen the teenaged boy on the beach. "I didn't realize he was a bird—hey!"

Arlo's arm tightened around her waist. "I think he has the right idea," he muttered into her hair, pulling her a step deeper into the water. Icy waves slapped against her shins.

Jacqueline squealed. "Not fair! Ooh, shoot, that's cold…"

She feigned trying to back up, then darted forwards, dragging Arlo with her. When he was balanced on one leg, she struck.

"Argh!" Arlo yelled as she tickled his ribs. He stumbled forward, splashing, and Jacqueline ran into the waves.

She winced as the water passed her thighs, then took a deep breath and dove. The sea enveloped her like an old memory, cold and achy but instantly invigorating. She kicked, remembering how good it felt to swim underwater when she wasn't afraid for her life. Sunlight sparkled through the water, reflecting off a million particles of sand suspended in the waves.

Jacqueline surfaced, gasping with the cold. She trod water, looking around. Kenna and Tally were ganging up on Eric, swimming up underneath him and bumping him out of the water with their heads. Dylan was racing in circles around them.

There was a splash and a rush of breath behind her, and then warm arms wrapped around Jacqueline's waist. Arlo nuzzled her cheek.

"They'll be happy here," he said.

"I know." Jacqueline turned around and kissed him. "Our family. Our pack."

"And you." Arlo cupped her face in his hands and kissed her again, slow and tenderly. "My precious mate. My love. None of this would have happened without you."

Jacqueline wrapped her arms around him and rested her head on his shoulder. The ocean stretched out around them, enveloped by the protective slopes of Hideaway Cove.

She'd been paralyzed with fear for so long, she'd forgotten what it was like to take action and ride the consequences through, whatever happened. But she'd finally done it. Everything could have gone wrong—but instead, it was going so, so right.

She kissed Arlo hard.

*I know what I want. And this is it.*

*Not just a fresh start—a whole new world to explore.*

*With my mate.*

# EPILOGUE

## ARLO

"**Y**ou'll get it all sweaty!" Kenna chided him.

"Ahh!" Tally added. "Yuck!"

Arlo clenched his fist around the small circle of metal. Kenna tsked at him.

"Give it to me!"

"Give what to you? Arlo, what—"

Jacqueline's voice broke off in a gasp of amazement as she rounded the corner. Arlo spun around, clasping his hands together behind his back. Kenna immediately started prying his fingers apart.

Arlo was too distracted by the sight of his mate to care.

It was three months since Jacqueline had come to Hideaway Cove and Arlo's solitary life had exploded. The bones of their house at the bottom of Lighthouse Hill had been built: a strong foundation for what would soon be the bustling home for their pack, half tucked into the hill, half stretching out over the water. Jacqueline had split her time between Dunston and Hideaway… until now.

Arlo drew in a deep breath. The white button-down shirt he'd borrowed off Harrison scratched at his throat. He'd told Jacqueline he had something important to talk to her about tonight. Had she guessed what he was planning?

She was wearing a flowing dress that made her look like a mermaid who'd just stepped out of the waves. Her hair was held off her face in a tumble of glossy curls. But it was her eyes that shone the brightest as she took in Arlo in his scratchy suit, the four children gathered around, and the covered table behind them.

"What's going on?" she asked, her lips curving into a smile. "Dylan, you said you had a surprise to show me before the party at Caro's?"

She was talking to Dylan, who'd led her in, but her eyes were locked on to Arlo's. He swallowed. Kenna pushed something back into his hands: a small box.

Eric cleared his throat. "We're going to head to Caro's soon. But first…"

They were standing on what would one day be the living room of their pack's home. Right now, it was more like a deck overlooking the water, with tarp-covered stud walls outlining where the walls and doors would one day be. Eric nodded to Kenna and they each expertly flicked the tarps away, revealing strings of glittering fairy lights wound around and between them.

Jacqueline gasped and Arlo's heart swelled. The kids had all made huge strides in their control of their telepathic abilities, but they couldn't keep their pride from leaking out as they watched Jacqueline take in their decorations. They had turned the work site into a magical grotto.

"This is amazing," Jacqueline breathed.

"We're going to head off now." Kenna tossed her head and sent Arlo a telepathic command so brusque and no-nonsense that he couldn't help a sudden bark of laughter. "The Menzies are doing a big sleepover after the party so we'll see you tomorrow, okay?"

She hugged Jacqueline and gestured for the others to all do the same. Arlo waited as Jacqueline hugged them all goodnight. She picked Tally up for a cuddle and a kiss, before handing her to Kenna.

Jacqueline raised her eyebrows at Arlo as the kids headed back to the main road to walk to the restaurant. "What did Kenna say to you?"

"You noticed that?" Arlo rubbed the back of his neck.

"I'm getting better at picking up on it, I think." Jacqueline slipped up to him and kissed him gently on the lips. Arlo's whole body thrilled.

"I'll tell you after," he promised.

"After...?" Jacqueline was practically glowing. Arlo gestured to the table.

"Dinner?"

He held out a chair for her. She sat down, a smile dancing around her lips. When he whipped the cloth off the table, she laughed with delight.

"Since you missed out the first time," Arlo said gruffly.

Dylan had timed Jacqueline's arrival perfectly; the delicate fish and fresh bread were still steaming, making small beads of moisture appear on the chilled bottle of wine. Arlo sat down opposite Jacqueline, hiding the box in his lap.

"Is this what you were doing out on the boat this morning?" Jacqueline asked as he filled her glass.

"Some of it."

"Ooh. Color me intrigued." Jacqueline flashed him a smile that made his skin thrill.

Arlo cut her a slice of bread and buttered it. The butter melted into the warm bread almost immediately. He felt Jacqueline's eyes on him as he added fish to her plate and handed it back to her.

"Thanks," she whispered, her voice warm. "Oh, my God, this is delicious."

"I wasn't going to steal you away from Caro's summer barbeque for bad cooking," Arlo pointed out.

"Good. *Mmm.* I can see why Tally hoovered her way through all of mine that first night."

Arlo watched Jacqueline eat. His heart felt so full, there wasn't room for it in his chest.

*How did I get this lucky?* he asked himself as they ate, savoring every bite.

"Dessert," he said next. Tess had delivered a batch of specially made ice cream earlier in the afternoon. He pulled it out of the cooler now and Jacqueline cocked one eyebrow.

"From Tess? Should I be worried?"

"She promised no experiments."

Jacqueline closed her eyes as she tasted the ice cream. "Oh!"

Arlo's skin warmed. "Good oh?"

"Yes." Jacqueline opened her eyes and gazed at him. "Here."

She held her spoon to Arlo's lips. He tasted it, not breaking eye contact with her.

"It's the same as the chocolates we had on our first date. Do you remember?"

*Thank you, Tess.* Arlo sipped his wine.

"I am sensing a theme," Jacqueline said cautiously, her eyes sparkling.

"Don't worry. I haven't arranged for Tally to start screaming in the distance," Arlo joked.

"Thank God."

Arlo let himself sink into Jacqueline's smile. He'd never imagined that having a mate would be like this. Thrilling and easy at the same time.

It was hard for him to think back to what his life had been like before Jacqueline and their pack were in it, but he had to.

"I've been so busy with the house, I haven't been out fishing since the day I met you," he said. "I was miserable then. I didn't even know why. I thought I knew how the world worked and how I fit into it, and everything I learned that told me otherwise hurt. I couldn't even admit to myself what the Sweets were really like."

"Arlo—" Jacqueline reached across the table to take his hand. Arlo folded his fingers around hers.

"And then I met you. And everything I thought I knew about the world and how I fit into it turned completely on my head. But it didn't hurt anymore. I finally understood what my own soul had been telling me."

He wrapped both his hands around hers. "Love is more important than fear. Openheartedness is more powerful than defensiveness. I was so scared of losing what I thought was my pack, I didn't realize they *weren't* my pack. You saved me from that. You showed me what love really is."

He took one of his hands away with hers and fumbled with the small box.

"You're the heart of this pack, Jacqueline." He kneeled down on one knee and Jacqueline gasped. "You've thrown yourself into this world with so much courage and so much love it takes my breath away."

"You're the strong one," Jacqueline protested. "You saved my life. You stood up to your parents…"

"I couldn't have done it without you at my side. And in my heart." He took a deep breath. "I know you've done this before and it hasn't worked out. But I need you to know that I'm yours. I want to be bound to you in every way. The mate bond, our pack… and in marriage." He opened the box. "Jacqueline March, will you do me the honor of becoming my wife?"

Jacqueline was completely still. Arlo's heart was in his throat. Then she made a noise that was half-laughter, half-sob, and slid from her chair. "Yes! Of course!"

She threw her arms around his neck and kissed him so hard he almost dropped the ring box. He exclaimed and fumbled for it and she grabbed for it, too, laughing against his lips. At last they both had their hands around it.

"I love you," Jacqueline whispered as he slipped the ring onto her finger. "Marrying you is the only thing I can think of to make our life even more perfect."

Arlo pulled her close against her. They sat together, gazing at the ring in the glittering light of the fairy lights.

"It's beautiful," Jacqueline whispered.

"The kids helped," Arlo said. "Eric came up with the design. Kenna and Dylan chose the stones. And Tally… Tally did a really good job of not swallowing any of the pieces, or anything else in the workshop."

"You made it yourself?" Jacqueline cupped her hand over the ring, treasuring it. But only for a second, before she had to look at it again.

"The guys helped. And the kids. And YouTube."

Jacqueline laughed. "It's perfect."

"It's not." Arlo's voice was rough. "It's—look, you can see where I slipped and took a groove out of the edge. And there's—Tally decided she likes hammers—I think I managed to buff out most of the dent, but you can still see it if you know where to look…"

She kissed him and he shut up.

"Shh. It's perfect. Dents and all."

She held out her hand and the fairy lights shimmered on the gold band with its cluster of tiny stones. The central gemstone was a dark sapphire with glints of lighter color in its heart, like sunlight on deep water. Around it were arranged four smaller London topazes.

"It's the pack," she breathed.

Arlo's heart swelled. Of course she'd understood. "Tally, Dylan, Kenna, Eric… and me," he said. "So you can always keep us close."

Jacqueline curled the fingers of her other hand over her ring and kissed him again. When she pulled away her eyes were shining.

*With happiness,* Arlo reminded himself as his heart thudded. *She only cries when she's happy.*

"What did Kenna say before she left?" Jacqueline asked.

Arlo rested his forehead against hers. "That I'd better not come find them until you'd agreed to marry me."

Jacqueline burst out laughing. "She didn't! No, God, of course she did." She sighed happily. "I suppose it will make things easier. Making it official, finishing the house—so we square up our little family with the authorities."

Arlo nuzzled her, brushing his lips across the soft skin of her cheekbones. "That's not the reason I'm doing this."

"I know." Jacqueline wiped her eyes. "What now? Back to Caro's?"

Arlo paused. There was a huge celebration waiting for them at Caro's, he was sure.

"There's one more thing I have to show you," he said. "On the boat."

Jacqueline raised her eyebrows. "We've missed sunset again," she pointed out.

Arlo looked up at the stars. "I know."

He rowed Jacqueline out to the *Hometide.* Her eyes were soft and happy, so different to that first time they'd rowed out together.

He helped her up on board and led her down into the cabin. Everything was freshly scrubbed and oiled, and the air smelled faintly of sawdust. Arlo lay Jacqueline down on the bed and propped himself up above her.

"What's doing that?" she asked, touching his face. Arlo raised one hand; colored lights danced over it. Jacqueline's eyes widened as she figured it out.

She rolled over, pushing herself up on her hands and knees to look at the newly repaired port window above the bed.

"Oh, Arlo," she breathed.

He pushed a stray curl behind her ear, letting the joy on her face wash over him.

"I figure with four kids, no matter how good our intentions, we're going to keep missing the real sunsets," he said, his voice rough. "But we'll always have this one."

He'd replaced the broken window with a stained glass picture. The sun, setting over the sea.

"I love it," Jacqueline whispered. She rolled onto her back and pulled him down on top of her, her curves molding to his body. "And I love you."

She kissed him, and Arlo knew: whatever happened next, every day of his life, his love for this woman would grow stronger.

# THE LIGHTNING DRAGON'S MATE

# APOLLO

Gemstones glittered in piles on the workbench's pitted surface. Dragon shifter Apollo sifted through them, admiring the play of light on the faceted jewels. They were every shade of the rainbow: brilliant citrine, rich garnet, lush amethyst, ranging from midnight hues to the barest blush of color.

*Come on*, he willed his inner dragon silently. Out loud, he murmured: "And here I thought *dragons* were obsessed with sparkly things. Is there something you're not telling us, Harrison?"

The brown-haired, broad-shouldered man standing next to him huffed. "Don't get any ideas." Harrison Galway's inner griffin glared out through his eyes, sharpening their mild hazel to something ferocious and possessive.

Apollo raised his hands in mock surrender. "Don't worry. My motives are entirely pure."

It was the truth.

And that was the problem.

He was a *dragon* shifter, for God's sake. If the other dragons he'd met were anything to go by, he ought to be in a constant state of half-crazed gold-lust, scheming to get his hands on as much treasure as he could carry, and then more. He should have seen Harrison's piles of glittery loot, snatched them up, and flown away cackling over the burned bridge of their friendship.

It wasn't as though he didn't look the part. In his dragon form, he was magnificent: serpentine body, powerful wings, and gleaming scales like sun-touched gold. His human form wasn't too shabby, either. He kept his long blond hair tied back, which drew attention to his aquiline bone structure and the unearthly gold of his eyes. The only other dragon shifter in his family—his grandfather—wore a three-piece suit for all occasions, but that wasn't really the vibe of Apollo's chosen seaside home, so he did his best with well-broken-in casual shirts and jeans that hugged his swimmer's torso and narrow hips.

Draconic vanity—tick. But...

*You're sure we don't want to steal his treasure? Even a little bit? Even just one piece?*

His dragon let out a bored sigh and shuffled its wings. Apollo tried not to let his own shoulders slump.

*Right. I get it. 'Treasure? What treasure?' It's only a pile of jewels, after all.* His chest tightened. *Why would we be interested in anything like that?*

"They're not for me." Harrison paced around the workshop, ruffling his hair with one hand and shooting unsure looks at the gemstones he'd scattered across the bench. "They're for the baby."

"Uh-huh." Apollo exchanged a look with Arlo, who was doing his usual lurk-scruffily-in-the-corner routine.

Harrison must have sensed doubt in their raised eyebrows. He shoved his hands in his pockets and said gruffly, "We don't know if the baby will be a shifter or not, but Lainie's dad was a magpie shifter. She wants to recognize that heritage. And I—"

"You're nesting." Arlo's sapphire-blue eyes sparkled.

"I'm *not* nesting."

"What do you call it, then? You've spent the last three months driving your mate up the wall re-renovating your newly built house, and now you're going to glue sparkly rocks up in the nursery?" Arlo crossed his arms and leaned against the wall, grinning. "Your griffin side's coming out. You're nesting."

"This from the man whose wolf rustled him up a ready-made pack."

Arlo's grin became wider. "Yeah. Great, isn't it?"

Apollo's eyes slid to the gemstones again.

Harrison and his mate Lainie were expecting their first child. Arlo had Jacqueline and their pack of adopted seal shifter kids.

And what did he have? Not even a hoard. Worse than that, he didn't even *want* a hoard.

He must have lost control of his cheerful expression for a moment, because as Harrison returned to the bench to grumble over his gemstones, Arlo pulled away from his corner and clapped him on the shoulder.

"Don't worry, Sparky. It'll be your turn soon enough. There's someone out there who wants to swim around in a pile of gold coins with you like Scrooge McDuck, and when it happens, we'll be here to heckle from the sidelines."

"What would I do without friends like you?" Apollo feigned the sarcasm his friend expected from him, but the words felt like sawdust in his mouth.

Arlo had hit on the exact thing that kept him awake at night, wondering what was wrong with him. The fear that his turn wasn't coming. That it never would. That he had no mate waiting for him. No perfect other half, a lover and companion precious beyond all others. No one to cherish, to protect and love and build a life with.

How else could he explain his dragon's lack of interest in collecting a hoard?

Dragons didn't collect hoards out of greed or a desire for shiny things. The whole point of having treasure was so that when they finally met their soulmate they could heap it at their feet, shower them with jewels and wonders and show they were worthy mates. The gold-lust was an evolutionary drive.

But Apollo didn't have any gold-lust. He had no instinctual need to gather treasure. His own hoard was still as pathetically small as it had been when he left home aged eighteen, as all dragons did, to seek his fortune.

He had put on a good act back then. Chased rumors of hidden treasures across the globe, raced other dragons to find long-lost caches of gold and jewels, because that was what you *did*.

But when push came to shove—when he had to choose between facing off against another young dragon in battle for some lost treasure and lying on a tropical beach—he always chose the beach.

That was how he had ended up here in Hideaway Cove, working with Harrison and Arlo. He had been chasing a story about a long-lost smugglers' treasure of gold coins and jewelry. And for once, he was the only dragon in search of it. He had told himself that was a good thing: no chance for his lack of gold-lust to take over and let him give it up to someone else. Once he found it, it would be his.

He had tracked rumors and stories and mentions in old newspaper clippings and local histories up and down the state. Finally, he had landed in Hideaway Cove. A small fishing village that from the outside looked no different from the other quaint little towns this far up the east coast. But once he arrived...

Hideaway Cove was a shifter town. A sanctuary for shifters, safe from the human world. In all his travels, Apollo had only rarely come across communities where shifters could live openly while keeping their true natures secret from the human world. He had swum and sunbathed in dragon form on hundreds of remote, isolated beaches around the world—but there was something special about doing so on a *non*-remote beach where you could buy an ice cream sundae afterwards.

Hideaway Cove wasn't exactly tropical, but it had a beach, and a great restaurant and incredible ice cream parlor, and friendly locals, and what with one thing and another, Apollo had never ended up finding the rumored smugglers' treasure and had never left, either.

And despite living in a shifter sanctuary town, he still kept secrets from his friends here. His lack of draconic instincts. His fears about not having a mate.

It would be one thing if he didn't want a mate. Some shifters didn't. They were content on their own. But not him. It had started as a twinge of jealousy when Harrison found Lainie, and the twinge had grown to an ache after Arlo found Jacqueline and their ready-made pack. He saw how happy his friends were, how their mates filled a hole in their lives they hadn't even noticed before they found them. He wanted that for himself.

But if he didn't want gold, treasure, a hoard worthy of offering the woman who was destined to be his… maybe she didn't exist.

He made sure none of his thoughts showed on his face. He was never one to turn down a pity party normally—he was famous for milking it when he over-extended his magical powers and exhausted himself—but this was private. He didn't want his friends' pity. He would rather they never found out at all.

Arlo shot him a watchful look. *Damn his wolfish senses.* Arlo was quiet, and often came off as sullen or grumpy, but he had a nasty habit of noticing things.

*Now would be a good time for that seal pack to come and distract their alpha.* Apollo closed his eyes briefly and concentrated on his dragon's magic.

Here was something he *was* good at. Something no other dragon he'd met had ever talked about, and which he'd never dared to ask his grandfather about. His draconic powers. Apollo had the ability to weave magic through the town he lived in, creating a shining web that strengthened and defended the town. His power shone from every light bulb and hummed in every wire. It made houses cozier and kept food from catching on the stove. It danced invisibly around the perimeter of the town, letting him know whenever someone was about to arrive—very useful for a town of people who didn't want to advertise the fact that most of them could magically turn into animals.

Apollo jerked. His dragon's eyes snapped open inside him, its sudden alertness an electric sizzle beneath his skin.

Someone was driving across the boundary right now.

He opened his mouth, ready to let Harrison and Arlo know they had a visitor.

And then shut it again as his dragon shrieked at him.

Every scale on its body was standing on end. It was trembling with excitement, pricking its claws against his ribs like an excited puppy.

*Go!* it hissed. *Quickly!*

Its urgency coiled around him, electric-sharp and so overpowering it took him a moment to figure out what it was talking about.

He sent a thin thread of his magic to examine what had just passed through the boundary. A car—modern, generic. And inside it…

Treasure.

Sparks crackled over his skin. He couldn't sense what sort of treasure was in the car—just that it *was* treasure. The most precious, valuable treasure he had ever found.

And he wanted it.

*At last.* Relief flooded through him, followed by a dizzy, buoyant energy. He wasn't broken, after all. His dragon was as gold-lust-y as the most terrifying dragon he had ever avoided meeting on his travels around the world.

He had finally found a treasure that he wanted to hunt down. He would have a hoard. And that meant there was someone for him out there. A mate. Someone who he could make as happy as Harrison made Lainie, or Arlo made Jacqueline.

He opened his eyes.

Arlo was staring at him oddly. "Hey, Sparky, are you okay? You look like you caught a two-by-four to the head."

"Fine. Good. Excellent!" He gathered his magic around him, ready to shift, and tugged his shirt off. "Must dash!"

"What are you—"

He didn't wait to hear the rest of Arlo's question. Ignoring his friends' confusion, he hurried outside. He tripped as he kicked his shoes off and almost face-planted on the driveway. Halfway to the road and halfway through pulling his pants off, he realized he had better warn them that—

His dragon *growled* at him and he almost fell over again.

*I'm not going to warn them about the treasure,* he reassured it. His heart leaped. Not only was his dragon focused on capturing this treasure, it was already jealous of telling anyone else about it, too? This kept getting better and better. All those draconic instincts he had heard so much about but never actually experienced—here they were. His. At last.

He heaved a deep breath and raised his eyes to the hills that surrounded the bay. Darkness made heavy by thick fog clung to the water and the hillside, broken only by the soft glow of the town lights. His town.

The fog clung damply to his skin for a breath of time before he shifted.

His dragon form was magnificent. It was pure gold, with long elegant wings and a gleaming crest that turned into a row of spikes down its spine. Its tail whipped the air and he leapt into the air, ready for the hunt.

# 2

# FELICITY

Felicity Park was on her way to ruin people's lives.

Back in the office, with her boss eyeing her from the other side of his sarcophagus-like desk, it had seemed simple. Palatable. *Doable*. But the further away from her workplace she got, and the closer to the lives she was meant to be ruining, the more she wondered if she'd made the wrong choice.

Which might have seemed like a stupid thing to wonder, but if the last five years had taught Felicity anything, it was that the only wrong choice was disobeying her boss's orders.

*But… people's lives.*

But it was her job.

*But literally people's lives, Fee.*

She bit her lower lip. The voice in her head sounded a lot like her friend Maya.

But Maya didn't work for Saint-John Montfort.

Montfort was the most terrifying person Felicity had ever met. His company, Montfort Industries, was the business equivalent of a bulldozer. It ground other companies to dust and sifted through the remains for anything left that was worth having. Saint-John Montfort himself was more like a shark. If you got in his way, then by the time he was done with you, there wouldn't be anything left to sift through.

Five years, she'd worked for him. She'd thought it was incredibly good luck at the time: a temp job as one of Montfort's rotating stable of personal assistants, assigned to his social calendar. Nobody lasted more than a week in the job. She lasted two. Then a month. Then, suddenly, half a decade, and it was too late to get out.

Five years ago, everyone except Felicity knew that if you lasted a week under Montfort, you got your pick of secretarial jobs anywhere else in the city, because people assumed that if you could cope with him that long, you could cope with anything. But that was then. These days, if Montfort got rid of you, good luck sifting through what was left of his competitors to find another job.

And it wasn't only her job that he controlled. Her chest tightened, a steel trap pressing harder and harder around her ribs. He owned her apartment building. She was pretty sure he'd bought out her student loan.

She shouldn't even be thinking this, because he had the creepiest habit of—

Her phone rang. She jumped, which was annoying, because she'd *known* this was going to happen, and tried to shrug off cold, prickling dread as she accepted the call on the car's Bluetooth.

"Good evening, sir."

"Lily," he barked. Felicity didn't even blink. She remembered Lily, a sweet white woman who'd smuggled Felicity a coffee on her first day and run sobbing out of the building two days later. She wasn't sure Montfort had even noticed. He certainly hadn't updated his internal Rolodex. "How long are you going to keep me waiting this time?"

It was important not to pause, or take a deep breath, or try to find your center. Montfort saw through that sort of shit in a hot second. The trick was to leap on board whatever horrible conversation he'd decided he wanted to have, run to keep up, and pick up the pieces later in your own time.

Oh, and ignore how every instinct in your body was screaming at you to run away, as though he was an ogre from a fairytale and not just a horrible boss.

*I'm fine. I'm totally coping.*

"I'm so sorry, Mr. Montfort. I haven't made as good time as I expected. I'm still on the road, approximately ten minutes away from the town."

At least, she hoped she was. The fog was so thick she couldn't see ten feet in front of her, which was why she was running late. Not that she could tell Mr. Montfort that. She just had to hope that *ten minutes* wasn't too optimistic an estimate.

If only her GPS were working. It had led her this far, from the snarl of city traffic to open highways to the all-but-invisible road she was on now, which was meant to be following the coast but felt as though it was turning back on itself in circuitous knots. Her car's location kept jumping back and forth on the screen as though it wasn't sure what was going on either.

It was too much to hope for that the phone signal would be as unreliable as the GPS, but to her surprise, Mr. Montfort took her excuse in stride.

"Fine. Don't call me as soon as you get in. Go prop up the bar, or whatever passes for a bar in a place like that. Get someone to buy you a drink and tell you their life story. We find their weak points, we know where to put the pressure."

*To make people uncomfortable enough to sell up.* Because they weren't. Montfort's usual tactics of buying up mortgages and forcing the owners out hadn't worked. His much less preferred tactic of offering cash for what he wanted hadn't worked, either. Which was why she was here. Because she had spent the last five years smoothing every feather he'd ruffled in a hundred-mile radius, so why not send her a few thousand miles to work her magic on some grumpy locals, too?

*What is it about this place?* Not that she could see it through all this fog. *Hideaway Cove.* Even the name made it sound like they wanted to be left the hell alone.

"Sir, if they don't want to talk to me—"

She froze. Breath locked in her lungs, hands locked on the wheel, eyes locked on the fog-wreathed road ahead, like she was a rabbit who'd stepped straight into the fox's jaws. Don't ask questions! She'd had five years to learn that.

*Maybe if he fires me, I can just stay here… in the fog…*

Mr. Montfort let out a hiss that she scrambled to classify. Annoyed? Amused? Distracted? Her heart hammered in her throat.

"Sure they will. You've got one of those faces. Kind of pathetic. You make people feel good about themselves, and that makes them talk."

*One of those faces.* Felicity stared at herself in the rear-vision mirror.

Her face was… her face. So familiar it was hard to think about what it was actually *like*. Hair: black, straight, shoulder-length bob. Skin, not as great as all the products she used on it promised. Her dad's Asian eyes and permanently surprised-looking eyebrows and her mom's small square jaw. Nothing special, she'd always thought, but…

*Kind of pathetic.*

She ducked away from the mirror, blinking.

Beeping noises were coming through the phone. Montfort was jabbing out a message at someone else, not bothering to remember she was still on the line. Well-trained by years as his PA, Felicity didn't even grimace. The words *What sort of asshole doesn't mute his phone's keyboard noises?* did not so much as appear in her mind.

She concentrated on the road. The whole ten feet of it she could see in front of her. There were hints of landscape either side of her—she'd glimpsed trees earlier, and according to the GPS on her phone the ocean should be close enough to see if she'd been able to see *anything*. The whole world narrowed down to the headlights pressing against the fog ahead of her, and the *beep beep beep* of Montfort texting coming through the car speakers.

"I know you know better than to waste my time, Lily." His voice made her jump. She resettled her hands on the wheel, licking suddenly dry lips.

Waste his time?

"I won't disappoint you, sir."

"Everyone's replaceable. Remember that."

"I'll remember, sir, I—"

Something was looming out of the fog ahead. Something large and flat and oblong.

A sign. When she got close enough to read it, she held back a sigh of relief.

*Hideaway Cove.*

"You know, sir, you always have perfect timing, and this is no different. I'm right on the edge of town."

"Finally, some good news." The slightest pause. "I'm impressed. You didn't have any trouble finding the place?"

*Other than the fog?* "None whatsoever," she replied promptly. "It's very—"

She took in the wall of white outside the car.

"—picturesque." That was a good hold-all word. If the town *did* turn out to be as quaint and adorable as the other old fishing towns along this coast, then she was covered. If it turned out to be a burned-out ghost town, she could claim she was being ironic. Mr. Montfort appreciated irony.

Sometimes.

"I hope I don't need to remind you to keep this little trip to yourself. If Blackburn discovers what I'm planning here..." His voice went tight and vicious, almost a snarl.

Corin Blackburn was Mr. Montfort's—Felicity hesitated to use the word 'nemesis,' but only because she was worried that once she started, she wouldn't be able to stop. He was also her best friend Maya's boss.

Maya. Her eyes stung. She hadn't told Maya about this trip. Six months ago, she couldn't have imagined keeping something like that from her. They both basically survived their jobs by swapping notes on what their bosses were planning and ensuring the two men never crossed paths.

Then Maya had her baby, and Felicity had done her best to help, but it was like a wall had formed between them. Their visits and messages had dropped from daily to every-other-day, to once a week, to rain checks, to nothing.

The truth was, there wasn't anyone else she would have told about this trip. Her parents only cared that she had a good job; they didn't care what it was or where it took her. Stomach tight, she forced herself to pay attention to the voice hissing through the car.

"—perfect opportunity. While he's hiding his face, I'll prove that Montfort Industries are stronger than ever."

And with that, he hung up.

Suddenly needing fresh air, she rolled down the window. Tendrils of fog curled in, touching her face with cold, damp fingers.

The air smelled of salt. She closed her eyes and breathed in deep. Something about it calmed her, which was strange, because all day the smell of salt whenever she got out of the car had only reminded her that she was out on this wild goose chase and not safely back in the air-conditioned office, where she understood all the plays Mr. Montfort made and how to counter them.

Now, though…

She opened her eyes and gasped.

Lights.

She blinked. No, she wasn't imagining them. A cluster of golden lights, soft and fuzzy in the fog, but still definitely *there*. How had she missed them before?

The lights were all below her—she must be on the edge of a hill or cliff, looking down on the town. There was too much fog to tell for sure, but she thought she could make out one longer curve of lights, like a main road, with smaller roads coming off it up the hill towards her.

*Like half a sun surrounded by sunrays.* She let the fanciful thought sit in her head for a moment, then shook it away. The important thing was that lights meant there was an actual town down there. No more driving blind through the night.

One week. That was how long she was meant to stay in Hideaway Cove and find out whatever it was Mr. Montfort wanted to know about it.

She glanced down at the lights again and warmth coasted over her skin. She shivered, from the strangeness rather than any cold. The strange warmth was like sitting in sunlight. Bright and glowing and… welcoming.

She blinked.

And something leaped up from the dashboard and bit her.

"Ow!" Felicity yelped and pulled her hands off the wheel. She stared at them. An electric shock?

The engine rumbled and she grabbed the wheel again, wincing against the strange, cold bite of static against her palm while her other hand scrambled to turn the engine off. The brake pedal jumped under her foot and the wheel spun itself around as though someone else was hauling on it. Another shock coursed through her, brittle-edged and sharp and *cold*.

She lifted her head just as the car began to hurtle towards the edge of the road—and a sheer drop to the town lights below.

# 3

# APOLLO

There was no time to think. Only react. Apollo shot from the sky like an arrow, flaring his wings a microsecond before he hit the ground. Fog exploded away with the force of his landing. He reached out with one massive foreclaw and grabbed the back of the car.

His dragon was almost insensible with gold-lust. As though all the instincts it should have been reacting to for the last decade were hitting it at once. Pure *want* hissed through his head.

Treasure. *His* treasure. Take it! Save it!

He dragged the car back towards the road. It fought back: the driver must have had the accelerator flat on the floor. What were they thinking?

The fog was rolling back in, smudging the edges of his wings and dulling the golden fire of his scales. He should have hidden himself in it. Instead, high on finally feeling like he wasn't broken in some way, he lowered his head to stare at whoever was trying so hard to take a vertical shortcut into town.

Black eyes in a pale face stared back at him from the rear-view mirror, and lightning crashed through his veins.

He froze. The woman froze, too, shock cascading across her features. Then the car lurched forward, and her mouth formed the words, "Help me!"

The car was still fighting him. But it was fighting *her*, as well. He pulled magic from the spinning core of his power and sent it into the car to kill the engine.

Something stopped it.

Another magic, magic already crackling through the car, already controlling it. Magic that sparked electric-sharp as his own power.

Apollo's lightning magic skittered over the car, unable to find purchase. He pushed harder.

*I have to save her!* His dragon's snarl was an echo beneath the urgency in his own mind: *Mine!*

The resistance disappeared. His magic broke through. The car was his. Its engine died at once, and one wheel popped as he pulled it securely back onto the road.

Apollo ran his magic through and through the car's systems, searching for the strange mirror-magic that had pushed it away, and found nothing.

The driver's door swung open.

The woman he'd seen in the rear-view mirror tumbled out. Apollo backed away, hiding in the thick fog. But his dragon stayed intently focused on the woman, its golden gaze piercing the blanketing white.

She was of medium height, with shoulder-length straight black hair. Her light sweater and jeans caressed narrow shoulders curving down to generous hips and powerful thighs. Her hair swung as she turned her head this way and that.

Searching for him.

Apollo's heart was thundering in his massive dragon chest. Sparks crackled at the tips of each of his wings and claws and he hunched down, concentrated on keeping them—himself—hidden.

Whoever this woman was, she wasn't a shifter.

He hadn't heard a single word of telepathic speech as her car dragged her towards the edge. Not even the wordless pulse of emotion that shifters could communicate when they were too young or too frightened to form words.

She wasn't a shifter. She was human, she had seen him—

She had asked for his help.

*Treasure,* his dragon breathed. Sparks rippled along his spine.

Apollo didn't spare even a glance for the car where, presumably, the treasure was stashed. Frankly, it wasn't his priority right now. He had to find out who this woman was, find out whether she had seen him in dragon form. He thought their eyes had met in the rear-view mirror. Could he have imagined it? If she somehow hadn't seen him, he would have to come up with some explanation for the three deep, claw-shaped gouges in the car's trunk. If she hadn't—he should shift back, shouldn't he?

She was still staring into the fog-filled darkness, desperation staining her face.

He wanted to comfort her. Tell her she was safe. Without him even thinking about it, his dragon curled its long tail in a protective circle around her, far enough away that she couldn't see it through the fog but close enough that it—that she—

*Treasure.* This time, his dragon's voice was more like a sigh.

*Forget the treasure.* Whatever was in the car wasn't important. And maybe that made him a bad dragon. Maybe it meant whatever instinct had brought him up here was a fluke, but he didn't care. This woman was—she was—

*Treasure.*

The word rang like a bell in Apollo's head. A warning bell come far too late.

She stepped forward, her dark eyes searching the fog. Her mouth shaped a silent word he couldn't make out.

*Go back,* he urged her silently. He could tell himself the same thing. Change back. Change into his human form, try to prevent the utter disaster he was headed for.

Instead, he stood like a statue. And when the woman took another step forward, and another, he stayed frozen until it was far too late.

Their eyes met for the second time.

She saw him. Her dark eyes widened; her lips parted in surprise. All the color that had been left in her face drained away.

If Apollo had been human, his face would have gone pale, too.

Wind swirled around them both, making the fog billow up and hiding him again. He shifted, pulling on his human form so quickly he stumbled as his center of gravity changed. Pants. Where were his pants? He was sure he'd brought them with him. They had been right there, in his claws. He needed to get dressed, and make sure the woman was safe and unhurt, and tell her—tell her—

His dragon had been wrong.

This woman wasn't smuggling treasure into Hideaway Cove.

She *was* treasure.

The most precious treasure he would ever find. His treasure. His mate. And he had no hoard worthy of her.

# 4

# FELICITY

Every nerve in Felicity's body was screaming at her.

She barely registered the scrape of gravel beneath her feet, or the clinging cold of the fog as she breathed it in. Light-headed wasn't a strong enough word. Her whole body felt strangely buoyant, ghostly, as though it wasn't really *real*.

As though none of this was real.

She stared up into the wall of fog where, a moment ago, she thought she had seen—

A dragon.

Impossible.

She ran her hands over her face. Her skin was clammy. That was a sign of shock, wasn't it? The moment this weird light-bodied feeling faded, she would start shivering uncontrollably. Or was she already shivering? God, she'd almost *died*. Her car had gone crazy and tried to drive her off the side of a cliff, and then something had stopped it, and then—

And then *she* had gone crazy.

"I'm going to count to ten," she whispered to herself, "and when I get to ten, this is all going to make sense."

Eyes closed, she made it all the way to seven before her brain started to fizz with self-doubt.

*Surely I couldn't have seen—*

*No, I definitely didn't, but if I did—*

*Why would my brain make something like that up?*

*And the car—that made no sense, either, and if that made no sense, then what if—*

"Ten," she gasped, and opened her eyes.

The first thing she saw was a naked man.

He was tall and athletic, with long blond hair and pale eyes, and that was as much detail as she registered before her brain cut out completely.

She blinked. He was still there. Still naked.

A naked man… was *not* what she thought she had seen.

"Excuse me," the naked man said, and backed into the fog.

She blinked again.

A *polite*, naked man was so far outside even the crazy she thought she had seen, that it made what she *thought* she had seen seem almost believable.

She took a shaking breath and stepped forward. Fog tugged at her hair, her throat, her lips as she opened her mouth. "Hello?"

No one replied.

A yawning emptiness opened inside her. Nothingness pressed in on all sides—that same strange feeling of there being nothing in the fog except more nothing, of being so close to the edge of the world that she had found it still under construction. Her hands started to shake. Once they started, they didn't stop.

"It's all right. You're safe. I've got you."

Someone touched her arm, and the touch was so warm that she leaned into it automatically and found herself staring up into pale golden eyes. It was him. The naked man.

Her eyes drifted downwards, past a tanned, muscular chest to washboard abs… and jeans. Plain, ordinary, faded blue jeans.

"You put pants on," she said, and slammed her hand over her mouth. "Oh god. I'm so sorry—I didn't mean—I mean, I thought—"

"I suspect it's best not to think at all in situations like this." The man's voice was a light tenor. It wrapped around her like sunlight woven into a blanket. "Although, most people who know me would advise against taking my advice, so…"

He trailed off. She tore her eyes upwards and found him staring at her. His eyes were strange—a pale yellow-gold that she had only seen in cats' eyes before, not people's.

"Hello," he said in his sunlight voice. "My name's Apollo. I would say I don't usually babble like this, but that would be a lie."

"Felicity." Her own voice was shaky. Her brain was still re-treading the last few minutes, trying to find sense in them.

She groaned and shook her head. Apollo's eyes sharpened with concern.

"Are you hurt?" He moved his hand to her elbow, helping her hold herself steady just as she realized she needed it.

"No, I—the car—"

"I saw. What happened?"

"I…" She bit her lower lip. What could she tell him? That it felt like something took control of the car, like it was possessed or something? That it *bit* her? That she thought a dragon had dropped out of the sky and rescued her? "I don't know. I must have lost control in the fog."

He made an urgent, concerned sound. "You should probably sit down."

He turned her around, heading back towards the car. Felicity jerked away. "No—not back there."

The rest of her was floaty and shivery, but the memory of the car getting away from her control was like a shard of ice straight through her chest. She wrapped her arms around herself. "And there was—I thought I saw—"

"What did you see?"

His voice was just a touch too casual.

*Wait a minute.*

She turned slowly towards Apollo, taking a step back to get a good look at him.

His skin was tanned to a golden sheen. A deep V cut from the low-slung waistband of his jeans to narrow hips. He was pure athleticism, slender but powerful, washboard abs leading up to cut-glass pecs. But it was his shoulders that undid her. A swimmer's shoulders, she thought dazedly, broad and strong. A sudden desire to lick his collarbone hit her so hard her head swam. And not just his collarbone. His neck, up to the sensitive skin beneath his ear… his earlobe, almost hidden behind a fall of long, golden-blond hair…

Her eyes lingered on the strong angle of his jawline, the surprising softness of his lips and the dusting of golden stubble around them.

Her gaze lingered, because she was putting off a realization that would rock the foundations of everything she thought she knew about the world.

*Get on with it.* Her internal voice was rough, but her mind was drifting on starlit clouds. Not out of shock, or shivery fear. Out of wonder and anticipation at what she would find in those strange yellow eyes when she looked into them again.

Slowly, she lifted her gaze.

His eyes were the same pale yellow that had made her think of a cat's eyes—but only for a moment. She held his gaze, and a deeper, richer color bloomed in their depths until they shone like pools of molten gold.

They were the exact unearthly shade as the eyes of the creature she had seen wreathed in fog. The creature that had pulled her car back to safety. Had pulled *her* back to safety.

Had saved her life.

Her heart thudded.

"I saw you," she whispered.

Understanding flickered in his eyes, warm and slightly rueful. "I thought that might be the case."

On an impulse that came from a part of herself she hadn't known existed, she lifted one hand and brushed a stray strand of golden hair away from his face. Where her fingertips kissed his cheekbone, a shock like but unlike static electricity crackled against her skin and filled her with the feeling of sunlight.

The weight of five years under Montfort's thumb and a lifetime of doubting herself lifted from her shoulders. She felt *free*.

She never would have dared dream something like this could be real. But here he was.

"You're a dragon."

# 5

# APOLLO

Felicity's eyes were like chips of jet. Like a starless night sky, velvety and welcoming. Like the sea beneath the starless night sky, reflecting its endless beauty.

They were the eyes of his human mate, who had seen him in dragon form and whose dark eyes were more than a little starry, now, as she gazed up at him.

Apollo's timeline for finding a suitable hoard had just become a *lot* shorter.

"I usually try to keep that particular revelation until the third date," he found himself saying, "but, yes. Apollo Jenkins, dragon shifter, at your service." He sketched out an ironic bow, but it didn't feel ironic. It felt like he should throw himself at her feet and beg her forgiveness for not being better prepared for her.

Her eyes widened, but when the question behind them burst from her lips, it wasn't about the dragon bit.

"Apollo. Like—like the god?"

"My parents had high hopes of me." Hopes that until now, he had thoroughly dashed. Guilt twisted in his stomach.

If he had only fought harder for those treasures he came across in his travels. He hadn't felt the gold-lust, but he could have pretended. Tried harder. Had *something* to show for himself other than...

His heart sank.

It wasn't true that he had *no* hoard. He did have one. A single piece of treasure, given to him on his eighteenth birthday by his grandfather, who had been reluctant to part with even that tiny fragment of his own hoard.

The gifted treasure was meant to spur Apollo's draconic instincts to hunt down his own, superior hoard. Instead, it was all he had.

He fought off an embarrassed wince.

"I usually go by Pol," he said. "Or Sparky."

Felicity's eyebrows pulled together, just slightly. It was the most beautiful thing he had ever seen.

"And you're a… dragon… shifter."

Apollo opened his mouth to explain—then closed it. Felicity had raised the hand she had brushed against his face again and was staring at it.

His magic had leaped between them at her touch before he could stop it. As she rubbed her fingertips together, he was caught by a sudden longing to know what it had felt like to her, the caress of his magic against her skin.

She swayed, and he took her arm to steady her again. Magic surged, the tiny star-like sparks flickering from his hand to her skin. Her eyes widened.

"You…" She shook herself. "That felt like…"

Slowly, carefully, she pulled her arm from his grip and squeezed her eyes shut. He let her go, although the small tremors in her hands made him ache to pull her into his embrace.

"What are the chances," she said, her eyes still shut, "that I'm imagining all of this? That it's just… shock. There's a sensible explanation for what happened to the car, and—what I just saw, and *felt*, and…"

She opened her eyes and lifted her arm. The last sparks of Apollo's magic whirled softly around her wrist before winking out one by one.

"…that," she whispered.

Apollo swallowed.

She wasn't a shifter. She was a human visitor, and part of living in Hideaway Cove meant keeping the existence of shifters secret from all humans.

But she was also his mate. He had already failed her more than she knew. He wouldn't begin by lying to her as well.

"The chances are not very high, I'm afraid."

"No. I didn't think so." She rubbed her fingers together as though she was trying to feel the just-vanished sparks again, and only an iron self-control Apollo didn't know he had stopped him from filling the air with more magic. He had already almost burned through his reserves. Much more and he would be running on less than fumes.

That self-control lasted exactly until she raised her eyes to his. Her face was still pale, but her gaze was lit up from within. "You're a dragon shifter. And you saved my life. I can honestly say I've never been happier to meet anyone in my whole life than I am to meet you, Apollo Jenkins."

The sound of his name on her lips crackled against Apollo's skin.

And the fog-choked darkness around them filled with light.

Felicity refused to get back into her car. Apollo couldn't blame her. He, in turn, refused to let her carry her own suitcase as they walked down the hill into town, their way lit by his wayward magic.

"Let me get this straight." Felicity gestured in front of herself, as though her thoughts were whirling around among the firefly sparks of Apollo's magic. "You're a dragon shifter. You turn into a dragon."

Felicity's eyes raked over him, full of curiosity, and he preened under her gaze.

"That's right. A lightning dragon shifter, to be precise."

"Hence the—" She gestured again, the movement taking in the lights around them.

"Among other things."

"Oh?" She leaned towards him, her face shining, then inhaled sharply. "No, don't tell me. My brain's about to explode already. And you live… here? Not in some ruined castle on a mountaintop somewhere, or, or a volcano or something, but here in this little town?"

Apollo cast his gaze around the fog-shrouded street and sighed. "It isn't looking its best at the moment, I admit, but it does have a lot to recommend it."

"I guess I'll find out over the next few days."

"You're staying?" Apollo blurted out, then slapped one hand to his forehead. "Of course you are."

"Well, it's not like I'm driving anywhere else tonight!"

His dragon jabbed him urgently with the pointy tip of its tail. Its wishes were so clear, Apollo heard them as his own thoughts. *Tell her she's your mate and she can live here forever!*

Apollo made a small, strangled noise, and did his best to keep his tone casual. "Yes, I can see how that might be a problem."

He couldn't tell her she was his mate. Not yet. Not two minutes after meeting her, after she'd almost *died,* and he'd already blown her mind with the small piece of information that he could transform into a dragon.

Besides, what would he say to her? *Hey, you're my fated soulmate—now please wait here while I fly off and gather enough of a hoard to woo you with?*

His shoulders slumped. No. He couldn't tell her, not yet.

Instead, he escorted her to the local bed-and-breakfast. He left her in the care of the landlady, bird shifter Marjorie Hanson, and promised to see to her car.

Felicity still looked shaken. She waited as Mrs. Hanson bustled upstairs to check the room and caught Apollo's arm as he was leaving.

"Be careful, will you?" She bit her lower lip. "I didn't say anything before because I wasn't sure I actually believed it had happened, but…"

"Here in Hideaway, it's best to believe what you see no matter how magical." He was hoping to tempt out another smile, but her expression darkened further.

"That's what I'm worried about. When I went off the road—it felt as though something else was controlling the car. The wheel spun around on its own and when I tried to stop it, something *shocked* me." She bit down harder on her lower lip. "If you're going to tow the car—do me a favor and actually *tow* it, in your dragon form if you have to. Don't try to drive it down. I don't trust it."

He didn't let his horror show on his face until he was outside, and the fog was creeping cold fingers along the back of his neck.

Felicity's warning had struck him like a bell. His ears were still ringing. Still, he didn't let himself fully believe the implications until he walked out onto the waterfront and turned to stare up at the town.

Hideaway Cove was a cluster of golden lights, like a handful of his magical sparks blown up to a thousand times the size. His house—the cottage his dragon had wanted him to take Felicity to—was in the middle of town. Dead center. Invisible in the fog, but all too clear on his internal, magical map of Hideaway Cove.

Dead center, and right below where Felicity's car had almost plummeted down the slope.

Her words echoed in his mind. She said that it felt as though something had taken control of her car. And he had felt it, too—that strange slipperiness as his magic came up against another active, electrical magic. He had been so distracted by discovering she was his mate, he had forgotten about it.

But he was the only person in Hideaway Cove with that sort of power.

Dread pooled in his stomach. His dragon hissed, unhappy with the direction his mind was going.

He didn't want to believe it. But the more he thought about it the more horrible sense it made.

Maybe there was a reason he hadn't hunted out a hoard to offer his mate all these years. It wasn't that she didn't exist. It was that they shouldn't be together.

He was meant to protect her.

Instead, his magic had almost gotten her killed.

# 6

# FELICITY

Felicity was dreaming of golden eyes.

It was a wonderful dream. The type she hadn't had in years. The type of dream that, if she was being honest, she thought had been stripped away with everything else that had disappeared from her life until only her job was left.

She didn't want it to end, and she was awake enough to know it was only a dream and that as soon as she opened her own eyes it would disappear. *He* would disappear. The man with golden eyes. Not hazel, or amber, or pale brown. A gold so rich they practically glowed. Surrounded by luxuriously thick lashes that turned every expression into a flirt.

Eyes that watched *her* with a combination of anticipation and wonder as though she was the dream that might disappear at any moment and not normal, ordinary Felicity Park. Eyes that cast flirtatious glances in her direction until she wasn't sure which way was up. Long-fingered hands that looked like they were made for doing wicked things. Like stirring sparks of magic out of the air and sending those sparks dancing across her skin. Each point of light pricked her skin, half kiss, half bite, warm and welcoming.

*Apollo Jenkins.* The name came back to her with a sudden, overwhelming sensation of the lips that had spoken it: soft and warm–looking and so kissable that she snuggled deeper into the bed, trying to get back to sleep and back to whatever was going to happen next in her dream.

It was a shame it wasn't real and that any second now, her alarm was going to go off and she would have to put on her work face and hurry to get to the office before Mr. Montfort, with his favorite coffee in one hand and a list of low-priority meetings for him to angrily tell her to cancel before he had his caffeine and could be gently directed towards the higher-priority actions for the day…

Felicity groaned and pressed her face into the pillow. She didn't want to think about Mr. Montfort. She wanted to think about Apollo, and his deep gold eyes, and the fact that his tan went all the way from his face to his jeans with no tan lines and how he could turn into a dragon.

*Wait just a goddamn minute.*
Her eyes shot open.

"It wasn't a dream." Her voice was muffled by the pillow. She shoved herself upright, and the first thing she saw was the view through the window above the bed.

The morning was bright and sunny and… welcoming. That was the only word for it. Everything seemed to be calling out to her to admire it. The sun glinting on the waves, the gentle curve of the walkway along the waterfront and the quaintly painted shopfronts—it was as though they were somehow waiting for her to look at them. Like the fog had been a sheet thrown over the town before its big reveal.

To either side of the bay, hills extended like arms curled around softly lapping waves. A lighthouse watched from one hilltop, and a road mean-dered down the other.

Cold crept down the back of her neck. The road looped back up the hill, heading out of sight behind rows of old wooden houses.

If she got out of bed, went down onto the road—would she be able to see where she almost crashed?

Where she'd first seen Apollo appear out of the fog?

*Apollo.*

She rocked backwards. The dragon shifter's name pulsed through her, heat flooding in its wake.

No wonder she'd had that dream. Apollo was… she didn't have words for what he was. He could turn into a dragon. The way his magic had danced through the air—she could still feel the echo of it on her skin. But that was nothing compared to the way his eyes had lingered on her, or the smile that had tugged at his lips once he made sure she wasn't injured.

He'd said to come by that morning to talk about the car, hadn't he?

She showered in record time, pulled on a fresh set of clothes, made it to the door, ran back and pulled on a different outfit—something that showed off more of her legs—and raced down the stairs.

Hideaway Cove might have shed its fog to put on a show for her, but it had a way to go to beat out the man who'd featured so prominently in her dreams.

At the bottom of the stairs, she almost ran into Mrs. Hanson and two other guests. Felicity stopped short before she bowled anyone over. Mrs. Hanson was the smallest old lady she'd ever met, and looked dainty as a dried leaf, though that hadn't stopped her hefting Felicity's suitcase upstairs like it weighed nothing before Felicity could stop her.

"Good morning, dearie. Have you met—no, of course you haven't. Felicity arrived late last night," Mrs. Hanson explained in not-particularly-hushed tones. "Antonia, Bruno, this is Felicity."

There was a pause. Felicity automatically took the opportunity to inspect the two other guests. They had to be shifters, right? What sort? Was there any way to know, without actually seeing them shift? Was it rude to ask? Was it rude not to ask?

They looked like ordinary humans, which was probably very rude to think, let alone say. Antonia was in her early fifties and clearly took an anxious pride in her appearance: her dark hair was shiny and healthy, her summery linen dress pressed to perfection, but the perfection gave away her nerves. Felicity got the impression she would spend more of her vacation brushing sand off her clothes than actually enjoying the beach.

Her son, Bruno, wasn't obviously anxious about anything—least of all hiding how much he begrudged being there. Whether that was there as in, stuck in the hallway while his mother chatted with the landlady, or there in Hideaway in general, wasn't clear. He had his mother's dark hair and a sullen expression and couldn't have been more than fifteen or sixteen years old.

Felicity held out her hand. "It's a pleasure to meet you. I hope I didn't make too much noise coming in last night. I had a bit of a shock."

"Felicity's car almost came off the road above the town!" Mrs. Hanson chirped. "You would have heard if that happened. Luckily, our resident dragon swooped to the rescue."

"Your dragon?" Antonia gasped. "I didn't know—goodness, I never would have thought—Bruno, did you see that last night? Bruno was out last night," she explained before her son had a chance to say anything.

Bruno waited an exaggerated few seconds. He didn't roll his eyes when he eventually answered, but Felicity thought it was a near thing. "No. Because of the fog." He hunched his shoulders and avoided her gaze.

"And I didn't even hear you come in!" his mother said brightly. So brightly, in fact, that Felicity guessed she was used to trying to make up for Bruno's grumpiness, like some sort of emotional seesaw. Poor woman, she thought.

Something like guilt flashed across Bruno's face—at least, until he caught her looking, and glared at her again.

She breezily ignored Bruno's glare and focused on his mother. "I'm glad I didn't disturb you."

"Now, Felicity, dear, did you want breakfast, or…?" Mrs. Hanson's eyes twinkled. The front door beckoned. Felicity was almost bouncing on her feet, she wanted to head out so badly. *Which Mrs. Hanson obviously noticed. Whoops.*

"I was thinking of going for a walk," she blurted out.

Mrs. Hanson blinked innocently. "To anywhere in particular, dear?"

"Er—"

"I'm only teasing. I imagine you'll be wanting to see young Apollo—about your car, of course?"

Yes. Yes, she was very much wanting to go and see the pants-droppingly gorgeous man who was named after a freaking Greek god, who could transform into a dragon and who had saved her life.

About the car. That was right. Definitely going to see him about the car. Yes. Absolutely.

Five minutes later, she was outside, arms laden with a basket of breakfast things Mrs. Hanson had insisted she take with her, saying the two of them would need to keep up their strength. Apparently, they took hospitality seriously here in Hideaway Cove.

She was glad not to be going to meet Apollo empty handed. Breakfast was small repayment for saving her life, but it was a start. Better than nothing. Better than—

Cold gripped her, so sharp and sudden it was as though the sun had gone out.

*Better than selling him out to Montfort.*

She *had* still been in a dream. A wonderful dream, where she really was on vacation, and the biggest thing she had to worry about was whether she was going to get laid or not. By a guy who could turn into a dragon.

Reality hit her like a bucket of ice. Montfort had sent her here to find out this town's secrets. And Apollo had already served them up to her on a plate.

She felt sick.

*I won't do it. I'll leave—*

In what? Her rental car was at the mechanic. With Apollo. Waiting for her.

Her eyes followed the wide promenade to the far end of the bay, where the stores and houses made way for a cluster of warehouses. One of those must be the mechanic.

Heart in her throat, she headed towards it.

She found the mechanic's—*Mackaby's*, according to the sign—tucked against the hill. It was an old warehouse with a newer concrete garage butted against one side of it. The garage's roller door was open, revealing Felicity's rental car raised up on a dolly.

Maybe she could still escape. Apollo could fix her car and she could drive and drive and never look back. If she never went home, Montfort would never find her, right?

The car didn't look too bad. A bit dusty. Nothing a good wash and polish wouldn't...

She walked closer and stopped dead.

*Not too bad* was an overstatement.

What she'd thought was dust was a constellation of blackened cracks in the paint. One particularly crackled mark arced down to the passenger-side wheel casing. The wheel was in ribbons.

Felicity swayed. No wonder she'd suddenly lost control of the car. What could have caused that?

A memory of sour-cold sparks crackling up her fingers made her shiver.

She wrapped her arms around herself and walked swiftly around the car. There they were: the three deep, jagged gouges where Apollo had grabbed the car and saved her life.

Strictly speaking, the claw marks of a giant mythical lizard should have been scarier than a busted tire. But as Felicity traced one of them with her fingertip, all she felt was relief.

"You're here."

Apollo's voice shivered across her skin. She was smiling before she even turned around - but the moment she saw him, the grin slipped from her face. "Is everything all right?"

Dark shadows lingered under his golden eyes. His intoxicating smile was brittle at the edges. "I didn't expect to see you—" He visibly pulled himself together. "—this early."

Felicity stilled. Her instincts had been honed by five years working for Saint-John Montfort and dealing with the sorts of people Montfort did business with; she knew how to hear what was left unsaid, and black-line what people said but didn't mean. And Apollo didn't mean 'this early'.

He hadn't expected to see her at all.

"You didn't want me to come?" She regretted the words as soon as they escaped. Her voice had a little-girl-lost edge that made her feel queasy.

*Kind of pathetic.*

"I wanted you to come more than anything." His voice was hollowed out. Had he slept at all last night? What the hell was going on here? Where was the confident, almost swaggering man—*dragon shifter*—from the night before?

He looked exhausted. Beaten down.

…Guilty?

She folded her arms. "Let me guess. Draconic claw marks are expensive to fix?"

His eyes jerked to hers. "What?"

"Because if you're thinking of feeling bad about saving my life last night, please don't. Whatever fixing the car is going to cost is more than worth not scraping myself off the side of a cliff."

"That's just it." Apollo took a step towards her. His magic, almost invisible in the morning light, danced in a halo around his hair. A ribbon of sparks twined around his wrist and reached out towards her—he hissed in a breath and clasped both hands behind his back.

Felicity stopped herself partway through stepping towards him. She hadn't even noticed she had started moving. "What's 'just it'?"

"I don't think I did save your life." He took an unsteady breath. "I think it's my fault you were in danger in the first place."

Guilt and misery warred on his face. Felicity closed the distance between them and froze, again, when he backed away.

"What are you talking about?"

His jaw worked. "My magic. You said you lost control of the car last night, that it felt as though it had a mind of its own. It didn't. It was taken over by my magic. It must have been. I can't think of any other explanation."

"You… magicked my car?" She rolled the idea around in her mind, trying to find a way for it to fit. "Why?"

"Not on purpose. I…" His head jerked. He was so obviously miserable, Felicity's chest pulled. "I haven't been entirely honest with you about my magic. How it works. What it does."

"You mean turning into a dragon?"

"I mean this." He waved one hand and lights trailed after it, a dancing ribbon of sparks. Felicity reached out, entranced. A spark buzzed against her fingertip, the same sunlight feeling from the night before.

And something else, too. Something warm, and safe.

Apollo's face paled, and he almost lost his balance. "Damn."

"Are you okay?" All thoughts of warmth and sunlight fled. Apollo looked a step from death's door. Was this why Mrs. Hanson had sent her with breakfast?

"It's nothing. I've let the tank run too low, that's all. And as a dragon I'm naturally allergic to admitting my weaknesses, so it's possible I'm subconsciously trying to make myself pass out rather than confess my guilt to you." His jaw worked and the amusement in his voice faded. "Yes, I can transform into a dragon, and I can do these little light shows. That is not quite the full story. I'm a lightning dragon, and my magic—"

He raised his hand again, but clenched his fist over the sparks that formed. "—my magic is electrical power combined with magical power. It's spread throughout this whole town. Every wire, every appliance in every house is touched by it. And it runs around the perimeter of the town and alerts me when a car passes over the boundary."

"Power and security system in one," Felicity murmured. "Is that how you knew I needed help?"

"It told me you when you crossed the border." His voice softened. "My dragon thought you were some sort of treasure."

"Sorry to disappoint." He was kidding, right?

"You didn't." His eyes burnt into hers. "But that's not all my magic did."

Unease tugged at her gut. She thought she could see where this was going, and it felt… wrong.

"I'm not in control of my magic once I imbue it into something. I can guide its purpose, but over the past few months I've had to admit to myself that it doesn't always obey." He lowered his clenched fist and looked away. "I tried to regain control of your car last night, but something stopped me. I've never had to fight my own magic like that before. And you can see what it did to the car. Those cracked marks. I can't risk something like that happening again." He straightened his shoulders, not meeting her eyes. "I understand if you prefer I didn't do the repairs myself. My colleague Harrison can fix your car. And please don't worry about the cost. I'm not going to charge you for being the victim of my magic's attempt to—to…"

"To what? You think your magic tried to kill me?"

His face twisted.

Felicity stared. A feeling that was familiar and yet strange unfurled inside her, like a long-dormant bulb producing its first flower. It took her a moment to recognize it.

Anger.

It rushed through her, a raging flood bursting the banks of a dried-out riverbed. And not just any anger. Anger about something that *wasn't right*. Anger and the burning determination to do something about it.

She couldn't explain it. Last night everything had seemed like a dream—Apollo, his magic, the cozy bed-and-breakfast. The fog gave the town a fairytale quality, soft and hidden, and she'd sunk into it like the softest mattress.

And today it was as though the sun had come out, not only on Hideaway, but on her mind. She hadn't felt this energized in years.

Five years, to be exact.

A chill prickled along her arms. How had she not noticed the effect Montfort was having on her? Hadn't she been fine? Hadn't she *coped* with everything he threw at her?

*Coping isn't living*. She stole a sidelong glance at Apollo.

And Montfort wasn't here now.

She'd stumbled from the nightmare of her car into a world that, instead of rejecting her, welcomed her.

If Apollo thought she was going to let him think there was something *wrong* with him?

Her head spun. "You're wrong."

Apollo looked at her, his expression unreadable. "I wish I were. But there's no other explanation for—"

"There must be. Your magic didn't try to hurt me." *It wouldn't. You wouldn't*. Her thoughts whirled. "Could it have been another dragon shifter?"

"I would know if another dragon shifter came anywhere near Hideaway Cove." His eyes flashed. "Even if there were any other dragons around, they wouldn't be responsible. No one else has magic like me." Apollo ran his fingers through his hair and shook his head. "The only other lightning dragon is my grandfather. I would know if he was here. Hell would have frozen over."

"And lightning dragons are the only people who could do something like this? Are you sure you're the only ones?"

"We're extremely endangered." Apollo's voice was dry. He was back behind his too-suave mask; only the tightness at the corners of his eyes gave him away. Anger surged through Felicity again. How *dare* he think that his magic hurt her? "One lightning dragon every two generations, which must be some sort of evolutionary self-defense because we can't stand to be around one another. Other dragons live in colonies; my dragon rattles its scales if I so much as see Grandfather Errol's contact details in my phone." He shivered delicately, as though to demonstrate.

"It must be something. It wasn't your magic. It felt *wrong*."

Apollo laughed hollowly. "I don't know what can feel right or wrong about a small electric shock."

"That's not what I meant."

"What does it feel like, then?"

He glanced at her sidelong and Felicity stopped, caught, her lips open to say something terribly, ridiculously true. Something like *it feels like sunlight*. Or worse.

Apollo kept talking as she searched for an answer that wouldn't make her sound like a complete lunatic. "My magic doesn't feel like anything. It's just... sparks."

"No, it isn't." What was he talking about? "What I felt in the car was cold, and nasty. Like dunking my hands into ice water. Yours feels... warm. And like it wants things to be—good, and safe, and..."

He was looking at her as though she'd just grown an extra head. Oh god. She'd really put her foot in it. *File this under 'things it's not socially acceptable to talk about with shifters.'*

The hell with it. She couldn't let him keep thinking he'd hurt her.

"It wasn't your magic I felt in the car, and I'll prove it."

She looked around. Apollo said he imbued his magic into the whole town? She should be able to feel it, then, shouldn't she, the same way she felt the warmth of the sparks he sent whirling around?

One wall of the workshop was lined with machinery. She dug up some names from school shop class. Grinders? Saws? And one massive metal beast that looked like a cross between a spinning wheel and a steam train. Something about it tugged her closer.

"Wait," Apollo burst out. "What are you—"

Felicity placed her hand on the strange machine. She felt cold, inert metal. *But there has to be more than that*, she thought, and *reached* with senses she didn't know she had.

Something leapt beneath her fingertips like a pulse. She jumped back, her eyes flying open.

"What is it?" Apollo was at her side, one hand on her waist. Her *waist*. Oh god. How was she meant to think of anything else when his hand was on her waist?

She twisted to look up into his face, and the expression she found there shocked away her sudden rush of heat.

He looked like he hated himself. "Let me guess. Cold and wrong?" There were walls up behind his eyes, but they weren't enough to hide the despair.

Anger swelled up in her again. What had happened to him, to make him think that his incredible, wonderful magic could have anything evil in it?

"The opposite. It felt alive." She reached out again, still holding Apollo's gaze. He grabbed her hand as if to stop her, but she was already touching the cold iron again. Their hands pressed against it together.

This time she didn't need to reach out. The magic was waiting for her, delirious at her attention. It sank into her, or she sank into it. The golden pinpricks of light formed images, impressions like constellations, suffused with emotion.

A young man with hazel eyes and something half-bird, half-lion in his heart fed a slab of butter-yellow metal under what she now realized was a massive hammer, under the watchful eye of an old man with a thatch of wild white hair. Across the room, a wolf used his human hands to sand a length of wood that would one day be part of a boat that could have taken him anywhere but which anchored him in Hideaway Cove. Years later, that same sapphire-eyed wolf was showing another young man how to send wood through a table saw so smoothly the blade seemed barely to kiss the wood until it fell away in two pieces. Sawdust settled like snow on the younger man's dark skin. And he was a bird, somehow, like the older guy was somehow a human and a wolf at the same time.

She knew what Apollo's magic was showing her. This was an important place. Years of skill passed down generation to generation. Men who showed their love and pride through the work of their hands.

She wanted more. Where was he? He had to be here somewhere.

*There.*

This was Apollo as she hadn't seen him. Younger, looser-limbed; she hadn't noticed the faint lines around his eyes until she saw him here without them. He was brimming with energy. His skin practically glowed. Then he reached out, his hand a ghostly echo over where his real hand was pressed against hers on the hammer, and light burst out of him.

Joy hit her like a freight train. Fierce, possessive joy. It was too much. Felicity's ears roared. Her skin was alight with sensation. She felt alive, more alive that she'd thought was possible, like a butterfly breaking free of a cocoon it thought it would be in forever.

The images faded, leaving behind a confusion of stars like the aftereffects of looking at the sun. Felicity blinked, then got the strong impression she hadn't *physically* blinked at all—that she was looking at this with something other than her eyes. Some magical sense she'd never used before.

The blinding luminescence faded, leaving a single star shining in Felicity's vision. Golden threads spun off it, held taut by something she couldn't see. She frowned. Was this what Apollo meant when he said his magic infused the town? This piece of machinery held the 'star', a whirling, sparking flame of his power, and those threads led—where? To other stars?

She turned slowly.

It was like standing on the edge of a constellation, too close to see the picture it made. Ribbons of gold light stretched between crackling vortexes. And where Apollo stood...

All the air vanished from her lungs. Apollo *glowed.* If these other magical hotspots were stars, he was the sun. Huge golden wings arced above his shoulders, and he was holding the threads of his magic like reins, twining through his fingers and stretching out to meet the whirling constellation of power.

And his eyes weren't warm gold anymore—they were sharp and glittering. Dragon's eyes. Her heart leapt into her throat.

*I'm going to see him in full dragon form again if it's the last thing I do.*

He reached for her. His magic followed, curling around her like shimmering wings. She tensed in anticipation—but the magic never touched her. It flowed around her like the light on water burbling over rocks in a stream. It shone over her, outlining every line and curve of her body, but stayed tantalizingly, achingly apart.

Longing swept through her, so intense her knees wobbled.

His fingers brushed against hers. Surely that must be what was needed to break the wall between his magic and herself, she thought.

Instead, he said her name, and the magical vision broke like a soap bubble.

She blinked. Apollo was staring into her eyes, his gaze taut with concern. "Felicity? Are you…"

Felicity took a ragged breath. "Am I what?" she said unevenly. She took another breath that seemed to fill space in her lungs she hadn't had before.

She had seen Apollo's magic. More than that. She'd jumped headlong into it, found herself facing the workshop's memories as though she'd pried into the old building's heart, and felt the steady thrum of his power enclosing the town like a protective cloak.

And she'd seen him, brilliant and shining, his human form barely containing the sun-like power of his magic.

It was incredible. Overwhelming. And the most erotic thing she'd ever experienced.

She was so turned on she thought she might die.

"I…" She froze her tongue just in time. *It's not possible to die from horniness,* she told herself as every atom of her being tried to melt into a puddle. *Think of something else. Anything else. Cold showers. Ice-cubes. Antarctica. Pluto. The frozen endless expanse of space.*

Apollo's eyes, shining warm gold and dragon-fierce.

She swallowed.

"I'm fine?" she croaked, and her cheeks flared red.

Apollo was holding her hand. At her words, he slid his hand up her arm, closing the space between them. He looked at her intently and the worry in his eyes narrowed to a mischievous glint. "You certainly look… fine," he murmured.

Felicity wasn't sure she'd heard him right over the hammering of her heartbeat. "I do?"

"Exceptionally so." Curiosity flickered across his face. "What did you do? You touched the power hammer, and I felt…"

Color darkened his own cheeks and Felicity's own blush was reaching critical levels. Heat throbbed between her legs. *That thing is called a POWER HAMMER? I touched his MAGICAL POWER HAMMER, and* this *is what happens?*

Apollo tentatively raised a hand to her face. His fingertips brushed her cheek. "You touched my magic," he breathed.

"Was I not meant to?"

"I have no idea. I didn't know such a thing was possible."

"And now that you do…?" She licked her lips, and his eyes tracked the motion. *Oh my God.* "Does it help to know there's definitely nothing, uh, nothing wrong with it? All the magic I… touched. It's all very, um. Good?"

"*Very* good?"

*So fucking good I am five seconds from tearing my clothes off and crying 'Take me, you sexy dragon man,'* she did NOT say.

But the way he was looking at her, it was like he'd plucked the words right out of her head.

The hell with it.

She kissed him.

He tasted like mint and sunlight and something that sent delicious shivers up her spine. His arms tightened around her and then he was kissing her back, hot and sweet and tangling his hands in her hair. She felt light-headed. Was this really happening? Was it part of the vision, still? The magic? Oh, God, the magic. He ran his hand down the side of her neck and his power whispered against her skin, electric-sharp with promise.

"Nghhh," she said, which was the wrong thing to say, because he stopped kissing her. "No, wait…"

Golden eyes blazed down at her. Apollo stared at her like she'd just stepped naked out of the ocean, not thrown herself at his magic and then at *him*.

She stepped back. "I'm sorry, I don't know what I was thinking."

"Don't be sorry." His voice was husky. She couldn't look away from his eyes. "Are you all right? You… glowed. I've never seen my magic cover someone like that before."

She'd been covered in his magic? No wonder she'd come out of it and dived in for a kiss.

As for whether she was all right… How to describe it? *I was so turned on my soul almost left my body.* No.

"Well, given my very little experience touching random men's… magic…" She drew herself up. "Everything seemed perfectly in order. Definitely nothing to do with what happened last night."

The teasing light vanished from his eyes. "How can you be sure?"

Felicity's stomach tightened. More than anything, she didn't want to lose the breathless, electric connection between them.

And she had a great idea how to keep that from happening.

"Hmm," she began, slowly, tipping her head back. "I guess I *can't* be sure, with so little evidence. Maybe we should investigate further?"

# 7

# APOLLO

All his life, Apollo had amazed people with his magic. Even other shifters were taken aback by the existence of what some of them called 'real' magic, as though their own ability to transform into an animal didn't count.

Listening to Felicity, he understood for the first time how they felt. She knew things about his magic he never even dreamed of.

*She can sense my magic.* Other people noticed his magic when he put on a light show to dazzle them, or zapped them with sparks as a joke, but what Felicity described was so far beyond that.

"I saw… memories, I think. Of people working here. It felt like—like it wanted to show me what it loved about this place. Sorry, that doesn't make sense. It was weird, though. The people I saw weren't just *people*, they were animals too, and—oh. I'm such an *idiot*. It must be because they're shifters." She hesitated, a beat that thrummed in Apollo's chest. "You were there, too."

"What was I doing?"

"You touched that… machine. The hammer thing."

The power hammer. All at once, he knew exactly what she had seen.

It was years ago, the first morning he'd set foot in Hideaway Cove. He'd flown through the night, willing himself to be excited about searching for lost treasure, forcing back the twist in his gut when the excitement didn't come. He had landed in the trees on the hill above town and walked down in human form. And then he'd seen it.

Hideaway Cove. A town so obscure it wasn't on most maps, and when it was, it was a tiny dot, its name picked out in letters so small you needed a microscope to read them. Any expectations he had vanished like sea spray the moment the town came into view: a scatter of jewels, bright, painted houses and glittering windows, tucked into the curve of the bay. Secret. Safe.

He'd half-run, half-skidded down the shaly hillside in his urgency to set foot in the town, and the workshop was the first place he'd come to. Old Mr. Mackaby had still been in charge then, but Harrison was ready to take over, and he'd been the one to greet Apollo.

He must have looked like a madman. Hair mussed from shifting, body stuffed into whatever clothes had been in the top of his bag. Harrison's griffin had glinted out through his eyes, wary of this crazy stranger, and Arlo had slunk around the door, and Apollo had laughed out loud. He'd seen their true natures at once. Other shifters, hidden away in this secret little town. *Hideaway Cove.* What a perfect gem of a name.

Harrison had asked who he was, what he wanted. Apollo had already forgotten he was here for Hideaway's hidden treasure. He put on his grandest voice, proclaimed he was here to help them out, and laid his hand and his magic on…

He rested his hand on the power hammer. It was an original, from when the town was founded. A huge, hulking cold iron brute, converted from steam-powered to run on electricity.

"This was the first thing I fixed when I moved to Hideaway. The first piece of my magic I gave away to the town was here. And you saw it." He was shaken. He'd never considered that his magic might be anything other than a sort of power boost for the town. "I had no idea that was possible."

"But… it's *your* magic." She looked at him quizzically.

"Yes. You'd think I would know more about it, wouldn't you?" His heart felt heavy. What else didn't he understand? Was this why he'd spent so long unable to gather a hoard?

"Maybe not, if you only have one lightning dragon in your family every few generations. I'm guessing from how you described your relationship that you don't spend time together swapping notes on your powers."

He winced. "Accurate."

"So…" Felicity's eyes danced. "This is the oldest piece of magic here, and it isn't all evil? I don't think your magic is the problem, even if you *don't* control it once you give it to the town."

He wanted to pull her into his arms and kiss her again. Two things stopped him. The guilty tug of his hoard, from wherever he'd hidden it in the back of some cupboard in his house; and the fact that Mrs. Hanson had sent her over with a basket to rival Little Red Riding Hood's. Which meant Felicity must not have eaten before she came over.

Sweeping his mate off her feet was all very well and good, but not if she literally swooned from hunger in the middle of it.

There were also, he soon discovered, selfish reasons to pay attention to his mate's well-being. Apollo was in heaven as he watched Felicity eat a stack of waffles.

Gratitude wasn't one of those emotions that dragons were meant to be familiar with, but he was grateful, his heart flooding open for this woman who was so determined to prove him wrong she had reached into his own magic and opened it up to inspect.

She cut her waffles into small, tidy squares, her movements quick and sharp. Mrs. Hanson had packed a feast into the food basket, and Felicity was demolishing it piece by piece, ferociously separating out fresh-cut strawberries, bananas and cream, and speared each in turn onto her fork. He wasn't sure how she managed to spear cream, but at this point he was willing to believe she could do anything. She drizzled syrup on top and darted the whole forkful into her mouth before any could drip off.

And when she bit down, the look of bliss on her face made Apollo's heart sing and his dragon whisk its tail with delight. Her forehead smoothed out and her eyebrows lifted almost imperceptibly as her eyes closed.

*I want to make her look like that.* The thought flashed through his mind. He shouldn't be imagining things like this. He shouldn't even be looking at her like this. He still couldn't let himself believe that his magic had nothing to do with what happened to her car.

"Right." Felicity's eyes snapped open, pinning him in place. Enthusiasm boiled off her like steam from the sidewalk after summer rain. She shimmered with energy, and it was the most erotic thing he'd ever seen. "With the benefit of hindsight and some food, I am willing to admit that marching up and sticking my hand straight into your magic might not have been the most sensible decision I ever made."

He inclined his head seriously. "It's certainly not a solution I would have come up with."

She tried and failed to fight off a smile. "It was worth it, though, wasn't it? Now we know the magic you've laid down in the town hasn't gone off like old milk. It's fine."

It was impossible to be miserable with the spotlight of her attention on him. His dragon preened as his shoulders straightened out, magic unfurling along his bare forearms.

*Stop that,* he told his magic sharply. It ignored him.

Her next words threw cold water on his mood.

"And anyway, if something *was* going wrong, you would have noticed problems before now, wouldn't you?"

He took a slow breath. "There have been problems before now, as it happens."

"What?" Felicity's eyes widened.

He waved a hand lazily, then hesitated. He was so used to skating over his true feelings that acting blasé came automatically.

*I can't do that now.* Dread prickled at his shoulders. *I have to tell the truth. Unvarnished. No dramatics.*

He put his hands on the table, fingers interlaced, and glared at them until the sparks flittering around them vanished.

He hardly recognized his own voice. "Last winter, during the big storms, strange things started happening in the next city over. Phone lines got crossed, power surged and cut at random… and cars took off by themselves." He forced himself to meet that spotlight gaze again. "I only knew because Jacqueline, my friend Arlo's mate, told me about it. She lived there. Apparently, it happens so frequently during winter storms that people joke about some sort of cryptid living in the city. And I had no idea it was happening. My magic was breaking free and causing chaos in the next town over and I had no idea."

Felicity had stopped eating. She reached across the table, then stopped herself before her fingertips touched his. "Did… anyone get hurt?"

"No." He shook his head, a sharp jerk. "But it was only a matter of time, wasn't it?"

"Do I look hurt to you? No. Next question." She ate another perfect portion of waffle, her eyes closing briefly. "Oh, god, these are amazing. I can hardly focus on—" Her eyes flickered open, and color rushed to her cheeks. "Anyway. Next question: are you sure it *isn't* a cryptid?"

"As far as most people would be concerned, I *am* a cryptid. So are most of my neighbors."

"You're neighbors with Mothman?"

"Sure, he has a beach house just down the street." A smile escaped him, so fleet and joyous he couldn't stop it. "No. No Mothman, I'm afraid."

"Just a dragon. Damn. So disappointing."

*Focus. You're not here to flirt.* But the longer this conversation went on, the harder it was to hold back. Felicity was like sunshine for his soul. He wanted to roll around in it.

On her. In her. Felicity's hair hanging across his face, her smile so close he could taste it, the sweet softness of her skin against his lips and under his hands.

Something must have shown in his eyes. Felicity's mouth opened, a perfect tiny *Oh*, and her cheeks raged red.

They both cleared their throats.

"Next question," Felicity squeaked. "Did you check whether there was any magic missing from the town, after your friend's, uh, friend told you about the problems?"

*My friend's friend?* Apollo backtracked through their conversation. *She means Jacqueline. Arlo's mate.*

'Mate' didn't mean 'friend' to shifters. He opened his mouth to explain, and just stopped himself in time.

Of all the conversations it was really quite important he *not* have with Felicity right now, the existence of soulmates was top of the list.

"I did check. Immediately," he said, remembering the horror that had crashed through his body when Jacqueline unknowingly told him he had lost control of his magic. "I couldn't see any gaps, but I shouldn't have expected to. When it comes to replenishing the magic I've put into Hideaway, I'm a tap that's always running. My magic comes from inside myself and I use it to weave and repair my spells."

She frowned. "That sounds exhausting. Is that why you're so run down today? Because you had to magic my car last night?"

That, and all the lying awake in bed, drowning in guilt and misery. "Yes." He narrowed his eyes. "You know, this feels an awful lot like an interrogation."

"That's because I'm interrogating you. You're the chief witness in me proving your innocence."

"Aren't you meant to be on vacation?"

A shadow passed behind her eyes. She pressed her lips together. "Do you want me to stop?"

*No.* "You should be lying on the beach, not trying to solve the mystery of the broken lightning dragon. Save the investigative skills for the day job. I'm assuming you're some sort of ace detective."

She snorted. "Hardly. I'm—" She fought off a shudder. "I'm a secretary. I organize my boss's social commitments, which means I run around putting out fires and dampening things down before he sets new ones." Felicity bit her lip again, her expression sobering. "Trust me, this *is* a vacation compared to that. But I can't just sit around and let you deal with this yourself."

"The power hammer is only one part of the town's magic. It's like a fishing net, or a piece of lace—hundreds of threads knotted together and spreading out to cover the whole town."

"Then we need to check the rest of the net? Make sure none of it looks evil, or suspiciously recently mended?"

*And spend more time with you?* He hadn't slept all night, checking and re-checking his magic, convinced that he would never see Felicity again.

His hoard still tugged guiltily at him, from wherever it was. But it could wait. He was a dragon shifter—but she was human. You didn't just throw gold at a human and expect them to fall in love with you.

But showing her the town, showing off his magic and giving her as many opportunities to kiss him again as he could manage?

"I think that sounds like an excellent plan," he said.

# 8

# FELICITY

"Right. Where shall we start?"

Apollo glanced sideways and her heart sank. She knew what he was going to say before he said it. And she knew he didn't want to say it.

*Total mood killer.*

"You think we should test the car next." She sounded deflated. Not *defeated*, but close.

"You don't want to."

She let out a surprised bark of laughter. "No shit I don't! That thing almost killed me. I don't even want to *look* at it again." She hugged herself.

"I can understand that." He lifted his hand as though he wanted to touch her, then ran his fingers through his hair instead. "It's all right. You've done enough. I appreciate you wanting to let me off the hook more than you know, but..."

"Let you off the hook?" Her eyebrows shot up. "You still don't believe me."

"No, that came out wrong. I'm letting *you* off the hook." When she didn't back down, he folded his arms. "Last night, the thought of getting back into the car terrified you."

*Last night, I didn't have a reason to. Now I do.*

From the way her heart was thudding, passing out might still be an option. She decided to keep that to herself, too.

"You're not getting off that easily," she said with a forced grin, and opened the driver's door.

It took a few deep breaths for her to gather the courage to sit down. Staring at the constellation of burnt, cracked paint above the wheel didn't help.

"Felicity—"

"Nope! I'm doing it!" She closed her eyes and got into the car.

Another deep breath.

The car didn't *smell* evil. It smelled like a long drive: stale air with a hint of old coffee and blueberry muffin from lunch on the go, sickly sweet overtones from the energy drinks she'd guzzled to stay alert in the endless fog…

But it made her think of Montfort. That was worse than the memory of the strange evil magic. Her throat tightened.

The sound of the passenger door opening made her eyes spring open. Oh god. Apollo was getting into the car. He was going to smell all the smells.

"You don't need to do this." His voice was soft. It wrapped around her, softening the hard corners of her determination.

"Yes, I do."

"Why?"

"*Why?*" Felicity sputtered. Except… she didn't really have a *why*. Not one she could tell him. *Because your magic feels like home in a way my real home never felt like. It can't be evil.* "You know why."

Apollo's eyes did their molten-gold thing again. Arousal spiked between Felicity's legs.

*Um. Now that I think about it… Why* does *he think I'm doing this?*

"Also, I'm suffering from a terrible crisis of confidence. I mean, you can turn into a *dragon*. How can I compete with that? I have to prove myself somehow."

"By proving me wrong." His voice rumbled against her skin. He didn't sound upset or disgusted. He sounded *delighted*.

*Sexily* delighted.

She stuck her chin out. "So, get ready to be proved wrong, dragon."

"I will prepare my most heartbroken pose."

"I look forward to it."

*When did I get so confident?*

She put her hands on the wheel. Exactly where they'd been the night before. This time, though, all she felt was room-temperature fake leather.

She closed her eyes again and concentrated. There was *something* there. A smile spread across her face.

"You *magicked my car*."

"What can you feel?" There was a hint of anxiety in Apollo's voice.

*What is he worried I'll sense?*

She had to find out. She reached further into the tiny spark of magic, like an impatient gardener poking around in the dirt to see if her bulbs had started to sprout yet.

She fell headfirst into another memory. Her own. Her own terror from the night before rushed at her—and was gone before her heart even had a chance to race, replaced by a deep sense of relief and… belonging?

And—

"Oh-h," she breathed. There *was* something else. A possessive, protective crackle of magic like logs settling in a roaring fire… or a dragon wrapping its sparking power around her. *Mine.*

She swallowed hard.

What was that about?

Felicity opened her eyes, half-expecting to see Apollo's dragon form wound around the car like it was some sort of magical treasure. But it was just the two of them, human-shaped still, sitting in the car like they were about to go for a drive.

"So, uh," she began, and caught her breath as Apollo trained his full attention on her. "No evil magic here. Should we keep going?"

"Are you giving me a choice?"

"I'm giving you the *illusion* of a choice." She leaned back in the seat and grinned. "Or, I could always go explore the town by myself…"

His eyes dropped to her mouth again. It was like he was having to constantly stop himself from staring at it. Had the kiss been that good?

*I mean, it was that good for ME, but he is a wizard who can turn into a dragon. I bet he's had some amazing kisses.*

"I think it's best if I join you." His voice was husky again and sent a jolt of anticipation up her spine.

By mid-afternoon, Felicity had learned several more things about Apollo.

First, whenever he got a woeful look in his eye, the best way to distract him was to praise the town in some way. She exclaimed in delight over the adorable wooden frontages, and he practically *preened*.

Second, he was friends with the whole town. Wherever they went, people greeted him with cheerful smiles and updates on how their families were doing, or what the weather looked to be up to, or how good the fishing was. When they asked how he was, they *meant* it, and when he breezed over his stress and exhaustion, they took one look at the shadows under his eyes and exchanged a glance with Felicity that said *You're going to make sure he gets some rest, aren't you?*

It shook Felicity more than she expected. She was used to people zeroing in on her when she entered a room, but when people asked her how she was, what they meant was *How can I use you to get on Montfort's good side?*

No one ever expected her to *help.*

They had checked half a dozen places by now, small businesses and delightful homes. Each time, Apollo told the owners that he was checking on his magic and they were happy for him to go ahead, as though he was doing something as ordinary as checking the gas or fixing a leaky pipe. Then Apollo cast his magic out over his—well, his other magic, she supposed, to make sure it was all where he'd left it. Only then would he step aside with a flourish and let her use her own magic.

*Her own magic.* It had to be. Her strange ability to look inside Apollo's power, to feel it on her skin and in her veins like sunlight. Somehow, here in Hideaway Cove she wasn't just plain, pathetic Felicity Park. Here where magic was real, *she* was magic.

And every time she reached for the dragon shifter's magic and felt it leap to meet her, the third thing she learned about Apollo became clearer.

He definitely, absolutely, one hundred percent knew how the touch of his magic affected her.

Her legs were weak as they left the fifth place they'd tested together. A corner store, the magic laden with memories of kids putting together their pocket money to buy supplies for summer adventures, of the cashiers having long gossip sessions on slow afternoons, and of Apollo, always Apollo, his smile like the sun glittering on the waves.

But in all the memories her magic showed her, he never smiled at anyone the way he smiled at her.

So many different smiles, and all just for her. Giddily pleased. Teasing and inviting her to tease him in return. And the sultry, sidelong smiles that melted into silent longing when he thought she wasn't looking.

The sun had heated up while they checked over the town's magic. And it wasn't the only one.

She drew a breath and had to concentrate on keeping it steady. "Where to next?" There. She sounded excited, but not *that* sort of excited, and perky, but not *that* sort of perky.

She looked down to where her cotton sweater hung loosely over her breasts. Okay. Maybe that sort of perky. So long as he didn't look…

Apollo's hand slipped around her waist. "How are you holding up?" he murmured, his mouth close to her ear.

*Kissing distance*, she thought. *No, stop it! We're doing important work here. I can't keep thinking about…*

About him. It was all him. Even without his magic flirting with her senses, she'd have been head-over-heels. With it? The soft sparkling touches that brushed her bare arms as he watched her push her sweater sleeves up, or the nape of her neck as she turned away from him, were driving her crazy.

She couldn't stop thinking about what it would feel like if his magic slipped beneath her clothes, instead of staying politely on her already bared skin.

"Um?" she managed to say. *Oh, wow. So eloquent.* Apollo laughed softly, his fingers tightening at her waist.

"I think we'd both appreciate a chance to cool down."

His eyes were molten gold as his arms around her waist turned into a caress. A promise that *cooling down* was really just one step on the way to really, really heating up.

"What did you have in mind?"

He took her to the ice cream place on the waterfront. A sign above the door proclaimed it to be *Sweets' Ice cream Parlor*. It was, like everything else in this town, freaking adorable, from the lacey net curtains on the windows to the pastel-colored chairs around dinky tables.

Even the woman behind the counter looked like she'd stepped right out of the pages of a magazine feature. One of those people who'd ducked out of the rat race in favor of spending their days hand-churning butter and perfecting their apple pies, made with apples from their own orchard, of course. A few days ago, Felicity would have had to swallow back envy at anyone who had the energy for something approaching a 'lifestyle' as opposed to her own increasingly narrow life. Instead, as Apollo introduced her to Tess Sweets, all she could think about was what type of shifter the woman was.

Tess Sweets had chocolate-brown hair swept back under a floral scarf and wide, smiling eyes. Her face was round and, beneath her matching sundress, her body was rounded too, with the sorts of curves Felicity could only dream of. Her shifter form must be something cute and cuddly too, Felicity thought.

Tess reached over the counter to shake her hand. "Welcome to Hideaway," she said, smiling. Even her smile was sweet.

Apollo explained that he and Felicity were checking over his magic. Tess's eyebrows almost hit her headband.

"Sorry, let me hear that again. You're taking her around to do *chores?*"

Felicity pinched back a grin at the expression on Apollo's face. He gestured, flustered, as he replied. "Well—not exactly…"

"Mm. Not chores. Your literal job." Tess grinned at Felicity. "Please tell me he's at least introduced you to people? Because I have to break it to you, in a small town like this, everyone's already heard about you and all the drama of your arrival."

"I've met some people," Felicity reassured her.

"Uh-huh. Everyone on his magical paper route?"

Apollo's arm tensed, almost imperceptibly. But she couldn't miss the protective whirl of his magic around her waist. "I'm concerned something might be wrong with my magic. Felicity is helping me make sure every-thing's safe."

Tess frowned. "I haven't noticed any problems here. You'd be the first to know if I did, you know that? Because if anything happened to my freezers, I'd kill you."

"God forbid your latest food atrocity not see the light of day," Apollo muttered.

She pointed at him. "Ha, ha. My ice creams are *delicious*. Which is why you brought Felicity here, isn't it? Using dessert to apologize for dragging her around on your errands?" Her expression faltered. "Though—seriously, Apollo, if you're worried about your magic…"

"We'll check the Parlor while we're here, Tess. Don't worry."

Apollo shot an easy smile at Tess, but there was tension at the corners of his eyes, and his arm seemed locked in place around Felicity's waist. She tucked her hand over his reassuringly and he sighed.

"I know I promised you ice cream, not…" His voice trailed off and Felicity's mind supplied the rest of the sentence. *Not… more infuriatingly sexy magic times?*

"I think I'll cope."

His eyes flashed, and he leaned closer. "Really?"

She could *smell* him. Clean and warm and masculine, with a hint of something hot that made her want to sit up and beg. *So not fair.*

Dammit. He *definitely* knew what his magic did to her.

# 9

# APOLLO

If he didn't make his move soon, he was going to catch on fire. Or possibly the building would catch on fire. Or the entire town.

Which would be a problem. Saving Felicity from a burning building would be terribly romantic, et cetera, but him causing the fire in the first place would really ruin the mood.

Unease jittered down his spine. Felicity was so certain that his magic wasn't behind her near-fatal accident, but what if she were wrong?

Selfishly, he wanted her to be right. It *felt* like she should be right. The way his magic wanted to curl around her, the way she reacted to it…

But he'd always been selfish before. And see where it had gotten him. No hoard, nothing to offer her except magic that seemed to have a life of its own.

And no matter how good it felt to have Felicity with him, here, opening his heart to her and letting her stitch it up again, part of him was waiting for the other shoe to drop.

Felicity didn't even need to ask him where to find the wellspring of his magic in the ice cream parlor. She found the seat at the window overlooking the beach, where the light reflecting from the waves below shimmered across her skin. He ached to touch her with his power, to make the reflected shimmer real.

To see her gasp as his magic caressed her, the tip of her tongue touching her teeth, the involuntary, delicious curl of her fingers.

*I need to take her home.* Urgency pulsed through him, spurred on by his dragon's silent agreement. He groaned and closed his eyes. *That, or throw myself into the ocean.*

Given his luck, the whole bay would probably boil dry.

Felicity closed her eyes. Her hand drifted to the windowsill—the same windowsill he'd rested his own forearms on, watching the waves while Tess and the others chatted around him. The Sweets' Ice Cream Parlor had been their unofficial poker night venue before Jacqueline and Arlo's kids turned up. Now it was even more the heart of their social group. He was surprised the seals weren't here now, laminating themselves to the glass cabinets as they decided on today's favorite flavor.

What would Felicity see here? What would his magic show her? He ached to know. The flicker of emotions across her face as she sank into his power wrenched at his soul.

His power, but not his power. He'd never thought of it like that before she came here: the separation between the blazing core of magic within him, with his dragon wrapped jealously around it, and the magic he sent out into Hideaway Cove.

And the way Felicity looked when she touched it…

God, he was jealous of his own magic. What sort of dragon was he?

Felicity sighed, long and slow, and blood rushed to his cock. *That* was what sort of dragon he was. The sort who tortured himself.

Any minute now, the other shoe would drop. Something would go wrong, Felicity would see that he had no idea what he was doing, and every sweetly painful moment they'd spent together would become a memory sharper than a butcher's knife.

Felicity opened her eyes. Her cheeks, already glowing, reddened further when she saw him watching her. Despite all his second thoughts about this being a good idea, he preened.

"No evil up there," she announced. "But I did get a strange feeling…"

She looked around and Apollo's second thoughts came back with a vengeance. Was this it? The ice cream parlor was the least evil place in Hideaway Cove—unless you got on Tess's bad side. But she was more likely to lace your ice cream with hot sauce than curse you, and at least forty percent of Hideaway Cove thought that was tasty, not evil.

It had to be his magic. This was it. The truth he'd been waiting for: his magic wasn't just out of control, it was dangerous.

"Lay it on me." He forced a light tone through the tightness in his throat.

"It feels—" Her blush crept down the soft skin of her neck. Guilt joined the anguish twisting in his soul. He'd tortured her, too, unable to keep from touching her, unable to keep the memory of that kiss out of the power that danced from his skin to hers. He should never have brought her into this.

Felicity cleared her throat. "—Um, well, apart from that. It feels—duplicated? But different? Wait." She groaned and rubbed her forehead. "I swear I am usually better at talking than this."

Her thoughts chased one another across her face—her mouth ticked down as she dismissed one idea, then firmed as she wrestled another into place, and at last she smiled.

He didn't let himself kiss her, even though it was suddenly the only thing on his mind.

"Hmm. Okay. How's this. It's as though there *was* another pattern there, and it's been erased, and replaced with a different one. In the other places we've been I could tell that you've reinforced the magic multiple times, but this one is like you changed your mind about… I don't know. About how important it is?"

"You're right." He couldn't even come up with a pithy joke to distract from his amazement. "That's exactly what I did. When I first moved to Hideaway Cove, Tess's grandparents still ran the ice cream parlor. They're away visiting family at the moment; you haven't met them. It was…"

He paused, trying to find polite words to describe how Mr. and Mrs. Sweets had run the shop. Felicity took advantage of his distraction to take his hand. Her hand was warm in his, her grip firm. As though nothing would make her let him go.

*Please*, he begged the universe, and kept talking.

"...I think it's possible entire generations went without ice cream in Hideaway Cove, because the thought of seeing Dorothea behind the counter was so terrifying." He listened carefully but didn't hear any disgruntled shouts from the back room; Tess must have gone on an errand while he was waiting for Felicity to complete her checks. "They were both important in the town, though—Mr. Sweets was mayor for years, before Harrison took over—so they insisted that the parlor be given the full magical treatment. I didn't want to cause a political incident, so I struck an appropriate pose and filled the air with mystical sparkles, but I couldn't make it stick. Not then."

"And that changed when Tess took over?"

"Yes, a few years ago." Now he was the one struggling to put words to the concept in his head. He'd never thought about it this clearly before. "The... *shape* of the town changed. The ice cream parlor was important in a way it wasn't before. People spent time here, and it made them happy. Tess stopped ordering in cheap bulk ice creams and started mixing her own witchy potions in the back room. So, I picked out all the fake glitz I'd done for her grandparents and wove it into its proper place."

Felicity hesitated. They were still holding hands; he felt the tremble that went through her body.

"That's incredible," she said softly. "I—I still half-thought I was making it up. But that *is* what I felt. And if it's real..."

She looked up at him, her dark eyes searching his. "I can't be the first person to be able to dig around in your magic like this, right?"

"You are. I don't think anyone else here even knows the full extent of my magic, let alone can sense it like you do. Or understand it." *Understand me*, he wanted to add. Because he wanted it to be true. God, he wanted that to be true.

He pulled himself together. "Which brings me to the other unique reaction you have to my magic. And what we're going to do about it."

"…Cooling down with some ice cream?" There was a hint of disappointment in her voice. She ran her free hand down her face. "I have to admit something to you."

"You can tell me anything."

A flicker of doubt, then she shook her head. "This… touching your magic. I feel like I'm taking advantage of you." Her voice came out oddly resentful, a soft, guilty purr that hit him like a shot of whisky.

She squirmed, uncomfortable. Apollo's magic stirred in response. "Taking advantage how?"

"I don't know what counts as going too far. With shifters. With magic. If all this is—too intimate…"

"It is incredibly intimate." Apollo brushed hair back from her face. "But *too* intimate? No."

The words came out in a rush, her cheeks reddening as she admitted: "I don't know if I could have stopped it even it was."

Desire coiled inside him, possessive and needy.

Felicity was his mate. She knew his magic better than he did himself. It responded to her in a way he'd never seen before.

It was time to stop doubting. If there was anything wrong, she would have seen it.

"What would you like to do about it?" Lightning laced his words.

She wet her lips. "You said something about ice cream?"

"That sounds like a good idea." There was no mistaking the disappointment in her eyes this time. He leaned over the table to whisper in her ear,

"To start with." Her short intake of breath made his dragon ripple its scales with smugness.

*Yes, yes, I know,* he told it airily. *I can get* some *things right.*

# IO

# FELICITY

*It can't just be the magic, can it?*

She'd never felt like this before. Desire rippled through her like raindrops falling on a still pond. Apollo looked at her—ripples. He stroked the back of her hand—ripples. He watched her lips as she licked strawberry cheesecake ice cream from her spoon—*tidal wave.*

She was fooling herself even asking the question. It wasn't the magic. It was him.

"I've been thinking," she said, scraping the last of her ice cream sundae from the bottom off the glass. "About last night."

His molten-gold eyes sharpened. His body language changed, from the languid tension of the crazy intense attraction between them to sudden, tense protectiveness. She should have felt bad for killing the moment. Instead, her heart soared.

No one ever wanted to protect her before.

"I think that was the best traffic accident I've ever been in." She hardly recognized her own voice. It was rough and smooth at the same time, lit through with laughter.

Was this what happiness sounded like? Her enjoying herself, not worried she would say the wrong thing and find herself in Montfort's path, like stepping out in front of a truck?

Because she was happy. Happy just being with him. She *was* glad her car had crashed, dammit, and glad she had a few days to spend with Apollo before—

A chill stole over her. The morning sun streaming in the window suddenly felt cold and clammy against her skin, like the fog from the night before.

She had a few days with Apollo, before she had to get back to her own life.

Back to ruining his.

Her fists tightened. *No.* She was free, here. Free from Montfort. And *happy.*

She wouldn't go back to that life. Even if she only had a few days here in Hideaway. Whatever the rest of her life held, she refused to spend it under Montfort's thumb.

Felicity let out a breath that took all the tension in her body with it.

Apollo's eyebrows went up. "You look as though you've made a decision," he said.

"I have." She grinned. She'd chosen happiness. And now that she'd chosen it, she wasn't going to let it go. "And I've finished my ice cream."

His eyes drifted down to her empty glass, tantalizingly slowly. "So you have."

"And, sadly, I think I've reached my limit of magic-testing for the day."

"That's a shame." He stretched lazily and dropped his hand entirely by accident—she was sure—next to hers. Their pinky fingers touched. "There's still most of the day left. Whatever will we do to pass the time?"

"More errands?" she teased.

"Be careful. Tess is right. I'll have you picking up my groceries next." A smile tugged at his lips. "This is your vacation. What would you like to do?"

His voice was layered with suggestiveness. She searched his eyes. Each time they tested a new location in the town, there had been real worry hidden behind his flirtatious smiles and hints. But this time there was nothing hidden behind his smoldering eyes except more smoldering. Even the deep exhaustion she'd noticed earlier seemed to have vanished.

Clearly, he had other things on his mind now.

Mouth suddenly dry, she licked her lips. Apollo's eyes tracked the movement. Oh god. If this went on much longer she would be a puddle on the floor. Which normally she would think wasn't possible, but magic was real, so who knew?

Better not to take her chances.

Felicity pressed her thighs together. "I want to see your dragon again," she blurted out.

Apollo's gaze heated up. "That can be arranged. Though I doubt it was part of your original vacation plan."

"Plans change," she told him seriously, and he laughed.

"What else? I could show you the sights. Take you up to the lighthouse. We could go swimming…"

She imagined swimming in the bay with Apollo, the water slipping over his bare skin.

"Yes," she said quickly. "That."

Apparently, shifters were all about skinny dipping—*And no wonder,* Felicity thought, imagining how annoying it would be to peel yourself out of a swimsuit either before *or* after you transformed into an animal form—but Apollo escorted her back to the bed-and-breakfast to get changed.

She'd barely glanced at the town as they went around checking Apollo's magic. All her attention had been on his magic, and on him. But now, walking along the waterfront promenade with him, the town seemed to be showing off again.

The night before, the town had been little more than a few strands of fairy lights strung through the fog. Now the afternoon sun blazed down on Victorian frontages painted to complement the surrounding sea and hills in blues, greens, and browns.

All except for one. High on the hill in the middle of town, one cottage was painted bright, summery yellow. Like a lone daffodil blooming in a field. She was strangely drawn to it.

*Not strangely,* she told herself, fighting back a bubbly, drunk feeling that threatened to burst out of her in a stream of mad giggles. *It's just making you think of something else that's shiny and yellow-gold…*

"What's caught your eye?" Apollo asked. He followed her gaze up the hill and color touched his cheeks. "Ah."

"Whose house is that?"

He raised one eyebrow at her. "I think you've already guessed."

"It's so…"

Apollo grimaced. "It's not exactly a rugged castle, or a cave at the top of a remote mountain, but it's mine."

"I love it," she breathed.

The daffodil-colored Victorian with white fretwork and abundant flowers cascading from the second-floor balcony wasn't what she'd normally associate with the word *dragon,* but for Apollo it was perfect. A bit fussy, but solid, cozy, and warm. Its hillside perch was right in the heart of Hideaway Cove, at the center of the curving hills that enclosed the water on either side.

It felt… right.

A look of relief passed over Apollo's face. "I'll have to invite you over sometime," he said blandly. Then their eyes met. The teasing heat in his gaze was so overwhelming she almost lost her footing.

She tucked her arm into his, feeling giddy. "That would be nice," she said, her voice as bland as his had been, and Apollo's eyes creased with silent laughter.

It took all her self-control not to invite Apollo up to her room at the bed-and-breakfast, and once she was up there, alone, she wondered why she hadn't.

Sure, they might not have gotten to the beach as quickly as they'd intended, but they would have…

Her phone buzzed and all the blood drained from Felicity's face as she realized how close she'd come to disaster. If that was Montfort—

It wasn't. She checked the caller ID and frowned, then picked up the call. "Mrs. Flores?"

"Felicity? Is that you? Is this the correct number?"

"Yes, it's me. How are you?"

"Have you heard from my Maya recently?"

Mrs. Flores' voice was tense with strain. Felicity's frown deepened. "No, but—"

"She is not answering my calls. I am so worried that something has happened to her. Or to Tomás."

Felicity swallowed.

"I'm sure they're fine, Mrs. Flores." But she didn't know, did she? She hadn't seen Maya in months. Her best friend, and she'd let her disappear out of her life.

"If you could go over and check on them—"

Felicity rubbed her forehead, borrowed guilt trickling into her stomach. She knew Maya found her mom overbearing; that was why she'd moved so far away from home. Sometimes she wished her own parents were as interested in her life.

"I'm sure it's nothing serious, Mrs. Flores. Maya is probably busy with her work. Most days she doesn't get a chance to stop and check—what?" She paused, sure she hadn't heard right.

"Maya left her job," Mrs. Flores repeated, with all the tragedy of a mother who knows her daughter has made wrong decision after wrong decision without consulting her.

"Since when?"

"Two months ago. I don't understand it, Felicity. My Maya? First she won't tell anyone who the father is, and now she is a solo mother, and no job…"

Felicity swallowed. "I had no idea. No, I—we haven't caught up in a while." Her voice sounded half-strangled. "I'm out of the city at the moment. My boss—I mean, my boss gave me the weekend off. But I'll get in touch with her and tell her to call you. I'm sure everything's fine," she repeated, hoping it was true.

When Mrs. Flores hung up, Felicity stared at her phone, worrying at her lower lip.

"I'm sure it's nothing," she said, utterly failing to convince herself. "She must be busy with Tomás. Or if she quit her job, maybe she's doing a digital detox."

It was one of the things they'd always said they would do if they got free. And now Maya had, apparently, and hadn't told her.

Something had to be wrong.

Her fingers flew over the screen, and she pulled up the encrypted messaging app they used when they didn't want either of their bosses to know they were communicating with 'the enemy'.

Felicity: *M what is happening? Your mom called worried sick about you. Call me???*

She paused, considering. "Don't hate me, Maya," she murmured, then sent another message.

Felicity: *If I don't hear from you in 10 I will call Blackburn and ask him!!!*

She forced herself to put her phone down. Staring at it wouldn't make Maya respond any faster.

Threatening Maya with her old boss was a low blow. Not as low as it would have been if their positions were reversed—Blackburn and Montfort were rivals, but Montfort definitely outranked Blackburn on the Total Evil Bastard scale.

Maya would understand, though, wouldn't she? They were friends. She was pretty sure they were still friends.

Felicity's chest hurt. Her world had totally turned upside down over the last twenty-four hours, but this shook her more than any of the rest of it. The thought that she had let her best friend slip away, that Maya had been in trouble and she hadn't even noticed—

Her phone trilled. She picked it up. Not a message—a call. "Maya?"

"Fee?" Maya's face appeared on the screen. Felicity's heart skipped. Maya looked *terrible*. Deep shadows under her eyes, hair a mess. But the room behind her was her own apartment. So why hadn't she been able to pick up her mom's calls?

"What the hell? Your mom thinks you've vanished off the face of the earth. What's going on?"

"Nothing's going on—" There was an odd shriek in the background and Maya's eyes widened. "Sweetie, no—"

The video swooped and went black as Maya dropped her phone face-down. Felicity was left listening to her murmuring soothingly, while the shrieks continued.

*Is that Tomás?* She blinked. The noises didn't even sound human!

"Shh, chickpea, it's all right. Look! Here's your—your thing. Your favorite toy!" There was a scrambling noise as she picked the phone up again. "Sorry, Fee, this isn't a great time. Tomás just woke up and he's always so grumpy after his nap." A pause, and then she added, sounding slightly frantic: "You didn't call Blackburn, did you?"

"I don't have a death wish."

"He's not—" Maya groaned. "Oh god. It doesn't matter. I'm never going to see him again."

"Your mom said you quit your job. Maya, what the hell is going on? I go on vacation for the first time in half a decade and you quit on me?"

A wobbly laugh. "You're on vacation. I quit my job. Maybe there's hope for both of us."

"I can't believe you're leaving me to deal with the terrible two by myself. Traitor. How am I meant to keep Montfort out of Blackburn's way without my woman on the inside?" Felicity kept her tone light, but she was on edge, searching Maya's face and voice for any hint of something deeper.

"I'm sorry, Fee. It's been… a weird couple of weeks." Maya's voice dropped.

"I bet. You would have had your work cut out for you, getting all your ducks in a row to leave Blackburn."

"You have no idea." Offscreen, Tomás started grizzling. "Fee, I really need to go…"

"Yeah, of course. I'll tell your mom you're not upside down in a ditch somewhere."

"Thanks. I really appreciate it. I just—I don't think I can stand to talk to her right now."

"Maya—" Felicity pressed her forehead against the edge of her phone, as though she could dive through it to her friend. "You're okay, aren't you? The two of you? If you need anything—I can set up another meal delivery thing for you, or if you need money—I feel so useless, being so far away."

"We're—it's complicated. We're fine. Money isn't a problem." Maya let out a shaky laugh. "And for the love of God, don't cut your vacation short on my account. This is the only time off Montfort has given you the whole time we've been friends."

*Except it isn't time off. It's a lie.* Felicity swallowed hard.

Maya's voice became wistful. "Maybe we should go on vacation, like you. Get out of the city for a while."

"Well, let me know, and I'll come meet you. I'm about a day's drive away, in this tiny place nobody has ever heard of."

"What's it called?"

"Hideaway Cove."

"Huh. You're right. I *haven't* heard of it. Weird. I thought Corin—um, Mr. Blackburn had me research all the resorts this part of the state for his family events."

"Hideaway isn't exactly a resort. It's more a… quiet getaway."

"Which is exactly what you needed. I still can't believe Montfort gave you time off for a vacation." Maya sounded more like herself; the stressed edge was gone from her voice.

Felicity took a deep breath. "Yeah, well, he's about to find out it's permanent."

Another pause. "Good. I'm glad you're getting out, too."

"If there's anything I can do—come over and help with Tomás, or…"

"Don't you dare cut your vacation short for me, Felicity Park. I'll murder you myself." Maya laughed, sounding more like her old self.

Felicity managed to keep her on the line for a few more minutes, long enough to convince herself that whatever crisis Maya was in, it wasn't an emergency situation. She slumped on the edge of the bed and stared at nothing.

"Felicity?" There was a knock at the door, and Apollo's voice. She wiped her hand across her face—what was that about, it wasn't like she'd been crying?—and invited him in.

He stood in the doorway. "You were taking a while. I wanted to see if there was any—are you all right?"

His eyes flickered across her face, full of concern. She shrugged. "I'm sorry for keeping you waiting. I had a call I had to take."

"A work thing?"

"No, thank God." But now the fear that Montfort would call was back. "A friend. She's—going through some stuff. I wish I was there to help her."

"Of course you do."

She frowned at him. "What do you mean?"

"It doesn't surprise me at all that you want to help her." Apollo sat down next to her on the bed, his weight making a dip in the mattress. She let herself sink against him. "The first thing you did when you found out about my magic problem was help me. Of course you want to help your friend, too."

"I feel guilty being here, having such an incredible time, when she's having trouble."

"You want to cut your trip short?"

She stared at him. *No,* her heart said, and she hated herself for it. "I want to be in two places at once," she said frankly. "How fast can your dragon fly?"

"Not that fast. And it's very shiny and visible. I don't know if I mentioned it, but we're meant to keep things like magic secret." He put an arm around her.

Felicity sighed. "She told me not to come charging to her rescue, anyway."

Apollo squeezed her. "Is there anything you can do for your friend from here?"

"I gifted her a meal service after her son was born. I can get that running again. One less thing for her to worry about." She pressed the heels of her hands into her eyes. "And I'll be back in a few days, anyway. I can check on her properly then."

She almost missed the shadow that passed behind Apollo's eyes.

"Then we'd better make the most of the time before you leave," he said, and pulled her to her feet. "Starting with our swim."

II

# APOLLO

Apollo was playing with fire. Every time Felicity had tuned into the town's magic, longing washed through him. He couldn't sense the power he'd laid down in the town without concentrating, but her presence in his magic echoed through whatever connection still existed between him and it.

He would have to be more of a fool than he admitted to not notice how it was affecting her, as well. The brightness in her eyes, the color in her cheeks. The way she looked at him and licked her lips, tentatively, as though she couldn't quite believe how much she wanted to eat him up.

He wanted to hand her a spoon and tell her to dive in.

But something held him back. He wouldn't call it honor; dragons weren't meant to be honorable creatures, after all.

*Shame.* His dragon whisked its tail, crouching protectively around the glowing heart of his magic. So close, in fact, you might call it hiding. Not that a dragon would ever *hide.*

Not unless it was, to take an example entirely at random, a dragon with no hoard, caught desperately between the urge to claim his mate and the painful truth that it *couldn't,* because again, no hoard. The reminder that he only had a few days to make her his only made his shame dig sharper.

Seeing Felicity envelop herself in his magic was excruciating, a blissful torture that would tear him apart and make him beg for more.

He had thought that a cold ocean swim would cure it.

He couldn't have been more wrong.

Half the town was on the beach or already in the water, but Apollo had eyes only for his mate. Felicity was wearing a halter neck bikini with tantalizing ties behind her neck and either side of her luscious hips. She was facing away from him, already calf-deep in the water, a light breeze tugging at her hair the way Apollo wanted to tug at those ties—light, teasing, drawing out the anticipation of the moment the clinging scraps of fabric would fall away…

A groan wrenched from him. *Down, boy*, he thought, clenching his thighs and willing his cock to behave.

Terrible, terrible idea.

"You know, I'm beginning to rethink this!" Felicity called. Her words so perfectly echoed his own thoughts, he wondered for a moment if he'd spoken aloud. She turned to him, a smile transforming her face. "You call this summer? The water's freezing!"

"You can't back out on me now." He made his way towards her. Icy waves lapped at his ankles. "Who was it who said she needed to cool off?"

"There's cool and there's hypothermic," she grumbled, her eyes not leaving him.

"You know what they say. It's best to dive in and get it over with." He strode forwards and she wavered towards him, wetting her lips.

"That's one option, sure," she shot back. "I'm all for throwing myself headfirst into trouble. You seem more of the edging in sort. Inch by inch." She stepped backwards, her grin teasing. "And you know the hardest part is coming, slowly, and the anticipation is almost worse than actually doing it." She stepped back again and a wave caught the backs of her knees, making her jump. "Am I right?"

Apollo's blood was on fire. "You're assuming I ever make it that far," he said. He'd aimed for a casual drawl, but his voice came out raspy. What were they talking about?

"Never?" The water was up to her thighs, now. Her enticingly plump thighs.

"Not often."

"You live right on the beach, and you never go… swimming?" Her grin broadened. They were definitely not talking about swimming.

"I don't usually find myself needing it so badly."

"Oh?" Her eyes were shining. One more step back, and the water surged over the tops of her thighs. She shivered, arms clenched around herself. "Oh-h-h…"

Apollo's mind whited out. His body was so overheated he couldn't feel the water around him as he strode forwards, intent on the delectable woman in front of him.

"Eek!"

Water splashed up in Felicity's face. Apollo's dragon snapped alert, ready to take action, until he spotted the culprits. Two dark shapes darted through the water at her feet, splashed her again and flitted away.

Felicity wiped her face, staring at the now-empty water. "What was that? I thought I saw—"

Giggles popped and bubbled in Apollo's mind, the psychic overflow of two shifter children having fun causing havoc. "Tally, Dylan, play nice!" he called.

Felicity wiped seawater out of her eyes. "Are they… seals?"

The two juvenile seal shifters wouldn't have been out of place on a Discovery program. They flew through the water, dark bodies sleek and nimble.

"A better description would be small, cheeky menaces." Apollo flicked water at the seal pups as they darted through the water towards him. "Begone, menaces! Go and bother someone else before I set my dragon on you!"

Gleeful laughter echoed in his mind. Felicity pushed her hair back off her forehead. "They're kids? Shifter kids?"

He glanced at her sidelong. "You seem surprised."

She shook her head. "If grownups can be shifters, it makes sense kids can be, too." She smiled wryly. "I guess this proves I don't always throw myself in totally headfirst. I could have figured out for myself that there would be kids who were shifters, and they would turn into adorable juvenile animals, but instead I'm just letting new bits of magical knowledge sneak up on me. Literally." Her eyes followed Tally and Dylan as they swam up behind their next victim. "Are all shifter kids one hundred per cent completely adorable?"

"They're even cuter in human form. Dylan can recite all the elements without drawing breath, and he *will* do it, and Tally has just learned how to run up to people, yell 'Fart!' and run away again."

Laughter exploded out of her. "You know them pretty well, then?"

"My friend Arlo and his mate Jacqueline are fostering them. They had a tough time of it before they came to Hideaway Cove, but they're here now. Them, their older sister Kenna, and their friend Eric."

"Arlo and his mate?"

"His… fiancée. You'll meet them later."

"I look forward to it."

Apollo glanced after the kids again. It was good to see them so carefree. All four children had blossomed since they started living with Arlo and Jacqueline—not that Eric counted as a child, at eighteen, except that Jacqueline had scooped him up in her mother hen act and he seemed perfectly happy to stay scooped up.

He concentrated. Arlo's little wolf pack were happy, splitting their time between his ship and their house on the water, but a little extra help never hurt. He sent his magic to the house, reinforcing the power that was already there and what it provided: warmth, security, reliable internet. Everything a young family needed.

"What was that?" Felicity was staring at him, her lips parted and her eyes wide with wonder. Every drop of water on her face looked like a star pulled from the sky. "I felt you do something. Your magic…" She licked her lips.

"That's the first time you've seen me put my magic to work, rather than putting on a light show." Something warmed inside him, along with a sudden, urgent curiosity. "What did it feel like?"

"Like…" Her cheeks pinked. *Oh,* he thought, inordinately pleased. *Like that, huh?*

"I was reinforcing the magic around Arlo and Jacqueline's house," he told her. "You haven't sensed any places I've only just used my magic on, have you? We could go over there, test it out…"

She was already shaking her head. "I think I'd prefer…"

"Swimming?" He moved closer to her until they were almost touching. The sun glanced across his chest, and he smirked as Felicity swayed towards him. "Or… swimming?"

She tilted her head back, regarding him through wet, sparkling lashes. "I never got a good look at your dragon last night," she said. "Show me?"

*Yes.*

His dragon surged up inside him, ready to take form. He held it back a moment; ghostly outlines of golden scales appeared on his skin, the promising crackle of power a cloak around his shoulders. The wonder on Felicity's face was more precious than a thousand perfectly cut diamonds.

His mate. His teasing, tempting mate. His joy and his anguish. He wanted to crush his lips against hers again, feel the wet hot press of her skin on his. But without a hoard, it would be only kisses. Only physical.

Not the magical claiming she deserved, the offering of all that he was at her altar.

"As you wish," he whispered. He kissed her, feather-soft, and shifted.

12

# FELICITY

The kiss lasted barely a heartbeat. Felicity's eyes flickered open as Apollo pulled away and the air around him began to shimmer.

The light rose to blinding brilliance. She tried to squint through it and gave up, covering her face as Apollo exploded in brightness. He was so close and his dragon form so huge that his transformation sent a wave washing over her. She lost her footing willingly, riding the swell backwards into deeper water, trying to get a better view of Apollo's dragon form.

Golden scales gleamed. A huge tail flicked through the water. Happy shouts filled the air. She wasn't the only one surfing on the dragon wave. All around, shifters were playing in the water, equally comfortable and wonderful in their human or animal forms. It was a magical, precious moment.

But she only had eyes for Apollo.

His dragon form was incredible in the water. With his wings tucked tight against his sides, he could have been some sort of mythical sea serpent. Dragons were meant to collect treasure, weren't they? Surely he wouldn't need any. He was like a treasure himself, shining in the afternoon sun.

Glorious. There was no other word for it. No wonder his parents had named him after a god.

*And he's all mine.*

She blinked. Where had that come from?

Apollo swung his massive dragon head around to look at her and she caught her breath. A feeling burst inside her that she couldn't name. It was giddy and sure and happy and terrified all at once. Like she couldn't breathe and was breathing the sweetest air on Earth at the same time.

But he *had* sent her spinning through the water when he transformed, so when their eyes met, she splashed him.

He tipped his head on one side and raised one massive foreclaw.

"If you *dare…!*"

She ducked under the water as he sent a wave crashing towards her. Still submerged, she opened her eyes to see his scaled flank gleaming in the light shining down from the surface. His tail curled protectively around her as he twisted in the water, his huge golden eyes concerned.

*I'm fine*, she wanted to tell him. More than fine. Exultant. More alive than she'd felt in years. If this was a dream, it was the best dream in the world, and if it was real…

*My Apollo. My dragon.* The thoughts shook her, but not as much as the certainty that accompanied them. She'd only known the guy for a day, and she'd never felt this possessive about any of her previous boyfriends. Where was this coming from?

*The same place that made me leap into his magic like it was my own private swimming pool?* Not just once, but over and over again, at all the places they'd visited that morning. He'd shown her so much of the town and so much of himself at the same time—all those memories locked away in the weft and weave of his magic.

And she wanted more.

She kicked away into deeper water. Past the breakers, the water was calm, with only a gentle swell. The yells and laughter from the other swimmers faded into the distance.

Apollo glided through the water at her side. Then he swam underneath her.

*Is this seriously happening?* Felicity barely had time to ask herself before he rose up beneath her. She straddled his spine and carefully grasped the spines on his back for balance. To her surprise, they were soft and flexible, not the sharp armor she'd expected.

A moment later she was skimming across the water.

*I'm riding a dragon*, she thought. Laughter bubbled out of her. "I'm riding a dragon!" she shouted, and stretched her arms above her head. "I—eek!"

She hit the water headfirst and tumbled around in a cloud of bubbles. Apollo turned around before she even surfaced, guiding her up with one massive foreclaw. She clung to him, holding back her laughter until there was air to laugh in.

Apollo's dragon eyes were huge and alien, more cat-like than human, but the warmth pouring out of them as he looked down at her was the same. She relaxed into his massive claw, feeling utterly at peace.

*This is where I'm meant to be.* She didn't understand it, but it was true as the sunlight on her skin.

The water out this deep was even colder. The first time she shivered, Apollo harrumphed out a cloud of sparks and put her back on his dragon-y shoulders. He cut through the water, swift and elegant, until they came to a small hidden beach tucked away around the side of the bay.

The only warning she got that he was about to shift again was the hum of magic against her skin. The air shimmered, his massive dragon form vanished, and she yelped as she dropped into the water.

Apollo was human again. Beautifully, nakedly human.

Beneath the flimsy fabric of her bikini, her nipples pebbled. The water was only partially to blame, just like her sudden dunking was only partially to blame for her breathlessness. She was intimately aware of just how close Apollo was to her. The icy water cut against her skin, but Apollo's nearness was a wash of fire that burned straight through it.

They were still far enough off the beach that her feet didn't touch the ground. She drifted, languid and longing, as Apollo's eyes found hers.

"How do you feel?"

*Like I'm about to lose my mind from wanting you.* "I don't think I should say."

Fire flashed in his eyes. "Why not?"

"How good is shifter hearing? Someone might hear. I'll get thrown out of town for public indecency."

The swell rolled her closer to him and her whole body ached with the nearness of his naked chest. His bare legs, kicking lazily beneath the water.

She wanted to run her fingers all over him. And her tongue.

His eyes darkened. He swam towards her, his movements slow and languid and oh, God, if she wasn't half-frozen she would be about to catch fire. He ducked underwater and light played over the muscles of his back as he moved around her like some sort of golden dream.

He surfaced, slowly, and blinked his eyes clear. His gorgeous, golden eyes. How had she ever thought they were a normal, unmagical color? They were all magic. *He* was all magic. She wanted to kiss every drop of sunlight on his face and feel his power crackle against her lips.

"Tell me," he whispered. "Or show me. Whichever you prefer."

Her skin felt too tight. There was too much raging inside her—too much need, too much heat, too much desperate, mindless *want*.

"I want this to last forever," she told him, lost in his eyes. "And I want to kiss you, and for that to last forever. And touch you. Like this."

She kicked closer to him, and her hands found his chest. He moaned at her touch. She stroked down the hard planes of his pecs to his abs, the deep V. *Mine.*

Apollo bit back a curse.

"I want you to touch me, too."

"How?"

"Everywhere. All over." Which wasn't the question he'd asked, but it was too late for that. He was already touching her, his hands leaving her skin on fire as he ran them over her waist, his thumbs drawing semi-circles on her stomach. He dropped them to her hips and she had a sudden vision of him holding her, hard, as he sank between her legs. A gasp broke from her lips.

"It's not fair," she complained, her voice ragged-edged with desire.

"What isn't fair?" He pulled her close, nuzzling her ear. Her breasts grazed his chest, her thighs brushed his and nothing mattered anymore except that he never stop touching her.

She struggled to remember what she'd been saying. "If you keep doing this," she said at last, "we'll both get so distracted that we drown, and then we'll never be able to do it again."

He laughed into her shoulder. His leg slipped between hers and oh, God, that had to be his cock, hard and solid against her stomach. She wanted him. Here, now, drowned, whatever.

Apollo took her by the hand and swam with her to shore. Her legs almost collapsed under her, weak with need and unsteady in the transition from water to solid land. The beach was a sickle of sand edged with water-smoothed rocks and grass silvered by the sun.

"Felicity." Apollo made her name sound like a prayer. "Will this do?"

"What is this place?"

"Another of Hideaway's secrets." He kissed her. His lips tasted like the ocean. "Soon you'll know them all."

Her heart jolted. She already knew too much. If Montfort ever found out even half of what she'd discovered here…

"Felicity." Apollo cupped her face. "If you don't want to do this, we don't have to. I know it's sudden." A wry smile played across his face. "It's sudden for me, too."

Her Apollo, who didn't go 'swimming' often. And had suddenly found him as far out of his depth as she was. A man who could turn into a dragon, whose magic held Hideaway safe as the hills, but who looked at her like she was the most precious person in the world.

She knew too many of his secrets. Too many of Hideaway's secrets.

*Montfort will never find out about this place.*

*I'll keep you safe, Apollo.*

She put her hands over Apollo's and pulled them away from his face. "Sudden can be good," she told him, and the answering light in his eyes made her giddy. "Want to know how much I want you?"

Hardly believing what she was doing, she slid his hands down her body, cupping them over her breasts, dragging them down her waist. His long, elegant fingers tightened as they reached the edge of her bikini panties. "Felicity—"

"Do you want to know?"

"Fuck. Yes."

She pushed his hand under the clinging fabric, gasping as his fingers found her slick and wet. He stroked her, his face buried in her hair, and she moaned and pressed his hand harder against herself.

God, his hand fit perfectly between her legs. His palm cradled her pussy, the heel of his hand a blunt pressure against her clit. She needed more. She wanted his fingers inside her, wanted their clever quickness pressing deeper, teasing pleasure, bringing her closer.

"Please," she begged, rocking against his hand, and Apollo swore under his breath.

He grabbed her hips, as strong and firm as she'd imagined, pushing her backwards until her legs hit stone. She lowered herself blindly onto a low, flat rock, Apollo guiding her down, his kisses like wildfire. He undid the tie of her bikini top and pulled it down, revealing what he must have already felt—her breasts heaving with each heavy breath, the nipples taut and hard.

"You're beautiful," he told her, his gaze worshipful. "All of you…"

His hands roved down her, retracing the path she'd led them, over her breasts, to the aching need between her legs. He hooked his thumbs through the ties on her bikini bottoms and pulled them down, groaning with satisfaction when she gasped.

"So beautiful." He knelt between her legs. "And you thought you were taking advantage of *me*."

Her own words took a moment to come back to her, and with them, a predatory, entirely sexual feeling of victory.

"And now you've got me on my back?" she purred.

His eyes caught her and pinned her in place. "I intend to take full advantage."

He kissed her inner thighs, long, torturous kisses that never quite got close enough. She moaned and writhed, but he stayed firm, capturing her hands when she tried to grab hold of his head and urge him further.

"Inch by inch," he reminded her, and she swore out loud. He laughed against her leg, and sparks rolled over his tongue.

Felicity cried out wordlessly. Apollo raised his head, blinking.

"That's new," he remarked, and a wicked light gleamed in his eyes.

She couldn't find the words for it. "*Please.*"

"Hmm." He kissed her again and static earthed itself in her skin. "Inch by inch, or straight in headfirst?"

He waited for her to answer. Felicity licked her lips. There was something feral about Apollo like this—naked and golden on this lonely beach, dragon-gold eyes burning in his human face. How far did she want to take this?

All the way.

"Straight in." Her voice was a prayer, rough with need.

He smiled at her, long and slow and wicked, and pressed his lips to her clit.

Lightning struck, fierce and unyielding. Felicity cried out, her body arching fully off the stone as an orgasm like nothing she'd ever experienced clamped down on her. Her vision whited out. Pleasure didn't roll through her, it *bit*, a single, bone-cracking bolt that left her shaking.

Apollo was above her, his eyes full of concern. "It was too much." His voice clipped with self-censure. "Felicity, I'm sorry, I didn't think—"

"Don't you dare be sorry." She grabbed his face in both hands and kissed him, brutally hard. "Holy fuck. That was the most incredible thing that's ever happened to me."

She was already rolling on top of him, pushing him flat on his back on the sun-heated rock. The lightning bolt of pleasure had filled her with another need or reminded her of what she'd wanted before. She wrapped one hand around his cock.

"I want you in my mouth," she told him. His eyes went dark with lust. "Please?"

Apollo licked his lips. "I feel like I should be the one begging you for that."

"Never." He jerked in her hand, and the expression in his eyes made her feel more powerful than she'd imagined possible. "I want to taste you. Please?"

"God." He dropped his head back and she grinned, positioning herself between his thighs.

"Inch by inch, or…?"

Apollo groaned, a torment of frustration and lust, and giddiness almost overwhelmed her. She was doing this to him. *Her*. Her hands and words had left him mute and groaning with need.

"Your cock looks so good," she told him, and his hands clenched into empty fists on the stone. "So big and hard. I bet you taste amazing." She kissed the head, her tongue flicking out. "I've been thinking about this since this morning."

"Oh god."

"I woke up dreaming about you, did you know that?"

"Felicity…"

"And when I kissed you, this morning…" She ran her tongue down the side of his cock, and up again. "Was that only this morning?"

"It was—it was—" Apollo swore. "Is this revenge? For the inches?"

She lifted her head to blink at him innocently. "Inches?" Still holding his gaze, she kissed the tip of his cock again, then slid her mouth down over him. She hollowed her cheeks, sucking hard as she pulled back. "Like this?"

"You're killing me."

"By inches?"

He half-groaned, half-laughed, and she took him into her mouth again. He tasted salty and masculine and sexy, and how the hell had she lived her whole life without knowing how incredible it felt, taking power like this?

Except it wouldn't have been like this. Not with anyone who wasn't Apollo. He was what made this perfect.

She took him deeper, thrilling at the noises he made, the taste and feel of him in her mouth, the furtive, desperate movement of his hands. When she finally gave in and put one of his hands on the back of her head, he gave a shuddering gasp that rolled through her like the tide. He kept his hand there, holding her gently, almost reverently, as she teased him over the edge.

Afterwards she nestled into his side, boneless with exhausted glee. He ghosted one hand over her side, his lips buried in her hair.

"That was…" He stopped, a strange look in his eyes like his mind had gone totally, blissfully blank. She recognized it. She probably looked the same, reliving what they'd just done.

She let her fingers trail down Apollo's chest. "Good?" she suggested.

He made a strangled noise. "So far beyond good I'm having difficulty finding the words for it." He picked up her fingers and kissed them, one by one. His magic danced in the air around them but didn't zap against her bare skin and she was actually relieved. She didn't have the energy for that right now.

Maybe later.

"The thing with your mouth," she said, musing aloud.

"Hmm?"

"I knew you could cast lightning magic with your hands," she said, twining her fingers around his. "But the mouth is new. Did you know you could do that?" She touched his lips.

"This was the first time." He kissed her, stinging her fingertips with the lightest kiss imaginable.

"Could you do it with your cock?"

Apollo stared at her and swore under his breath. She grinned at him. "Well?"

"It isn't something I've ever experimented with," he admitted, teeth gritted.

"So..." She pushed herself up on her elbows and his eyebrows snapped together. "I'm just thinking, in the interests of really, thoroughly investigating your magic..."

"How the hell did I live before I met you?" Apollo sat up, pulling her into his lap. His cock was half-hard already, pressed against her behind. "And what did I do to deserve you falling into my life?"

"Saved my life," she reminded him, and his eyes darkened.

Certainty gripped her, as hard and unforgiving as the orgasm that had ripped through her body minutes ago. *I'll never give you up to Montfort. You or Hideaway. I don't care what it takes.*

Her future, which had once stretched out in front of her, cold and frightening in its endlessness, faded. She didn't know what was coming next—only what she *wasn't* going to do.

She wasn't going to go back to Montfort Industries. Because it didn't matter how sexy and confident and powerful she was here. Montfort would tear all that away. One terrifying look from him and she would tell him everything, and he would destroy Hideaway Cove.

*I won't let that happen. I've got savings. I'll run away. Disappear.*

But first, she was going to enjoy the hell out of whatever this thing was between her and Apollo.

*My dragon.*

"So… now that I've fallen into your life…" She wriggled, barely bothering to pretend she was trying to get comfortable and not just enjoying the feeling of his cock rubbing against her.

He kissed her—then stood up, picking her up bridal-style. She squealed and he gave her one of his roguish smiles.

"If you're going to be like that," he drawled, all impervious golden smirk, "you can at least buy me dinner first."

Reluctantly, Felicity had headed back to the bed-and-breakfast to freshen up for dinner. There was a message from Maya waiting on her phone when she got out of the shower. Relief unspooled inside her as she read it.

Maya: *Sorry about earlier! Things crazy. Call tonight?*

It was followed by a photo of Tomás beaming from his highchair, a spoon in one chubby hand and something shiny in the other. He was shaking it so excitedly, his whole arm was a blur.

"Hey, chicky," Felicity murmured, smiling at the photo. She hadn't seen Tomás in weeks. It felt like years.

Felicity: *He is so big!!! Rain check on call? Going out tonight.*

Her phone pinged again a few minutes later, as she was pulling clothes out of her suitcase.

Maya: *Montfort not happy you are quitting? Sorry not there to run interference.*

Felicity: *Not work! Having dinner with a guy I met on vacation.*

Maya: *A DATE*

Maya: *TELL ME EVERYTHING*

Felicity wasn't sure whether she wanted to laugh or cry. Talking with Maya like this was so *normal*. Like a window into another life.

Felicity: *Tall. Blonde. Amazing kisser.* Amazing at everything that came after kissing, too, but she wasn't going to say *that* over text. *Tell you more tomorrow.*

She and Maya messaged back and forth as she got dressed and put on her makeup. A strange hiccup-y excitement filled her. Which was ridiculous. She and Apollo had already had sex. On a beach. In the middle of the day. Sex with *magic*. A dinner date—*with his friends*, she reminded herself, so it wasn't even like they were going to be alone—should have been a step down on the anxiety scale. So why did she feel like a teenager waiting to be picked up for prom?

On Maya's urging, she sent her a selfie of her all dressed up.

*SEXY,* Maya sent back at once. And then: *Have FUN girl. You deserve this.*

Did she?

Felicity looked at herself in the mirror. The woman who looked back wasn't the terrorized office-worker she usually saw staring back at her. She was fresh-faced and excited.

She didn't look like a woman who'd had sex on a beach a few hours ago, either. She still ached slightly; a warm, delicious physical reminder of what it had been like to throw caution to the wind.

What would she look like later tonight?

Anticipation twisted sweetly in her core. She tossed her phone in her bag, smoothed her hair one last time, and headed out to find her dragon.

# 13

# APOLLO

It was Saturday night in Hideaway Cove, and that meant the whole town was descending upon Caro's Hook and Sinker, the best—and only—restaurant the town had to offer.

Apollo was lingering at the bar, where he'd arranged to meet Felicity. Caro had set aside a table for them on the mezzanine, but in a town like Hideaway he wasn't going to get away with spiriting his mate upstairs away from prying eyes. The prying eyes would come right up after them. Besides, he wanted her to meet his friends. Harrison and Arlo were both bringing their families tonight.

And they were all under strict instructions not to mention the word *mate*.

Guilt needled his heart. They'd all understood, and so had his dragon, after a little internal debate, but keeping the truth from Felicity still felt wrong.

*I can't tell her before I have a hoard worthy of her*, he reminded himself. *That would be worse than not telling her at all. 'Hello, most beautiful woman I've ever met. We are fated to be together forever, but not just yet, because I have to do some shopping first. And by shopping, I mean grubbing around in the dirt on some distant, deserted island, trying to find a chest of lost treasure before some other bastard dragon digs it up first.'*

Yes. That would go down well, wouldn't it?

Not that he'd told the others the real reason not to bring up the existence of soulmates. And they hadn't asked. They all accepted that telling your human mate they were fated to be with you was awkward at the best of times, and it was best to let him take things at his own pace. Same as they had done, more or less.

Less, really, but who was counting?

His stomach rumbled. Caro, who was in the kitchen directly behind the bar, snorted and shoved a plate at him. "I've got you," she said.

Apollo opened his mouth to thank her, but she was already turning back to her work. The no-nonsense orca shifter was oddly tetchy about people noticing she actually cared about her customers, despite the fact she'd been doing it for years.

*Thanks, Caro,* he said silently.

*That? It's just insurance to make sure you don't pass out and fall over the railings, right onto someone else's dinner.*

*Very forward-thinking of you. I appreciate it.*

She'd given him a plate of mozzarella sticks. He munched absently on one, watching the door.

He had eaten already, of course. A rushed, regretful meal of half-heated leftovers. More a fuel stop than an actual meal, meant to stop him from doing something embarrassing like keeling over unconscious during dinner if too many people drew on his magic too quickly. His shifter metabolism, combined with the extra energy his magic required, meant he would be starving again by the time their starters came out.

The mozzarella sticks would help. They always did. He suspected Caro ordered them by the pallet-load just for him.

"Those for the table?" Harrison shouldered his way through the crowd to the bar. Apollo was about to snatch the bowl away from the griffin shifter when he saw who was behind him. Harrison had been nudging the crowd aside to make room for his fiancée, Lainie. Lainie was short and curvaceous—extremely curvaceous at the moment, as she was heavily pregnant.

"Take them," he said, pushing the bowl towards her. She gave him a tired smile.

"Thanks, Pol. We won't stay long tonight. I'm dead on my feet."

He got out of his seat and Harrison helped her into it. She was so short he had to boost her up. She leaned against him and closed her eyes. "Now I'm stuck up here. If I fall off…"

"I won't let you fall."

The love on both their faces made Apollo's heart yearn. Harrison and Lainie were perfect together. That should have gone without saying—they were soulmates, each the other's perfect pair—but Harrison and Lainie had a connection that was more than magical. They trusted and cared for each other implicitly.

"Mozzarella sticks! Thank god." Jacqueline strode through the crowd, a small girl with tousled dark-blonde curls on her hip.

"Swim me! Swim me!" Tally shouted insistently. Jacqueline heaved the little seal shifter over her shoulder and zoomed her up to the bar. Tally opened her mouth wide.

"Aaaah!" she squealed as Jacqueline leaned her over the bowl. "Aaaaah…. chomp!"

She raised her head and grinned, her mouth full of deep-fried cheese.

"Excuse *you*," Apollo remarked. He tipped the bowl to look into it. "Do you want the rest of the ones with teeth-marks in, or…?"

Tally giggled maniacally and ran away without answering.

Arlo arrived a few minutes later, the rest of his pack in tow. Lanky, dark-skinned Eric, still growing into his limbs; teenaged Kenna, constantly lurching between surly and giggling; and Dylan, who could, and would, tell you to the minute how long until he was ten years old.

Apollo found himself watching them. Arlo and Jacqueline had a different sort of connection, too. They were one another's anchors, the calm center of the storm of chaos that was their young pack.

Would he and Felicity be like that, one day? Or would they be something new, something purely them? What could they make together?

He remembered the look on Felicity's face as she took him in her mouth and blood rushed to his cock. *Apart from that*, he thought automatically, but—that was part of it too, wasn't it? Finding joy in one another.

God, he hoped he could make her as happy as she made him.

The door opened again. Nothing else changed—there was no falter in the hum of conversation, no dramatic swoosh of air, no parting of the crowd between them. But he knew Felicity had arrived before he turned to look.

There she was. His mate. When he'd left her at the bed-and-breakfast after their swim, she'd been a salt-bedraggled elf, her hair in tangled ribbons, sand drying between her fingers and toes.

Now she was a dark angel. Her hair was a shining black waterfall pouring over one shoulder. Her eyes were starless black diamonds. Her mouth was a mouth he desperately wanted to kiss.

Slight anxiety creased her face as she scanned the room. He waved to her and the moment their eyes met, happiness overflowed and poured out of her.

His mate. His Felicity.

She slipped through the crowd like one of the tiny fishes that darted around the marina at night, chasing moonbeams. He met her halfway, catching her hands in his.

Felicity smiled up at him. "Long time, no see."

"It's been almost two hours. I'm amazed either of us survived so lengthy an absence."

"I'd better catch you up on everything you missed." Her smile turned into a grin as she slipped her arm around his and they made their way back to the bar. "Had a shower. Got dressed. Lay down on my bed, thinking about… swimming." She sighed deeply. "Had another, colder shower."

Apollo's magic rippled at the thought of goosebumps prickling over her skin under the cold spray. He knew exactly how to heat her up.

"Who's having cold showers?" They'd reached the bar, and Lainie had caught the end of their conversation. "Pol, you can't let that happen! Can't you do something about the hot water?"

"Yeah, Apollo, can't you do something to warm me up?" Felicity asked, her smile pure evil. He put one arm around her shoulders.

"Dinner first, remember?"

"Spoilsport."

"You say that now. You haven't tried Caro's cooking yet." He introduced her to everyone, and the conversation idled through the usual visitor small talk—how she was finding Hideaway Cove, whether she'd been to the ice cream parlor yet, an invitation up to see the ruined lighthouse.

"Someone said your car almost crashed on the way in." Jacqueline's forehead creased with concern. "The fog last night was so thick we couldn't see the water from on deck. That must have been terrifying."

"It was an adventure, for sure." Felicity leaned her head against his arm. "I'm lucky Apollo was there. Wings and everything."

"That's one way to let out Hideaway's secret," Arlo murmured, and Jacqueline poked him.

"You're one to talk," she said. "Remember?"

His sapphire eyes softened as he gazed at her. "I'll never forget."

Jacqueline shook herself, like she'd forgotten the rest of them where there. "But you're all right now?" she asked Felicity.

"Oh, yeah. We sorted it out."

Cold washed over Apollo's skin. Had they? They'd spent the day exploring his magic and Felicity's strange and wonderful connection to it, but they hadn't actually figured out what had happened up there on the cliffs.

His jaw tightened. *I never change, do I?* He'd met his mate, and here he was, slipping into bad habits. Instead of protecting her, he'd let himself be dazzled by her presence. Instead of figuring out what had almost *killed* her, he'd…

The beach. He almost groaned aloud at the memory.

Tomorrow. Tomorrow they would do things properly. He would find out what caused the crash, and make sure it never happened again.

# 14

# FELICITY

The others had left early, as promised; now it was just the two of them, hidden away in the mezzanine nook above the restaurant's main floor. Most of the restaurant's booths and tables had views of the water, but this one was designed for a different view: staring into the eyes of whoever was sitting opposite you.

Which was obviously why Apollo had chosen it. He was making the most of it, too. They had ordered their meals and now the gentle light from the tea candles on the table flickered softly over his features, turning his golden eyes molten. And he was gazing at her as though she were the most beautiful woman he'd ever seen.

It was, she realized with a jolt, the same way he'd looked at her last night. And this morning. And at the beach. She just hadn't recognized it before now.

"I hope that wasn't too much of a chore," he said, pouring her a glass of sparkling wine. He'd snagged the bottle from behind the bar before they came upstairs. "They're lovely people, but they can be a bit much. And anyone new is exciting, in a town like this. You'll be the top story for all the gossips tonight."

"That's slightly terrifying." More than slightly. She took strength from the knowledge that nobody knew why she was really here. Apollo's friends had been curious about what brought her to Hideaway, but she'd given

449

them the same story about picking a random place for her vacation, and they'd accepted it.

No one needed ever find out the truth. Not now that she'd decided she wasn't going back to Montfort.

She just had to figure out how she was going to escape him.

Without letting Apollo know anything was troubling her.

She glanced at him, more than half expecting to catch him making sultry eyes at her. To her surprise he was looking away, a strange expression on her face.

Her stomach fell. She recognized that expression, too. It was the same one he'd worn that morning, after he'd convinced himself his magic had hurt her.

She cleared her throat. "You're looking serious again." Taking a leaf out of his book, she sighed dramatically. "Let me guess. You're feeling bad about the whole mind wipe thing?"

Apollo had been nodding along. She assumed he was waiting for the right moment to step in and reassure her, no, of course nothing was wrong. Instead, she watched as his brain caught up with what his ears had heard. He frowned. "Wait. What mind wipe thing?"

"There's got to be something, right?" She propped her elbows on the table and leaned forward. "You have this secret town full of secret, magical people. How do you keep it from getting out? I figured either you have some Harry Potter-style mind wipe spell you can use on outsiders so we don't run off and spill the beans, or…" She smiled mischievously. "You're a dragon. I'm still holding out for a secret tower where you stash everyone who wrongs you."

"Wizards have towers," Apollo informed her, faux-serious. "Dragons have—"

"Hoards? Caves full of treasure?"

His mouth twisted. "Something like that."

*That hit a nerve.* She was deciding whether to prod him further when he smoothed over his expression and smirked at her. It was a sexy smirk and under normal circumstances she would have happily let it melt her into a puddle, but—something was still disturbing him, no matter how much he was trying to hide it.

He reached across the table and took her hand, turning it over in his as though it was a precious jewel. "No tower to imprison you in, no hoard… I'm sorry to be such a disappointment."

She gave him a hard look. "You are *not* a disappointment. Nothing about this day has been disappointing."

"It's understandable you would think that. You don't have any other dragons to compare me against." He gave a long-suffering sigh that made her want to smack him and dissolve into giggles at the same time.

Instead, she rolled her eyes. "Fine. I'll bite. Who are these other dragons, and where would *they* have taken me… swimming?"

Golden eyes flashed and his hand tightened around hers. "They wouldn't have taken you anywhere."

"I'm glad we've got that straight." She took a long, slow sip of her wine and watched Apollo watching her lips. "So, what do these other dragons bring to the table, then?"

"The usual. Gold. Riches. Treasures beyond imagining." Apollo slumped in his seat, apparently bored by the whole topic. But there was a sharp glitter in his eyes that told her otherwise.

And… his magic was responding to his words. Or his emotions, maybe. She couldn't see any sparks, but she could *feel* his power twisting around them both. Waiting for something?

"I don't know. I can imagine some pretty huge piles of gold, and if there really were dragons sitting on piles of treasure like that, I think I'd have heard about it by now."

"Absolutely not. Any dragon worth his salt keeps his hoard secret and safe." Apollo was still playing absently with her hand, drawing patterns on her palm with his long, gentle fingers. "It's the circle of life. Dragon finds hoard. Dragon hides it. Another dragon attempts to steal it…"

"Sounds tedious."

"Oh, not at all. It's what dragons are meant to do. The lust for gold is an integral part of our DNA. We're proud of it."

He didn't sound proud. He sounded exhausted.

And what had he said? *No tower to imprison you, no hoard…* No wonder he seemed uncomfortable, if hoarding treasure was so important to dragons and he didn't have any.

She wrinkled her nose. "Well, forgive me if I don't run off to find any of those other dragons. I've had enough of rich assholes for one lifetime."

He shot a look at her, incisive and questioning, and her heart pounded. She was reassuring *him*, damn it. Not airing out her own issues.

"Here are your entrees!"

Felicity sent up a silent prayer of thanks as the waitress interrupted. Whatever Apollo had been about to ask vanished as they tucked in. The meals were delicious: smoked fish pie in pastry that flaked like a dream, accompanied by crisp, sharp salad that perfectly cut through the creamy, smoky decadence.

She closed her eyes. When was the last time she'd had food like this? No, that wasn't the right question. She'd been to more than her fair share of expensive restaurants during her time working for Montfort.

When was the last time she'd *enjoyed* food like this?

Magic brushed her skin, and she opened her eyes to see Apollo watching her, his eyes hot, and there was her answer.

When was the last time she'd enjoyed a wonderful meal with a man who made her heart melt?

Never.

It was the dessert course that finally broke her. They hadn't ordered dessert, but apparently the chef had decided they were getting some anyway. And according to Apollo, you didn't say no to the chef.

"If I've learned nothing else in life, it's that you always want to keep on the chef's good side, especially when the woman holding the knives is also a killer whale shifter."

Felicity's eyes widened. "She's an orca shifter? The woman who was practically force-feeding you mozzarella sticks before?"

"Believe me, with Caro, *killer whale* is the more appropriate term."

"I wish—" she began, and stopped herself too late. Apollo raised his eyebrows at her.

"Go on."

To put off answering, she pressed the tines of her fork into her cake. Caro had sent up two slices of orange almond cake with cream on the side. Decisions, decisions. Where to start?

The outside of cake usually went dry first. Start there and work her way to the inside. *And be amazed, again, at how it feels like a treat to be able to enjoy my food. To think, 'I'll make sure to save the nice bit for last' and not worry that Montfort will turn the table over before I get to it.* The waffles this morning, perfect squares of cream and syrup and fruit. The fish pie. And now cake.

It wasn't that she didn't *eat*. Meals were for vital fuel, keeping her going between meetings. Sometimes they were part of the meetings. Vendors bribing her to add them to Montfort's diary—or take them off it. But never to be enjoyed. And never, really, for *her*.

She shaved off a portion of cake from the outside of the slice. *Delicious.* The crumb was rich and decadent, the orange perfectly juicy. It wasn't dry or overcooked at all; the crispness at the edge was crystalized sugar.

"This is amazing." She took a forkful from the inside corner, just in case it was *too* moist. Nope. Still perfect. "I can't believe no one's poached your chef yet."

"Well, there aren't many places that can offer her full control over the menu *and* the opportunity to swim around in her killer whale form after she clocks off."

"See? Amazing. Not just the meal. This whole place. It's like a fairy tale. I wish—*dammit*." She scowled at herself, then caught sight of Apollo's expression and put her fork down.

He raised his hands in surrender. "Let it be put on record that I didn't push you to tell me what it is that you're wishing for, even though it's my heart's desire to know the answer."

"You just let the cake get past my defenses for you."

"I know my limitations. They're far more limited than the vast power of cake." He leaned forward, resting his chin on one hand. "Take another bite."

She narrowed her eyes at him and did as he said. Sweet, bright citrus burst on her tongue, perfectly cushioned by the soft crumb of the cake and smear of cream. "I wish I could stay here forever."

"Then do."

Felicity shook her head. "After everything I've seen here—I don't want to go back to my old life. I *can't*. The thought of going back into the office, doing the same thing I've done every day for the past five years, knowing all the time that there's magic like this just out of sight... I couldn't do it."

"Then don't go back. Stay."

His words finally registered. "Stay?" It took her another moment to add, "Here?"

"Why not?"

There were a million reasons why not, and all of them were Montfort. Felicity licked suddenly dry lips, her whole body heavy and aching with longing. Not the hot, exciting need that had roared through her veins like wildfire earlier, but something deeper, sadder.

*I wish I could.* But she couldn't, and she couldn't even explain to him why.

# I5

# APOLLO

Apollo woke in a bed that had never seemed cold and empty until he met Felicity, and she wasn't in it.

She'd stayed at the bed-and-breakfast the night before, saying she had some work stuff to take care of. But they had arranged to meet again that morning.

And before he saw her again, there was something he had to do.

He would do anything for his mate.

Even call his grandfather.

Apollo's Grandfather Errol was the only other living dragon shifter in his family. He lived in the penthouse apartment of a skyscraper in Singapore. The closest thing a dragon could get to a tower while still being a part of the modern world.

Memories of the one time he had met Errol in person bubbled uneasily in the back of Apollo's mind as he made his way back to his own small cottage. Apollo had been eighteen and about to start his treasure-hunting travels. His first stop had been to pick up the starter hoard his grandfather had reluctantly indicated he would, because of their family connection, be willing to offer him.

His grandfather had given him a single scrap of gold, and all but chased him out of his apartment building.

He found his grandfather's contact details hidden deep in his email. He plugged the numbers into his phone and waited for the call to connect while his dragon hissed, disgruntled that he was crawling back to his grandfather to help him find a hoard.

But Errol was his best chance. He kept repeating that to himself.

Then his grandfather picked up.

With a video call.

Apollo bit back a groan and quickly smoothed back his hair. His reflection in the phone screen looked like something out of a horror movie, all deep shadows under his eyes and haggard gray skin.

His grandfather, of course, looked flawless. His silvery hair was swept back from a widow's peak like he was ready to step onto a production of *Dracula*, and his golden eyes were clear and sharp.

"Good day, Apollo," he intoned.

"Grandfather." Apollo resisted the urge to bow. He could see a little of Errol's apartment at the edges of the screen: plush velvet hangings, glowing pendant lights and rows and rows of glass-fronted cabinets displaying his grandfather's collection of antique men's jewelry. His hoard.

Errol's nostrils flared and he zoomed in his camera so that only his face was visible. Draconic hackles prickling, Apollo adjusted the angle of his own phone so that the camera only showed the wall behind him.

Wonderful. Less than a dozen words exchanged, and they were already practically snarling at one another. Apollo took a deep breath, searching for inner peace.

What he found was his dragon, hissing angrily.

"What are you calling for, kid?" Errol sniffed. He peered out at him, his eyes narrowed suspiciously.

"Can't a grandson call his only draconic relative just to say hello?"

"No."

"Ah, well."

Apollo moved restlessly around the room. He almost ended up leaning against the living room window until his dragon snapped at him that it did *not* want his grandfather to catch a glimpse of Hideaway's lights through the glass.

"Get on with it, boy! If you've got something you want to say, say it. I have an appointment with a fence in ten minutes that promises to be very… profitable." A toothy smile spread across Errol's face. "For me, at least."

"Speaking of," Apollo began, and hesitated. He sat down on the sofa, slowly, the pain in his head a heavy throb. "Er. About… hoards."

His grandfather's gaze became even more suspicious. "What about hoards?"

*Why do I feel like a misbehaving schoolboy whenever I talk to him?* It had been the same every time his parents called Errol at Christmas and birthdays growing up, to ensure that Apollo had *some* draconic influence in his life, and it had been unbearable when he turned eighteen and actually visited the man in person.

It wasn't as though he even *wanted* the old man's hoard. His mate was a woman. What would she do with hundreds of solid-gold tie pins?

"I was wondering if you'd heard any more rumors about potential hoards in North America," he managed to grit out from behind an entirely unconvincing smile. "I find myself at a loose end, and—"

"Hah! Finally decided to make a move on a hoard of your own, have you?"

"The quicker the better."

"We agree on that, at least." His grandfather's gaze turned inwards.

Apollo stayed silent, feeling once again like an errant schoolboy waiting for the principal to lay down judgment on him. He resisted the urge to scuff his feet.

At last, his grandfather roused himself. A slow, reptilian greed gleamed from his eyes. "Conveniently," he drawled, "I have only today heard a delicious piece of gossip…"

Apollo leaned forward. His grandfather let the silence stretch out, clearly enjoying every minute.

"Well?" he burst out when he couldn't take it anymore. "What is it?"

"I couldn't possibly say. Not without confirming several key details first." Errol sat back, folding his hands over the gold-topped cane he was never seen without.

"You're not even going to tell me?"

Errol fixed him with an icy glare. "I do have my reputation to consider, hatchling. Do you know how embarrassing it has been, watching you flit from failure to failure? I was the laughingstock of the club. Until I cleared out the president's vault, of course." He inspected his fingernails. "I will make a few inquiries and be in touch when I have something foolproof to give you."

*'Fool'proof being the operative word.* Apollo just managed to keep his shoulders from slumping. "Very well."

"Hah! As though you had any other options." Errol sniffed. "Try not to embarrass me any further while you're waiting for my message."

Apollo's mouth was still hanging open, waiting for his brain to supply words, when Errol ended the call.

Well.

That could have gone better.

And something about his conversation with his grandfather gnawed at him. Not the barely veiled insults. Those were to be expected. But his dragon hadn't even turned a scale at the brief glimpse of Errol's hoard.

His own exhaustion he understood, but shouldn't his dragon be champing at the bit to snare whatever gold it could get its claws on? Every time he so much as glanced at Felicity, it nudged him to give her his hoard, but it had never pushed him to get one in the first place.

In the karst country of Vietnam, the Jordanian desert, the Vespa-clogged streets of Rome, his dragon had been as gold-hungry as himself. That was: not very. Whenever they had faced the choice to fight for a treasure or let it go, they had let it go.

*Care to explain yourself?* he asked it.

It whipped its tail uneasily. The shame of its hoard being not enough for Felicity was still raw, but its testy mood was more than that. It was... confused.

He sighed. His magic was still playing up, his dragon was having an identity crisis, and his headache was getting worse, but he had achieved one thing today. He had a lead.

And he had Hideaway. For the next few days, at least. He would not leave it in chaos from his broken magic. He reached for the shining web he had painstakingly woven across the town and winced as pain shot through his head. The magic frittered out of his grasp.

He was too tired, he told himself. That must be it. If he could only rest a little longer, everything would feel right again.

Sleep beckoned, but he had something more important on his agenda. The most important thing of all.

It was time to find his mate.

# 16

# FELICITY

"Oh! Hello—Felicity, wasn't it? How are you today?"

Felicity put down her coffee with a pang and turned to smile at Antonia. "Great," she half-lied. "And yourself?"

"Oh, well, you know—and it's not that—well, everything's lovely, of course…" Antonia sat down opposite her, and Felicity tried not to let her heart sink. "Bruno was out late again last night. I hope he didn't disturb you when he came back?"

"He must have been quieter than a mouse," Felicity replied promptly. But of course, that wasn't the conversation Antonia really wanted to have.

Despite her best efforts, her heart did sink. *I really do have one of those faces. One look and everyone wants to tell me their secrets.*

She had sent her resignation to Montfort the night before. She wasn't his spy. Not anymore. But somehow, that just made her feel worse. Now that she wasn't here to betray Hideaway, shouldn't she admit that was what brought her here in the first place?

"I hoped he would be able to relax more on vacation." Antonia's fingers kept flittering around, from her earrings, to her hair, her necklace, to the table, and Felicity thought Bruno wasn't the only one who needed to relax.

"It's this job of his. Is it a job if they're not paying you? His *internship*. Really, if they're not paying you and they're working you so hard you can't sleep even when you *are* on vacation, is it the sort of job you want to get? But he's so proud of getting his foot in the door, and he's worked *so* hard…"

"And now he can't switch off?"

Antonia gave a relieved smile. "Exactly!"

*Sounds familiar.* Felicity hid a grimace behind a big gulp of coffee. "Where is his internship?"

"Oh, you know, one of those big firms. He won't tell me about it. He thinks that if he doesn't talk about it, he can ignore how badly it's affecting him, but that *never* works." Antonia sighed. "The stress just gets bunched up inside until it *explodes*. It was the same when he was a baby. I wish he would let me work on him, but I can understand him not wanting his mommy's elbow in his gluteus."

"*Pffngh!*"

Felicity winced as hot coffee shot up her nose and halfway across the table. "Augh, I—sorry, I—your elbow in his *what?*"

The other woman blinked and then gave a giddy laugh. "Hah! Golly, yes, I can see how that might have sounded strange. I'm a massage therapist. I can practically *see* where poor Bruno is tying himself up in knots, but he'd be so embarrassed by me offering to do something about it, it would only make the problem worse."

*A massage therapist?* Felicity was actually on Bruno's side with this one. She couldn't imagine the nervous, twitchy woman in front of her soothing anyone's muscular issues, even without the added horror of his mom being the one to work all the tension out of his butt. She made a sympathetic noise and drizzled maple sauce on her waffles.

Antonia sighed. "At least he can shift freely here. That should help, even if his boss *does* keep bothering him. On the weekend! Changing our shape, you know, you can leave all your worries in your old body and try not to pick them up again when you shift back."

"You don't get the chance to shift much back home?" She still had no idea what sort of shifters Antonia and Bruno were.

"Oh, well, splashing around in the bathtub can't compare to actual fresh water." Antonia blinked rapidly. "I—well—neither does the sea, but there are a few small rivers, nearby, and if we stay in the mouths of the rivers where it isn't *too* salty then it won't cause any problems that a little moisturizing won't fix."

"It must be such a relief." Freshwater animals—or fish? Were there fish shifters? Felicity remembered the fish pie from the night before. Now *there* was a whole world of awkward she hadn't even thought about.

"Oh, it is. Such a relief. That is exactly what it is. If only Bruno…" Antonia shook her head. "He would tell me to stop worrying about *him* and focus on my own relaxation."

Felicity couldn't imagine surly Bruno worrying about anyone's feelings except his own grumpy ones. She was casting about for something friendly to say in response when the now-familiar tingle of Apollo's magic washed over her skin, from the back of her neck coming around to lap against her collarbones and the tops of her breasts. Her breath hitched.

She twisted around in her seat just in time to see him hopping over the railing at the other end of the patio.

He was wearing his hair loose, and the sun turned it into a waterfall of shimmering gold that fell across the open collar of a light shirt that was so well worn it was practically transparent. The sleeves were rolled up, giving her an eyeful of firm, muscular forearms and those incredible hands. Felicity dragged her eyes up again.

She'd stopped breathing when she felt the touch of his magic, and it wasn't until she met his gaze that she remembered to start again.

"Damn," Apollo murmured, a lazy grin spreading across his face. "I didn't even manage to get into position. Are you sure you're not a shifter?"

No way she was going to tell him she sensed him coming because his magic gave her a sexy shiver. "Pretty sure I would have noticed if I'd started turning into an animal. Or my workmates would have."

Apollo came around to the table and Felicity un-twisted in her chair. A muscle twanged behind one shoulder blade and she winced. "Oh, and I would *definitely* have taken advantage of—what did you call it, Antonia? Leaving all your stress behind when you shift between forms?"

"If you'd like me to take a look," Antonia began, but Felicity held up her hand.

"What were you just saying about being on vacation? I am not going to make this a working holiday for you." *And I don't want to give Bruno any more reasons to glare at me, if you're right and he really does care about you getting a chance to relax.*

She reached back to rub the knot, but Apollo got there first. He ran his thumb along the line of her shoulder-blade.

Her eyes fluttered closed. *Oh, god, that feels…*

"Is that the spot?" Apollo's lips brushed her ear and Felicity's thoughts went from PG to R18. She bit back a groan.

"What did you mean before, about not managing to get into position?"

"Ah." He sat next to her with one arm around her shoulder, his thumb making hard circles over the tight muscles. "In my continued quest to make a good impression on you, I planned my first appearance this morning to the finest detail. By the time you turned around, I would be lounging—there—the morning breeze combing my hair, the sun outlining all my best attributes…"

Felicity's gaze dipped down below the table. His *best* attributes? Did he mean…?

By the time she got control of her eyes and hoisted them up again, Apollo was practically glowing with smugness. He made a very visible effort to look humble as he added, "It would have been considerably more dignified than you catching me in the middle of hopping over the fence."

Had he looked undignified? Felicity shook her head. "Sorry. You'll have to give me some warning next time. I'll be sure to ignore you until your grand entrance is ready."

"Thank you. I would appreciate it."

"Can you let your magic know your plans too, though? It's how I could tell you were coming."

He stared at her. For a moment, Felicity thought she'd actually struck him speechless, until he managed to force out: "My magic?"

"I'm pretty sure it was. I, uh, felt it enough yesterday, I think I can recognize it by now."

He still looked dazed. "That's incredible." He leaned closer, his hand flattening across her back. "I had no idea…"

"Gosh, is that the time? You know, I think I'll take my breakfast to go." Chair legs scraped as Antonia stood up.

Felicity jumped. "Oh, shoot, Antonia, I'm sorry. I—"

She was aghast. She'd completely forgotten the other woman was there. As though the moment Apollo came into her orbit, everyone else in the world vanished.

"No, no, don't trouble yourself. Excuse me, lovebirds." Antonia nodded to Apollo and hurried off, almost knocking another chair over in her haste. Felicity stared after her, embarrassed and horrified.

She groaned and covered her eyes. "I can't believe I forgot she was there. That was so rude of me."

"Don't worry. She's a shifter, she'll understand. I'll go and apologize to her."

He strode after Antonia and caught up with her at the far end of the breakfast room. Felicity watched as he introduced himself. They were too far away for her to hear their words, but she could fill in the conversation:

hello, I'm Apollo, I'm Antonia, sorry for breezing in and acting like you didn't exist…

Antonia sparkled in Apollo's presence. Of course she did. *Everyone* did. Even Felicity.

She found herself wondering if anyone else sparkled as *literally* in his presence as she did, and was surprised by a sudden stab of jealousy. She shoved it away. What, did she think she was the first person he'd taken 'swimming'? He'd had a lifetime of being magical. She'd only known magic existed for a day and a half.

*But it would be nice to be special*, she thought, and the pang came back, sadder and more painful than before. Harder to push away, too. *And he did seem surprised that I could sense his magic. What if…*

She shook her head before her imagination got any wild ideas. All Apollo needed from her was her ability to tell whether his magic was secretly turning evil, and she was happy to provide.

Inside, Apollo finished his conversation with Antonia and farewelled her with a blinding grin. When he turned back towards Felicity, his smile changed, too, from the theatrical megawatt grin to something that was somehow both subtler and infinitely more… heated.

*He doesn't* only *want me for my magic-sniffing powers*, Felicity reminded herself, remembering how he'd lingered at her doorstep the night before. Maybe he would be interested in delving even deeper into exactly how well she could 'sense' his 'magic'.

She wouldn't say no. Not when this might be the last day they spent together.

# 17

# APOLLO

Felicity turned her head so that her nose tickled the triangle of bare skin above his collar. Her breath ruffled his shirt. Magic twisted around them, new and old; the magic he'd embedded into the building around them and the magic that filled the air around him in his mate's presence. He closed his eyes, reveling in the sensation of Felicity interacting with his magic. When she touched his magic, it felt like she was looking at him. Seeing him in a way no one else did.

The fact that it turned him on was an added bonus.

The fact that they were pressed together in a cramped closet… well. Bonuses all around.

Felicity hummed. "I'm sensing…"

"Hmm?"

She tipped her head back, resting her chin on his chest. "I'm sensing you don't actually need to be in here for me to do this."

"What gives you that idea?"

There had barely been room for the two of them even before he shut the door. Felicity shrugged, and her breasts rubbed against him. Because there was so little space, he had no choice but to let his hands slip around her waist, and from there down over the generous curves of her hips.

Felicity snickered. "Just a feeling."

"What else are you feeling?"

"Hmm…" Felicity straightened. "Magically speaking? Everything's fine, again. And with all the places we've checked, it feels…" She gestured blindly and her hand rapped against the side of the cupboard. "Ouch. It feels like we're almost… done."

Apollo's stomach dropped. "Done?"

Felicity made a frustrated noise. "As though… I've looked at all these separate places, but together, they form something that's almost… complete?" She tapped her fingers on the side of the cupboard, deliberately this time. "You described your magic as like a net over the town, right? It *feels* like I've visited almost all the knots holding it together. I'm just missing the… the… one piece that holds it all together." Her voice became amused. "I don't think that's how nets work, generally, but maybe it's how your magic net works."

*Maybe it is.* He had to ask, even though it would mean an end to this strange investigation-flirtation. "Do you have any ideas about where this last piece might be?"

"Just the one." She smiled up at him and he tried not to let his heart sink to join his stomach. So long as they'd had this game to play, he could avoid what he needed to do next.

"Oh? Do tell." His voice was light and teasing and no longer sounded like his own.

"It's up on the hill." Felicity stood on her tiptoes to whisper in his ear. "Painted like a certain dragon I know."

*His house.* Buttercup-yellow, not gold, but… "Shall we go there now?"

"In the interests of continuing our investigation?" Her eyes glittered wickedly. "I—"

Her phone chimed and she slapped her pocket.

"Excellent timing, whoever that is," Apollo murmured, then stopped at the look on Felicity's face. She was pale, her eyes wide and features frozen. His magic jerked towards her. "What's wrong?"

"Nothing! It's—" She fumbled for her phone, her other hand pressing wildly around for the door. He opened it for her, and she stumbled out. In the full light, her terror was only more obvious.

Draconic possessiveness rose up inside him, a strange, dizzying counterpoint to his human concern. He wanted to comfort her; the teeth and claws inside him wanted to find whoever made her react like this and hurt them. What use was a dragon who couldn't keep his mate safe? "Felicity—"

"It's fine! It's nothing. It's—" She finally looked at her phone, as reluctantly as though she was staring into something awful, and her face relaxed. "Oh. It really is nothing." She rejected the call with a quick swipe. "A spam call. Talk about the real world intruding on… not that this isn't the real world, but—"

"I won't be offended if you call Hideaway a fairy tale," Apollo reassured her.

She smiled, relieved. "It is. It's this magical, golden, fairy tale world where spam callers don't belong." She waved her phone at him. "Can your magic do anything about that? Stop spam callers?"

"I'll look into it." He frowned as she pocketed her phone. "Who did you think was calling?"

Felicity hesitated before answering. "My boss." She grimaced. "This is the part where you make a joke about all bosses being awful."

"Yours must be out of the ordinary, if he makes you react like that."

Felicity opened her mouth, then shut it. "Yes," she said, her voice wavering. "I didn't realize how bad it had gotten until I came here. He's like… like a fog pressing in all around. You know he's out there, somewhere, you just don't know where. I spent so much time preparing myself for whatever he might do next, even when I wasn't on the clock. It was inescapable. Until I came here." She snorted gently to herself. "I guess that's why the spam call was such a surprise. I thought, hey, if your magic can tune out Montfort's Dracula aura, *surely* it must block spam as well."

*Monfort.* Something about the name was familiar, but Apollo was barely able to spare a thought for it before his dragon roared to life within him. "If this Montfort makes you so miserable—"

"I didn't even *know*." Felicity shook her head, cutting him off before he could say *then you never have to see him again.* "It all became so normal. The friend who I was talking with yesterday, Maya? Our bosses hate each other. They're famous for it. Maya and I spent most of our time arranging their schedules so they would never meet. My first year in the job, the chef at the most exclusive restaurant in the city sent me a bouquet the size of my desk because they'd gone six months without any property damage."

"What?" His dragon pressed beneath his skin, sending lightning crackling along his arms. "What sort of job is this?"

"Personal assistant to the sort of man no one says no to." Felicity shook her head. "Well. Until now." She went slightly pale again and powered off her phone. "There. Try getting through that," she muttered, almost viciously.

Apollo slipped one arm around her waist, and she leaned into his embrace. "I can see why Hideaway seems like a fairy tale compared to working for someone like that."

"Too good to be true," she sighed into his chest.

"Excuse me. Hideaway Cove is exactly the right amount of good to be true, and I put a lot of work into making it so."

"Hah." She cuddled against him. "I wish—ah, forget it. Where were we, before I got spooked by my phone?" She tipped her head back and their eyes met. "Oh. I remember."

Something stirred inside him. "I was taking you home."

# 18

# FELICITY

The walk up the hill to Apollo's house took approximately a thousand years and was over in no time at all.

By the time they were outside his front door, Felicity felt as though her feet weren't touching the ground. Not even the sight of grumpy Bruno, hiding around a quiet corner and muttering with apologetic desperation into his cell phone, could bring her down. She hoped that whoever he was talking to—his boss, was her first thought—he could leave it behind like she was going to leave Montfort behind, and enjoy his vacation.

She was leaving Montfort behind. *That* was what didn't feel real.

*And I'll have to leave Hideaway, too.* The thought threatened to dim her brilliant, buoyant happiness. She pushed it away and looked up at Apollo's house.

"It's perfect," she said, with absolute sincerity.

She'd seen it from the waterfront promenade the day before: the daffodil-yellow walls with white trimming like decorative curls of icing on a cake, the brilliant pink and purple flowers spilling over the veranda that made her think of exotic far-off countries—Italy, or Spain.

The front door had a stained-glass window set into it. At first, she thought it was an abstract design. Then it hit her. The pattern was a replica of the cove: blue sky above, green hills making way for pale rocks and sand, and the sun-flecked sea.

"You've got the cove right on your doorstep," she told him, touching the glass. Magic pulsed against her fingertip and Apollo slipped his arm around her waist.

"The moment I saw that window, I knew this was the place for me." Apollo opened the door and ushered her inside. "Of course, at the time, I wasn't intending to stay quite so long."

"Lucky for me you did."

He blinked. "Yes. I hadn't thought about it like that before." A line appeared between his eyes.

*Shoot. I'd better change the subject before the specter of my car crash raises its ugly head again.* This whole flirtation-via-magic thing had started off as a way to check on Apollo's magic, sure, but as far as she was concerned they'd left that behind long ago.

Even though 'long ago' was only… *Yesterday?* How could it have only been *yesterday?* She felt as though she'd known Apollo for months.

And his house…

Light streamed through the stained-glass window, casting colorful lights into the entranceway. Felicity looked around as she took off her shoes.

"This is… it's very…" She turned to him, and her heart felt as though it was filling with stars. "It feels like… home."

The words slipped out before she could stop them. They were too true, that was the problem. She didn't know whether it was the magic or the fact that this was where Apollo lived, but the house's atmosphere wrapped around her like a warm blanket.

A tumult of emotions crashed across Apollo's face. Surprise, first, breaking through like a ship plowing through the waves. Delight: hesitant, hopeful, and something inside her echoed in harmony.

"Shall I give you the grand tour?" He leaned closer to her so his voice whispered against her skin and she shivered deliciously.

"That depends. How long will it take?"

"The full experience?" The double meaning was clear. His fingers danced up her neck, coming to rest caressing the back of her head. "That depends. The house has many fine features. Hardwood throughout, newly renovated bathroom with *very* good water pressure in the shower, an excellent view from the living room…"

"And the bedroom?" She relaxed into his touch. Sparks prickled on her skin.

"Another excellent view. More hardwood. A small balcony, for your morning coffee."

She opened her eyes comically wide. "The house tour's going to take so long, I'll still be here in the morning?"

"Oh, no. You've found me out." His magic and his arms wound around her, intoxicatingly powerful. "Turns out I *do* have a tower for trapping princesses in, after all."

"Very sneaky, dragon."

"I am, aren't I?" He kissed her, slow and gentle and suddenly hard and passionate.

His arms and the house's magic were still gentle around her, a careful caress as though she were some precious thing that might break, but she wasn't. Her hands tangled in his hair. She dragged him down and pushed herself up on her tiptoes, wanting to climb him, wanting all of him to be touching all of her.

Apollo's breath rasped against her lips. "My magic—" he forced out.

She only had a day more in Hideaway. She had sent in her resignation the night before and lain awake in terror, as though she was worried Montfort would tear across the country to destroy her for daring to quit her job.

*As though he even reads his own emails.* She had until Monday, easy. The poor assistant who was covering for Felicity while she was on 'vacation' would either have read her resignation email last night or this morning. It would take them at least twenty-four hours to muster the courage to tell him. If they were smart—and she'd trained them, so she hoped they knew their business—then they would wait until Monday, when the office was full. By then, Felicity needed to be gone.

So if Apollo thought she was going to waste *any* of the time she had left here in Hideaway with him—

"I don't need your magic. I only need you. Now."

One more day until she left and took Montfort's attention as far away from Hideaway as she could. She wasn't going to waste a minute of it.

# I9

# APOLLO

Felicity's kiss was a bolt of lightning. Magic crackled through his veins in sharp counterpoint to the softness of her lips, the gentle tease of her tongue against his, the drift of fingertips against his cheeks, his jaw, the column of his throat. She gasped something wordless and needing against his lips and he deepened the kiss, claiming her mouth as he wrapped himself around her. She was soft and pliant, her body shaping to his.

She was *his.*

He lifted her against the wall and pushed his thigh between her legs. His cock throbbed, jutting hard against her stomach.

"Oh…" Felicity rolled her hips, and he felt the rush of pleasure it gave her in the clutching of her fingers in his hair. They were on the edge of a precipice. He felt its pull, the sweet temptation to let himself fall and take her with him. "Apollo…"

At her whispered plea, he broke the kiss. Yes. There was more they needed to discuss. The mate bond. His hoard and the special magic it provided to seal the mate bond. He should tell her, now.

Her face was hazy with desire. All other thoughts vanished from his mind.

"See?" she whispered, a teasing glint breaking through the fog of arousal. "No zappy magic required."

She was right. His magic was still coursing through his body, stinging his nerves from the inside. He hadn't let any of it out as he kissed her.

He saw the question in her eyes and asked it for her. "And with magic?"

Their second kiss was more tentative. This new aspect of his magic was still so new to him. But his magic knew what it wanted. What *he* wanted. His dragon sighed with satisfaction as power flowed down his arms, tracing patterns on his bare skin and filling the air around them with golden pinpricks of light.

As the first spark landed on Felicity's skin, she startled. He held her close and she relaxed in his arms. Another spark touched her, and another. She trembled, her kisses becoming more frantic. He cradled her jaw in one hand and her pulse beat staccato against his palm.

Apollo pulled his magic to his hand and let it drift slowly down her neck. Golden light traced a path over Felicity's soft skin, reflecting off the sheen of sweat at her collarbones. He stroked lower, to the very edge of her sweater. Beneath it, her nipples hardened into lickable points.

"*With* magic," Felicity stammered. "It's—oh god. How are you doing that?"

"It's you." He bent his lips to her collarbone and pressed a kiss that sparked with power. "All you."

Felicity moaned. "Don't stop."

"Are you sure?" There was something else they were meant to be doing here, he was sure. Something other than pleasuring his mate, here, in the heart of his magic.

"Yes, I'm sure. I've never wanted anyone in my life as much as I want you. If we stop now, I'll never forgive myself."

"If we don't stop now, I don't think I'll be able to."

"Good. *Please.*"

Her words tore away the last of his hesitation. He kissed her again, possessive and exultant. She wound her arms around his neck and her legs around his hips. Her meaning couldn't have been clearer. She was staking her claim on him, the same way he was on her.

The layers of fabric that separated their bodies were maddening. He thrust against her, his cock hard and ready, and she gasped. "God, that feels good. Do it again."

He did, his magic teasing the insides of her thighs, and she cried out. "Too much?"

"Never." Her eyes danced as she tugged at the buttons on his shirt. "Not while we're still dressed, at least."

His shirt fell to the floor. Felicity ran her hands down his chest. She spread her fingers wide as though she wanted to touch as much of him as possible and his magic followed her touch, leaping and dancing.

She let out a shaking breath. Her eyes shone, dark and wonderful. "I suppose you're used to this."

"You suppose wrong."

Her fingers stilled. "When you said no one sensed your magic like I did…"

"It's the same for this." He kissed her, another jolt of whisper-soft lightning. "And this. And this…"

He drew her sweater over her head, revealing a pale lacy bra and lush, soft breasts. Easing her legs off his hips, he pulled the lace away and sucked one hard nipple into his mouth. Her back arched. Fingernails dug into his shoulders, and he swirled his tongue, glorying in the effect he was having on her.

*My mate.* He should tell her. But his mind was aflame with her soft moans and cries, and he couldn't find the words to let her understand. If he'd begun earlier, explained more about how shifters worked, about why they were drawn to one another like magnets, like moths to a flame, like summer rain to a parched, sunlit earth…

Then she was begging him, her voice half-broken with need, and he couldn't think anymore. He fell to his knees and kissed her stomach. Her shorts were in the way, and then they weren't, his senses full of the intoxicating scent of her arousal. He stopped, admiring how beautiful she was, her folds slick and darkly pink.

She tasted like sin in heaven. Sweet and feminine and bewitching. He licked and sucked until her legs trembled, then pulled away, nibbling on her inner thigh as he dragged her shorts and panties all the way to the floor. Then kissed and tasted her again, then stopped, and again, until her pleas weren't words anymore but helpless sighs and moans. He pulled one of her legs up, licking along the inside of her thigh as he laid it across his shoulder, and pressed his tongue and fingers into her in one smooth motion.

She came like a whip cracking. Her body tensed, back arching off the wall, leg like a vise over his shoulder. Her inner muscles clenched around his fingers over and over as he worshiped the perfect nub of her clit with his tongue.

He couldn't hold on much longer. Half-thoughts bounced against the inside of his skull and disappeared into nothing, like the sparks of his magic. Could he ask her to use her hand, or her mouth?

The thought of Felicity's mouth around his cock made his balls clench. Then she was pulling him up, her hands frantic at his fly and then wrapping around him.

He braced himself against the wall. "I don't have any protection."

*Again.* Idiot.

"I don't care." Felicity pulled him to her. Her eyes were dark and wild, her cheeks flushed, her lips red and wet and bruised from kisses. "Let me handle that. I want you inside me."

She put her legs around him again and he held her up against the wall. The tip of his cock brushed against her folds, just for a moment, then she groaned and tightened her legs and he sheathed himself inside her.

A curse forced its way out of his throat. She was so tight and hot and wet and took him all the way in. His perfect fit. He pulled out, slowly, and Felicity tipped her head back, eyes at half-mast, lost in sensation. She whimpered. He plunged back in, again, hooking his arm under one of her legs and pushing it higher up so the next time he thrust into her the angle was different, deeper, tighter, *perfect*.

Felicity came again, a crashing sob she tried and failed to bury in his shoulder. It tipped him so far over the edge the world went white. He stayed buried inside her as his orgasm ripped through him.

She was his. His mate. His treasure.

But something was missing.

Felicity sighed, long and satisfied and ending in a ripple of laughter. She slid her legs back down to the ground, bracing herself on his chest as though she didn't trust them to hold her up.

"Oh my god," she breathed. "That was…" Her head dropped against his chest as she caught her breath with a rush of laughter. "What did we come in here for? I'm sure it wasn't that, but I'm not complaining."

Nor was he, but something wasn't right. His dragon should have been sated and smug, but instead it scratched its claws, frustrated. Something was *missing*. He'd been so close…

*My hoard.* Understanding struck with a bite of guilt. His hoard was *right there*. Abandoned on the floor with his trousers. Felicity was his everything; he should have told her the truth and mated her properly, not let himself be swept away by lust.

"A house tour," Felicity giggled, her breath ruffling against his chest. "That was what we were meant to be doing, wasn't it?"

"Oh, yes." He held her close, not letting any of his conflicted feelings show through. "Are you enjoying it so far?"

"Definitely. I'm very impressed by—uh—what room are we in, again?"

*The wrong one.* He couldn't offer his hoard to his mate in the entranceway, under the accusing glare of his work boots and coatrack.

He nuzzled her ear. "We could continue the tour in the living room, if you like? Or the kitchen?"

"Good idea. We'll need supplies to keep our strength up, if this *tour* continues the way it started."

# 20

# FELICITY

The tour did, indeed, continue as it had started. By the end of it, she was sure she wouldn't be able to say a single thing about Apollo's décor, or even the house in general, except that the vanity in the bathroom was a very convenient height and his bed was the coziest thing she'd ever been thrown onto.

They lunched naked in the living room—an activity ripe for causing distractions, which of course it did—and spent the early afternoon in a blissful dream. The sun was just starting to dip towards the horizon when Apollo glanced at the clock and groaned.

Even fairytales had some downtime, Felicity decided. Apollo had work to do—boring work, he'd assured her, nothing that her strange talent for piggybacking on his magic could benefit from.

She got the sneaking suspicion that what he actually meant was, the boring work would suffer from her being around and distracting him from it. Which as well as making her blush like a fire engine, she had to agree with.

She had decided against staying at Apollo's while he was away, pining like some maiden in a tower, and was instead sitting in the ice cream parlor on the pier, watching kids play on the beach. *Also, it's good to have a break before I literally catch fire from how hot he is,* she reflected as she dug a spoon into her ice cream sundae.

"Holy shit," she muttered as she tasted it. "This is delicious."

Behind the counter, Tess Sweets laughed. "I'm sure Apollo warned you about my flavor experiments."

"Yeah, but he said they were weird. This is *amazing*. What is it?"

"Spicy mango," Tess announced triumphantly. "If you're here for Halloween, you should try my ghost pepper ice cream. It's a real treat. Especially if we can trick Apollo into eating it."

*Spicy mango and ghost pepper?* Those sorts of flavor combinations made Felicity think of crazy food fests in the city, not a small-town ice cream shop. How the hell had Tess not been lured away from Hideaway already?

*Because she's a shifter, duh. Hideaway Cove might not have many adventurous palates to offer her, but it is a safe haven where she doesn't have to hide what she is.*

"Ghost peppers at Halloween, huh? I look forward to it," she said out loud, and then wondered why her automatic reaction was to not even question the idea that she would still be here at Halloween.

"Morning, Tess!" a woman's voice called out as the bell above the front door tinkled.

"Lainie! How are you feeling today?"

"Ready to blow."

"That bad? Well, you know, my offer still stands."

Lainie shuddered. "Okay. I revise my statement. I feel like a whale that's learned to walk on land and immediately regretted it, but I am *not* ready to try and evict baby Galway by eating mystery ice cream."

"Shrimp." Tess's eyes glittered with mischief.

"You did *not* make shrimp ice cream."

"No, I made shrimp sorbet."

"How. *How* did you make…" Lainie put her hands up. "It doesn't matter. I'm not going to eat shrimp sorbet."

"Come on, you were crazy for shrimp crisps earlier in your pregnancy!"

"And now, I am sane." Lainie caught sight of Felicity for the first time and waved at her with a smile. "Back me up, please? Shrimp sorbet is not a thing. And if it is a thing, it shouldn't be."

"Hmm," said Felicity. "I mean, I wouldn't say no *immediately…*"

"Oh, god, you're both ganging up on me! Have mercy. And a bowl of sour cherry and lemon, please." Lainie came over to Felicity's table. "Do you mind if I join you?"

"Go ahead."

Lainie relaxed into the seat opposite her. "You've picked the best table. When I don't think I can move another step, I sit here and watch people running around on the sand and give myself fomo."

"You should go swimming!" Tess chirped from behind the counter.

"Sure, if I want to freeze this baby out!" Lainie smoothed her dress over her baby bump and sighed. "Apollo let you out of his sight, huh?"

Felicity's cheeks warmed. Were they that obvious? "He has work to do."

"Well, at least one of them still remembers they have a job. I swear Harrison's barely stepped foot inside the workshop since I told him I was pregnant." She leaned back in her chair and closed her eyes. "I'm sure he's racing through whatever he's got left to do so he can come sweep you off your feet again."

"Oh, is that what he's expecting to do? Do I need to set up another dramatic situation for him to rescue me from?"

"Hah!" Lainie giggled. "I recommend wandering around a ruined lighthouse in a storm. Worked for me. Or falling into the ocean during a storm. Or… we're really big on romantic storms around here, I guess."

"Here I thought the fog was atmospheric enough."

"For a first rescue, maybe. You'll need to step up your game for the next one."

Lainie's laughter was contagious. Felicity burst into giggles. When was the last time *anybody* had wanted to just hang out with her like this? Back home, everyone who knew she was Montfort's assistant always had an ulterior motive in spending time with her. Except for Maya, but she had her own life. Lainie didn't want anything from her except fun conversation.

*I wish I could stay.* Her chest hurt suddenly, and she found herself gripping the edge of the table.

The bell above the door dinged again.

"Oh, hello! You're one of our other visitors. I think I met your mother yesterday," Tess called to the newcomer. Bruno sidled through the door reluctantly as though he was scared the pastels would jump up and attack him. "Come on in."

"Mom said you do thick shakes?" he asked, suspiciously.

"That's right. Any ice cream flavor you want, just let me know."

Felicity waved at Bruno when he caught sight of her, but he scowled and looked away. *Okay, geez,* she thought. *Nothing in the world is as embarrassing as being caught ordering a thick shake for your mom. Got it.*

She turned to look back out the window at the beach and saw Antonia stabbing an umbrella into the sand. She had a foldable recliner out already, and... a paddling pool?

Felicity stared as Antonia went through a quick series of yoga stretches, shrugged off her linen wrap, and disappeared.

*What?*

Something went *splash!* in the paddling pool. Felicity rubbed her eyes. Antonia had shifted. Of course. That made sense. She'd shifted into something smaller than her human form, that was all. Some sort of fish or... eel, maybe? And now she was relaxing in her travel pool.

"Wow," she breathed, sitting back. Lainie grinned at her.

"I'd say you get used to it but honestly, it still takes me by surprise sometimes. And I'm always suspicious when a seagull tries to steal my lunch that it's actually someone I know."

The conversation at the ice cream counter was still ongoing—mostly one-sided, as Tess tried to tease out her customer's preferences and he remained stolidly grumpy—but something pinged Felicity's senses and she started to pay closer attention.

"I'm sorry, that one's been declined too," Tess was saying in a sympathetic undertone.

"Try again." Bruno's voice was throaty with embarrassment. He hunched his shoulders.

There was another merciless beep from the POS machine. "I'm sorry," Tess said again. "Do you have another—"

Felicity caught Tess's eye and waved her own card. "I'll cover it!" she mouthed.

"Actually, that's okay. We've got it covered!" Tess told Bruno.

He turned and saw Felicity before she could put her card away again and his scowl turned thunderous. "You're offering to pay for me?"

"Well, yeah…"

"No! God, it's bad enough—"

"Hey." Tess prodded him in the shoulder. "She's not paying. She *offered*, but I'm giving you these for free, because you're clearly having a terrible day. Call it a vacation special. This is your first trip to Hideaway Cove, let us treat you."

"That's *worse*." He seemed about to say something more, then groaned, grabbed the thick shakes, and fled.

All three women blinked after him.

"I guess that's what I have to look forward to in a few years," Lainie said at last. "Seriously, what was that about?"

Tess shrugged. "As a former shitty teen myself, could be literally any-thing."

Felicity was still staring at the door. There was something about Bruno that was strangely familiar. She just couldn't fix on what it was. She shook her head. Either it would come to her, or it wasn't important.

What was important? Was the gleam of sunlight on a certain someone's shining golden locks as he made his way down the road from the direction of the workshop.

She pushed her chair back. "If you'll all excuse me…"

Tess and Lainie's laughter followed her outside.

Apollo invited her back up to his house. Once again, they barely made it past the front door before tearing each other's clothes off. Felicity hooked her legs around his waist, aching for him already.

"You're not even going to ask me what ice cream flavor I chose?"

He groaned and kissed her neck. "God, no. Then I'd have to live with the fact that I love a woman who willingly eats seaweed-flavored sorbets."

Her heart leapt. *Love?* Did he really mean—

Apollo froze. "Wait."

*Oh. Okay. He didn't mean it. Good?*

"Did you hear that?"

*Or maybe he isn't talking about the fact he just sprang the L-word on me?*

Apollo frowned. He kept his arms around her, but his embrace changed from sensual to protective.

And then the front door crashed open, smashed off its hinges by an eagle the size of a car.

Apollo leapt in front of her. "God dammit, Harrison! Get *out!*"

Golden scales appeared on his skin and the air around him shimmered. Felicity blinked. The shimmer was the shape of giant wings, stretching out from his shoulders.

Was he going to transform into his dragon shape? *Here?*

*He'll destroy the whole house!*

She grabbed his arm. "Apollo—"

The giant eagle turned its massive head, fixing one hazel-gold eye on her. It reared back, looking oddly humanly embarrassed, and she saw it had the back half of a lion.

"Out!" Apollo shouted again, picking up what was left of the door and shoving it into the doorframe. The creature's front-end claws tangled with its back-end paws as it backed up.

There was a rush of air on the other side of the damaged door, and a man's deep voice said: "Sorry, Sparky. I didn't realize you had company."

"What the hell, Harrison? I don't answer the psychic telephone for two minutes and you break down my front door?" Apollo whirled around, digging his fingers through his hair to his scalp.

Felicity ducked to pick up her clothes. She held her sweater in front of herself, an entirely insufficient modesty shield. When she'd thrown off all her clothes the moment they came inside, it had seemed like the most natural thing in the world. But now…

Apollo searched her face. "I'm sorry about this. My friends usually have more manners."

His magic curled around her. The home-feeling intensified. She felt safe and protected, as though the outside world couldn't reach her here.

Despite the smashed front door providing evidence to the contrary.

"Pol!" Another male voice yelled from outside. "Hurry it up in there!"

Apollo growled. Actually *growled*. Felicity bit her lower lip to stop from giggling.

"Half the town lost power a minute ago. We thought something had happened to you!"

Apollo straightened. Color drained from his face. "What?"

"Hell's bells, Sparky," another voice growled from the other side of what was left of the door. "We thought we'd find you passed out in here, not... you know."

Apollo put a hand over his eyes as their words sank in. "Shit."

"Here." Felicity handed him his jeans. He started pulling them on.

"Half the town?" He ran one hand across his scalp as though he was checking for bumps. "That should have almost knocked me out. Strange. I didn't feel..."

He muttered to himself, and his gaze turned inwards. Felicity felt the pull of his magic and let herself fall into it. Her new magical senses let her follow Apollo as he sent his awareness out over the town, carefully checking the knots and threads of his magic. The closed-off, secure feeling of the house faded, as though he'd flung all the doors and windows wide open.

The entranceway light flickered. Outside, one of the guys swore. "There it goes again."

Apollo gasped. His eyes snapped open, he took a step towards Felicity, reached for her—and collapsed.

Felicity screamed. The door shot off its hinges again. Harrison and Arlo barreled in. Felicity barely glanced at them. She was beside Apollo, rolling him onto his side and staring desperately into his face.

"Apollo! Can you hear me?"

His eyelashes flickered and he groaned. Relief rushed through her. She tucked one hand under his head, cushioning it against the hardwood floor, and put the other against his chest. His heart thudded reassuringly against her palm.

His lips parted. "How embarrassing," he murmured. Eyes still closed, he braced his elbows against the floor and pushed himself up. "I swear this doesn't usually…"

He fell back with a grunt.

"Half the town," he muttered, his voice aghast. "And you were right. It's… cold."

Ice clutched Felicity's heart. *Cold?*

The magic she'd felt in the car. It hadn't been her imagination.

It was real, and it had hurt Apollo.

Ice wrapped around her lungs. She'd been so distracted by all the wondrous things about Hideaway, and protecting it from Montfort, she'd forgotten about the danger that had brought Apollo to her in the first place.

Harrison was kneeling opposite her. "Let's get you on your feet again and you can tell us all about it," he said.

Together, the two men helped Apollo through to the front room. He recovered quickly enough to grumble at them every step of the way.

Felicity tagged behind, feeling exposed and helpless. The front room was full of sunlight and warmer than the entranceway, but it was a normal, physical warmth, not the comfort of Apollo's magic. It only made the uneasy chill inside her worse. She clutched at her shirt, reassuring herself she'd managed to put it back on.

She caught a glimpse of herself in the reflective surface of the TV mounted on one wall. She looked beyond debauched. *More like deranged.* Her hair was mussed, her clothing obviously barely thrown on, her lips and cheeks red and her eyes dark holes in her face.

*Like a little lost girl who has no idea what she's doing.*
*Pathetic.*

"Felicity," Apollo croaked. She jumped. He was sitting on a plush oatmeal-colored sofa, holding out one hand to her. Sick with guilt, she took it and sat next to him. He pressed a kiss into her hair and rested there a moment, his head heavy on hers. "Sorry about this," he murmured. "I told you that the magic exhausts me sometimes."

"*Exhausts* you?" Arlo burst out. "This is beyond that, Sparky." He growled under his breath and stalked out through another door. Felicity heard a fridge opening and crockery banging together.

"Don't pretend you've never seen me play the damsel in distress before," Apollo joked weakly. Harrison frowned.

"*Playing*, yes. Not like this."

Apollo's face twisted. He levered himself further upright, wrapping his arm around her waist. She stiffened and he softened his grip on her, then looked at her closely. "Are you all right?"

"Are *you?* You collapsed. It was so sudden."

He shrugged one shoulder, a half-smile on his face. "It happens. You'll get used to it."

"I doubt that."

"Don't worry." There was a hint of bitterness in his voice. "I'll give you plenty of practice."

Felicity opened her mouth. No words came out. *How long does he think I'm going to stay here?*

And why did he sound so resigned? Her stomach lurched.

A mug appeared in front of her, and the scent of hot chocolate filled her nostrils. "Here, you two." Arlo waited until she wrapped both hands around the cup before he let go, which was smart, because even with both hands it trembled a bit.

"What's this?" Apollo blinked at his own mug. "Don't tell me Jacqueline has you house-trained, Arlo."

"Stranger things have happened. You kept muttering about it being cold, so I thought a hot drink might shut you up."

"Food would shut me up even better."

"You're worse than the kids, you know that?" Despite his gruff tone, Arlo headed back out. A few minutes later he returned with a plate of sandwiches.

Apollo offered her the plate and when she waved it away, inhaled three sandwiches in quick succession. The tension in his shoulders eased. "That's better."

"Now." Harrison sat down in a squashy armchair opposite them. Arlo prowled by the window, darting occasional glances down at the water. "You want to tell us what the hell's going on, Sparky?"

"It's my fault."

All three men looked at her. Apollo's arm tightened around her, and he shook his head. "That's not—"

"It is. I'm the one who got us distracted playing around with your magic instead of investigating what happened in the car. I was so determined to make you believe it wasn't your fault, I forgot there was any danger in the first place." She swallowed. "And now it's hurt you, whatever it is."

Harrison sat back and folded his arms. "I think you'd both better explain what's going on."

Between them, Felicity and Apollo told the full story of what had happened the night she arrived in Hideaway Cove. Her voice faltered as she described how the strange, wrong coldness had washed over her as her car spun out of control.

"And you're sure it's not your magic?" Harrison looked at Apollo.

"Yes, we're sure," she snapped before he could answer. "It isn't his magic. I can tell."

"But you're not a shifter. How can you know?"

"She can sense my magic."

Surprise flashed in the others' eyes. Arlo nodded slowly.

"Makes sense, if she's—"

"*Don't.*" Apollo's voice was harsh with some deep emotion. Unease twisted Felicity's stomach. What had Arlo been about to say?

*It doesn't matter. You're leaving tonight anyway, aren't you?*

"It isn't Apollo. Whatever made my car run off the road and affected the town just now, it's…" A puzzle piece she hadn't known had been missing suddenly slotted into place. "Oh, no."

Apollo's eyes met hers and a silent understanding passed between them. They'd both come to the same conclusion.

Apollo's magic wrapped protectively around her. His voice was grim.

"You were right. Someone else out there does have magic like mine. And they're attacking Hideaway."

# 21

# APOLLO

He should have listened to Felicity from the beginning. He'd thought it impossible that someone else could be using magic in Hideaway Cove. But there was no other explanation.

"You're sure it isn't a technical issue? Ordinary power surges?" Arlo asked.

He shook his head. "Ordinary electricity doesn't feel like that."

"It exhausts you like that, though. Not the first time you've overdone it."

"*Really.*" Felicity knitted her eyebrows. He squeezed her hand reassuringly.

"Don't worry. From now on I won't faint in front of anyone except you." He gave her a sunny smile that said he was joking—that he was fine, really, that everything was fine—and she returned him a look that told him exactly what she thought of his pretend carelessness. He gave her another, wryer smile, and turned back to the others. "As for whether we can tell it's a different power, consider this. Could you tell the difference between falling into your bed at night, and falling into what turns out to be a pile of dead fish? Yes? It's that obvious. My own magic is…"

"Warm," Felicity said softly. She squeezed his hand. "Protective, and comforting."

"And whatever this new magic is, it's none of those things." *Protective? Comforting?* He knew Felicity found his magic exciting—there'd been no missing *how* exciting—but to know it was more than that touched something deep inside him.

Arlo rubbed his forehead tiredly. "I can think of a few kids for whom falling into a bed of dead fish would be a lifelong treat," he said dryly, "but I take your point."

Harrison's expression darkened.

"We're sure, then. Someone's targeting Hideaway. How much danger is the town in?"

"From someone who can use magic like I can, but to break things, not fix them?" A muscle in Apollo's jaw twitched and he ran his thumb along the back of Felicity's hand, reminding himself she was safe. "They would have killed Felicity if I hadn't gotten to her in time."

And he'd forgotten that. He'd let himself drift through the joys of spending time with her, oblivious to the danger she had been in.

"And you can't sense when they're attacking."

"It appears not." His face twisted. He didn't bother trying to hide it. "I didn't sense them take over Felicity's car. I could tell something was pushing against my own magic, but I needed to concentrate to even sense that. And I didn't feel anything before you burst through the door, either."

"To be fair," Arlo drawled in his gravely voice. "You *were* distracted."

"For God's sake, Arlo, I know this is bad. As soon as you said something was wrong, I tapped into the town magic. I thought I could at least track where the attack had come from. Instead, I was right there the next time they hit, and I couldn't do anything. The power drain was too much and it was—well. You saw." Tension ratcheted up his spine, turning his neck and shoulder muscles to steel hawsers. "If I can't protect the town, what's the point of me even being here?"

Arlo looked shocked. Apollo didn't blame him. The wolf shifter had been joking, trying to ease the tension, and he'd exploded. He sighed and ran one hand down his face. "Arlo, I…"

"We're going to find them." Felicity's voice was low, but sure. His heart ached at her faith in him.

"I wish I could be so confident." His voice was grim. "You were right. This other power is cold, and… wrong. I thought facing it would be like taking back control of your car. Difficult, but possible. But whoever we're facing must have given way deliberately then. This time it was actively attacking. It surrounded me. I couldn't…"

He looked away, not fast enough. Whatever Felicity saw in his face, it made her eyes widen.

"If it had been like that before, I don't know if I could have saved you."

The room was silent.

"But you did save me. I'm here, and we're going to figure this out," she told him. "There must be some way we can use our abilities to hunt down whoever did this."

"I can't ask that of you."

"You're not asking. And I'm not offering, so you can't say no. I'm *telling* you I'm going to help." She took his face in her hands and pulled his head around until he was looking at her. "None of this is what I expected to find here, Apollo. My life is so different to how it was two days ago. Being here, helping you—you've given me a chance to be a different person. A better person." Her voice dropped. "I'm not going to waste that chance."

*A better person.* The same way her being here gave him the chance to be a better person. He'd thought it was a disaster, meeting his mate before he had a proper hoard. But she was right.

It wasn't hopeless. They had each other.

*And I do have a hoard.* He had a hoard, and the first thing he was going to do with his chance was find it and make Felicity his. If Hideaway was under attack, his mate needed to know he would protect her with everything he had.

He remembered the bone-deep cold of the other magic and repressed a shiver.

The conversation turned to what they were going to do next. Harrison sent out a telepathic warning to the rest of the town, telling them to be wary of further attacks, and reported that no permanent damage had been done. Apollo was relieved.

"Do you want me to check the protection spell?" Felicity asked.

"No!" His voice came out in a bark. Grimacing apologetically, he added, "The attack disrupted my magic briefly, but there's been no damage done."

"How can you be sure?"

*I'm not. But I'm sure enough that I don't want to put you in our enemy's sights.* He waved one hand lazily. "The power drain. The spell is drawing on my magic to replenish itself. It wouldn't do that if it was broken."

"Unless it's so broken it's like trying to fill a sieve." Felicity's mouth set in a mulish line. Before he could stop her, she closed her eyes.

His heart wrenched. "Felicity—"

Magic hummed all around her. Not the showy sparks he made to impress people; the invisible weft and weave of his spell, crooning as she swept her magical sight across it. His throat went tight. "Be careful."

"I am," she told him absently. Her expression went distant.

*I can't lose her.* Fear sent ice down his back. *I can't—*

He reached for her; his hand touched hers, and with a lurch, he followed her into the spell.

It was like coming home. Magic flowed past and through him, tangling briefly in the blazing core of his power where his dragon lived and continuing on its way.

He'd described his protective spell to Felicity as a net because that was how he saw it. He'd never seen it like this. A constellation of stars connected by gold threads. A garden of sparkling blooms, with shining paths between them.

And Felicity was walking among them, running her hands through the flowers.

A shock wave passed between them. She turned back, her eyes meeting his with a look of surprise. *Apollo?*

Her voice was in his mind. Not like shifter telepathy; something closer, more intimate.

He didn't remember moving, but the next moment, he was next to her. There was a strange, shimmering aura around her body; around his, too, he noticed belatedly. *Is this what you see every time you check on my magic?*

*Yes. Isn't it what you see?*

He looked around. When he looked at the spell himself, he felt like a fisherman checking his net for snags and holes, darning needle at the ready. He had thought Felicity must have experienced it the same way. A bird's-eye view, distant and all-seeing.

But it hadn't been all-seeing, had it? He'd never seen any of this.

*I had no idea my magic could look like this,* he told her honestly. She smiled up at him.

*It just keeps surprising you, huh?*

His mate had never looked so beautiful. His dragon stretched its wings—and the magic around him swirled, as though buffeted by them. Felicity took his hand.

*Full of surprises and in excellent condition,* she said, mock-stern. *I don't need to worry about you draining yourself to fix it.*

She was right; the star-garden around them was complete and brimming with power. There were no tears, no dull spots or broken-off ends. Relief washed through him.

*No sign of whoever attacked it, either. I was kind of hoping they would have left a trail,* Felicity admitted.

*The spell is safe and there's no sign of the intruder. Let's go back before anything else happens.*

An odd reluctance pulled at him, despite his firm words. He didn't want to leave the shining star-garden of his magic. Something stirred inside him, like a memory from a dream he'd long forgotten. There was something he had to do…

*Protect Felicity. Keep her safe.* Who knew what their unknown enemy could do to her if it struck while she was here?

Felicity squeezed his hand. *Back to the real world, then.*

He blinked and was back in his body. His hand was clasped in Felicity's; Harrison and Arlo were staring bug-eyed at them.

"What the hell was that?" Harrison demanded.

Felicity slipped her hand out of his. Her cheeks were a familiar pink. "Magic," she replied primly, then ruined it by giggling. Her dark eyes were even darker with desire and Apollo saw the effort it took her to push the feeling away. "It—uh. We were making sure the protective spell was secure. And it is!"

"For now." Apollo was still unsettled by the strange reluctance he'd felt to leave the star-garden, even though being there put Felicity in danger. "And there was no way of telling where the attack came from."

"Do we have any suspects?" Harrison asked. "It has to be someone in town, doesn't it?" He gritted the words out, clearly hating that he had to say them. His own mate had been accused of wanting to destroy Hideaway Cove. The thought of accusing one of their neighbors of the same thing must bring back ugly memories.

Felicity shook her head. "Or outside the boundary. The spell covers the whole town. They could be sitting right on the perimeter, sneak attack, and run off without Apollo being alerted by them crossing the border." She swallowed. "If the first attack was my car... well, that's where it happened."

"So, it's either someone in town or someone anywhere else in the area. That narrows it down," Arlo said wryly. He nodded to Felicity. "What about you?"

Felicity flinched. "Me?"

"You're accusing Felicity?" Apollo's dragon reared up.

Arlo raised his hands. "No. I'm asking if she's sensed anything out of the ordinary."

"More out of the ordinary than a town full of magical people who can transform into animals, and my sudden ability to go traipsing through dragon spells, which also exist?" Felicity asked shakily. "No. I haven't sensed anything."

"That points towards it being someone out of town."

"Or someone here who's been keeping their head down until they knew you were distracted," Harrison suggested.

"Mrs. Hanson has two other guests at the Innlet, doesn't she?" Arlo asked.

"The two shifters from out of state?" Harrison raised his eyebrows. "It's a possibility."

Apollo was already shaking his head. "Not unless they've spent their winter vacations in exotic Dunston the last few years. Jacqueline said the troubles started there, remember?"

Arlo nodded. "I'll ask her more about it. Could be a delivery driver or someone else who comes through so often we don't notice it." He looked at Apollo, who shrugged.

"I haven't noticed anyone. But I don't pay as much attention to people who regularly come and go as I could." *Like having a security system and not bothering to switch it on.* Guilt burned his throat.

"That's somewhere to start, then." Harrison watched him for a moment, then punched him lightly on the shoulder. "You thought we would let you do this on your own?"

"It's my magic. I'm the one who should deal with it." He sounded exhausted. He *was* exhausted. And he knew he should hide it, but...

"The magic that fixes anything in town that's broken, lights the way for people out walking or sailing at night and warns us when someone's arriving in town? That magic?" Harrison gave him another friendly shove. "You've put yourself on the line for Hideaway ever since you moved here, Apollo. Time for us to join you there."

Apollo blinked. He hadn't thought about it like that.

Harrison and Arlo stayed for a few minutes more, planning their next steps. Apollo said he would go with them to discuss the danger with the rest of the town, but one look at the dark shadows under his eyes and everyone else disagreed.

Secretly, he was glad. Yes, he needed to protect the town.

But he had to protect Felicity, too.

# 22

# FELICITY

Apollo flopped back into the sofa at the sound of the front door being propped closed. "I don't think Harrison has ever called me 'Apollo' before," he said mildly. "I don't like it."

"What does he usually call you? Sparky?"

"Or Pol."

"Would you prefer it if I called you one of those?"

He looked at her quizzically. "No. I like that you call me Apollo."

"Because it makes you feel appropriately divine?" she teased. He'd looked so haunted ever since the attack, she was desperate to see him smile again. A *real* smile, not one of his performance ones.

"Because..." He hesitated. "You make me want to be more than I am. More than I have been, here."

Felicity felt as though the ground was crumbling beneath her feet. Determined not to show it, she forced a smile. "More than being able to turn into a dragon, and use magic, and give me the most mind-blowing orgasm of my life given less than a moment's notice?"

"Yes." His eyes turned a richer gold and he bent to kiss her—then groaned and leaned back, resting his head on the back of the sofa. "Though right now I'd settle for being able to move my head without the room spinning around. I'm afraid you'll have to give me more than a moment's notice if you want a repeat of earlier."

"It's that bad?"

"I always get migraines after significant power drains. Food helps. I'll be fine in a minute or two, once those sandwiches work their magic. You're worried about me?" He managed to look wan and smug at the same time.

"Of course I'm worried about you. You collapsed." She nestled against him. "And I'm worried… about other things, too."

She forced herself to meet his eyes. His beautiful, golden, dragon's eyes. *I should tell him everything. About Montfort, and why I'm really here. It can't be connected to this, but…*

But what if Arlo or Harrison or someone else made the connection while they were chasing leads about the town's mysterious attacker? Would they see that she worked for an infamous developer and put two and two together? Her chest seized at the thought.

"I am, too." His magic reached for her, and she reached back, instinctively. "I haven't been fair to you. You deserve answers to all your questions, and more." A wry smile twisted his face. "Questions you don't even know to ask. I shouldn't have any secrets from you."

She shook her head. "I've already pried into enough of your secrets."

"Not quite enough." His voice dropped. "I've been half terrified you would figure out the truth. You seem to have figured out everything else about me. My magic. How I play the fool when something's worrying me. You see me more clearly than I do myself."

*And I keep my own self hidden.* Felicity bit her cheek.

"But there's one thing about shifters that you don't yet know." His magic coiled around her.

"There must be thousands of things about shifters I don't know," she responded. Magic lapped at her skin and mirth bubbled inside her. *Seriously? Wasn't he just complaining about having a migraine?*

"One thing in particular." His lips twitched. Not with humor—*Is he nervous?* She scootched closer to him and he seemed to brace himself.

"Out with it," she told him, mock-stern.

He smiled wanly at her. "I can't stop you from diving into my magic whenever you please. I have no idea how we're going to find whoever's behind the attacks, let alone what we'll do when we do track them down. But I do know it's my duty to keep you safe. And I can't do that by keeping you in the dark." He closed both hands around hers. "When shifters meet someone who we're meant to be with, we... know. At once. Except it's not someone, it's *the* one. The only one. It's part of the magic all shifters have. Turn into some sort of animal, talk to each other telepathically, and find your soulmate. Someone we can make happy. Someone who, if we're together, makes us so much more than we are apart. Like Harrison and Lainie, or Arlo and Jacqueline."

*The person you're meant to be with.*

And the two couples he'd mentioned were shifter and human. Like her and him.

He couldn't be saying...

"It's you, Felicity. It's been you since the moment you drove into town, and it'll be you for the rest of my life. No one else."

Felicity's breath caught in her throat. Her skin tingled. It should have sounded like some sort of scam. But it felt right.

"Me?" she said, in case she'd gotten it all wrong again somehow.

*But I'm leaving. I have to leave.* Leave Hideaway, and leave this time with Apollo as a perfect, magical memory, unscathed by reality.

His eyes glimmered like a mirage rising from hot asphalt. "You. You're my soulmate, Felicity. That's why you can step inside my magic. Why it seeks you out like a cat seeks sunlight. Why—" He paused, almost imperceptibly. "Why I've been head over heels for you since the moment we met. You felt it too, didn't you?"

"Yes." She hadn't had a name for it, but she'd definitely felt it. That strange, wonderful attraction. But— "Wait. Are you saying the way I feel... it's because of the magic?"

"No. The other way around. My magic behaves the way it does around you because of the way we feel. It's not a trap, or a compulsion. It's… two hearts, finding each other, despite everything the world throws at us."

Her own heart felt like it was about to choke her. Despite everything? *I can never tell him the truth now.* He wouldn't be looking at her as though she hung the moon if he knew why she was really here.

She was Apollo's soulmate. No matter what, she had to make him not regret it.

"I want to protect you, Felicity. More than anything in the world. I want you to be safe, and happy. And—selfishly—I don't want to be apart from you for a moment more. I don't want to hide this connection between us. I want to claim you as my mate, so that everyone who sees us can tell that I'm the most fortunate dragon ever to live, with the most perfect mate."

"*Claim* me?" That sounded… possessive. Part of her rebelled at the thought.

Part of her thought *Oh, god, yes.*

"Make you mine. Officially." Apollo's voice dropped to a purr, and the gleam in his eyes was pure dragon. The part of Felicity that rebelled against the idea of being possessed thought again. "Every dragon has a hoard. A treasure to offer their mate. When she, or he, accepts the hoard, the mate bond forms." He paused. "I don't know what that means for us, practically speaking. What difference it will make to your ability to sense and affect my magic. But you'll be mine. I'll be yours. It's a promise that I will protect you and cherish you, whatever happens."

"That kind of sounds like getting married."

"Oh, no. There's nowhere near so much paperwork." He checked himself and rubbed his face. "I'm sorry. I shouldn't joke. This is serious, and—and terrifying…"

*Because he thinks I'm going to reject him,* she realized with a shock. He thought *she* might reject *him.*

Longing flooded through her, as overwhelming as it was sudden. Yes, she wanted to be his. She'd wanted it since the moment she set eyes on him. Everything she felt about Hideaway Cove—the warmth, the sense of safety, the quiver of excitement—was all because of him.

She wanted to be Apollo's more than she'd ever wanted anything.

But she had to leave. That was the plan. Abandon her job, abandon Montfort, and then abandon Apollo.

Once she thought about it that way, there was no question.

"I'm not that scary, am I?" she teased, and won a smile from him.

"The thought of letting you down is." Shadows passed behind his eyes. "I should shower you in gold and jewels."

"Didn't you just say that was what you were going to do?"

"My hoard isn't that expansive."

"Well, good. I was imagining piles of treasure. I couldn't imagine where you kept it all."

"You'd be surprised. Hideaway Cove is riddled with smugglers' caves. But—no." He seemed to come to a decision and drew himself up. A muscle in his jaw twitched. "My hoard is a token. One piece, to fasten us together."

"A ring?"

"Er... not quite." He looked suddenly rueful. "I told you dragons are thieves, didn't I? My treasure is from my grandfather's hoard. His collection is... very particular."

She shot him a questioning glance.

"Cufflinks," he clarified, blushing slightly.

"Well," she said, drawing it out. "It's a good thing I decided to wear a blouse today." She lifted her wrists to show him the tiny imitation-pearl buttons that held the cuffs together.

Hope lit his eyes, but didn't quite chase away the shadows. She smoothed the muscle in his jaw, and kept her hand there, caressing him.

She was a new person since she set foot in Hideaway. A person she actually liked. And Apollo was why.

*His soulmate.* It should have sounded crazy. Instead, it was like finding a missing piece of her own heart.

He leaned forward, his eyes gleaming, his mouth kissably close. Felicity brushed the edge of her thumb against his lips.

"Why don't you try giving me your hoard now?"

# 23

# APOLLO

"Right now?" His mouth was dry. "Right here?"

Felicity nodded. Her dark eyes gleamed. A thrill went through him, quick and sharp and delicious, and his exhaustion vanished.

"I'll have to find it," he said, his tongue fumbling over the words. "It's… hidden. Somewhere in this house."

"I can wait."

The memory of Felicity's shining eyes chased him out of the front room.

His hoard was somewhere in his house. But where?

This was the problem with being so ashamed of something. He'd ignored his hoard so steadfastly for so many years that he'd forgotten where he'd hidden it.

His dragon fretted inside him, scratching his claws like it wished it could dig itself into the center of the Earth and never have to show its face again. "Don't tell me you don't remember where it is, either!" he groaned.

His dragon let out a sad puff of sparks and hid its head under its wings. "Argh!"

He racked his brains. Somewhere safe. He wouldn't have hidden it in the kitchen or the living room. Too much risk of one of his friends finding it while they rummaged for a fresh glass or a book to borrow. It would be in the back of a cupboard somewhere, jammed tight beneath some other box he hadn't touched since he moved to Hideaway.

Storage—he ran through the options in his head, absently leaving a trail of chaos behind himself as he tripped from the kitchen up the stairs. The top of the linen closet? Or in the bathroom…

Finally, in the bottom of an old trunk in the back corner of his attic, he found it. An old, black-lacquered jewelry box. Hardly a treasure chest, and hardly overflowing with gold and jewels, but it was all he had.

A complicated tangle of emotions surged up as he held it.

*Baby's first hoard.*

The old embarrassment rose bitter in his throat. And guilt. He had lied to Felicity.

He kept the box closed as he scrambled back down from the attic, folded away the ladder, and made his way to his bedroom, where he slumped down on the side of the bed.

No one would mistake it for a treasure chest. It was too small to hold a hoard of any importance. That was the point. Grandfather Errol had reluctantly given him this starter hoard when he first left home. It was meant to spark his draconic instincts to find more treasure, and to collect and protect a hoard of his own. Instead, it was a reminder of his failures.

Until now. Now, it was the only thing he had to offer his mate.

He flicked the jewelry box's lid open with his thumb. There it was, nestled on crimson velvet.

A single, solid-gold cufflink with a ruby set into it.

He waited for his dragon to crow over it. It had shown more gold-lust when Felicity drove into town than ever before. He had hoped that seeing his *actual* hoard again would inspire some of the same glee.

Apparently not.

Apollo sighed.

He was going to need to do better than a single starter-hoard cufflink. But for now, it was his only hope.

The cufflink in his pocket burned so hot he half expected Felicity to see it the moment she walked back into the front room, the same way she was so attuned to his magic. A bright, betraying glow.

But she only had eyes for him. "Any luck? It sounded like you were tearing the house apart up there."

"My hoard was *very* well hidden," he drawled, sitting next to her and putting his hand in his pocket. His fingertips bumped against the cufflink, outlining its polished gold setting, the crisp angles of the stones set into it. It was cool to the touch, and he buffed it on his shirt to bring out the shine before cupping it in his hand.

His dragon was so tense he was almost trembling. The cufflink wasn't the hoard it had dreamed of, but his mate wanted it. That made it special. Didn't it?

Apollo pushed away the glimmer of doubt with a joke. "I feel like I should go down on one knee."

"We're already sitting down."

He jumped to his feet. Felicity tipped her head back. Her dark eyes melted into his with a combination of warmth and desire that made his masculine pride gleam like purest gold.

He dropped down on one knee.

Excitement and amazement warred in the corners of her mouth and the tiny creases at the edges of her eyes. Her whole face shone as, just for a moment, she looked as though she couldn't believe any of this was happening.

Then he closed the gap between them and raised one hand to cup her face. He was still an inch away from touching her when the world tipped around him.

Apollo froze.

This was it. This was *it*. Everything he'd been waiting for his entire life. Not a trick or evasion. Not avoiding his responsibilities and hoping, somehow, they'd never come back to bite him in the ass.

This was everything. His only chance.

"Are you sure?" His voice was rough.

Felicity put her own hand over his, not touching, oh, god, still not quite touching. All the caresses they had shared before, his hand in hers, her fingertips brushing his face, faded into the distant past. With his hoard and his heart on offer, each almost-touch was imbued with painful importance.

She ran her fingertips almost along the back of his wrist, down his arm, up to his shoulder, still with that empty inch of air between her skin and his. Apollo's breath caught somewhere in his chest, trapped by the thrum of his heart.

"I've never been surer of anything in my life. Which you've completely turned upside down. I never knew I could be as happy as I am with you." Felicity's eyes were shining. The dark of her irises was almost completely taken over by the deeper black of her pupils. Her lips were slightly parted, and for a moment he couldn't think of anything except how much he wanted to kiss those lips. To feel them part further, slip his tongue into her mouth, press his body against hers and re-learn the soft curves of her body with his hands.

He couldn't stop babbling. "It feels fast. But at the same time, I feel as though I've been horrifically slow. As though I'm barely keeping up and if I get even one thing wrong, I'm going to fall behind and never catch up again."

"Are you planning on getting this wrong?"

"No."

She leaned back, slowly, and he followed, slowly, his whole body crackling with electric anticipation. They still weren't touching. Even as she nestled back into the sofa and he followed her, they didn't touch.

He curled around her, close enough to make his skin spark but still not actually touching her. Not yet. It should have been ridiculous, this tense distance after they'd made love only an hour ago, but instead it was electric. Her breathing quickened, her breasts pressing against the thin fabric of her shirt.

"I have something for you," he whispered.

"Oh?" Her smile was a lure, pulling him closer.

He opened his hand so that the cufflink gleamed. Again, he waited for the shiver of draconic whatever that he was meant to feel when he looked upon his hoard.

Again, he felt nothing. All he saw was a piece of jewelry. Gold, yes. Gold was always nice. Rubies—lovely. No one ever complained about rubies.

But there was no shiver. No frisson. No *magic*.

He looked at Felicity. *His* Felicity. His mate.

There was the magic. In the teasing darkness of her eyes and the hot anticipation of her smile. His own magic swirled under his skin, longing for her.

He cleared his throat. "I suppose you're wondering why I brought you here," he said, putting on an air of lordly mystery.

Her lips curved into a smile that cut straight through his act and was just for him. Why was he putting on this ridiculous pantomime? Why in God's name was he pulling out all the stops to delay and delay, even now, on the brink of his heart's desire?

Because he wanted this to be special, not hurried along like something to be gotten over with?

Or…

*Because I'm scared. I'm terrified.*

"Apollo." Felicity's eyes locked on to his, dark and enticing. "I won't lie to you. This is the weirdest thing I've ever done. But…" She took his hand, the one not holding his hoard. "Nothing that's happened to me since I arrived in Hideaway has been anything like I ever experienced before. And every moment of it has been wonderful, because you've been at the heart of it all. And I'm glad your hoard is this single cufflink, because it means I can keep all of it with me, all the time."

And all at once his heart was on display again. Of course she'd understood what had made him hesitate.

She tipped her head back. Her neck was long and golden in the afternoon light, her collarbone marked out by shadows that he wanted to bury his face in.

"Give me your hoard, Apollo."

Nothing she could have said would have been sexier than that.

Electricity raced through his veins. He groaned as his cock hardened. Felicity's eyes widened. God, he couldn't take this anymore.

"Take it," he whispered, and tipped the scrap of gold into her hand.

She took the gold and his hand, too, winding her fingers around his. The touch shocked him. His pulse thundered in his ears, a beat of need and desire so intense he couldn't hold back anymore.

He leaned over Felicity, his free hand curving around her back as he pressed their joined hands and the hoard into the cushions. Felicity raised her hips to meet his. Her cheeks were flushed, her hair a black halo around her perfect face. One of the buttons on her blouse had popped open. His cock throbbed as she pressed against him.

But…

Something still wasn't right. Deep inside him, in the heart of his magic, something felt unbalanced.

Where was the cufflink? Gold glittered at the corner of his eye and he snatched it up.

"I don't want you to lose this," he said, and threaded it through her top buttonhole. The heavy gold nestled against her collarbone, rich and decadent next to the pale silk of her blouse and the delicate blush of her skin. "There. Perfect."

He let his fingers slide down the sliver of bare skin just visible where her blouse had come unbuttoned. He undid another button and glimpsed the curve of her breast, the lacy edge of her bra. Power thrummed beneath his skin.

Felicity chuckled, a low, sultry sound that went straight to his cock.

"You're beautiful," he whispered.

"Says the Greek god."

"It's only a name." An embarrassing one. His parents' names were Jane and Bill. But the only lightning dragon for two generations needed a fancy name, so they lumbered him with this one. "What about yours? Felicity. That means happiness, doesn't it?"

She went still. "It's only a name. Not exactly an accurate one either, until I met you."

Her eyes skidded away from his and all thoughts of hoards and dragons and magic gone from his mind. The only thing left was the need to comfort her. He cupped her face in one hand and kissed her.

Her lips were perfect. Soft and warm, instantly giving beneath his—and then pushing back. Taking. She wrapped her arms around his shoulders and held him in place as the kiss deepened. His hands clenched in her hair, on the curve of her hip, one thumb reaching out to brush her cheek as her tongue slipped between his lips to taste him.

His breathing was ragged by the time he pulled back. She stared dazedly into his eyes. He moved his hand to the back of her head, holding her gently.

"You make me happy," he told her. "And I will do everything in my power to make you happy. Starting now."

# 24

# FELICITY

When she had first seen Apollo shirtless in the fog, she had told herself off for staring at him. Every second since then had chipped away at her shame over how attracted she was to him. She'd thought, after the beach and—oh, geez, right up against the wall in the hallway—that it had all been worn away, like the sea eroding cliffs.

She had been wrong. Like a flower unfurling within her, she discovered new levels of giddy delight in this strange, wonderful man who had turned her life upside down. Being with him felt sinfully good, like a stolen treat, or sneaking peeks at gifts on Christmas morning. She wanted all of him, every dramatic posture and shamefaced smile when she caught him out, all his protectiveness and joy. All of his fucking amazing sexy body.

For a year, she had been numb to the world and her own responses to it, and now she was alive again.

Now she couldn't get enough. But she also couldn't *see* enough of him. Not now he had his clothes back on. She could only feel the heat of his skin, the smooth movement of muscles under her fingers, the jolt of her own heart as if every time it beat, she was realizing for the first time that this was real. It was happening. To *her*.

He was claiming her as his mate, and god, she was ready to be claimed. Or she might have to do some claiming of her own.

She pulled at his shirt and managed to get half the buttons undone before he groaned and tugged it over his head. His chest needed to be kissed. She obliged, and sparks danced against her tongue.

"Sorry," Apollo gasped as she licked his nipple and was shocked again. "I'll try to control it—"

"Don't."

"Oh, well, if you insist…"

He collapsed onto his back, and she climbed on top of him again. Sparks followed her fingers as she ran her hands up his chest and through his long, shining hair. They swirled over her skin like fireflies and sent little static shocks racing across the sensitive spots on her wrists.

"You're sure it doesn't hurt?" His eyes were wary.

She traced a circle on his chest and sparks encircled her lower arm in return. "Not even slightly." When the sparks finished teasing her, they floated off into the air and faded out. Some strange part of her wished they didn't. She wanted more. *More than what he did to you on the beach? What would that even look like?*

He unbuttoned her blouse. The cufflink hung heavy against her chest. Surely something so magical shouldn't feel so solid and real. But Apollo was magical and he was here, his hips hard against the inside of her thighs. His cock was even harder. She ground against him and he moaned deep in his throat.

"You're so beautiful."

Felicity looked down at herself. She was just the same old her. Flattish chest and increasingly not-flattish belly and hips. She had never thought she was anything special.

But Apollo always looked at her as though she was the most gorgeous woman in the world.

She slid her blouse off her shoulders and his eyes went dark, with only a ring of gold around the outside. Then she undid her bra. Her nipples were already hard, and they ached to be touched as the soft lace of her bra brushed over them.

"May I?" He reached up tentatively.

She let her hands drop and he slowly pushed the straps of her bra down. It wasn't covering much, but he still sighed as he uncovered her breasts. He caressed them gently, the pads of his fingers barely brushing her skin.

"Use your magic," she whispered.

His eyes flashed. Sparks ignited from his fingertips, blazing across her breasts. Her back arched. Every time was like the first time. His magic was a teasing, tantalizing shock against the sensitive skin of her nipples, leaving her breathless.

She couldn't wait any longer.

She dived down to kiss him, one hand tangled in his hair and the other struggling to take off her trousers. He was there at once, pushing her pants over her hips. By the time she raised herself up to kick them off completely he was already naked. His lean, golden body stretched out beneath her.

She paused. His cock was magnificent. It deserved a pause. It jutted against his stomach, hard and thick and hot. She wanted it inside her, and told him so, which made him swear under his breath.

She sank onto him, reveling in the slick heat of her body against his. They were perfectly aligned. The hard ridge of his cock against her soft, wanting heat.

Apollo groaned. His eyes were pure darkness now, with jagged sparks of gold like distant lightning. "I don't want to hurt you, so soon after we…"

"How many times do I have to tell you, you're not going to hurt me?" She kissed his lips, then his jaw beneath his ear, then licked slowly down the hard cord of his neck. He groaned again. "I should be the one asking you if you need us to go slowly. After the other magic attacked you, you looked—"

"I'll never let it hurt you." His eyes were intent on hers. "I swear, Felicity. You're mine and I will protect you."

Her mind, horribly, went straight to Montfort. She banished the thought instantly. Montfort was out of her life. He was never going to hurt either of them ever again, and Apollo didn't need to know that had ever been a risk.

"We're in this together, Apollo. You'd better let me protect you too."

"I doubt I'll have a choice." He kissed her hard, then pulled back and gazed at her, his eyes full of tenderness. "I never imagined it would be like this. Finding my mate."

"What did you imagine?"

His mouth moved wordlessly. "Not this."

"Oh? What bit of *not this*?"

He groaned wordlessly and flexed his hips beneath her, grinding his cock against her wet heat. "My imagination isn't always up to the task at hand. I couldn't have…" He cupped her breast, running his thumb over her puckered nipple and then raising his head to suck on it until she cried out. "My imagination couldn't compare to this."

It was as though a dam had broken inside him. His hands roved all over her, exploring every inch of her body. She kissed him as her own hands claimed his chest, his shoulders, the deep V that brought her tantalizingly close to the velvet hardness she ached for.

His fingers slid inside her thigh and just touched her slit. She gasped. He went further, pressing two fingers inside her so slowly she whined for more and her own hand found his cock. Apollo choked out her name like a prayer.

He pushed another finger inside her and she gasped.

"Is this okay?" he asked.

"Yes. God, yes."

It was more than okay. It was fire in her veins, a longing for more and harder and deeper that she had never felt with anyone before.

Hell, it didn't matter how deep he went with his fingers, it wasn't going to make her ready for his cock. She already knew how much she was going to ache later, and the thought made her want him even more.

She rolled her hips against his hand, pumping him slowly at the same time. He pushed his fingers deeper into her and she mewled softly. "More," she begged.

"Oh god," he gasped. His fingers curled inside her and she almost lost it. "I need you."

She needed him too. She rearranged herself on top of him and he pulled out of her, gripping her waist with both hands.

His touch, the heat in his eyes, his shy tentativeness and sudden confident need, all of it was intoxicating. He was taking her somewhere she had never been before.

She lined his cock up against herself and lowered herself slowly onto him, letting her body adjust even though every part of her was crying out to go faster, harder, more. Apollo closed his eyes. His eyelashes fluttered.

"God, Felicity, you're so… so…"

He was so big. She was still tender from before and he eased into her with a delicious ache that made her legs shake. One inch. Two. She let out a sigh that was almost a keen. Apollo's fingers tightened on her waist. He flexed his hips, slowly, and she met his movement with her own, until he was fully inside her.

They were meant to be together.

She rocked against him. He swore under his breath. Then his eyes were on her, and his hands, and his lips, and the hugeness of him inside her all came together to sweep all her thoughts away. Their bodies sang in concert with each other. Each movement, each breath, brought her closer to a rush of sensation that promised to overwhelm her. Her body clenched in anticipation, nerves wired tight, heart hammering. Apollo thrust inside her again and she ground herself against him. Almost there, almost—

Pleasure crashed into her like a tidal wave. Light burst behind her eyes and she cried out without words. Apollo groaned and flipped her over, driving into her again and the new angle sent ecstasy spiraling through her again. He filled her, over and over, and it would hurt in the morning, but it was incredible now. She wanted this forever. She wanted to drown in it, this overwhelming, blinding happiness and passion.

"I love you," she gasped out, and he stiffened above her, just for a second, then kissed her as though his life depended on it. He thrust into her again and she rose up to meet him, holding him tight as he spilled inside her.

Her whole body tingled, a strange, drunk combination of dazed happiness and intense sensation. Apollo's breath shivered on her neck.

"That was incredible," she whispered. Her limbs wanted to relax, to bathe in satisfaction like a cat in a sunbeam, but instead she curled into him, unwilling to lose the connection between them.

Apollo let out a long, ragged breath. "God. Yes. It was. It was incredible. You're incredible. You're..."

He lifted his head and kissed her. Her brain went fuzzy again. This wasn't one of the tentative, questioning kisses from before—it was confident, loving and just on the edge of proprietary. As though he was saying her lips were his to kiss.

Then he stopped. His eyes opened, confusion dawning in the gold.

A cold shiver of doubt twisted inside her. "What is it?"

Apollo looked away. Eyes desperate, he cast around until he found her blouse, abandoned on the floor, with the scrap of gold still strung into the buttonhole. Still not speaking, he took her hand and closed it around the scrap of gold, his own hand white-knuckled over hers.

"What's wrong?" she asked.

He licked his lips. She saw his automatic response, to deny anything was wrong—and watched him force himself into the truth.

"It didn't work," he breathed.

"What do you mean?"

He still wasn't looking at her. "My dragon is telling me it wasn't enough. That I still haven't given you my hoard."

"But you did?" She tightened her grip on the cufflink. "I have it. Right here."

He hesitated. "What can you sense? My magic? You're already so attuned to it. If the mate bond had been successful, you must know."

*I don't feel any different.* She bit her lip before the words came out. But it was true. There hadn't been anything *magical* in their lovemaking—no more so than usual. Just joy and delight and pleasure.

*Right. 'Just' all those things.*

And apparently they weren't enough.

With the feeling of the world crumbling away beneath her feet, Felicity closed her eyes and concentrated.

Magic hung in the air like dust motes in sunlight. The protective net of power was as strong and unbroken here as it was everywhere in the town. When she reached out to it, it responded to her attention, the same way it always did.

But... wait. She frowned. "It feels like it's waiting for something. Like... the curtains have opened, but the stage is empty."

Her words barely touched the surface of the strange, taut expectation that filled the world around her. She opened her eyes and the expression on Apollo's face made her heart sink.

The last few days had been such a headlong rush of wonder and happiness. She should have known it wouldn't last.

"Is it me?" she asked, her voice small. "Was I meant to do something?"

"No!" He shook his head sharply. "No, you're—you're perfect. It's nothing you've done."

"Then—if it didn't work—" She cast around for something, anything to say to make this better. It was like trying to catch the tide in her hands. It just kept slipping further and further away. "We can try again? Maybe there's something we're missing. It's—the wrong place, or the wrong phase of the moon, or… you're a lightning dragon, so maybe we're meant to wait until a thunderstorm, or…"

"It's not that." Apollo's voice was final.

Suspicion twinged in her gut. She swallowed hard. "You know why this didn't work."

He hesitated before answering.

"All my life I've known I wasn't what a dragon was meant to be." Before she could speak, his face twisted, a bitter expression more grimace than grin. "Oh, I look the part. Dashing good looks. Showy magic. Dragon like a pile of gold brought to life. But I'm not—I've never…"

He stared at the cufflink as though he wanted to wish it out of existence. As though he hated it. Then his expression cracked and, oh god, it wasn't the *jewelry* he hated. It was himself.

Her heart broke for him.

"I lied to you. A hoard isn't meant to be a *token*." He spat the word out. "It's supposed to be a treasure beyond value. Something worthy of our mate's attention. Something to prove that the dragon—that I—have value." He turned away from her, shoulders hunched. "I should have told you the truth. I knew it wouldn't be enough. I should have spent my whole life gathering a hoard worthy of you. But my dragon was never—"

His confession came out in a rush, a tidal surge of misery. How his dragon never had the requisite gold-lust that was meant to drive all dragons. How his overseas travels weren't the carefree adventures he'd made them sound like, but failed attempts to track down lost and hidden treasures for his own hoard, and how he'd failed every time.

Shame was clear in the tight line of his shoulders, the angle of his neck, the way he couldn't bring himself to meet her eyes.

"I wanted to be able to protect you. But I might fool myself, I might lie to you, but I couldn't trick whatever power it is that bonds a dragon to their mate. I just—I thought…"

*Oh, Apollo.* Her bright, wonderful dragon. She wasn't the only one who'd been running headlong, not stopping to look where they were going or make sure there was solid ground beneath them.

She slipped closer and placed one hand on his back, her palm flat against his skin.

"You told yourself a story. A fairytale where everything had gone wrong, but somehow, it all worked out in the end." She smiled wryly. "I do the same thing. I just never knew it. I thought I was on top of everything. I was always the one looking ahead, figuring out all the terrible ways the story could go, and making sure they didn't happen. That was why I kept my job for so long. I filled my head every day with all the things my boss could do to make everyone's lives hell and ran myself into the ground fixing problems before they happened."

She stepped closer to Apollo again, resting her cheek next to her hand. His heartbeat thudded against her ear, strong and agitated. "It's only since I got here that I realized *that* was the story. A story about the girl who could do anything. I was so focused on pre-empting every problem before it happened that I missed the big picture. I wasn't winning anything. I was stuck like a mouse on one of those little wheels. The problem was the *job*, and I couldn't even see a way out until I met you."

"And now I've let you down." Apollo turned, his face a mask of bitter regret. "I can't even save you from your job—"

Laughter escaped her, too sudden to stop. She cupped Apollo's face in her hands before his guilt could sharpen into shock. She wasn't laughing at him, but he was bruised and hurting, and she couldn't bear to make him hurt worse even for an instant. "You already did. I quit."

He stared at her, uncomprehending.

"I quit days ago. Before any of this mate stuff. I already knew I wasn't going back." She ran her thumb along his cheekbone. Apollo's eyes searched hers.

"I hadn't asked you to stay yet."

"I know. I was going to run away. See the world, like you did."

"Not like I did." His lips twitched downwards. "I imagine your escape would have involved less digging for treasure."

"It's going to involve *more* digging for treasure." She lifted her chin and gazed up at him. Apollo stared back, tentative hope softening his gaze; and his dragon watched her, too, sharp and intense, the golden disks of its inhuman eyes underlaying Apollo's sunlit irises. "You need a hoard. And if a massive pile of lost treasure is what it takes for your dragon magic, or whatever, to consider us a done deal, then I want you to have a hoard. And I want to help you get it."

Wonder and disbelief flashed across his face. "You would come with me?"

"To fight a bunch of other dragons and steal their treasure?" she punched him lightly in the arm. "Try to stop me."

His lips twitched again. Properly, this time, not the half-wince from before. "I couldn't possibly. I never managed to stop any of the other dragons getting to treasure before me. I'd have no chance against you."

"You distract them with your dashing good looks, I'll run in and grab the goods."

He dropped his forehead to rest against hers and let out a huff of breath that might have almost been a laugh. Then his expression sobered. "We can't go. Not while Hideaway's in danger."

His magic responded to his words like a cat hearing its name—smug, accepting of its due worship, but not giving anything away. Felicity grinned. "Of course not. You've gotta save the day before you get the girl. That's how it works, right?"

Apollo sighed dramatically. "That sounds terribly cliché. But I shall attempt to prevail."

She kissed him and his sigh turned into a hum that sent shivers up her back. "I'll prevail *quickly*."

"You better." She nipped his bottom lip. "And I'm going to help with that, too. My magic has to be good for something other than draconic quality assurance."

"No." His arms were firm around her. "You saw how the cold magic affected me. The last time you encountered it, you hadn't found your own power yet. If you use your magic and it attacks you again—"

"I can handle it."

His lips found her ear. He nibbled it teasingly. "Let me take care of it."

"Take care of me, you mean?"

"Always." His voice burred against her skin. "Mate bond or no. I will always care for you."

# 25

# APOLLO

Felicity didn't let him brood on his failure. He was grateful—until he took a second look at her, and the tightness at the edges of her eyes as she teased and cajoled him out of his own gloom.

She'd quit her job for him. And would have left him without ever telling him how much she had sacrificed for him.

He would spend the rest of his life trying to live up to that.

The next few days were a whirl of activity. Harrison organized a group of volunteers to keep watch for anything unusual. Apollo woke each morning with Felicity in his arms. Not as his mate, magically bonded to him, but as the woman who had chosen him. Chosen *him*, with all his failures and frailties.

Love was a blossoming flower in his chest, the first rays of morning sun on still water, the subtle relief of going home at the end of the day. Wondrous and delicate and comforting. Strange and familiar.

Magical.

Felicity moved out of the bed-and-breakfast and into his house, and everyone assumed they were properly mated. By the customs of normal shifters, they were. It was only because he was a failure of a dragon that he—

"Stop it." Felicity prodded him in the ribs. "You're glooming again."

"I'll have you know I gloom very prettily."

"You do," she agreed, "but Caro's on her way over and might think you're glooming about her cooking."

"Thanks for the warning." He straightened as Caro passed by their table. It was pizza night at the Hook and Sinker, and she was rushed off her feet.

It was late evening, and he and Felicity had finished their own sweep of his protection spell as well as physically walking the perimeter. The part of the perimeter that was on land, at least.

"We'll swim the rest tomorrow, right?" Felicity asked.

"Why do I get the feeling I'll be doing most of the swimming, while you laze around on my back?"

She chuckled and rested her head against his shoulder. "I'll be keeping lookout."

"Sunbathing."

"*And* keeping lookout."

"Frolicking around in my magic…" He gave a long-suffering sigh, and she stole his last slice of pizza.

"I'll be frolicking, sunbathing, *and* watching the perimeter, and all you have to do is swim. Sounds to me like you got the good end of this bargain."

"An excellent point, well made." He waited until she laughed again, then stole his pizza back.

"Hey!"

*Caro, can we get another couple pies over here?* he called out telepathically as he and Felicity wrestled over the last slice. *The pepperoni, and—*

Ice spiked against his senses. He leapt to his feet, Felicity right beside him.

"Did you feel—" They said at the same time.

Felicity bit her lip. "The workshop."

"I—"

"*Don't* tell me not to come with you."

He nodded curtly, and they both ran.

Streetlights brightened as they sprinted past them. His power strained ahead, searching for danger, but there was no time for him to search his protection spell for weak points now. All he knew was what they'd both felt: the sudden shock of acid cold, like jaws clamping around your leg underwater, and the deep knowledge that something was about to go seriously wrong.

He called to the others as they raced towards the workshop. If they could catch the culprit in the act—

They were a dozen yards from the building when he smelled the telltale tang of too-hot metal.

He flung himself in front of Felicity. The workshop exploded. Heat and fire bloomed out one side of the building, a massive, white-hot flower, its petals stained by dark marks. *Bricks and piece of wall.* His dragon reacted before his mind could properly register what he was seeing and he shifted, curling around Felicity to protect her from the debris.

Fire and rock blasted his side, but the pain was nothing compared to the freezing burn of his magic tearing apart.

He couldn't catch his breath. Felicity was shouting something, but he couldn't hear her past the ringing in his ears. He collapsed to the ground, collapsed out of his dragon form back into a human body that was too heavy. Her arms were around him, her eyes black pits of horror and her mouth still silently shouting.

Energy flowed out of him. The blazing core of his power spun down and guttered as the protection spell tried desperately to replenish itself.

But there were too many broken ends. He was emptying out. *Like a sieve,* he thought vaguely. Who had said that? Felicity. Felicity had said that, after the last attack, and then she had…

She closed her eyes.

*No!* he tried to shout. She couldn't go into his magic now. Not while the attacker was still so close. It was too dangerous.

He gathered what was left of his strength and followed her.

The star-garden was breaking apart. The light that had once been the heart of the workshop was gone, and the orderly golden paths had become swift-running rivers.

And Felicity was ahead of him, arms outstretched, fighting against the current.

He was with her in a thought. He planted himself strongly in the center of the raging river, arms wrapped around Felicity to keep her from being swept away.

*I have to stop it!* she cried into his mind. *Cauterize the pathways, tie them off somehow—it'll kill you otherwise!*

It would kill them both. It would kill *her.*

But if it swept him away first, would she be spared? If he was gone, the whole spell would collapse. There would be nothing left to pull her in.

She struggled against his grip, as though she'd heard his thoughts. *Don't you dare!*

*If it keeps you safe—*

*No! I'll never forgive you! I can SEE what I need to do. I just—I can almost feel it—*

She stretched her hands out towards the endless rush of power as though she could twist it between her fingers. But the pull of the broken spell was too strong. Her face twisted. *It won't listen to me! Apollo, you can do it. Block off all the pathways to the workshop!*

The workshop. The first magic he'd laid down in Hideaway, and the place where he'd spent so many happy days, learning to work with his hands, building friendships stronger than any he'd ever had before. The loss tore at his heart.

*Better it than you,* Felicity growled, grabbing him by the shoulders. *Take your magic back! Now!*

He'd always given his magic, before. He'd never stripped it away. It felt like heresy.

He focused on the pathway they were standing in.

*Like cauterizing a wound,* he thought. Scales rippled beneath his skin and his dragon hissed its displeasure. Abandoning the workshop wasn't like cauterizing a wound, it was like chopping off a part of himself.

But it had to be done. His vision doubled: he was standing in the star-garden, arms around Felicity, and at the same time he was sitting cross-legged, the net of his protection spell spread over his hands. The broken part needed to be fixed, no matter how much it hurt. He twisted strands around his fingers, bound them together, and pulled the knot tight.

# 26

# FELICITY

The magic stopped.

It hit her like a blow to the chest. One moment Apollo's power was pouring through the broken spell like a river disappearing down a hidden sinkhole, the next she was staring into pure darkness. There was no afterimage of light in her vision, like if she'd been staring at a lightbulb and it turned off. Just… nothing.

She clutched at Apollo, pulling his arms closer around herself as though to prove to herself that he was still there. He sagged against her.

*Did that fix it?* His voice was little more than a whisper in her head.

She stared out at the darkness. It seemed wrong that the dense nothing meant it was *fixed*, but… *Yeah,* she told him. *Let's go.*

She hugged him close and opened her eyes. The real world crashed in around her: people shouting, urgent voices, the roar of fire. She was leaning against something warm and strangely textured. Scales?

"Apollo?" she murmured faintly, shaking her head and trying to focus.

He was in dragon form, his massive, scaly body curled around her. Legs wobbling, she pulled herself to her feet. Which way was his head?

Huge wings blocked out the sky. Her dragon stared down at her, the sharp gold of its eyes tinged with concern. She put her hand on his muzzle. She'd meant the touch to be comforting, but the world tipped around her and she had to lean on him for balance.

He shifted back, a dazzle of golden sparks, and took her in his arms.

"It worked," she gasped into his chest. His hand cradled the back of her head, holding her close as though he was terrified she would disappear. He didn't say anything.

He didn't need to. She'd felt it, in those last moments they'd been together in his magic. The broken spell had been killing him—but in stopping it, it was as though he'd carved out a piece of himself.

She barely noticed what was going on around them. Arlo's mate, Jacqueline, bundled blankets around them both and took them back to the restaurant. Someone pressed a hot drink into her hands, but she had no idea who, and couldn't have even said what the drink was after she finished it. Any attention she could have given to it was attention she would have had to take away from Apollo, and she couldn't do that.

He still hadn't spoken. She had to prompt him to finish his drink, and the food that someone else placed in front of them. His eyes were haunted.

It could have been hours or minutes before he finally stirred himself. His arm, which had been around her waist since Jacqueline sat them down, tightened.

"Hey," she said gently. "Are you back with us?"

"I could say the same about you," someone said. She jumped. Arlo, Jacqueline, Harrison and Lainie were all sitting around them. She hadn't even noticed they'd arrived.

Jacqueline acknowledged her look of surprise with an understanding smile.

Apollo shook himself. "I'm… fine," he said slowly, then grimaced. "You can all tell that's a lie, can't you?" He made an attempt at one of his brilliant smiles, but it quickly faded. "I'm better than I would be if we hadn't done it."

"What exactly did you do?" Harrison asked.

"Let it go." Apollo looked as exhausted as he felt. Felicity tucked her hand into his, wishing she could give him her strength the way he gave his strength to the whole town. "The explosion wasn't just physical. It tore apart my protective spell over the workshop. I didn't have enough power to fill the gaps, so I…"

He was ashen. Felicity squeezed his hand and finished explaining for him. When she was done, the mood in the restaurant was even gloomier.

"They're escalating," Arlo said gruffly. "The fire's out now, but that explosion took out a whole exterior wall. It's a good thing we've been storing most of the gas for the forge in the other shed."

"Was anyone hurt?" Felicity asked.

"No. Eric sometimes works on his own projects in the evenings, but he decided to stay home tonight." Arlo rubbed one hand over his face. Eric was the eldest of his foster children. "Thank God."

Felicity shivered as she realized just how much worse it could have been.

"I couldn't stop it." Apollo's voice was hollow. "There was no warning, or if there was, the explosion masked it. And then it was too late. It's as though whoever they are, they know exactly how to get past my defenses."

"It has to be someone familiar with the town—"

"Are we sure it's the town they're targeting?" Lainie's voice was hesitant. Her dark eyes flickered around the group. "Pol is right. It's not the *town* that's being attacked, it's his magic. And attacks on his magic hurt him."

"Why would anyone attack Apollo?" Felicity demanded indignantly. "His magic protects this town."

"Maybe they want to drive him away." Lainie bit her lip. "I've got some experience with that. Chip away at someone's personal connections to a place until the people that once wanted you around can't wait to see you go… it's effective." She put a protective hand over her bump.

Arlo frowned. "People aren't going to start hating Sparky because someone's attacking his magic."

"What if I can't stop it?" Apollo went very still. "How long are you all going to put up with me failing to protect the town?"

"Nobody's going to drive you out," Harrison growled.

"They blew up the workshop, Harrison!" Apollo snapped. "What next? Will they attack the restaurant again? What if next time, it's not only property damage?"

Silence fell around the table.

"Who needs an angry mob when you can just convince someone to drive themselves out?" Lainie murmured, her mouth a thin, angry line.

Harrison spread his hands. "We're all tired. It's been a hell of an evening. The situation is under control, for now. Let's all call it a night and see how things look in the morning."

Apollo drew himself up and Harrison shot him a look that was so sharp, Felicity was surprised he didn't sprout a griffin-ish beak. "Tomorrow, Sparky. You're all out for today."

Outside, the crowd was dispersing. Felicity didn't want to look at the half-destroyed workshop, but she couldn't keep her eyes off it. Even when she turned her back, walking with Apollo the other direction along the promenade, it hung in her mind, a dark, empty husk with one wall torn out of it.

They passed the bed-and-breakfast. Felicity hadn't been back there since she started staying over at Apollo's, though she'd seen Mrs. Hanson and the two guests every day she'd been in Hideaway—in a town this small, it was impossible not to.

All three of them were standing on the front stoop, staring worriedly down towards the workshop. Mrs. Hanson was her usual perfectly turned-out self; Antonia was wrapped in a plush dressing gown, as though the explosion had interrupted her in the bath, and Bruno was wearing an old t-shirt and a disgruntled frown.

"Of course it was an accident, Mom. There's nothing to worry about."

"Oh, but I hate to think—how awful—I just keep remembering what happened at—"

Mrs. Hanson petted her on the arm.

"Nobody was hurt." Bruno looked pale under his frown. He caught sight of Felicity and Apollo and his expression tightened briefly, then he called out: "That's right, isn't it? Nobody was hurt?"

Felicity reassured him and he relaxed. "See, Mom? It was just an accident. Someone probably... left some gas tanks too close to some matches, or something."

Apollo stiffened beside Felicity, and she hurried on. When they were out of earshot, he murmured, "Left some matches next to a gas tank? If Harrison heard that he'd blow his top." He sighed. "Better not further worry visitors by reassuring them it was a mysterious villain attacking the town and not a mere accident, though."

When they reached Apollo's house, he fell into bed at once, fast asleep the moment his head hit the pillow. Felicity watched him for a moment, with a strange sense of foreboding. Sure enough, he hadn't been asleep for more than a minute before he began to stir.

"Can't sleep," he muttered, sitting up. "Have to stay alert. They might—"

Felicity pushed him back down. "*Sleep,*" she urged him. "You're exhausted. The best thing you can do is rest."

"If they attack again—"

"I'll wake you if anything happens."

Exhaustion hollowed out his face. He stared at her imploringly. "Don't go into the spell without me. If something happens—"

"I promise."

She watched him give in to weariness, letting it drag him down into a sleep that she feared wouldn't be as restful as he needed.

He curled against her as she arranged herself around him, sitting up against the headboard with his head and shoulders in her lap. The fine lines around his eyes and mouth relaxed a little, but even in sleep he was still tense.

*Maybe Antonia can give him a massage.* Or maybe *she* should. Felicity ran her fingers along the stress lines, gently smoothing them, then moved her attentions to his scalp. He sighed softly as she stroked his temples, then the hard knots at the back of his neck.

She wished she had been more help. When she'd dropped into Apollo's magic, she'd seen how to fix it—but she couldn't actually *do* anything. Frustration boiled through her. Apollo had offered her everything, and she couldn't even take one small part of the load from him. She was left fretting on the sidelines or jumping into danger herself and needing to be saved. It left a sick feeling in her throat.

*Someone wants him to leave Hideaway.* It made a sick kind of sense. If she wasn't here, Apollo would have been convinced he was the one endangering Hideaway. He would have left rather than risk hurting anyone.

But who would want him to leave town? She hadn't wanted to say anything in front of the others, but she had a few theories why. Another dragon might be after his hoard—they wouldn't know he didn't have one, but the way he behaved, sitting pretty in one place all these years, it must look to other dragons like he was guarding a goldmine. Or another type of shifter might be jealous of his magic. Or...

Her mind went to Montfort, for some reason. Not that he could possibly be involved, but—Montfort wanted to develop Hideaway. Transform it into his own playground or sell it off in pieces. What if that was their enemy's goal? Drive off the dragon who protected the town so they could take it over.

The day started to catch up on her. Her thoughts drifted through her fingers. Their enemy was after the hoard, or after Hideaway, and either way, her dragon was hurting.

If Apollo was the real target of the attacks, then how much worse was this going to get? He'd given Hideaway Cove years of his life, at the cost of building his own hoard. He loved the town, but these attacks were injuring him, body and soul. Cutting off the workshop, even when it was killing him, had broken something inside him. If their mysterious enemy wanted Apollo gone…

Mingled guilt and anger filled her heart. Lainie was right. If this went on much longer, someone *would* drive Apollo out of town.

And that someone would be her.

# 27

# APOLLO

Apollo woke to the smell of sizzling bacon and fresh coffee, in the bed he shared with his mate.

For one blissful moment, everything was perfect.

*It's gone.*

Blood roared in his ears. He sat upright, eyes wide. He was in his room. Felicity wasn't there, but he could hear her, humming to herself in the kitchen. So what was—

*Gone. Gone.* His dragon was wrapped tight around the core of his magic, wings spread, eyes watchful and unblinking. A sliver of magic crackled loose from the core and the dragon snatched it back, herding it into the core again and then checking over the whole blazing inferno.

Apollo groaned and pinched the bridge of his nose. *We're hoarding magic, now? Isn't it a bit late for that?*

His dragon ignored him.

*You make an excellent point, as usual.* He stretched. His dragon did have one thing right: he should be checking on his magic, too. They still didn't know—

He'd spread out his awareness across the net of magic without remembering what had happened the night before. The hole where his workshop had been hit him like a blow to the stomach. He steadied himself against the wall.

"Are you all right?"

Felicity was standing in the door, a breakfast tray balanced precariously on her hands. She looked one fainting dragon away from throwing it to the floor and rushing over to him.

"Don't come to my rescue so quickly that you abandon that breakfast," he warned her. She huffed at him and put the tray on the bedside table, then came around and hugged him.

Apollo let his head drop onto hers. Her hair smelled of smoke. So must his, he realized. Neither of them had washed up or changed after the explosion. No wonder he'd woken in a panic.

A memory rose to the surface of his mind: him falling asleep the night before, exhausted and shellshocked, and Felicity with her arms around him, one hand on his chest as thought she was holding him in place. Anchoring him.

*She has no idea how true that is.* Since she arrived, he'd felt more… grounded. Perhaps that was a bad thing for a dragon who was meant to be planning to leave on another grand treasure hunt, but it was a good thing for Apollo. She'd shown him a side of his magic he never considered before. Made him see his powers, his abilities, in a whole new light.

He wanted to relax into her arms again but knew he couldn't. Even last night had been a luxury he shouldn't have allowed himself. If he let his guard down now, and Felicity or anyone else in Hideaway Cove got hurt, he would never forgive himself.

He must have tensed, because she stroked one hand down his spine. "Last night catching up to you?"

"Somewhat," he admitted. He could still smell her beneath the smoke; sweet and tantalizing and feminine. His Felicity. His mate.

*She trusts me. Even though I've done nothing but disappoint her.*

Shame thickened his throat, but he forced his voice to come out light and wry. "My dragon's brooding over my magic like a nervous hen."

"No wonder, with the attack almost draining you last night." She raised her head and placed one hand against his cheek. "Harrison was around earlier. He wants to discuss what our next steps will be—"

"Then we should go and see him."

"—*after* you've recovered. Breakfast first." A shadow passed behind her eyes. "And… there's something I'd like to run by you before we see the others."

They ate on the balcony outside his bedroom, staring down over the roofs of his nearest neighbors to the water spread out below. Silence filled the bay; it was still half-dark, a calm interlude between the town's early risers—the fishing boat crews, and Caro, putting the day's bread on to rise—and the beginning of the day for people who had set their lives up to start after daybreak.

The morning was still and peaceful, but the hint of red stretching across the sky as the sun rose behind them suggested that wouldn't last long.

"Harrison dropped by earlier?" It wasn't even full light yet.

"Yeah. He didn't look like he'd gotten much sleep."

*And there I was, snoring away.*

Felicity smacked him lightly on the arm. "If you're going to say you feel terrible for actually getting some rest after what happened last night…"

"I wouldn't dare."

"Good." She sipped her coffee. "Because that's how I felt when I woke up to him knocking on the door. And that's enough dumb guilt for both of us."

"Did he say if they found anything?"

She didn't ask *anything what*, just shook her head.

They sat quietly for a few minutes, eating breakfast before it got cold.

Felicity hugged her mug of coffee to her chest and stared up at the sky. "It's nothing to do with everything that's happening, but… I can't remember the last time I was up for the sunrise," she said, her voice oddly strained. "I mean—I've been up *before* sunrise loads of times, but I never actually saw it. I'd be hurrying to work, or head-down in my laptop, and suddenly it would be daylight instead of dark and I wouldn't have noticed."

"The more I hear about your job, the less I like it," he told her, frowning.

"You can say that again." Her lips quirked. "In fact, I think you've already said it."

"It bears repeating."

"Yeah." She stared out to sea, her gaze unsettled. "It feels like another lifetime. Like another *me*. And… doesn't it seem weird to you, this whole thing? We're fighting this evil magic, we're apparently soulmates, but we hardly know each other."

Something must have shown in his face. She raised her hands. "This isn't me trying to let you down gently. It's me saying that I don't even know… I don't know. Do you have any siblings? What did you do before you came to Hideaway? Is there a school for dragons?"

He relaxed. "No dragon schools. Frankly, the thought is terrifying."

"Right. You just all head out into the world to steal each other's treasures, which isn't terrifying at all."

"Imagine how much worse it would be if we'd had any training." He wiped up the last scrap of yolk with his bread and popped it into his mouth, chewing slowly. "It was bad enough as it was."

Felicity looked at him out of the corners of her eyes. "You want to talk about it?"

"No, but I will, anyway." He sighed and resettled himself in his seat. "You said you would go with me to find a hoard, so you deserve to know what that means." And he needed to convince himself that going treasure-hunting with her was still going to happen, even as everything that happened seemed to push it further into the distance. "I wasn't very good at it."

"I gathered that much."

"I mean I was terrible at it. Hopeless. Utterly ineffectual. A lost cause." His fingers tightened around his coffee mug. "Sharing the locations of poorly defended treasures is a hobby for a lot of dragons. Where's the fun in sneaking off with some treasure if no one knows you're doing it? Older dragons who already have respectable hoards bet on who's going to lose their treasures to whom."

"That's crazy. This is going on, all the time? How is there enough treasure to go around?"

Apollo shrugged. "There isn't. That's why we're always stealing it off one another."

"There can't be *that* many dragons in the world. I'll accept that shifters have existed under my nose this whole time, but not that I've missed a freaking war between dragons."

"Hardly a war. More a series of thrilling heists. And there aren't many of us, that's true. Just enough to keep the whole circus running."

"Constantly stealing each other's treasures."

"And hiding our own treasures, turning our backs, and—whoops! There it goes again!" He grimaced. "What I'm saying is that if you want to find some treasure, knowing where to look isn't the hard part."

He took a deep breath. Here was the hard part.

"Most dragons have this sense of... gold-lust. It makes sense, I suppose, evolutionarily speaking."

Felicity raised both eyebrows. "It does?"

"Our magic compels us to offer a hoard to our mate. So it's only fair that it should give us an instinctual kick in the backside to gather that hoard too, right? That's the gold-lust. It kicks in when we're in the presence of treasure. At least... it's meant to. I've never felt it."

He paused. Felicity was staring at him carefully. "Okay."

"It isn't, though. It isn't okay. I went all around the world, hunting tales of lost treasures. And every time I got close, I… stopped. I thought maybe if I concentrated hard enough, or waited until the time was right, my gold-lust would spur me on. It never did. And while I was hesitating, another dragon swooped in. Every time."

Felicity put down her cup. She stood up and pulled her chair closer to his, so that when she sat down again, she could lean against him. He put his arm around her shoulders, breathing in her sweet feminine smell, willing the warmth and closeness of her body to ease the tension in his own.

"You're worried the same thing will happen when I'm with you?"

"I want to think that surely, surely now that I've found you, I'll be fixed. But what if I'm not? What if even with you beside me, I can't summon enough gold-lust to win a hoard for you?"

"Apollo, you're not broken."

He laughed mirthlessly. "By dragon standards I am."

"Then we'll make our own standards." She raised her chin and looked him in the eye. "I've walked in your magic. It's the most beautiful, wonderful thing I've ever experienced, apart from waking up next to you in the morning. There's nothing broken about it. If you've never felt any gold-lust—well, not every human feels love and attraction the same way. Maybe it's the same for dragons."

He stared at her. *The most wonderful thing I've ever experienced.* Her words hung in his heart. "Do you think so?"

She took his hand. "Or maybe it was waiting for me to turn up. I'm going to grab the treasure and run while you distract anyone else around, remember?" She kissed him, slow and sweet. "We're going to make this work. But—are there any other dragons in your family you've talked to? Maybe you're not the only one. I mean, if all dragons are meant to feel horny over gold, then you're not going to go advertising the fact if you don't, right?"

"Gold-lust isn't—never mind." He narrowed his eyes as she smirked. "You want me to believe that it's all a myth?"

"Well, have you ever talked to another dragon about it?"

"I've listened to a number of dragons crow far too excitedly about their newly acquired hoards, if that counts? But dragons aren't particularly social creatures, outside their own clans. The only other dragon shifter in my family is my grandfather, and he's very strict about draconic traditions. I cannot imagine a world in which he would admit to *not* feeling something as inherently draconic as gold-lust."

"No siblings or cousins?"

"My family doesn't branch out very far in any direction. It's deliberate, I think. Lightning dragons only show up once every few generations, and since there's never been more than one of us per generation, cutting siblings and cousins out of the equation is… easier, I suppose."

Felicity sighed. "It sounds like a lot of pressure."

"…Yes, now you mention it."

"No wonder you worried about your hoard so much."

"And dealt with my worries by ignoring the problem for most of my adult life."

"Very mature of you."

"Thank you, I try." He brushed his hand along her arm, turning it over to stroke the soft skin of her inner wrist. "And… thank you. Really. You've given me some new ways to think about it."

"And I didn't even need to break into your magic. Again."

"You're more of a sneaky dragon burglar than I am, it's true." He twined his fingers through hers. "While we're delving into either our deepest secrets or interminable small talk—What about you? Any siblings?"

He was relieved that she'd taken his revelations about his lack of gold-lust well—and determined to find out more about her. His sparkling, brilliant mate.

"No siblings. Same pressure. Well, not the *same*, but…" She made a face. "My parents expected me to get a good degree and a good job, and I did, and then… that was that, I guess. They never wanted to hear about my studies or my work. It was just something they could tick off a checklist."

"And meanwhile your boss was making your life hell."

"Aha, but I didn't *notice* he was making my life hell, so it was okay, actually. And I would have gone on deluding myself that it was okay if he hadn't—" She made a face. For a moment, she seemed on the edge of saying something that scared her, and then her expression cleared. She clinked her coffee mug against his. "And now I never have to see him again. We're going to sort out this evil magician, then disappear off to the sunset hunting treasure, and I'll never have to look at Saint-John Montfort's smug face again."

"Cheers to that," Apollo agreed.

"It's a plan, then. We find whoever's wreaking occasional magical havoc here," she said a while later, tracing loops on his chest.

"And I chase them out of town?"

"I was thinking Caro could put the scare on them. That woman is terrifying whatever form she's in."

He frowned. "What do I do while Caro's lurking in the shadows with her knives, then?"

"Don't worry. I have *plenty* planned for you." Her smile promised the exact sort of wickedness he was hoping for. "And once Hideaway is safe, we go treasure-hunting. If dragons are always needling each other over their finds, there must be some sort of dragon-y grapevine where you all share treasure maps or something, right?"

"Yes," he said, with more certainty than he felt. His grandfather had been ominously silent on the topic of treasure—as distinct from his usual frosty silence on all other topics—but it wouldn't take much to hook back into other dragon clans' gossip networks. He'd made a start already and it was all exhaustingly familiar. Clan elders bragged about the thinly veiled 'opportunities' their grandchildren were chasing across the globe or made snide remarks about coming across other clans' 'lost property'. The younger generations were just as bad. Sure, it was years since he'd last been on the hunt, but had his fellow dragons always been so… blatant?

*When did I start to feel so old?* he had thought, scanning through photos and videos of smirking dragon shifters in front of ancient ruins and abandoned caves—and rappelling down the sides of fortified high-rise buildings, and breaking into the occasional bank vault. *Maybe Felicity's right. Time to start gumming sadly on toast and complaining about my back.*

Felicity pressed her palm against his chest. "Don't worry," she told him, smiling gently. "Hideaway first. We can break out the treasure maps later."

He opened his mouth to say *That wasn't what was worrying me*—then closed it. She was right. He *had* been feeling sorry for himself about treasure-hunting, but as soon as she reassured him they would ensure his town's safety first, something eased inside him.

"You don't mind putting it off?" he asked.

Felicity frowned at him. "No. Of course not. I would never ask you to abandon everyone you care about here when they need your help. And anyway… this way, I can enjoy the anticipation."

Around them, the town was beginning its second waking. Curtains were being drawn, lights turning on. A lone seagull winged its way out towards the horizon; one of the White girls, he assumed, carrying a message to one of the fishing boats that had gone out of telepathic range.

A surge of protectiveness tightened his chest. This was his *home*. And the peace suffusing the morning was an illusion.

Felicity caught his eye. "What are you thinking?" she asked. "I can feel your magic reacting to it."

He grinned at her. "I'm thinking it's time we went and sorted out this evil magician."

# 28

# FELICITY

Sorting out the evil magician was easier said than done.

While she and Apollo had been filling up on eggs and toast, Arlo had gone over the site of the explosion with his finely honed wolf nose. He found nothing. Even if there were any clues to be smelled, the rank scent of burning overpowered everything else.

It was the same with the magic. She and Apollo delved tentatively around the newly stitched edges of his spell, but there was nothing to find in the darkness where his magic no longer touched. She'd hoped they might find some traces of *something* in the remaining spell—the equivalent of magical footprints—but again, nothing. Maybe the rush of power had flushed the evidence away, or maybe there hadn't been anything to begin with.

"Nothing," she said as she opened her eyes back into the real world. Apollo had grasped her arms as they went under; he loosened his grip and gave her a tense smile. "I know you're worried about us getting attacked while we're in there, but at this point I swear, whoever this asshole is, if he comes at either of us, I'm going to kick him in the head. I don't care how magic he is."

"You have my full support to do so."

"I just wish there was *more* I could do. When I tried to stop the power drain after the attack on the workshop—it was like I could almost hold your magic, but it kept slipping out of my grasp. I wish I could—" She broke off and flushed. "Sorry. It's *your* magic. It's bad enough I go rummaging around in it without wanting to take the reins myself."

"I'd be happy to hand over the reins if it meant seeing you run down whoever is attacking our town." There was a glint in Apollo's eye, and she couldn't tell if it was teasing or deadly serious. "Besides, my magic bothers you enough. Serves it right if you steal it away from under me."

"You're right," Felicity said as his magic began to fill the air around them, thrilling at their attention as much as she thrilled at its touch. "It *does* bother me. Almost constantly."

"That's terrible." Apollo leaned closer to her, his voice almost a purr. "Maybe we should do something about that?"

Anticipation sent shivers up her spine. As if that wasn't enough, Apollo trailed one finger down her arm. Electricity sparked against her skin, hot and full of promise.

"Sounds like a sensible idea," she murmured, completely failing to control the pleased grin spreading across her face. "Shall we—"

Apollo's head jerked back. Frowning, he cast a glare back along the promenade. Harrison was jogging towards them.

"At least shout out loud so Felicity knows who's responsible for the interruption!" Apollo called to him hotly.

"Sorry," said Harrison, but it sounded more automatic than authentic. He nodded to Felicity. "Didn't want to attract too much attention. We've got a possible lead. Jools saw a ship round the coast—far enough away your spell wouldn't sense it, Sparky, and out of sight from the town."

"A ship?" Felicity frowned.

"Yeah. A leisure yacht, Arlo says. I'll leave you to imagine the look on his face as he said it."

"I'm sure he was marvelously pleased." Apollo's voice was light, but a muscle jumped in his jaw. "I don't care if it's outside my perimeter. I want to check it out."

"Are you crazy?" Felicity tugged him to look at her. "You're going to what? Fly out?"

"Swim."

"I don't know if anyone's told you, but you're not exactly inconspicuous. The water just makes you shinier. We don't even know if this yacht has anything to do with the attacks! I mean, why would someone go to all the trouble of attacking you, leaving no trace of how their magic works or who they are, and then just hang out around the corner on a fancy boat?"

It didn't make any sense. The hairs on the back of her neck prickled.

Apollo's mouth twisted. "I can't just sit here and do nothing."

"It feels—"

She stopped. Last night, she'd sworn that if it meant getting Apollo out of harm's way, she would convince him to leave town.

Could she really go through with that?

Guilt carved through her. *I've been lying to him the whole time I've been here. What's one more betrayal?*

If Apollo went out to confront this ship, and was seen—he would have to leave Hideaway, wouldn't he? To distract attention away from the town, at the very least.

That was how she would sell it to him. If he were spotted by outsiders. The best solution would be to lay a trail of breadcrumbs away from Hideaway Cove—more sightings, more glimpses of golden scales beneath the waves, until whatever urban legend grew up around him was completely dissociated from the town.

He would do it. Of course he would. He was too noble and self-sacrificing to risk his friends' safety, and the sanctuary offered by the town, to stay, if she convinced him that staying meant endangering them.

*One more betrayal.* Her throat felt thick.

"It feels like a trap."

Both men looked at her. Her cheeks went hot under their stares, but she kept her chin up. Now that she'd said it out loud, she was sure she was right.

Something was wrong with this situation. "The attacks escalate, and suddenly there's a sitting duck on the horizon?" The magic of Apollo's protection spell rippled around her, and she clutched automatically, as though she could grab it. "I don't like it. I know you feel helpless, and frustrated. They must know it, too. What if it's some sort of trick to get you to leave Hideaway? Remember when we wondered whether they were attacking the town, or you? Maybe they want you out of the way so they can do something worse here."

There. She felt all crumpled up inside, but she'd done it.

One more betrayal would be one too many. She couldn't trick Apollo into leaving his friends.

Apollo and Harrison exchanged a look. "Jools said she'd be happy to head back out and check them out again."

"She's a kid. I'm not sending a teenager into danger." Apollo sounded appalled.

*They both believe me?* Felicity's heart thudded. She was used to taking control of situations in her old life, where people knew her well enough to take her advice on how to stay out of Montfort's warpath, but she didn't have that sort of rep here. Apollo and Harrison just… trusted her judgment.

Even though her judgment was based on a random hunch.

*Thank God I didn't try to trick him into leaving*, she thought, and shivered.

"If Jools catches wind that we want someone to take a closer look, we might not be able to stop her," Harrison mused.

"We could tell Caro." Apollo's lips quirked. Harrison nodded.

"Two birds with one stone. She'd make sure Jools stays put, and I bet she'd like the chance to scope out our visitors if there's any chance they're responsible for shutting off her kitchen the other night."

The decision was made. Harrison left to talk to Caro, and Felicity slipped her arm around Apollo's. "I know you hate not being able to do anything. It's just a hunch, the whole trap thing, but…"

"It feels like bad news to me, too." Apollo sighed. "And I'm more use here than I would be outside Hideaway's borders. Though *more use* is still little enough." His mouth twisted bitterly, and Felicity nudged him gently with her elbow.

"So you can't hunt this asshole through your magic. Who cares? We'll root them out, or Harrison will, or Caro, and then you can transform into a *freaking dragon* and beat them out of town."

He tipped his head to one side and regarded her. "True. I hadn't thought about it like that."

"You said you never fought other dragons over treasure. Well, I bet you would fight them over Hideaway."

His eyebrows drew together. "I bet I would, too," he murmured, his voice strange.

"Not that we know it's even another dragon we're facing. Could just be some dude who's good at breaking stuff. A little slug shifter with a thing for short-circuiting mains power and setting stuff on fire."

"And who wields a magic that bites like frost."

"Like a bucket of nasty ice, yeah. The sort you get at a dodgy bar where you decide you don't need a cold drink that badly after all."

Apollo heaved a deep breath. "A slug shifter. I hope you're right." He hesitated. "Felicity, I know you've said you'll stay with me, that you'll wait until I can gather a hoard…"

"There's a 'but' coming, isn't there?" She narrowed her eyes at him and he smiled wanly.

"Quite. *But*. If you—" His phone buzzed and he slapped his pocket. "Dammit. What now…"

He stared at the screen and his frustration faded. When he looked up at her again, the smile that danced around his lips was genuine. Excitement crackled in his eyes.

"Maybe I won't have to keep you waiting after all. That was my grandfather. He's sent me a tip about a stolen treasure. The thief is on the move… and they're heading straight for Hideaway."

# 29

# APOLLO

Of course, the old dragon hadn't put all the details in his message—just enough to pique Apollo's interest.

To find out more, he would have to call him.

Felicity didn't seem to understand why that was such a bad thing.

"I know you said he's a grouchy old dragon," she said, watching him with an air of bemusement as he carefully arranged his phone screen so that the video wouldn't show anything but plain wall behind him. "But isn't this a bit much? You don't even want him to see where you *live?*"

He didn't know how to explain the weird, vulnerable sensation he'd had during their last call when he'd realized his grandfather could see the town in shot behind him. "It's a dragon thing," he said at last, dismissively.

Which felt strangely accurate, actually.

At last, he had the background to his liking: a wall in a back room, utterly featureless, away from any windows.

"I'm surprised you aren't hiding yourself away in a wardrobe," Felicity muttered.

"An excellent idea. Why didn't you mention it sooner?" He kissed her as her eyebrows shot up. "No. This will do."

His grandfather must have been expecting his call; the old man picked up after only a few too many seconds, no doubt carefully calculated to make Apollo doubt he was going to take the call at all.

"Well?" Errol barked as the video stream started. Apollo was amused to see that his grandfather, too, had chosen his background carefully. There was no trace of his hoard. Instead, he was standing in front of… a tropical island?

*A digital background.* Apollo hid a sigh. *Why didn't I think of that?*

He cleared his throat. "I got your message."

"Yes, yes, I gathered as much." Errol's eyes glittered. "Well? Are you going to go for it, or not? A piece of one of the largest American hoards! I'd go after it myself, but…"

His eyes twitched sideways, scanning the gathered treasures hidden by his digital background. The classic draconic conundrum: once your hoard reached a certain size, the risks of leaving it undefended to gather *more* treasure began to outweigh the benefits.

"I'll have to take what glee I can from the fact that another of my clan is the one to take it from them," Errol hissed. "*If* you can manage it."

*Thanks for the vote of confidence, grandpappy.* Apollo raised one eyebrow languorously. "It would help if you told me what it is I'm meant to be managing to do."

"Someone—no one knows who—managed to get past the clan's defenses. They tried to hush it up, of course, but couldn't keep it quiet forever. Now the thief's on the run, and their new lordling is taking chase." Errol made unconscious grasping motions with his hands. "I had it from Harkford, who had it from the Esperanzas, who still have a mole in the clan's staff, that they're heading in the direction of that trifling fishing village you've been rusticating in. They're—oh, a few hours away, at most."

"*What?* You couldn't have alerted me earlier?"

Errol sniffed. "Two hours' warning should be *more* than enough time to plan a daring theft. If you're clever, and cunning, you can slip in and steal the treasure from under the thief's nose *and* slip away before the fools know they should be chasing you instead."

Apollo clenched his fists. *If* he was clever and cunning enough. Errol's lack of faith in him was clear. And given his history, Apollo wasn't sure he had any more faith in himself than his grandfather did.

*That was the old me. It will be different this time. It must be.* He needed a hoard. Something to prove to Felicity that he was hers. *And that I deserve the trust she's put in me, staying in Hideaway despite everything.*

He glanced behind the phone to where she was sitting, quiet and out of sight of his grandfather. She rolled her eyes as Errol kept ranting on about the other dragon clans and how he wished he was still young enough to go and show them a thing or two, then winked at him. There was no sign of any trepidation in her expression.

Her confidence lit something in his own heart. *I won't let you down again. Sneaky and cunning? Let's do it.*

"Really? We're going to go after the treasure? We don't even know what it is!" Felicity folded her arms and worried at her bottom lip. "I don't know..."

"It's important." *Let me do this for you.* The words were on the tip of his tongue; he had to bite them back. It was too close to begging. He had to be strong for her. "It's..."

"More dragon stuff?"

"Dragon stuff. Magic stuff." He reached out and brushed his thumb over her lower lip until she stopped chewing on it. "A hoard is about to practically fall into our laps. No dragon worth his salt would let it get away again without at least trying to steal it."

She still didn't look convinced. "But if you have to leave Hideaway to get it—"

"Not necessarily." He put his arms around her and she leaned against his chest. "The last time a treasure came my way, I intercepted it at the border."

She narrowed her eyes, but a smile twitched at her lips. "Hmm."

"I mean you."

"*Hmm.*" She sighed. "It can't be a huge treasure, right, if whoever stole it from this dragon clan is hightailing across the country with it? Like, we're probably talking jewelry, not two tons of gold bullion."

She was coming around. Hope curled tiny tendrils around his heart.

"But…"

Or not.

She made a frustrated sound. "Stealing? Going off in search of buried treasure is one thing, but actually stealing off someone…"

"If it helps, it's not considered a crime by dragons. Just an embarrassment if done to you, or something to crow about if you're the one doing it."

"Do we really want to end up with an embarrassed dragon hanging around in Hideaway? Exactly how fiery do dragons get when they're embarrassed?"

"Plenty." Felicity jerked her head back to stare at him, outraged, and he smiled seductively. "Which is why we'll have to make sure that neither the thief nor the clan pursuing him know that the treasure has changed hands until long after they've all left town."

"And if we get it wrong, we're left with not only one, but potentially how many angry dragons?" She made a face. "Weren't we worried enough about the mysterious slug shifter?"

"You said that you could *almost* control my magic." She stopped scowling and stared at him, suspicion and curiosity warring in her eyes. "What if the mate bond is all it takes to turn that *almost* into reality?"

Her lips quirked. "If dragons don't like it when their hoards get stolen, what is the usual dragonish reaction to someone stealing your magic?"

"I have no idea. But *my* reaction is that I would like it very much, if you were the one doing the stealing." He brushed a kiss between her eyebrows. "This might give us the edge we need."

She sighed long-sufferingly. "All right. Let's steal a stolen treasure off a dragon before some other dragons steal it back first."

"Exactly. I'm glad you've come around." She huffed, and he added teasingly: "And we have all of two hours to come up with a plan."

"Oh, that won't be a problem." Felicity straightened her shoulders, a glint in her eye. "Dragon nonsense is still new to me. But last-minute crazy plans? That is one hundred per cent my wheelhouse."

Her positivity was catching. Apollo's dragon uncurled its tail, loosening its grip on the core of his magic for the first time since the explosion.

The next hour was a bustle of activity. Apollo had heard of people being described as 'like poetry in motion' before, but that wasn't right. She was like the conductor of a symphony where at any moment, the strings might all break or the wind section blow entirely away. If one crescendo failed, she had another in the wings; if the melody wavered, she had a whole new sheet of music ready to replace it.

She was incandescent, and Apollo had never been more attracted to her.

It was impossible to keep his admiring glances secret. She caught one of them, then another. Then too many for him to continue pretending he didn't find her organizing ability incredibly hot.

"It's just project management," she told him, going red in a way he found very pleasing. "This is what I spent the last five years doing. My whole adult life so far." Her eyes shadowed, but she shook herself and smiled up at him. "And you're a *big* improvement on my last boss."

One day, he wanted to meet this Montfort, and tell him exactly what he thought of the sort of man who made fear and anxiety echo across his mate's face.

Early afternoon found them on the outskirts of town, just inside the perimeter of his protection spell. A hundred yards or so in front of them, the few scattered roadside trees thickened to forest cover; behind them, the hill dropped away, giving the impression that the road ran straight into the Atlantic.

They were fewer than fifty yards from where Felicity had almost run off the road the night she arrived in Hideaway.

This was the first time Apollo had been back here. Being near the site was too close to reliving it, and the ice that clenched around his heart when he realized he'd almost lost his mate before he ever knew her.

Which was why this had to work. He needed a hoard, to pledge himself to her properly.

But his magic kept itching against him, telling him something was wrong.

"What's up?" Felicity asked.

He smiled. *No point trying to hide things from my inquisitive mate.* "I'm not used to being this close to the perimeter. It's … itchy."

"The spell is like an additional sensory thing for you, isn't it? A sort of magical sixth sense. Having it suddenly drop off a few yards away must be weird." She squeezed his hand. "Come on. We only have to trick a dragon out of their stolen hoard, and then we'll be home safe. Honestly, I don't know what you're stressing over."

"I'd feel happier if you were back in town," he told her plainly.

She narrowed her eyes at him. "Is there any point me telling you *I* would be happy if *you* were back in the middle of your protective magic, Mr. Fainted-from-Exhaustion?"

"Absolutely not."

"Then I won't. And don't you say anything annoying like 'Oh, but I'm a strong and mighty dragon, and you're a mere human who can't even fly' because I already realize that, thanks."

"I wouldn't dream of it." He wrapped his arms around her and spoke into her ear. "Even though I *am* a strong and mighty dragon, and you are a small and graceful human who can't fly."

"Pah. You just want to steal this treasure for yourself. I see right through you, you sneaky dragon—"

Her phone rang. She slapped her pocket. "Damn it. Who's—Maya?" She put the phone to her ear, eyes wide. "Maya, what's—where are you? What's all that noise in the background?"

Apollo's sensitive dragon hearing made out Maya's voice and the frenzied squawking overlaying it. "Fee, everything's gone wrong. I don't know where else to go. This is—you're going to think I'm crazy, but Tomás—I can't even say it."

"What happened? Is he okay? Are you okay?"

"Yes, he's okay, we're both fine—for now—but… Oh, God, Fee, I've messed everything up so badly. I need any dirt you have on my boss. Anything at all."

"Dirt on your boss? But—"

"Or—shit, I don't even know if I'm driving the right way."

"You're *driving?*"

"I have to! You have no idea, Fee. I feel like I'm trapped in a nightmare. Tomás stole—I don't know *how* he got it, but he did and he won't give it back and I don't think Corin would even *take* it back, and now we're being followed and—I'm sorry, I don't want to lead them to you but I don't have anywhere else to go. You said you were in Hideaway Cove. There can't be more than one within a day's drive, right? But I don't even know if we're going in the right direction—oh, honey, no, *please* put your wings away while we're driving—"

There was one more staticky squawk and the call cut off. Felicity was ashen-faced.

"She's coming here to Hideaway? Oh my god. She sounded terrified."

"She told her son to put his wings away while they were in the car?" Apollo frowned. "You didn't tell me your friend was a shifter."

"She's not." Felicity stared at her phone. "Or… I don't think she is?"

"Unless I eavesdropped that conversation entirely wrong, I think at the very least her son is a shifter." Suspicion was beginning to build in Apollo's mind. "A shifter who stole something from a Blackburn, and is now being chased across the country."

"Oh no. No. It *can't* be Maya we're chasing." Felicity searched his face as though she was desperately trying to find an answer there. "Or Tomás. We can't be here to steal something off a *baby*."

"A baby who already stole from one of the most famed dragon clans in the country."

"Don't be ridiculous. The Blackburns aren't dragons. They're…" Felicity ran her fingers across her scalp. "Corin Blackburn? Corin Blackburn is a dragon?"

He nodded. "Famously."

"And now he's hunting her down." Determination flashed across her face. "Screw waiting here, we have to go find her now!"

She sprinted for the car. Apollo was right behind her.

Even if it meant leaving the protection of his spell, she was right. A baby shifter and his mother needed sanctuary.

He had to help them.

# 30

# FELICITY

*Maya's in trouble. I have to help her.* Felicity's fingers were white-knuckled on the steering wheel as she navigated the forest road. "Can you try calling her again?"

"I think it's safest she not answer the phone if she's on the road," Apollo told her diplomatically.

"Well, can you—I don't know, magically reach out and let her know we're coming to find her?"

"I could if she were a shifter."

"No. No way. I told you already. Maya isn't..." Her voice trailed off. *Could* Maya be a shifter?

"Then I'll try to contact her son." He sounded doubtful. Felicity didn't blame him.

"Good luck. He's one. I don't know if one-year-old shifters are any better than one-year-old humans at intelligent conversation."

"In my experience it's mostly screeching and giggles." Apollo closed his eyes.

Felicity waited to feel the tug of magic around her, but there was nothing. Of course. They weren't in Hideaway Cove anymore, and Apollo wasn't the only one feeling the absence of his spells.

"Aha," he said after a few minutes.

"What?"

"I can sense somebody. A little telepathic wildfire."

"Tomás? How is he? Can you tell if he's okay?"

"He's not scared. He's determined, and a bit bored."

"Okay. That's good, I guess?"

Apollo frowned. "I'm not so sure. A bored baby shifter who can already shift, stuck in a car on a long drive? Sounds like a recipe for mayhem."

Felicity swung the car around a winding bend. "I've had about as much mayhem as I can handle," she muttered.

"We're getting closer. They're—hah! Very close. Pull over."

"Here? But—"

Another car swung around the next corner, straddling the center line. Felicity veered out of the way and slowed down. "Is that them?"

"That's them!"

"Shit!"

She pulled a quick U-turn and hauled after the other car. It was an unremarkable silver sedan. She couldn't see inside, but—

"I'm going to drive up alongside them! Try to get her attention!"

Apollo swore. "That's a terrible idea!"

"Maya! Maya, it's me! Pull over!" Felicity rolled down her window and waved madly at the other car. She got one glimpse of a shocked dark face staring back at her and her heart leapt. "Maya!"

They both pulled over. Felicity hit her hazard lights and jumped out of the car, Apollo a half-second behind her.

The driver door on the other car opened. Felicity could barely believe her eyes.

But there was no way she wouldn't recognize her friend.

Maya steadied herself on the door. Her medium brown skin was grayish with stress, and tension pinched the muscles around her mouth and eyes. Worry twisted in Felicity's stomach. Maya usually dressed her curves down with severe suits at work and bulky sweaters on her days off. Even postpartum she'd managed to look as though she was holding everything together. But right now she was wearing a stained scoop-neck t-shirt and leggings with a line of holes in the knee. Her usually sleek hair was falling out of a rough ponytail, her face was bare, and she wasn't wearing any jewelry.

"Fee?" she whispered, eyes wide.

Felicity hurried towards her and pulled her into a bear hug. Maya shivered once and then collapsed against her with a sigh that was almost a sob. "How are you here? I don't understand."

"We came as soon as I got your call. It's okay, Maya. We know what's going on. We're going to take you back with us and make sure nothing bad happens to you or to Tomás."

"Oh, god, Fee. You don't know how bad it is. I…"

She twisted to look back at her car. A frustrated wailing was coming from the back seat.

"You have a dragon shifter baby?" Felicity suggested.

Maya stiffened. "How can you know that?"

Felicity gently turned her around until they were both facing Apollo. He was standing in a ribbon of sunlight pouring through the tree cover. *Another well-orchestrated entrance*, Felicity thought with mingled fondness and an internal eye-roll.

"Because I've got a dragon shifter boyfriend," she told her friend.

"Apollo Jenkins." Apollo stepped forward, hand outstretched. "You must be Maya."

"Maya Flores." She reached out an uncertain hand. "You're… a dragon shifter? Another one?"

"*Another* one? How many have you met?" Felicity asked.

Maya winced. "That's a complicated subject. I—"

She was about to shake Apollo's hand when an indignant screech cut through the air. Maya swung round. "Tomás, no!" she cried out as something exploded out of the door she'd left open.

Felicity gasped. A dragon was flying towards them—a tiny, flame-colored dragon. It landed on Maya's shoulder and hissed furiously at Apollo.

"Hello to you, too," he said politely.

The tiny dragon hissed again and clung to Maya's hair, wings flapping unevenly.

The dragon was the size of a house cat, though its wings made it seem larger. Its scales were white-yellow on the belly, shading through orange to brilliant red on its wing-tips. A gold wristwatch was hanging around its neck like a pendant.

And it was glaring at Apollo as though he'd personally insulted it.

"Tomás?" Felicity gaped.

The dragon baby peered at her and let out an excited squeak. Then it got back to glaring suspiciously at Apollo, front claws clinging to its golden necklace.

He sighed. "I'm not here to steal your hoard, dragonlet."

*Well, not anymore, anyway.* Felicity swallowed hard. So much for that plan. They would have to find another way to get Apollo a hoard.

Tomás hissed at Apollo again, and his eyebrows shot up.

"Yes, it's a *very* nice hoard. But it's yours, and I think your mother would be very upset if I tried to steal it off you. No offense meant, Ms. Flores, but you look upset enough already."

"You've got that right." Maya juggled Tomás into her arms. "The last few days have been a nightmare. I—I don't mean to cause any trouble. I didn't know where else to go."

"You picked exactly the right place. Hideaway Cove is a sanctuary for shifters. You'll be safe there." Felicity glanced at Apollo. "Right?"

Because suddenly, she wasn't sure. Hideaway was a sanctuary for shifters away from the human world. But what about when it was other shifters they were running from?

"Felicity's right. You'll be safe there. Both of you. No matter how many people come knocking to follow up the rumors of a stolen dragon treasure."

Maya went pale. "Oh god. How many people know?"

"It's made its way along the grapevine." Apollo looked apologetic. "But there aren't many draconic clans in this part of the country; very few close enough to be bothered chasing down a stolen hoard, at least."

"Oh, great. Then I only need to worry about Corin." Maya's voice broke. "I can't believe he—"

"We'd better move quickly," Apollo interrupted her, staring past them to the road. "Someone else is coming."

Felicity hadn't noticed the sound of another approaching car until he mentioned it. As soon as he had, though, she couldn't not hear it.

"I can't put him in his car seat when he's like this." Maya's voice rose. "Not until he's back as a human baby again and that might be hours when he's all worked up like this."

Felicity's mind raced over their options. Apollo could fly Maya and Tomás back to Hideaway—but would the little dragon accept being flown around by another dragon? He barely seemed to be coping with Apollo on the ground. And would Apollo accept leaving her here to face whoever these other dragons were?

Did *she* want to be left here to face the other dragons? If the dragon Tomás had stolen from was who Felicity suspected… would that make them easier to deal with, or worse?

She turned to Apollo. "I don't know what to do," she admitted. After the way he'd looked at her while she fired off plans earlier, she was afraid he would be disappointed in her.

Instead, he looked at her as though she'd just offered him the world. "Then it's a good thing you have a dragon around," he said. "I can sense them coming."

His stance changed. His spine was straight, his shoulders back—but it wasn't overdone, or ironic, like most of the poses he put on. Felicity wondered if he even knew he was doing it. Suddenly he wasn't the loose-limbed, relaxed man who'd slipped his way into her heart. He shimmered with power.

Her lips almost hurt, she wanted to kiss him so much.

"You and Maya get behind me." Apollo's golden eyes burned into hers. "The Blackburns won't get past me."

Blackburns. Holy crap. She still wasn't over that. She wasn't sure she ever would be.

Felicity's eyes slid sideways towards her best friend. *How did your son end up stealing treasure off another dragon… who's also your boss?*

# 31

# APOLLO

*The Blackburns won't get past me.*

The crazy thing was, he actually believed his own words.

Maya was terrified for her son. They needed Hideaway's protection. And what Hideaway protected, he protected.

Still… heroics or not, he couldn't keep his mind from wandering. How had a *baby* managed to steal a piece of a fully grown dragon's hoard?

Assuming the dragon he had stolen it off was fully grown. Perhaps Grandfather Errol had it all wrong, and this whole wild goose chase was the result of a shifter play date gone terribly wrong.

Except Maya seemed too scared for that to be the case.

Never mind. No dragon was going to get past him.

Felicity drew Maya back between the two cars. They provided a small amount of cover, and if Tomás calmed down enough to shift back into human form, they could strap him into his car seat and leave.

Of course, the chances of him calming down around even more dragons when he'd been set off just by Apollo were vanishingly low.

"How long do we have?" Felicity called over to him. "Fog's coming back. Maybe it'll help this time."

She was right; fog was creeping in through the forest, bringing with it the scent of the sea.

Apollo tipped his head on one side. "A few minutes. If you change your mind about driving with Tomás in dragon form—"

"No. I've made that mistake before." Maya bit her bottom lip.

The cars were getting closer. No question that this was the Blackburn clan. When he'd been telepathically searching for Tomás, the little dragon's mind had been like a single spark in the darkness; this was more like a wildfire bearing down on him. At least half a dozen fully grown male dragons, in human form.

He reached for his power automatically—one hand to the magic inside him, one to the magic outside—and swore. No outside magic. Right.

Its absence was more of a handicap than he'd expected. If he somehow lured the Blackburns back to town…

His dragon rustled its scales and hissed angrily. If he lured them back to Hideaway, then these stranger dragons would be in Hideaway. And he didn't like the thought of that at all.

Awareness burst against his senses. Even off his home turf, he could tell when another fully grown dragon was close, and this one was closer than the others.

He stalked forwards. The farther away from Felicity and the others he met the dragon, the better. He'd just rounded the corner when another car loomed out of the fog.

It rolled towards him, not with brakes squealing like Maya's vehicle, but completely controlled.

Because the driver had sensed him, too.

Apollo moved his weight forward, balancing on the balls of his feet and keeping his shoulders and arms loose so that he was ready to spring into motion. Whether that was shifting, leaping out of the way of an oncoming car, or both.

The new car rolled to a stop ten feet away. It was a high-end model, gleaming and out of place on the rugged forest road. Its engine was completely silent; it didn't even purr, though it looked like it should.

Apollo sent out a tendril of magic—not enough to be noticed, but enough to tell him if the car was about to start moving again.

He didn't recognize the dragon shifter who stepped out from the driver's seat. The shifter's human form was in his mid-thirties, with a streak of gray in his black hair and piercing blue eyes. He scowled as he felt Apollo's appraising gaze, and Apollo felt the same way as the other shifter looked him up and down. If they had been cats, they would have been hissing at one another.

"I'm afraid I can't let you go any further." Apollo kept his voice light, an almost-insolent drawl. The other man's hackles went up at once.

"And who're you?" His voice was cultured American.

"Excellent point." Apollo's drawl intensified. "Yes, let's do the proper introductions. That way I'll know what to carve on your tombstone—no, that's a bit dark, isn't it? Let's say, so when I'm telling people later how I wiped the floor with your wings, I can give a name to the mop instead of just referring to you as *that other one, you know, with the dry skin.*"

The other dragon's hand twitched, as though he was about to lift it to rub his face. Apollo allowed himself a moment of petty smugness.

"Since we're on my ground, I'll start the pleasantries, shall I? Apollo Jenkins. It isn't a pleasure, but of course pleasure isn't why you're here, is it?"

"You—" The other dragon *almost* snarled, but managed to hold it back the same way he'd managed not to check his face for flakes of dry skin.

He thrust his shoulders back and started to stalk around Apollo. Apollo thrust his own shoulders back and stalked right back at him.

"Corin Blackburn. The pleasure's all mine. Because retrieving a piece of my stolen property is *always* a pleasure."

Apollo raised one eyebrow. "This happens to you a lot, does it? Losing track of your hoard?" His feet barely made a sound on the road as he circled around Corin, away from—shit. Away from Felicity. If he moved much further, he'd let Corin get between him and his mate.

He reversed direction, sneering as though he'd meant to do so all along.

Corin sneered back. "One takes these risks when one isn't afraid to wear their hoard on their sleeves." He tugged on his cuffs, neatening the crisp white fabric of his shirt where it peeked out from beneath his suit jacket. The white and the dark cloth both shimmered in his car's headlights.

Apollo's dragon blinked in astonishment.

*Gold?* This other dragon was literally *wearing* his hoard. How had he managed that? Was it woven into the cloth? It must be terribly heavy. And how did you even start to go about washing a shirt imbued with gold thread? Half his hoard must go on dry-cleaning bills.

What about his underwear? Was he packing gold-thread boxers underneath it all?

Apollo was so distracted that he didn't pay attention to what his mouth was saying.

"You *wear* your hoard? No wonder you're so used to losing pieces of it. What do you do when one of your socks goes missing, wage war again the launderette?" He narrowed his eyes. "Anyone would think you did it on purpose. Like you were trying to get Maya into—"

"*Don't say her name!*"

Blue fire flared in Corin's eyes. His dragon was so close to the surface Apollo could almost see it, a huge, ghostly outline made of flames in the glow from his car's headlights.

Apollo rocked back on his heels. Not because he was intimidated. To reinforce to this Corin Black-whatever that growling and letting your dragon almost physically manifest *around* you—which, really, *how* was he doing that?—was both extremely un-cool and not particularly draconic. And definitely not something he wished he could do.

Being a mouthy little shit, however, was a draconic tradition with centuries of history. So he raised both eyebrows innocently and said, "Whose name? Maya?"

"You dare—" The fire in Corin's eyes sharpened until it was almost painful to look at. Apollo refused to look away. That would count as backing down, and he was never going to back down again. Even if it left him blinking away sunspots for the rest of the night. "How do you know Miss Flores?"

The ghostly flame-shadow of his dragon stared at Apollo with eyes that shouldn't exist.

He shrugged, keeping his expression carefully casual and not gulping even slightly. "Of course I know Miss—Maya. Why would I be out here, keeping you away from her, if I didn't?"

"If you've done anything to her—" The dragon shifter surged forward, fists clenched. The ghostly flames around him brightened.

Apollo raised one eyebrow, trying to look as though his pulse wasn't racing a mile a minute. His dragon was prickling for a fight. Just one little bite, it begged him. Or one really big zap.

"If *I've* done anything to her? You're the one who's been chasing her across the country. All because you couldn't keep your hoard safe from a tiny baby?"

"You don't know what you're talking about." Scales shimmered on Corin's cheeks.

Apollo readied his own dragon. Sparks crackled beneath his skin. His dragon was champing at the bit to get some action, and his own heart was pumping at the thought of—what?

He'd never been a fighter before. Not even for gold, let alone to protect another dragon. Another dragon who, at less than a year old, was a more accomplished hoard-thief than he was. What happened?

Felicity happened.

Felicity, with her sharp smiles and sharper mind, the way he could make her laugh and how that laughter uncurled something hidden and wicked inside of her. Felicity, who always knew exactly what to do and say no matter what sort of trouble he had gotten himself into.

Felicity, who didn't believe that he was a failure of a dragon. Who believed in *him*.

The other dragon stopped. His flames paled. "You *don't* know what you're talking about, do you?" The anger was gone from his voice, replaced by a wary suspicion. "How do you know Miss Flores?" His nostrils flared. "Someone else was here."

*He's talking about Felicity.*

Apollo tensed. The sparks beneath his skin started to spread on top of it, outlining claws where his fingers were. "Stop right there."

"There *is* someone." Eyes the color of ice fire burned into his. Corin's nostrils flared as he glanced past Apollo. "A woman. Another—good. This makes things easier." His shoulders relaxed. The burning shadow behind him winked out. "Apollo, was it?"

Corin might have relaxed, but Apollo wasn't going to let a feint like that fool him. He focused on his dragon, bringing it so close to the surface that it would only take a moment to shift.

"There's no need for that." Whatever conclusions Corin had come to about Felicity, they'd given him an insufferable look of confidence. "Listen, the others will be here soon."

*Others?* The moment he said it, Apollo heard the roar of distant engines again. Far less distant than the last time he'd heard them.

"Actually, this is perfect." To Apollo's horror, Corin *smiled*. It even looked genuine, albeit slightly predatory. "You won't let me pass, you said?"

"Er. Yes." Apollo gave up pretending he hadn't lost the thread of the conversation. "Wait, what?"

"Let me guess what happened here. You and your lady friend know Maya somehow. You're offering her sanctuary in your territory?" He nodded past Apollo's head, towards Hideaway Cove. "That explains why the whole place feels so… anyway. It's as good an explanation as any. The thief outsmarted us but got himself trapped in another dragon's territory. We'd be idiots to throw ourselves in after him, just for a single watch."

Scales twitched around his eyes as Corin's dragon objected to the idea of its stolen hoard being labeled *a single watch*. But Corin wasn't bothered. He rolled his shoulders back and stretched his arms.

He didn't look like a shifter who'd just walked back a challenge to another dragon.

He looked like he'd *won* something, damn it all. And Apollo had no idea what they had been competing over.

"Look, what are you—" he began, when three SUVs suddenly burst out of the darkness.

Two dragon shifters tumbled out of each one. They all looked like cheap knock-offs of Corin, with slight variations in height, weight and coloring. Apollo's dragon hissed in anticipation. What was this, the whole clan?

*A whole dragon clan and none of them are at each other's throats?* That had to be some sort of miracle.

A miracle that was about to crash down on him like a tidal wave.

The closest of Corin's backup shifted the moment their feet hit the ground. Their dragon forms were smaller than Apollo's, but stockier, more powerfully built. Their scales were dark: mainly blacks, grays and blues, with the odd vivid lime-green stripe like lightning.

He glared at them. Lightning was *his* thing.

His dragon weighed up their chances as all six of them shifted. He was still the bigger shifter—but they had strength in numbers. And whatever draconic abilities their clan possessed. Other dragons he had met could turn invisible, or breathe fire, or didn't need to breathe at all. He had no idea what sort of powers these ones could be packing.

He couldn't rely on his electricity magic being able to take them down.

Still, he let his power simmer in the air around him. Let them know he wasn't going to make this easy for them.

Corin advanced towards him, his face settling into grim lines. His own dragon was an almost physical force behind his eyes, the way Caro got when someone disrespected the Hook and Sinker.

*Fire*, he thought, seeing the flames around the other man's shoulders. *Their powers are definitely something to do with fire.*

The ground nearby was still damp from last week's rain. But that hadn't been a heavy fall, and it had been a dry spring. What if the trees caught fire? What if it spread to Hideaway?

His shoulders ached with the pressure of wings straining to break free and stop these invaders before they could harm his town.

And then they did. A mighty shudder went through his dragon and suddenly its wings *were* spreading from his shoulders—wings made of brilliant golden light.

Corin stopped a few inches away from him. He could count every scale shimmering beneath the other dragon's skin. Apollo readied himself. The other dragons were a solid wall of scales and claws around them. But if he was fast enough, if he shifted first, he could pin the other dragon down, shock him with enough power to stun him and—

"Fine," Corin growled. Frustration and resentment poured off the single syllable. "You win. We'll leave—for now. But if you think you've heard the last of the Blackburn clan…" He stepped closer, danger radiating from every pore in his body and his eyes in particular. "Next time, you won't see us coming."

He raised one hand in a sharp gesture to the dragons crowded around them. "Let's head back to the tower. There's nothing worth our time here."

The solid wall of dragons around them dissolved as the other dragons shifted back into human form.

The other dragons shouldered their way back into human form and back into the black vans, pausing only to pick up their shredded clothes with short, sharp movements that made it clear they'd rather be punching. One of them actually did punch what was left of his jacket, then hastily bundled it under his arm and hustled away.

Only Blackburn stayed where he was.

Apollo narrowed his eyes. His own dragon was still flickering close to the surface, using up precious energy sending phantom golden scales whirling behind his shoulders. White-scorched darkness flared out like wings behind Blackburn, but if it cost him anything, Apollo didn't see it.

At last the road was empty. Just him, and Blackburn—and hidden, but still too close, his Felicity and her friend and the precocious dragonling.

Too close and too far away. He should have been clearer: they needed to be in Hideaway. They would be safe there.

*My mate.* The pride of it rang through him, stronger than the fear. His fearless, sharp-eyed mate, who saw so much and used what she saw to help people.

That explained why he was having trouble keeping a smug look off his face. It didn't explain Blackburn.

The other dragon's teeth gleamed white as he smiled. "That went about as well as we could have hoped for. Shall we exchange a few blows for the look of things, or leave it at that?"

"What?"

"You'd better have your hoard well locked up. Not that it'll make any difference. That dragonling is going to swipe it from under your nose before whatever old Rustback is planning comes to fruition."

Blackburn looked inordinately pleased for a man who'd supposedly hunted Maya and her son across the state for the crime of stealing a portion of his hoard. Apollo would have narrowed his eyes further, but he didn't put it past the other dragon to ask, all concern, if he had something in his eye. Instead, he gave a lazy shrug and even lazier sigh.

"If you rely on locks to keep your gold safe, no wonder an infant made off with it," he drawled, as though his own hoard wasn't looped around his mate's neck, barely thirty feet away. Probably less than two feet away from the dragonling, come to think of it.

He tried not to let his sudden worry show.

"No, you've got some other trick, don't you?" Blackburn turned to gaze in the direction of the city and as his expression clouded, Apollo's magic sizzled. But this far from Hideaway, there was no answering call from the magic he'd laid down in the town. "Whatever you've done to keep your hoard hidden is effective. If it keeps Rustback on his toes and out of my city, all the better."

Rustback? Apollo spread his arms. "Hideaway is a haven to shifters of all sorts. If this Rustback wants to spend his retirement playing sentient metal detector along my beach, he's welcome." Distaste flickered at the corner of Blackburn's mouth. "As for you… don't think that your little act just now makes up for threatening my mate's friend."

"I never threatened—" Corin broke off as a muffled noise came from behind Apollo. His eyes snapped past him.

Recognition froze his face. Apollo didn't need to turn around to know what he'd seen.

Maya was standing at the corner, Tomás in her arms and Felicity trying to pull her back behind the trees. She was staring at Corin.

The expression on her face was… not fear. Not exactly.

Corin's mouth outlined her name. The phantom wings at his shoulders wavered.

"I think it's time you left," Apollo suggested. "Before the rest of your clan notices you've fallen behind."

Corin glared at him. Just as he was about to turn away, the other dragon's psychic voice brushed against his mind.

*Tell Miss Flores—* He grimaced, heavy eyebrows lowering over his glittering eyes. *No. Don't tell her anything. But you'd better look after her.*

He nodded to Apollo and made his way briskly back to his own vehicle. Apollo waited until it disappeared into the distance before he let out a relieved breath.

He wasn't the only one who'd been waiting. Behind him, Felicity's voice darted out: "What was *that* about? Maya, is he…?"

# 32

# FELICITY

Whatever Blackburn was or wasn't to Maya, she wasn't telling. As soon as Felicity asked, Maya's face started burning, and her eyes got that *stop-looking-at-me-please* look.

Felicity knew she shouldn't ask. She had to ask. She nodded at Tomás and whispered: "Is he Tomás's—?"

"*No!*" Maya hissed at once, then shut her mouth with a click. She glared at Felicity. "It's—complicated. Okay? And weird."

"Weird and complicated, okay." Felicity slung one arm around her friend's shoulders.

In front of them, Apollo turned around. The strange echo of his dragon was fading, briefly replaced by the familiar glimmer of golden sparks; then he stopped in front of them, magic hidden, nothing but his strange and wonderful self. Her heart tugged towards him.

"Weird and complicated. I get it."

"An apt description for whatever just happened, I agree." Apollo pulled her close for a kiss. "I never realized that I was missing the perfect draconic accessory: a pack of mini-me goons. I've heard of the Blackburn clan, of course, but I had no idea they were—"

He broke off suddenly and raised his head.

"What is it?" Felicity asked.

Apollo's face was tense. "Something's wrong." Sparks darted from his fingertips, heading in the direction of Hideaway Cove before sputtering out. "I—"

His phone rang. He grabbed it. "Arlo?"

The wolf shifter's voice was garbled and staticky. Felicity couldn't make out what he was saying, but Apollo's expression turned grim. "I'm on my way."

He ended the call and passed one hand over his face. "Something's happened."

"You need to go?"

His eyes met hers, equal parts worried and grateful. "Arlo managed to get that ship on the radio. The captain decided to come into town to talk. Arlo wanted to let me know he's on his way, but…"

The hairs on the back of Felicity's neck rose. "You already knew."

"Something strange is going on." He reached for her and she took his hand automatically. Magic pulsed between them. Not the tantalizing electric tingle she was familiar with, but a warm, reassuring caress.

At least, it should have been reassuring. Instead it petered out, making Felicity ache for the magic-rich air of Hideaway. From the haunted expression in Apollo's eyes, he felt the same way.

"Apparently this *captain* is familiar with shifters." Apollo's lips were white-tinged.

"Good. That means you can fly over and find out what the hell's going on." Felicity leaned over and kissed him. "It's only a few miles, and those clouds should be thick enough for you to hide in. You go and we'll catch up to you in the car."

Apollo wasted no time. Felicity watched him launch himself into the sky, golden and shining, a bolt of lightning transformed into a creature so beautiful it made her heart ache to look at him. Part of her was already coming up with mitigation plans if he was spotted—*call it an atmospheric mirage, or storm activity, there must be something we can use, especially if there's no video footage*—but most of her attention and all of her heart was out there with him, riding the darkening storm clouds.

*We should never have left Hideaway undefended*, she thought, and shivered.

They took Maya's van back to town. Tomás had transformed into human form—an adorable mop-haired toddler—and was busy blowing raspberries to himself in the back seat, and Maya drove, which left Felicity free to worry.

*I'm sure it's nothing,* she told herself. Over and over again.

Maya glanced at her. "I hope we haven't caused any problems for you."

"God, no. Don't even think it."

"I can't believe that you're on vacation in the same town that I was running away to." Maya shook her head, eyes back on the road, then laughed tiredly. "I've been so—exhausted and terrified. What if they didn't want us? What if Tomás decided not to shift, and I couldn't prove he was a shifter? What if it was all a hoax and I ended up revealing Tomás to a group of random strangers, in the middle of nowhere?" She gulped back a sob. "And suddenly—you're here, and you understand, but I'm making trouble for you…"

"You're not making trouble for me. Someone else is making trouble for me. And for you! Fuck 'em all," Felicity said firmly.

Maya went bright red.

*Ah ahhh,* Felicity thought. *And exactly who did you have in mind when I said "Fuck 'em", huh?* "So," she said out loud, all innocence. "Blackburn…"

Maya groaned.

"…is a dragon shifter, too?"

"Tch. That isn't what you were going to say."

"Oh, I'll still say it."

"Don't…"

"Is there something between you?" The way Blackburn had looked at Maya—she knew that look. She'd seen it in Apollo's eyes. "You're *sure* he isn't Tomás's—"

"No!" Maya yelped. She sighed. "No. He isn't. And that's… it's complicated."

Felicity took a deep breath. *Complicated like being the mate of a dragon who's convinced he isn't good enough for you?* "Tell me about it."

"I'd rather hear it from you." Maya shot her an encouraging smile. "How long have you known about shifters? Oh my God. Don't tell me forever. If I could have told you about Tomás months ago, I'll scream."

"I only found out a week ago, when this gold-colored dragon screamed down out of the sky and saved my life." *Only a week?* It felt like so much longer.

A week of not being terrified of Montfort. Of not tiptoeing around in her own life like she was terrified of knocking something over and drawing his attention on herself, even when she wasn't in the office.

Ever since she'd set foot in Hideaway, she'd been free. And now Maya and Tomás would be, too.

They had just emerged from the trees. Fog was rolling in from the sea, and the clouds overhead were looming lower and lower, but it was still clear enough for Hideaway to gleam like a pile of jewels. The strange before-the-storm half-dark only made the lights shining from windows and streetlamps more bright and cheerful. Felicity's heart swelled as she began to point out different locations. They weren't yet over Apollo's perimeter spell, but they were close, and anticipation prickled across her skin.

"The beach is amazing. Don't get me wrong, the water is *freezing*, but it's worth it to literally go swimming with dolphins and seals and everyone else in their shifted forms. And the ice cream parlor! Tess's ice creams are amazing. Look, you can just see the restaurant where everyone practically lives on Friday and Saturday evenings, and that's—"

She broke off. Her throat tightened. There was a big yacht in the bay, just within the mouth of the cove. That must be the boat Arlo was talking about. But that wasn't what made fear shiver down her spine.

A crowd was gathered on the main road. Apollo was there, his hair a golden beacon in the stormy gray; Harrison and Arlo were with him. Jacqueline was there, too, and Lainie. Mrs. Hanson was standing next to Antonia, who was wringing her hands about something, and in front of them all, Bruno was shouting about something.

Dread pooled in Felicity's stomach.

"Slow down a bit," she urged Maya.

They crossed the boundary. Apollo's magic spun around her, and she caught her breath. It was like coming home. The air was a little brighter, a little warmer. The whole world was more welcoming. And the town lay below, a tumble of lights and happiness, hidden and precious, like…

Whatever she'd been about to think was knocked out of her head as they drove down the hill and got close enough for her to hear Bruno's shouts.

"All I did was short a couple of fuses! Nobody was meant to get hurt!"

Felicity's heart thudded. *Bruno? Bruno's behind the attacks?*

"You did a fair bit more than that." Apollo's voice was more serious than she'd ever heard him. The air tasted of danger.

This was her dragon in his element. Surrounded by his own magic, ready to defend what was his. The hairs on the back of Felicity's neck stood on end.

"What's happening up there?" Maya asked.

"Um—" How to explain that the sanctuary Maya so desperately needed had been under attack? "Another… shifter thing."

"Another fight?"

"I hope not. Could you park here and stay back? Just a bit?"

She got out of the car.

Antonia was trying to put an arm around her son, but he kept pushing her away. "I'm sure this is all an awful misunderstanding," she said, her voice brittle. "Maybe there was an accident? Bruno's been working so hard. This vacation was a reward from his college program for doing so well—"

Bruno's voice burst out again, shrill with something that sounded almost like panic. "Nobody was meant to get hurt! If you'd revealed where your treasure was at the start, I wouldn't have had to keep going!"

*Apollo's treasure?* Frowning, Felicity strode forwards. What would Bruno want with a dragon's hoard?

"It wasn't my fault!" Bruno sounded hoarse. Felicity almost felt sorry for him, until he saw her through the crowd. Something unpleasant flashed behind his eyes. He pointed at her. "She's the one you want! She's been spying on you this whole time!"

Felicity stopped breathing.

Apollo let out an exasperated hiss. "Good God, must we go over this again? Every time anything happens in this town, it's *Ooh, they're going to sell off half the town to outsiders,* or *Ooh, they'll reveal Hideaway's secret to the world and endanger us all.* Please, find a new playlist, I *beg* you. The Sweets played this one out years ago."

"Ask her." Bruno thrust his chin out. "Go on. Ask her why she's *really* here. I didn't want to do any of this! *She's* the one who's been working for him for years! *She's* the one he sent to screw you guys over!"

"Stop trying to deflect blame. You almost burned down the entire building! Felicity has nothing to do with—Felicity?"

Apollo stared at her. Her face had betrayed her. She knew that, in a distant, cold way. As distant and cold as everything felt at that moment.

Even Apollo's magic. And that was a good thing, wasn't it? Because she didn't deserve the comfort of his power right now. She never had. She'd stolen her way into his life on false pretenses and taken what was never meant to be hers.

Her breathing was shallow. The world tightened around her.

"Felicity." When did Apollo get so close to her? She needed to explain. Apologize. There was no point trying to *explain*. Why would he believe she'd only been trying to protect him, when Montfort… "Felicity, it's okay. Listen to me, and breathe." His fingers were gentle on her cheeks.

"I wasn't," she forced out before her throat closed over again. She fought against it, ribs aching. "I never—"

"I know."

He cupped one hand behind her head, the other caressing her cheek. She was too numb to tell if his magic was holding her, too.

She searched his eyes, terrified of what she would find in them. "You know? How can you know?"

"I know you." Warmth filled his eyes. "I know you're fierce, and kind, and that coming to Hideaway was like taking the first deep breath you'd had in a long time. Whoever sent you here, you left that life behind the moment you set foot in my town."

"You—you trust me." She could barely make herself say the words.

"Of course I trust you. I love you, Felicity. You're the best thing that ever happened to me."

The steel trap digging into her ribs released her. She gulped in breath. "Montfort did send me here. But I never told him anything. Coming here, meeting you—it was like I'd been trapped underground my whole life and I could finally see the sun. I would never betray you. I just didn't want you to know that I almost had." Rain pattered on her face. "But if Montfort—wait. Montfort sent Bruno?"

Apollo's jaw tightened. "He admitted to it just before I arrived, apparently."

"But that means…" She turned to Bruno. "He already knew, didn't he? He knew what was special about Hideaway. He knew about shifters. That's why he sent you, to… try and find Apollo's hoard?"

"He said that if I caused trouble, the dragon would try to protect his hoard, and that would let us know where it was and he could come and take it!" Bruno's face twisted.

The raindrops came down harder, cool at first then shockingly cold. The light was fading. She wrapped her arms around herself. "How could you do that? You're a shifter. Hideaway is meant for people like you, and you know what he'll do if he gets a foothold here!"

"Do you think I don't know that? It's not like I had any choice!" Bruno spat as his mother tried to get him to calm down. "No, Mom, you don't get it! This vacation wasn't a reward, it was a way for him to get me here to do his dirty work. *She* was meant to make everyone suspicious of her being a human asking questions in Hideaway Cove, while I found out where the treasure was!"

*I was a decoy.* Felicity's chest thudded as she realized the true extent of Montfort's duplicity. She'd thought she was the spy. But she was a distraction, set up to take the blame for the mysterious attacks while Montfort got closer to his real target.

Except it hadn't worked out that way. Instead, she'd almost died, and Hideaway's biggest secret had flown out of the fog on golden wings to save her life.

Her fists clenched. "It was you. My car going crazy that first night—you did that."

Bruno looked anguished. "I didn't mean for that to happen! He told me to check whether you really were there. And—" He hunched back into himself. "—and to give you a shock. He said… he said he was sick of you always acting like you knew what was going on, and you needed a taste of not being in control."

Felicity felt sick. "Of course he did," she whispered. The rain was getting heavier. "I bet he was just freaking overjoyed when you told him what happened.

"He said it was good. That when things started going wrong, everyone would suspect you. Like you'd planned the whole thing."

"Right. Of course." Felicity's jaw ached. She couldn't tell whether it was from the tension of stopping herself from crying, or stopping herself from screaming in frustration and anger. She'd known Montfort was a monster, but this…

Apollo wrapped his arms around her. Bruno watched them both warily, as though he expected them to attack him.

His mother took a deep breath. "Why didn't you *tell* me, Bruno?"

He turned frustrated, desperate eyes on her. "Because you were so proud of me! When I got the scholarship, and the internship, and…"

*The good job.* Felicity's stomach sank. That was all her parents had cared about. That the job with Montfort was a *good job*. No matter that it was destroying her from the inside.

But Antonia was shaking her head. "None of that matters. I don't care how important this guy is. How dare he treat you like this!" She pulled him into a hug. "I wish you'd told me."

"It doesn't matter now, anyway," Bruno muttered into her shoulder.

Felicity dashed water off her face. The clouds were so thick that even the light was changing, turning sallow and yellow-red. "What do you mean, it doesn't matter?"

He gave a miserable shrug and pushed away from his mother. "It's too late now." His shirt started to collapse in on itself.

"Hey! Stop shifting and answer the question, you—hey! Come back!"

A vividly colored eel the length of her arm slithered out of the pile of clothes. Felicity took chase, splashing across the road, but was too slow to stop him from vanishing down the drain.

She blinked water out of her eyes, not sure whether it was rain or angry tears. "Damn it! You can't just run away!"

*Even if you're terrified?* a voice whispered in her head. *Even if running away is the only thing left you can do? Like when you quit your job and pretended you could leave everything from your old life behind you?* Her breath caught in her throat and she swore. "Bruno, wait. I'm sorry. We both—"

"Fee!" Maya had parked the car and was standing on the road with Tomás in her arms. She was shading her eyes with her free hand, staring out over the water. "What's going—oh no. Oh *no*."

Her eyes widened. Behind Felicity, Apollo swore. She spun around to see him staring into the storm, confusion and outrage mingled in his eyes.

"Felicity." Apollo's arm closed around her shoulders, and his voice was more serious than she'd ever heard it. Her heart quailed. "Get everyone inside."

Did he really think they would listen to her? After everything Bruno said? She steeled herself, ready to start trying to convince them regardless, but the words froze on her tongue.

Rain fell in sheets against her face, but she didn't stop staring out towards the sea.

Those weren't just clouds.

There was a *dragon* riding the storm.

What she'd taken for strange red clouds were huge wings the color of old blood. The dragon faded in and out of sight as rain crashed around it, so thick it was as though the ocean had leapt up and was crashing back to

Earth. Teeth flashed, then vanished. Cruel red eyes flashed in the gloom and were gone.

Cold gripped Felicity's heart.

*"Everyone get inside!"* she screamed.

In retrospect, it wasn't the deftest way to handle the situation.

Half the people present started to argue. The other half started to argue with the first half. If they'd been in animal form, there would have been bristling feathers and puffed-out tails galore.

And then a solid wall of rain hit them, and the dragon landed.

It was huge. The rain was too thick to see how far its wings spread out before it folded them against its sides, or how long its body and tail stretched out along the esplanade, but Felicity knew without a doubt that it was the biggest creature she'd ever seen.

And the expression in its dark red eyes was somehow, horrifyingly, familiar.

Felicity took an inadvertent step back. Apollo's arm tightened around her shoulders and wings of golden flame erupted from his shoulders, wrapping protectively around her.

The dragon shut its wings with a clap like thunder. Its neck shot forwards, bringing its head close enough for blood-red eyes to stare imperiously at their small group.

Fur and feathers exploded as Harrison and Arlo shifted. Felicity tensed, but Apollo didn't transform. His arm stayed wrapped around her, as though they weren't being stared down by a massive fucking dragon that had just appeared out of nowhere.

He squeezed her shoulder. Felicity remembered to breathe. Then he shot her a quick, sly smile, and she forgot how again.

"This is all very impressive!" he shouted, somehow managing to drawl lazily while yelling over the storm. "Welcome to Hideaway Cove. Well done on picking the most dramatic day of the year to visit! However, I'm afraid to inform you we've already had our allotted draconic stand-off today. You'll have to come back tomorrow."

The dragon hissed. Smoke poured from between its teeth and was immediately swept away by the pounding rain.

Apollo tipped his head to one side. "Now, far be it from me to dictate how anyone chooses to comport themselves," he said, his lilting voice underlaid with iron, "but perhaps you'd consider shifting into a form where everyone can hear you, not just the shifters among us?"

Scaled lips peeled back. Teeth gleamed.

"Apollo Jenkins," the dragon sneered. "*Draco foci.* I've heard stories about your people. I didn't expect much from a hearth-dragon, but I did expect more than this." Concrete cracked under its heavy claws.

For a moment, there was no sound but the roar of the storm.

Felicity's mouth fell open. "I'm not the only one who heard that, right? The talking dragon?"

The rain was too heavy for anyone to have heard her, but Apollo's lips brushed her ear. "You are not the only one. And may I add, in my capacity as the resident dragon: what the *fuck*? First a baby dragonling, now a dragon who can speak in shifted form? How am I meant to compete with that?"

She giggled, hysteria bubbling up too fast for her to catch.

The other dragon sneered. "Enough from you, Miss Park. You've done your job well enough, preparing the way for me. Now make yourself scarce."

Everything went still. The dragon hadn't even glanced at her, but she was pinned to the spot.

*It can't be…*

"Let me introduce myself, little hearth-dragon. I am *draco terribilis.* A warrior dragon." Dried-blood scales surged in the darkness, closing around them. "And thanks to you not understanding your proper place as a jumped-up foot warmer, I'm here to claim your hoard for myself."

Felicity's hand flew to the scrap of gold at her neck. He couldn't mean *this*, could he?

But that wasn't the worst. The worst was that she recognized that voice, even overlaid with smoke and ash.

"Montfort," she whispered.

# 33

# APOLLO

*M*ontfort. Felicity's fearful whisper told him everything.

Apollo stretched leisurely, flexing his wrists. "You know, only a few hours ago, I was thinking how much I would like to give you a piece of my mind about your treatment of my mate." His teeth flashed with the gleaming confidence of an apex predator. "But like I said, we've reached our quota of draconic grandstanding for the day. Which leaves me with nothing to do but show you the door."

Montfort sneered. "You don't stand a chance against me, you puny, flameless—"

Felicity squeezed his hand. It was all the encouragement he needed. Apollo soared into the air, transforming into his dragon form in a flurry of golden sparks. His magic danced beneath his wings. In less time than it took for Montfort to hiss in a breath, he whipped his tail around to slap him into the water.

Waves surged and Montfort lunged up with a roar of indignation.

Apollo was ready. He snapped his long neck forwards, lightning-charged teeth clashing shut an inch from Montfort's snout. Driving him deeper into the water, away from the buildings and the shifters who didn't have teeth and claws to defend themselves.

Montfort flailed. Saltwater sheeted off him as he gathered himself to leap into the air. His dragon form was larger than Apollo's. His scales were a dark, stale-blood red, his frame heavy-set and muscular compared to Apollo's lithe, sinuous shape.

*Speed versus brawn.* And he'd never actually fought a dragon before. But there was no avoiding this fight.

And he didn't *want* to avoid it. His dragon was ablaze with ferocious indignation and a white-hot hatred for the dragon who'd invaded his town. It boiled with rage.

*Defend Hideaway. Protect our mate.*

Apollo harried Montfort deeper into the water as the larger dragon struggled to get its wings clear. Other forms slipped into the sea: Caro and Tess, their shifted forms cutting wakes through the waves, and the dolphin shifter Menzies. Apollo felt a sudden urgent jab at the edge of his mind—Arlo convincing his kids not to follow the other water shifters.

**Get them away from the main street,** he sent to Arlo.

**On it. And the others, too. Your girl's looking after Lainie.**

Relief flooded through him. Felicity making sure Lainie got somewhere safe meant she would be safe, too.

While he dealt with Montfort.

**What are you hoping to achieve here, exactly?** Apollo spoke directly into Montfort's mind, hoping to goad him into being too angry to think straight and put up a useful defense.

Montfort roared. Flames burst from his mouth—but Caro knocked him sideways, and the fire sizzled into steam as it hit the water.

**Felicity told me about your little problem with keeping your temper. If you wanted to get into hot water, surely you didn't have to come all the way here?**

**That's not why I'm here! Idiot!**

**What is it you're after, then?**

"What is any dragon after?" The sound of Montfort's human voice growling out of his dragon mouth sent a shiver of strangeness down

Apollo's spine. "Your treasure. The thing which gives your existence value. And I'll take it. Starting now!"

He burst upwards, huge wings pounding the air as he took flight. Apollo wheeled out of the way. But Montfort wasn't the only one who'd taken wing. Mottled gold and brown flashed through the driving rain—Harrison in his griffin form.

Montfort was completely focused on Apollo. He shot towards him, breathing out another spear of flame.

Apollo dodged. Montfort whipped his neck around.

*Shit,* Apollo thought. *He doesn't need to out-fly me. I need to out-fly his fire.*

*Or at least keep his attention until Harrison can get his claws into him.* With his vicious talons and powerful beak, an attack from Harrison could easily disable one of Montfort's wings. Given the choice between floundering in the water and being rescued and firmly escorted out of Hideaway Cove, surely even a dragon would accept they were defeated.

Apollo's own dragon bared its fangs. A polite dismissal was too good for a creature like Montfort. It wanted to see the other dragon crawling on its belly. Conquered and shamed and powerless. Montfort deserved nothing less, for tormenting their mate and threatening their home.

*The longer he's here, the more opportunity he'll have to hurt the town,* Apollo reminded it. His dragon hissed with displeasure.

Apollo taunted Montfort, dodging fireballs as Harrison flew higher and higher. When Montfort turned back towards the town, he shot lightning at his tail. Montfort swung low, and Apollo swore. He couldn't risk sending lightning into the water—not with Caro and Tess and the others in there.

A huge black and white shape hurtled from the water and slammed into his side. Caro's orca form was nowhere near as large as Montfort's dragon, but her blow was enough to knock him from the air.

Enraged, Montfort turned on the orca shifter, but she wasn't his only problem. One wingtip brushed the water and he snatched it back with a shriek. An alligator hung from it for a second, then dropped back into the water.

*Be careful, Tess!* someone called from the beach.

Frustration rolled from Tess's mind like water overflowing a dam, but she stayed silent. Apollo could sense her lurking beneath the water, waiting for her next chance.

With all of them working together they could tire Montfort out until he was ready to surrender. Apollo broadcast his plan to the others and glanced back to shore.

Where were they? He reached out with his magic.

*There.* The inhabitants of Hideaway Cove were taking the advice of the town's name. The cliffs were riddled with caves—perfect hiding places. More flameproof than the town's wooden buildings. He sensed Arlo herding the kids along, and a dozen other families, most of them shifted to animal form to move more quickly.

Felicity wasn't among them. She was in a car, speeding up the road leaving town. She wasn't alone: Lainie was with her, and Maya and Tomás.

Leaving town. It made sense. The farther away from Montfort his mate was, the better. And Lainie—Harrison wouldn't be able to live with himself if something happened to her. As for Maya and Tomás, the last thing any of them needed was for the little dragon to decide he wanted to fly away from mama and join the fight.

But it still hurt. His mate, leaving him. Leaving his magic. Leaving his town.

*I'm supposed to protect them all. Instead, they're fleeing.*

Frustration rippled over his scales. He snapped at Montfort and darted away, drawing the red dragon further from the shore. Harrison was circling high above them; the rain was so heavy, he was sure Montfort hadn't seen him.

Montfort shot flames at him. Apollo swerved away and he turned his flames on the water. Steam billowed as he breathed a line of fire into Caro's path.

*Now!* Apollo called to Harrison.

The griffin dived towards Montfort.

Th red dragon was distracted, chasing Caro through the water with his flame. Harrison shot through the rain like an arrow from a bow, fearsome beak and claws ready.

And then Montfort twisted around and breathed fire over him.

*No!* Apollo screamed. Harrison gave one pained jerk and tumbled through the air. His psychic shriek of pain cut off partway through.

Time stood still. Apollo flattened his wings against his sides and raced to catch his friend. It took an eternity. Even his heartbeat felt like it had slowed down. And Harrison was falling. Too far below him. Too fast.

And then suddenly he was close enough to wrap his claws around him. Apollo beat the air with his wings, hovering a scant few feet above the waves. The smell of burned feathers hit him.

Harrison groaned.

*Shift back to human form!* Apollo commanded.

A black fin cut through the waves. Caro was coming up fast beneath them.

Harrison groaned again. *Working on it. Leave me with Caro and go kick that asshole's face in for me.*

He shifted slowly, gritting back pain. Apollo lowered him carefully into the water, where he grabbed hold of Caro's dorsal fin. His human form wasn't burned, but he still winced as the saltwater lapped over him, pain echoing through his body.

"Apollo!" Felicity's voice soared over the water.

His head snapped around. Why wasn't she in the car? She was running down the hill, hand raised to point at—

Montfort. The attack on Harrison had been a distraction.

He had already reached the town.

The massive dragon landed heavily on the promenade, smashing the railing with his armored tail and cracking through the concrete with his claws.

And Felicity was running towards him.

Apollo roared and flew towards them both. His mate was standing between Montfort and the rest of the town. Why? Then he saw it. A tiny streak of color on the sidewalk. Bruno. He must have crept back out of the pipes when Montfort flew off.

Felicity was protecting the person who'd attacked the town?

*Who was bullied and terrified into doing it. The same way she was.*

The memory of Felicity's face when Montfort revealed the truth was burned into his mind. She had actually thought he would reject her for it. For surviving for years under Montfort's hideous influence—and as soon as she was free, doing everything she could to protect the town he had in his sights.

And now she was facing down the monster. Alone. One human against a dragon.

His magic bunched around her fists. As though it wanted her to use it, but something was preventing it. Apollo raced towards her as quickly as he could, weaving magic as he flew—a new pattern in the protective spell that covered the town.

He'd never been skilled at weaving spells in dragon form. Bolts of lightning, yes; protective magic, no. The pattern stretched and twisted, but his attempts to shape it into something useful were as fruitless as Felicity's. *Damn it!*

"You think you can stop me?" Montfort hissed. "I'll take what I want from this town, and you'll beg me to give your job back."

"There's nothing you could ever offer me that I'd want," Felicity told him, her teeth bared in a snarl. "And there's nothing here for you! Leave us alone!"

"You still think you can lie to me? I know your pathetic boyfriend has a hoard here. I can smell it. I'll find it and then you'll both pay for your disloyalty. You and that slimy vermin hiding behind you."

"There's no gold here! No treasure!"

"No. Not gold." Montfort drew a slow breath, as though he was savoring the taste. "Something *better*. Something I've never smelled before. No wonder all the stories of hearth-dragons talk about their strange treasures. Treasures they should give up to real fire dragons! I *will* have it!"

Apollo landed beside Felicity. He curled his tail around where she stood and sent sparks into the air, an electric barrier between her and Montfort. Delicate spells were beyond him in this form, but a wall of lightning he could manage.

But Montfort wasn't going after Felicity. Bruno was back in human form and had crept around as Apollo landed. The teenager was wide-eyed and bow-backed with terror, but he held himself steady as he and Montfort circled one another.

"It's a little late to play the hero, isn't it?" Montfort sneered at him.

"You leave him alone!" Antonia stormed up, her hair and dress plastered against her body but her expression blazing with ferocity. "You *monster*. How dare you make a teenaged boy do your dirty work!"

"His talents were going to waste!" Montfort whipped his tail. Heavy and covered in knobbly spikes, it looked like it belonged on a dinosaur, not a dragon. "And you weren't complaining when I plucked him out of that terrible school you sent him to and put him on a path to becoming someone *worth* something. I remember how you primped and preened when I said I'd pay for his college fees. *Pathetic.*"

Antonia's eyes flashed. "You—"

"You're even more useless than he is. And even his little tricks are only good for one thing."

"Leave her alone!" Bruno yelled back, his voice cracking. "And leave this town alone! These people were good to me. I won't let you destroy their home!"

"More than you already did?" Montfort snapped his jaws at Bruno.

Antonia ran between them and Montfort smacked her out of the way with one of his wings. She fell heavily and Bruno ran to her side. "Mom!"

Montfort's tail lashed the air. "Stop wasting my time! If you're going to do something, do it!"

The air around Bruno shimmered. He bent over, his spine twisting sinuously.

Apollo's dragon rattled its scales in warning.

He braced himself. Bruno had already torn through his magic twice. Whatever his electrical powers were, if he used them to attack Montfort, would it damage his magic as well?

Electricity crackled around Bruno's fists and Apollo tensed. There was his answer. His magic skittered away from the other shifter's powers like magnets put the wrong way round.

Bruno stuck out his chin, stared up at the red dragon—and ran.

Montfort's voice thundered as he chased him. "Coward! You betrayed me for this? A pathetic town, clinging to existence at the edge of the world? You'll crawl through the dirt to beg my forgiveness!"

*He's leading him away from his mom.* Antonia had gotten to her feet but was leaning heavily on one leg. She stared after her son with an expression of horror.

Montfort's huge tail swung behind him, smashing one of the struts holding the pier up. A shudder rocked through Apollo as his magic swelled around the break, reinforcing the threads around the ice cream parlor.

It wasn't enough. The pier creaked and collapsed into the water, taking the ice cream parlor with it.

The destruction hit Apollo like a blow to the chest.

Montfort didn't need to attack him. If he destroyed any more of the town, he'd take out Apollo, too.

Unless he dismantled his spell first.

Magic poured through him, the same unstoppable drain as before. He pulled on the threads of his spell. They didn't move. He wasn't altogether surprised, in a vague, panicked way; it was always easier to weave the protection spell in his human form. His dragon mostly enjoyed looking over it, but never actually wove or mended it. The same must be true for unraveling it.

His dragon fought the shift. Its shriek of indignation echoed in his head as he finally returned to human form with a force of effort that sent him to his knees.

"Apollo!" Felicity crouched beside him. "I understand what Montfort was saying now. You have to—"

"Remove my protection spell. I know. It's the only way I'll be able to defeat him." He gasped as his dragon raged inside him. Scales rippled over his arms as it fought to get out. "It—I—I can't fight him if all my power is going into healing the spell."

Did he have time? Montfort was still chasing Bruno. A distraction, whether the young shifter intended it or not. Apollo closed his eyes and sank into his magic.

The spell lay across his lap, part fishing net, part tapestry of golden threads. There was a tear near the ice cream parlor. Of course, he'd already unraveled and rewoven that part already, hadn't he? Unraveling the whole thing should be simple. Just pull it to pieces and don't put it together again. Take all the magic he'd put into the town over the years and put it…

The ruby cufflink glinted in his memory. Put it into a hoard? Yes. That felt… right.

He concentrated and tugged on the broken strands, and they unraveled more. Yes—that was it. Like watching Marjorie Hansen frog one of her hand-knitted cardigans halfway through because she'd messed up her stitching.

The pattern came undone. The spell dissolved. He wound the unraveling power back over itself like a skein of yarn, adding it back to the core of magic in his soul.

And then Felicity was in front of him, gripping his wrists with all her strength. "Stop!"

# 34

# FELICITY

**"S**top!"

Felicity threw herself headfirst into the spell. The constellation of stars around Apollo was already dimming as he took his magic back. She looked down into his arms and her vision doubled. She was standing in his spell and seeing it in his arms at the same time; the star-garden around her and a woven net of pure magic that Apollo was holding and pulling apart like a piece of knitting.

His head snapped up. "Felicity?"

"Don't destroy the spell!"

"I must. You heard him. He thinks my hoard is hidden somewhere here and he'll tear the town apart to find it. The power drain will destroy me. I won't be able to protect anyone." Desperation tinted his eyes. "I won't be able to protect *you*."

*But it's wrong.* She knew it, bone-deep, like she knew how to breathe. And just like knowing how to breathe, as soon as she started to think about it, it got away from her.

She gritted her teeth. For one shining, terrifying moment, as she felt Apollo begin to unravel the spell, it had all made sense. How?

Something Montfort had said…

*Flameless whelp.*

*Not Draco terribilis. Not terrible, but… a little hearth-dragon… With a strange treasure unlike anything else…*

*Treasure.* But Apollo didn't have any treasure.

He only had his magic, and Hideaway, and—

Her golden dragon's words echoed in her head. *I thought some great treasure had come to Hideaway. And I was right. You are my treasure, Felicity.*

No, that wasn't it. Not yet.

*It's not gold. It's better than gold.*

*Little hearth-dragon.* A hearth was part of a house, wasn't it? The fireplace where food was cooked and the family gathered for warmth and companionship.

What had Apollo said about visiting his grandfather, the one who collected men's jewelry… and apartments in his expensive high-rise? That he could feel his grandfather nipping at his heels as he left. Like he was being pushed out by an invisible force.

What if a hearth-dragon's hoard wasn't gold, but something else? And their magic… not fire magic, not destructive, but something that protected people, kept them safe…

The old man had it wrong. He'd never given Apollo any of his hoard, because his hoard wasn't the lifetime supply of cufflinks, it was the *building.*

And the cufflink wasn't Apollo's hoard, either. He could have stolen gold from a thousand dragons, and it still wouldn't be his hoard.

"I have to protect Hideaway," Apollo said. His dragon screamed behind his eyes. "I have to protect you."

"Then don't let him hurt the town or your spell. Don't let him even *touch* a single brick!" She moved her hands from his wrists to his hands, holding them together in hers. "Like Tomás with his watch."

He frowned. "But—"

"We were wrong. You do have a treasure. It's been here all along. Hideaway is your treasure, Apollo. Hideaway is your *hoard*. Now *throw him out!*"

# 35

# APOLLO

*Hideaway is my hoard?*

It should have sounded crazy. Instead, it was completely right. Like he'd been looking at the world through a clouded window and Felicity had just wiped it clear.

Apollo stared down at the gleaming tapestry in his hands, and the shining star-garden around him. He'd told Felicity that dragons were sneaky, and conniving, but he'd never truly felt the truth of that until now.

Montfort had almost tricked him into giving up a hoard he didn't even know he had.

His dragon rose up inside him, fierce and angry. *Hideaway is my hoard.* The town he'd protected for most of his adult life. The town where he'd made his most precious memories, and watched his friends make treasured memories of their own. He'd watched Tess transform the ice cream parlor from the world's most terrifying dessert counter to a vital part of summer afternoons. Hideaway was where Arlo had transformed from a gruff loner to the alpha of an eclectic pack, and where his mate had blossomed as adopted mother of three seal children and an ibis shifter. Where those kids had not so much blossomed as exploded with the confidence that came from having a safe home where they were loved. Where Harrison was about to become a father to a tiny baby whose parents had both known loss and pain, but who would grow up among friends and neighbors who had rejected the cruel secrecy that had hurt Lainie so much.

Of *course* Hideaway was his horde. He'd never cared about gold, because gold wasn't the treasure that called to his soul. This was: a home for those who needed it, a sanctuary where people with no place in the outside world could be free and safe.

And there was no way in hell he was going to let Montfort take it from them.

He opened his eyes. Felicity was kneeling in front of him in the same position she had been in the spell. Her hands tightened over his and her voice was little more than a whisper, tight with urgency. "I'm right, aren't I?"

"Always." He kissed her, fast and passionate, and his magic sang an aria over her skin. *Yes, yes, I remember why I wanted a hoard,* he told it. *Give me a minute to save the day first.* "Sweetheart?"

"Yes?"

"I'll be right back."

He stood and shifted at the same time. His dragon form took up the full width of the promenade, his wings like two shining sails. The sun was still hidden behind forbidding storm clouds, but his magic burnished his scales to a blinding gleam, making him the perfect target for the dull red dragon at the far end of the road.

He shouldn't have been surprised when Felicity scrambled up his foreleg to sit on his shoulders.

"You're not going anywhere without me," she said. "Now let's take the trash out."

Apollo grinned, lips curling back over sharp teeth. He couldn't talk to Felicity in this form, but he didn't need to. His magic formed a lacework over her skin without him even thinking about it, like a harness to hold her on his back. There was none of the usual awkwardness of spell casting in his dragon form. He and his mate were one, and his magic knew it.

*MONTFORT!* he roared. Across the bay, the red dragon's head rose. Murderous thoughts poured from his mind as seagulls dive-bombed him.

Apollo laughed. The other shifters weren't all hiding. Even the smallest had come out to defend their town.

"Cowardly whelp! What sort of dragon hides behind *birds*! And—" He shook one massive back leg. "Damned alligator!"

Apollo laughed. *Ready for round two?*

He didn't give Montfort a chance to respond. With a quick telepathic message to the other fighting shifters, he leapt into the air.

Rain crashed down around him as he took to the sky. The air was taut and heavy with the promise of lightning. On his back, Felicity hollered with delight.

Montfort shook off his attackers and flew towards him, rain sheeting off his massive red wings.

Apollo wheeled up, fighting the storm for altitude. Lightning speared down, thunder rippling a scant few seconds later. Montfort laughed. "You couldn't fight me with a griffin on your side. You think you have any chance alone, with your mate on your back? Give up now before I roast you both alive!"

Montfort's shouts were barely audible over the storm, but his telepathic voice crept into Apollo's mind with crystal clarity. *Or maybe I'll only roast your mate. Isn't it a shame, how humans are so bad at healing themselves?*

*I won't let you touch her.*

Mocking laughter echoed in his skull. *Didn't your griffin friend's fate prove to you I don't need to touch anyone to get what I want?*

Apollo whipped around as Montfort breathed a lance of fire at him. The flames hissed and boiled as they hit the rain. Steam filled the air and heat ghosted along one of Apollo's wings.

Felicity swore. Apollo shot lightning at Montfort and grazed his side, trying not to think what would have happened if he'd been a second slower.

He wheeled up, gaining altitude as the storm raged around them. The lightning strikes were getting closer; thunder tumbled with each shattering crack of light. Soon the heart of the storm would be on top of them.

And Apollo's attention would be split between defending his hoard from lightning strikes and driving Montfort off.

Even as he thought it, a tremor went through his magic. It was as though leaving town earlier had weakened his grip on his spell—or weakened the spell's grip on Hideaway. It had made unraveling it easier.

But he didn't want it to unravel anymore. He needed more power. More control.

How far above Hideaway did his spell reach?

Montfort was rising to meet him. The protection spell twanged like a too-tight string, and suddenly Apollo understood.

*Montfort* was weakening his spell. Every second the enemy dragon spent within Apollo's hoard, his connection to it weakened.

But how to get him out?

The answer was so obvious he laughed with delight. His spell was wound as tight as a bowstring; all he had to do was let it loose.

He dove through the driving rain. Montfort wheeled out of his way and began to circle him, slow but utterly confident that he was unstoppable. Steam billowed around his jaw as he readied another flame.

Lightning flared. Thunder roared as electricity arced from the sky, seeking the highest point to ground itself in. Apollo grabbed its power and twisted it around himself, a crackling, luminescent edging to the cloak of his own magic. Felicity shouted something he couldn't hear above the rain, but he didn't need to; her fierce heart thrummed within the blazing core of his magic, and he felt her clutching for the reins of his power. *Now!*

*All yours,* he told her silently, and together they let his magic loose.

White lightning streaked towards Montfort. The other dragon's flame had been a lance; this was a god's fury given form. The rain around it didn't steam, it vanished, blasted out of the way by Apollo's power.

The bolt hit Montfort dead on and sent him tumbling through the air. He struggled to regain his wings but the magic was relentless. It poured through Apollo, white-gold and shining, transforming the power of the storm into a magical sword that pinned Montfort and drove him out over the sea.

When the magic hit the boundary of Apollo's hoard, it vanished. Montfort dropped like a stone. The splash he made sent his yacht rocking in the swell. Water boiled around his head as he surfaced again, wings and claws scratching at the waves.

*You'll pay for this, whelp!* he screamed. Then his outstretched claws hit the boundary, and his scream of rage turned into one of pain.

He couldn't get through. Whenever he touched the invisible barrier between Hideaway and the outside world, there was a sound like metal on concrete and he reeled back, screeching. Apollo's dragon let out a roar of triumph. He had protected his hoard.

For her. For Felicity. And for everyone else who made Hideaway Cove such a treasure.

He stretched his wings wide. All the power he had drawn from the storm—and since when could he do that?—had cleared the skies, and warm sunlight shone down on him and Felicity.

She stroked his neck. Sparks danced where she touched him.

His dragon sighed with satisfaction. Its muscles ached pleasurably, like after a long flight, or like his human body did after a lot of physical activity. Ah. That was a bad sign, wasn't it? Using so much magic at once always drained him. And…

Exhaustion weighed down his wings, as much mental as physical. Beneath him, the tremor that had run through his spell was growing more intense.

He coasted back down to land on the promenade. Felicity slid from his back and his shifted into human form in time to catch her in his arms and whisper a brief prayer of thanks that he wasn't the one who needed catching. Any moment now his magic use would catch up with him and he would need to crawl off and hide with a migraine.

His magic thrummed. He groaned aloud.

"Hey." Felicity cupped her hands around his face. "You okay in there?"

"Just waiting for my heroic aura to fade and leave me with a murderous headache," he muttered. Damn, damn, *damn* his migraines. He didn't want to lie down in a darkened room—well, he did, but not with a damp cloth over his eyes. With his mate. Arousal surged restlessly within him.

"I don't think that's going to happen." There was a smile in Felicity's voice. She opened her eyes. There was a smile on her face, too. It took him a moment to remember she was probably talking about him having a migraine, rather than where his mind had immediately gone.

"I'm afraid there's no escaping it. That was more power than I've ever used at once before. It's… shaken something loose. The whole spell is rattling around like a car engine on its last legs."

"Is it? That's not what it feels like to me."

He stared at her. Felicity's dark eyes were shimmering with a secret so delicious he wanted to kiss her to find out whether he could taste it on her lips.

"Listen," she urged him. "Listen to your magic. What's it telling you?"

Listen to his magic?

He closed his eyes.

The spell was still there. The storm hadn't burned it away, and his final attack on Montfort hadn't torn it to pieces. His magic had settled back into the net he'd woven and rewoven during all his time in Hideaway. Each thread, each knot and pattern, was familiar.

It told him that Harrison was singed, but not badly. That Tess was still soaring with adrenaline from fighting a *dragon*. That he'd been right about the risk of Tomás wanting to join the fight, too. He and Maya were perched on the very edge of his spell. They hadn't left after all. They were all safe.

But something was different about his magic. It was delicate, trembling. Wait…

He took a deep breath and, instead of reaching out into the weave to investigate it, let it settle over him. His skin hummed, and Felicity was right—his magic wasn't *trembling*, it was dancing. Singing, a chorus of bells made of pure light, of joy at being where it belonged. His hoard, acknowledged for the first time. So why did it feel as though it was on the edge of changing forever?

"Do you get it now?" Felicity asked gently. He looked down at her. The hint of a smile was teasing at the corner of her lips.

And he got it. Oh, God, did he get it.

"Oh," he said, eloquently.

"Oh?"

"I have the strangest feeling," he said, drawing it out to watch the mirth in her eyes sparkle brighter, "that there is something I have left unfinished."

"Really?"

"Mmm." He kissed her, experimentally, and the shiver running through his magic intensified. "Correct me if I'm wrong, but it was both of us who gave Montfort the shove before, wasn't it?"

"It certainly felt that way." Felicity tucked her smile against his chest.

"I gave you some of my power." He kissed the top of her head. "My… hoard."

Now it wasn't only his magic shivering. Felicity trembled, a gasp catching her, and the mingled wonder and pleasure suffusing Apollo's heart heated into something sharper and more longing.

He pulled her face up to kiss her again and she wrapped her arms around him, deepening the kiss until he thought his magic would shake itself apart with frustration.

All around them, the town gleamed under a layer of fresh rain. Water ran in shining rivulets down windows and rooftops. Everything was clean and cool and bright. Apollo stood with his mate in his arms as the last clouds wisped away.

He reached out with magical senses. *Harrison? Arlo?* he called out. *Is everyone—*

*Fine, Sparky.* Arlo's telepathic voice was husky and wolfish. *A few bruises, that's all. Ms. Flores and her son are with us. So's Antonia and that poor kid Bruno. We'll make sure they're looked after.*

A few bruises? *Harrison—*

*Swear to God, if you start fussing over me too...* Harrison grumbled. *My wing feathers got singed off. That's all. Lainie's taking it harder than I am.*

Of course she was, Apollo reflected silently. She'd just seen her mate almost burned out of the sky. Harrison knew that. He could tell by the tinge of embarrassed pride in the griffin shifter's psychic voice. Pride in the love his mate had for him. Embarrassment for causing her worry.

*Well, I hope you enjoyed your experience of dragon-repelling heroics, because there's not going to be a repeat of it,* he informed the others primly. *Montfort is gone for good.*

He opened his eyes.

"Just checking again?" Felicity asked, a smile dancing on her lips.

"Everyone's safe. Arlo's looking after Maya and Tomás. They couldn't be in better hands."

"The ice cream parlor is smashed—"

"Buildings can be rebuilt. And when it is, we can re-weave the spell there together.

Wonder danced in her eyes. "Together?"

He cupped her face in his hands. "Yes, together. My love. My perfect, fierce Felicity. You found me my hoard after all. And I think it's time I gave you the rest of it. Quickly." The last word came out in a possessive growl.

Felicity's happiness bubbled over into laughter. Apollo kissed her again, then shifted and leapt into the air with her on his back. Even the clouds were gone now—the sun beamed down on them, turning the still-water-swept town into a jewelry box. His little house was the central link in a necklace of glittering jewels, gold-bright and beckoning.

He landed on the balcony outside his bedroom, angling himself so that Felicity could slide easily from his back. The shock of magic on his skin as he shifted was dizzying, but not as intoxicating as her lips.

Magic humming through his veins, his hoard safe around him, he took Felicity in his arms, looked into her eyes, and said, "Felicity, everything I have, I offer to you. Will you take it, and be my mate?"

# 36

## FELICITY

Apollo's body was hot and strong against her, his muscular arms holding her firmly against the balcony door as he kissed her. His kisses. She would never get enough of his kisses. His hot mouth, tasting slightly of saltwater now; his tongue; the teasing drag of his teeth across her lips…

And the sizzle of magic as he pressed against her, leaving her aching and desperate.

"Inside," she managed to gasp as they both broke for breath. Her hand fumbled at the balcony door, and it swung open. Apollo lifted her before she could fall. She wrapped her legs around him, marveling at the naked glory of his body. Sun-burnished and glowing with power, wet hair sizzling with electric sparks, he was a god in human form.

And he was *hers.*

Wonderfully, gloriously hers.

He carried her to the bed and laid her down as carefully as if she were made of spun glass, then kissed her with a wild passion that made her thoughts fracture. "Apollo?"

"Yes, my love?"

*My love.* Her thighs clenched together. "It's not fair. You're naked and I've still got clothes on." As he pulled back, she rose with him, whispering in his ear: "I don't know what *giving me your hoard* entails, but I'm hoping it involves not being dressed."

He pushed her down onto the bed and stared at her. His golden eyes went dark with lust as his gaze lingered on her lips, her neck, her breasts and between her legs. His gaze was so penetrating it was as though she wasn't wearing anything at all.

"Yes," he said, his voice hoarse. "Take them off."

Magic thrummed around her. Felicity's breath caught in her throat. Slowly, with Apollo kneeling above her, she stripped off her clothes. Her t-shirt was soaking wet and there was no hiding the hard tips of her nipples even before she wriggled out of it. The goosebumps racing across her bare skin had nothing to do with being wet or cold. She reached behind herself to undo her bra and gasped.

Apollo wasn't touching her. He was still straddling her, his eyes hot with desire, but it wasn't his hands tracing patterns on her skin. It was his magic, caressing her with aching tenderness.

"Apollo…" she whimpered.

"Yes, my love?" Teasing fire sparked in the depths of his molten-gold eyes. "My *mate.*"

"You…" She gasped and cried out softly as his magic brushed across her lips. "How am I meant to concentrate with you doing that?"

He lowered himself over her, planting strong arms either side of her head. "Concentrate on what?"

Her fingers fumbled on her bra's hooks. "You're impossible."

"I'm a dragon." His smile promised wonderful, terrible things. "And you're my treasure. I want to enjoy every last inch of you before you finish unwrapping yourself."

His magical touch ran down her spine. She arched her back, letting out a frustrated moan as he moved just out of reach. Agonizingly tender touches brushed against her neck, then her lips, each one a tiny spark.

By the time she got her bra off she was taut and trembling with need.

Apollo's magic descended on her bare breasts. She moaned as it lapped over her nipples, teasing and nipping with sharper and sharper bursts of power. "Damn you," she moaned through gritted teeth, fighting with her jeans. At last, they slipped down over her hips.

And Apollo's magic followed.

Her hips bucked as his magic slipped between her legs. She strained towards him, desperate for the shimmering, ghostly sensation to become harder, more real, and he groaned with lust.

"You're gorgeous." His magic responded to his words, spreading out across her stomach, wrapping around her waist. "I can still hardly believe that you're mine." His magic tightened all around her. "My mate."

"Apollo—" She pleaded, finally kicked off her pants and reaching for him. Her arm didn't move. She looked at it and gasped. Sparks surrounded her wrist, tethering her to the bed. The other arm, too. "What is this?"

"I told you dragons carry maidens off to our towers and ravish them, didn't I?" He leaned over her, golden fire in his eyes. "If my hoard was gold, I would tie you up with it. But my hoard is…"

"Oh-h-h," she gasped as the manacles around her wrists sparked.

"…a little more complicated," he finished, a smile dancing on his lips. "You showed me that. Are you okay with this?"

His worried concern made her heart sing. Her Apollo, her dragon, was worried she wouldn't want literally the best thing to ever happen to her?

"More than okay," she reassured him. "Only… I can't touch you?" She couldn't keep a hint of complaint from her tone, and Apollo looked unreasonably smug. "I want to touch you."

"Say that again."

"I want to touch you, Apollo. My mate. My dragon. I want to kiss your lips, and your chest, and your cock. I want to make you come."

He let out a wordless groan and buried his face in the pillows by her head, still not touching her. "All in good time, my love."

She laughed. She couldn't help it. It was too much—too sensual, too wonderful, too more than anything she'd ever imagined. "Business first?"

He lifted his head and grinned at her, possessive and predatory. How could he have ever thought he wasn't a good dragon? "Business first."

Maybe because he was a very bad dragon. That made sense. As much sense as anything made, when her body was crying out to be filled.

"How do we do this?" Her own voice shook.

"I…" Despite how confident he had seemed until now, doubt edged in at the corners of his voice. But this… this was right. She knew it was, deeper than bone-deep, and as she stared into his eyes, she saw he knew it too, more instinctually than any draconic instinct he'd ever had in his life.

Slowly, carefully, he made a beckoning gesture with one hand, his wrist flexing as though he was conducting an orchestra.

And the sparks that had teased and tormented her followed his hand, streaming together into a ribbon of light.

"This," he said, and touched the backs of his fingers to her cheek.

She gasped.

When Apollo had touched her with his magic before, it had been like brushing up against a live wire. Thrilling. Exciting, with a hint of danger, and thoroughly erotic.

This was different. The magic still stung as it entered her, but then it grew, blossoming into an energy that hissed through her veins. She cried out, arching her back, as he continued his slow caress, tracing his fingers down her back to her collarbone, between her breasts, the curve of her belly…

Every touch was like a fire blazing across her skin. Every spark a new burst of power inside her.

This was what his magic had been singing about. This was what it had been waiting for. What it was all for. His magic, his hoard… *her.*

Apollo ran his fingertips up the insides of her wrists. His breathing was ragged; his eyes were fever-bright. It took her a moment to realize they weren't lit from within. The gold shining in his gaze was reflected.

It was her.

His magic had entered her. Golden light shimmered just beneath her skin, the way she'd seen scales glimmer beneath Apollo's skin when his dragon was close to the surface. The power that had touched her skin as a crackling fire now rolled through her.

Her awareness flashed out through the town. The magical bonds at her wrists were suddenly the only steady thing in a whirl of movement and sensation. His magic was so ecstatic to show her everything. Every window and every sunrise that had flowed through them. Chimneys that had seen the smoke from countless wood fires and captured the laughter and happiness of the families that had gathered around their warmth. Handrails and doorknobs worn smooth by generations of friends and families and welcome strangers. Layer upon layer of all the small ways Hideaway Cove had welcomed the people who lived in it.

"Felicity?"

Apollo's voice was an anchor line drawing her back to herself. She breathed in and the scent-memory of woodsmoke and home cooking and muddy shoes vanished, replaced by Apollo's scent of fresh sweat and magic.

"That was…" she began, and shook her head, unable to put words to it. "It worked. I don't know what it was, but it worked."

Apollo kissed her. "My mate," he murmured against her lips, and the buzz of his voice on her skin sent shivers through her.

"All yours," she whispered back, and he thrust into her.

His magic entered her in a storm surge that left her emptied of everything except need. She strained against the manacles holding her to the bed as he buried his cock inside her. She wrapped her legs around his waist, the only touch the claiming would allow her. His hips flexed beneath her thighs, and she drew him closer, harder, more, *more.*

One of his hands dug into her hips, the other cupped the back of her head as he kissed her, claiming her entirely. Every touch was a torment. Every touch was bliss. She cried out helplessly. When he pulled out, she was adrift; when he filled her ,she was overwhelmed.

"My hoard. My life. Everything I have. It's all for you." Apollo's voice was ragged, cut through with moans. He kissed the side of her neck and his lips stung with magic. "Yours."

It was too much. Too much magic. Too much sensation. Too much love. She was going to come apart at the seams. Apollo pushed inside her again, tilting her hips up to thrust even more deeply into her, and it sent her over the edge. Her whole body shook, her hands clutching at nothing. She gasped her mate's name.

Apollo kissed her again, gently, bringing her back down to Earth. She sighed against his lips.

"How do you feel?" he asked.

He was still hard inside her. Little tremors shivered through her thighs. She blinked, looking down at herself. "I'm not glowing anymore?"

"You are to me." His dragon rose up in his gaze, sharp and predatory, and Felicity licked her lips.

"And—"

She lifted one hand, then the other. The golden manacles were gone. And inside her…

*Magic.* A cascade of white-gold blossoms, twining around her heart.

Apollo stared down at her with his soul in his eyes. "It's yours, now."

"No." She pressed the back of her hand against his cheek, an echo of how he had touched her. "It's both of ours."

Magic flowed between them. She felt Apollo's surprise and delight through it and hoped he felt the same from her—the wonder, the happiness, the sheer fucking relief that they had each other. It had worked. Her crazy gambit had come through.

"Wait," he said, eyebrows creasing. "Crazy gambit? You mean you weren't sure that—"

"Shh," she told him, pressing a finger to his lips and tipping him backwards. He sprawled elegantly beneath her as she straddled his hips, not willing to lose the connection of his cock deep inside her.

He hadn't come yet, and she intended to fix that.

She trailed her fingers down his chest, marveling at the sparks that followed her touch. Apollo groaned. His cock twitched inside her and she dug her fingers deeper into his pecs, riding him until heat began to build inside her again.

"You're incredible," Apollo whispered, meeting every roll of her hips with his own. He held onto her waist, his hands firm and gentle at the same time. Magic sparked everywhere they touched and she sent it curling and teasing over his skin until both their breaths came in desperate gasps. "My love. My Felicity. My mate." Draconic gold gleamed sharp and possessive in his eyes. "*Mine.*"

She clenched herself around him and he came with an earth-shattering groan. He reached up and kissed her, his breath hot on her lips, his pleasure catching her and tipping her over the edge of another orgasm.

"*Mine,*" she whispered to him as their hearts beat as one, and magic wove itself in new patterns around them. There was no question the bonding had worked. Apollo's power didn't just shiver at her attention, now; she could weave it the same way he had. To protect Hideaway. "My dragon."

"My mate. My hoard is yours now." Apollo sighed and pressed another kiss into her hair. "My magic…"

"Is *ours*. Not mine. And the hoard is *ours*, too." She pushed herself up on her elbows and sank into the spell, pulling him with her. "See?"

The star-garden lay spread out around them, warmed by two glowing suns. One in Apollo's chest, and one in hers.

"Ours," he murmured, surprised and happy. "I thought…"

"That I would take it all?" She smiled. "No. We're in this together, my dragon. You can't offer me your everything and not expect me to share it with you."

"That's not very draconic of you." His voice was little more than a whisper, soft with pleasure.

"We make our own dragon-y rules, remember?" she reminded him, and kissed him again.

# 37

# APOLLO

They couldn't lie in bed all day. At least, that was Felicity's argument. He reluctantly gave in.

"We can't stay in the shower all day, either," she said sometime later. Apollo gazed up from where he was kneeling between her legs.

"No?"

"I—*mmph*—No! We have to go and… ahh…" Her hands fell against his head, fingers clenching briefly as he kissed his way along the crease of her thigh to her clit. "You make a very compelling argument," she grumbled at last.

"I do, don't I?" He hummed against her, reveling in the taste of her pleasure. Her soft gasps—and then much, much louder ones—fed his pride.

*That might become a problem*, he thought later, while they were both getting dressed. *I was unbearably pleased with myself even when I thought there was something wrong with my dragon. What am I going to be like now?*

"Intolerable," Felicity laughed when he shared his thoughts with her. She pulled him close for a kiss, then jumped away before he could keep her there. "Come on! We have to go and help with the cleanup. And I want to go explore my hoard." She spun around and sparked shimmered down her arms.

Apollo's dragon purred with satisfaction. "As you wish, my mate."

She laughed and took his arm. "*Our* hoard. Our town."

"You know you don't need to go down into the town physically to check in on our hoard. What does your magic tell you?"

She stared at him, wide-eyed. "Oh. Oh!" With a shaky gasp, she closed her eyes. Magic tugged and rippled around her, and Apollo fought the urge to sink into the spell of his hoard alongside her and watch her make her way through the avenues of her star-garden.

"Everything feels… wonderful," she said with a happy sigh. "It's like the town itself is happy. The town or your magic, maybe. Things are broken, but apart from that… everything's as it should be. The *people* are safe. That's what's important."

Apollo checked in with the others telepathically as they walked arm-in-arm down the hill. The older local shifters were quick to reassure Apollo that for all Montfort's bluster, he hadn't done much more damage than some of the bad winter storms that had carved through the town before Apollo moved in.

"I get the feeling they're actually excited about the opportunity to dig in and rebuild," he confided in Felicity as they walked. "I'm hurt. All the effort I put into keeping the town in one piece all these years, and what they really wanted was an annual barn-raising after an ice storm took someone's roof off."

Felicity laughed. "Maybe you'll have to roll through and shoot lightning at things every now on then. In the interests of community spirit."

Something scratched at the edge of Apollo's mind. Whenever he tried to focus on it, it disappeared, like he'd seen something in the corner of his eye and turned around to find it was a shadow, or a reflected flicker of light, or nothing, or—

*Or a baby dragon testing his boundaries,* he thought as they followed the sound of laughter to the promenade.

Maya was sitting in the middle of an adoring crowd, glowing with pride and awkwardness as Tomás crouched on her lap. He was in his dragonlet form again, with the gold watch hanging around his neck like an amulet. The curiosity prickling at Apollo's mind was the little shifter reaching out telepathically to what must be the biggest group of other shifters he had ever met in his short life.

Apollo sighed. "Arlo said he was looking after them. Of all people, I'd have expected him to know that doesn't mean throwing them to the tender mercies of a pack of baby-loving shifters."

The atmosphere couldn't have been more different to the crowd that had gathered earlier. What seemed like all the local kids were gathered around, as excited to meet Tomás as he was to meet them. Their parents were juggling stopping them from straight-out swarming Tomás and Maya, and keeping their own curiosity under control.

"How old is he?"

"And he started shifting *when?* And you didn't even know he was a shifter?"

Maya could barely start answering one question before another sprang up. "Just turned one—no, I didn't even know what shifters were—"

*Hello, dragonlet.* Apollo nudged Tomás's mind with the psychic equivalent of a head-pat and the little dragon fizzed with excitement. He clutched at his watch and stood upright on his hind legs, eyes wide.

Maya looked up and caught sight of them both. "Felicity!" she called out, sounding more than half relieved.

*Ah,* thought Apollo. "Time for a rescue mission?" he murmured in his mate's ear.

They gently extricated Maya and Tomás from Tomás's adoring fans and made their way down to the beach.

"Maya, I am so sorry," Felicity burst out as they found a driftwood log to sit on. "I completely abandoned you. I don't know what I was thinking."

*I think I know what you were thinking,* Apollo reflected silently.

"I think I know what you were thinking," Maya said at the same time. She narrowed her eyes mischievously at Felicity, then yelped and struggled with Tomás as he tried to wriggle out of her arms and escape back to his admirers. "Your friend—Arlo?—got us settled at the bed-and-breakfast. The woman who owns it was very… informative… about where she thought you had gone."

"Oh my god," Felicity moaned, and Maya laughed.

"Fee, I swear, if you try to apologize one more time." She looked back at the town, a strange expression in her eyes. A yearning, like she'd only just let herself admit what she wanted when she'd already arrived at it. "You've found me something I never thought could exist. A place where Tomás can be himself, and I can learn what the heck that means. And you're out from under Montfort's power. Don't be sorry. This is the best thing that could have happened for both of us."

The last traces of tension lifted from her face and Apollo reached over and squeezed Felicity's hand.

She looked up at him, her eyes full of light, and Apollo's heart sang.

This was what his magic was for. All those years of worrying there was something wrong with him because he wasn't interested in gold and jewels, when the real treasure was right in front of him—Hideaway Cove, this place of warmth and community and safety.

All he'd needed was Felicity to show it to him.

It didn't take long to clean up the immediate debris from the fight and the storm. Many hands made light work, even when a lot of the hands were wildly gesticulating as their owners retold how they'd bitten or swarmed at Montfort, instead of carrying broken boards and chunks of concrete. But even when the ruin of the ice cream parlor and the broken sections of the promenade were cleared away, Apollo's work wasn't over.

Because Hideaway—his hoard—was a place of warmth, and community, and safety, there was one more person they needed to talk to.

A few minutes later, he knocked on a door inside the B&B.

Antonia answered. Her face was drawn and anxious. "Don't worry," she said quickly when she saw him, with Felicity at his side. "We are leaving. We won't trouble you anymore. I can't tell you how sorry I am—and Bruno, too, he…"

Her face crumpled. Bruno stuck his head around another door in the room behind her, scowling. "Mom, who's—oh."

Apollo's heart twisted as he saw the effort Antonia took to pull herself together. "Bruno, dear, it's okay. I've told them we're going to be out of their hair in two shakes of a bunny's tail."

"Antonia," Apollo began, and Bruno strode forwards, fists clenched at his sides.

"Mom didn't have anything to do with this! If you want to take it out on someone, it's—it's me! I'm the one who did everything. I got the internship with Mr. Montfort. I told Mom this trip was a reward from the company because of my hard work. Like the research trip to Dunston last winter, except that was a practice run for this, wasn't it?" His scowl deepened, but not before Apollo glimpsed the misery it hid. And the self-hatred.

*Poor bastard*, he thought. *That explains Dunston, though. It was Bruno the whole time.*

Which meant the kid had been only a few miles away last year. So close to somewhere he could have been safe from Montfort's machinations. Anger rolled through him. *If I'd had any idea…*

"This is all horribly familiar." Felicity gave Antonia a lopsided smile. "I'm so sorry my asshole ex-boss got his claws into your life, Antonia. And you too, Bruno."

The teenager stuck his chin out. "Why're you apologizing to me? I'm the one who—"

"Who Montfort bullied and conned into doing his dirty work?" Felicity met his bullish look with one of her own and folded her arms. "I bet he didn't tell you before you got here that he expected you to blow things up. He kept that nice and quiet until you were already here."

Bruno's shoulders slumped. Antonia looked close to crying. "That doesn't matter, though, does it? Because when he did tell me to start breaking things, I did it. Isn't that why you're here? To throw us out and make sure we never come back, like you did to him?"

Apollo remembered the way Bruno had thrown himself in Montfort's path yesterday—one small teenage boy, desperate to do anything to make up for what he'd done. And he didn't think it had been enough.

*They're going to leave, and he's going to think he's a monster for the rest of his life.*

Apollo put on his most brilliant smile and spread his hands. "Actually," he said grandly, "I was hoping you would join us for dinner."

38

# FELICITY

Beneath his playfulness and overblown dramatics, and even beneath his thoughtful and kind interior, Felicity's mate had a cunning streak that made her love him all the more.

He took them all to have lunch at Caro's. Not upstairs, hidden away in the little mezzanine nook, but on the main floor by a window. Out in the open.

As soon as he picked the table, Felicity knew what he was planning. He wanted Bruno and his mother to be safe in Hideaway, too, and was beginning his campaign by showing everyone who walked by that he was welcoming them with open arms.

Antonia figured it out, too. The look of thankful relief she sent at Apollo made Felicity's chest ache for her.

It was only Bruno who hadn't yet caught on. Being sixteen and neck-deep in misery, she supposed she couldn't blame him for that.

Especially because she would have been the same, a few years ago. Even a few weeks ago. And she wouldn't have had the excuse of being sixteen.

"So," said Apollo before Bruno could gather enough half-scared, half-belligerent courage to speak up. "You're an electric eel shifter of some sort? That's one hell of a defense mechanism you have there. I thought for sure we were dealing with another magic user."

628

For a moment, Bruno looked as though he might explode. Then his shoulders sagged. "Why are you drawing this all out? I know we have to leave."

"Nobody's going to make you leave," Apollo said gently.

Felicity had been putting two and two together. "You're from the Young Achievers' Program, aren't you? I should have remembered sooner." The program had been a short-lived attempt at salvaging Montfort's social capital—short-lived because it had quickly become apparent that exposing smartphone-loving teenagers to Montfort's outbursts was a quick way to worsen his reputation, not fix it. "I thought we shut that down last year."

"He told me I made such a good impression, he wanted to keep me on. And this vacation was a bonus for doing so well." Bruno sunk into his chair. "But it was just my electric abilities, right? He just wanted to use me. And it worked. At first, he just asked me to tell him about what businesses were in town, how everyone got on with each other, and then—when you arrived… I didn't mean for the car to go crazy like that! I was only trying to short out the engine!"

Felicity's breath quickened as the memory of that night washed over her like ice water. She forced herself to breathe normally.

Apollo touched her arm. His magic flooded through her, driving away the cold.

"And of course, after that, Montfort leaned on you harder," he mused out loud. Felicity nodded. She was thinking the same thing. "If you refused to do what he said, all he had to do was threaten to reveal that you'd almost killed my mate, and I—another terrifying dragon—would have murdered you in cold blood."

Bruno looked confused at his contemplative tone. Apollo raised his eyebrows.

"Sorry, were you expecting me to go into a wild rage *now* at the fact that you endangered my mate? I already tried that when I thought I was the one responsible—well, it was more of a grim puddle of misery than a towering rage—and she didn't like it at all. I'm sorry to disappoint." He squeezed Felicity's wrist. "Frankly, even if it wasn't completely clear that all blame for the situation lay with Montfort, I don't think my mate would be very happy with me if I went after you."

"You've got that right." Felicity smiled at him, then turned back to Bruno, careful to keep her expression serious, but still friendly. "Montfort preyed on both of us, Bruno. If Apollo can forgive me for turning up in Hideaway with the intention of selling everyone out to my asshole boss, I can't turn around and hate you for doing the same thing."

"But you didn't actually *do* anything!" Bruno insisted. "That's why Montfort got so angry! As soon as you got here, you started lying to him about the town. He could tell you'd chosen them over him. And he said—he said we could make it look like *you* were attacking the town, and it would never be traced back to me! And when nobody turned against you, he told me to make it worse, and I thought the workshop was far enough away that nobody would get hurt but I didn't expect it to blow up like that, and…" His face twisted. "What am I meant to do now? Montfort gave me a scholarship to college. He owns our apartment building. He gave Mom a deal on the lease for her new studio."

"He crept into your life every way he could until he controlled everything around you." Felicity felt sick. No wonder Bruno's powers had felt so ice-cold and nauseating. He'd been trapped and hated every cruel thing Montfort threatened and goaded him into doing.

Antonia clicked her tongue. "I'm sure it can't be that bad," she said, not sounding sure at all. "It was such a good deal on the lease…"

"From the guy who just did his best to burn down this entire town," Felicity pointed out. Antonia winced.

"What are we meant to do?"

"It sounds as though you're both going to extend your vacation," Apollo said. He reached over and patted Antonia's hand. "Don't worry. You're safe here. Between my magic, and Felicity's insider knowledge, we'll figure out a way to deal with Montfort."

*Huh.* A surprised smile crept across Felicity's face. She hadn't thought about it like that before. She *did* have insider knowledge—all the intricate details of Montfort's business, and habits, and weaknesses. She'd spent five years using that knowledge to help him.

*Time to use it to undermine him instead*, she thought with a spike of savage glee.

The rest of the evening went by in a sunlit dream. Caro's was the beating heart of the town that night. Tables spilled out over the promenade, taking over the road for the evening. Darkness fell while they lingered over dinner and dessert. Fog blanketed the cove, a wooly comforter over the golden lace of Apollo's magic. *Their* magic.

Apollo introduced Maya properly to Harrison and Lainie, who started off talking about housing options and rapidly ended up talking baby. Lainie was overjoyed to have another non-shifter woman around who had experience having a shifter child. Bruno resentfully accepted that all was forgiven and swore to help repair the damage he'd caused. Conversations buzzed about the fight, and Apollo's strange magic, and how exciting it was to have another dragon around.

Montfort's revelation that Felicity had been sent to undermine Hideaway Cove hadn't gotten any traction with her new friends—especially after she'd helped drive him out of town.

She couldn't stop reaching out with her new magical powers. Every time she did, the realization she'd had during the fight with Montfort became more and more obvious.

Hideaway was a treasure. And Apollo's magic—*their* magic—was meant to protect it.

Felicity tucked her arm in Apollo's as they walked slowly along the promenade after the meal. Magic whispered to her as he closed his eyes briefly and followed the threads of power through the town.

She knew what he was seeing: Everything was as it should be. Every shining thread in the weft and weave of the town's magic glowed contentedly.

"Checking in?" Felicity rested her head against his arm.

"Like a mother hen counting her chicks," he declared, and stopped dead.

Felicity hid a grin, knowing what he'd found. His magic *wasn't* as he'd left it.

Every thread in his spell was doubled. Tiny flowers blossomed along the lacework net, delicate but full of life.

"You've been busy," he murmured, his eyes shining.

Felicity traced a line down his face. Sparks followed her fingertip, dancing on Apollo's skin. "I've got a lot of catching up to do," she told him. "There's the workshop to fix, and we really ought to double-check how far the spell goes out to sea. And—"

Apollo caught her mouth with a kiss. She let him, for a few very pleasurable moments, then played her ace.

Sparks shivered over her lips, sharp and hot. Apollo made a *very* appreciative sound.

"And there's this," she said innocently.

"Intriguing," Apollo murmured. He kissed her again and she teased magic along her tongue. "I think I'd like to hear more about... *this.*" He ran gentle hands down her spine, magic swirling in their wake, and Felicity moaned.

"Home?" she whispered, unable to keep a begging tone out of her voice.

Apollo's eyes burned gold in the foggy night. "Home," he agreed.

Home to their buttercup-yellow cottage on the hill, with the sea hidden beneath its blanket of fog below and the hills curled protectively around. Her secret, perfect sanctuary. A treasure to share and protect with her mate.

# EPILOGUE

## APOLLO

**"I** know what you're doing," Apollo's mate murmured sleepily from bed.

Felicity was lying on her stomach, one hand outstretched across the pillow where he'd been lying beside her until a few minutes ago. Her hair was tousled, and she hadn't actually opened her eyes yet, so he had no compunctions about continuing what he was doing.

"I know you know what I'm doing," he told her. "Now hush and let me do it."

"Sneaky dragon," she murmured, and yawned.

He looped one finger through the chain around her neck. The fine gold links shimmered as he ran his finger along until he found what he was looking for. The chunky, hideous cufflink he'd once thought was his hoard.

He had better plans for it, now.

Felicity lay patiently as he undid the necklace and pulled the cufflink free. Then she sighed and rolled over, fixing him with a loving, if slightly bleary, stare.

"Very sneaky," she informed him.

"Thank you, I thought so too." He picked up her hand and kissed it. "Go back to sleep."

"So you can keep being sneaky?"

"Precisely."

She closed her eyes. The temptation to stay with her was strong—the night before had involved very little sleep for either of them and for truly excellent reasons that Apollo intended to repeat many, many times—but he had a mission to complete.

It was a month since he'd claimed Felicity as his mate. Maya and Tomás were settled in with Maya's new job helping Mrs. Hanson at the B&B, and with Felicity's help Antonia was extricating her finances from Montfort Industries and preparing to move herself and Bruno to Hideaway Cove. Yesterday, the repairs on the workshop had been completed.

Which meant it was time to transform his shameful old hoard into something wonderful.

Harrison and Arlo were waiting at the workshop. They had the forge hot already, and everything ready to go.

"It might not end up perfect," Harrison warned him. "Jewelry is fiddly."

"I know." Apollo rolled the cufflink around on his palm.

"It doesn't have to be perfect." Arlo handed him a pair of pliers. "It's the thought that counts. Just don't do so bad a job it falls apart on her finger."

"If it goes that badly, I'm relying on you to help fake my death," Apollo told him, and began to work the ruby loose from its setting.

He'd been working on the design ever since Felicity moved in with him permanently. After talking with Harrison and Arlo, he had assumed it would take him a few attempts to come up with a design that felt right, but the first version that sprang up under his fingers had been perfect.

Turning the design from an idea on a page into a physical object—that was the challenge.

It had taken Apollo several attempts at carving the design in wax and test casting it in cheaper metals before the object in front of him matched the vision in his head. He'd carved the final version last night and it had been like a hot coal sizzling in the weave of his magic ever since. He was surprised Felicity hadn't sensed it. Quite possibly she had. The same way she'd known what he was doing that morning.

Once the ruby was loose, he melted the gold cufflink in a crucible and put both crucible and plaster cast into a centrifugal caster. The spinning of the centrifuge forced the molten gold into the cast. It was a special kind of magic; all that was visible of the ring was a little gold plug. The rest was hidden.

Apollo held his breath and submerged the plaster cast in water. The plaster melted away and his fingers traced the outline of a ring. It was ring-shaped; that was an excellent start. A complete circle, with the plug at one end and a smaller flattish surface at the other, where he would re-set the ruby. If it had all gone well. If he wasn't about to lift it out of the water and discover something had gone horribly wrong.

"Get it over with, Sparky." Arlo clapped him on the shoulder.

He lifted his hand from the water. Gold sparkled between his fingers. A perfect circle of precious metal.

"Oh, good," he said unevenly. Arlo squeezed his shoulder.

"Now for the fun part."

The "fun part" was hours and hours of sawing, sanding, and polishing. Gold dust peppered his fingertips by the time the ring was smoothed to his satisfaction. He'd made a hard task for himself, with the intricate pattern woven into the ring, but it was worth it. At last he set the ruby into the bezel and carefully secured it in place. It was finished.

As though on cue, magic brushed against his jawline. Felicity's scent filled his nostrils. She couldn't communicate with him telepathically even with her new magic, but she could do this—send tantalizing hints of herself to seduce his senses until he got the message and ran to her side.

He put the ring in the box he had ready for it and took the hint.

Felicity was waiting for him on the balcony of their house, sitting tucked into the wickerwork loveseat with a warm blanket around her shoulders and her arms around her knees. Her eyes shone as she looked up at him and he remembered the night they first met. How the fear and uncertainty had melted from her beautiful dark eyes as she took him in, and despite the foggy sky he'd sworn her eyes were full of stars.

They were full of stars now; reflected points of gold and white-gold light, as their shared magic strained to cross the space between them. He ran the back of his hand against one of her arms, delighting in the way she shivered as their powers met.

"Hello, love," he said simply.

"Hello." She tipped her head back and gazed at him. "Coffee's in the pot. And Tess popped by, so there are Danishes. There are even Danishes that Tomás didn't nibble on."

"Lucky us." Apollo tucked himself around her and the blanket around them both and reached for a pastry. Tess had been working out of Caro's kitchens while they waited for insurance to get sorted for the ice-cream parlor and making the most of Caro's mentorship. Her pastries were as delicious as her ice creams, but thankfully, much less adventurous. He inspected the Danish for bite marks. "How is Maya?"

"Oh, the usual. Apparently, Tomás has mastered flying up to the ceiling fan, but not down yet, so she had to borrow a ladder off Mrs. H. It sounds like that sort of thing is normal for flying shifters, though." She shot him a questioning glance.

"No comment." He bit into the Danish. Apricot with mascarpone, and no surprise chunks of seaweed or licorice or God knows what else. Delicious. "Any word on…?"

Felicity made a noise that was half-sigh, half-groan. "Whether she's ever going to tell me what the hell is up between her and her old boss, or not? That's a big nope."

"Give her time?" he suggested innocently.

"It's been weeks! And the *last* time I gave Maya time, she turned out to be hiding the fact that her baby could transform into a *dragon*. If I give her any more time *this* time, who knows what'll happen?" She threw her hands in the air. "I can't believe I have all this magic and I can't even use it to spy on people or bully my friends into telling me their secrets."

"It is a terrible shame," he agreed gravely. She snorted. "You'll have to make do with… hmm. What was it again?"

"A wonderful home." She sighed deeply. "A perfect, idyllic town. A man I love so much I sometimes think I must be living in a fairytale. Being able to fix things around town before they break and pull the power out of storms to keep the bay still and safe for sailing." She considered. "A regular supply of the most incredible, literally magical sex I have ever had in my life."

"And delicious pastries."

"And delicious pastries. Hmm. I *suppose* I can live with that." She curled against him, her hands sneaking up to run his chest under the blanket. "But, you know, if you had anything else in mind to help sweeten the deal…"

Her magic nipped at his fingertips and earlobes. He pulled her close for a kiss.

"I think I have just the thing," he murmured. He pulled the box from his pocket. His dragon stirred inside him with a feeling like coals settling comfortably in a fireplace—satisfied, and with the promise of heat and roaring flames if the right ingredients were supplied.

Was this love? It felt like it. Not only the heady, drunken joy of attraction and sex and magic, but long evenings on the balcony or lying on the roof, watching the town's lights reflected on the water, talking until their words overflowed their minds and filled the sky. The roaring flames and the banked coals that kept the house warm overnight.

"Felicity Park," he said, opening the box to reveal the gold ring inside, "will you marry me?"

Felicity bit her bottom lip, but her smile shone through anyway, breaking through every attempt at restraining it. "With all my heart," she said, and her magic sang the truth of it to Apollo's soul.

"Hello, Grandfather." Apollo grinned as his grandfather zoomed in his camera until there was nothing visible on the screen except his face. He'd arranged his own phone so that Hideaway lay spread out behind him and Felicity—the perfect backdrop.

Now that he knew Hideaway was his hoard, he understood why his dragon had gotten its hackles up before about his grandfather seeing it. No dragon liked to reveal his hoard.

As for why it was purring with smugness now, instead of trying to keep all sign of Hideaway from the video call…

*Because it's not* my *hoard anymore. My greatest treasure is sitting beside me… and I'm never going to stop wanting to show her off.*

"Apollo!" Errol's eyes narrowed suspiciously. "And who is this?"

"Grandfather, meet my mate, Felicity Park. Felicity… my grandfather, Errol Jenkins."

Felicity didn't mention that she'd already encountered Errol when she listened in on their previous call. "It's a pleasure to meet you, sir."

"Your mate? Your mate? Good God, don't tell me you actually managed to steal the Blackburn hoard."

"Certainly not. What do you take me for?" Apollo retorted promptly, then relented. "Actually, that's something I'd like to talk to you about.

Felicity and I made the strangest discovery about my dragon's hoard. You see…"

As he explained that his dragon hoarded the safety of a town and its people rather than gold and jewels, Errol's expression flitted from disbelief, to confusion, to consternation.

"But that's absurd!" he protested. "A town? Who ever heard of hoarding a *town?*"

"Or a high-rise apartment block?" Apollo added innocently.

"Or—" Errol's eyebrows snapped together. "You think… my building?"

"How much of it do you own now?"

His grandfather's hands clutched claw-like at the air. *I don't think he's even aware he's doing it.* "Not enough."

"And if you had to choose between finally getting your hands on the retail space on the lower levels, or your cufflink collection…"

Errol's eyes gleamed. "You've made your point." *Now stop talking about my retail space,* he might as well have added, with electricity glittered along his eyebrows to drive the point home. He scowled—then his face fell. "But this is terrible news. You're getting married! I assume you're getting married. You did propose to her, didn't you?"

Felicity lifted her hand and Errol nodded approvingly. "Excellent. You're exceeding my expectations more than I ever hoped would be possible, boy."

"I'm so glad," Apollo murmured, and Felicity stifled a giggle.

Errol waved a hand irritably. "Defending my gold hoard while I traveled to celebrate your wedding would be one thing. Any fool can keep a few shipping containers safe."

*Shipping containers?* Felicity mouthed to Apollo.

"But an entire building? I can't transport thirty-four floors of steel and concrete across the globe! And if I leave it unguarded…" His claws raked the air again.

"But no one else will know it's your hoard." Felicity's smiled was like the sun rising. Even Errol looked stunned to be on the receiving end of it. "Most dragons will assume the cufflinks *are* your hoard. You can use them as a decoy while you're traveling."

"Yes… yes. I could! Lead them on a wild goose chase…"

"There is one dragon who might know," Apollo reminded her. Her eyes sparkled.

"Yes. Saint-John Montfort might figure it out, after he targeted Hideaway. But he also knows what happens when another dragon sets foot in a lightning dragon's domain and he isn't wanted." She gave Grandfather Errol a conspiratorial look. "If he does come calling… I expect you'd enjoy magically knocking him on his ass as much as Apollo did."

"I think I would, young lady. I think I would enjoy that *exceedingly*."

After they hung up, Apollo leaned back with a sigh and stared blankly at the wall for a few minutes.

"You know," he said eventually, "I'm not sure it was a good idea, telling my grandfather he can magically boot people out of his hoard. You should hear how he gets about people subletting their apartments. We could have started something terrible."

"Is it bad that I almost hope we have? Your granddad looked like a kid in a candy store when you told him about Montfort." Felicity stretched and curled around him, anchoring him on the sofa. "Grandfather Errol's coming to our wedding? Shoot. We'd better start planning it, then."

"Lucky for me, I engaged myself to an excellent project manager."

"Lucky indeed. And this is a project I'm going to enjoy *very* much."

She wrapped magic around them both. "For a theme, I'm thinking… stars?"

"Flowers."

Her kiss was like starlight strung through with lightning. "How about both?"

# FLY AWAY HOME

# I

# SHERRYL

Hideaway Cove was exactly as Sherryl Eaves remembered it, and so different it broke her heart.

She should have been paying attention to the speeches. Tonight was her daughter Lainie's wedding rehearsal dinner, and all the happy couple's closest friends had gathered in the cozy, fire-lit warmth of the local restaurant. The air was full of laughter and the smell of good food. Lainie was radiant, in a dress that floated over her baby bump. Outside, the moon hung bright and full in a clear sky speckled with stars.

Which meant there was no avoiding the sight of the old lighthouse at the top of the hill. The place that had been the backdrop to the most wonderful and most awful parts of Sherryl's life, and still left a shadow on her heart.

Hideaway Cove, this tiny, hard-to-find coastal village, was a haven for magic of the sort she never would have believed existed if she hadn't seen it with her own two eyes. Almost all the town's inhabitants were shifters—people who could turn into animals. It was like something out of a storybook. Shifters lived secretly all around the world, dotted among the human population, but in Hideaway Cove they didn't need to hide their true natures. The kids who ran wild on the beach really did run *wild*, shifting back and forth from their animal forms as easily as putting on a shirt. Houses were built with easy-unlatch windows and dog doors, not because people here were crazy about their pets but because who wanted to bother shifting to human form just to go in or out?

So much magic. So many happy families, living free of the fear of their magic being discovered and abused by the human world.

And now her daughter was going to be married. Here. In Hideaway Cove. The same town that had cast her out—had cast them all out—when Lainie was born human, like her, instead of a shifter like her father.

Every fairytale had its dark side. All the princes who hadn't made it to Sleeping Beauty's tower; all Bluebeard's wives who hadn't escaped. Moms that died to make way for evil stepmothers. Tragic backstories that made the hero and heroine's happily-ever-after all the sweeter.

*Anton.* Sherryl squeezed her eyes shut. Her fated mate had been declared legally dead years ago and had disappeared so long before that the thought of him shouldn't still bring her to tears.

But her heart didn't know that.

Anton was a magpie shifter. His family had been Hideaway royalty—one of the founding families who had banded together to create the sanctuary town. She had met him in the human world, in their first year of college, and it was like falling into a storybook. Magic was real, and the most handsome boy she'd ever met was head-over-heels in love with her.

And then…

They'd exchanged letters when he went back home over summer—actual stamped, posted letters, which seemed unbelievably old-fashioned now. Phone calls had been rare and treasured things, hushed conversations in the hallway, constantly alert for the sound of a foot on the stairs. It had all been so Romeo and Juliet, and she hadn't even known why until their own wedding.

His parents hadn't approved. That was putting it lightly. And what should have been the happiest day of her life had been the beginning of the end.

She kept her eyes tightly closed until the treacherous heat behind them faded.

*Things are different now.* Lainie had told her so, and because this was Lainie, she'd backed up her case with solid evidence. Her little girl—*Not so little anymore*, she had to keep reminding herself—wasn't the only non-shifter to be welcomed to the close-knit community. When she arrived last night, Sherryl had met the other women who'd followed in her footsteps and found themselves magically connected to the men of Hideaway.

*Not exactly in my footsteps. In Lainie's footsteps. Thank goodness.*

Lainie's heart wouldn't break like hers had. The magic wouldn't die for her.

She wouldn't find herself alone and somehow still in love with the man who left her.

"Mom?" Lainie's voice pulled Sherryl from her thoughts. "Are you alright?"

"Oh, don't mind me." She shook her head and smiled as one of the groomsmen stood up and raised his glass to the happy couple.

Lainie wasn't convinced. Her dark eyes, so much like Anton's, were bright with concern. "If you want to head back to the house..."

Back to the house? Lainie and Harrison had built their home next to the ruins of the old lighthouse where Anton grew up. His family home. She couldn't go back there now. Not with her head trapped in the past.

And she could *not* let Lainie know that was why she was getting all weepy.

Anton had left them. He'd disappeared one night after his family had made it clear he had to choose between them or his non-shifting wife and daughter, and he'd never come back. End of story.

"I'm fine. Moms are meant to cry at weddings. I'm just getting a head start." She nodded towards the groomsman. "Now shush and listen to your friends saying nice things about you."

Lainie grimaced, then smiled and turned away. Sherryl managed not to sigh with relief.

How could she explain to her that, despite everything, she still loved Lainie's father? That, despite everything, she still missed him?

*It's easy to love a ghost.* Maybe that was why. If he were here in the flesh, alive, the man she'd loved so much it tore her apart, who left without even a look back…

But he was dead. There had been no sign of him for almost twenty years.

Loving him was safe.

Sherryl let the groomsman's speech roll over her. *Apollo*, she remembered; the dragon shifter. He was making a big act of it, gesturing and sending golden sparks flying through the air. He made a joke, and everyone laughed. The tug of the past loosened its grip. This wedding was already nothing like hers and Anton's, and Lainie's marriage would be nothing like theirs, either.

Mid-speech, Apollo paused. He exchanged a look with the dark-haired woman seated next to him, his mate Felicity. Sherryl tensed. What was happening?

Harrison leaned over to explain: "Someone must have passed the town boundary. Normally I'd wonder why Sparky was letting something like that interrupt his storytelling—" He raised his voice, and Apollo snorted dramatically. "—but we're all on higher alert after what happened recently."

"What happened recently?"

"Nothing!" Lainie squeaked. Sherryl fixed her with a hard look.

"Lainie—"

"It's not another dragon, is it?" Lainie asked Apollo hurriedly.

At the end of the next table, the boy who was their ring-bearer perked up. "Another dragon?"

"*Not* a dragon," Felicity informed him, and he slumped back in his seat.

"Aww. I want to see another fight!"

This was getting worse and worse. "Another *fight?* Lainie—"

Lainie cursed under her breath. "It's nothing, Mom."

The boy's foster-father, a shaggy-haired wolf shifter called Arlo, gave him a warning look. "One dragon fight was bad enough."

"But I barely even got to see it! We all had to hide!"

"There was a dragon fight, and you all had to hide? Lainie, what is he talking about?" Sherryl's voice was tight. "When did this happen?"

"Just—a while back." Lainie winced and rubbed her bump. "Ow. Stop kicking, bubba."

*You're not going to distract me like that, young lady.* "When were you going to tell me about it?"

"Um … In a few years, when it turned into a funny story?"

Her heart was beating too hard. Something inside her reached out for a warmth, a reassurance, that hadn't been there for years, and found only cold emptiness. "Sweetheart … you told me things had changed here."

"They have. I promise, Mom." Lainie saw her expression and squeezed her hand. "What happened to you and Dad will never happen again. But we need to protect what we have here, and sometimes that means a teeny, tiny little dragon fight."

Harrison muttered something that sounded like "Teeny tiny property damage," and snorted.

"I thought that was storm damage!" Sherryl objected.

"There was a storm, too. Of a sort." Lainie grinned at her, but there was a tightness around her eyes that made Sherryl instantly suspicious.

"What else aren't you telling me?"

"Nothing!"

*You said that too quickly*, Sherryl thought.

"If you really want a close-up look at a fighting dragon, try eating an ice-cream in front of Tomás and not sharing," Felicity called out.

The boy rolled his eyes. "I know better than *that*."

*Let it go*, Sherryl told herself, despite the thudding in her chest. Whatever Lainie was hiding was her own business. And this was her wedding. She didn't need her mom prying.

Apollo cleared his throat and raised his glass again. "As I was saying. Here's to you, Harrison, and you, Lainie. Hideaway Cove's griffin interloper and prodigal daughter. As an interloper myself, albeit one of a more recent vintage, it might not be my place to say this, but the two of you finding one another—"

CRASH!

Glass shattered. Something smashed through the picture window at the front of the restaurant. Chair legs shrieked on floorboards as people leaped to their feet. Fur and feathers burst as some guests shifted in shock. On the floor between two tables, black wings beat the air.

Sherryl's body turned to stone.

The clamor died down, but she still couldn't breathe.

Lainie turned to her. "Mom, it's okay, no one's hurt. Are you okay? You look like you've seen a ghost."

Black and white feathers. The magpie flailed splay-winged on the floor. Something deep inside Sherryl cracked open. *This can't be happening. Not here. Not now.*

"Mom?" Lainie sounded worried.

*Lainie hasn't seen him.* The world splintered. For one awful, lurching moment, she imagined darting to the broken shape on the floor and gathering it in her arms and running away, so that Lainie wouldn't have to deal with what had just happened.

But she couldn't do that.

"It's fine," she reassured Lainie, even though it was anything but.

Around them, the chaos that had followed the broken window was fading. Everyone would be looking for someone to take charge. Lainie's mate, Harrison, was the obvious choice. That was another option, she supposed faintly. Don't grab him and run; give up. Let someone else take over.

She stood up. Maybe she was making a fool of herself. Maybe he was already talking with the other shifters, in that way she couldn't hear.

But she was his mate. The mother of his child.

The only family he had left.

She ignored the pain in her chest and called out.

"Anton!"

Silence rippled out through the room. Lainie's gasp, and the shaky breath that followed it, lodged in her heart next to the unwanted pain.

On the floor, the bird raised its head. One dark eye inspected her, then the other, as he flicked his head from side to side.

Feathers shivered into shadows, and melted into flesh.

Anton's coal-black eyes pierced her. The lost part of her soul, the absence she always reached for in times of stress or worry, the piece of her heart she had plastered and papered over and yet always found herself scratching open again—he was here.

She'd been wrong. He wasn't dead. He was here, sprawled on the floor, staring at her as though she was the sun rising after the longest night of his life, and it hadn't been safe to still be in love with him after all.

"Stop everything. This wedding can't go ahead," he rasped, and fell to the floor unconscious.

An hour later, the brittle silence that followed Anton's announcement was still scraping against her skin.

The rehearsal dinner had fallen apart. Anton had collapsed from exhaustion. Now they were in the guest bedroom at Lainie's house—the nest her mate had built for her with love in every plank and nail, a testament to his loyalty.

Only a few dozen yards from the ruins of the lighthouse. The guest room didn't have a view of the old place; Lainie, sweet, thoughtful Lainie, had been careful to ensure that. But it didn't matter. She could feel it, a shadow at her shoulder, reminding her of everything that had happened.

They couldn't take Anton to a hospital. The nearest one was hours away, and anyway, what if he shifted again in front of strangers? But one of the wedding guests was trained as a nurse, and she reassured Sherryl that Anton was only exhausted, not injured.

*How can she tell?* Sherryl reached out, hesitated, then brushed the hair back from her mate's forehead. His breathing was steady. His pulse was strong. But he was so pale, so thin, and he hadn't woken up…

It was easy to love a ghost. A man who'd been gone so long the law and her heart had both decided he was dead. But a man who was alive, whose every breath and flickering beat of his heart tugged at her own? Who had been alive all this time?

Who had only come back to ruin Lainie's happiness?

"Where were you?" Sherryl whispered.

"Mom?"

Lainie was at the door, pale-faced in a way that had all her mama alarm bells ringing. Harrison was at her shoulder. Sherryl exchanged a look with him. She might not have shifter telepathy, but one glance was enough to tell her everything. Yes, he was aware Lainie was at the end of her rope; yes, he had suggested she sit down, eat something, drink something, and so on; and no, her dear stubborn daughter wasn't listening to a word he said.

How could she, when her father was back from the dead?

"Come in," Sherryl said, beckoning. "He's sleeping."

"Still?"

"No change yet. Caro said he was exhausted, remember? And that shifting must have taken the last of his energy."

Lainie tiptoed in, suddenly the same little girl who used to sneak back into the living room when she was meant to be asleep in bed. The tightness in her eyes was back; whatever she was hiding before was bursting to get out.

"What is he doing here? Why is he..." Lainie's voice trailed off. Sherryl put her arms around her.

"I don't know, honey. We'll have to wait for him to wake up."

"He hasn't said anything? To you, or..." Lainie's eyes went to Harrison. He shook his head.

"I've tried to reach him telepathically, but he's not responding. Your mom's right. The best thing is to let him rest." He shook his head again. "I don't know where he came from or how long he was on the wing to get here, but, if you ask me, it took more than he had to spare."

"I wrote him an invitation," Lainie blurted out. Her shoulders shook beneath Sherryl's arms. "I didn't send it—I couldn't, I had nowhere to send it to—but I wrote it, I—"

Sherryl held her tight. "It's okay, hon. It's not your fault."

It was theirs. Hers, and Anton's, and all the truths they avoided until it was too late.

Bit by bit, she and Harrison convinced Lainie to go to bed. Sherryl watched them go, Lainie with one hand protectively over her baby, Harrison with his hand over hers.

Eventually, the house was quiet and dark. Out the window, she could see the sea whispering far below, and the town like a scatter of glowing pearls. From this distance it seemed silent, too, though she was sure that wasn't the case. Anton Eaves, back from the dead and forbidding his daughter's wedding? The gossip machines would be up and running.

"Sherryl?"

Her heart stopped. She turned. He was exactly where she had left him: too-long hair a tangle of dark weed against the pillow, one arm awkwardly stretched out on top of the coverlet. His other hand was clenched over something, his fingers locked so tight that even asleep, he hadn't let it go.

But his eyes were open. Those black, bewitching eyes. He reached for her. How could she not take his hand?

His skin was dry, the bones of his hand more prominent than she remembered. But his grip was sure. He held onto her like he would never let go.

The same way he used to. *And we both know how that ended up.*

"You're here." His voice was the same rasp as earlier, like an old tool worn thin from use. Or lack of use. She looked for the water jug and glass Harrison had laid out, but before she could fetch it Anton tried to sit up and she had to put a stop to that before he fell out of bed and the thud brought Lainie running.

Or so she told herself as she sat down next to him. Her weight made a dip in the mattress and he leaned towards her, weary but resolute.

"You're here," he said again. "You're real." He traced the outlines of her face with his gaze, his eyes so intent her skin prickled under his inspection. "I'm not too late."

"You arrived in the middle of the rehearsal." Now her voice was the one that sounded old and worn-out. "Some people might call that too early."

He looked confused, and she added, "Traditionally, you're meant to make your objections during the ceremony itself."

He still looked confused—and worried, as though he was missing something. He shook his head. "The wedding," he muttered. Why did she feel as if he was holding onto that one word out of all she said as though it was a lifejacket in a storm? "We can't—it'll all go wrong, Sher. I promise I'll give you everything you want, but—not here. We can't be here."

"Anton—"

"Not here. This is where the end starts. Let's go away. Find a courthouse. Don't let them—" Something ragged and lost passed behind his eyes. "Don't let *me* ruin this. I never should have brought you here. I should have kept you safe."

Staring into his desperate face, Sherryl forgot how to breathe. She wet her lips. She had to be careful about this; the world was plummeting around her.

"Anton … whose wedding do you think we're here for?"

2

# ANTON

He had thought he still had a chance. A way to make everything right. *It was all a dream*, he'd told himself as he flew. *A nightmare.* He'd been wrong. It had all been real.

Dark wings beat inside his mind, tearing at his memories the harder he tried to hold on to them. Only the pressure of his mate's arms around him kept him from falling away with them. Back into his magpie's simple mind, and the oblivion he'd created for himself.

Images whirled through his head. Sherryl standing on a kitchen stool with her wedding dress pinned around her, her face alight with laughter, yelling at him not to look. The floaty puff of a veil. Flowers. Bright, shining images, like treasures kept under glass.

But—other images surged up from the depths of his mind. The dream, he'd told himself. The future he had to protect. A tiny baby, her face wrinkled with displeasure. A little hand clinging to his. Sherryl again, still laughing, all three of them covered in flour and sugar after a baking day gone wrong. Lainie's ecstatic shrieks as he tossed her in the air, and the words he'd said so easily, not knowing the misery they would prophesy.

*My little magpie. You'll get your wings soon, won't you?*
Not much more laughter, after that.
And it hadn't been a dream.

655

"Where have you *been*?" Sherryl's voice was ragged-edged. "Where—how can you come back here now, objecting to the wedding—how did you even know there was a wedding?"

"I—"

"You left. How can you come back here, now, like this, after you left us?"

He had to fix this. Wasn't that why he'd come all this way? All this way from … where had he been?

*I left them. That wasn't a dream. Where did I go?*

He swallowed hard. "I never meant to leave you. I thought—I could convince my parents. About the wedding, and about…"

"You did convince them." Sherryl's voice was quieter. "With your silver tongue. You told them it would all be all right. Our daughter would be a shifter."

Daughter. Lainie. But when… "It's all out of order in my head. I thought … when the invitation arrived, I thought I must have dreamed it all, that I was getting another chance…"

But how could he have remembered Lainie, if it was a dream? How could he have known all the misery he wanted to avoid, if he hadn't already lived through it? "I wanted to get it right this time."

"That doesn't make any sense."

He laughed hollowly. The torn pieces of his mind were knitting themselves together, and he did not want to see the shape they were making. "Yes. I'm beginning to see that."

"No, I mean—how could you have known about the wedding?" Sherryl's eyes were worried, but there was a hardness in them he didn't remember. His heart lurched. *My mate. What did I do to you?*

"I was invited," he said, uncertain. "Here."

It was still in his hand. How it had survived him shifting, he didn't know. He remembered clutching it in his talons, flying, and then…

He uncurled his fingers one by one.

It had been card when it arrived. Thick and unbending, eggshell-white—as though it was already old, a relic bleached colorless by the sun except for the gleaming gold lettering that looped like a magic spell on its face. Now it was limp as a scrap of washed cotton. Most of the gold had peeled off. Only a few words were still legible.

Mrs. Eaves ... invite you to celebrate the wedding of...

"I thought it meant my parents. But ... you kept my name?" It felt like a gift. One he didn't deserve.

"It was my name, by then." She frowned at the invitation, distracted. "When did you get this?"

"I don't know. Time is—difficult."

She glanced up at him, her eyebrows coming together. He swallowed again.

*Make it better. Don't let her worry.*

"You know what my magpie is like. It saw something shiny and picked it up. It didn't know the shiny bits were words, and by the time it remembered—I remembered—this was all that was left." Instead of being reassured, she frowned more deeply. He was missing something—a flicker of a thought, gone too fast for him to capture—but he kept talking. "I shouldn't have come back here to try to convince my parents." Was that what he'd done? "That's where it all went wrong." Was it? "I'm sorry."

The truth.

"Where have you been?" Sherryl asked gently. The hairs on the back of his neck rose. *Something's wrong. Something isn't adding up.*

It was her voice. It was calm and soft, the way it got when she was trying not to upset anyone.

She was trying not to upset *him*. The thought made him want to laugh. It made him sick. He should be her strength, not the other way around.

He braced himself. "I managed to convince them the first time, didn't I? They couldn't want you gone so badly. There had to be a way to make them change their mind."

"You came back here after you left us."

"It didn't work. I thought I could make them see—you're my mate. I couldn't forsake you. I told them I would look after you both, but they told me they would disinherit me."

Sherryl stiffened. "And then?"

He shook his head. He'd lost track again, of something, but this shame cut too deep to mislay. "I don't have my own money, you know that. It's all tied up in the family business. I don't know how I'm going to provide for you. I was going to fly home to you straight away, but I couldn't bring everything they'd said back with me." His head swam, and he clutched it. "I needed to get my thoughts straight. If I could only figure out a way to make things right for you…"

*Weak.* His father's voice echoed through him. *Weak-minded and weak-hearted. Of course you won't break the mate bond. Not even now you see what a mistake she is. Both of them! You betrayed your own family, and for what?*

He hadn't wanted to risk even a whisper of his father's words passing his lips when he went back to Sherryl. If she'd asked her what his parents said—no. She could never know how deep their hatefulness ran.

So *he'd* run.

And then—

No.

He straightened his shoulders. He couldn't lay this on Sherryl's shoulders. He was her mate; he was meant to protect her, not trouble her with his own failings—

"Stop that."

"Stop what?"

"This—" She gestured at him, then rubbed her hand over her forehead. "It's the same as when we were married. You're keeping something from me for my own good. Like I'm some delicate glass doll. Well, I've got some very old news for you, Anton. Keeping things from me did not work out well last time."

He stared at her. The careful gentleness was gone from her voice. As though reading his mind, she pressed her lips together and visibly calmed herself.

It was too much. She deserved so much better than what he had been. Let alone what he was now: a broken shell of a man whose own mind had turned against him.

"I broke," he said simply. "I failed you. I failed Lainie. Everything I was meant to be as a man, as your mate, I failed. I couldn't even keep you safe in my own nest. When I left again, to clear my mind—I lost myself." He took a shaky breath. "I meant to come back. I'm sure I did. I don't want to be the sort of man who wouldn't have wanted to come back to you."

He looked down at the scrap of paper in his hand. *Whose wedding do you think we're here for?*

"This … called me back. I couldn't even read it at first. How does that happen? Even in magpie form, I still have a human mind. Had. Have I … been in magpie form too long?" He hesitated. "I can't remember shifting since I left here that night. I think … I think this is the first time I've been human since then."

"That's impossible." Sherryl was white-faced. The prickling feeling of something not being right was back. He didn't want to ask.

*Mrs. Eaves invites…*

"Sher," he said slowly, "Whose wedding is this invitation for?"

"Anton, you—" Her mouth moved without words for a moment. "Lainie is getting married. You know—you know what that means, right?"

"Lainie," he said dully. Sherryl had said the words, but he couldn't make them make sense in his head. "It's … it's Lainie's wedding?"

It couldn't be. His little Lainie. He remembered—how much? Childhood. An energetic, stubborn pre-teen. Her first years of high school and the growing stress as she stayed perfectly human, his parents peering over his shoulder at his non-shifter child, their judgement a constant weight around his heart. And then … college? She must have—but he didn't remember…

*My memories are out of order*, he told himself desperately. *I've misplaced the ones of her growing up. That's all.*

Except the whole reason he'd gone to plead with his parents was that she wasn't a shifter, and that must have become clear before she grew up.

He swallowed.

"She—she's young to be getting married, but if you're happy for her, then—"

"She's not young to be getting married, Anton. She's older than we were." She hesitated, and that moment of silence held all the horror his brain was so desperately trying to hide from him. "She's only a little younger than you were when you left us."

"No." His voice was coming from a long way away. "No. If that's true, I must have been gone…"

Years. Too many years to contemplate.

"Please," he whispered. "Don't tell me I missed that much."

Feathers beat behind his eyes again, and he lost track of his thoughts.

"Anton!" Warm arms wrapped around him. Around his human shoulders, his human head. If he shifted, he would lose them.

*Not again. Not again.*

# 3

# SHERRYL

Sherryl held her husband as he shook. Feathers pricked beneath her fingers, then melted away, until he gave a gasping breath and turned his face to nestle in the crook of her shoulder.

Her insides felt like they were made of ice.

Anton was her mate, back from the dead. She knew how strong the mate bond was. His parents had made sure of that—and that she knew how disappointed and disgusted they were that fate had chosen *her* for their son. The mate bond was practically sacred to shifters, and she'd desecrated it just by existing.

Anton had always told her they were wrong.

But now...

Maybe his parents had been right after all, because, from the moment he woke up again, she had all but pushed him away and it turned out he'd been so psychologically destroyed by being cast out by his parents that he hadn't even been able to stay *human*. All these years. He hadn't been dead. He'd been lost.

"I'm sorry," she whispered against his hair.

He lifted his head, his jet-black eyes searching hers. "Why?"

"I haven't been a good mate to you." She swallowed. "I thought you abandoned us. You didn't. You were lost, and I didn't find you. Your parents told me you didn't want anything to do with us anymore. I shouldn't have believed them. If I were a proper mate, and not—"

"You are a proper mate. You're *my* mate." He smoothed her hair, the same way he used to. She choked back a sob. "If you'll take me back—"

"Of course I'll take you back. How could I not?"

Their lips crashed together like they were teenagers again. The taste of him flooded her memories. His mouth softened against hers, testing, tentative—and something inside her finally melted.

*He's still here. I haven't lost him.* The man who'd filled her life with magic. She deepened the kiss. It was like coming home, like Hideaway itself—intimately familiar and different in so many ways. He was unsure in his human body, gentle and loving. She was sure in hers—but sure of its practical capabilities, not its romantic ones. She knew how long she could sit at her computer before her shoulders ached and how long she needed to stretch after the gym so she wouldn't regret it the next day, but she didn't know…

It really *had* been a long time.

Afterwards, she couldn't stop staring at him.

"You're really back," she whispered.

He gave her a crooked smile. Their lovemaking had returned some color to his face, but he was still exhausted. *More* exhausted. "Did I not just prove that?"

"I could still be dreaming."

Pain lanced behind his eyes. "You dreamed of me?"

"I didn't let myself, for a long time. Until…"

She couldn't say it, so he did. "You thought I was dead."

"Safely dead." Saying it out loud felt like another betrayal.

"A dead man couldn't hurt you." He rested his hand against her cheek, gentle as moonlight. "But I'm alive again, so all bets are off?"

"That's not—" She broke off, and tried again. "You know that isn't—"

"Isn't it?" His eyes searched hers. "I promised to love you forever. Instead I left you, and now I've come back to you a broken man. I can't even remember the time I've lost and I know I can't make it up to you. I wanted to be strong for you, and instead I've made our mate bond into a millstone around your neck. The bond is meant to be a blessing, not a curse."

She returned his caress. "Loving you has never been a curse."

"You only say that because I've done what I always did, and tumbled you into bed instead of talking about what's wrong."

"We're talking now, aren't we?" And suddenly they were: talking like they hadn't even when they were together the first time, as though their years apart had torn down barricades they hadn't even noticed they had built in those early days together.

There was so much to talk about. Everything he had missed. His parents had passed several years ago, and he grieved them, but grieved more that he hadn't seen how conditional their love was until he let it tear their family apart.

He was amazed that Sherryl would support Lainie moving back to Hideaway Cove, after what they had been through. She found herself repeating the arguments Lainie had made to her, when she announced she'd found her mate and was moving in with him on the old Eaves property.

"Hideaway has changed. She changed it, her and Harrison. And she isn't the only human to make her home here. If a Hideaway shifter has a human mate, they don't have to leave town anymore. And if Lainie's child isn't a shifter—this will still be their home."

"I still can't believe she's having a child. Our little Lainie."

"Not so little anymore. Even I have to keep reminding myself of that."

He smiled sadly. "I came here thinking I could save our family. But she's saved everyone already. Are you sure this isn't a dream?"

"If it is, it's a happy one."

"I'm afraid to fall asleep." He laughed softly, mirthlessly. "Which I shouldn't admit to you, because you're not the one who disappeared in the night. I—"

"I'm not going anywhere." She covered his hand with hers. "And neither are you."

"Of course the wedding is going ahead," Sherryl said, breezy and with the slightest hint of disbelief, as though her husband hadn't just returned from the dead.

She said the same thing to half-a-dozen callers already that morning. It was a nice change from having to find a polite way to say *Yes, that's right, it's me, the woman who destroyed the Eaves family.*

"Do they all need to physically come to the door? Couldn't they ask telepathically, rather than coming all the way up here?" she grumbled, closing the door.

"Ah, but then they couldn't snoop," Anton replied.

"Lainie's meant to be getting ready for her wedding, not warding off gossip!"

"Speak of the devils…" He stalked to the front door and opened it before the group behind it had a chance to knock. "Good morning. Yes, I am alive, and yes, the wedding is going ahead, but it going ahead does require giving the bride and groom time to at least brush their teeth before the big event, so if you don't mind…"

The three people at the door—two blonde women in their early twenties and a ginger youth—blinked at him.

Sherryl smiled and tugged Anton gently out of the way. "Morning, everyone. Anton, this is Jools and Jilly White, and Adrian Mackaby. Come on in."

"Good morning, Mrs.—uh, Sherryl," Jools said, barely tripping over the correction. She beamed at Anton. "We're here to help get ready! I'm hair and makeup, Jilly's photos—well, she's setting up for Dad, but she is meant to be here—and Adrian's—"

"Caro sent me up with food," Adrian explained. "It's my job to make sure Lainie doesn't faint from hunger during the ceremony, or she'll put my head on the wall and use it for darts practice," he recited solemnly.

Anton stepped back to let them past and shot Sherryl a wry look. "I suppose I deserved that," he said. "Who's Caro?"

"She owns the restaurant in town."

"What, the old diner?"

"Oh, no, that's long gone." She put a hand on his arm. "Another change."

"You keep telling me things are different. It's like my brain doesn't want to accept it." He looked over his shoulder down the hallway, but Sherryl knew where he was really looking: his gaze took him into the past, through plasterboard and wooden cladding to the ruins of the lighthouse at the end of the bluff.

"Despite everything … I wish I could have seen them again. Or maybe … maybe I wish they'd been the sort of parents I could wish I'd seen again." He gave his crooked smile again. In the living room, Lainie's voice rose in welcome to the newcomers. "The bar for parenthood in my family is so low I'd have to dig a hole to reach under it."

"But you're still scared?"

"How could I not be?" His smile lost some of its crookedness as he gazed at her. "It's not my parents I have to live up to. It's you."

She took his hand. "Then let's go in together. Some of my shine might rub off on you."

# 4

# ANTON

His little girl. Not little anymore. A grown woman, with another life growing inside her, on the threshold of the same step that had sent him and her mother hurtling into disaster.

He didn't know how to talk to her, this sparkling stranger he'd last seen as a worried teen. But Sherryl did, and she helped him find his way back into the nest over breakfast.

Caro, whoever she was, had been right to send the kid with food. Nobody was in a mood to cook. Lainie was alight with joy and nerves, and her fiancé was no better, though he did a good job of hiding it.

Anton inspected his future son-in-law as the two of them told the story of how they'd met. He approved. The man was besotted. You could almost see his feathers puffing out with broody satisfaction as he looked down at Lainie beside him.

But there was a firmness—not quite a hardness, but close to a warning—in his eyes when he looked over at Anton.

*Good.* His daughter deserved a mate who would protect her from anything. Including her feckless father.

A griffin shifter, though. That was new.

Part eagle, part… He couldn't remember his mythology. Horse? No, that wasn't right.

"Lion," Harrison said when he asked.

"I didn't even know that was possible. Mythical shifters?" He shook his head.

Harrison grinned. "Wait until you meet the dragons. We've got two of 'em. Apollo's lived here almost as long as I have. Tomás is a recent arrival."

"His mom's human," Lainie put in.

"And his father?"

"Not in the picture. Though…"

*If this is a dream, I hope I never wake up.*

After dinner, the group split. Sherryl and Lainie headed for her bedroom to start getting ready, and Harrison to join his groomsmen down in town.

Anton followed him outside. There was something he wanted to check.

"Sherryl tells me Hideaway Cove has changed."

"You don't believe her?"

Outside, there was no escaping the sight of the lighthouse. Even from the other side of the house, it was visible, a broken wreck looming up into the sky. Why the hell hadn't Lainie gotten rid of it?

"I believe her," Anton said, his eyes still caught on the old lighthouse. "I believed it myself once, too. Or at least I thought I could change it. But you live here. You see your neighbors every day. I want to hear it from you."

Harrison nodded. "I lived here my whole adult life before I met Lainie, and never heard a word about what happened to your family. No one spoke of it. The old lighthouse was a haunted house, not somewhere you would think people had ever lived, let alone not even a generation ago. What your parents did, didn't help anyone here. It made them scared and ashamed."

"And now?"

"The people who were scared, aren't. The people who were ashamed—well, there's something to be said for learning you were right to be ashamed." He followed Anton's gaze. "I won't promise you everything's perfect. The people who never regretted their choices—they don't now, either."

"I think I can guess the ones you mean," Anton said grimly.

"But this is a good place to make a home now." Harrison's face softened as he looked back at his house. "A good place to nest."

"Thank you."

"For what?"

"Doing what I couldn't. Fixing Hideaway."

"Thank your daughter, as well. Lainie has been the heart of the changes here." Harrison eyed him carefully. "What are your plans now?"

"You two have already rescued the town from the mess my generation made of it. What's left?" He answered his own question. "Only the hardest thing of all."

"I'm glad we're on the same page about that."

"Regaining the love of the two most important people in my life."

Harrison looked at him strangely. "That's not it."

"What?"

"You already have their love. Sherryl and Lainie. That's what makes it so dangerous." Harrison nodded over Anton's shoulder to where his groomsmen had just pulled up in a truck. "You have to earn their trust."

# 5

# SHERRYL

Sherryl and Anton had been married in a church, under the judgmental gaze of his parents. Lainie got married in the sunlight, on the clifftops overlooking the ocean, surrounded by the love of her friends and family.

The original plan had been to have Sherryl walk Lainie down the aisle, but, with Anton back, Lainie asked both of them to do it. Sherryl felt as though her heart would burst. Lainie and Anton had talked privately that morning after Harrison left, which felt like a hell of a risk on Lainie's wedding day, but they'd both come out of the conversation weepy yet happy.

"It's the first day of the rest of her life," Anton explained when she asked what they'd talked about. "I told her I won't miss this one. This is a new start for me, too."

Now they were halfway down the aisle. Lainie was wearing a floating white gown that made her look like a heavily pregnant angel, with a coronet of blossoms holding her veil in place. Harrison was standing waiting for his bride and looking like he was about to cry, and Lainie was absolutely already crying under her veil, and Sherryl had to blink far too often to keep her own eyes clear.

A dream, Anton had said. This was better than a dream.

The wolf shifter, Arlo, was officiating. *Finally, one person who isn't crying,* Sherryl thought. Though his voice was noticeably huskier than it had been the last time they'd spoken.

At last it was time for the vows. Lainie and Harrison stood staring into one another's eyes as though nothing else in the world existed.

"I, Harrison Galway, take you, Lainie May Eaves…"

"…for better or for worse, in sickness and in health…"

"…to take strength in your love, and use that strength to cherish you…"

"…as long as we both shall live."

Harrison raised his hand, palm-up. "Give me your hand and let me be yours forever."

Lainie placed her hand in his.

"You may kiss the bride," Arlo said, his voice hushed as though they were all intruding on a private moment.

Lainie stood on her tiptoes to kiss her husband, and golden sparks flew through the air around them. Apollo, standing to one side, flicked his hand to transform the sparks into an arch of magical glowing flowers.

"I was worried," she admitted to Anton in an undertone. "I was sure something would go wrong. But now … she's safe. She's loved. I can leave her here and not feel I'm throwing her to the wolves."

"The wolves seem remarkably well-behaved," Anton murmured, nodding to where Arlo was patiently waiting for the newlyweds to stop kissing. "Would you consider staying?"

"Staying?"

Lainie and Harrison finally broke apart. Cheers exploded from the gathering, and for the next few minutes Sherryl was swept up in the whirl of joy and celebration. Champagne corks popped, glasses were raised, and excited shifter children who'd spent the whole ceremony wriggling with impatience burst into their animal forms and raced along the lawn.

Baby seals, and a *dragon*. This was the magical world Anton had described to her so long ago. The one she thought she had been exiled from forever. That she would never be able to even think about without hurting.

Watching this—seeing her daughter glowing with happiness, the joy of her friends and neighbors, the children changing shape as naturally as breathing, happy and free … it didn't hurt.

Could she stay here?

In a month or so, she would be a grandmother. There would be another little Eaves in the world. A griffin, or a shifter, or a human—and whatever they ended up being, they would be safe here, and cherished.

She meant to find Anton and give him her answer at once, but everywhere she turned, people wanted to congratulate her. *Her*. Sherryl Eaves, whose only other visits to Hideaway Cove had been marked by secrecy and shame.

At one point, Apollo Jenkins, the dragon shifter, pulled her aside. He wanted to reassure her that dragon fights weren't a common occurrence in the new and improved Hideaway Cove. She was distracted at first, but as Apollo described how his and his mate's powers kept the town safe—would keep her daughter and grandchild as safe as the most valuable treasure—she found herself enraptured.

Magic could still amaze her, after all. And more than that. What Apollo described would keep Hideaway safe in a way Anton's parents' scheming never could.

It wasn't until after the reception that she was able to have another quiet moment with Anton. "Yes," she told him, the moment they were alone. "If staying is an option, I want to stay."

"Good."

She tensed. Something in his voice…

*He's hiding something.*

All the joy of the day washed out of her like the tide going out. It was going to be the same as before. Everything was going to go wrong, and Anton would keep it from her until it was too late, and—

"I need to talk to you about something." His voice was low and urgent.

"What?"

"It's important." He drew her aside, to the shadows at the edge of the property. The lighthouse loomed above them. A few dozen yards and a thousand miles away, Lainie and Harrison danced beneath magical whirling lights.

"Something isn't right," he said, and the tide rushed in again. He paused, looking into her face.

"Go on," she said, almost giddy with relief. Whatever was wrong, he wasn't hiding it from her.

Things *had* changed.

"Everyone I've spoken to today has said it's a miracle I'm here," he said slowly. "But I was invited. All this time, someone knew where I was, and they chose now to bring me home."

Sherryl frowned. "Lainie told me she wrote you an invitation, but never sent it."

"Someone must have." His jaw tightened. "I talked with Harrison earlier. He said public opinion on Hideaway's old shifter-only policy has changed. Some people are ashamed of what they did, or what they silently supported being done."

"Maybe one of them had a change of heart."

"But—now? Of all times?" He gave her a weary smile. "Call me paranoid, but our marriage broke my family into pieces. I can't help but think that invitation was a very sparkly lure cast out to bring me back so I could do the same again."

Sherryl opened her mouth to protest—and closed it.

"I can't stop thinking about it. Someone knew where I was, all this time. They might have even come to see me. The—place where I was. A human could have lived there. I must have meant to be human there, and sort myself out, not lose myself to my magpie." He ran his fingers through his hair, tugging it into a mess of curls. "But I can't *remember*. Did I tell anyone? Did they visit?"

"Where was it? This place?"

He stared at her, eyes wide, and slowly his gaze became distant as he looked inside himself. "An old fishing cottage. I think … it was livable when I first went there, surely. Then the invitation arrived, and I looked around, and it was a ruin. Roof falling in. Windows broken. A suitcase open on the floor, everything inside it wrecked by the rain…"

"But you said you were in magpie form when you left Hideaway that final night. How did you have a suitcase?"

His eyes refocused on hers. "Someone knew where I was."

Rage boiled up inside her. "They came and saw you, saw how unwell you were, and did nothing?"

"I don't remember…" His voice faltered. "If it was my parents…"

"I'll dig them up and kill them again," she spat.

He kissed her. "No need," he whispered against her lips. "Just stay with me."

She held him, but her mind was still a firestorm of anger. "Your parents can't have sent the invitation, though."

"Not without rising from the grave. But they weren't the only ones who might have known where I went." His arms tightened around her. "Or, from Lainie's story of how she and Harrison met, the only ones who still feel that casting you both out was the right thing to do."

He looked into her eyes. "The night is young," he said. "Shall we visit some of my parents' old friends?"

6

# ANTON

The Sweets' house was just as he remembered it. The Eaves lighthouse loomed; the Sweets' home lurked.

A light was on in the front room. He sighed. "Another lure."

"Are we walking right into their trap?"

"I expect so." He linked his arm around Sherryl's. "But if we thrash hard enough, we might manage to break free."

He knocked on the door. A few minutes passed, and it opened.

"Anton?"

"Dorothea." He smiled. "It's so good to see you again."

*And I thought I got old.* Seeing her was more of a shock than seeing his own face in the mirror had been. Dorothea Sweets and her husband had been a constant in his childhood: they and his parents were close friends, and he'd spent countless days playing with their daughter Elaine. Both sets of parents had hoped they would end up as mates.

"Is Elaine around? I didn't see her at the party."

Dorothea's mouth pursed. "Elaine doesn't live around here any-more."

*So she escaped. Small mercies.* If she'd ended up like her parents—that would be another knife in his heart.

"Won't you invite us in? There's something Sherryl and I would like to say to you. And I doubt you want us shouting it on the street where everyone can hear."

675

Dorothea narrowed her eyes and stepped away from the door with a huff.

*I've been gone decades, and it looks exactly the same.* A shiver went down his back as he followed Dorothea to the living room. The one at the front of the house, for 'show'.

She snapped the curtains shut. "So, you finally decided to come home."

"I wouldn't call it a decision." Mrs. Sweets didn't offer him a seat, but he took Sherryl to one anyway, and sat next to her. The firmly upholstered, floral-patterned sofa creaked beneath them. "A week ago, I wouldn't have said there was enough of me left to decide on anything, let alone remember how to come home."

"Your mother lost her mind before she went. Did you know? Poor, dear Iris. Sitting there all alone in the nursing home, calling out for the son who abandoned her."

He went perfectly still. Beside him, Sherryl was trembling with rage. Her anger warmed him.

"If only there'd been someone who knew where to find me." He kept his voice deceptively light, but he wasn't fooling anyone. "But someone did, didn't they?"

Dorothea's eyes sharpened. "I have no idea what you're talking about."

"That's a shame, because I want to find whoever it was. I want to thank them."

Dorothea blinked. "You what?"

Not *excuse me*, or *I'm sorry*, or any of the other mealy mouthed politenesses she'd drilled into his and Elaine's heads. Pure, honest shock.

Sherryl caught on. She twined her fingers through his. "That's right. It might be a bit late, but that's understandable. Perhaps whoever discovered they still had Anton's address after all this time is having memory issues, too. But in the end, they brought Anton back to Lainie and me. They let us be a family again."

Her voice was saccharine, and frustration glinted behind Mrs. Sweets' eyes. He could almost hear her complaining that fake sweetness was *her* game.

Complaining to who, that was the question. And the answer made a noise like a landslide from the armchair in the corner of the room.

"Overrated," Mr. Sweets barked gruffly. "You and Elaine. Disappointments. Waste of our effort."

Dorothea tensed almost imperceptibly. "Elaine will come to her senses," she declared.

Of course. Elaine had gotten away—but her parents would do what they did best. Lurk. Sit quietly and innocently, until everyone forgot what big teeth they had, and then they would strike.

They must have gotten quite good at it, while he was gone, if Harrison was right and there hadn't even been rumors that they were part of the reason his family had split apart.

"I can see how the temptation was too great to resist," he said, understandingly. "Another human–shifter wedding. An *Eaves* wedding, at that."

Dorothea smiled kindly. "You have been gone a *very* long time, Anton. You must be confused. Why, Alan and I weren't even invited to the wedding. Can you imagine? Your parents' oldest friends."

"It hardly seems fair, I agree." He matched her tone of gentle regret with his own and her eyes flashed with irritation again. "When you went to so much trouble for the happy couple."

No one else could have known where he was. No one else would have sat on the information for so long until they could use it to finish what they started all those years ago. The invitation he'd received had his address on the envelope, but no name; it would have been easy enough to steal it from someone else's letterbox and send it on its way, a lure cast out to bring him home.

"I'm sorry to be such a disappointment once again," he said softly. "I hope that coming here tonight makes up for it. Like I said, I wanted to thank you for sending that invitation. And I understand your secrecy, not telling Lainie what you'd done. No ambush predator wants to reveal their hand before they are sure everything is lined up properly. You knew what leaving my mate had done to me, but you couldn't know how I would react to coming home. Would I be broken? Violent? So far gone there was no human left in me?"

"You weren't supposed to come back at all!" Mrs. Sweets' voice was pure bile. "There was nothing left of you. No telepathy. No shifting. You were nothing but a bird, nesting in that godforsaken old shack. You should have stayed there!"

His stomach went cold. Beside him, Sherryl hissed in a breath.

*It was all true.* Those pecked half-memories hadn't been a result of his madness. They'd been real.

Dorothea and Alan, his parents' old friends, had come to find him … and had left him there.

"But I didn't." His voice seemed to come from far away. But there was no shiver of feathers in his mind, no temptation to avoid reality by losing himself in his other form again. Sherryl's warm presence at his side kept him anchored. "I arrived in time, after all. I got to see my little girl get married and be welcomed by the people of my hometown as one of our own again. And it's all thanks to you."

He'd lost his family because of these people's cruelty. He'd lost years of his own life. His mind, his memories.

Black-billed magpies weren't predators. They didn't hunt, or lay ambushes. They pecked at bugs and scavenged other animals' kills—and maybe that was why his parents and the Sweets had gotten on so well.

But he had spent too long being nothing but his bird's instincts. It was time to be a man again.

One of his hands was still holding Sherryl's; he reached out to Mrs. Sweets with the other, his face stretching in a smile an alligator would be proud of. "Not even the best-laid plans survive reality, do they? But don't worry, Dorothea, Alan. I'll be sure to let everyone know you were the ones who tracked me down." He let that hang in the air a moment. "I won't tell them about your visit. Let's keep that between us for now. I wouldn't like to take attention away from Lainie and Harrison's big day. Let's say … how horrified you were when you realized you'd had my address all this time, tucked away in some forgotten notebook. Or perhaps in the things my parents left behind?"

Mrs. Sweets had taken his hand automatically. He squeezed it reassuringly, his smile still in place.

"I'll make sure the story adds up," he said, staring into Mrs. Sweets' pale blue eyes. "And you'll make sure of it, too. Because if you don't, the real story will come out. How you knew what had happened to me and did nothing. How you brought me back so that my only daughter would have to face the wreck her father had become, during what should have been the happiest time of her life. How easily you hurt the boy you'd known from when he was in the cradle."

He paused, and that was a mistake, because in that moment he wasn't standing in front of his parents' old friends: he was standing in front of his parents themselves, half a lifetime ago, hoping with a broken heart they loved him enough to accept his decision to stay with Sherryl and Lainie.

And something told him this was about to go just as badly.

And here it was. Mrs. Sweets' face twisted. "You want us to let everyone think we brought your family back together on *purpose*? That what we did was wrong?"

Sherryl's voice was low and calm. "Everyone already thinks you've made your peace with the way Hideaway is now. Arlo's mate, and now Felicity and Maya—"

"The red-headed trollop is barren." Mrs. Sweets dismissed Jacqueline with an irritated wave. "We won't see any human children from *her*. As for the dragon's mate…" She ground her teeth. "We all make compromises."

She said it like it was a dirty word. And she'd said the other word—*barren*—like it was a reason for celebration.

He felt sick.

"Do you feel the same way, Alan?" Sherryl asked, by all appearances unruffled.

Mr. Sweets was still motionless in his armchair. A wave of wariness rustled feathers Anton didn't have. Even with his shifter hearing, he had to concentrate hard to hear the old man breathing.

Dorothea Sweets was easy to deal with, in her way. Sweet on the outside, rotten inside. But her husband … something about him made Anton uneasy on every level, man and magpie.

"Of course he agrees with me," Mrs. Sweets snapped.

"Letting people live with the people they belong with—that's a *compromise?*" Sherryl was losing her grip on her calm voice. Anton's heart swelled. He wanted to know what would happen if she let it go completely. "And what do you call leaving Anton to die in his magpie form? Knowing you could help him, and choosing not to?"

Mrs. Sweets' lip curled back. "Another compromise. One we wouldn't have had to make, if you'd respected his parents' wishes."

His blood went cold. Before he could speak, Sherryl stood up. She wasn't tall enough to loom over the Sweets, but she didn't need to.

The years had changed them both. And the wide-eyed, sweet but anxious girl he'd known had grown into a formidable woman.

Sherryl smiled, but it didn't reach her eyes. "Let me make this simple for you. I don't owe you anything, but let's pretend that I do, since even if bringing Anton back was the last thing you planned—that's what you've done. You brought my mate home to me, where he belongs."

"Where we *both* belong." Anton stood with his mate, his hand in hers, and a golden glow he hadn't felt in years unfurled in his chest. The mate bond, healed at last.

"I have a deal for you. No compromise required. No need to play-act to your *dear* friends and *beloved* neighbors that you've softened your anti-human stance." Sherryl paused. "You leave Hideaway."

"Don't be absurd, you—"

"Your reputation remains intact. No one knows you'd send their children to the slaughterhouse to keep control of this town. And our grandchild will not grow up in the shadow of what you did to our family."

She turned to leave, and Anton soared with her.

"How is that not a compromise?" Mrs. Sweets snarled.

"Because your only alternative is that everyone here learns the truth about you, and you *still* leave." The smile had reached Sherryl's eyes now, but the gleam in them was anything but friendly. "I've had some very interesting conversations with Lainie's new friends today. The dragon shifter, Apollo, particularly. You know—the one whose dragon powers skip a generation, so any children he has with his mate are guaranteed to be human?"

Mrs. Sweets' mouth shut with a click.

"I think he and Felicity could make life *very* uncomfortable for you if they knew that you still thought human children were an unacceptable cost for Hideaway to bear. And I'm sure you'd rather leave on your own terms than be magically tossed out on your ass."

In the corner, Alan Sweets stirred like something old and rotten emerging from a swamp. "You dare to threaten us?"

Anton swept in front of his mate. The Sweets might be alligators—hunters—but he was faster than they were. His beak and claws against their—

"Of course!" Sherryl said brightly. "Of course I dare to threaten you. I'll dare anything, now that Anton's back. Because, for all these years, I thought I was a bad mate for him. And now I see how to be a good one—and it's not by standing aside and letting him handle the shifter side of things alone. I will protect him the way he protects me, and together, we'll defend our nest from anyone who would hurt it. Even if that means siccing a dragon on them. Now—it's been lovely to see you again. *Truly.* I appreciate it more than you can imagine. But I think our absence is going to be noticed soon. We'd better head back to the celebration."

"You—" Mrs. Sweets stayed frozen in her seat, glaring up at them, apparently too angry even to speak.

In the corner, her husband stirred again. "Not worth it," he muttered. "Blasted dragon magic. They're right."

Back outside, Sherryl's fingers clenched around his. He felt light-headed.

"They knew." Speaking the words made it more real; he wanted to un-say them. He wanted to rewind twenty lost years. "All this time—"

Sherryl wrapped her arms around him. "You're home now."

He rested his head on hers, inhaling her scent.

*Home.*

"What if it happens again?" More words he didn't want out in the world, but he'd promised to himself that he wouldn't hide things from his mate anymore. "If I lose myself."

"You won't. I won't let you. And if you do, I'll come find you." Sherryl turned her head to kiss the side of his neck. "I meant what I said in there. You shouldn't have shouldered the burden of facing up to your family alone. We're together. Whatever happens next, we face it as true mates."

*My mate. She wants to build a nest with me again.* Anton held her tightly.

"Though god knows *where* we're going to stay," she went on, resting her cheek on his chest. "Lainie and Harrison will want their space. And I am *not* moving back into that wreck of a lighthouse. It's—too full of ghosts."

"We'll figure something out. Apparently, there's a godforsaken old shack somewhere within flying distance that I found livable enough."

"Don't you dare. I bet it isn't even baby-proofed."

He stiffened. She looked up at him, her eyes bright. "Scared of becoming a grandfather?"

"Terrified," he admitted.

"I am, too. Do you know what I thought when I got here, and kept seeing your shadow out of the corner of my eye? I thought, at least it's safe to love him, now he's dead. And then you came back."

"I turned your world upside down again?"

"You turned it back the right way up." Her jaw hardened. "And I am never going to let that change. Those Sweets were right to be scared of what a human could do. If they do anything to hurt you or Lainie, that dragon shifter will have to make do with whatever's left of them."

She looked up into his eyes and blushed. "I'm sorry," she said. "I know that's not a nice thing to say. But—"

"It's the best thing you could have said to me. Except for one other thing." He twined his fingers in hers. "My love, you've already said you would stay here with me. But would you start over with me? Properly?"

"What do you mean?"

"I came here to stop our wedding. But I was years too late for that. Instead … would you marry me, again? Let me get it right, this time?"

She gazed up into his eyes. Her face was so much older than he remembered, made all the more beautiful by the laughter lines around her eyes and the silver in her golden hair. His human form was different, too; a new version of himself to learn as he learned every soft curve of his mate's body again.

"Of course," she whispered. "So long as you let me get it right again, too."

She kissed him, soft and loving, as though they had all the time in the world.

Because this time, they did.

9 781991 196811